BIRTH
OF
WIND

STEPHEN FRANCIS MONTAGNA

Printed in the United States of America
Published by: Stephen Francis Montagna

ISBN: 978-1-970301-00-7 PB
ISBN: 978-1-970301-01-4 HB

For my Dad, Frank. For the living years

PROLOGUE

The Heaven and Earth weren't separated at the very beginning of the world. Together, they formed the chaotic mess of the past and the future all in one. The pure air and land mass pulled away from the impure and heavier particles that made up this turbulent mass of confusion, and these pure forms shaped the Heavens, while the more dense particles continued to float through the Universe aimlessly. Heaven formed, and Heaven's first deities gave birth to the Brother Izanagi and the Sister Izanami. These two great Japanese gods would become man and wife, and would give birth to what would soon become known as the eight islands of Japans.

In the beginning, the Universe was a non living baron place. The deity Izanagi, whose name means the Male who Invites and his sister Izanami, whose name meant the Female who Invites, drifted aimlessly through the Heavens in pure thought. Izanagi searched the Universe looking for the site he intended to create. He was sent on this mission by his father, and his search lasted thousands of years. Unable to find the proper place he was looking for, Izanagi gave in to his boredom and driven by his father's desires, he created the earth.

With a thunderous clap, the earth was created in the wake by drawing the floating particles together in one wave of air created by the hands of Izanagi, and the earth was covered by water on its creation. Even with this creation, Izanagi continued to be bored with his existence in the floating world.

Izanami, his beloved sister realized Izanagi's dilemma, and talked him into creating land masses on the bubbling curdling and forming earth. Izanagi agreed with his sister's suggestion and together, Brother and Sister, Man and Wife stood on the last step of the Floating Bridge to Heaven. They dipped the fabled Amenotamaboko, the Celestial Jeweled Spear and phallic symbol of pure birth, in the swill which was the basis that made up the earth as it was at this time. Together they pushed the Jeweled Spear in the forming earth until it pierced the spine of the great Ocean covering the surface of the forming planet. Together they stirred the untidiness until the brine and froth gave forth with a thundering and curdling gurgle.

When the waters and mud and floating particles boiled in a swirling, moving and forming mass, the two deities withdrew the sacred Spear, and Izanagi held the Jeweled shaft to the Heavens as a gift offered to his honored father. His father allowed the drops of soupy mix to fall from the tip of the Spear of Birth. The drops crystallized and floated on the swirling water, thus creating the Japanese Island of Kyushu which the deities named Onogoro. Onogoro later became the birth place of the honored Japanese race.

The deities soon grew tired of floating on the clouds, so they descend from Heaven and erected the fabled Eight Fathom House with a Central Pillar. This gave the forming earth the World Spine or center core; this swill would be used to build on. When the deities moved to the island they performed the ceremony which would forever make them Man and Wife, by circling this Central Pillar twice, meeting face to face on the other side.

As other drops of mud dripped from the Spear, the deities Izanagi and Izanami gave birth to the other Seven Islands to make up Japan. Together the islands made up the

Ohoyashimakuni, the land of the Eight Islands of Japan. Thus endearing the number eight to a scared significant to the future race of the Japanese population.

Ninigi was the next deity to leave the Heavens and take residence on the newly formed earth. His task was to direct the development of Japan, insuring his future grandson, Jimmu Tenno would become the first of divine Emperors to rule the islands of Japan. And to insure his future offspring's would rein Japan forever, by instilling the honor of Emperor on his grandson Tenno.

This greatness bestowed on the Eight Islands of Japan, did little to make Izanagi content with his work or existence in the new world. He searched his mind for other ways to improve his creation. Izanagi went on to finish his work, before creating the indispensability's needed to make Japan the true seat of creation on the earth, and the future populations of the world.

Izanagi shaped Onogoro by using drops of his sweat, and turned them into the forests of trees. His breath which he blew across the baron lands turned into a mighty sea of grass. Tears of happiness turned into lakes which gave birth to crystal clear streams crisis-crossing the Eight Islands of Japan. A second thunderous clap of his hands gave birth to the animals which walked on his creation. A third reverberating clap, gave birth to birds that replaced him and soared among the Heavens, along with the sea animals that prowled the ocean's depth.

Izanagi grew weary of the toils of his creation and wanted to rest, but the entire expanse of the eight Japanese Islands was flat. His sister Izanami felt bad for her husband's weariness, and with a sudden stomp of her foot, appeared a central mountain range. Thus from the depths of the earth, Mt. Fugi was born. The Mountain rose until it was the height to offer Izanagi a great chair on which to rest his body upon. With a wave of her hand the clear blue sky was instantly dotted by soft fluffy clouds. The hot temperature dropped, making Izanagi rest more comfortably on his mountain chair overlooking his vast creation.

When the Eight Islands of Japan were formed to Izanagi's desires, Izanagi and Izanami decided their work was completed on the earth, and they considered returning to the Heavens. To give birth to the future deities who would follow them in the hearts and minds of the proud and respectful Japanese people.

The birth of many Japanese deities was a most stormy and violent task, with many arguments developing between the deity Izanagi, his wife, and gods they created to rule the earth he created. The first Kami's born was the Heavenly Blowing Male, later known as Fujin, or the God of Wind. The sea kamis, Foam Waves, Foam Calm, and Ocean Possessor, and Heavenly Water Provider followed then Izanagi gave birth to the deities of the earth solid. Mountains, passes and valleys had their kami's or god like guardians, along with the grass, crops, and rock kami's.

The sea gods were called Watatsumi, or sea children. But the war between the gods didn't end at their creation. Izanami gave nativity to the fire god Kagutsuchi. This fiery deity caused the death of his mother and his wife and sister of Izanagi. With the death of Izanami terribly burned by this kami's birth, Izanagi's heart became filled with grief and hatred. In his rage he drew his ten grasp sword and chopped the head of Kagutsuchi from his body, Izanagi proceeded to chop Kagutsuchi's body into three pieces, and each severed piece became gods themselves.

Other gods were born from the blood splattered on the rocks and ground from the slaughtered god. Blood dripping from Izanagi's sword became the gods Kuraokami, the Dragon of Valleys, and Kurayamatsumi, the Lord of Dark Mountains, and Kuramistsuha, the Dark Water Snake.

Before his beloved sister and wife Izanami died, she grown ill and her vomit gave birth to gods, her urine gave birth to Mitsuhanome, or the female water snake. The other deities Izanami and Izanagi gave birth to were of the fearsome dragon family, Mizuchi, or water fathers sometimes referred to as horned deities. Wani, one of the last gods born, was a mighty dragon who resembled a mix between a crocodile and shark. It was believed Toyotamabime, or Abundant Pearl Princess took a human lover, and she transformed herself from human shape to a dragon, and forever retained the shape when her child died at birth, as anger and punishment for her sharing a mortal lover.

After Izanagi slaughtered Kagutsuchi, he longed for his dead wife and sister. Izanagi set out to find his wife residing in the land of the Underworld. Izanagi found his sister living in the land of gloom and darkness. Seeing him standing outside the Parturition structure, Izanami raised the door. Izanagi ordered her to follow him, saying the Islands they created weren't complete without her presence. But Izanami refused to follow him to the world of the living and light, stating she doomed herself to this place of loneliness for eternity, because she ate from the food of Yomi. Izanami desired to return to the land of light and told Izanagi she would speak with Yomi while Izanagi remained waiting outside.

Izanagi waited and then entered Izanami's sacred Parturition dwelling against her will. Upon entering the dwelling he saw his wife lying in a rotting state with the gods of thunder eating from her decaying body. Shocked by what he witnessed, Izanagi pulled away from his loving wife and sister in disgust. Izanagi broken the sacred taboo of seeing his wife dwelling in the Parturition House, the specially erected one room structure where the honored Japanese women of respect went to have children unobserved by anyone in the mortal world.

Outraged by this indignity committed against her person and coupled with a great loss of face to Izanami, she became humiliated and commanded the Ugly Females of the Yomi to arise from their graves and hunt down and slays her once beloved husband and brother Izanagi.

Izanagi hearing this command to the lowly gods of the underworld, he fled the sequestered house being pursued by the angry Female gods. He slowed the horde of pursuing evil gods by throwing articles of clothing behind him, which formed obstacles too great to be overcome by the pursuing gods. Thus stopping the evil deities in pursuit of him. Izanami, finding the Female gods failed on their mission to kill her brother and husband, unleashed other pursuers from the dark side of the underworld. The eight Thunder deities she gave birth to were sent after Izanag, with a thousand, five hundred warriors of Hades to assist them.

Izanagi was able to escape the Even Pass of Hades by swinging his ten grasp sword, forcing the pursuing demons back in the depths of the dark and foreboding cave and doorway of the underworld. Izanami took up the pursuit of Izanagi. Seeing her rapidly approaching from within the depths of the dark cave, Izanagi blocked the mouth of the Pass of Yomi with a massive boulder that would take a thousand men to move.

Enraged by this blocking action of her brother, the screaming Izanami threatened from within the mouth of the cave to kill a thousand men from the land of light and living. Izanagi yelled back threatening to give birth to a thousand five hundred men to exceed the number threatened by her death order. The great bolder held Izanami at bay in the dark cave forced her to forever become the Yomotsuohokami, or Yomi's Great Deity. Upon Izanagi's return to the land of the living, Izanagi performed the honored ceremony of the purification of the body.

Izanagi went to the river and bathed. Two evil demons were born from the filth of Hades washed from his battered and exhausted body, and floated down river to escape Izanagi's wrath. Izanagi washed his left eye, and from it he gave birth to Amaterasu, the goddess of sun. He washed his right eye in the pure waters of the river, and from that he gave birth to the god of the moon, the great Tsukiyomi.

Izanagi ordered the sun deity Amaterasu to rule over the great Plains of the High Heavens, and ordered the moon god Tsukiyomi, to rule over the night Heaven. Susanowo, born from Izanagi's spittle, was decreed by Izanagi to become the brother of the war like and fearsome Fujin, the always angry god of Wind, and he was ordered to rule the immense depths of the unending Sea he created with his own hands.

The god Susanowo defied Izanagi's order and wept, unleashing an evil poisonous rain to wash over the lands of the sacred eight Islands of Japan. Seeing this evil rain was destroying what he created for the children of his breath, the angry Izanagi confronted the god Susanowo, and demanded to know why he wept so. Susanowo replied he wanted to join his mother dwelling in the honored land of the dead in the cellar of the underworld.

Enraged by Susanowo's defiance of his command and destroying of what he created, Izanagi banished Susanowo to Afumi, the fresh water lake. Izanagi hoped the pure waters of the lake would do something to wash away some of the evil thoughts from the angry god's mind. Izanagi returned to Heaven for a rest.

Susanowo rose in the air as a bellowing and ferocious dragon, and caused the lands of Japan to be violently ripped apart by crippling earthquakes. The Sun goddess Amaterasu came to her brother's side. There they pledged faith and love to each other, with Amaterasu requesting Susanowo's sword before she would consider having his children. Upon receiving the sword from his right hand, Amaterasu broke it in three pieces.

Amaterasu removed five hundred curved jewels from her hair and washed them in the pure waters of the Pool of Truth in Heaven, then crushed them and with her breath, blew the fine jeweled dust to the Heavens. The deities of the Torrent Mist Princess, the Lovely Island Princess, and Princess of Torrent were born from the crushed jewels and Amaterasu's breathe.

Susanowo who dearly wanted to have children with his sister, asked her for the remaining five hundred six foot long curved jewels from her hair. He washed them in the waters of the Pool of Truth in Heaven, and crushed them in his hands and just as his sister had done moments before him, he gently blew the fine jewel dust towards the Heavens. From his breath came forth the birth of the gods, the Truly Conqueror, I Conquer, Conquering, and Swift Heavenly Great Ears, and the god Amenohohi, along with the god Prince Lord of Heaven, and god Prince Lord of Life, and lastly to be born from this dust, was the god of Kumano who came forth from the glittering dust as it drifted to the surface of the earth. Thus, the gods of Japan were given their birthright in the hearts and minds of their loving people of Japan forever to be loved and respected.

CHAPTER ONE

Thus throughout the great history of Japan's turbulent beginning, starting with the end of the Prehistoric Age, life was a savage struggle at best for the children of Izanagi. This struggle extended to the birth of the religion of Buddhism, born from the influences of the Chinese civilization which filtered into the development of Japan. True growth began in earnest in Japan around the time of the sixth century, and extended to the feudal times of the Middle Ages. But Japan's development was plagued by many rivalries between the ruling clans. Clashes occurred frequently between the different clans making up the haphazard Japanese lifestyle. A period of violent wars began with the conquest of the northern section of the emerging country against the fearsome Caucasian type Ainu Aborigines, and continued with great battles breaking out between the rival families of nobility.

Early wars caused hopelessness among Japan's citizens, the conflicts undermining the national consciousness, and the only way citizens felt security from their leader's wrath was by belonging to a group. Groups, city, or military districts sprouted up throughout the islands. This need to belong coupled with the want for security against the bands of Ronin, the masterless samurai warriors or highway men, or wave men and criminals roaming Japan. Created the need for the birth of Seii TaiShogun. Shogun means the barbarian suppressing commander in chief, or military dictator. To rule over their domain, the Shogun with his retainers developed a bakufu or central government to rule Japan. They were forced to employ help and developed daimyos or provincial governments to protect the bakufu. Daimyo means great name.

These ruthless feudal sub leaders or provincial lords, were merciless dealing with farmers (hyakusho), artisans (shokunin), merchants (akindo, chonin), and outcasts (eta, himin). Peasants lost their lives to the killing sword for such minor infractions as not bowing properly.

The need for protection from criminals robbed the uneducated of initiative to better themselves, insuring no disturbances from the inhabitants of the bakufu. There was no reason for them to better themselves or escape servitude, when they didn't realize the situation they were in.

The emergence of the Japanese culture suffered more hardships and setbacks through countless years of unrest and strife, with the worst beginning in the year 1051 and extending to 1062. This was the time of the Early Nine Year War, which witnessed the emergence of the warrior Yoshiie Minamoto who eliminated the Abe clan in northern Honshu. 1083 to 1087 was the time of the Later Three Year War which witnessed many warriors from Yoshiie Minamoto destroying the opposition from the Kiyowara clan who took over northern Honshu, when the Abe clan was destroyed in war. 1095 was the year that beheld the marauding sohei monks as they descended from Mount Hiei, and attacked Heian Kyo.

The continuing years of fighting and hatred caused disruption in Japan, and when Kiyomoni Taira emerged from the masses, it was hoped he would be the answer to Japan's problems. But it wasn't to be, he was the worst. In 1156, Kiyomoni Taira of the military aristocracy in the provinces took control of the civil government of Kyoto. This period became known as the Fujiwara period, which extended from 866 to 1160, and led to the beginning of the Taira period of rule, 1156 which gives birth to this story.

THE KAMAKURA PERIOD, ELEVEN EIGHTY FIVE TO THIRTEEN THIRTY SIX

The beginning of the Kamakura era marked a turning point in Japan's history. During the time of the tenth and eleventh centuries, aristocratic Fujiwara clan was the ruling power of Japan. The Fujiwara clan enjoyed unlimited control of the capital of Kyoto, Japan's seat of power and ruling center of the country. But the foolish Fujiwara leaders allowed themselves to fall victim to the perils of good life, the absolute power and stagnation offered Japan's rulers. They became involved in the pleasurable pursuits of culture, grand rituals and leisurely pleasures of court life, and forgot how they had to fight to become the leaders of Japan. Rulers of the Fujiwara clan neglected martial arts, and relied on independent warrior clans controlling the outer provinces for their maintenance of the political structure of Kyoto, sowing the seeds of their demise.

By the beginning of the twelfth century saw the rise of two powerful rival clans to rule the lands of Japan. The clans owed their strengths to the weakness of the bored and unsuited Fujiwara government leaders. Forced to appoint the Kiyomuri Taira and Yoshitomo Minamoto clan leaders as daimyos of the land south and north of Kyoto, because of their military strengths and knowledge of war making abilities. This appointment made it possible for the warlords to mass powerful armies of feared samurai warriors for future wars to rule the land of Japan.

The Kamatari Fujiwara government not possessing an army of its own was compelled to call on these clan leaders to put down constant uprisings plaguing its government. The government wasn't aware samurai warriors were mostly responsible for the uprisings. The leaders of the these clans, Yoshitomo Minamoto or Genji, and Kiyomori Taira or Heishi or Heike, took advantage of the needs of the government to savagely attack each other's camp. Making it necessary for each side to reinforce the size and strength of their armies with more samurai. Terribly savage wars between these armies arose from the political foundation of Kyoto, and gave birth to a class of samurai to fight for the opposition against the rule of the aristocracy. This new class of warriors began to revenge themselves on the capital city trying to control them.

The final battle between the clans occurred in 1160, when Yoshitomo Minamoto attacked the Imperial castle in the proper of Kyoto with five hundred warriors. They overran the castle, taking the Emperor Goshirakawa cloistered in the castle and imprisoned him in an ill fated attempt to regain power. A month of fighting took place in Kyoto until the forces of Taira overwhelmed the Minamoto warriors. The Taira set out on a mission of revenge by ordering executions and retribution of unparalleled savagery to be carried out against surviving Minamoto clan members, until the clan was hunted down and on the brink of extinction.

For a period of time in Japan's stormy history, the Taira clan enjoyed absolute authority under the harsh leadership of Kiyomori Taira. Kiyomori Taira was a ruthless general of courage and brilliant military leadership who succeeded in ruthlessly crushing his enemy without mercy, and leader of the Minamoto clan. Kiyomori trapped Yoshitomo in a valley and butchered the rival leader with many military leaders and family members. Others adherents were scattered and without a true leader to guide them, they took to roaming Japan looking for a safe place to settle. Yoshitomo's two eldest sons were put to the sword, sharing the fate that took their parents. But one fatal mistake was committed, a mistake that would come to haunt Kiyomori forever. He allowed the third son of the feared Yoshitomo Minamoto to survive.

Yoritomo Minamoto, leaving his isle after fleeing the slaughter of his family, headed for the province of Mino and from there, he attempted to head for Kwanto or east provinces and safety this region offered him. But he was unable to elude the armies sent to capture him. Yoritomo was captured by the Taira commander General Kunekiyo, who brought him to capital of Kyoto. Yoritomo was dragged before Kiyomori where he was asked if he was ready to meet his fate. The child's fearless demeanor ruled his actions and he replied proudly he was ready to die by his own hand if ordered, but added he would rather live, for he was the only one of his clan left alive to pray for the souls of his relatives. His words and plea for prayers to his relatives softened the stout heart of the fearless Taira leader, and Kiyomori spared the child's life, and placed him in the care of two trusted retainers.

Once Kiyomori's clan defeated Yoshitomo's armies, he established the supremacy of his rule over Japan, by putting his rivals and troublemakers to the sword. This purge of Japan lasted months, and when Kiyomori grew weary of the slaughter he ordered a stop to the killings. But instead of returning to the woods where the Imperial Court and Emperor of Kyoto felt he and his followers belonged, Kiyomori moved to the heart of Kyoto and settled and surrounded himself with his best generals and captains and counselors, who served to strengthen his position.

These positions of government were occupied by prominent members of his clan. Kiyomori's power became so absolute over the Fujiwara government; it was believed the Taira leader was unworthy of belonging to the human race. So soaring was Kiyomori's ambition that the cloistered Son of Heaven, the Emperor, felt threatened and declared his own position in control over Japan was in jeopardy. Realizing his power was soaring, Kiyomori dared to take the title of grand chancellor, and taking a page from Kamatari Fujiwara's rise to power, he married his daughter to the Emperor. The couple produced their only heir who would occupy the throne.

THE RISE OF THE FIRST TRUE SHOGUN

In the year of 1180, the Minamoto clan was being led by one of the greatest generals in Japan's history, and who would later become a statesman.   Yoritomo Minamoto appeared on the horizon. He was a surviving son of the great leader of the Minamoto clan, Yoshitomo, assassinated in 1160 after his bid to overthrow Kiyomori failed. Kiyomori's clan would have ruled Japan if it wasn't for one fatal mistake. Instead of slaughtering all surviving children of Yoshitomo, Kiyomori allowed two sons to live. One child was Yoritomo Minamoto, although he was raised by Taira guardians, Yoritomo grew to hate Kiyomori for what he done to his family. He rose to become a most ambitious leader of opposition against the Kiyomori leaders.

Rallying the surviving members of the Minamoto clans together who took safe harbor on the far east coast of Japan, Yoritomo Minamoto established a formidable army to rise up and challenge the Taira ruler over Japan and her subjects.

Shortly after the death of Kiyomori Taira, the eldest Minamoto son, Yoritomo seized the opportunity and rose in rebellion against the Taira clan, launching the beginning of the great Gempei War, which lasted from 1180 to 1185. The war was one of the longest in Japan's history. Not only did the war last for an extended period, but it was Japan's most savage and bloody conflict, witnessing the deaths of thousands of loyal warriors to both sides.

The Gempei War began in the spring of 1180 when Yorimasa Minamoto, an aged Kyoto courtier and relation of the banished Minamoto clan, plotted to overthrow the Taira leader and establish on the Imperial Throne the disqualified Prince Mochihito. Mochihito was overlooked as the successor in favor of Kiyomori Taira's infant grandson, the Emperor Antoku.

The plot was discovered and it ended with the deaths of Yorimasa and Prince Mochihito, with their heads being lost as a result of their crime. The incident served to incite Yoritomo and his clan and he rebelled from his place of exile on the Izu Peninsula.

The animosity that fostered between the Taira and Minamoto clans erupted in one breath of the dragon, and unleashed the fires of hell on the lands of Japan in the war between the two clans. Late 1180 on the twenty eighth day of the twelfth month, Shigehira Taira, one of Kiyomori's sons set fire to the temples of Kofukuji and Todaiji. These temples were regarded as powerful centers of Japanese religion and cultural beliefs, and a forceful seat of anti-Taira sentiment.

In one rampaging night of unmasked destruction and hatred, these remarkable structures, along with the Buddhist statuary of the temples once believed to be the spine of Japan since the eighth century, were reduced to ash. Shigehira Taira realized he committed a foolish act against the heart of Japan. He killed himself, but his rash act aroused the abhorrence of the pure men of conscience throughout Japan. Taira clan's future was sealed in their demise.

After the Nara fire that destroyed much of Kyoto had been brought under control, restoration work on the sacred temples and shrines began at Todaiji on the sixth month of 1181. The Taira clan retreated, and on the third month of 1183, the Taira clan was pressured in abandoning Kyoto. Their retreat was, with the Minamoto forces maintaining pressure on the retreating Taira troops. The fleeing Taira army was slaughtered almost to the last warrior two years later, in a sea battle off the coast of Dannoura.

Minamoto's forces were aided by a shift in the tide which caught the Taira army depleted by hunger and desertions by surprise, and the raging tide capsized warships carrying thousands of Taira fighters. So many weighted down warriors were drowned that the sea in this region ran red with blood from the slaughtered Taira soldiers. The massacre of the Taira clan was so complete the daughter of the clan's leader, and infant son and future Emperor of Japan, Antohu, were drowned. When found, they were hacked to pieces and their body parts were scattered along the beach, having been refused a proper burial.

YORITOMO MINAMOTO, NOW THE UNDISPUTED MASTER OF ALL OF JAPAN

The true Emperor was so pleased when he was informed Kiyomori Taira and his family were destroyed; he bestowed the highest privilege of Seii TaiShogun, on the head of Yoritomo. The barbarian subduing general was honored for his accomplishment of destroying the Taira clan. Thus establishing the duel system of government that would rule Japan for centuries. Yoritomo learned not to repeat the same mistake of allowing his enemy to survive, only to come back sometime in the future to wage war on his rule.

When Yoritomo received the title of Seii TaiShogun from the Emperor in the third month 1192, he became the master of his fate. By the time this honor was bestowed on him, Yoritomo controlled half Japan with the outlying provinces swearing loyalty and allegiance to his leadership. With this honor placed on his head, the decree rendered the Emperor's authority to be overshadowed by Yoritomo rule. His need for money and troops linked the new Emperor to the Yoritomo clan. The Emperor agreed with the arrangement, he knew he had no choice, because Yoritomo was so powerful a force to deal with. If he decided to make a claim for the Emperor's seat, the population would have served it up to him on a silver platter.

The Shogun Yoritomo made certain he didn't commit the second fatal mistake of his career, by taking residence and living in Kyoto. Before the collapse of Kyoto, the city was known as Heian Kyo, translated as the Capital of Peace and Tranquility. Heian Kyo went out of use and the capital's name changed to Kyoto. If he stayed in Kyoto, Yoritomo was worried he might fall victim to the glorified ways of life, and luxuries of the Imperial Court that trapped many leaders before him, and doomed them to the pitfall of stagnation. Yoritomo set up headquarters at the military site at Kamakura in the Sagami (Soshu) province, at a town resting on the shore at the mouth of Edo Bay. Upon establishing this capital city, the wise Shogun Yoritomo made his loyal henchmen, daimyos and stewards of the land, and then sent them to govern their provinces, which he bestowed on them in his name for their loyalty to him and his rule.

The daimyos were placed in command of provincial armies, thus sowing the seeds of the samurai caste. The daimyos duty was to instill the loyalty of these soldiers to their Shogun. This was the development of the Bushido, the Code of Conduct and Chivalry, the Way of the Warrior which governed the soul of samurai, and enslaved them to the steadfast belief in their Shogun and his will. The Shogun's honor was raised up to a living god like reverence, forever bonding the samurai's body and soul to their leader. This insured the Shogun there would never be any uprisings against any Shogun from the ranks of soldiers, while the daimyos ruled the royal estates they were placed in command of by the Shogun.

The samurai class took years to establish firmly before these warriors could assert themselves in the army of the Shogun. The Shogun was forced to take them on if he wanted to remain in power. Years of unpredictable changes, battles, and political and social disorders, added to the strengthening of the rising samurai class. Japan thus entered its most active and alternating phase of history. It was as if Mount Fuji had awakened after lying dormant for thousands of years. Japan was poised to erupt into a greatness that still rules her nature today, hundreds of years after the true meanings and the beliefs of Bushido came into being.

With the unwavering backing of his samurai, Yoritomo Minamoto set up a military dictatorship with the samurai becoming his most important class of personage. Yoritomo was swift enough to realize his Shogun's power rested on the shoulders and loyalty of his samurai. Their loyalty was vital to his rule and he did everything to insure their happiness. He established a section of his Kamakura bakufu to deal with the samurai's problems. A ruling samurai dealt out the duties of every samurai, and recommended promotions, and other different forms of rewards for the warrior's accomplishments on the field of battle, or to the protection of the Shogun's lands. This ruling samurai determined the punishments against any infractions of laws and controlled the home life of each samurai. Yoritomo didn't want unhappiness among the soldiers. Tea Houses were established to service the samurai who felt the need to pillow a woman. Everything to further the samurai's comforts was pursued.

The Shogun Yoritomo Minamoto demanded unwavering loyalty from those who served him, and was ruthless to all he dealt with or was against him. His treachery was so compelling he trusted no one, not even his brother. Yoritomo tried to have his brother assassinated when he suspected he was becoming too great a general and threat in his right, and beginning to usurp his rule. Yoritomo's brother was the popular Yoshitsume, the ninth and youngest son of the slaughtered leader, Yoshitomo, Yoritomo's father.

Stories of his brother's deeds in battle were spoken among the campfires of samurai. This mounting respect for his brother clouded Yoritomo's mind until he turned against his brother in the closing days of the Gempei War. Yoritomo arranged for his brother's murder, but the assassins were clumsy and discovered. Yoshitsume and his servants and vassals escaped the attempt on their lives.

Yoshitsume fled Kamakura and rushed to the protection offered by Kyoto whereupon he appealed to the Emperor. Yoshitsume was ordered to arrest his brother and bring him to the capital for justice. But Yoshitsume lacked the support of samurai to carry out this order by the Emperor. Yoshitsume was forced to sail for the western provinces to raise the army he needed to place his brother and Shogun under arrest. He went to Mutsu and Dewa and pleaded with his friend Hidehira Fujiwara for help in finding the soldiers he needed to defeat his brother.

While his brother Yoshitsume wasted time raising an army to go against the ruling Shogun, Yoritomo Minamoto marched an army of samurai to the heart of Kyoto. There demanded an audience with the Emperor, whereupon Shogun Yoritomo insisted the Emperor change his order of arrest, and forced the Emperor to grant Shogun Yoritomo a new arrest warrant, this one was to arrest his rebel brother, Yoshitsume.

Late in the fifth month of 1189, Yoshitsume's palace at Korumogawa came under siege once it was discovered Yoritomo's brother moved into this palace with the army he massed to go against the Shogun. Under crushing attacks from Yoritomo's samurai, Yoshitsume's bakufu crumbled. Yoshitsume, seeing escape from the bakufu was impossible, ordered his second in command, General Kanefusa to kill his wife and children while he committed seppuku.

Once Kanefusa was certain Yoshitsume and his family was dead, he completed the orders from his master. He set out to torch the palace before he died, but not until he carried out one final act of defiance. Kanefusa, his body ablaze ran from the burning palace and he wrapped his arms around a general from Yoritomo's armies and dragged him into the flames, causing the general's death with his own. No samurai reacted to this act of defiance carried by the enemy general because it occurred so swiftly. The siege ended with this act of bravery with the samurai of the opposing side paying homage to the memory of General Kanefusa.

With the defeat of Yoshitsume and the destruction of his palace, Yasuhira Fujiwara who recently succeeded Hidehiru, committed suppuku once he ordered his soldiers to march with Yoshitsume. Yasuhira was so eager to prove himself to Yoritomo, ordered the execution of his brother for helping Yoshitsume's army. The head of his brother, along with the head from Yoshitsume's body was taken, and sent to Kamakura as proof of his loyalty to the Shogun.

Shogun Yoritomo Minamoto searched his mind for a way to wreak revenge on the two he believed to be, rebel provinces. He was angered over their compliance with his rebel brother Yoshitsume's attempt to take him in custody. Upon receiving the courier sent by Fujiwara, and viewing the heads resting on the wooded plates, Yoritomo faked outrage over what he deemed to be a terrible deed committed by Fujiwara. Yoritomo used this outrage as a reason for war and he sent out his samurai who destroyed the provinces of Mutsu and Dewa, while taking thousands of heads as the massive armies marched through the enemy provinces. This set an example to any who dared to go against the Shogun, Yoritomo's will and rule.

There were other uprisings plaguing Yoritomo Minamoto's reign, but he was successful in crushing them. When Yoritomo died 1199, the power held by the Minamoto clan was transferred, and now being wielded by the Hojo family. Hojo Tokimas was the father of Yoritomo's wife, and he took over the military post of Regent. The Hojo family, whose members were once steadfast loyal vassals to the destroyed Taira clan, was rewarded by the seat of Regent and absolute power, and he ruled the troubled period of the Kamakura era. Although the Hojo rulers continued to rule in Kamakura, they exercised absolute rule over the realm, but no Hojo clan dared to assume the title of Shogun. They were content to be known as Shikken, Power Holders or Regents to the realm. The worse challenge to the Hojo rule came in 1274 with the first of the Mongolian invasions of Japan.

THE WAR BETWEEN KYOTO AND KAMAKURA

When the bloodline of Minamoto became extinct with his death, the Hojo clan rose to power over Japan, and they would hold this power for years. The reign of the Hojo clan in Kamakura began. However, the idea of Hojo Regents being in command of Japan didn't sit well with the Emperor, who wanted to move the seat of power to its rightful place in Kyoto. The Emperor Go-Toba availed himself of the disturbances in the military government of Kamakura to overthrow the Hojo clan, and reinstate the Imperial Power in the capital of Kyoto. The Emperor Go-Toba infuriated the military followers in Kyoto, and once he was assured of their backing, he declared the Hojo clan and their followers to be traitors to the realm and its rule, and he assembled a great army with one objective, to destroy Kamakura as the current seat of power in Japan.

In the year 1221, a mighty Imperial army was dispatched from Kyoto, thus initiating a new confrontation against the Kamakura leaders. The ill trained and poorly equipped Imperial army was soundly defeated and forced to capitulate in one month's time to the seasoned, better trained and equipped samurai of the Hojo of Kwanto, made up of samurai from the Yoritomo clan. This insured Kamakura would remain the seat of power over Japan. The Jokyu Disturbance as it came to be known brought down the curtain on Kyoto as the main stage of natural affairs for Japan.

All the nobles who took part in this short lived and soundly routed uprising were put to the edge of the sword. Heads were taken and placed on the Gunyokis, the small spiked wood platforms specially designed for the displaying of severed heads of one's enemy. The estates of the vanquished were confiscated by the Hojo and divided between the loyal daimyos that made up the Kamakura bakufu defenders, and they backed the Hojo in this uprising. The heads were displayed before the Hojo leader and this act was elevated to a sacred ceremony of right, the viewing of the heads of their enemy.

The severed heads of the enemy were prepared by the women of the defeated who washed the battlefield grime and blood from them, and then the heads were set on the Gunyokis with the spike holding the heads in place for viewing. The heads were marched through the samurai ranks for viewing before being placed on the ground in patterns around the victor. In this case, Hojo viewed the heads for a moment, before ordering them to be brought to the beaches where they were placed on bamboo spears, and left for the birds to eat, or rot in the sun.

The Imperial family was treated harshly for their actions in this Jokyu disturbance, with Emperor Go-Toba receiving the rare punishment of being exiled to the barren and rocky island of Oki. He suffered there for three years of sequestration before succumbing to the toils of trying to survive under the harsh conditions. The rest of his family allowed to survive the slaughter of the disturbance, were married to mere peasants and farmers for their punishment.

THE MONGOLIAN INVASION LEAD BY KUBLAI KHAN: 1274

Another event held significance in shaping Japan and made the ruling Hojo Regent Tokimune, the 6th Regent of the Hojo clan, one of great distinction. This acknowledgment began in the fourth month 1274 when the Mongolian hordes in the backwash of their great invasion of most of Europe, attempted to ride this wave of success with the first of their invasions into Japan.

This race of outcast mixed blood Chinese Nomad warriors called Mongols, received their reputation of being great warriors by possessing highly maneuverability and employing surprise attacks against their enemy. They spread across developing Asia lands as a mass of deadly humanity. Like a plague sweeping the region, the Mongols attacked nations bordering their own. Within a few years the aggressive Mongols were successful in overrunning the Empire that made up the Chinese world, adding to their conquests, Korea. Although the Mongols had a number of leaders in their time, one great leader would be remembered as their greatest. Outside his grandfather Ghenghis Khan, it was Kublai Khan who ruled the Mongolians the longest.

Kublai Khan was the first grandson of Ghenghis Khan, who possessed a warring heart and as such, his mind always looking for the next nation to conquer, the next war to fight. The Khan turned to the rich Islands of the Japans. Klan sent spies to Japan long before he intended to invade, and they reported Japan were ripe for invasion, sighting the wars and uprisings plaguing the Hojo leadership. The discontent of the nobles in Kyoto added to the beliefs the time was right for invasion.

Kublai Khan, operating under the advice from his generals, decided he was going to bring Japan into the Mongolian Empire and dispatched six emissaries to the Japanese Emperor, demanding homage and gifts of tribute be paid to the Chinese empire. When the Emperor refused, Kublai Khan ordered the defeated Koreans to construct an armada of five hundred ships. In the eleventh month of 1274, the armada carrying twenty thousand Mongolians crossed to the island of Kyushu, and landed at Imazu in Hakata Bay, almost unopposed except for a few samurai who were the village's only military presence.

The demands leveled on the Kyushu bakufu officials concerning the problems facing the samurai defenders and peasant farmers of Kyushu, resulted in the uncertainty of maintaining law and order on the island. This forced the officials to turn their backs on what was happening in the waters off Japan, China, and Korea. Coastal waters were visited by Japanese pirates believed to be using Tsushima, Ikishima, and Kyushu as their safe ports in which to operate from.

The Mongolian leader sent to Japan the first of six intermediates to address this fact with the Emperor of

Japan, demanding the officials of Kyushu place a stop to the pirate raids in his domain. When there was no response from the Emperor to his demands, Khan decided to make a number of new demands of tribute from Japan. Khan demanded to be paid to replace what was stolen by the Japanese pirates. The sixth ruling Hojo Regent, Tokimune, was capable of defending Japan from invasion by the Mongolians, and in this crucial point in Japanese history. The islands that made up Japan were relatively free from civil strife and war. Making it possible for the ruling Hojo Regent to muster his force of samurai for the defense of Kyushu.

Kublai Khan's army began his conquest of Japan by building his forces with the lesser trained Korean fighters, and his first attack occurred when his armada landed on Tsushima, which lay half way between Korea and Japan. Once this island was defeated, Khan aimed his army at Kyushu. On the island, Khan forces encountered a force of samurai numbering five hundred warriors commanded by So Sukekumi. These samurai as all Japanese warriors were trained fought courageously for hours before Khan's outnumbering forces broke the defenders down by overwhelming them and slaughtering the garrison.

After this victory of Khan fighters was completed, the Khan armada moved on until it came across the second island, and the outer most defenses of the mainland. The Khan forces attacked Ikishima which suffered the same fate as her sister island miles before her, defeat at the hands of the Mongolians, ending with the slaughter of those who dwelled upon the island.

Khan began his attack on the Japanese mainland by landing his forces on Kyushu. Upon hearing of this attack, the Hojo sent his samurai to do battle with the invaders.

When the samurai defenders arrived on the site where the Mongolians landed, the Mongolian aggressors launched a hail of arrows at the massed samurai who stopped and waited orders. The samurai beat on their shields and yelled battle cries, giving notice to the Mongolian hordes of their intent to do honorable battle.

The Mongolians replied to this threat with a deafening drum roll lasting throughout the battle yet to come. This constant drumbeat so terrified the samurai horses they bolted uncontrollable, with many steeds breaking free and fleeing their masters. Gathering the remaining herd for battle, the samurai mounted their steeds and rode at the Mongolians, proudly announcing their names and making challenges to the invaders of single, honorable combat by the sword. The Mongols were aware of the samurai's devotion to honor and opened their ranks to the advancing Japanese, making them believe they would receive their wish. The Mongol warriors allowed the samurai to enter deep in their army before closing ranks, trapping and savagely slaughtered the samurai to the last man, by attacking the warriors in force in great numbers.

The samurai defenders showed one tactic employed by the Khan wasn't going to work on them. The campaign of creating panic in the enemy defenses was wasted on these samurai. Another cry of anger and beating of their shields rose from the remaining ranks of samurai; they were stunned by this barbarian act committed against their attacking warriors. They massed another hundred samurai horseman who rode fool hearted forward as did the first wave of samurai, against their less than chivalrous Mongolian adversaries. Ninety nine of these fearless warriors were butchered outright by the overwhelming enemy fighters who attacked the samurai in large packs rather than one on one, leaving the commanding officer of the samurai to carry on. The samurai were unprepared for this style of mass attack warfare. The Bushido, the samurai code of law laid emphasis on their individual challenge and the combat of the soul of the warrior.

With the drums freezing the Japanese in place, the Mongols advanced on the samurai defenders, using a new weapon the Japanese never seen before. The deadly cross bow which sent enemy arrows further and with more power and accuracy. They advanced in huge bodies of troops so packed tightly in massive detachments no light passed them. The Mongols opened the attack by firing showers of arrows at random into the defending samurai ranks. Realizing there were no gallant antagonists to challenge to individual combat, just mass of Mongolians marching against them. The samurai aroused from their stupor and offered heavy resistance before fighting fiercely and bravely.

The Mongolian hordes fought the samurai wielding swords. The samurai sliced and hacked into the leading elements of Mongolian forces. The Mongols resorted to fire giving exploding weapons launched by catapult, knowing the Japanese warriors' fear of fire and destruction fire could bring to their cities and towns made mostly of wood and paper. The samurai being soldiers of training and discipline, adapted to this tactic of fighting, and they attacked in controlled waves from different angles at a time. After a time, the fighting skills of the samurai forced the Mongolians to make a tactical retreat to the sea from whence they came, but not before setting the village ablaze as they retreated from Japan. Once their armada was out to sea, a great storm arose, capturing the enemy fleet and causing much damage to the invaders of the Khan. Sinking many warships and losing countless soldiers to the roaring surf. and breaking the back of their first invasion of Japan. The survivors were forced to return to China.

Undaunted by his defeat at the hands of the samurai defenders, Kublai Khan sent more emissaries to Japan demanding homage and loyalty to his ever growing and expanding Mongolian empire in China. In both instances the Mongolian embassies were killed. Infuriated by this action ordered by the Emperor of Japan, the Khan planned his second attack on the Japanese islands. He amassed an army ten times the size of the first invasion fleet. Armed with two thousand ships and one hundred and fifty thousand troops and horses, the Khan's troops set off for the islands. On their journey the invading Mongolians attacked the smaller islands off the coast of Japan. This time to their surprise, they found Tsushima and Ikishima deserted.

In the summer of 1281, countless soldiers from the Khan's second invasion army landed, this time on the northern coast of the Japanese island of Kyushu. But by the time of this second invasion, the samurai had plenty of time to fortify their coastal defenses against the new horde of invaders. In some cases the Japanese defenders constructed long stone walls running the length of the shoreline from which the samurai launched thick clouds of arrows of their own, thus stopping the invasion forces from landing on their land and trying to fight from their boats.

With the ability to stop the enemy armada from coming ashore, vast numbers of samurai were afforded time to swarm to the island's defense. The Japanese harassed the invaders before they could approach the main coast. Samurai boarded small fishing boats and sailed out to meet the invaders head on, mounting daring hit and run attacks on the larger ships with arrows, using the cover of darkness to make good their escape.

As the enemy ships approached Japan's coast, large numbers of samurai swam out to attack the vessels. The daring attacks destroyed a number of enemy ships at sea. On one occasion, forty samurai swam to one troop ship floundering in the surf and chopped the heads from the crew and fighters left aboard the stricken ship. Then the samurai swam to shore with the heads clutched in their teeth by the hair, and placed them on wood spears on the beaches to serve as warning to the Mongolian army waiting to invade the island.

All the attacks against the Khan's mighty armada served the purpose of forcing the Mongolian invaders to remain at sea for long periods of time at the mercy of pounding surf and turbulent tides, and stifling under the heat from the summer sun. Water and food provisions became a serious problem to the Khan's invasion forces trapped afloat on the ocean, and the Mongolian invaders were soon forced to slaughter and eat their horses for food, and drinking their blood for life giving fluids.

After fifty days of fierce battles on the ocean and land with the Mongolians able to fight their way ashore, the outcome hung in the state of indecision. The summer days of warring gave way to the dreaded typhoon season. The once clear bright sky held the darkening and threatening clouds of the typhoon spell. Then, in the early morning hours of August 14th, 1281, the prayers of the samurai were answered when the first of the mighty storms wracked the islands of Japan.

A fierce storm made its way on shore capturing the remaining fleet of Mongolian invaders in the open seas. For two days raging winds blew, mauling the enemy ships at sea and buildings on shore, sweeping soldiers on shore out to sea, and drowning those trapped in the ships on the water. On the closing night of this immense storm, the worst winds blew. The kamikaze or the divine wind blew hard and long, surpassing the destructive winds of the storm of the day before. It smashed the once great Mongolian armada, destroying many remaining ships and scattering the others to the far off corners of the four winds.

When the storm blew itself out and calmer weather returned, thousands of enemy troops were washed ashore. Many alive but unable to fight due to exhaustion. The samurai marched the shore, dispatching enemy warriors they came across. The enemy who had fight in them after their ordeal of battling the kamikaze winds, tried to carry on with their fight, but they were forced to surrender and fell to the way of the sword.

THE DOWNFALL OF THE HOJO REGENTS, THE END OF THE KAMAKURA ERA AND THE RETURN OF POWER TO THE CAPITAL, KYOTO

With the defeat of Kublai Khan's second invasion forces, the samurai united as never before. For the first time in Japan's courageous history, many samurai from different clans fought side by side as one against a foreign enemy. After the war ended, the samurai demanded pay from the Regents. The Hojo Regent Tokimune unable to tax the people further had no other way to raise the money needed to pay his samurai for their services. The war with the Khan armies was different than wars carried out on the mainland of Japan. Here, with the end of this war there were no captured lands to divide among the samurai or their feudal land owners, no caches of captured food and valuables to be used as payment, and no women to give away.

The demands from the warriors who defeated the Mongols placed a strain on the economy of the Hojo government based in Kamakura. The Hojo made requests for monies and food from the land owners, the daimyos he appointed to govern the lands he gave for their services, and his pleas fell on deaf ears. With the neglect of the samurai who fought on his behalf, and after the discovery there was no place to give for these samurai who demanded land for payment of their services, bands of Ronins formed. These criminal samurai were from many defeated clans who weren't absorbed into the ranks of the conquering clans.

In 1284, the leader and the last great generals, Tokimune Hojo died. The leader of Japan whose military mind led hordes of samurai in the defense of Japan against the Mongols was gone. With his death, the demise of Kamakura began. Tokimune Hojo's successors failed to lead the country in this time of need. They lacked the man's inspiration and abilities of leadership, and the drive that carried Tokimune Hojo on to his greatness in his rule over Japan. Just as they did during the short time of the Jokyu Disturbance, the Imperial Family understood the weakness of the Kamakura bakufu as an opportunity to make their move against the ruling Hojo government and leadership, and their want to restore Kyoto as the seat of power for Japan.

From the beginning of 1318, the Imperial throne belonged to Emperor Go-Daigo, the second Emperor in the Go-Daigo line to rule the throne of Japan. The latest Go-Daigo to assume the Imperial throne was an ambitious man who once made up his mind. He showed by thoughts and actions he was going to end the existence of the outlying bakufus and bring the seat of power to Kyoto. The Go-Daigo made sweeping changes in the beginning months of his rule, abolishing the hallowed belief in the Cloistered Emperor. He made it clear to those who observed his government he was determined to rule Japan as its Emperor. Thus insuring the independence of the Emperor through his action. The lack of affirmative military action by the Kamakura bakufu, or outlying bakufu's, incited the Emperor to challenge the Kamakura bakufu's dominance.

When the Hojo Regent realized what the Emperor was attempting, he sent out an army from the Kamakura bakufu to challenge the Emperor's orders. Emperor Go-Daigo received advance warning of this army from Kamakura's approach, and it gave him time to prepare for the attack. Go-Daigo requested and received help in the form of samurai from the warring monks of Mount Hiei Buddhist bakufu, because the Emperor appointed his eldest son, Prince Morinaga, to become Abbot to the sohei monks. In this way he maintained control of the unpredictable monks. The Emperor had the wherewithal to make monetary offerings to the Buddhist bakufu of Nara. This was wise on his behalf because it inked the bakufu who controlled the high lands on which the army from Kamakura had to travel upon against his seat of power in Kyoto.

But as before in the turbulent history of Japan's warring past, the plot of the Emperor was uncovered by spies sent from Kamakura. In the early days of September of 1331, the Go-Daigo was forced to flee Kyoto under pressure, and he headed for the safety of the Todia-ji in Nara. Again the Emperor didn't leave Kyoto before taking with him the symbols of the Emperor's sovereignty, the Imperial Regalia. The highly regarded Imperial Regalia consisted of three honored objects which forever insured the holder the throne of Japan. These were the Mirror, the great Sword, and the comma shaped Jewels.

The dangerous Todia-ji monks informed the Emperor they wouldn't be able to fight off the attack from the Kamakura soldiers marching on their bakufu. So Go-Daigo was forced to move to the safety of Kasagi where another bakufu of monks let it be known they would protect the Emperor of Japan. The monks welcomed Go-Daigo and set out to reinforce their defenses for the pending attack from the Kamakura forces, but this attack never came about. Instead, the Kamakura army attacked the sohei monk bakufu at Mount Hiei, destroying the bakufu and forcing Prince Morinaga to flee, isolating Go-Daigo at Kasagi. The decision to attack the monks on Mount Hiei dealt a blow to the feared monk's bakufu where the Go-Daigo took refuge. These warrior monks were depending on reinforcements coming to their aid from Mount Hiei. Now, with their destruction the monks worked by themselves protecting the Emperor in hiding.

After the attacks on Kasagi began, the ruling party of Kamakura tried through political means to force the Emperor to abdicate his Imperial throne. When he refused to step down, the Hojo leaders made the extravagant decision to raise a member from the Imperial family loyal to the Hojo's rule, to take the throne of Japan in the Emperor's absence. Go-Daigo was officially deposed by the Hojo Regents, but the newly appointed Emperor was still unable to be elevated to the throne of Japan, because the ruling Go-Daigo had the Imperial Regalia in his possession.

Infuriated he was unable to install his choice to rule Japan, the Hojo ordered attacks on Kasagi intensified, in an attempt to capture the Emperor and seize the Imperial Regalia. Upon hearing of the attacks, a samurai rose from the ranks of the soldiers, to take up the fight for the Emperor. Samurai Masashige Kusunoki, a renowned fighter prized for skills at warfare and loyalty to the Emperor, fought from his stronghold of Akasaka in the province Kawachi, in the western foothills of Mount Kongo. Masashige gave refuge to the Emperor's son Prince Morinaga, and together defended his camp against the warriors sent to destroy the Emperor from Kamakura.

The loyalists, who served the Emperor faithfully, fought bravely against the Kamakura samurai. Short on troops and supplies to keep the few he had fighting, Kusunoki had only the terrain to stop the over running of his defenses. The inevitable happened in the eleventh month of 1331 when the resistance waned and collapsed. Instead of committing seppuku as samurai are taught from the day they were born, the two Go-Daigo defenders escaped to Akasaka.

Once the Emperor was informed without reinforcements of sohei monks from Mount Hiei, the task of protecting the Emperor was seriously in doubt; Go-Daigo fled the monk's protection and tried to make his way to his son's side. On his way to join his defenders, Go-Daigo was captured by a scouting party sent from Kamakura, and brought to the Rokuhara bakufu in Kyoto. After a trial, Go-Daigo was exiled to the baron island of Oki, to live out his years far from any army who might pick up arms for his cause.

Samurai Masashige Kusunoki returned to his stronghold, but this time he built a stronger and easier defensible camp higher up on the steps of the impenetrable south side of Mount Kongo. From this stronghold he and his samurai inflicted devastating losses on the army sent from Kamakura. The inexpertly strong resistance from so small a defending army surprised the Regents, and the leaders were left with no choice but to reinforce the attacking army.

In 1333, three massive armies were massed, and sent out from Kamakura in an attempt to purge the rebel Imperial defenders from their stronghold once and for all. The first army was to be led by Aso, ordered to attack the enemy encampment at Kamiakasaka along the main Kawachi road. The second army being led by Osaragi was ordered to attack Yoshino. Once these two armies were successful in destroying the resistance from these positions, they were to join forces with the third army, creating one massive Kamakura army scheduled to attack Kusunoki's stronghold at Chihaya on Mount Kongo. They were to take the warrior alive.

Kusunoki withstood every assault mounted against his fortification. He enjoyed success fighting the army of Kamakura using not only his warrior's skills, but the terrain. Huge boulders were sent crushing down on the attackers, caving in mountain passageways and cutting them off from their army. Kusunoki dispatched all trapped troops of his enemy. He launched clouds of arrows to rain down on the enemy working their way up the rough terrain of the side of the mountain. Kusunoki's stronghold was never breached by the soldiers from Kamakura, and they were fought to a standstill. Stories of Kusunoki's stand against such an overwhelming force, along with tales of his defiance and honors bestowed on him by the attacking enemy. Spread across Japan, and were instrumental in forcing the exiled Emperor to return to the mainland.

In the fourth month of the year 1333, the true Emperor of Japan, Go-Daigo landed on the Hoki Province on the coast of the Japan Sea, west of Kyoto. The response from all who met the Emperor's reappearance on the mainland distressed the Kamakura Regents. Seeing this as a threat to their rule, the Kamakura bakufu sent two more armies with orders to destroy Emperor Go-Daigo and his followers.

General Takaie Nakoshi, a highly respected Hojo relative was to lead the massive army mounted from the east, and General Takauji Ashikaga, a direct descendant of the

Minamoto clan, and leader of one of the most wealthiest families from Eastern Japan, led the second army to its targets. The armies set out in different directions from Kyoto to destroy the Emperor.

On his way to attack Hoki, General Takaie Nakoshi was felled upon by a superior army led by the rebel Samurai, Norimura Akamatsu. The general was killed in the exchange. The remaining forces from Nakoshi's army returned to Kyoto where they joined forces with the second army commanded by General Takauji Ashikaga, in command of Kamakura soldiers in western Japan. Being a wise general, Ashikaga realized the opportunity his to command. He was aware with his family's royal lineage; he alone would be able to demand his rightful call to become Shogun of Japan. He was certain the long sought after title would be bestowed on him from the captive, grateful Emperor if the soldiers under his control were used properly.

General Takauji Ashikaga knew his future rested with Go-Daigo, and not with the weakened Hojo Regents. He knew Samurai Kusunoki's army was demonstrating the weaknesses of the Hojo armies to the rest of Japan. So he seized on the moment and changed his alliance from Hojo Rule, now supporting Go-Daigo. He wisely turned his army from the pursuit of the Emperor, and attacked the army defending the Kamakura bakufu headquarters at Rokuhara at Kyoto. Ashikaga's forces overwhelmed the Rokuhara defenders and resistance collapsed, allowing his forces to capture the city in the name of the Emperor. Go-Daigo was returned to his throne, but not before he allowed the Emperor who was supported by Hojo to live.

When the news of the collapse of the Kamakura bakufu at Rokuhara reached the Imperial defenders led by Samurai Kusunoki at Chihaya. The siege ended with many Hojo samurai going over to the Imperial defenders, thus allowing Kusunoki's rapidly enlarging army to descend from his stronghold. With the Hojo strengths lying only in eastern Japan, its demise were soon written on the clouds hanging over the Kamakura capital bakufu.

On the six month of the year 1333, the Kamakura bakufu finally fell under staggering attacks mounted against the defenders by an Imperial army led by Samurai Yoshisada Nitta. This fearless leader organized other leaderless rebel clans, and the large groups of samurai who floated around the Kozuke province looking for direction. Together, this new army descended on the Kamakura bakufu. Yoshisada Nitta used the tactic of splitting his army in three forces, and together the three columns fought through the narrow mountain passageways, which afforded Kamakura much of its natural defense.

It was said by many samurai the forces of Samurai Yoshisada Nitta's army might have enjoyed divine intervention, mainly from the Sun Goddess, Amaterasu. It was also said Yoshisada offered his blood soaked sword to the Sun Goddess, who took it with reverence, and in return she rolled back the waters of the Ocean, affording Yoshisada and his army a dry coastal route to attack the defenders of the Kamakura bakufu. From this direction his army could easily attack the bakufu from the least possibly defended position.

After nine days of savage hand to hand combat through the tunnels making up the defenses of the Kamakura bakufu, the remaining bakufu defenders who numbered less than a hundred strong, along with their deposed leader Hojo, retreated to a Buddhist temple to make their last stand. Totally cut off from reinforcements or supplies, and seeing their situation as hopeless, the last warriors of the Hojo clan committed suicide, while Kamakura burned about him.

The collapse of the Kamakura bakufu marked the end of the Hojo rule, and it brought the Imperial capital of Kyoto back in focus for all who dwelled in Japan. Go-Daigo's restoration to the Imperial seat of power was complete and installed where it truly belonged. In Kyoto.

THE RISE OF THE ASHIKAGA SHOGUNATE

The early Muromachi period, as the Shogun General Takauji Ashikaga time of rule became known by, began in the year of 1333 with the return of Japan's rule to Kyoto after the collapse of the Kamakura bakufu and the installation of the Emperor Go-Daigo as supreme ruler over Japan. But his return to power was far from what the Emperor envisioned. As many Hojo Regents before him, his administration was soon plagued by hordes of samurai making demands of land rewards for returning him to the seat of power in Japan. The samurai were disappointed and displeased when they received no bounty for their service to the Emperor during the Hojo wars. Of all samurai, none had more to be rewarded for, and none were more disappointed than General Takauji Ashikaga was.

In reading the unrest written in his eyes, Emperor Go-Daigo decided to remove him from the capital by ordering him to mass an army, and capture the Kamakura capital which had recently been conquered in the name of the Hojo ruler by one of his surviving sons. General Takauji Ashikaga did as ordered and within a short period of time, he vanquished the young rebel son and his small army, making Kamakura his own bakufu to rule over.

The upset general took command of the old headquarters and word filtered back to Go-Daigo the general was acting suspiciously to his rule. Emperor Go-Daigo paid little attention to this problem, he was satisfied to have the trouble making general out of the capital, and he never imagined he would dare to raise an army against his rule. But during the second month of 1336, it was reported to the Emperor that General Ashikaga was marching a great army against Kyoto with one idea in mind, to place General Takauji Ashikaga as the next Shogun of Japan.

Ashikaga was a clever general, and he seized on the rivalries still existing between the warring monks of Miidera, and supporters of Go-Daigo, the sohei monk Ninja's of Mount Hiei. He allied himself with these fierce and respected fighting monks who were in the midst of carrying out another one of their unending squabbles against the sohei monks of Mount Hiei. Ashikaga underestimated the Miidera monk Ninja's hatred of the Mount Hiei sohei warrior monks, and they outright refused to support his army and or his current ambitions.

The general's march on Kyoto was further plagued by countless attacks from these fearsome warrior Ninja monks, and his forces were soon so depleted his once great army was defeated by the Emperor's larger armies. His army was driven out of the capital and were pursued by Go-Daigo's army into the narrow straits separating Honshu from the Kyushu province, where General Ashikaga was forced to cross over to the southern island for support and protection.

The wise general began to raise a series of suspicions against the Emperor and his rule over Japan, and he was able to unite these suspicions with new complaints of Kyushu samurai who fought so bravely for the Emperor, and they received nothing in return for their loyalty. A number of angry clans were talked into supporting Ashikaga, and his soldiers swelled after the swift victory of his forces enjoyed over the defending army of the Emperor at the battle of Tadara Beach. By the sixth month of 1336th year, he felt his army had grown to the numbers needed to afford him success in challenging the army defending the capital city of Japan.

The general began his assault on Kyoto with a joint attack from land and sea. The vastness of his offensive caused panic in the Imperial Court and a fearful Emperor ordered a stand to be taken by his army on the shores of the Minato River, at the fork where the river flows to the sea. The samurai responsible for the fall of the Kamakura bakufu, Yoshisada Nitta had his army stationed at this position by the time Ashikaga's army appeared.

Samurai Masashige Kusunoki, who fought bravely against the Hojo army from his stronghold, warned Go-Daigo not to engage the superior forces of Ashikaga in pitch battle at Minato. He suggested the Emperor leave the capital for the safety offered by the sohei monks of Mount Hiei. Kusunoki also offered to engage in a harassment campaign in much the same way he attacked the Kamakura forces on Mount Kongo. He would fight against Ashikaga's troops until he could wear them down to a much more defeatable force.

But fueled by past victories over all who challenge his rule, the Emperor decided against fleeing the capital, and went against the suggestions of Kusunoki. The Imperial Court with the backing of Go-Daigo, decided on the original battle plan and he ordered the armies of the Emperor to march out. Not wishing to go against the Emperor who he valiantly fought for in the past. Kusunoki had no choice but to agree, and rode off to share the fate as the rest of the Emperor's army, defeat at the hands of the Ashikaga's more powerful armies.

THE GREAT BATTLE OF MINATOGAWA

The great battle of Minatogawa began on a hot, humid and stifling sunny day in the middle of the seventh month of 1336. Samurai Masashige Kusunoki made his stand with the river Minato to his rear, against the powerful onslaught being fought by Tadayoshi Ashikaga, General Ashikaga's favored son. As his force made its opening attack from the river's edge and tried to force a landing of troops in the middle of the Imperial army's flanks. Kusunoki realized this attempt against his forces and fought the attackers to a standstill while the outcome of the full battle still hung in the balance.

Kusunoki's forces could have won the battle if it wasn't for the mistake committed by Yoshisada Nitta. Instead of fighting alongside Kusunoki's troops, Yoshisada decided to withdraw a number of troops from the frontline, when this army from the river landed in his flanks. Yoshisada was hard pressed between two enemy armies, and he was driven from the battlefield suffering horrendous loses to countless warriors who resisted the enemy samurai so fiercely. With the collapse of Yoshisada's warriors, the openings the defeat created, crumbled Kusunoki's defenses. The defeat of Yoshisada allowed the armies of Ashikaga and his son Tadayoshi, and the army from the river led by Hosokawa, to cut off Kusunoki's army.

Cut off from reinforcements and military supplies, and pressured from all sides by an overwhelming Ashikaga army. Kusunoki watched in horror as countless brave samurai were slaughtered in uncountable numbers. Masashige Kusunoki, the famed samurai who defeated the army sent from Kamakura months before on his mountain encampment, decided to commit suppuku. He chose this course of action instead of allowing himself to be taken alive by the enemy forces, and marched through the streets of Kyoto as a common criminal, only to be crucified at the end of his long march, was too much for him to endure.

Kusunoki hadn't committed suppuku in the previous battle when he was surrounded on Mount Kongo, because he was instructed by the Emperor to keep fighting for his cause against all odds. This instruction had the samurai fighting from the mountain tops until Ashikaga turned the tide of war by going over to the Emperor's side, for the short time he was defending the Emperor before turning against him again. But here, on this flat outpost at Minatogawa, the warrior was unable to defend himself properly. The Emperor instructed Kusunoki to fight until there was no hope left. This instruction from his lord and master, opened the door for him, and also allowed Kusunoki to commit the final act of honor and obedience towards his Emperor, suppuku.

Kusunoki sealed his name with many legends of Japan's past. He died the death beloved and sought after by all samurai of respect and honor, motivated by unwavering loyalty and devotion to his Emperor, and commander of life. When the armies of Ashikaga located his body, it was locked in the honored sitting position with his legs crossed under his body, to stop his body from pitching forward in death. His stomach ripped open from one side to the other, and his innards spilled on the breast plate of his armor, resting before his knees on the ground before his body.

The attacking samurai from Ashikaga's army didn't separate his head from the body; instead the warriors accorded his honorable death the final act of honor. The once enemy warriors built a great pyre and there upon it they respectfully laid the body of the honored warrior dressed in his battle armor in the center of the heap. The soldiers laid his breast plate across his chest and set the pile ablaze. Many warriors from Ashikaga's army knelt and paid homage to the fallen samurai, and they kept watch until the fire consumed every part of his honored body.

The wise Ashikaga was driven not by thoughts of deathlessness. His driving force was his family, and for the title of Shogun, once this title was bestowed on him for his deeds in battle, it would live to be passed on from one family member to another for the rest of Japan's future.

After the defeat of the Imperial armies defending positions at Minatogawa, Go-Daigo had no choice but to flee, and once more took up refuge on Mount Hiei under the protection of the feared sohei monks. Upon receiving this information, he ordered his forces to the mountain stronghold of Hiei, with orders to destroy the troublesome monks, and take the Emperor captive. After months of savage fighting with both sides suffering many losses, the Emperor was captured when Ashikaga sent word he was going to allow the deposed Emperor to live out his remaining days in peace in the Tosa province.

Weary of countless years of unending wars and the innumerable deaths suffered by loyal samurai fighting under his name and banner, the Emperor capitulated to the trickery of the military officer, and surrendered to the Ashikaga samurai. He was marched to Kyoto where he was held captive in the castle until he was able to escape in 1337, when he fled to the mountains of Yoshino where he ruled as Emperor over the southern domain of Japan. Yoshino was ideally suited as a defensible fortification, and with his son

Prince Morinaga, the Emperor remained in safety, defeating any small army sent by Shogun Ashikaga to capture him.

The Go-Daigo died in 1348, but Prince Morinaga never came to succeed his father to the throne. The prince died the year before his father. This left Prince Norinaga to rule the southern domain until it was decreed the northern and southern courts should make an alliance, joining the two Japans together forever.

CHAPTER TWO

ASHIKAGA SHOGUNATE, THE GREAT TIME OF DARKNESS

From the years of 1337 to 1392, spanning fifty five years of two ruling Imperial Courts of Japan, each serving to keep the islands of Japan in a state of unrest and mistrust. The lines of Ashikaga Shoguns never returned to Japan's history of once strong feelings of national pride and trust. The Ashikaga's were never powerful leaders and they were unable to control the provinces. This led to fighting between the feudal lords Ashikaga appointed to power.

Unlike the Minamoto clan leader, Yoritomo who was smart enough to remove himself from the trappings of the Imperial Court in Kyoto. Ashikaga fell in the trap of setting up his Court in the city. The reason for this decision was so he could keep an eye on the court and decisions governing Japan's future. Unfortunately the pleasurable way of court life appealed to the new Shogun more than his usual manner of fighting for survival in the provincial headquarters.

When General Takauji Ashikaga proclaimed himself Shogun, he insisted his seat of power be installed on the same site formerly occupied by Yoritomo's mansion. In the twelfth month of the 1336 year, the Shogun left his bakufu in Kamakura in charge of Kwanryo, and after setting up headquarters in Kyoto, he lavished luxuries and magnificence on himself and his closest supporters. In the following months Shogun Ashikaga turned his back on his old bakufu, allowing it to grow in any direction the Governor General chose to take it.

Kamakura rose up from the ashes from the invading Emperor Go-Daigo army. In a short time, the Kamakura bakufu became a second base from which laws and regulations were decided, and administrative code of ethics of Shogun Ashikaga were decreed. Even though enough power returned to the bakufu at Kamakura, it would never return to its original splendor or power. Kamakura never recovered from the slaughter Samurai Nitta's forces visited on the occupants of the old Kamakura bakufu.

In Kyoto, he erected magnificent palaces in the Muromachi quarter of the old city. The Shogun became possessed with one thought, to make Kyoto the cultural center of Japan. He spent great sums of money to entice artists and craftsmen to return to Kyoto to construct and paint the luxury goods demanded by the city. To pay for these extravagances, unprecedented taxes were levied on the shoulders of farmers and merchants. For the first time, discontent rose from the lower classes who once tolerated their position in silence.

The government of Shogun Ashikaga took its true shape between the years of 1338 to 1392. A change in the way

Japan was governed was evident under his rule. The Shogun's regional daimyos served as high officials of government, and also as local military governors (shugo). This change of power lead to the competition for power between regional lords, thus opening the surrounding towns and provinces to many years of unrest, and invasions by regional lords trying to increase their vast wealth and fief, and it also caused the burning and destruction of many small surrounding towns and villages.

The Shogun realized what was happening in the outermost provinces, and tried to put a stop to the unrest by creating dominance over this coalition of shugo houses. Outside the capital, it was the shugo who ruled their province in the name of the Shogun Ashikaga.

By 1392, Ashikaga claimed authority over the coalition of shugo houses numbering twenty members, who held jurisdiction over the forty five provinces making up central region of Japan. The shugo of the ten eastern provinces were made accountable to the shogunate headquarters at Kamakura. The eleven provinces of Kyushu were placed under the supervision of one of their own members appointed Jito, an official accountable to the Shogun. With this power to govern parts of Japan dealt out to so many, the seeds of unrest were forever sown.

THE UNREST

The more Shogun Ashikaga ignored the outer provinces, the more they began to pull away from his rule. He didn't mind this as long as those provinces remained relatively peaceful and paid taxes. Occasionally, he would allow a daimyo to attack an unruly province leader, when he made certain threats against his rule. He had no idea how serious this situation was developing in the sixteen eastern provinces.

Provincial Lord Takehiro Kawasomeru, steadfastly loyal to Ashikaga's rule, was in command of the provinces of Shinano and Kazusa, and had problems with Provincial Lord Motoshige Wakatsuki, constantly trying to pull away from the Shogun's rule, and become a powerful ruling Shogun of Far Eastern Japan. Wakatsuki was in command of Echigo and Shimotsuke provinces. The contention of the problem was Lord Wakatsuki was trying to talk the Daimyo Akihito Takashina into joining his future plans and ambitions. The reason this created interesting problems for Lord Kawasomeru, was because his province was bordered by Kai. Soon, the Provincial land barons were trying to ally sides against each other.

Lord Kawasomeru sent a messenger to Kyoto to inform Shogun Ashikaga of what was transpiring in the eastern provinces. But the Shogun was too busy to organize an army to help his loyal retainer out of the dilemma. He sent a reply stating this was a situation handled best by the daimyos in command. He warned if he was unable to control the provinces under his command, he would have him removed from power, and install a stronger daimyo placed in his stead that would control the eastern provinces better.

He was enraged by the Shogun's lack of concern for his province's loyalty to him. Realizing he wasn't going to get help from the Shogun, he organized the daimyos loyal to the Shogun and himself. He sent messengers out, ordering the daimyos from Kozuke, Nobuhiko Anjoh, Masashi, Terukiyo Meguro, Sagami, the Kamakura bakufu leader, Norimitsu Onishi, Izu, Koichiro Saitow, Kazuza, Haruo Tamaki, Totomi, Asahiko Shiina and Suruga, Taro Murate, to appear before him on the third week of the forth month of the 1339th year, to speak of war against the outcast Lord Motoshige Wakatsuki and his followers.

He waited in Engakuji Castle for the daimyos to appear before him. The castle was ordered increased to its great elegance, paintings were touched up, copper works polished, and carp pools restocked, rock gardens repaired and plantings ordered. The overlord masterminded the layout and construction of his city and castle. Engakuji Castle was separated from the city by a twenty foot wide moat twenty feet deep. The only way to access Engakuji Castle was by three massive gates guarded by a force of samurai. The gates could be closed during times of attack on the castle. Once visitors entered over the moat, they had to pass through the samurai private living quarters separated in three compounds, separating the class of samurai.

The foot soldiers dwelled in the farthest area of the enclosure, the samurai occupied the center compound, and the samurai horsemen and stables occupied the third and largest compound area well away from the castle keep. Before any visitor came upon the main gate, they would see an impenetrable stonewalls rising fifteen feet in the air. All the time the visitor walked through the warrior compound for the castle, he walked up a series of steps or slight inclines.

Engakuji Castle was constructed on top of a man made hill fifty feet above the samurai compounds. From the third floor of the castle which had eight floors prepared to warn the master if treachery was about? The floors were built in the old ways; the fabled Nightingale floors were employed. The wood of the deck was attached to beams in such a way if any assassin dared to tread upon the floor in the dead of night. Specially placed nails and small metal wedges allowed the wood to move barely noticeably. When the boards moved, the pieces of metal would move together, and they would sing the songs of the Nightingale. Each board made a certain note so the master of the castle would know where the assassin was at all times in his castle. From the third floor, the lord could look over his city and watch his servants as they toiled through their work. In the heart of the castle was the well from which they drew drinking water.

Visitors to the castle were forced to go through heavy gates, each laid out to cause the visitor to take a long way to the castle keep. This was to expose assassins to the alert samurai guards before they could reach the master's quarters and do him harm. In the castle were stored enough food, water, and weapons and provisions to withstand a long siege. The master would direct any defense of the castle from the top floor, giving him time to commit suppuku if he found himself cut off and his armies depleted, and he was about to be captured alive by his enemy invaders.

The castle was enormous; covering over two acres, and the main floor was dotted with large reception rooms and kitchens. The second floor was used for visiting dignitaries, families and servants, and personal temples and shrines. The third floor was used for special meetings and quarters of those who the lord wanted separated from the others, and his personal temples and shrines. The fourth and fifth floors were used for the servants and personal guards of the castle. The sixth and seventh floors were put aside for the lord's personal use. The eighth floor contained the Master and Lady's living quarters, and his many consorts and personal guards.

Outside the castle and warriors compound elevated above the town, on the other side of the moat laid the townspeople's district. Narrow streets separated living quarters of the town workers, town samurai and protectors, merchants, and store owners, lay stone fences in the farming areas used as the first line of defense if the castle came under siege by an enemy army. An elaborate fresh water drinking system consisted of a series of moats and canals which carried drinking water to the castle, and human waste out of the city to the stream which went to the river and out to sea. The water from the moats not used for moving human waste was used for irrigation of crops to feed the townspeople and castle dwellers. The large compound housed over thirty five thousand civilians, and everything about the complex was geared for the protection of the castle first, and then the samurai and civilians. His castle was one of the better laid out and most protected zones of Japan.

The Daimyo ordered his servants to prepare the set aside living quarters on the second floor of the castle for the visiting daimyos. They were to be aired out and freshened up, and fresh flowers placed in the rooms. The faint sent of cherry blossoms could be detected on the slight breeze drifting through the castle rooms. The preparations for the meeting had been carried out, and during the second week, all he could do was wait and scream at any who dared to cross his path. This included his pregnant wife who he hoped carried the next heir to his command. Lady Mineko was attended by Kawasomeru's favorite consort, the beautiful Lady Yuko Takenaka.

The overlord was a strong man of thirty three years of age, tall for a Japanese man at six foot three with a barrel chest and stocky legs. His girth was showing signs of spreading, but he was still a man who possessed great strength, and he commanded the utmost respect from his mere presence, and who was well schooled in the ways of the sword and arrow. He had been married for fifteen years to Lady Mineko who was twenty nine, and in perfect shape for a lord's wife. She was with his third child, the first two were daughters, and this one was believed to be a boy child. Lady Mineko's seer informed her so, and he was now under the threat of death if he was wrong.

His first consort, Lady Akiko Hashimoto was of the highest class of women from the Minamoto clan. She was twenty one years old, and blessed with large breasts and a waist and he loved to wrap his hands about. His fingers almost touched when he did this, showing him and all who observed it, she was blessed with a narrow waist. She had long slender legs which made her stand nearly as tall as her master. He was a happy and well contented man who fought with his Shogun master's son, Tadayoshi Ashikaga against Kusunoki and Nitta warriors at the battle of Minatogawa. He was savagely wounded by a blade but managed to fight on and win the recognition as a great fearless warrior. Many times it was heard shouted by him when he began his attacks on the Imperial warriors. "You fools will wish you were born a dog rather than risk my wrath falling on your god cursed foul souls."

ON THE FIRST DAY OF THE THIRD WEEK OF THE FORTH MONTH OF THE THIRTEEN THIRTY NINETH YEAR

The powerful overlord's closest friend and fellow daimyo from Kozuke, Lord Nobuhiko Anjoh, fought side by side with him on numerous occasions, appeared at the main gate to his castle. He had the most to lose if war broke out between the provinces if he didn't ally himself with Lord Kawasomeru. His province was bordered on both sides by Wakatsuki's provinces, and the warlord made no secret he wanted Kozuke for his own, so he could join his provinces together.   Then he would have Lord Kawasomeru's provinces and those loyal to him, bordered on their western flank.   A desired situation in which his enemy would be trapped and defeated.

The narrow street leading to the main gate of the castle was lined by the best of his samurai dressed in full battle gear, paying homage to Anjoh and his party as they rode into the capital. Lord Anjoh's caravan who held many shuttered palanquins, foot soldiers, warriors on horseback and women in serving, stopped at the foot of the gates of Engakuji Castle. Lord Kawasomeru and his Lady with his generals and field officers greeted Lord Anjoh. He bowed politely and Anjoh returned it equally.   The powerful lord was surrounded by his Mononobe palace guards, spread out his hands and welcomed Anjoh as he called out in his booming voice commanding respect. "Lord Anjoh. Ohayo. (Good day) Ikagadesuka?" (How are you?)

"Domo genki desu. (Quite well, thank you.) He replied kindly to Lord Kawasomeru.

"Do itashimashite. (You're welcome) It's a pleasure and honor for me to welcome such a wise old friend on such a fine day. Shall we walk Anjoh-sama? You'll pay me honor to walk with me. Share together the beginning of this fine and glorious day." The overlord said as he bowed and led the way by waving his arm in the direction of the stream leading to the sea.

Lord Anjoh left his party with the castle personnel showing them to their quarters. His samurai were fed and shown to a place where they could relax. Soldiers from both sides never came in swords length of the powerful leaders, as they headed for the stream which fed the moats and canals of his castle. A squad of twenty warriors dressed in armor from both lords, trailed them. All had their hands resting on the tsuka, the hilts of their swords which were cracked two inches out of their scabbards, so the weapon could be easily drawn for action. The guard's eyes searched the area for treachery. Lord Kawasomeru had the wherewithal to order his archers to scout out the area where he intended to walk with his friend. Each warrior took up positions among the trees, rocks, and bushes, showing their presence to the two leaders.

When the two reached the water's edge, Lord Anjoh bent down as he done throughout his life, and picked up a stone and skipped it in the water before speaking. "Lord Kawasomeru, forgive my lack of manner and directness, but it's with a sad heart I'm forced to listen to the worthless threats, and counter threats from those who supported the Shogun to the south, Ashikaga. What is to become of Japan if this talk is allowed to continue unchecked?"

"Ahhh... Lord Anjoh you're a wise man indeed I offer. This is why I have summoned you and the other loyal daimyos to my castle, to discuss this present threat from Wakatsuki's filthy hole." He omitted the sama or lord from Wakatsuki's name, to show Lord Anjoh he was in contempt with the actions of the rebel daimyo.

"Yes Lord Kawasomeru, his words are troubling indeed to my worried mind, and to the minds of my people. The evil words he speaks from his pile ridden arse, makes it difficult to sleep peacefully at night, not knowing what kind of treachery his madness might take next, and when he might unleash it on my province. He's talking like Shogun Ashikaga's sworn teki (enemy) and is upsetting the great Wa (Harmony) of the land."

"Ieeeee! The words from his anus that should be filled with dung should upset you so, but what can you expect from a man who drinks his own urine. Lord Anjoh, you know he has plans for your province." Lord Kawasomeru grunted, his province was blessed with rich deposits of akome (iron ore) necessary for the making of swords for their warriors. This wealth made him the most powerful of the provinces, and no other daimyos would dare attack him unless forced to. It caused the other daimyos to swear loyalty to him for fear of having their akome cut off.

"Ieeeee Lord Kawasomeru, the son of a dog wants to take my land and drive me from it. I piss on him and his ill begotten ancestors. For weeks the dung eater sent raiding parties to my land. They attacked my important villages and towns bordering his foul provinces, and his warriors taking their worth and leave slaughtered civilians in their wake. Lately, every day I'm forced to commit more samurai to defend my borders against such evil raids. I sent messengers to Wakatsuki-sama, complaining of these troubling raids on my lands, and his reply is always the same. The raiders must be Ronin manure eaters hiding in the hills. In his messages, the dung eater assured me none of his soldiers carried out these raids. He offered to send armies to my lands to help protect my villages against further attacks from these supposed foul Ronin dogs."

"What did you tell him of this foul offer, Lord Anjoh?" He asked the other warlord.

"Ieeeee, I'm not an addle leader my Lord, what do you think I told the manure heap born from inhuman ancestors and a foul arse hole? I told the Ronin to greet his dead ancestors and I'd be proud to open the doors for him to travel through. I'd be nothing more than a eta peasant (eta's are the lowest of the low, the ones who prepared bodies for burial and did tasks no one else in Japan would perform) if I allowed myself to be talked into allowing an army of his worthless warriors in my province. I know once Lord

Wakatsuki has an army of dogs in my country, he'll turn them on my people, and I'd be hard pressed to stop the slaughter."

The overlord rested his hand on Lord Anjoh's back as he mumbled. "Lord Anjoh, you don't have to worry about further threats from that dung eater. This is the reason I sent for you and the others loyal to me. I intend to join the provinces loyal to Ashikaga-sama and myself, and go after this fool and all who follow him, and erase them from the earth as it should have been done during the Minatogawa war. If only Ashikaga-sama would've listened to me when I suggested this. Bah, Karma." He cursed and spat on the ground and kicked dirt over it.

"Kawasomeru-sama! It is a great honor. I cannot tell you how pleased I am over this news you shared. If you didn't bring the subject of this dung eater up, I was going to ask a great o negai (favor) of you, because I intended to breach this subject. It's time to do something about this evil to our northeast before he becomes too powerful, and we're unable to stop his growing ambitions." He picked up another rock and sent it skipping across the water.

"Lord Anjoh, the others coming today to join us facing the same problems raised by this dog eater, will receive the same offer of protection as you received. Anjoh-sama, join forces with me and I'll forever erase the evil of those who so dishonor the Shogun, and all loyal rulers of the Eight Provinces. This is the reason I sent for everyone, to ask where your toda chu (loyalty) lay. As you stated, it's time we do something to the one which gives refuge to the lowly bands of Ronin filth creating unrest throughout our provinces."

"Ieeeee, this is great news for my old ears to hear Lord, but how long do you think it'll be before you're ready to mass our combined armies, and attack on the slime dweller?"

He laughed over Lord Anjoh's calling Wakatsuki a slime dweller. It was a great insult leveled on any Japanese person of nobility, let alone a leader as Lord Wakatsuki was supposed to be, as he offered. "Lord Anjoh, it should take me no more than a year's stick of time to organize the troops and supplies I'd need, to carry out a successful campaign against this dog. I hope my attack will be a surprise against him and his lowly Samurai."

"Ieeeee, I doubt that could happen my Lord. Lord Wakatsuki's spies are as thick as head lice on an eta's cursed head I fear." Lord Anjoh exclaimed as he threw his hands over his head. This move made the guards flinch. All were nervous of a sneak attack leveled against the two powerful leaders. Each samurai knew he would meet a slow and painful death if he allowed anything to happen to the overlords as they spoke.

Anjoh realized the stress he caused the guards and smiled. He was one who demanded his warriors remain alert to danger. Many times during his rule of Kozuke, he would disappear in his castle, and make his guards go wild searching for him while he shared tea with his consort in a hidden room, only he and his consort and wife and children knew about.

"Lord Anjoh, how do you feel the others of the regions will vote? I invited the seven provinces I feel I can trust the most. I know Hitachi, Shimosa, Awa, Kai, Hida, Mino, and Owari will go against us when we make demands on Lord Wakatsuki. I'm not to certain of Mikawa, and I was tempted to invite Lord Saburo Okamuda to the meeting to find out where his toda chu stands." Lord Kawasomeru took a quick breath as they watched a quail flutter in flight.

"Ooooyyyyaaaa!" He grunted as he pointed to the quail fleeing from beneath a bush as the two leaders approached it from the path, and from out of nowhere two bamboo arrows flew, both hitting their target and causing the quail to tumble to earth. "It's good to keep my archers sharp, one never knows when they may be needed for protection and defense. This area is great to hunt, neh? (Isn't it) Anjoh-sama, were you wise enough to bring your hunting falcons on this trip to my castle, my old friend?"

"Ieeeee, I'd be nothing more than a worthless fool if I dared went anywhere without my prized birds accompanying me, Lord Kawasomeru." He roared with a wide grin.

"Good, we'll hunt tomorrow at sunrise. I'll send out my beaters before we arrive to warrant a good hunting day for us to enjoy. It'll be good to see your birds in action again." Lord Kawasomeru allowed a smile to cross his lips over the thought of hunting with his bird.

"You pay me personal honor when you know as well as I my Lord, my birds are unworthy to soar in the same skies as your birds. Lord Kawasomeru, need I remind you your birds won every competition since the provinces began holding hunting sessions between each of the provinces."

"Lord Anjoh, it'll give me honor if you'd allow one of my birds to mate with one of your proud birds. Old Leather Eyes would be the one I'd pick for the mating."

"Ieeeee, Old Leather Eyes! Mate with one of my unworthy birds. He's your prized bird. The honor you offer me is too great, one I could never return. The bloodline you'll introduce into my bird's lines, I'd forever be in your debt Lord Kawasomeru."

"Your minor debt will be paid in full if you back me against this common teki (enemy) of ours to the east, along with the rest of the trusted Lords coming to my castle for this meeting, Lord Anjoh. And with that debt being paid in full, it'll also come with the promise of my armies protecting your province, along with all others who'll side with us, Lord Anjoh." He rested his hand lightly on Anjoh's shoulder again.

"Ieeeee, this is impossible, you pay me to great an honor to be paid back in this lifetime. I'll accept this offer of the mating of our birds, forever linking our provinces together through the blood of these young birds, only if you allow me to offer you a blade made in my province by my master blade maker, Ninagawa-san. He's the best in all the provinces."

"Lord Anjoh, now it's you who offer to great an honor. To receive such a fine blade of wealth created by Master Ninagawa-san, is payment for a whole province. I'll accept this Katana if we're even, and I'll honor it all my days. It'll be handed down to my heirs, to remain in my family for all time." He bowed to Lord Anjoh who returned the bow, happy he pleased him.

Their conversation was interrupted by a samurai who rushed up to their side and assumed the position of obedience by kneeling, and placing his weight on his legs, placing his hands palms up and opened. So the lords could see he had no weapons. His neck was exposed in case they didn't want to be interrupted, and either decided to separate his head from his body. The warrior remained in this position with his eyes cast down until he was addressed by his master.

Lord Kawasomeru glared at the young warrior before grunting. "Report! Isogi!" (Hurry)

He looked up and stated Lord Meguro and his procession arrived at the castle's main gate.

"I hope he was offered proper hospitality by you, young fool." The lord snarled at him.

"Hai! (yes) My Lord, Meguro-sama and his travelers have been taken care of by your Castle help. Dozo (Please) take my cursed eyes if this is not a honto (fact), Lord Kawasomeru. I swear this upon my oath to you." The warrior cried in an excited voice to his master.

"Save your worthless eyes fool, I expected they would've been well taken care of. Show Lord Meguro to the reception room on the first floor of the castle, and have him wait until I arrive to meet with him. Anjoh-sama and I'll be up shortly." The lord dismissed the young samurai with a quick wave of his hand, while turning back to Lord Anjoh.

They watched as the samurai almost broke his neck running up the footpath to the castle. Anjoh picked up another rock and bounced it in his hand a couple of times, feeling its weight and balance, then sent it skimming across the stream again, and he smiled.

"Anjoh-sama, you seem pleased with yourself on this fine day, my old friend?" The powerful overlord remarked with a grin on his lips.

"Hai, very Lord Kawasomeru, I received the answers I hoped for. Your backing of my province of Kozuke, and the support of your troops to defend against any invasion of my province. Though I must inform you I'm pleased you didn't invite Okamura to this meeting, I have foreword his sympathies lay more with the lowly dog of the east, Wakatsuki and the pig Lady Etsuko, his foul wife." He snapped as he looked for another rock to launch.

"Iye! (No) I was unaware of this. Are you certain Lord Okamura will go with the manure eating Wakatsuki? I hoped to use his army to cut off support from Owari, using the sea to attack Surrugi or Sagami, to get enemy reinforcements to Kai for support against us. This is disturbing for my ears to absorb, Anjoh-sama. This forces me to change my plan of attack. I'll have to keep the province of Kai cut off from support, or be forced to protect my province from two fronts, Kai to the south and Echigo from the north. Not to mention Kai if it's allowed to be supported by the enemy troops from Owari and Mikawa provinces will be able to send troops against us to flank our soldiers in Musashi, Suruga, and Sagami, and that will leave our provinces of Totomi and Izu open to attacks from the sea.

"But my major concern is Kazusa, this province is surrounded by Shimosa to the north and Awa to the sea. Kazusa is opened to attack from the sea. I'm worried about this province, if we allow it to be over run, Wakatsuki's forces will have us surrounded from sea to sea, and we'll be pressed to keep his forces from attacking wherever he so chooses. I'll send troops to Kazusa to support them, and stop this from happening against me. I can use the excuse I'm in the midst of changing soldiers garrisoned at Kazusa, to keep Wakatsuki off stride. Now I'm forced to court Etchu province to cut Hida off from linking up with Echigo, so I'm not forced to defend three fronts against our enemy. Lord Ichimatsu Fukuyama is a hard man to work with. He's of the nature of defending his lands by himself, and not seeking nor accepting help from anyone."

"Ieeeee, this is true Lord Kawasomeru." Lord Anjoh snapped as he hawked and then spat in the stream. "He's a stubborn but wise leader in Japan, my old friend."

While they spoke and walked up the path leading to the main gate of Engakuji Castle. Before they knew it they were on the street standing before the gate, as the fourth caravan of visitors came down the road. Both lords turned to face the arriving caravan of Lord Norimitsu Onishi from Sagami province and seat of the old capital, Kamakura. His unending procession had numbers of elaborately embellished palanquins. Onishi's province was the second richest of all eastern provinces. Lord Onishi clumsily climbed out of his palanquin because of his wide girth, and walked up to Lord Kawasomeru and Anjoh. All three lords bowed to one another, as Kawasomeru made a series of grunts and hand signals, and his samurai helped the other members of Onishi's cavalcade to their sleeping quarters for their visit to Engakuji Castle.

Onishi introduced the liege lords to his wife and when they drifted away from Lady Tokie, Onishi knew Lord Kawasomeru wanted to speak with him, and he sent her with the others.

The three leaders entered the gate and walked up the road to the castle. Everyone in the compound got out of the way of the lords, all dropping to the ground and bowing, touching their foreheads to the ground. Even the samurai not part of the soldiers guarding the lords, knelt and remained that way until the three lords passed them.

Lord Kawasomeru was the first one to enter the castle, and noticed Lord Meguro was being served Sabazuki. (Sake-rice wine) He rose and bowed to Kawasomeru who returned his bow as graciously. He didn't mind allowing Lord Meguro to wait alone, his province had the least to offer to his plans of war against Wakatsuki. He had no wealth from Akome, and his warriors were poorly trained and ill mannered, and Meguro always needed assistance from the other provinces. If he had his way he would have Meguro replaced. The only use his province served, was to keep Wakatsuki's troops from being able to strengthen Kai troops. No matter, he was bound by loyalty to be friendly to this lord until he was in a position to have him replaced.

He was positive the only solution to the problems facing him and his allies was war. Besides, it was too long since Japan was involved in a good, honor creating war. His warriors were becoming complacent and lazy, and with this complacency and sloppiness. They were becoming apparent, and that would surely lead to certain defeat on the battlefield. The concerned Lord Kawasomeru waited for the niceties to be concluded so he could speak to the three lords. Outside the castle, caravans from Suruga and Totomi province joined and arrived. Lords Asahiko Shiina and Taro Murate entered the reception room, led by palace warriors in all their regalia. Again, the niceties delayed his meeting and Kawasomeru was growing upset. Finally he gave in and had Sabazuki. He decided to wait for the missing Lord Koichiro Saitow from Izu. He turned to the samurai guarding the way to the sleeping quarters on the second floor and nodded. The guard rushed over and remained on his feet but bowed politely.

"Find out where Lord Saitow's caravan is at, fool. I want to start this meeting, I'm unable to begin with these interruptions. Find him and get him here, even if you have to carry him on your foul shoulders!" He hissed in a low harsh voice.

"Immediately my Lord Kawasomeru." The samurai ran from the room. In moments he returned with the information. This time the warrior knelt in the proper position when making his report once he realized Kawasomeru moved from the others. "Lord Kawasomeru, Lord Saitow is one hour's ride from the Castle. I dispatched horsemen to ask the Lord to hurry his pace. I gave instructions if he is riding in a palanquin, he's to get on horseback and leave his caravan, and arrive at the Castle at his earliest convenience. I offered Lord Saitow twelve guards from our palace ranks to ride with him in his haste, I hope I served my master properly."

"Yes, you have done very well indeed. That was very wise on your part young Samurai, I'll increase your wealth by one koku a year." A unit of rice measurement, one koku was enough rice to feed a man for a year. An increase of this much wealth would enable the samurai to afford a second consort if he so chose.

The samurai lowered his head as thanked his lord for the increase of his wealth.

The overlord kicked the samurai, a signal made to show he was dismissed and he should get back to his position. He held up a finger and a servant brought sake. She bowed politely and offered the cup and he growled for show. "Next time one of these fools wants more sake, take your time bringing it and keep it low. I don't want them too drunk and useless until after this meeting's been completed with the fools, and I took all I want from them."

"Hai, Yes, I'll do as ordered Lord Kawasomeru." She offered politely to her master.

"Have the foolish musicians stand by. I want three women to dance for our guests. Remind them I want to see plenty of skin while they dance for these fools. Have them not wear under kosodes, I want to keep their attention glued to them for as long as I can command it, woman."

The servant didn't respond instead she smiled, knowing what her master wanted from the dancers lent to him by the Mama-san of the Third Tea House. "It shall be as you ordered."

He turned to the province rulers when he heard his name mentioned. He walked up to Lord Anjoh and bowed, showing the proper respect for indoors. Meguro, the obnoxious one was already feeling the effects of the rice wine and was acting like an ass. He displayed bad manners by grabbing one of his servants in a most rude of manners. Lord Kawasomeru walked to the other lords and spoke with Anjoh and Onishi who told them of the damage done to his city by Samurai Nitta, when he laid siege to the old capital. He ignored his endless complaints, knowing Onishi was happy when he was giving Sagami.

Lord Saitow strolled in the room guarded by samurai. He was surprised to see the other rulers gathered in one room. He was unaware the others were summoned to the castle. He was under the impression this was a private summon between him and Lord Kawasomeru.

"Ahhh... Lord Saitow, I see by the expression written on your face, you're surprised with everyone attending the meeting. All will be explained to you in due time. Sake?"

"Hai, dozo (please) Lord Kawasomeru, I'd like sake yes. I must also attend to personal needs for the immediate moment, my Lord of the land."

"Forgive my bad manners, of course you have to attend to yourself and your staff. I'll have sake waiting when you return." Lord Kawasomeru bowed graciously to the trusted liege lord.

Another fifteen minutes of small talk continued while the warlords got reacquainted, some hadn't seen each other in a year. When everyone was assembled in the reception hall, he called the meeting together. Again he had to wait until the daimyo's generals entered. He wanted input from everyone, even the warrior leaders who would control the fighting. The generals were on one side of the room with the wood double covered coffered ceilings, the cedar beans with copper inlaid work, and carved dragons on each end of the beams supporting the roof. There was a central wall with nothing but highly carved and decorated columns holding up a half wall, which came down from the fifteen foot ceiling, forming the center support structure of the room. The floor was covered with thin kneeling tatami mats, they were for the daimyos, and the straw unpadded mats were for the generals and other warriors attending their generals.

Any lord or general within ten feet of Kawasomeru was unarmed. An honor guard of eight of his best sword samurai, sat protectively at the base of the six inch high platform where the lord sat. The samurai rested their hands on their tsuka (hilt of their sword) and cautiously eyed the gathered nobles, each searching the group for signs of treachery.

The respected overlord took his position on the platform and sat on an overstuffed silk mat more a pillow. Before him rested a lacquered bamboo table which had a ream of rice paper along with brushes and ink and his gunsen, a folding war fan.   Behind him mounted on the wall was his gumbai uchiwa, a non folding war fan. The appearance of the fans left in the open as they were, left no doubt in anyone's mind why the lords of his provinces were summoned. To his left, his battle armor was displayed on the wood stand and his heavy, two handed no-dachi sword was crossed by a kihuchi yari one sided spear.

He was dressed eloquently in a light green silk under kosode with a heavier darker green kosode. He wasn't wearing the usual kataginu, the stiffened wing like jacket which lay across his lap. His swords tucked in his sash as he knelt on the mat. One was his katana, the fighting sword which was said to have been forged in the fires that raged in Mount Fuji, by the master sword maker Sugahara. The other was his wakizashi, the shorter stabbing sword forged by the same hand. To his right sat Old Leather Eyes. His hair and beard were perfect.

Two lords hadn't taken time to change from their travel kosode, (Kimono) they were Anjoh and Onishi. The other lords were given time to change into more comfortable kosodes, while he spoke with Lords Anjoh and Onishi outside the room. Even Lord Saitow took time to change from his travel clothes before the meeting was called to order. The lord's soldiers were dressed in battle dress, adding to the splendor of the meeting, and giving it the proper importance.

The powerful Daimyo surveyed the dignitaries and trusted military officers before he spoke to them. He remained seated, but grunted every word in his loud booming and commanding voice, as his threatening gaze shifted from one lord to the other. "Huh trusted Lords of the realm, we find ourselves faced with the dangerous threat to face our eight provinces in many years past. Everyone gathered here knows full well that the worthless outlaw Lord Wakatsuki and his hordes of lowly Ronin filth have been sending armed raiding parties to Kozuke and Kazusa provinces. I have information of his treachery." Lord Kawasomeru held up a folded scroll and shook it rapidly then continued with his words. "This paper before me has information from my spies in Owari province. It states Wakatsuki ordered Lord Yoshizawa of Owari province to assemble a sea faring army to conduct raiding parties into Totomi and Izu provinces."

A roar arose from the lords and generals of the threatened provinces. He received more support than he dared hoped, the rest of the lords and their military officers joined in on the demonstration of anger aimed against Wakatsuki. Lord Kawasomeru knew no one would dare challenge the paper he held aloft, although it was barren of printed words. He continued waving it around to infuriate the leaders further.

"I have certain information that states Wakatsuki plans to create much havoc between our peaceful provinces while inciting the outer provinces to join his foul cause against us, just as I am trying to organize the inner provinces to combat this upcoming threat to our peace. I have further information once this filth eater organized the outer provinces to rise up against us, he will attack Kozuke with his forces. So he can unite both of his foul Echigo and Shimotsuke provinces together, and drive a deep wedge into the middle of our defenses."

An angry grumble rose through the ranks of the gathered, but he held up a hand to silence it as he offered. "Once this manure eater has driven this wedge in place, he'll attack Musashi and Kazusa provinces, linking his defeated provinces with Kai and opening up our eastern front to attack. He plans to unite Hida, Mino, and Owari provinces, and attack our remaining provinces from the east. If this lowly filth eater is successful in his ambitious foul plans, we'll be helpless to defend or stop Wakatsuki's aims. I figured in three years of fighting, all our provinces would belong to Wakatsuki, along with other provinces he organized against us.

"Once we're destroyed, his plans are to attack his allies as a vicious dog would attack a helpless cat. Wakatsuki will not be happy until he owns the entire eastern region of Japan, and then he'll ordain himself Shogun of the East. This I'll not allow to happen as long as there is breath left within me!" Lord Kawasomeru bellowed as he leaped to his feet and rested his hands on his hips. He glared harshly at the gathered lords, ignoring the generals off to his side.

Lord Anjoh rose and bowed towards Lord Kawasomeru who recognized him to address the members of the meeting. "You have something to add to this war council, Anjoh-sama?" He growled as he stared at his lifelong friend, hoping he took the subtle message he tried to convey when they were speaking by the stream earlier in the day.

"Hai Kawasomeru-sama, I have information." He said as he bowed then added. "I'm aware Mikawa province plans to join forces with the godless Wakatsuki, and the Lord plans to send sea going troops to attack Suruga and Sagami from the sea and is planning to…"

"The son of a motherless dog would not dare to attack my province! I'll see his head resting on a spike, and I'll piss on it for considering this cursed course of action against me! Kamakura is a province of respect and vast wealth. To attack my province would not only be fool hearted, it would be a serious insult to the other provinces of Japan. This action would bring down the wrath of Shogun Ashikaga and his countless troops on the worthless head of this Ronin filth eater." Lord Onishi growled as he rose and interrupted Lord Anjoh's words.

Lord Kawasomeru picked up a second scroll and held it high. "Here is Shogun Ashikaga's response to my request he send troops to help defend the eastern region of his realm against Wakatsuki invasions. The Shogun states he's too busy reconstructing Kyoto to send troops to our defense. He orders me to organize the army needed to maintain peace in the region. It seems his castle and shrines mean more than the eastern realm." The angry Daimyo threw the paper at the feet of Lord Onishi who in return, stared at it until a general from his ranks rushed over and retrieved it so he could read it.

Lord Onishi opened the folded rice paper with the broken Imperial seal on it, and read what he just spoke. He refolded it and placed it in the inner folds of his kosode and returned to his kneeling position of respect at his feet.

A murmuring arose in the meeting room with the other excited lords and generals trying to figure out what their next move would be. Lord Anjoh rose and turned to Lord Onishi and grunted in a harsh tone. "Speak Onishi-sama! Is it as Lord Kawasomeru stated to us? Ashikaga-sama has bestowed unto Kawasomeru-sama's hands the defense of the eastern realm!"

Lord Onishi remained kneeling and his eyes cast towards the ground as he grunted loudly. "Hai! It is as Kawasomeru-sama has stated."

More murmuring from the dignitaries and their generals filled the large meeting room until Lord Kawasomeru raised his hand and waited for silence to return. He remained on his feet staring at the lords who stared back with questioning, worried faces. He allowed himself to be pumped up for his next speech.

Lord Meguro couldn't take the suspense and jumped to his feet, causing the palace guards to pull their swords as a warning his move caused alarm to their lord, and he better be seated before he lost his head. The guards left their position of watch and scurried between Lord Kawasomeru and Lord Meguro. Lord Meguro ignored the threat from the guards as he bellowed for all to hear. "What is it we're to do to defend ourselves against the overwhelming forces under Wakatsuki's foul control? We lords of the smaller provinces are in no position to defend ourselves against an attack from so many enemy provinces, especially at the same time. What are we to do? Sure, you're comfortable with the knowledge that you have the ability to defend yourself and your provinces against any threat from an enemy force leveled against you, no matter how large it might be. Lord Kawasomeru, you have the wealth and massive army to defend your two provinces. How do we defend ourselves?”

Lord Kawasomeru grunted an order and his guards relaxed, knowing Lord Meguro was no threat to their lord and master. Lord Meguro was upset, and he was depending on this weak minded warrior who could no longer control his water, to be the driving force to give the emphasis to his next speech. The guards returned to their positions of protection at the foot of the platform. The remaining guard wouldn’t move until Lord Meguro returned to his position. Once he did, the last samurai returned to his place. But never took his eyes from Lord Meguro, nor took his hand from his tsuka. His sword remained half out in case it was needed.

“Ahhh… Meguro-sama of course it would be you who would demand we act. To offer what has ruptured your stones.” Lord Kawasomeru decided to give Lord Meguro face by making it seem he was responsible for his words. “The reason I requested you to appear at this audience is so I can do what Wakatsuki is attempting before he’s successful. He’s trying to organize the outer provinces against us. It’s my intention we, the inner provinces do the same, and organize to defeat this Ronin before he’s powerful enough to overwhelm us. Once we’re organized, we, all provinces loyal to me will mass our armies to one, and we’ll send smaller armies from the one army to protect Kozuke from invasion. The smaller provinces, such as Izu, Sagami, and Totomi, will have enough samurai from this army to defend against any enemy attack…”

Lord Meguro called out from his kneeling position. "Lord Kawasomeru, what about my province? Will I be afforded this protection you speak of?"

This time he glared at Lord Meguro for daring to interrupt him. "I'm willing to overlook your bad manners of calling out. If it happens again it'll cost you your head."

There was a protest raised from the generals of Lord Meguro, but a glare from Lord Kawasomeru brought the protest to a swift end as he continued with his threat. "And the heads of his Generals if they so choose to interrupt me again."

When quiet returned, he began his words anew. "Meguro-sama, your province is strong enough to offer troops to the smaller provinces I mentioned. It's the cost that makes your bowels loose and churning. You have nothing to fear if you, and the other liege lords assembled here, back me faithfully in this upcoming war with Wakatsuki and his godless foul followers."

One after the other, each provincial lord stood and removed their compliance fans from the cuffs of their Kosodes, and opened and held them over their heads. Each general on the other side of the hall rose, and grunted as they held aloft their army's battle banner which showed their liege lords the generals were behind this decision to back Lord Kawasomeru.

He allowed the soldiers and lords to get their blood hot before he went in his final act of whipping them into a frenzy. When the lord felt the others were angry enough for him to continue with his words of war, Lord Kawasomeru stepped back three paces until he was even with his table, and he picked up his closed Gunsen war fan and raised it to his chest.

The hall quieted with the leaders and officers watching every move he made. With a swift hand movement he snapped the fan open, causing everyone even the guards to roar in compliance with his defiant act. When the reverberation ended, he lifted the fan before his eyes at arm's length, turning his body to the side so all could see his fan, and roared as he lifted his foot in the air, and brought it down heavily on the platform with a thud.

"Ooooyyyyaaaa!" He bellowed deeply and raised his foot a second time. He hesitated a brief second then stomped it with a resounding beat. At the same moment his foot struck the platform, he repeated his roar in his loud, booming voice. "Ooooyyyyaaaa!"

He repeated the battle cry one more time for the gathered. "Ooooyyyyaaaa!"

This time all the lords and generals in the room answered his bellow. "Ooooyyyyaaaa!"

The generals snapped to attention and rattled their battle banners, making a racket as the angry lords repeated the battle cry. The powerful Daimyo stood as one imposing presence, alone and proud on the platform and his hands resting threateningly on his hips. The fan protruding from his hand and streams of sweat streaming down his face. His expression was locked in a sneer as he stared at the others gathered before him.

"I want everyone to commit five hundred warriors and sent them to the masters of your land for training in the art of making war. Each samurai will be raised to rank of warrior leader, so they can control a regiment of samurai. In this war it's my belief the foot soldiers will be more important than horsemen. This war will be fought close to the ground with small bands of fighters engaging in warfare, rather than huge armies engaging at the same time in battles that would bring this war to a speedy end. You'll increase the trained samurai's pay one koku of rice to insure their loyalty to me."

A grumble filled the meeting hall coming from only the seven lords this time.

"Need I remind you how you'll grumble under Wakatsuki's rule. One koku of rice is a small price to retain your province in your control. I want some samurai to be schooled in mountain archery and attack tactics in mass, as the Mongolian devils employed against us at Kyushu. Other soldiers will be trained in tactics of the sword, and the rest will be trained in fighting from horses, using Yumi (Bows) riding at gallop. They'll be trained on how to carry three arrows in their teeth as they fire one, so they can reload their yumi quicker. There are new tactics developed by the trainers over the years we haven't been taking advantage of. It's a waste of money and time to send these masters to China and Korea to learn new strategy of war making if we don't take advantage of them. If your master trainers are unable to handle these retainers, let me know and I'll speak with them."

A strained chuckle came from a few generals, they found hilarity in this statement. The generals knew if Lord Kawasomeru spoke to any master over a problem about following his orders, it would be a complete disaster to the master's health. The angered master trainer would find his head resting on the ground separated from his body. Then Lord Kawasomeru would simply replace the dead master with another.

Lord Kawasomeru ignored the interruption and continued. "This war might be of five years or more because I'm certain once Wakatsuki finds out we're aware of his treachery, he'll change them. I would, and I'd turn to light raids and swift attacks, and fleeing before reinforcements arrived on the scene. My purpose would be to keep the provinces I wish to attack in a constant state of fear and agitation. If I'd resort to these tactics, you can be positive Wakatsuki will. No matter what filth he has sunk to, he's a great tactician, and will do everything in his power to defeat us, whether it be all out war, or a war of attrition, wearing down our will to fight.

"This is why we must count on a long war continuing for many years once we committed to this. I order each of you to have your chonin, (townspeople) your ichiryo gusoku, (rustic samurai) and samurai under your command, to point out it's their hombun (duty) to make male babies to replace the fearless soldiers on the battlefield certain to fall in the upcoming battles."

The lords agreed and gave their pledge to have the retainers prepare for training. When he was assured all were behind him, he snapped his war fan closed which caused another round of 'Ooooyyyyaaaa' to arise. He replaced the fan in his kosode. He next slapped his hands together and five women appeared from each corner of the hall, carrying trays covered with cups of sake and handed them to the lords then generals. There was something about these servants. They were dressed in outer kosode's with no under kosode's. Every time they bent to offer sake to the lords they were exposed. This had the effect he wanted, in no time the leaders were more interested in receiving sake to see naked breasts than worrying about what they had agreed to.

He wanted a breath, the atmosphere in the room was stale, and went out the side door, followed by guards. Other samurai stationed on the balcony sharpened their eye for treachery.

Lord Anjoh watched as Lord Kawasomeru left and follow him. As he entered the terrace area the guards who followed their lord, spun around and removed their swords and aimed them threateningly at Lord Anjoh, until they realized who he was. They bowed and relaxed their stance, placing their katanas in their sayas, (scabbards) but neither warrior set the blade home so they would be able to withdraw them at the first sign of treachery.

A female appeared carrying a tray and two cups of sake, her kosode was resting on her arms, exposing her breasts. She was tall, slender and child like as she stood waiting to be acknowledged by her lord which he didn't do. Instead, he spoke to Lord Anjoh. "Ahhh... my most trusted old friend, I was wondering how long it'd take for you to follow me outside. How do you think it went with the worthless fools in there?"

"You received great face with the others my Lord, and you forced them to come to your side, if they want to retain their leadership over their provinces. It was genius on your part to hold up that blank scroll, and swear it was evidence of Lord Wakatsuki's treachery planned against us when he attacked our provinces." Lord Anjoh hawked, and spat over the rail of the terrace.

"I didn't realize you discovered my attempt at falsehood, but it was necessary. Did this have anything to do with you allying your province with mine?" He asked with a grin.

"Iye! I would've backed you to the fires of Mount Fuji if asked." Lord Anjoh bragged.

"Shall we piss on the deal, in that way we can seal it forever between us, my old friend?"

Both lords stepped closer to the rail and pissed over it, laughing and grunting like children as they passed wind, belched and fumbled getting their members back in their fundoshi, (loincloth) never once considering the young woman standing close by them as they urinated. Lord

Kawasomeru took a cup of sake and offered it to Lord Anjoh as a further honor to him. Anjoh took the gesture as what it was meant for, the honor of being offered the first cup from Lord Kawasomeru. He rightly refused as manners demanded it as he took the remaining one, and slurped the cooling rice wine loudly.

"I must say Kawasomeru-sama you certainly do have an interesting way of serving sake to your special friends." He said as he greedily cupped the young serving girl's small breast.

"It was something I learned from the barbarians when they dared to invaded Kyushu. Every one of our women taken captive were forced to serve them almost naked. It's a pleasurable way to drink. Do you not agree Lord Anjoh?" The powerful overlord said as he fondled a breast. The young woman didn't flinch as the lords paid attention to her body.

He smiled when he realized Lord Anjoh was getting carried away with the young beauty. "Anjoh-sama, it's a shame you chose to bring your wife and consorts. I been experimenting with a Tea House (House of Women) and the Mama-san teaching her Willow Women in the ways of giving pleasure to men. Some women will take your honorable member in their mouths and make the mountain erupt in a most exciting way using only their tongues."

Lord Anjoh stared at Lord Kawasomeru in disbelief before crying. "Ieeeee! I heard of this novel way of erupting one's essence, but I never had the honor to experience it. I must visit this honored Tea House so I can experience this pleasure first hand."

He let out a bellowing laugh as he announced. "Anjoh-sama, you don't have to wait to visit such a house, standing before you is one of the Mama-san's most experienced of disciples. Look, I'll show you how they do this pleasure."

"You?" Lord Onishi cried as he swayed, the sake starting to take effect on him.

"Iye, not me you great fool. She'll show you how it's done properly. Kinue?" Lord Kawasomeru asked more than said to the young woman, not sure that was her name.

"Hai my Lord!" The young beautiful Japanese woman replied politely.

"You heard what I told Anjoh-sama of your fine abilities of giving man pleasure with your mouth. He wishes to witness this experience, and I ask you to show him."

For a brief second, fear showed in Kinue's beautiful eyes, but when her lord next spoke, she immediately obeyed his orders without further hesitation.

"Kinue, on your knees and show Anjoh-sama how you give the special pleasure to a man."

She moved her hands and allowed the kosode to fall from her body and stood naked before the lords and guards. She knelt before Anjoh and fumbled with the front of his kosode until she found him and pulled him free of his loincloth. He was hard as she drew him in her mouth. In what seemed to be less than a heartbeat, he erupted amidst moans and curses, weak in the knees. When he finished, she wiped him dry with her kosode and disappeared in the castle.

The overlord ignored the smile on the guards who dared to watch the act as he asked. "Well, what do you think of this new style of pillowing?"

"Ieeeee my Lord! It's like soaring among the clouds in the Heavens. I must employ this act in the many Tea Houses that serve my province." He announced proudly.

Lord Kawasomeru laughed as he fumbled around in the loose sleeve of his kosode until he found the slip of paper he was looking for then offered it to Anjoh.

Lord Anjoh took the folded paper and stared at it as he asked. "Kawasomeru-sama, what is this you offer me?"

"Anjoh-sama, I took the liberty of absorbing Kinue's contract before you arrived at my Castle. She belongs to me and I happily give her to you as a o negai (favor) for your loyalty. I couldn't begin to make these demands on the other Daimyos, without your support, old friend." He bowed to the stunned Anjoh who looked up at the powerful lord of the eastern provinces, and smiled and returned the bow.

"Kawasomeru-sama, you opened my eyes to new pleasures women of the Soft World offer a man. But as your overly kind offer to breed your prized Falcon, old Leather Eyes to Free Soaring, my prized Falcon, this contract is far beyond earthly worth. I'd find myself not being able to return such a favor." He cried as he refolded the contract and tucked it in his kosode.

Lord Kawasomeru smiled as he watched Lord Anjoh put the contract of Kinue away, knowing he forever linked Lord Anjoh's province to his no matter what happened in the future as he added. "You honor me with your friendship and loyalty. This is enough payment for the few worthless gifts I gave you, Anjoh-sama." He rested his hand on Anjoh's back as they turned and headed to the party in the reception room.

The visiting lord's ladies weren't allowed in the hall during the meeting, so they were unaware of the servants of the Soft World serving the lords more than sake. The generals were shown out the doors before the party began, and the cerebration of the agreement to back Kawasomeru by the lords of the eastern provinces, lasted well in the early hours of morning. There were more servants brought in to insure the lord's pleasures and wants were satisfied. The drunker they got, the more daring they became with the beautiful servants, especially with Kawasomeru explaining and demanding the servants show the lords the moist world of the mouth as he called it.

Come the next day, the servants were gone and the exhausted lords rested on the kneeling mats, nursing hangovers and suffering dry mouths. The morning was jolly as some lords relived the moist world of the mouth with the others. Some vowed to have their courtesans taught this new way of giving pleasure which, unbeknownst to many of the overlords, was shared by many samurai and hemi (commoners) of Japan for years.

The meetings lasted three days, with one ceremony and meeting after the other, each carried out with one purpose in mind, to keep the lords in a state of drunkenness and susceptible to Lord Kawasomeru's demands. On the last day visit to the castle, the women and wives of the lords and generals were allowed in the reception hall. Everyone was served sake and an endless flow of cooked fish, kelp, seaweed dishes and rice cooked in different fashions.

The ladies were shown a night of majestic dress and fine food. They enjoyed speaking with the other ladies of the realm, sharing lovemaking stories and abilities and telling of how their servants disobeyed them. They spoke of how their husbands were always searching for new courtesans to make their nights pass enjoyably. Each lady wore kosode's made from expensive silk imported from China. Each tried to be the center of attention by having the most exquisite kosode draped over their bodies. The last night was the most impressive with the party lasting late. Some lords made for their sleeping quarters on the second floor. The outer edges of the hall were lined with each lord's samurai, dressed in kosodes as they stood guard over their lords.

For the most part, Kawasomeru stayed apart from the other lords, always surrounded by Anjoh and Onishi who his existence depended on, more than the others. It was decided he would allow five hundred retainers from the two lords to enter his lands, and be trained by his Master Trainer, Nitaro Tanizaki-san. He was the most feared and respected teacher and warrior in Japan. He was responsible for military training of special palace guards for Shogun Ashikaga in Kyoto.

He sent a messenger to Etchu to court Lord Fukuyama to his side. If successful, he would win the war by stopping Lord Wakatsuki's forces from linking up on his western frontier, forcing him to defend his realm from three sides. Lords Anjoh and Onishi swore allegiance to Lord Kawasomeru no matter what the outcome of the war. They, as well as the other overlords knew if they didn't back him in this war, they would eventually be overrun by Lord Wakatsuki's forces. They and their families would then be slaughtered, and Wakatsuki would be ruling their lands and the entire eastern province. This they would not stand for a moment.

The next morning the lords were scheduled to leave the castle. They were assembling their caravans for the long trek to their provinces by the time Lord Kawasomeru rose for the day. He was only interested in speaking with Anjoh and Onishi before they left. It was his wife, Lady Mineko who talked him into waking so he might visit the lords before they left his lands.

Exhausted, he walked down the steps of the castle to the caravans as if his life was about to end, and addressed the generals, lords, and ladies as they started out the gate of

Engakuji Castle. He made certain Lords Onishi and Anjoh were the last caravans to leave, so he could spend more time with them. By the time Lord Onishi's caravan was about to leave, he was his old self and greeted him honorably. As his caravan walked out the gate, Lord Onishi stood with Lord Kawasomeru. He asked when he expected to have his soldiers come to his land for training.

"Kawasomeru-sama, it'll take my caravan seven sticks of time to get to my province. It'll be two sticks of time until I clear my state affairs before I assemble the soldiers I'll pick for this training. This task should take another week and another to get them to your lands. I'm forced to say in three to four weeks, my warriors will appear at the gate of your Castle."

"Taihen yoi, (very good) this will give me time to assemble my troops who I wish to have trained. I'll march them personally to Master Trainer Tanizaki-san's village, along with the other warriors from Anjoh-sama's army." He proudly announced.

"Ieeeee Kawasomeru-sama, this is a great honor you'll bestow on my unworthy warriors and I'll make the lazy fools aware of this fact." Lord Onishi bowed to him and his wife, Lady Mineko standing by him. Both returned the bow graciously as Onishi moved off to catch up with his caravan which cleared the gate of the castle.

He watched as the caravan filled the streets under the shadow of his castle. He was unaware Lord Anjoh, Lady Enko, his courtesan of old, and the new courtesan Kinue, walked beside him. They were watching Onishi's caravan as they walked down the streets to the outer section of the city, lined with his samurai dressed in their light weight battle armor.

Lady Mineko drew his attention to Lord Anjoh standing to his right. He smiled at Anjoh as he waved his arm over his head, and a samurai broke ranks and rushed at the lords. The warrior dropped to his knees and adopted the position of obedience the moment he reached his lord and held out his arms. Lying across them was a red silk wrap three and a half feet long.

He grunted as he picked up the wrap. The samurai didn't lift his eyes, he held the wrap in one hand and allowed the contents to slide out the open end of the tube. A sword came in view, its polished black lacquered zutsu (scabbard) with silver inlaid appeared before the ivory handle. There was a collective gasp from the crowd as they viewed the magnificent sword.

Lord Anjoh was impressed by the sword when he removed the blade from the decorative wood scabbard, he knelt on one knee to pay greater homage as he stared at the weapon.

"Anjoh! Ikaga desu ka?" (How are you?) He omitted the sama which meant Lord as he addressed his old friend on purpose, to make him feel he was displeased with him.

"Yoi!" (Good) Lord Anjoh replied as he stared at the great killing blade before him.

"Anata wa yoku nemutta hu?" (Did you sleep well?) He asked while drawing out the suspense of what he was going to do with the great blade of honor for a while longer.

"Domo, genki desu." (Quite well, thank you.)

"Do itashimashite. (You are welcome) Anjoh-sama, I ordered this sword constructed for you. It was created by my master swords smith Sugahara of the First Village. He worked on it since I called the loyal lords of Shogun Ashikaga to my castle. The sword's steel has been heated in the fires of Mount Fuji, tempered to hardness by the sweat of his brow. It's a sword with no equal in all the civilized world." He respectfully offered Lord Anjoh the priceless sword.

A grumble rose from the samurai who watched Kawasomeru hand Anjoh the sword. Some pounded the chest plate of their armor as they called out in compliance of the gift offered Anjoh.

Lord Anjoh took the unsheathed sword and held it overhead for all to see. The sun glistened off the highly polished steel, and sent a blinding flash over the warriors and members of his caravan. A second roar of approval and admiration for the finely crafted sword, arose from his caravan and among Lord Kawasomeru's guard. Even Lady Mineko paid homage to the sword as Lord Anjoh took the scabbard and placed the sword in it.

The wise Lord Kawasomeru produced the Wakizashi stabbing sword, the twin but shorter sword which was the exact match to the Katana Lord Anjoh was holding in his hands.

"A matching pair! By the Kami great and small who make up the Heavens and earth and beyond. What have I done in my poor efforts to deserve such great honor. I'm not worthy of such an honor, Kawasomeru-sama. You're too kind to such an unworthy tomo. (friend) I'm in your debt for the years I'm allowed to walk this earth." Lord Anjoh bowed again to the smiling Lord Kawasomeru who nodded at the homage he was paying to his gift and himself.

The pleased overlord watched the first members of Anjoh's procession start down the walk leading out the main gate. "I'll wait for your warriors to appear in my land, so I can bring them to my Master Trainer. How soon will it take to have the summoned soldiers at Engakuji Castle?"

"The honor you pay me is far beyond my earthly worth, and I fear I could never..."

"The sword is yours as my gift, old friend. The honor is well deserved, Anjoh-sama. I'm more interested in when your warriors will arrive in my realm." He snapped, his irritation rising to the point it was bordering on bad manners.

Lord Anjoh smiled, allowing the rebuke to pass as he replied, holding the sword as if it was hot in his hands. "Kawasomeru-sama, I sent a runner two days past, with instructions for the Warriors I listed on my scroll, to assemble and set out for Engakuji Castle as per the night of our conversation of war. I believe my runner should be in my land, and the Warriors should be assembling." He looked to the sun, thought for a second then added. "My Warriors should be on their way for Engakuji Castle as we speak. Hmmm... I figure they should arrive in the next week. As I discussed on our prior meetings, I'm behind you in your decisions Lord Kawasomeru, and to be supporting you means I must have my troops where you want them, when you want them. You ordered Onishi-sama and myself to have five hundred Samurai report to your Castle, and that is what I ordered." His attention went back to the great sword in his hands.

"Ahhh... Anjoh-sama! It's I who am honored by your unwavering loyalty to my decisions. I decided to make you second Roju (President of Shogun's council) of the eastern provinces in command over loyal Daimyos of the eastern provinces. I'll have this decree delivered to your Castle when I get the favored reply from Shogun Ashikaga which I assure you will come, old friend of too many years to count." He offered, knowing Shogun Ashikaga would back his decision to elevate Anjoh to second Roju of the eastern provinces. After all, was it not the Shogun, who ordered him to do what was necessary to retain control of the eastern provinces.

"leeeee! Lord Kawasomeru, I was wondering who you were going to appoint to the post of Second Roju of the eastern provinces now you dishonored Wakatsuki, and you removed the fool from the position of the Second Roju. I dared hope for the title to be bestowed on my worthless head." He bowed politely one last time to the well liked Kawasomeru as he cast a quick eye on his long caravan nearly out of the main gate of Engakuji Castle. He knew he had to leave immediately if he was going to take the lead of his caravan back to his province as was his duty.

He picked up the glance from the older lord and smiled before continuing his conversation. "Lord Anjoh! I believe it's time you leave my Castle and catch up with your people before they're out of sight. You more than thanked me for the few worthless gifts you so rightly earned, which I bestowed on your head. I'll send a messenger to your Castle, the moment I hear of your appointment to the Council of Lords, from Shogun Ashikaga." He bowed politely and handed Lord Anjoh the silk tubular scarf which surrounded the sword and provided protection from marring nicks and scratches the sword might pick up if it wasn't protected by the soft scarf.

The powerful overlord turned to his wife and spoke quietly to her, as Lord Anjoh slid the swords in the blood red scarf then tied the ends together so they wouldn't slip out of the exquisite silk protection. This was done so he could end this conversation he felt Lord Anjoh was going to carry on, until he died of old age. It was a less than polite way to dismiss the lord, but he had to do something, for Lord Anjoh was in danger of becoming a royal pest of himself.

CHAPTER THREE

Lord Kawasomeru smiled as he watched Lord Anjoh increase pace to catch up with the lead horse. He saw him mount and take command of the procession marching out of the city before his samurai and townspeople. He let out a sign, he was pleased he had his castle to himself. He turned to his wife and said. "Is Lady Mineko feeling well on this great day?"

"Hai my Lord! I'm fine, domo for asking about my health. I'm sorry to be such a burden on my Lord and Master, but the baby's carrying low and is putting much pressure on my body. It'll pass soon enough when the baby is finally born I assure you my devoted husband. I wish there was a way to move the process along though." She apologized with great humility to her concerned and attentive husband. She was a beautiful young woman to behold, with her hair up in the traditional Kami no sagari way. The front of her hair neatly trimmed at the ends, allowing her hair to fall pleasantly to the breasts, while the other section of hair was long and hung loosely over her back below her rearend. Her head was surrounded with a thin braid of woven hair, and there were braids woven throughout her magnificently shining hair. Long silver strands hung exquisitely from the braid around her head. Hanging from each strand were small gold shapes of the specially chosen kami she worshipped.

"I learned long time ago to leave Karma to Karma, Lady Mineko. It's good you're with child, I pray it'll be a healthy male. I have a feeling we'll need more young men to lead our armies in battle before Lord Wakatsuki is defeated. The gods must be angry with the people of Japan, to allow such an inhuman to challenge the rule of right." Lord Kawasomeru complained and walked to Engakuji with his wife and courtesan following. Six samurai walked him to the castle. Once inside, he left his wife to be attended by her servants, and went to the third floor to watch Lord Anjoh's caravan go over the hillside and disappear from his view.

THE SECOND WEEK OF THE FIFTH MONTH OF THE THIRTEEN THIRTY NINETH YEAR

The samurai sent from Lord Anjoh's Kozuke province, arrived as a column of neatly disciplined warriors. Kawasomeru ordered them to be housed with the other soldiers he picked from his samurai for training by the Master Trainer, Tanizaki of the Ninth Village. He had to wait for Lord Onishi's warriors to arrive before leaving for the ninth village. He figured it would be around seven sticks of time before he marched with these retainers to Tanizaki's village.

The days passed slow as Lord Kawasomeru waited for the warriors from Sagami to arrive. He was bored with the wait, he was a man of action, and being forced to wait turned him into an angry ruler, one who barked at anyone appearing before him. The feeding of troops was no problem, his capital was rich beyond counting. He continued with the matters of his province and sent a messenger to Wakatsuki's Chiyoda Castle, requesting an audience with the ruler of Echigo and Shimotsuke provinces. The messenger was to take his time delivering the request, because he wanted to appear before Lord Wakatsuki, after he returned from the ninth village, and deposited the retainers for training from Tanizaki.

The overlord wasn't certain Wakatsuki would entertain his request for an audience, and he was unsure if he would pay the visit if invited. He was aware of the treachery practiced by the untrustworthy Wakatsuki and his unscrupulous followers. There were many visitors invited to Chiyoda Castle over the past years, with many disappearing forever. Others were attacked and slaughtered by roaming bands of Ronin, who operation in Lord Wakatsuki's provinces at will.

He sat on the third floor of his castle staring over his city, as his mind wandered through his troubling thoughts. A flock of birds scattered and his attention was drawn to it. The birds were scared to flight near the road leading to his city. His eyes narrowed as he strained them to look over the distance to the sloping main road. After moments of staring, he picked up the first battle banners of the column of samurai marching up the nakasendo (central highway) to his Castle.

"At last, the pack of worthless fools arrived!" He bellowed to no one in particular as he leapt to his feet and headed for the staircase to the main floor of the castle. His sudden moves made the palace guards assigned to his protection jumpy, as they followed the rushing in haste leader of their land. As the concerned Lord Kawasomeru moved to the vast courtyard, he bellowed angrily at his guards. "You worthless fools, open the cursed gates, the Samurai from Sagami province have arrived! Now we can concentrate on preparing to head for the Ninth Village."

The massive gates were swung open and an honor guard rushed out and quickly lined the courtyard. Lord Kawasomeru waited as the approaching warriors marched towards him. The powerful overlord didn't move a muscle as the general in command of the column of warriors, held up his hand and barked. "Stop!"

The exhausted warriors stretched outside the gates, and the ones forced to wait in the streets of the lower city, weren't able to hear anything being spoken by Lord Kawasomeru or the general.

General Tadayoshi Miyamoto bowed before Lord Kawasomeru, who returned his bow as graciously then spoke. "Who are you General?"

"I'm General Tadayoshi Miyamoto of First Army of Sagami province, Kawasomeru-sama."

"General Miyamoto-san, are you here for added training?" The lord asked.

"Iye Lord Kawasomeru I am not. I'm trained well. I've been ordered to march these chosen worthless Warriors of Lord Onishi to Engakuji Castle, and no further."

"General Miyamoto-san, what do you intend to do while these fools of soldiers you brought, are being trained by my Master Trainer of the Ninth Village?"

"Kawasomeru-sama, I'll remain if invited until the Samurai's training is complete. I have orders from Lord Onishi to turn myself over to your army if needed,

Kawasomeru-sama. I'm also instructed to follow your orders as if they were issued by Lord Onishi." The general offered a neatly folded scroll and snapped to attention while he unfolded the paper and read the message.

"Ahhh... General Miyamoto-san, it seems you're correct. Lord Onishi offered your contract to me to do with as I please. General, I believe it good if you went through this training with your Samurai. It'd be wise if all generals were trained along with their Warriors." He smiled as he stared at the general to see how he felt about his decision.

General Miyamoto's facial expressions didn't change a bit as he bowed and offered to the master of the province. "If my Lord so chooses, I'd be honored to go through the training with my Samurai, Lord Kawasomeru."

"General, your loyalty will be noted in the hall of records, you're hereby raised five kiki's of silk which is to be paid by Onishi-sama. I'll so inform him of my order."

The general was stunned by the warlord's words, five kiki's of silk was a daimyo's fee. He bowed as he offered. "I'm unworthy of such a fee, I'll earn the belief you bestowed upon me."

"General Miyamoto-san, you come to me with a note boasting of yukakasa, (having high value) I have no doubts before this war with Wakatsuki has run its course, you'll earned this fee and more. Look after your men, have them prepared to march for the Ninth Village in two days. You may garrison them with the other armies to be trained in the Ninth Village. Takashi Hara!" He grunted, not turning to the warrior he called.

A soldier broke ranks and rushed to his lord and the general, and dropped to his knees. He bowed until his head touched the ground, and held it until he was addressed by Kawasomeru.

"Stand on your feet Samurai Takashi-san!" The overlord ordered.

When the warrior stood, he ordered him in a commanding tone. "Takashi-san! You'll escort the General to the barracks area and make certain he and his Samurai are fed and looked after."

"Hai, my Lord." Samurai Hara said as he bowed and turned to the general and waved his hand in a motion bidding him to follow. General Miyamoto turned and bowed as he offered to the leader in a polite tone. "Lord Kawasomeru, you're generous in many ways. I'm certain my Samurai and myself will be treated honorably."

He returned the general's bow then turned from him as he addressed the guards. "You have carried out your duty honorably today, you're ordered to your posts to stand watch." He started up the steps of his castle as Miyamoto barked at his warriors to follow Samurai Hara.

He stopped and spun around as he grunted. "General Miyamoto-san!"

The warriors froze in place, his bellowed words still echoing throughout the castle walls. All eyes went to the warlord standing on the third step with his hands resting on his hips, staring at Onishi's general as if he was insulted by him.

An insult to a liege lord could cost the general his life if it wasn't too serious, but if it was a major infraction, it could cost the lives of the retainers, and Onishi's honor. Even Kawasomeru's guard froze in place and snapped to attention, waiting for their master to address Miyamoto. Many guards were preparing for an attack on the general's column if ordered by their liege lord.

"Kawasomeru-sama?" The concerned general replied.

"General! When your Warriors are taken care of, you'll report to the reception room on the second floor with the other officers in your column. I'll have the officers from Anjoh-sama's Warriors there as my own appear at this time. I give you one feather of time to rest and I'll begin my meeting with, or without you." He spoke no more as he turned and continued his way up the eight steps leading to the door of his castle.

A collective sigh came from General Miyamoto's warriors, and Lord Kawasomeru's guards, as the general's warriors followed Samurai Hara to their assigned places again.

The lord enjoyed a chuckle as he remembered the face of General Miyamoto and his men, when he barked and he mumbled. "It'll teach the fool never to let down his guard in my presence." He headed for the hall on the second floor, commonly used for meetings between him and his officers. He sat on the six inch high platform as three female servants attended his needs, wiping sweat from his brow and bringing him a new kosode change and spraying him with perfumed water. Sake and cups of water were placed on a table along with a folded war fan.

The bamboo shutters were opened to allow breeze in. Although the room was cool, by the time the officers entered and conversations began, it would not take long for the room to become stifling. He sipped the sake, it was impolite to drink anything in the presence of another person, unless they were drinking also. His officers were the first to appear and assumed the important seating then officers from Lord Anjoh's army began to filter in, and the last were General Miyamoto and his officers. Once the officers were present, He spoke. "I ordered you to appear before me for this discussion. As officers, I'm holding you responsible for the actions of your soldiers while they stay in the Ninth

Village. I'll make certain the Warriors to be trained have enough food to eat and sake, but I'll not stand for molesting of the female population of the village. I'll order a Willow House to be established before your troops arrive. All soldiers will make use of these accommodations, and only become involved with the local females if they so choose. Any soldier who forces himself on a woman, will pay for this insult with his head.

"The Ninth Village is an important village, and its security will be vigorously defended by me and my Warriors. Also, I expect you as officers to maintain control of your soldiers. They're to listen and obey Master Trainer Nitaro Tanizaki-san, as if the orders he spits out come from me. Any Warrior who gives him a hard time will lose his head. I warn every officer, I'll be looking for someone to serve as an example to warn these Warriors never to insult Tanizaki-san, or any member of the Ninth Village. I order each of you to keep an eye on the retainers. Watch the Warriors carefully, anyone who is not interested in this training will be removed from the classes, and he'll be ordered to the ranks of himin, and put to work carrying shit from the latrines.

"I'll not put up with insubordination from the trainees. I'm bestowing on every officer the capability of ending ones training any time he may chose. I don't want anyone uninterested in this training disrupting the other retainers who want to learn from my Master Trainer. I need my Samurai trained in the ways of properly waging war if I hope to be successful against Wakatsuki, and his army of Ronin dung eating fools, and it's your responsibility to safeguard this training."

The overlord took a quick breath and stared at the officers as he breathed deeply and began again. "The upcoming war will be a long bloody one, but it'll forever shape Japan's future. Each of you received a substantial pay increase and to retain that increase, I expect loyalty to me and my Trainer, and to the village he lives. I'll not hesitate to remove any officer and have him reduced to himin. And if I'm forced to remove an officer, his family will suffer the same fate, and be reduced to the filthy himin class to serve in the world of shit for their entire lives. A well trained army of the future is all I'm concerned with, and to insure this need, I'll lop off the head of any foolish Warrior or officer who stands in my way!" He snapped as he jumped to his feet and stared at the officers. Eyeing each, trying to shake their confidence.

No officers flinched as they stared at the angry lord with scowls on their faces as they looked straight ahead. The officers barely breathed as sweat ran down their faces, and they knelt ridged on a most uncomfortable and coarse thin straw mat.

"I'm of the belief every one gathered before me are honorable men, and if I was to ask you where your loyalty lay, you'd answer me truthfully."

The officers grunted 'Hai' and nodded in agreement with the lord.

"This is why you were picked for this yoshi gi." (duty) He clapped his hands and servant women appeared with trays of cups and handed them to the officers. He waited until each had a cup then offered. "Officers of Lord Kawasomeru's army, I salute you."

"Oooooyyyyyaaaaa." Was repeated by each officer as they drained their cups. Each realized the honor he bestowed on them by saluting them with sake, this ceremony was usually retained for nobility. Pride swelled in their chests as the officers stared at this lord so defiantly standing before them with his hands resting threateningly on his hips.

Suddenly, one of the officers called out in a booming voice. "Kawasomeru-sama."

It was picked up by the other officers who likewise chanted his name proudly.

Over and over the officers repeated his name until the walls of the room vibrated. Many samurai rushed in ready to defend their lord, not knowing what they might be facing. They surrounded the officers with their naginata yaris (six foot curved bladed spear) ready to hack them to pieces, if their lord's life was in danger. Other guards rested their hands on the hilts of their swords and stared at the officers as they called his name. It was uncommon for chanting to occur in a meeting room. Usually, this chanting was reserved for the battlefield before engaging the enemy, it served to pump up the warriors before they battled.

He saw his guards disperse with five guards taking position between him and the officers chanting his name. He ordered the guards to put up their spears, indicating he was not in danger. The guards looked from the officers to Lord Kawasomeru then back to the officers who continued to call his name, paying little attention to the samurai threatening them.

Finally, they stopped chanting as the lord stepped from the platform and lifted a naginata spear. He sent it flying and it stuck in a cedar cross beam. A roar rose as the officers admired the mighty heave, and the spear vibrating in the beam. He barked at the guards. "You'll leave that spear where it is for the life of this Castle. Leave this room so I can speak to the officers, allow no one to enter until I'm finished." He made this order to show the officers he placed his life in their hands as he turned to the door leading in the room. He saw his wife being restrained by guards who did not know what was happening in the room. He stared at her until their eyes locked and then turned away, informing her he was all right and she was to leave. She did so after receiving the silent order.

Once the guards left, the officers again rested on the mats and waited until he was on his platform speaking again. "I accept this honor you offered, and apologize for my inconsiderate guard's bad manners displayed before you. Most of the fools are young, but they too will go through this training, to turn the addle minded ill mannered heaps into proper guards. Dozo, (please) it's my fault for their poor efforts of guarding me and interrupting us."

The officers from the two provinces ignored his apology, their heads swollen by the salute offered by him. He could have ordered them to commit suppuku at this moment, and they would have gladly obeyed after this great honor.

The wise Lord Kawasomeru realized this and quickly changed his tactics. "This is all I have to speak to you about unless any have something to add to this conversation. I call this meeting to conclusion." He waited for the proper amount of time to lapse then added. "I remind each of you, I want the Ninth Village to be left in better condition when you leave than when your troops appeared in the village. The training of the Warriors are up to you as well as it is up to the Master Trainer. I'm tired, leave, and make sure your Warriors are ready to leave by first light two days from today." He bowed to the officers and they almost broke their necks to stand and return his bow as he turned and disappeared through a side door.

The officers were left looking at each other and reliving the salute offered them by Lord Kawasomeru. They grew bored by the conversations, each officer dared not admit, but they wanted to get back to their troops and brag about the toast from Kawasomeru. Each officer rushed from the castle and headed out the gate to the barracks and their troops. Sake flowed as the officers bragged about the salute. It was a good strategy, because when the officers returned to their troops, they had them policing the area, and cleaning debris and raking the sandy soil. The warriors were in good moods because of the officer's happiness, everything served to make the samurai comfortable and eager to please the three powerful lords.

The two days passed with the overlord keeping an eye on the samurai assembled for training. He was pleased the warriors were respecting his lands and cleaning up after themselves.

Early on the third day, he woke in a good mood and prepared for his ride to the ninth village. His wife, Mineko helped him dress in his traveling kosode and takaashidas (high wooden clogs). When he was dressed he kissed his lady and tapped her on her rear which caused her to purr sexily then he headed down the staircase. He walked out the door and was surprised to see the retainers in the courtyard ready to leave. The officers were mounted and waiting for him.

He bowed to General Tadayoshi Miyamoto who was one horse from his and nodded to his general, Yoshinobu Shimbo. "General Shimbo-san! Are the Warriors ready?"

"Hai my Lord!" The wise general replied proudly.

"Yoi!" (Good) He held up a foot and a servant rushed over and removed his clogs and placed his riding boot on. He lifted his other foot and the servant repeated his duty. He had a light over kosode on which he used as a riding coat. He grabbed the side of the wood saddle and with a heave, pulled himself on his horse. He pulled the reins to the left and started his horse walking, two samurai rushed up and walked a few yards ahead of their lord, their naginata's pointing up, and the wood shafts held inches from the ground. General Shimbo moved to his right side, with General Miyamoto moving up to his left one step from his lead.

The warriors left Engakuji Castle in silence, only orders barked by the officers broke the harmony of the city. The chest of Kawasomeru swelled with pride as he rode out the courtyard through the main gate, and traveled through the fifteen foot high stone walls. The taller watch towers which protected the castle from attack, held samurai on daiban yaku (guard duty). He guided his horse down the avenue to the nakasendo (central highway) and as he rode out he glanced to his right. There he noticed his ninjuden, his living quarters where he stayed if there was a problem with the castle, or he wanted a change of scenery. As the lord rode, his caravan crossed numerous small streams by means of wood bridges in the upper class area of the city.

This area extending through the prime region and encompassed the first to third avenues closest to the castle walls that made up the elite section. The streams which flowed from the canals offered the city drinking water, and fed the gardens of the upper class villas. At the end of this area, the streams served to wash human waste from this section of the city out to the sea.

He smiled as he sniffed the sweet fragrance of blossoming cherry trees as he passed the houses of the well to do of his city. Midway, the market place served as a separation of the upper class from the middle class and less fortunate lower classes. After the lord passed the stores and warehouses, temples and shrines, the appearance of the city changed.

Dogs barked, hawks and owls cried the end of another night of hunting. A child could be heard crying in the distance, obviously hungry and only quieted when offered a teat from which to suckle. Great rows of long houses lined the length of the road he rode. The purifying steams no longer crossed in this section of his realm, instead they veered off to the sea. These long houses were the homes of the lower class, they were simple structures consisting of a single door all occupants used, and a low pitched thatched roof. The structure had single room apartments in which sometimes up to ten members of the same family lived, barely leaving room for them to lay out on the rough cut wood floor, with no windows in the structure. With the lack of running streams through this section to wash away the human waste, the area smelled terrible.

As he neared the end of his city, the foul smell grew more intense. Again he vowed to do something about the living conditions of his lower class. Soon, his caravan was out of the city and on the open road, and the air was again filled with the fragrance of flowers. The ride was enjoyable, he loved being free of the pressures of the city. He left his pregnant wife behind, attended by one of his favorite concubines Lady Kumik, a young beauty seventeen years of age. Lord Kawasomeru was thirty three years old, and he surrounded himself with the youngest and fairest and most beautiful concubines. The first day's ride took him through three smaller villages, but the lord refused the village ruler's offers of hospitality if he chose to remain in the village overnight and continued riding, taking the minimum of time to visit the village head, and also the lead samurai of the village before riding off.

He entered an area of his province dotted with small inns, he headed for one in particular, and took over the structure of eleven rooms. The samurai on foot were instructed to bed down in the open fields. He, his lover, and the officers stayed in the building enjoying hot food and lodging. He allowed Lady Michiko to work out the payment for the inn with the keeper. It was beneath him to deal with money matters, unless he wanted to try his hand at wheeling and dealing, which gave him pleasure. Throughout his province, he earned the reputation of being a hard man to receive proper payment from, and enjoyed the reputation.

It didn't matter to the innkeeper who paid him, as long as he received monetary profits from Lord Kawasomeru's brief stay in his establishment. It was an honor for the lord of the province to single out one's inn. This honor would bring the innkeeper many travelers wanting to use his establishment, who would pay the higher fees he would charge after his visit.

He allowed Lady Michiko to please him in the way of the mouth and slept, knowing his samurai were outside his door. He slept alone and woke refreshed and ready to go, the air of the country invigorated him. He walked out the inn and was happy to see the army assembled and waiting his presence. He went inside and had his morning meal while his horse was prepared for travel. When he, the officers, and Lady Michiko finished eating, they mounted their horses. Lady Michiko was traveling in a shuttered palanquin carried by four kagamen of the lower class.

The May morning was cool, a good day for travel. He figured they should reach the ninth village by late that night if he pushed his retainers. He headed down the road, making the warriors rush to turn their columns to catch up with him. The officers headed off in a gallop to catch up with him. He grinned over the mayhem his rash moves caused his soldiers and guards.

Shimbo rode up to Kawasomeru's side who grunted at him. "General Shimbo-san! Perhaps this will teach these worthless Ronin to be ready for anything at any time." The smile remained.

The general returned his smile as he announced. "Lord Kawasomeru, I believe after this move, the foolish Warriors will be ready for anything. They lost face at being caught off guard as they were, and I'll not allow them to forget the insult they offered to you."

"Yoi, this is good General. I want these fools trained properly, my province's safety will rest in their warring abilities." He barked as he stared ahead. The rest of the day, the ride was completed in silence. The foot soldiers felt the faster pace, and marched through mid time eating while no one dared to complain about not stopping to eat. As the sun began to lower, he saw the first signs of the ninth village a plowed field.

The general pointed out a column of warriors marching out to them. "Kawasomeru-sama! They must be the Ninth Village Samurai sent to escort you to the village."

"Hai! General Shimbo-san! You'll ride ahead and order them to line up on the side of the road and wait my column to pass the fools. Then, they'll follow us to the village."

"Hai my Lord." He rode off in a gallop, his horse kicking up a dust cloud as he pulled on the reins and made his horse stutter step, kicking up more dust. He remained mounted as he bellowed orders to the lead warrior, who in turn issued orders to his men. They separated on each side of the road and stood at attention. The general turned his horse and rode back to Lord Kawasomeru, and resumed his position of honor riding on the right side of his lord.

When he came within ten feet of the samurai standing on either sides of the road, they dropped to the ground and bowed until their heads touched the ground, and they stayed in that position until he rode past them. They got up and silently fell in step behind the column, as they entered the ninth village.

Burning torches lit up the road to the village. Lord Kawasomeru, before entering the village, took a few moments to dress in his battle armor as did the officers. He was an imposing presence perched on his horse decorated in her armor. The magnificence of the procession of officers and warriors dressed in armor with samurai marching behind their lord and the banner men, was an impressive sight. He was clad in his armor which became shiny towards the sircoat, it had a striped under dress and wide, short breeches of heavy cotton reinforced heavy silk.

On his chest plate he had four pair of extraordinarily detailed dragons representing the Eight Islands of Japan, facing to the center of the breast plate, looking up at him. His kabuto helmet was adorned with lofty plumes of feathers, and a brass U shaped set of kuwagata horns. The helmet was constructed of one piece of iron, coated with a layer of black and polished lacquer. His shikoro neck shield was made of eight pieces of plate iron held together by silk roping which encircled his neck and curved outwards, so as not to hinder his sword movements. His brass hoate face mask was fearsome and threatening. His katana and wakizashi blades were made by the master sword maker Sugahara, decorated with Ivory and inlaid silver.

On his back was an ebira, an open quiver with eight hirane ne, flat broad headed bamboo shaft arrows and his eight foot decorative yumi (bow) clutched in his right hand, crossing his chest and held ready for action. His left hand was protected by the leather gauntlet worn to draw the bow. Amidst rattling, he rode past the chonin, the common townspeople as they bowed, with him ignoring them. He continued riding through the village leaving his generals behind, until he rode to the center of the village and came to the home of the Shoya, headman in charge of the village.

On one side of the Shoya, Toru Sanaki stood the commanding samurai leader, Yoshio Kobayashi, on the other side of the Shoya stood Master Trainer, Nitaro Tanizaki. They bowed and held it as he rode up to them. The townspeople were ordered to line the main street and pay homage to their lord. They bowed as Lord Kawasomeru rode passed and held it until they were told to get up by a samurai in the column.

His samurai rode and marched in step in lines of three across, all wearing various armor of their choice, designating their rank in service. Until the lord held up his hand, whereby they stopped and stayed where they were, leaving over a hundred and fifty meters between them and the lord still moving ahead of them on horseback.

The powerful Daimyo rode up to the heads of the ninth village and pulled back on the reins and his horse reared mightily, and waved its legs in the air as if searching for something to get a footing on. Then the horse's legs returned to the earth, as a samurai rushed over and took hold of the dropped halter. He swung his leg over the steed and dismounted. The lord walked up to the Shoya as if to separate his head from his shoulders, as he grunted in a harsh tone. "Toru Sanuki-san! It's an honor to see you again. It's been too long since the last time we spoke. Perhaps you might see your way to visit my city, Shoya." He bowed politely to the old Shoya.

Sanuki looked up and straightened as he offered. "You pay me great honor my Lord. May you live a long and prosperous life. I'd be proud to visit your honorable city."

"Yoi, I'll have Lady Michiko work out the details of your visit with Lady Tokie." He turned to the warrior and grumbled. "Kobayashi-san, it's a pleasure. How are your old wounds healing?"

He was wounded when merchants he was leading to a village, were attacked by Ronin filth. He was staggered in battle but not before he slaughtered five, and wound uncounted others who fled.   It was Kawasomeru who forbade him to commit suppuku, and ordered the village doctors to heal his wounds under the threat of their deaths.

He bowed as he replied. "Lord Kawasomeru honors me with his interest in my worthless welfare. My wounds are healing well, the village doctor has assured me my wounds will not be permanent or hinder me in any way, my Lord. He states I should be back to health in a few week's time." Again, he bowed to his liege lord.

"Your doctors have treated you well, Kobayashi-san?" The lord asked.

"Hai my Lord.   Well indeed, thank you for asking Kawasomeru-sama."

He turned to the Shoya and barked. "Sanuki-san! I want the village doctors given ten koku increase in rice for their work on Kobayashi-san.   His health is important to my provinces. I'll help pay this increase in fee by increasing your yearly proportion of taxes, and I'll give you a land increase of five hundred square Ri."

"Lord Kawasomeru! This is a Daimyo's fee. I'll be honored to absorb the doctor's increase in pay myself." Toru Sanuki offered to his lord.

"You returned my honor with a greater honor Sanuki-san, I made my decision and you'll live with it. Sanuki-san, I have need of one of your citizens, and with this need will place tremendous pressures on every one in your village." He turned to Tanizaki and grunted. "Master Trainer Tanizaki-san!" The great lord bowed to the old trainer of samurai.

The bow took the trainer and everyone standing before their lord off guard. It was an honor to have the lord of the province visit the village, yet alone bow to you before he began to address you before the village inhabitants.

"Master Trainer Tanizaki-san, I brought you fifteen hundred worthless retainers to be trained in your ways of making war. I made preparations for feeding these foul lot of soldiers, their housing will be left to your village to provide them. I know I never sent a messenger, asking permission to train these worthless Warriors, forgive my foul manners. But I knew once I traveled to your honorable village to request your training of these Samurai in person, you'd not dare refuse my impolite request of you, old man."

"Kawasomeru-sama! There's no request you could make of me I'd dare show ill manners to refuse, I'm not a worthless eta. My life, my blood is yours to command or take."

"You're truly one of my most loyal Warriors, Tanizaki-san. It's a shame I cannot talk you into leaving this village to move to my unworthy city. So I can better look after your health, Tanizaki-san." He offered as he straightened up his back some.

"Lord Kawasomeru! Am I now an old woman I need my Lord to look after me? Iye! I can look after these old bones myself. Soon, I'll visit my worthy ancestors in the Ukiyo, (the floating world) where these old bones will no longer cause me honorable pain. Until that time, I'll remain in the village that gave me birth."

"What makes you think your ancestors will welcome such an old grouch as you, my friend?" Sanuki grunted with a smile as he ordered more torches to replace the ones that burned out.

"Tanizaki-san! I wish you'd reconsider and move to my city. I know you like to live in the peace and harmony this village offers, but I have need of your wisdom and ability. Shinano and the seven provinces are on the verge of war with Wakatsuki. A war which will last well into the next decade I fear. Many Samurai will fall victim before the swords as does the wheat in the field to the blade. I ordered an increase in our children. I need many Warriors born to the realm to fight on long after our old bones failed our worthless skin. Tanizaki-san! I need you to train these worthless soldiers of the future, and it'd be easier on everyone if you'd move to the city. So I can keep you going with a steady stream of Warriors who need to be trained in the way of the Warrior." He took the offered cup of water as darkness of the night closed in.

"Lord Kawasomeru! We're facing war with the foul dog eaters to our east I see?" The well aged master trainer offered to his lord.

"Hai! I'm fearful that's a true fact you speak, Master Trainer Tanizaki-san."

"How soon?" His mind was already working on the problems he would face in the training of these warriors. He needed to know how much time he'd have to accomplish this feat.

"Master Trainer Tanizaki-san! I'll not engage in warfare with the lowly Ronin Wakatsuki for at least a year's time, maybe longer if I can put it off. I don't intend to engage his well trained forces until I have the proper numbers of better trained Warriors in my armies."

"Kawasomeru-sama! Has anyone offered to speak with Wakatsuki to see if we could talk this problem out, rather than go to war? I grow wearily of the many years of war. The killing of our youth must stop. It has to stop if Japan wants to come out of the dark ages and join the civilized world." Sanuki mumbled, showing his disappointment of the news the eight provinces of the eastern realm would be fighting with the leaders of the outer provinces loyal to Wakatsuki.

He glared at Shoya Sanuki for daring to interrupt his conversation with the master trainer, and the insult was driven home when he didn't respond to Sanuki's question.

The stunned Shoya took the harsh silent rebuke seriously, and took a step back as if struck across the face, allowing Kobayashi to fill in the void he created.

The overlord saw the movement by the two and cursed Sanuki under his breath for displaying his weakness to his village. It would have been proper for him to repeat his question once he didn't respond, but paused before he chose to speak to the master or lead warrior. But his bowels turned to water and his knees to rice paste, and now he was even less a man in his lord's eyes.

"Kawasomeru-sama! It grows late, should we now be forced to continue this conversation in the open like lowly insects, or shall we retire to the privacy of Shoya Sanuki-san's humble home, and talk like civilized humans of the future of the realm and what we intend to do about Wakatsuki's ambitions?" The old Master Trainer Tanizaki growled, giving into the pain the night's coolness was causing to his old bones.

"Ieeeee! Master Trainer Tanizaki-san is correct with his words of wisdom, Lord Kawasomeru! May I offer the hospitality of my unworthy home for the lack of comfort it offers to my Lord, and his honored guests." Sanuki offered weakly as he waved his hand out before him to the door of his modest home. His wife and their servants were standing on the front porch waiting orders.

"Tanizaki-san is correct, we're civilized people and civilized people don't carry conversations in the street like old women talking against each other. But I'd rather go to

Tanizaki-san's home where I'll spend the night. General Shimbo-san! You and General Miyamoto-san settle the Warriors. Take them to a field we past entering the village, and have them set tents. It'll be the living place until their training is completed, unless Master Trainer wants them someplace else. General, take charge of the Warriors." He barked without facing the general he issued orders to.

"Hai Kawasomeru-sama!" General Shimbo spun on his heels and snapped orders to the trainees. They quick marched out of the village in formation, followed by the cavalry.

All four men watched as the samurai left the center of the village, marching in step.

"I hope my unworthy village will be able to sustain the abuse this many Warriors will cause."

"Sanuki-san! Fear not, your village will weather my Warrior's presence. My Samurai received orders not to cause damage to your village or grounds, or it'll cost their heads. They have himin to look after their waste and repair damage to the earth or village they might cause."

"Lord Kawasomeru! You're a great and wise man." Sanuki offered with a polite bow.

The trainer was stunned over the information his home would house Kawasomeru during his stay in the village. He couldn't fathom why the master was bestowing on him such a great honor.

He realized the bewilderment of the trainer and brought Tanizaki's mind back to the conversation by asking. "Tanizaki-san! How is your lovely wife Lady Emiko doing?"

"Lord Kawasomeru! She's well, but I'm afraid she's with child again my Lord."

"Ieeeee Tanizaki-san! This is good news for my troubled ears, it shows me the peerless pestle will work well into the years of old. How many children does this make for your family?" He words of praise for Tanizaki's sexual powers made the four men chuckle.

"Eight children to my honorable family my Lord." He proudly announced.

"By all the Kami who travel the night's darkness, you better take up fishing, or I might be forced to increase Sanuki-san's trivial fief. So his honorable village will be large enough to house your many offspring, Tanizaki-san." His words made the leaders laugh. Suddenly, the warlord yawned and passed wind and scratched between his legs proudly.

The master trainer picked up the meaning of his moves and offered. "Lord Kawasomeru, you must be exhausted from your long journey to my village. Please my Lord, allow me to offer you the unworthy comforts my home has to offer." Tanizaki bowed to his lord.

The Daimyo bowed as he acknowledged his offer and replied. "Tanizaki-san! I'm positive your home will offer me many comforts far greater than I enjoy at Engakuji Castle."

"Huh Lord Kawasomeru! You offer me far too great an honor. One I'm sure I'd not be able to live up too. Please, if you wouldn't mind, may I show you to my unworthy home?"

He turned to his guards and grunted. "Take ten of the best men and secure Tanizaki-san's home. These guards will remain throughout the training program."

The old Tanizaki was quick to realize the honor his lord bestowed on him. To be offered a guard of fourteen samurai to protect your every move was a daimyo's reward. He knew once the training courses were completed, this honor guard would remain behind.

"Master Trainer Tanizaki-san! I'm looking forward to some of your wife's special dishes of eel and ayu. (fresh water fish) I remember and cherish fondly the first time your Lady made these dishes for my delight." Lord Kawasomeru grunted as he rubbed his belly.

"Lord Kawasomeru! My worthless wife has been supervising cooking of meals since she was informed of your visit. Lady Emiko prayed to Buddha, hoping you'd honor my home by a visit."

He belched and announced in a commanding voice as he swatted at a mosquito trying to get a meal from the lord. "I must make room for this great feast. Is it too late to expect such a feast? It's an impolite time of day to begin eating."

"Kawasomeru-sama! My wife would commit suppuku if you dared to turn in for the night without eating what she prepared for your honored visit to my lowly village, my Lord. Especially since she's been supervising the cooks while they were preparing the meal for her Lord." Master Trainer Tanizaki offered politely to the leader of the eight provinces.

"Well then Master Trainer Tanizaki-san. I don't wish to insult your wife any longer by not appearing before her. Shall we go? I'm empty of food." He glanced at Shoya Sanuki and knew he wanted to speak privately with the master trainer.

"Kawasomeru-sama! I have important matters I must attend to, and I must beg to be pardoned from this meal and your presence." Shoya Sanuki bowed graciously.

"This is terrible news, Sanuki-san. I was looking forward to sharing a meal with you. If your matters of state is so important they must be attended to then so be it. You have my permission to handle your matters. I'll make your excuses to Lady Emiko, Sanuki-san."

Another honor was bestowed on Master Trainer Tanizaki when his lord referred to his wife as Lady Emiko. An honor which was usually reserved for the higher nobility of the capital.

The samurai took positions around Master Trainer Tanizaki's home, and Kawasomeru nodded to the samurai in command as they stopped before the main door. Emiko and her lady in waiting were kneeling on the front porch, and bowed as he stopped before the door, and removed his riding boots and left them resting on the stone planted in the ground for this reason.

"Ahhh... Lady Emiko, it's certainly a pleasure to set my weary eyes on you again. You look as beautiful as the morning sunrise after a night of pleasant rain. Yes Lady Emiko, it's been a long time since I last saw you. I believe you were with child then also."

Emiko giggled as she bowed and thanked the lord for his kind honor. She couldn't believe her lord was calling her Lady Emiko.

"You honor my province with so many healthy children Lady Emiko." He offered as he returned her bow. Then noticed the stream running alongside the building. He remembered the ornamental lake fed by this stream, and the beautiful garden Emiko had and he ordered himself to enjoy the serenity the garden offered him before he left the village.

The lord took a second to view Tanizaki's shinden. (main house) The roof was covered with wood shingles of hand hewn Cyprus with the steeply sloping roof peaking over the verandah of the front door, offering cover from the rain when removing clogs before entering the building. The building's first floor was suspended three feet above the ground by heavy wood piles tied to the floor by corbels. This offered sufficient movement to resist strong winds of typhoons, or by movement by slight earthquakes. The building owed its stability to the weight of the roof and wood piles resting on foundation stones set flush in the earth.

The outer walls were constructed of bamboo mats between the main wall supports, a heavy coating of plastered over the mats gave the interior a bamboo wall, and the outside a hard crusted masonry, making the wall waterproof, and the building far less drafty during the cold days of winter. A small metal oven was set in the corner of the main room, and was the only means of heat for the building during the cold winter months.

Lord Kawasomeru looked under the house to the hygienic space which offered protection from the humidity of the wet season. The first floor was constructed in a manner allowing the floor boards placed end to end to be easily removed, so Tanizaki could keep the ground under the house clean and free of destructive debris or rot. Emiko took his helmet as he entered their home. He saw straw cushions used for sitting and smiled at their simplicity. There was a three way folding screen separating a section of the sitting room.

Everywhere he looked, he observed fresh cut flowers resting on top of bamboo chests, the only furniture in the building, or in vases propped in nooks and crannies. Hand carved toys and dolls rested here and there, and the pleasant smell of food cooking, made his stomach growl in anticipation of the delights he would soon enjoy.

The trainer led the lord in the largest room of the first floor to the tokonoma, the main receiving area for honored guests set in the best room of the house with a slightly raised floor. There were two pieces of furniture on the platform. A small, over stuffed straw sitting pillow covered with the finest silk he ever saw, and a table for him to eat at.

When he was seated, Emiko clapped her hands and her three daughters served him. One young beauty carried a proportion of smoked eel wrapped in seaweed covered with baked rice and Tamari. The second of Tanizaki's daughters carried a tray of fresh water fish baked with a cooked wheat mat underneath. The third daughter carried other delicacies for their lord's enjoyment. The trays were placed on the table before Lord Kawasomeru who studied the dishes. The proud Tanizaki sat on the lower section of the floor with his wife, as his daughters carried other trays of food and cups of sake.

"Lady Emiko! You must be proud at how lovely your fine daughters are, they serve well and act properly. A fine example of womanhood." He announced as he bowed to Emiko's eldest daughter, honoring her and causing her to cover her mouth in order not to insult her lord, by baring her undarkened teeth before him.

"Tanizaki-san! You'll honor me by taking the first piece of eel? I insist and I'm too tired to argue with you." He offered kindly.

"Ieeeee! My Lord, I'm unworthy of enjoying the best of the meal prepared for your enjoyment. That honor is yours to be enjoyed. Please Kawasomeru-sama, it'll be an honor to my unworthy wife, if you'd enjoy the first and best of the meal she prepared for you, my Lord." Master Trainer Tanizaki begged, as he bowed slightly while sitting with his legs crossed beneath him.

"Hai! Since you put it that way." He grumbled as he took some eel and placed it on his plate and took a piece of fresh water fish, and covered all with rice and Tamari. As hungry as he was, he knew it was terrible manners if he ate everything placed before him. It was great face to Emiko if he took just so much of everything on the table. He dared to look at Emiko, it was ill manners to look at anyone while they ate. He saw the pride swell in her when he offered her the plate of eel before she offered it to her husband. Although it was a slight insult to Tanizaki, the lord offered the food to his wife first. He felt Tanizaki would understand the honor he was aiming at his wife. An almost hidden smile informed him Tanizaki was pleased over the honor he bestowed on his respected wife. It was bound to give her and him face throughout the village.

Tanizaki's daughters and sons ate in the outer room, far from the lord and their father.

When he finished his meal, the daughters instantly appeared without being summoned and cleared the dishes and leftover meal as the warlord offered to his master trainer. "Tanizaki-san! You have polite daughters, I'll start their worth by giving each of them five koku paid to them from my personal vault."

"Ieeeee! Such a vast sum of worth for my daughters my Lord! They'll be sought after by every young buck in the village." Tanizaki-san cried as he looked from the lord to his wife, who was trying to hide the fact she was crying over Lord Kawasomeru's kind offer.

"They're worth it my old friend. I decided to have your sons come to my city and be trained in the ways of the nobles, and have them learn to read and write. I have many heads of state overdue of replacing." He picked at his teeth with a bamboo sharpened shaft.

"Lord Kawasomeru! I thought you'd want my lazy sons to serve in the field of battle. Two of them are well trained for battle, and I was planning to train the other sons when they're old enough to begin my training program, my Lord." The trainer offered.

"Huh! The two sons you trained in the art of warfare, I'll put to work as officers with my Mononobe Castle Guards. The other sons I'll have trained as public servants. I made up my mind, I don't want your sons dying in the field of battle.

Hmmm... maybe I'll reconsider and allow you to train the son your wife carries in her belly as Samurai. This way he'll be the one chosen for greatness on the battlefield. If this boy is marked for Samurai, you'll not waste time training him in any other manner, as you done with the others of the village. Yes Master Trainer! This is my decision, your eighth born will bear the sign of greatness, and be Samurai. I order you to train him well, when you decide you had enough of this way of life, I'll allow your eighth son to replace you as Master Trainer of my Warriors. He'll be given every honor you enjoy."

He turned from the aged master trainer to his elderly wife then back to the old trainer as he offered. "I have a feeling about this child hidden within Lady Emiko's belly. Any eighth child born to a household will be a lucky one, and I feel this one is destined to be one of greatness and worth. Lady Emiko! When is your child due in this world please?"

"Lord Kawasomeru! The village doctor assured me he'll be born within the next thirty sticks of time, no longer. I have my parturition building prepared and my sisters and daughters will assist me with the birth. Of course, my old Warrior will be waiting outside drinking sake and bragging with the other villagers, of his great powers of making me with child, my Lord."

He let out a body shaking laugh as he looked to Tanizaki and grumbled. "It seems your wife has enough of your potent and dangerous faucet, which drips the flow of life between her legs. It'll be as I ordered, your eighth son will be trained in your ways of warfare. I promise you I'll look well after this one, long after you have gone to visit your honored ancestors in the Floating World of the hereafter. At the risk of displaying bad manners, I must brag Lady Mineko is also with child. This one makes my fifth, but I fear I'll never be able to catch up with the master of the golden faucet, who turns out children as does the cherry tree turns out blossoms to bear fruit."

"Lord Kawasomeru! It's a great honor to learn that Lady Mineko is with child. I promise I'll not produce another child until you catch up with me my Lord. After all my Lord, is it not written on the divine winds that blow in from the sea that the Lord of the provinces will have as many sons as there are villages in Japan."

"Ahhh... Tanizaki-san! You should be a poet, you were born with a honey coated tongue whose words are wasted on this old fool's ears. I'll stay with you one night, I must visit the boring Sanuki, and be on my way back to my city. Between Lady Mineko being with child and threat of Wakatsuki demanding war between the inner provinces and his, it's an ill time to be away from the city. I'll make preparations for the provisions of my troops then I'll be expecting them to be well trained, and back to me in how long a time, Master Trainer Tanizaki-san?"

"Kawasomeru-sama! It depends on the training you want me to teach the fools. The more training you want them to understand, the longer it'll take to teach them, my Lord."

"Huh Tanizaki-san! I know this well. I want each Samurai to be taught in the ways they are lacking. I brought you a mixed batch of fools. Horsemen, foot soldiers, spearmen, and swordsmen. Each Warrior has his one discipline mastered, but it's as I stated, they're trained in only one discipline. I want each Samurai to be trained in the four disciplines of warfare. That way I can have any arm of my army replace with another, and their fighting abilities will not suffer from this change. With the changing times Japan is suffering, my armies and I must be like the willow branch and bend in the wind. With each Samurai able to do the others discipline, I'll accomplish this desire. I'm of the mind to believe a soldier trained in more than one duty, will better be able to perform all his duties."

The trainer stared at the bamboo wall for a moment going in thought. Kawasomeru decided to allow the wise trainer the moment to sort through his words and thoughts. He amused himself by watching a bird trying to land on a branch blowing in the light wind. Finally, the bird gave up and fluttered away at the same moment the trainer chose to speak to his lord.

"Lord Kawasomeru! I see the way you're thinking and I applaud this thought. But I fear I'm mired in thoughts and ways of the old style of warfare. It's important to be a master in one discipline, to be perfect in all of one's moves than to be a poor master in four fields. Please forgive my thoughts Kawasomeru-sama, I don't believe it's wise to train the foolish Warriors in all four fields of honor. Perhaps, two, at the most, three, but never four my Master." He cast his eyes to the floor waiting for his lord to explode for he dared to go against his thinking.

"Tanizaki-san! You have skillfully failed to answer my question of you old man. I'll repeat it so your old ears cannot say they didn't hear my question properly. How long will this training in all four disciplines take you to complete for these worthless Samurai that I bring before you?" He snapped angrily at the old man.

"Please forgive my foul manners and addle mind for not answering your question my Lord. I can have most of them trained within six months, seven at the most if they're badly addle minded and of slow learning."

"This time limit includes all four disciplines you teach, Master Trainer Tanizaki?"

"Hai Lord Kawasomeru! The added thirty sticks of time I'm speaking of taking, is in case I have to train them in the art of Kyushin, my Lord." (Close hand to hand combat)

He stared at the older man kneeling before him thinking of what he told him. There was a shuffling by the door to the rear of the building, and Kawasomeru saw Emiko standing in the door with cups and a pot of warm sake resting on a small tray. She was staring at him, begging her lord with her eyes for the right to serve him. He smiled at her as he nodded and she moved forward. Her movement caused Tanizaki to turn to her and he was the one who exploded.

"Foolish old woman who entered this room without permission! How dare you interrupt Lord Kawasomeru and myself when we're speaking! If it were not for you being with child, I'd have you beaten and the offending hair shaved from your worthless head and offered to the Lord Buddha to burn in his boiling pot. This is a terrible insult to Kawasomeru-sama. I'll have to apologize to him with my worthless life." Tanizaki stood and lifted his hand.

Emiko dropped to her knees and prepared for a beating from her husband, still holding the tray in her hands. She didn't protest his anger, knowing it was Kawasomeru who nodded her forward. She was prepared to take a beating if the lord chose to allow this to happen. All she kept repeating was, "Hai!" As her husband belittled her in front of the lord.

The trainer moved at Emiko ready to strike, but was stopped in his tracks when Kawasomeru bellowed. "Tanizaki! I was the one who called your obedient wife in the room. She's only guilty of doing her duty of serving me as I requested. She'll not be beaten for obeying my request, or for anything else for the rest of her life by you, or anyone else who walks upon the soil of Japan. You're not an uncivilized Ronin filth eater, so you'll not act as they and beat your wife needlessly! Especially if her insult to you was she was serving me as requested! Lady Emiko! You'll stand up and serve me as I asked of you. I am thirsty, domo."

Emiko didn't dare to raise her eyes from the floor as she replied to her master. "Hai!"

The concerned Lord Kawasomeru watched her struggle to her feet and smiled when her youngest daughter rushed in room to assist her to stand. "Yoi!" Good! He grunted, he waited until Emiko handed him a cup of sake and smiled to her, causing Emiko to blush. Then she handed a cup to her husband and filled it for him. Tanizaki nodded politely to his wife, who caused great relief to overtake her, and she dared a quick smile at him.

"Lady Emiko! Domo! Domo! You take good care of your worthless old Lord. I know Tanizaki-san will take excellent care of my Warriors. Tanizaki-san! I gave thought to the words you spoken. I agree with them, but I'll not change my mind on this matter. I decided to have these cursed Warriors trained in the four disciplines, and that's what will be done with the fools. It's wise to have Samurai trained in four honors. I have enough trained in one, more than enough." He bowed to the old master trainer.

"Lord Kawasomeru! It'll be as you demand, my Lord!" The old trainer replied as he offered him a polite bow to further his honoring of him.

"Fine! Enough of this talk, I'm tired and want to know what's happening in your honorable village, Master Trainer. Tell me of your fine children, and of your devoted wife, old man. Domo, more sake please Lady Emiko." He grunted as he held his empty cup at arm's length, and smiled at the trainer's lovely wife.

The youngest daughter rushed in the room and refilled the two cups as Kawasomeru grumbled. "Ahhh... Tanizaki-san! It's easy to understand why you chose to remain living in this honorable but small village." He mumbled as he listened to the frogs calling for their mates in the brisk night air by the stream, and added. "It's truly peaceful here. Will you honor me a short walk through your garden, Tanizaki-san?"

He bowed and stood without word and led the way to the garden for them. The second he requested to go for a walk, a number of Tanizaki's servants rushed to the garden, and lit torches, so the two masters would see where they walked in the darkness of night. The torches would also serve to keep the mosquitoes away as they strolled around. The overlord was unaware and less concerned about Michiko and her sleeping arrangements for him. He knew Tanizaki would make certain she and his important vassals and soldiers were taken care of in the village.

They walked in the garden, both were enjoying the sounds of night, and soft breezes which filled the air with sweet fragrance of flowers in night bloom. His three daughters prepared the honored place of the tokonoma, where the lord would sleep for the night. Folding screens were set in place to separate the tokonoma from the rest of the room, so he could enjoy privacy in peace and free from household interruptions. Soft, silk covered mats were placed on the floor for his added comfort and pleasure, and a vase of fresh cut flowers was placed at the head of the room. Along with a jar of water spiked slightly with honey for his pleasure and enjoyment.

Mosquitoes made the lives of the two warrior's miserable, but neither wanted to be the first to leave the pleasures of the garden. Lightening bugs danced in the air before them in the cool night air, drawn near by the torches, making an interesting and peaceful sight to watch.

As the mosquito swarm intensified, they gave in and return to the house, and protection the structure offered from the biting insects. It was past midnight before he turned in for the night, and wiggled under the silk sheets and allowed himself to relax. His troubled thoughts turning to Wakatsuki and the treachery he was about to unleash on the realm. A soft breeze entered the room and it sent a chill to his bones, he turned his back to the wall and ordered himself to sleep.

A soft rustling sound caught his ear and he stealthily unsheathed his wakizashi blade, and the master of the realm prepared for a night attack. He was ready to lunge at who entered the room, when he noticed the fine sent of Michiko's perfume, and reset the stabbing sword in its scabbard as he whispered softly to the unseen person. "Lady Michiko?"

"Hai my Lord. It is I Kawasomeru-sama." She replied to her master.

"You may approach Lady Michiko. It's well you chose to be with me on this night I'm chilled to the bone and I curse this cold for what it does to my bones, when it assaults me like this." He offered as he lifted the sheet and allowed Michiko to wiggle under the cover. She was naked and her warmth chased the chill from his bones as he fondled her breasts. They made love then she remained the night, each keeping the other warm on the cool night.

The next morning without waking Lord Kawasomeru, Lady Michiko crawled out from under the covers and over saw the making of the morning meal for the household. Though naked when she slept, she wasn't unarmed. She was a well trained and disciplined samurai woman, and as such she was allowed to carry certain types of weapons on her person. She carried a kogai, a skewer type weapon carried in the scabbard of a katana, it was tucked in her long jet black hair. She was prepared to protect her lord's life, even if it cost her own.

The morning sun shone brightly in Lord Kawasomeru's eyes and this caused him to stir and wake even though he was still tired from his ride to the ninth village. He sat up, warmly remembering the pleasures of the night he shared with Lady Michiko, as he stretched and moaned aloud. He slipped in his silk kosode and went on the verandah to enjoy the rest of the morning sunrise. To his surprise, Tanizaki was sitting on the front verandah, and the lord walked over to the old man sitting with his legs crossed under him, enjoying the wonderful sunrise.

"Tanizaki-san! Please excuse this unworthy intrusion to your Wa, your harmony and peace of mind. Will you allow this fool the honor of sharing the birth of this day with you?" The warlord asked the trainer politely, it was needed, for he interrupted the trainer's meditation.

He half turned his head. "Lord Kawasomeru! It'd give me great pleasure to share the beginning of such a beautiful day with you. Dozo, dozo, please sit and be with me and be comfortable. It's a beautiful sunrise to enjoy my Lord."

"Domo Tanizaki-san, you're most kind to share this beautiful of sunrises with this unworthy man, Tanizaki-san. Ieeee! My mind's deeply troubled old man." He offered as he stared at the sun as it left the grasp of the earth.

"I can understand this fear you're suffering, my Lord. One would think the warlords of Japan would have grown tired of this death and destruction by this time, and they might have found some way to live in peace and harmony with the earth, and with each other. But I see my prayers to Lord

Buddha have not reached his ears. Many times in the past I considered leaving this veil of tears for the filthy life of a cursed monk, so I could pray for Japan's lost sons and daughters who perished by the tongue of the sword of indifference for the want of land, or for the want of worthless valuables and other trinkets of sin and lust. I'm at a loss over how easily we allow our children to perish on the battlefield with little thought." He was deep in thought as he spoke, but he didn't look at the lord as he continued to stare at the soaring sun. He was one of the only people in Japan who would retain his head for daring to speak this way before his master.

Something Tanizaki said aroused his interest, and Kawasomeru grunted. "Tanizaki-san! What was it you meant by the word warlords of Japan? I fear this is a new word for my ears to digest."

"Lord Kawasomeru! I'm sorry for uttering that word before your presence. It's a term some younger Samurai of the Ninth Village use when referring to the great lords of the provinces of Japan. Domo, please forgive my stupidity for using a word that puzzled your mind. I didn't intend to insult my Lord with my poor choice of words. If you'd like, I'll shave my head of offending hair and enter the Buddha way of life to forever fo..."

"Dozo Tanizaki-san! Save your hair please, it's far too little and too white to please Lord Buddha, old man. Besides, if you banished yourself to the Buddha way of life, who will be left to train my worthless Samurai? Iye, I'm not insulted by this word Master Trainer, it's a fine word to be used when referring to the lords of the eastern provinces. Maybe it'll serve to make us think once in a while, do we really want to be known in history as warlords? No Tanizaki-san, I'm not displeased by the word, I'll adopt this word until we can live in peace with one another. Then, and only then will I have this word struck from the Japanese culture, a lovely sunrise neh?"

"Hai Lord Kawasomeru! A most enjoyable sunrise to behold with one's eyes, and whose beauty is further enhanced many times over, because I was allowed to share it with my Lord." He bowed to the sun, the warlord joined in the homage he offered the sun goddess Amaterasu.

A soft bell rang twice, and Tanizaki rose and announced. "Kawasomeru-sama! I believe it's time we eat. I'm certain by this time, the fool old Sanuki-san is losing his water waiting for you to appear at his home on this glorious day. Would you like me to attend this meeting, my Lord?"

"Ieeeee! Of course I want you to attend this meeting with that one who I don't like much, Tanizaki-san. I want you presented at every meeting I attend in your village, before I leave your town for the safety of my Castle. I'll be leaving by the high noon sun, and you'll notify me when your wife delivers my next Warrior to this world of the living, old man?" He asked more than ordered the master trainer this time.

The trainer bowed as they headed for the morning table covered with different fruit. They ate in silence with their eyes cast to the table. When they finished eating, Lord Kawasomeru belched loudly then left after eating the proper amount of food, not too much to insult his host, but enough to honor her meal. He put his heavier kosode on, and prepared to leave Tanizaki's home. He made certain he addressed Tanizaki's three daughters before leaving his home. Then the lord of the realm ordered the oldest boys to present themselves at Engakuji Castle in thirty sticks of time then bowed to Emiko who returned the bow as politely as he added. "Lady Emiko! You'll take care of my little Warrior hiding within your belly?"

"Hai my Lord, hai. He'll be well taken care of even before he's born to the life in Japan, Kawasomeru-sama. May you enjoy a life of the crane my Lord." Emiko bowed again, pleased with the honor she spoke to Kawasomeru, for the crane was the Japanese symbol of longevity. She was attempting to repay some honor he bestowed on her, he bowed to her first, and the gracious bow took place on the verandah.

The act was carried out in plain view of the entire village even though not one person was visible outside their homes. Emiko was certain everyone witnessed the kind gesture offered to her from their lord. If any fools missed it, they would be informed by the others who seen it when they went to draw water from the well. She smiled because of the face the lord's bow brought her. She watched as Lord Kawasomeru and her husband headed for Shoya Sanuki's home for their meeting with the village leader.

The meeting with the Shoya went quickly, with Lord Kawasomeru promising to have food provisions delivered to the village tomorrow morning for the samurai to be trained by Tanizaki. With much fan fare, he prepared to leave, his armor placed in its carrying case and samurai supplied by Sanuki who joined his samurai to join in the upcoming war, he left for the castle.

Lady Michiko was in her shuttered palanquin, and would be carried back to the castle, her feet were not made to touch the dirt of ground of Japan any longer. She was above that insult.

CHAPTER FOUR

Master Trainer Tanizaki waited until the caravan was out of sight before he went to the field where the samurai were garrisoned. The troops were beginning to stir and he barked at the officers assembled before him. He was angry the soldiers remained at rest late in the morning. He issued orders from this day the warriors were to be up exercising before sunrise.

The crafty trainer allowed the trainees one day of rest, before the training was to begin. He had the officers order hinin to construct a narrow canal to bring clean drinking water to the encampment, and to wash away the human waste then he stormed back to the village. Every samurai received orders they weren't allowed to go near the village proper unless invited by the trainer, or Shoya. The officers dispersed and bellowed at their warriors to carry out the orders of the trainer. Each officer knew they were bound to obey every order given by the master trainer, as if the order came from Lord Kawasomeru himself.

The trainer reported to Sanuki for the last time before assuming command over the village, the samurai and surrounding area. The trainer knew he would order some townspeople to move from their homes, and have them leveled to make room for the training area. As of that day, and during the rest of the time the warriors were undergoing training, he was the master of the village, and everyone was bound to listen to his demands and orders without hesitation.

When he returned home, he was surprised his wife left the home without informing him where she was going. His daughters didn't know where she disappeared to, and he was concerned because she was so close to delivering her baby. He entered their home and went to the bamboo chest where he removed his armor, weapons and notes he accumulated over the years, explaining the art of warfare. No one in the village besides Toru Sanuki, Yoshio Kobayashi, himself, his wife, one daughter, and two sons, were able to read or write. Samurai Kobayashi's abilities of reading and writing were limited.

He laid out his scrolls and drawings, and picked through them to put aside the ones he needed for training. He was proud he was doing something more than training small numbers of samurai, for defense of villages and towns from attack by the roaming Ronin filth. The old man unwrapped his no dachi, his favorite weapon a six foot long two handed sword from its silk wrapping. He removed his katana and wakizashi blades and placed his everyday carrying swords in their place. The trainer pulled the blade out, noticing the many nicks and discoloration from blood which dried on the blade before he clean it. He smiled as he remembered his last battle at Minatogawa, where he stood shoulder to shoulder with Shogun Ashikaga, and received a gash which crossed his chest and nearly cost him his life. He remembered how proud he was when the Shogun helped him to his feet, and made sure he was all right. His fingers ran gingerly down the length of his katana, feeling the nicks and chips from his enemy's blade striking his sword. The edge was surprisingly sharp and menacing. He sighed, knowing days of battles were only lived in the mind. The battlefield forever changed since the days of invasions of the Mongols.

Emiko rushed out of the home seconds after her husband and Lord Kawasomeru left. She went to the far end of the village to the home of the old, hated and feared seer Hachirobe, to have him search his world of wonder for the answer to her feared question held in her mind. If the child she was carrying was truly a boy. She carried two branches of the willow along with a tray of rolled eel, his requested payment for this sought after information. She knelt before his door and from within she heard him bid her entry. She feared this man greatly; she didn't like him, he was so mysterious and smelled terribly, and was always filthy. He was of the old monk's world, where men went months before bathing until their noses were unable to stand themselves.

She entered the dark room with covered windows and knelt in the center of the room. From a dark corner of the same room, a deep voice called. "And what is this visit about?"

"Dozo, I'm concerned about..." Her words were cut off by the old seer.

"You're concerned about the sex of the baby you carry inside you, Lady Emiko?"

"Hai honorable one of the lost days and night!" She answered politely, she was scared to her soul the seer knew what it was troubling her so.

"Lay down on the floor and open your Kosode, woman. Do not hesitate."

Shocked by the order, she slowly laid on the floor knowing if she opened her kosode, she would be in his gaze, a terrible insult to her husband. She was caught in a dilemma, she knew she wouldn't sleep until the baby was born if she refused to open her kosode, and the seer refused to tell her. If she allowed this filthy man to see her naked, she would betray her husband's trust. Slowly, she stretched out and opened her kosode. She knew she had gone too far and had to know the sex of her baby, or be driven mad with doubt and concern. If only Lord Kawasomeru would have given consideration to the possibility of the child being a female then she wouldn't have to be defiled as she was about to do.

After she laid on the floor and had her kosode open, Hachirobe crawled to her, his legs grotesquely bent from battle. His body odor reached her before his filthy hands ran over her stomach and breasts. It was clear he was enjoying himself as he searched the wonder world for the answer she searched for. His touch almost caused her to wretch. His examination felt as if it were taking an eternity then it ended with Hachirobe crawling back to his dark corner.

She stayed frozen while on the floor, she was afraid to move or breathe.

"Close your kosode woman, you're with a male child, woman. Go from me at once woman!"

"Hai! Domo Hachirobe-san, domo." She cried as she closed her robe and struggled to her feet, happy beyond happiness she was with a male child. She was pleased for the honor her husband would receive, once the province became aware Tanizaki's son would be an officer in Kawasomeru's army, and be destined to become the new trainer for his realm. As happy as she was, she still felt the terrible touch of this filthy, wretched old man. She wanted nothing more than to rush home and take a yu, a hot bath. She rushed to bathe, surprised Kawasomeru hadn't taken advantage of the natural Kamiyu, the hot waters bubbling up from the depths of the earth naturally heated. She entered her house and noticed her husband examining his weapons.

"Lady Emiko! Where were you hiding? I was worried about you my Lady."

"Sunimasen, (I am sorry) I went to see the old and foul Hachirobe."

"Why in the name of the good Kami who give us life would you want to see that pile of filth and waste?" He demanded angrily as he painfully stood and glared harshly at his wife.

She dropped to her knees and bowed, not daring to allow her eyes to meet his. She was filled with shame over the examination she was forced to endure as she answered. "Husband! I wanted to know if he was able to tell what child I was carrying in me."

"What child you carry?" Tanizaki grunted as he relaxed and looked at his weapons again.

"Yes my husband, what child. Whether the child living in me is that of a male or female child." She cried while staring at the floor, ashamed of her actions.

"Ahhh... I see Lady Emiko. And what did the pile of filth have to say about the child to you?"

"My most honored and loving husband, he informed me I am with a male child."

He couldn't hide the smile that crossed his lips as he rushed to his wife and helped her to her feet as he called out. "Estsuko come at once. Your mother needs assistance.

Enko, make your mother cha. Attend your mother who'll bring forth the next master trainer to the world."

His eldest daughters rushed to their mother's side and helped support her weight until she was steady on her feet. They led her to the outer room and prepared tea. Emiko whispered to Estsuko, her oldest daughter she wanted to take a Yu, and she offered to bathe her before she entered the hot waters. Emiko smiled at her eldest as she ran a finger down the side of her face, knowing she understood the vile examination she endured, to find out the sex of the child. "Estsuko, you'll make some foolish Warrior an honorable and attentive wife."

Estsuko smiled at her mother, proud she was her so wise mother, and rushed out of the home to prepare the bath for her.

The master trainer was happy as he separated a number of charts and scrolls and put the ones he wouldn't need back in his chest. He was overjoyed Emiko was with a male child, he never gave a thought to the examination she endured, for the old Hachirobe to see into the strange world of the seers. Once he had his supplies sorted out to his satisfaction, he shoved the chest against the wall and placed his equipment on top of it. Then he began the arduous task of preparing his mind and body for the disciplines that would be placed on his aging body and mind, during the training of this Ronin filth Kawasomeru delivered to his village. He allowed himself to enjoy a smile in the knowledge that soon, this bunch of dung eating shinigurai (crazy to die) warriors would be transformed into one of the best fighting and disciplined armies in the world. An army who would know the world of the four disciplines, Aisu-kuge swordsmanship, Hozo-in spearmanship, Kajima archery and the last, horsemanship.

For the rest of the day, he mentally and physically prepared himself for the countless toils of training the warriors. Night closed, and he drew peace from the frogs crying by his pond. His wife prepared his night meal, and they ate with the children. He finally turned in, looking forward to the night's sleep, and working with the men on the next day.

LORD KAWASOMERU'S CARAVAN

It took three days for the now warlord to arrive at Engakuji Castle. His city was operating properly as he entered before daylight. He waited in the woods outside his castle, refusing to make his entrance at night. Again, the warlord rode to the gate over eight wood bridges, his horse's hooves clapping loudly, informing all of his arrival. He appeared dressed in full armor and roasting from the heat of the high morning sun, and heavy armor.

Before meeting with his second in command, the warlord checked on his pregnant wife's welfare and then he undressed and took a hot bath and dressed in a cool, light kosode. He appeared at the large reception room and opened the meeting. General Satsuki Okumura was sitting in the center of the room, ten feet from him. He stayed silent until he was noticed and recognized by the powerful Lord Kawasomeru.

He allowed General Okumura to wait while he welcomed his Falcon old Leather Eyes, offering him a sliver of raw meat which the bird devoured greedily. When he finished with his falcon, he turned to General Okumura and grunted. "Ichi, (first) have we heard from that dung eater?"

Everyone knew he was referring to Wakatsuki. The general made a scene of clearing his throat and shifted his weight as he grunted. "Hai Kawasomeru-sama! Lord Wakatsuki sent a messenger with a scroll." He handed the neatly folded scroll to his lord and continued. "I opened and read it. He states now is not a good time for the Lord from his west to pay a visit to Chiyoda Castle. He further states there are many problems he must settle in Hida province, and would not return to Chiyoda for weeks. He further stated he would deem it an honor and privilege, if you'd pay a visit to his Castle after he returned from his toils."

"Ooooookumura-san! What are some of these problems the fool refers to?" He growled, glaring at General Okumura as he drew out his name.

The general bowed as he replied. "Kawasomeru-sama! Upon receiving this scroll, I sent spies to Hida to see what the problems might be. Yesterday the first spy reported by means of pigeons. He states Hida and Mino provinces are having a problem with the Ronin Omi province, part of Mino and the Lord from Omi spoke to the lesser lords of Iga, Yamoto and Yama. Lord Muraoka is angry with Lord Yonezawa, and vowed to separate his province from Yonezawa's rule."

"Ahhh... this is good. What does the lowly worm eater say about that threat?" He growled, unable to hide the pleasure he received from the two warlords threatening each other.

"Lord Yonezawa's unhappy at the thought of having his provinces ripped out from under his weather beaten feet. He has openly threatened to separate Lord Muraoka's head from his body, and destroy his civilians and take his province over by force if needed, in an attempt to bring peace to the other provinces. It was said he complained to Lord Muraoka he was not the enemy, but Lord Kawasomeru was the real enemy in this region."

He laughed as he thought of the dilemma Wakatsuki was mired in as he mumbled. "Ahhh... This is good, Okumura-san! Very good to know indeed. So I'm the enemy am I? To think the filthy hinin waste was days before threatening to attack my provinces. How long do you think it'll take for the fool to gain control of his rebel provinces, General Okumura-san?"

"Lord Kawasomeru! My spies assured me there are no way these warring provinces will ever come to peace on their own accord. It's believed by our generals once Lord Wakatsuki turns his attention to the provinces to our south, his provinces to the north would take advantage of this opportunity, and will wage war between themselves. We know it's only Lord Wakatsuki holding the cursed provinces together in the northeastern and southern region. I think we should sit by and watch the lowly dogs happily eat at each other's worthless flanks."

"General Okumura-san! Is there any chance we might get one of Wakatsuki's provinces to cross over and join forces with us, before war starts between the sixteen provinces?" He asked his second in command as he stared at him while waiting his reply.

"Hai Lord Kawasomeru! I believe there's a chance we'll win our battle over Echizen province. Jomyo Chosokabe-sama keeps changing sides with the wind that blows. One day he's supporting us, the next day the fool is speaking to Lord Wakatsuki again, and I..."

"The fool has to check his bowels and make them strong; the waste of a man has no backbone in his body. It's a wonder he still remains in control of his province. I would've thought by now, at least one of his worthless Samurai would have stepped up, and dispatched the old woman. Even his worthless Warriors are not to be trusted in this world." The warlord grunted as he waved his hand, dismissing the ugly thoughts about Chosokabe with his general.

"Hai Lord Kawasomeru, perhaps someday one of his worthless soldiers will show his mettle, and will remove this foul dung heap from his rule over them."

"What about the rest of the provinces under Lord Wakatsuki's foul thumb and breath?" The warlord asked his general with concern.

"Iye! Not a chance of that happening, and we're worried if war does break out between the smaller provinces under Lord Wakatsuki's control. It might spread to our allies of Ise and Kii provinces, my Lord. They're the most unstable provinces of the Eight of our house, Master. I'm worried Kii might go to Lord Wakatsuki's side if Lord Saito is offered the proper inducements from the despised Ronin Wakatsuki, my Lord."

"Perhaps you might want to dispatch a few of our Warriors, and have them pay a visit to his camp, and order them to point out the dangers he'll face if he backs the wrong warlord in this upcoming war." He barked as he hawked and spat into a bowl.

Okumura bowed deeply, but remained silent as he waited for Kawasomeru to add to his words.

"What is it now Okumura-san?" He snorted as he stared at his general.

"Lord Kawasomeru! You used a word I'm unfamiliar with, my Lord."

"Huh!" He grunted, not realizing he used the name for the lords of the provinces.

"Warlord! What is meant by this new word warlord you speak of? Kawasomeru-sama."

"Hai, warlord. Warlord is another and proper name to call land barons. It was spoken first by the Master Trainer from the Ninth Village." He replied, pleased that he caused distress to his second in command. "What do you think of the fine word?"

"I like it, it's a worthy word to call a great Lord. Shall I order it to be added to the rolls?"

"Hai! So it is ordered. General Okumura-san! Keep your spies working day and night in the cursed provinces to our south. If the loathsome Wakatsuki seems to be gaining control and settling the provinces down, you'll order your spies to create an incident in the region. I want to give the fool much unrest and countless problems to deal with, so he'll not be able to concentrate on organizing his worthless forces against us. This is a gift sent to me by the Kami, General. I order an offering to the monks at Ryi.

"I'll do this at once my Lord." The general bowed, stood and left the meeting hall.

THE NEXT MORNING IN THE NINTH VILLAGE.

The excited Master Trainer Tanizaki was the first in his house to awake. He ate little as he hoisted his armor on his shoulders, and tucked the swords in his sash and struggled down the stairs of the verandah to his front garden. None of his family or samurai offered to help the old man as he struggled to open the gate. They knew it would be loss of face if anyone thought him too old to carry his armor and weapons. It was still pitch black as he went down the street, leaving the gate open and the shinren, the protective cords tied to the gate gently swaying in the soft breeze. These four cords were hung by his wife to protect the occupants of their home, and anyone who used the gate against evil influences The old warrior was followed by seven of the fourteen guards. The rest were ordered to remain and guard his family from all ill.

He struggled, not daring to stop and take a breath; his guards moved closer in case they were needed. Each saw the struggle being fought, and it gave him great face which was surely going to be spoken about at the camp fires of the young trainees. He arrived at the encampment as he desired, before the soldiers began to stir from their sleep. He dropped his armor on a chest, and drew in a breath and bellowed as he picked up a bamboo staff and beat on anyone sleeping. He charged in tents, beating and yelling at the soldiers, all the while gaining his strength. "Get up worthless piles of manure, the best part of this day is over and you dogs snore as if you were old men waiting to die. Get up before I shave your heads, and order you to follow Buddha."

Startled samurai ran in all directions while dressing and retrieve weapons and horses. Officers and samurai picked up his scream, and yelled at their wards and trainees.

The old warhorse was swamped by the horde of samurai running in all directions and he got out of their way by moving to one of the larger tents where he spotted General Shimbo, as he stood grinning at the trainees rushing around. The instant General Shimbo saw Tanizaki he bowed. He returned the bow and assumed his position by the general's side. They were joined by the second General, Miyamoto. Samurai Kobayashi joined the group, and Master Trainer Tanizaki introduced him as the general who would be overseeing his orders. The two generals bowed to the samurai, overjoyed he just appointed Kobayashi a general.

General Shimbo bellowed for the warriors to assemble before him, and Tanizaki ordered a platform constructed as a viewing station. He ordered a building erected where most tents were pitched. In the back of his mind he looked to increase the size of the ninth village, and would use the energies of the soldier as laborers who neither he nor Sanuki had to pay. He pointed to a canal and ordered Shimbo to divert water from that canal needed for drinking and waste removal. When everything quieted down and the soldiers were assembled, he asked which soldiers were trained in what discipline. The soldiers trained on horseback were moved to the left of the formation. His spearmen moved to the left center of the group, and archers moved to right of center, and swordsmen to their right. Most of the samurai was trained swordsmen already.

The trainer asked the samurai if any were trained in hand to hand combat to speak up and about everyone grunted. He realized his training would be easier to accomplish than first expected, because so many samurai were trained in this discipline. His next order was for the soldiers to dress in armor and assemble before him once this was accomplished. While they waited for the soldiers to return, the officers along with Tanizaki had something to eat. General Shimbo asked when the soldiers would be fed and Tanizaki snapped shortly, "Night time."

"Master Trainer Tanizaki-san! You want the Warriors to go the full day without food?" General Shimbo asked.

"Without water also General Shimbo-san. They are Samurai, and they'll act like Samurai."

"This is wrong; the men need to eat. They were marched two days without eating properly, and you want to deprive them of food and water for an entire day. I'll complain to Lord Kawasomeru over this foul treatment of his Warriors. Tanizaki-san! Fear his unfettered wrath, he'll order the taking of your head for this insulting way of treating his soldiers trusted to you."

"Ahhh... General Shimbo-san! If only you would listen to the words which pour forth from your mouth and soil my ears. Kawasomeru-sama has trusted me with the training of these dung eating soldiers. I'm in command of them, and if you don't like how I train them, you're ordered to commit suppuku, and I'll request to have you replaced, that simply. I have no problems with my orders for the Samurai, General! What is it we request from our soldiers? We need them to be prepared to fight whenever a situation arises. Do you think we'd put off a war because our soldiers have not eaten yet General, neh? The soldiers I train will learn to go days without eating, and days without rest, and more days of being able to war without complaining. Any soldier who has a problem with these orders, will be allowed to go over to that, err..."

He scanned the tents until he settled on the one he was looking for. "Hai! The tent where I'll have a filthy monk take up residence, and he'll shave the heads of any soldier who fails to complete my training as ordered. The soldiers will be given two options, suppuku, or endure the life of a monk. Shimbo-san! You're free to be the first to go to that tent and become monk."

When the general's chest heaved and he stiffened his backbone, Master trainer Tanizaki added to his orders for his officer. "Very good General Shimbo-san! I knew you'd make the right decision. I want, no correct that, I demand that tent be feared by all warriors. I want them to be willing to be hacked to pieces rather than be forced to visit that tent, and live that foul way of life. I want that tent hated more than they'll hate Wakatsuki."

He then asked General Shimbo what his discipline was and he grunted. "Swordsmanship." Then the trainer asked General Miyamoto's discipline and he replied, "Archery." He was aware Kobayashi was a master at spearmanship. The trainer was a master at the four plus three more disciplines. He thought for a moment then barked. "This is good. Shimbo-san, today you'll take the archers and teach them swordsmanship. General Miyamoto-san, you'll take command of the spearmen and teach them in the ways of the Yumi (Bow). General Kobayashi-san! You'll train the archers in the way of the spear, and I'll train the horsemen in the ways they'll wage war in the future. Every day, trade groups with one another. We'll teach the dung eating youngsters the proper way in which to fight, and win the war or they'll be filthy monks. Begin!"

He watched as each general took charge of his warriors, and moved them around the training field. The spearmen set up targets and attacked them, archers did the same, and swordsmen attacked each other with wood swords. Each general screamed at their wards. The trainer dressed in armor, mounted his horse almost as old as he was, and addressed his mounted warriors in a commanding tone. He wanted them to learn to guide their horse with their legs rather than the reins. He showed them what he meant and they tried to do the same. He was thinking of allowing the swordsmen to attack his mounted warriors later in the week. The horsemen were his favorite, and he would invest his best training and time in them.

The day proceeded long and back breaking for Tanizaki, he once fell off his horse and made light of it. He paid the price for his stupidity for the rest of the day, with a pain stabbing him in his back. The day was helter skelter at best with no organization for the trainees. When he saw the messy way his program was being carried out, he spent the rest of the week making better targets and obstacles to challenge his soldiers. He ordered wooded areas leveled for an archery field away from the main part of the training field. Horsemen moved to the other side of the village which was level to a good field to gallop on. The field they used today would remain the sword and spear field, along with the soldier's sleeping quarters. He decided to have his carpenter's help the warriors build their permanent living quarters while in training.

The trainer looked at the lowering sun and informed General Kobayashi he was turning in for the day, and left him in charge of the troops. He ordered him to have the warriors work on the training field and start the construction of their living quarters. He informed the new general any soldier who balked at his orders, was to be directed to the monk who only hours ago took over his tent in the middle of the encampment. This did the trick, no warrior would dare complain once the first warrior was told he could go see the monk and have his hair shaven clean.

The old trainer dragged his aching exhausted body home, leaving his armor with Kobayashi for tomorrow's use on the field. His wife had a hot bath waiting, and his daughter washed his body as he stared at the ceiling of the bath house, and prayed for death to overtake his aching and battered body. It didn't and he turned in for the night, not bothering to eat. His wife slept with one ear open in case her husband woke and was hungry, but he sleep through to the morning.

Lady Emiko had to wake her husband Tanizaki and tell him the sun was about to rise. He ate in silence, the pain he was suffering from yesterday's training program kept his tongue quiet then he rushed for the camp as quickly as his old bones allowed him to move. The soldiers and villagers had cleared the new archery field as ordered. He was surprised to see the warriors were in assembled waiting his orders. He walked up to General Kobayashi and General Shimbo. He bowed to each. "My Generals do honor by their accomplishments on our training field. Where is General Miyamoto?"

General Shimbo immediately returned the bow as he replied. "Master Trainer Tanizaki-san! General Miyamoto-san has taken the spearmen out to the archery field, and is having them hit stationary targets with spears."

"I intend to allow the men to enjoy a morning meal on this day, General Shimbo-san."

"This is out of the question Master Trainer Tanizaki-san, we issued orders to start work on the horse field, while the carpenters of your village take what warriors they need to start on the housing for the trainees. It was wise to order that monk to take the first tent. Ahhh... the worthless warriors are so afraid of being sent to visit the filthy man, they run passed his tent as if the Devil Kami dwelled within. I'll suggest this same treatment be adopted by Kawasomeru-sama when I return to Engakuji Castle, Master Trainer Tanizaki. It's a novel way to maintain control over these worthless manure heaps we're trying to shape them into worthy warriors." General Shimbo snarled as he warily kept an eye on one warrior he intended to make an example of, sending him to visit the hated monk and have his hair cut.

It was an enjoyable time when it was the swordsmen's turn to try their hand at riding a horse. Tanizaki watched with amusement as the warriors were sent flying as they tried to mount their horses. He stared as other warriors able to mount their horses, were bucked and bounced off. It was mayhem at best, but it proved to be a source of jokes and laughter, as other trainees stopped what they were doing and watched the swordsmen being abused by the horses. The weather didn't help, this was the first day of constant rain and thunder claps.

By the third week of training, the buildings were constructed, fields were leveled and areas picked for training were squared away so the training could begin at first light every day. The trainer changed the warrior's time to eat and rest, he went through a night attack, even though these attacks were usually reserved for the Ninja warriors. Days blended to weeks as he carried out his mission of training the samurai delivered by Kawasomeru. He had no idea war between the two warlords was put off, because Wakatsuki was having trouble with the few provinces he was depending on to attack Kawasomeru's southern flanks, and force him to split his forces to defend a two front war. Nor did he care, he was only interested in training the warriors.

After the third week of training was completed, Master Trainer Tanizaki decided to change his lessons again. He was concentrating on riding skills every day, and was able to get the swordsmen to become good horsemen. It was Saturday, and he was weary from the long days of training with no breaks. His wife was in pain and the night before he thought his son was going to be born, but it turned out to be a false alarm. Having been up most the night and was exhausted, and in his mind he already gave the soldiers Sunday to rest. Convincing himself he was doing this in their best interest, not his. As he dragged himself home he decided it was time to move to the next level of training for his horsemen using bows.

The archer exercises consisted of hitting four sets of three targets, while running across the field. Monday, he planned to put these archers on horses and have them gallop while firing arrows at the same targets. If the archers were able to hit their targets, he planned to move to the next level of training, using dogs as swift moving targets to hit. He walked down the street to his home, when he reached the gate he heard his youngest daughter playing the shakuhachi. (flute) He listened to the enchanting music, and his chest swelled with pride, knowing his daughter was able to bring tranquility to his soul with her music.

The old Shoya Sanuki was out and walking about his peaceful village. It was believed by many villagers that he walked the night in hopes of catching young women of the village undressing. Everyone in the village was aware of this and ignored it, with some of the more daring women giving him a show when they knew he was about. Shoya Sanuki walked up behind Master Trainer Tanizaki, and placed his hand on his shoulder. He was detected by the old man and three guards who brought his attention to the old man with subtle grunts and guarded head movements. For a moment, he toyed with the idea of allowing his guards to challenge him, maybe scare him from his nighttime walks, but decided against it.

"Master Trainer Tanizaki-san! The music of your daughter fills my honorable village with such delight and calmness, even the birds roost on roofs and pay homage to her outstanding abilities with the flute." Shoya Sanuki brought his attention to five robins perched on the fence and seemed like they were listening to the music.

"Hai Sanuki-san! I believe you're correct with your kind words. They truly look like they're listening to her music. Why are you out and about on such a cool night, old man?"

"I was watching the stars when I noticed you walking home from the training fields, and wanted to know how the training of the Warriors was going. You know it'll give our village great face if you train those worthless slobs, and make them well trained Warriors. There'll be no end to the gifts and honors that'll shower on us from Lord

Kawasomeru, if he's pleased with your abilities to train his army of Samurai."

"Fear not for the training of the worthless Samurai, Shoya Sanuki-san! You'll receive the honors that you seek from our Lord and Master. The training of the fools is going better than beyond my thoughts. The Warriors are learning by leaps and bounds, and soon they'll be complete soldiers for their Master." He let out a sign.

"Tanizaki-san! Don't fear to ask for help if you need it. I'm prepared to lend you number..."

"I fear nothing of this life, Sanuki-san!" He snarled as he shoved the gate aside and stormed through it. His guards took the suddenness as a threat and they assumed a defensive posture as they stared at the old Shoya, until he walked away from his home.

The exhausted master trainer didn't enter the house right off, instead he walked to the rear of the building and strolled peacefully through the garden. His daughter's music and the serene tranquility he enjoyed from the garden, and other soothing sounds from the small pond and crying frogs, invigorated him. When the trainer had enough peacefulness, he entered the rear of his home from the garden area.

He took his wife and daughters off guard by entering the house from the rear door. When they saw him, the daughters rushed over and helped their father out of his clogs which he failed to remove outside the home. He looked to his wife and apologized for the insult he offered by entering their home with his clogs on. She smiled at her exhausted husband, trying to hide the pain she was receiving from the child within her.

"I have a meal prepared for my honorable husband." His wife offered.

"Forgive my impoliteness, but I'm too tired to eat on this foul night. I'll go to bed and take tomorrow off to rest myself. I'll give the Warriors a day off before I change their training to the next level. I sent Ogino-san off to inform General Kobayashi-san of my decision. I'll sleep in tomorrow and enjoy the sunrise from my bed." Ogino was one of his samurai guards.

The day off was a beautiful one for early May. The temperature was warm and the explosion of blooming flowers and almost constant chatter of hordes song birds, added to the beauty of the day. The trainer's daughter was practicing her flute again, and the sweet smell of the morning meal assaulted the old man's nostrils. He yawned and stretched as he threw the silk sheet aside and stood naked. He didn't remember washing last night, but he found himself clean this morning. He looked around and saw the basin wasn't in the room and realized his wife must have washed him while he slept. It was his eldest daughters who washed him, Emiko was suffering from the tossing child, and hadn't gone to sleep.

He dressed in a clean fundoshi (loincloth) a lightweight kosode and nothing else. The old trainer intended to spend hours in the bath to steam away some pains from his body. For the first weeks he willed the minor pains from his body, by the third week proved how worthless his mind's orders to his body were. He entered the outer room and asked how his wife was feeling. Looking at her answered his question. "Emiko! You're in pain I can read in your face. Do you wish me to send for the worthless doctor to attend to your needs? He can give you herbs to ease your pains. Maybe he can start the baby early."

"Iye! I'm no worthless whore of the Pillow World incapable of carrying her baby to time of birth. I have the midwife stopping by today to see what is happening, and how soon before this stubborn little one will decide to leave my worthless body. He's acting like our other sons when I carried them. Ieeeee, the daughters came out with no pain, but the boys. Ieeeee, they have given me such pain and discomfort. It's true, boys create pain to their mothers even before the day they're born to the world. I should've had daughters and avoided this discomfort." She cried as she lifted her shoulders and drew in air to help take away some pain this child was causing her.

"Lady Emiko! It was wise for you to have seen that filthy seer the other day so the great fool could lay your mind at easy you carry a boy child. I know of the embarrassing examination you endured. But I allowed you to endure what was intolerable, so you could rest your troubled mind. I know you'd never have rested peacefully until the baby was born, if you didn't visit the foul seer." He mumbled as he sipped his tea.

"Ieeeee! But what if he was wrong with his vision? What if the child is that of a girl child? Think of the disgrace that'll befall our home if that happens. Lord Kawasomeru has given you great face for a boy child. My mind still worries so much." Emiko complained.

"Emiko! You worry needlessly, you know this old seer has never missed on his picks of the child's sex. Think woman, you said yourself this child is being carried as a boy child. I have witnessed your carrying and I too have seen the similarities between the boys and my daughters, in the way you carried them. Lady Emiko, I have no doubt he's a male child so rest your troubled mind, you have enough to worry about without thinking of more to worry about." The old trainer grumbled as he flicked his hand, dismissing her worries as he sipped his tea again.

"What if he was wrong this time my wise and old husband?" Emiko cried again.

"If he's wrong, I'll take his miserable head and have it placed on a spike." He snapped harshly as he jumped to his feet and stormed out the room to the garden.

She was shattered she upset her husband's Wa so terribly. She rushed for his katana and ran out the door and dropped to her knees before his feet and offered him his sword.

"What is this foolish old woman?" He said as he took the offered sword from her hands.

The moment he did, she stretched her neck so he had a clear swipe at it.

"Emiko! What is this foolishness about you offer me on this foul day, woman?"

"I have insulted you my husband, I have disrupted your Wa. I'm a miserable old whore who failed her duty to make her husband happy. I don't merit the right to remain on this earth, taking up space with my poor efforts at making my husband happy. I don't deserve to continue to live if I cannot make my husband..."

He tossed his blade to the guard standing nearest him, and reached down and helped his wife to her feet as he complained. "Emiko! I order you to have this baby. I believe he's driving you mad, and in return, you're driving me insane. Emiko! You're a good wife, worthy of remaining on this earth as long as the Kami see fit to allow you to visit it. I'll have no more of this nonsense. Where is this foul midwife of yours?"

"Husband, you're not upset with me for my stupidity of upsetting your Wa?" She cried as she wiped at a tear seeping out of the corner of her eye.

"I could no more be angry at you than I could be at the sun goddess for giving us this most delightful day to enjoy. Lady

Emiko! It'll please me greatly if you would accompany me for a quick walk through your wonderful garden. Together, we can watch as the flowers awake from a long winter sleep."

They walked to the rear garden, with Emiko leaning lightly against her husband for added strength. Calm again returned to the home of Tanizaki, but it didn't last very long. As they peacefully strolled through the garden together, Emiko suddenly suffered more pain than the night before. She believed it was because she was upset, but when it continued she blamed her moves when she rushed for the sword. Everything she blamed for the suffering was in vain, her baby was preparing to come.

They stopped by the pond and she reached down and pulled a petal from a flower and pitched it in the water, a carp came to the surface and snapped it up. This caused her to turn to her husband and smile as she offered. "It's truly beautiful out here my husband."

"Yes." He replied with a smile as he turned and his face clouded over with worry as he stared at her. Her color was wrong and there was a slight trace of blood in the corner of her mouth. Not wishing to worry her, he said that he wanted another cup of tea, and started to guide his wife towards the house. As they walked, she suddenly doubled over in pain, but she refused to allow her husband know of her pain. It would be most insulting to exhibit any form of pain from child bearing before her husband.

"Emiko! Are you all right? Is the baby giving you trouble inside?" He snapped at her as he lifted her on his arm, making her walking easier to bear.

"I'm fine my foolish husband. But I think the time for this child coming is nearing." She replied in a weak voice to her concerned husband.

"I'll carry you to the parturition house then."

"Nonsense. What will the Samurai and our neighbor's think of my failing, if I allow you to carry your worthless wife who cannot have her baby like a worthy wife. I'll not be carried like a sack of rice going to market. I'll walk like a true Japanese woman." She announced with as much pride in her voice as she could muster under her great pain.

"Emiko! I care not one grain of rice what these manure heaps think of me or you." He growled as he scooped up his wife in his arms and carried her towards the house.

When the guards to the rear of the building saw this and their commander's struggle with his wife. They rushed to his side and to his surprise, they helped him with his ailing wife. His eldest daughter Estsuko rushed out of their home to her mother's side, fearing her father ignored Lord Kawasomeru's orders and beaten her for some infraction. When she noticed the trace of blood on the corner of her mouth, she was sure her father beaten her mother. She dared to shoot an angry look at her father who ignored it, and allowed his daughter to takeover carrying her mother.

He noticed his second daughter staring at them and growled. "Enko! Go and fetch the midwife for your mother. I think it's time for your brother to arrive in the world of true life."

"Hai father." The daughter raced off as ordered, showing pride as she ran for the midwife. Only the young such as she would be tolerated this way.

He supervised the samurai and his daughter carefully carrying his wife into the home. He rushed in before them and threw the straw mat on the floor in the main room, and ordered them to place his wife on it. When this was done, his daughter rushed to the kitchen to make some tea with willow bark to ease the pain.

Enko came in the house with the mid-wife. She checked Emiko's condition then ordered. "Estsuko, you and Enko help your mother to the parturition house. Tanizaki-san! Fetch the foolish Shinto priest and have him start his worthless prayers, it's time for your baby to come forth. I'll send for Lady Emiko's sisters and your relatives, they'll assist with the birth." The midwife was the only one who had the power to speak to Tanizaki or Kawasomeru in this manner. She was in control of his home for as long as it took for the birth of his son to occur.

He watched as the women walked Emiko to the rear of his property and entered the parturition building he constructed for the birth of his children. It was a great loss of face to Emiko, if her husband or any other male saw her in the time of pain of child birth. It was as much a loss of face to him if he or any other male saw his wife in this manner.

The master trainer tapped a guard on his shoulder, and ordered him to go to the place of worship and bring back a priest. The warrior rushed off without question. He prepared his position on the verandah where he would remain until the birth of his child.

From out of nowhere, Shoya Sanuki appeared and sat next to him on the porch, and the trainer grumbled with a snap. "Huh, I knew it wouldn't be long before you arrived to bother me. Sake my honorable friend?" He offered, knowing the Shoya would show up anytime sake was to be served and enjoyed by anyone in the village.

"Tanizaki-san! It'd be a great honor to share some of your private sake for this special occasion." The Shoya announced proudly to the master trainer.

"Huh torturer of the truth, you want me to waste my finest sake on the likes of you?" He grunted as he ordered his youngest daughter to bring a bottle of his red. The finest sake in Japan.

"Tanizaki-san! I'll absorb your insults gladly, to get a cup of your private sake." Shoya Sanuki grunted with the broadest of smiles plastered on his weathered face.

"You'll get your wish of sharing my prized sake, old fool. I'm honored you chose to be here and willing to sit with me until the birth of my son, Sanuki-san."

"Iye Tanizaki-san. It's my honor to be allowed to sit with you and share the birth of your eighth child to my honorable village. Eight, Ieeeee what a lucky number for my village to have born to it. What an honor to be placed on your eighth born child to have secured a position in Kawasomeru-sama's army of becoming the next Master Trainer of the Ninth Village, once you chose to cross over to the Floating World for forever. I hope you'll talk your eighth son into taking residence in my village like you done over these passing years. Ieeeee, the prestige the village will enjoy if this soldier remains in our village as did his honorable father. You'll speak to him when the right time comes?"

"Control your water Sanuki-san! My eighth son will have my same beliefs, old fool. I believe he'll have no problem and be proud residing in the village of my birth for his life. If not, I'll suggest he remain in the village as I done."

A noise from the birthing building drew their attention. The two powerful men of the ninth village stared at the small structure, with Tanizaki trying to see thought the wall. He wanted to make certain his wife was all right. The old trainer was concerned about his wife's health, he didn't want anything to happen to her during the time of this child birth.

CHAPTER FIVE

In the midst of the harshness that made up the daily life of the people of Japan at this time of shaping Japan's future. The early years were a constant struggle for survival, beginning with the birth of their children. The unyielding law of natural selection dealt harshly and with savage finality with most newborn children. The severity of the climate was responsible for uncountable deaths of the children even before life-giving oxygen entered their lungs.

The birth of the young was carried out in a specially built sequestered one room building called parturition huts, constructed for the purpose of child birth. If the family was unable to build a birthing building, these and the poorer families sequestered a single room in the house.

Many times during a pregnancy, the people of the village didn't know for sure if a woman was with child, and when the child was being born no spectacle was made of the event. Everything pertaining to the birth of a child was kept quiet to preserve the order of the day, not drawing attention to any one person living if the village. Face and honor forced women to suffer through pains of childbirth in silence. Keeping the pain of the birth to themselves was the accepted way.

The trainer sat outside the house on guard duty on the back terrace, trying to show little concern over what was taking place in the parturition building where his wife was delivering his eighth child. Alongside the grumpy trainer's side, sat a Shinto priest from the village temple, plucking at a tattered bow string, the symbol needed to drive off evil spirits, and unwanted underworld kami whose wandering attention might be drawn to the commotion of child birth.

Master Trainer Nitaro Tanizaki glanced at the priest making a racket on the string held between his fingers, and the other end looped over his big toe. He wrinkled his nose as he grumbled over the foul odor being emitted from the priest's filthy body. The trainer didn't believe in priests, religious beliefs, or gods and kami for that matter. He only believed in what he could see with his eyes and kill with his sword. He felt the reason the priests were around was to beg donations and food from the villagers. He hissed, angered this lazy fool of a priest lived better than he. Before this priest sat and made himself comfortable as he plucked on his string, he setup a table on which he placed seven cotton strips with writing on them, they were kami offerings, prayers for the purification. He cursed the priest, and told himself he would lop his head off if he hummed again like he was moments ago.

As if hearing the trainer's thoughts, the priest began to hum and rock as he made hand signals and moved rocks he placed on the step of his terrace before beginning his prayers.

He angrily rolled his eyes and shifted his weight as he glared at the priest again. Then he looked to the Heavens to see if he could see who the priest might be praying to. Sanuki moved his cup from hand to hand and looked at Tanizaki, and gave him a smirk and nod. He saw the empty cup and knew Sanuki wanted another cup of his prized sake. He bellowed without taking his attention from the outer house. "Tsutomu! Sanuki-san is out of sake! I'll have another cup also. You must make certain we never run out of sake until your brother arrived in the world."

Normally the male child would never be expected to serve sake, but since his daughters were helping their mother with the birth, it wasn't shameful for a male sibling to pitch in and help with household chores. The youngest of his male children came out with a bottle of sake and poured the cups full. He grunted at the child who stared at the building as if trying to see through the walls. He was of his beliefs, and felt he should be with his wife at this special time. But because Sanuki chose to attend the birth of his child. He was forced to adhere to the old ways of Japan's beliefs, which ordered the husband to stay away from his wife until the child was born.

There was a noise from the front of the building and the trainer heard one of his samurai challenging someone who chose this time to visit him. He got up and rushed to the front of his home, only to see his guard giving General Kobayashi a hard time. He rushed up to the guard and ordered him to put up his sword. He bowed to General Kobayashi while announcing a birth was taking place in his home. This was to warn the visitor an impure act was occurring, and he was at his own risk if he entered the property.

The general bowed as he replied. "Tanizaki-san! This is the reason for my visit. I was made aware of this birth, and come to keep you company. I ordered Shimbo-san to take care of the training for the days we'll be attending the birth of your child. Such a great event as this is worthy to witness, I'm prepared to stay as long as it takes. Shall I send for Sanuki-san?"

"Iye! The manure eater has appeared and is drinking my sake. The fool thinks I didn't see him sucking it out of the bottle before. The greedy fool would drink his own urine, and not be aware of it. Between him, Sanuki-san and myself, we drank four bottles and opened the fifth." He moaned as he bowed to his guards and led General Kobayashi to the back of his home.

"Ieeeee Tanizaki-san! I hope there's some sake left for me to enjoy, it's the true reason I stay friends with such an old man as you." He grunted with a smile.

"Do you think me a foul mannered worthless host General Kobayashi-san? I have enough sake to float all of Engakuji Castle, and sail it out to the endless sea, my General."

The two men took up positions on the low terrace, and began to speak. The smiling General Kobayashi spoke with Sanuki and Tanizaki at the same time, and the filthy priest continued to pluck away on the bow string and drinking his best sake.

Unbeknownst to the trainer, his wife was locked in a squatting position on top of a heavy tatami mat, covered by a clean quilted white rice paper covering. She was being attended by her daughters, her sisters, and two other close female relatives. Emiko was sweating heavily as she strained and pushed trying to deliver her eighth born child to the world. She was so looking forward to the birth of this child who would certainly bring great face to the Tanizaki family.

Emiko's youngest daughter Enko was hiding behind her older sister Estsuko, who herself was trying to support her mother's weight in this position. Emiko was ordering herself not to cry out in pain, or she would lose face before the other women, but she was crying and this scared Enko who never seen her mother cry. The women were bound to this small house for five sticks of time (Five days) if the child came on this day. The only way the women would be allowed to leave the parturition building, was after they were purified by a priest, and their clothes changed and their bodies cleaned of any fluids from the birth mother.

The Lady Hiromi Ikeda was a close friend to Emiko, she was her brother's wife and of the same age as her sister-in-law, the two were inseparable friends. Hiromi was the midwife of the village. She bent low and checked to see if she could see the baby's head. There was no sign, just a trickle of blood. Not even the water had burst, Hiromi hoped this wasn't a false alarm, if so they would be forced to remain in the building until the baby came, even if it took another week, two weeks, or a month. She looked in the sweat covered face of her friend and patted it dry with a clean cotton cloth, and smiled as she purred at her sister-in-law. "Lady Emiko! I fear you made it too comfortable for the little one to want to leave the warmth of your body."

"Please excuse my stupidity Hiromi!" Emiko replied while panting heavily and sweating. "But will my baby come to the world of light on this day?" She fought against another spasm of pain wracking her body. Her cheeks swelled and were red, and she let out her breath in a rush, sending spittle flying everywhere.

Hiromi wiped the face of Emiko again and dried herself as she cried. "My Lady Emiko congratulations! Your most honorable child will make his appearance on this fine day."

She didn't hear Hiromi as she fought through another spasm of pain. Her lower body was naked, but the thin kosode hung below her squatting position, offering her some modesty.

Outside the trainer shifted his weight for the umpteenth time as he grew angry and his rearend pained him from sitting on the wood of the veranda. He wanted to know what was happening in the birthing building. He wanted to be with his wife. He wanted to see his eighth child born, the lucky one. He wanted to be part of the birth of the one who would replace him as master trainer of the village, when he stopped teaching the future soldiers of Lord Kawasomeru.

General Kobayashi had known Master Trainer Tanizaki since his birth. The old trainer had taught his father to be a soldier for his master's father. The general never really knew his father, he died while he was a young child at the battle of Minatogawa where his father fought on the side of Ashikaga, Shogun for Japan. He raised his hand and brought it down lightly on the old man's shoulder and offered in a calming voice. "Huh Tanizaki-san, I know what you must be going through. If you'd like, I'd be glad to take Sanuki for a walk with this dung heap of a priest. That way you may sneak in the sequestered building and check on Lady Emiko's health." The general shared his feeling towards the priests.

"General Kobayashi-san, I can always rely on you to be with me at my times of need. You do me honor to stand by my side. Maybe later I'll ask you to do as you offered when the child has come. I'll see my child the day he's born. I'll not wait the five foolish days, stupid laws dreamed up by priests who have nothing to do but to stick their filthy eyes into other people's business. One day a wave will come and perhaps wash the priests from the islands." He grumbled as he stared at the birthing house.

He watched as servants went in and out of the building carrying pots of hot water and other necessities for the birth of a child. The trainer saw attendants hanging around outside the building in case they were needed, because once they entered the building they would also be impure and would have to stay in the building for the proper time, before they could leave again. Stupid laws he continued to think.

Inside the birthing building, things were happening quickly. Emiko's pains were coming quicker, almost continually. The tatami mat was soaked by the water sack which burst and relieved some pressure on her body. Her oldest daughters were supporting her weight in their arms as she squatted to give birth. Her youngest daughter was hiding behind one of the other attendants, scared at what was happening to her mother who seemed to be in much pain.

With one mighty shove, the eighth child came. Emiko's daughters moved their mother to a mat where she laid waiting the afterbirth to be delivered. The birthing paper mats were picked up and discarded in the small pot burned to ash. Other attendants went about cleaning the room as Hiromi cut the umbilical cord with a bamboo knife, which she placed in a pot of hot coals as tradition dictated. She removed the baby from the mother and cleaned the mouth and ears, and wiped blood and wax from the body. All signs of the birth were gone from the baby by the time Hiromi surrendered the naked baby to Emiko's breast. She looked at her friend and announced. "There you see Lady Emiko! You have brought another fine sister into this world of honor. May she live the life of a crane."

Her sister-in-law couldn't understand the horrified look which crossed over Emiko's face as she stared up at her friend and cried. "Lady Hiromi! How could your words be true to my worthless ears? There has to be some kind of mistake you made with the sex of my child. The seer, the cursed old fool told me I was going to have a boy child."

"Lady Emiko! Don't tell me you believed the foul words of that manure heap?"

"Hiromi! You don't understand what this means. Tanizaki-san is expecting a boy child. Lord Kawasomeru is expecting a male child. He set aside a position for the eighth child of my husband as a Warrior, and later, trainer of his armies. By the Kami great and small, I brought dishonor on my husband's shoulders, my Lord and village. I don't deserve to live. Hiromi! I beg for a blade so I can perform my yoshi gi (duty) and commit suppuku, and put an end to my worthless life, and end the life of this child who betrayed the words of the seer."

Her sister-in-law laughed and patted her friend's hand as she cooed. "Dear Lady Emiko! You speak like a woman who lost her mind, rather than a woman who just gave birth. You haven't brought dishonor to your husband or master. The birth of a child is Karma, and we must leave Karma to Karma. No earthly form has control over Karma. I'll make the announcement."

Emiko grabbed her hand and pleaded. "No! Put off the signal until I had a chance to kill the child, and prepare myself for death. Please, don't send up the signal yet. I have to carry out my duty before you announce the birth of the child."

"Calm down Emiko or you might hurt yourself. It's too late to stop it, the signal's prepared and must be sent to inform everyone your child is within the world of the living, but is still not alive until the thirty sticks of time are over. Lady Emiko! You must think of your husband, it's your duty to allow the announcement to fly. Your honorable husband Tanizaki-san is a wise and understanding husband. He'll explain to Kawasomeru-sama who is an understanding liege lord and you'll see, everything will be fine. The birth of a child is an honorable deed, and must be celebrated at the proper times, or the Devil Kami will enter the Karma of the village, and we'll all be destroyed by his hatred. I'll send the signal and you'll not harm your baby." Hiromi hissed, getting irritated over Emiko's strange reaction.

She nodded to her sister-in-law and sent the signal kite out the window to make the announcement of a successful birth. A second attendant hung the bamboo sign on the door, warning all no one was to enter the building. The building was considered impure, and according to customs, all who dared to enter the building would be thought of as impure. Hiromi stared as Emiko cried and clutched her child to her breast. She didn't understand the problem and decided to talk to the master trainer so he could put Emiko's mind at ease.

The old master trainer was in such a trance staring so intensely at the building he failed to notice the kite soar to the Heavens in the bright cloudless afternoon sky. General Kobayashi was the first to see the kite and pointed it out to the others on the terrace. The Shinto priest babbled his prayers and plucking away on the toneless bow string, as Tanizaki stood and stared at the tiny purple and yellow kite fighting the swift currents of the air to stay airborne.

Forgetting his pride he raised his hand to the sky and bellowed. "Ieeeee! I have a son, the eighth born son, the lucky son who'll bring pride and honor to the Ninth Village, and Shinano province and Kawasomeru-sama." He turned to the priest and added in a harsh tone. "I don't know what good you did in the birth of my son, but as your reward. I'll build a shrine at the entrance to the village, and this will be your living quarters until the day you leave to meet the foul Kami who you pray so much to."

He stepped from the terrace and walked to the birthing building then caught himself and turned away and saw the stunned faces of Sanuki and the priest, who thought he was going to break taboo and enter the building. When he turned, he growled. "By the fearsome wrath of Fujin, the god of Wind, sake for the entire village on this most proud of days."

The wise General Kobayashi got his cue from the trainer and bellowed. "A great honor has been bestowed on the Ninth Village of Shinano province. We must celebrate properly. Shoya Sanuki-san, priest come with me. We must pass out the gift Tanizaki-san offered the village. We'll celebrate the birth of Master Trainer Tanizaki's new son."

He watched as General Kobayashi led the fools away and spun around and came face to face with Hiromi who walked up behind him as the others left. She knew him well enough to know he planned to visit his wife in the birthing house, even though he knew it was against the law. "Come Tanizaki-san! I'll introduce you to your new child. Don't smile at the poor child though, I don't want you to scare the poor thing." She didn't tell him if it was a boy or girl child, it wasn't her place to do so. That honor was left up to the child's mother.

He left Hiromi as he charged in the building, causing a gasp from the women still inside the birthing building. He knew Hiromi would swear them to silence under the threat of death. He pushed the white curtain aside and looked at his wife who looked upset as the child resting peacefully on her chest, suckled her breast. The baby was naked, but Emiko's hand rested in a position so he was unable to tell its sex.

The aged trainer looked threatening as he stood over his wife staring at her. He was dressed in his light kosode and had his swords tucked in his sash. His hair was disheveled and he looked excited as he announced. "Lady Emiko! By the Kami of the day world, you made me the proudest man in Japan. You done well to bring to this world my eighth child, a boy child who is destined for great things. I'm honored at your effort and gift my Lady." He bowed to his wife who started crying uncontrollably again.

"What is this you offer me Emiko!" He grumbled as he spread his hands apart, shocked at his wife's ill mannered display of emotions. A wife would never shed tears in front of a man, especially her husband. It was a sign of weakness and in Japan, weakness wasn't allowed.

She didn't listen to her husband's warning as she continued to cry.

"Emiko! What is this foolishness? There are people here so stop this foolishness. You're bringing loss of face on us. This is a time of happiness not sorrow and womanly weeping."

She looked at her husband, sobbing and still didn't say a word.

He wrote it off as common birth problems as he scooped up the child from her chest and raised it to the ceiling as he bellowed. "This is my eighth child, the boy who'll become a man, and a man who'll become the future Trainer of the Ninth Village for our Lord Kawasomeru."

The child screamed at being taking away from her mother's warmth and breast.

He brought the child to his chest. He stared in the angelic like face looking at him through green eyes, and smiled at the child. His smile quickly disappeared as he looked between the child's legs and saw no stem. Anger instantly replaced the smile and he dropped the child from waist height on her mother's chest. She brought the child to her breast and protectively wrapped her arms about the child to shield her from his wrath and anger.

His mind raced to the moment he knew this child was conceived, and remembered the strange omens. While making love to his wife at the instant he ejaculated, the earth rumbled beneath them and a breeze stirred, gently moving the wind chime. The wind became strong enough to rattle the bamboo shutters. Then, a sparrow, the owner of day wind landed on the window edge, it was joined by the strange and rare sight of a bat, owner of the night wind standing on its legs.

Both animals stood together on the window sill and stared at them as he finished making love to his wife. Both were members of the wind. He shuddered to think what gods were lining up to guide this lucky eighth child. A warm breeze crossed his cheek and he couldn't help but plea, 'By Fujin's angry breath, what am I to think'. When he finished making love, he looked out the window and saw the breeze pick up, and wondered what this child had to do with the only kami he knew. Fujin, the always angry God of Wind.

Even though he was thinking this child had divine links to the fearsome God of Wind, he was beyond anger and wise thought. He couldn't believe that he was being so ill mannered as to display such a weakness before his wife. He knew better and was better disciplined to control his temper. No matter what his mind told his soul to do, he just couldn't control his rage. He unsheathed his sword and it whispered the song pure steel emitted as it was dragged against the sheath, and he raised it over head and roared.

Everyone in the building moved to the edges of the room, fearing they would be next to feel the cold steel of his sword ripping their bodies apart in his fit of anger.

Emiko cried as she raised her head lying on the clean tatami mat with her baby suckling at her breast. She extended her neck to give him access at her throat with his blade and said. "Tanizaki-san my beloved husband of countless years! I'm sorry I dishonored you so by bringing forth a worthless daughter for the eighth child to your home. If you choose, I'm prepared to do the honorable thing and put the child to death then commit suppuku if you'd allow me."

"Ieeeee! You brought disgrace to our family, to our village and importantly to our Lord by having this bitch child as my eighth born. I'll kill it then you, then I'll beg our Master's forgiveness for the other members of our family, by offering to commit suppuku." He hissed as he held the sword overhead. The weight of the blade made his arms ache and the blade swayed.

She noticed the hesitation and plead for her child's life, by trying to rationalize with her fuming husband. "Dear Tanizaki we can have another child." She lied, knowing this child had so badly hurt her innards, she would never be able to have another no matter what she tried.

"Foolish woman! What good would having another baby do. I need to offer this one in fifteen years at Gembuku, the ceremony of entering malehood. To have another baby would put this off by a year's time, and Lord Kawasomeru would have my head for deception. No wife, I must make amends for this insult against our Lord and his lands. Curse you woman, you must have insulted the gods of good judgment for them to punish our family so. It's your fault, if you were not in so much pain I'd beat you for this insult. You offended me with this bitch child. Are you sure the filthy thing is mine? Your seer! That manure heap shitted out by the gods of the dark world. I'll find this piece of filth and kill this enigma. I swear by the ancestors of my line."

"Kill me if you must but spare the child. She's special my husband." She cried with surprising strength as she tried to get up, displaying outright defiance against her husband.

"NO!!!" He bellowed as he moved the sword around in his hands.

"Husband! The eighth child has the mark from the gods, she's special and deserves to live." She dared to yell at her husband as she cast her eyes to the floor again.

"The mark? She has the mark of the foolish gods on her body?" The trainer mumbled more to himself than to his wife as he lowered the sword slowly. His demeanor changed to one of understanding after hearing about the mark blessing his daughter.

"Yes honorable husband, the mark of the gods is on her body." His wife moved her hand and there on the tiny wrist of the sword arm of his daughter, his eyes beheld the mark of the gods. A small birthmark which looked more like a shooting star making its way through the Heavens was visible on the small wrist.

"The mark, by the Kami who waste their time floating around the Heavens doing nothing, she has the mark upon her body. She's a chosen one, the mark of a pure Samurai, marked by the gods for greatness in her lifetime." He growled as he laid his sword beside his wife and child.

She knew she had his attention and pushed her luck, and force him to a rash decision. She knew once he decided on a course of action, nothing this side of the afterlife would change it. "Ieeee! I must make up for this disgrace I brought upon our house."

"Disgrace! Disgrace? Foolish woman who put up with me for so many years for reasons I do not understand. There's no disgrace to bring forth a daughter if she's so blessed by the gods with the mark of their greatness on her person. I'll see her and this mark of the gods."

The trainer took the child tenderly this time, and brought her to his chest as he looked in the beautiful face. The child stopped crying and looked in her father's eyes with the greenest and happiest big eyes. "Ieeeee! She is beautiful old woman."

"Yes husband, and I'll begin to bind her feet so they'll forever remain small. I'll start as customs demand of me on the third month of her life."

The trainer immediately glared at his wife lying helpless on the mat and growled. "Foolish woman, you'll do no such thing, I forbid this treatment of my chosen eighth child."

"But my husband, it's the proper ways of the past, it's custom to bind a female child's feet from birth." She cried, smiling inside knowing she was leading her husband down the path she wanted him to travel upon, and forcing his decision to allow the child to live.

"I care not one worthless grain of rice for what is the way of the past of Japan, woman!" He growled as his mind flashed to the keeper of the births. He was hoping he would be able to talk the fool into allowing him to do what he was planning with the child he had to register in the birth records. If he would not help him then the trainer was going to kill the keeper.

"But my husband, if she's to serve her master faithfully, she'll need small feet. Or she'll never be allowed to please a man and will be shamed for life."

"She'll not please a man unless she chooses to do so. She'll be trained in the ways of the Warrior. I'll train her myself and she'll be raised to a position of authority. She must live to fulfill what the gods decreed for her. I'll train her for her destiny, not as a female but as a male Samurai." The trainer raised the child over his head by one arm and leg and prayed. "I offer the gods who chose to mark my child. May you guide her deeds. Woman! You brought this house great honor. You'll teach her of what she'll need to know about being a female, but as little as possible. She must be free to think and act as a male Samurai."

"Husband, what will Lord Kawasomeru think of you once he discovers that the male child you presented to him at Gembuku, is that of a female child?" She warned him.

"Old woman, by the time I present this child to the Lord of the realm at Gembuku, she'll be so well trained even he wouldn't care if she was a two headed pigeon. Emiko! Don't worry about our Lord, or the foul keeper of the births, or anyone else for that matter dwelling on the soil of Japan. I'll handle everything. I'll be responsible for this child and her destiny, and you'll cut her hair in the way of the trainees. I'll speak and teach her as if she were a male Warrior. I'll make her the greatest Samurai Japan ever witnessed in her history." He handed his wife the child again and watched her as she put the baby to her breast.

"Wife of many years! I must leave before Kobayashi-san returns with the dung eating heaps, Sanuki and the Shinto filth of a priest. I'm not worried about them, they must be seeing two times by now, and if I know General Kobayashi-san and the effects of my sake on one's head. He'll insure they're too drunk to know what's happening about them. I must leave before I'm forced to remain for five days. Emiko! You done well, well in deed. I'm honored wife."

She closed her eyes and bowed her head, a tear betrayed her inner feelings.

He caught the tear in his fingernail and put it in his mouth and smiled as he picked up his sword and slid it in the scabbard and put it in his sash. Normally, a sword which shared the bed with a woman who gave birth would have to be destroyed by melting. But he didn't obey the laws of the land, he obeyed the laws which governed his life. He did what was best for his master and for his family and his soldiers. The laws of the gods didn't interest him.

The trainer took one long look at his new child and his wife, then headed for the door. He was stopped by Hiromi who warned him the three men returned. She suggested he sneak out the window that faced away from the main house.

He wasn't amused as he snapped at the wife of Emiko's brother. "Hiromi! Am I to act like a filth eating Ronin sneaking out a window like the common criminals they are. No woman! I'll walk out the front door and anyone who doesn't like it or what I done, let them unsheathe their sword and we'll settle it on the field of honor. These foolish laws are dreamed up by lazy good for nothing priests who have nothing to do with their lives but force everyone to live their lives the way they want them to, mean nothing to me or my life." He made a spitting sound as he added. "I spit on their laws and their foolish gods. I live my life for Kawasomeru-sama and Tanizaki and my family, and no one else. Out of my way old woman." He rudely shoved her aside and marched out the door with his hand resting on the hilt of his sword. His walk dared anyone to challenge him leaving the birthing building.

Neither Tanizaki nor Emiko gave consideration to the loss of face he caused his wife and the attendants, by seeing her in the birthing house. She was relieved he entered the building, she believed the same as her husband. Though she obeyed most priest's warnings, and the ways to offer her family protection from evil kami who floated the earth hunting victims to corrupt.

He came out of the birthing building like he owned the world and came face to face with the stunned priest, who spoke in a flood of rapid words. The trainer paid little attention as he growled. "Fool of the waste land, if you want your head to remain on your shoulders, and that temple I promised. I order you to come up with a prayer that'll cleanse the impurity you say stains my soul, and threatens my home. Then swear yourself to secrecy or I'll order your tongue removed, and your hands cut from your body so you can't communicate with anyone."

The priest gained control over his thoughts and bowed. "Tanizaki-san! A prayer is what I was working on. I'll chant it three times and you'll be cleansed after you have a cup of tea. As for my secrecy, I'd be the fool to go against your wishes. I already forgot what I did not see."

"Huh! I thought so worthless old man. You priests are all the same. Out of my way before I have you skinned and roasted over an open pit, fool." He pushed aside the priest and headed for Sanuki staring at him as if he was the devil himself.

"Close your mouth old man before a bee flies in it, and the foul thing stings your worthless tongue. I bring you news of my new born eighth child, Shoya Sanuki-san."

Sanuki's mouth snapped shut with an audible click as he stared at Tanizaki. He was unable to speak because of the shock of seeing him come out of the birthing building.

He next turned to the new general. "General Kobayashi-san! You'll accompany me, I have a pressing duty to carry out." He turned back to Sanuki and hissed. "Shoya Sanuki-san! You can announce to the village Lady Emiko has given birth to my son. Send a runner to Engakuji Castle and have him report this news to Lord Kawasomeru in person." He bowed to Sanuki and looked at General Kobayashi and added. "We leave now!"

Sanuki couldn't wipe the grin from his lips as he forgot about his transgression visiting his wife in the birthing house, his mind counted the honors this boy child would bring to the village and himself, as he replied. "Tanizaki-san! I can't tell you how pleased I am Lady Emiko delivered a boy child on this day. I'll order her elevated to the Village Lady. I will…"

"You'll do what I ordered and nothing more Sanuki-san! I'll explain more when I return from my mission. I intend to settle with that filth eating animal we call village seer. Emiko informed me of the terrible inspection he carried out on her body, and I'll seek honor from him for this insult. General Kobayashi-san! We go while I'm of the mind to deal with a waste of a man?"

He walked out the sidewalk to the road. His speech was made more for his samurai's edification who he knew would report this news by pigeon to Kawasomeru. He had to be honest with Sanuki when he returned. He didn't worry about the attendants in the birthing cottage. If they spoke of his deception they would have to admit he entered the building and by honor, they would be forced to commit suppuku, and he knew none of the women would want to leave this world. He wasn't concerned about his daughters, Emiko would swear them to secrecy.

They were passed by Sanuki who they knew was going to try and be the first one to get this news to Lord Kawasomeru. He stormed to the end of the village and with the height of bad manners, pushed his way in the seer's filthy home before being granted entry. The stench that assaulted their noses when they entered was overpowering. The interior was pitch black and free of furniture or decorations.

His eyes searched the corners of the building for sign of the filth that dwelled in the walls of the building. From the north corner of the room his ears heard the shuffling of naked feet on the floor. He unsheathed his sword and waited.

Hachirobe spoke softly before Tanizaki's eyes fell on his earthly form. "Ahhh... Tanizaki-san! I see you have come to destroy me, neh? You're angry because I told Emiko she was going to have a boy child, and she failed this honor. I told her what I believed she wanted to hear. If I told her she was going to have a female child, she might have destroyed herself rather than bring this child to the world of the living, and dishonor you. Master Trainer Tanizaki-san! Normally, I wouldn't care about my death, but I read the stars and Karma of this child is one of greatness. Greatness on the scale of a Shogun, greatness which will be impossible to measure in earthly terms. This child had to be born, it was demanded by the Kami, even if it cost my life. Even if it cost you your life, and the lives of every villager of the Ninth Village.

"Master Trainer Tanizaki! It's a wise decision to bring this child up as a male, a Samurai. But this decision was not yours to make, it was written on the clouds of destiny. You would never have been able to bring the sword down on the child or your Lady's neck. The gods wouldn't have allowed it, they would have struck you dead before you could strike out against this eighth born child. Her place in the history of Japan was preordained, and nothing you could do would changed her destiny and fate. Tanizaki! You can kill me to silence me if you wish, but I assure you that'd not be necessary, I'll prove to you by deed I'm no threat to your secret, and the fate of your child. That in fact, I'll do everything in my power to help you and your chosen child, so she might succeed on her mission for Japan's sake."

He was stunned the old seer was able to see everything he did, and what he would do in the future. Suddenly, he feared this filthy animal. He ignored the ill manners Hachirobe paid him by omitting the san from his name. At the moment, he didn't care if this fool called him a dung eater, as long as he continued his words. He asked through shaking lips. "Hachirobe-san! You seem to be able to truly see into the future. What is it the foolish gods have set on my child's shoulders? What would be the sign of her greatness?"

He bowed to Tanizaki the best his bent and battered body would allow him to move, acknowledging the honor the trainer had just bestowed on him. It was countless years since anyone addressed him as a person. "Tanizaki! I thank you for your honor. Your child who is a woman yet not a woman. Will be the one person in all Japan who'll stop the war threatened between Lord Kawasomeru and Lord Wakatsuki, and through her deeds the eight provinces will be spared uncountable deaths threaten in the future. Her deed will be the turning factor in the drama which must be begun in the future, to shape Japan's unfolding for generations to come. Her name and yours will be honored until the Gods decides we have polluted this earth long enough, and calls us home. More than this I cannot and will not tell you."

His chest swelled with pride at the knowledge his child was destined for greatness. But one question puzzled him and he found himself compelled to ask. "Hachirobe-san! How will my child bring greatness on my name and to Japan and her Lord? What will she have to pay for this greatness promised? The gods are parsimonious with gifts they bestow on us. To receive a gift from the gods, one must be prepared to repay these self-seeking idols many times over."

Hachirobe's face changed to a mask of sorrow as he suddenly shifted his weight from one crippled leg to the other, preparing to answer the question asked of him. "Tanizaki! She'll repay the gods debt by her early death."

"Death?" He snapped before he realized he said it.

"Yes Tanizaki. Death! Her death is the price they have set for her greatness."

The trainer's shoulders sagged and his mind screaming. Your beloved new daughter will die for the sake of Japan. What better honor could be placed on any proud Japanese warrior? His sad eyes turned to the seer and he asked softly. "How long will she walk upon this earth?"

"Ten plus fourteen years, no more, but it could be less. Fear not, her spirit will return to the world of the living many times after her honored death, to carry out the next and next Shogun's demands after her death has been accomplished. Tanizaki! Your daughter is meant for greatness even after she crossed to the land of the great waiting. Ask no more of me, if I were to speak more, I'd betray a trust by the Kami. If you'd allow me to prove my want to serve you and your blessed daughter, I'll demonstrate my loyalty for you now."

He didn't respond, he merely nodded at the old crippled seer, as he stared at him with a stunned expression locked on his face.

Hachirobe produced a razor sharp cutting sword and stuck out his tongue and before the trainer's mind could register what he was about to do, the crippled seer sliced off most of it. The thing that made Tanizaki shudder the most was the fact no blood came from either end of the slivered tongue. Without a cry of pain, Hachirobe picked up the slivered end of his tongue, and walked across the room and placed it in the hot coals he used to heat the room. A soft puff of smoke and the end disappeared. The seer could no longer speak well, so he would never be able to betray the secret Tanizaki's child was female.

Kobayashi moved closer to Tanizaki and allowed him to lean on him for support. He saw how shaken he was over what he witnessed, and carried out by the seer. Although Tanizaki sheathed his sword, the general remained with his hand on the hilt of his blade, and the sword was pulled half way out so he could easily draw it for action. It was the way any samurai would stand if he was threatened. To remove the blade further than half way of the sheath, would commit him to action. To remove a blade more than half way and not use it, was dishonoring the blade, something no self-respecting samurai would dare to do to a weapon his life depended on.

Once he placed his slivered tongue in the coals, he returned to the center of the filthy room to stand before Tanizaki and Kobayashi.

The trainer forced his mind to think, to register what he heard and seen. It was overwhelming as he fought to give strength to his Naijo, the inner help. He drew a breath as he got control of his mind. He looked at the filth known as the seer and offered. "Hachirobe-san! I order you to move to my home. I'll order a room added in which you'll live, and watch over my chosen one. Guide her on the path the gods destined her to travel. Since you're entering my home you'll live by my rules. My home is a clean house and you'll bathe regularly, every night after a day of toil. I'll feed you and take care of your earthy necessities. I warn you seer, if you can truly see in the future, you'll know what I'll do if you betray me, fool." He warned as he glared at the seer.

The old seer bowed greatly to Tanizaki and his general.

"Good. Now that's settled. Hachirobe-san! Once you leave this building of filth and constant darkness, I intend to have it dismantled and the foul wood of the cursed structure burned to ash. I can't believe you have allowed this structure to fall in such disarray. General Kobayashi-san! Shall we leave this world of filth and fears and wonders?"

"Hai Master Trainer Tanizaki-san! I feel in need of a hot bath, I feel my skin is trying to leave my bones. This filthy structure is covered with lice and varmint." He snarled, showing his displeasure Tanizaki was taking the village manure heap into his home.

"General Kobayashi-san! My daughters will show the seer the errors in his ways, once they bathe and scrub years of filthy from his body. The lice will die as will the layers of filthy skin. Let's leave this cesspool." They left, but not before Tanizaki left a paper pinned to the door stating the building wasn't to be entered. The three walked down the street to his home.

Shoya Sanuki standing on his front porch noticed them walking down the center of the street and followed to see what this was about. He quickly caught up to Tanizaki and asked what the meaning of walking with this filth was about. When the trainer informed Sanuki he was going to allow Hachirobe to live in his home and care for his child, the stunned Shoya stopped walking and stared at the trainer in disbelief then grumbled in a shaking tone. "Has your memory gone along with your wits of age, Tanizaki-san?"

He stopped walking and stared at Sanuki. He sent Kobayashi along with the seer so he could speak with him. "Have you sent a runner to Lord Kawasomeru?"

"I sent a runner and three pigeons with the same message, in case my runner is set upon by Ronin filth. This doesn't answer my question, Tanizaki-san. Why in the name of the clean gods that make our lives pure, are you allowing this vile filth to live in your home?"

"Shoya Sanuki-san! Clear the manure from your clogged ears and listen carefully to my words. Emiko hasn't had a male child. My eighth born was that of a female child."

He was stunned to his soul as his mind raced. He knew the message he sent to his lord sealed his fate. If the feared lord found out this child was a female born, he would order his death for daring to lie to him. Sanuki's mouth hung open as he stared at his friend, wishing he was consumed by the angry god of the underworld. Then he stuttered.

"Tanizaki-san! Has your mind slipped out of your ear? Can your eyes no longer tell the difference between a male and female child? Were you not able to notice the missing stem on this child? You have risked the wrath of our Lord and Master, I fear his justice will be swift and harsh. If you wanted to commit suppuku, why did you not go down that path without taking me and the rest of the village with you? By the gods I want to live, but you made that impossible. I'm bound by honor to send another message to Lord Kawasomeru. Then I must trust my future to his wisdom and mercy. I suggest you commit suicide before he arrives to slaughter you for bringing dishonor to his eight provinces. Ieeeee! The dishonor, we're doomed, the village, and all because your eyes are too old to see no stem where one should be."

"Be still and hold your foul water and stand tall old fool, or I'll dispatch your worthless life from you where you stand to stop you from weeping like an old whore who has past her prime of serving man. My eyes are not too old to oversee a missing stem on any child that is brought out before me I assure you. I have started this great deception against our Lord and Master because my child has the mark of the..."

"The mark!" Sanuki interrupted. "By the gods who protect us from evil. A female has the mark of the honorable

Samurai imprinted upon her body. What type of foul curse have the gods plagued the Ninth Village and my head with? Never before in the history of Japan has a female child ever been born with the mark of the Samurai on her body. Something is amiss here I fear. I swear to the gods this must be the work of the old seer. He has drawn the wrath of the Kami down upon our heads. Not only have we betrayed our Lord, we…"

"Shoya Sanuki-san, hold your bowels before you soil yourself and I'm forced to order you to remove your worthless tongue as Hachirobe done, to honor me and this new born child." The master trainer warned the concerned old Shoya.

Shoya Sanuki's hand went up to his mouth as he moaned between his fingers. "The filth eater has cut out his foul tongue and the old fool still lives in this world? Ieeeee! How is this possible? What Kami protect him?"

"Huh Sanuki! Hachirobe-san has shown me the strength he possesses, a lesson you should pay a little closer attention to I suggest. Shoya Sanuki! I intend to train this female child as if male Warrior. The seer has looked deep in the future of life, and assured me that this daughter of mine is destined for greatness in her short lifetime, and we must do everything in our power to protect and prepare her for the countless battles she'll fight in the honored name of Kawasomeru-sama in the future." He saw the look in Sanuki's eyes and added. "Yes Shoya Sanuki-san! We must protect this female Warrior until her task is completed on this earth."

"You speak as if this child is not long for this world, Tanizaki-san." He complained as he removed his hands from his mouth and stared at the old master trainer.

"Sanuki-san! I fear that her fate has already been sealed for her, though her life will be but a short stay, she'll return to the earth many times in the future to carry out the Shogun's needs and desires. She's been chosen to honor our Lord even in death. She's the one the sacred scrolls have written about for years past time. I'll protect this child of the gods, even if I must move from the eight provinces, and carry out her training in the ranges of Mount Fuji. My life is hers, and I'll teach her everything locked in my old worthless mind. She'll be a greater fighter than I ever was. A greater fighter than she has not yet been allowed to walk the ground which makes up the eight islands of Japan. Her name will be as it has been predicted by the worthless gods. The greatest name in all Japan's proud history."

"If all is as you speak Master Trainer Tanizaki-san then we have a great task that has been laid out ahead of us by destiny and the gods. But our foul deception will be discovered when we bring forth the child before the keeper of births, Tanizaki-san. You know he'll not see a child unless the child is laid naked before his weather beaten old eyes. I know of no way in my power to make what is not there, suddenly appear."

For the first time since this conversation began, the old trainer gave a laugh. "Nor have I found a way to make what is not there appear, Sanuki-san! But this deception will not be necessary, I know the keeper for years, and know I'll be able to talk him into recording the birth of my eighth child as that of a male child. Especially if he knows his life depends on his support to my deception. I saved this old fool's life on the battlefield more times than I can count, and know he'll honor me with this memory by helping me with my plan. I'll show him the mark and that'll be enough to enlist his aid and silence to our plan."

"The mark, yes I must remember the mark is upon your child, Master Trainer Tanizaki-san. It has to be as you have stated. If this young child has the mark of Samurai bestowed on her body by the gods who control our lives, and the cursed seer was able to see wonderfulness in her short lifetime. We must insure the way for her the gods demand she must travel upon." He thought for a moment then added. "I'm sorry your eighth child will have a short life upon this earth."

"Yes Shoya Sanuki-san! It's the curse of the worthless gods to outlive your child. But that's something I must live within my soul and mind. I have to offer the life of my daughter to the gods who demand so much from our lives."

"I must stop the messengers I have sent out to our Lord and Master. Maybe there's still time for me to save my life over this matter. If the Master has no knowledge of this child he will not know the male is a female." He offered to the master trainer.

"No, allow the messengers go on as ordered. Lord Kawasomeru must be made aware the eighth child of my family had been born to his province." He snapped at the concerned Shoya as he headed for his home and wife and new child. The old man wanted nothing more in life than to be near his child and wife, he also wanted to protect them from harm. In his mind he seen many assassins coming after his new born child in the middle of the night.

CHAPTER SIX

ENGAKUJI CASTLE IN SHINANO PROVINCE

When the runner from the ninth village arrived at Engakuji Castle in an exhausted state, Lord Kawasomeru couldn't have been less interested in the information he carried. His meeting with Wakatsuki never took place as figured. Wakatsuki was trying to hold his southern regions together and stop warring with each other. Mino province has open warfare taking place with Omi province, and Wakatsuki was trying to stop the situation from spreading to the rest of the provinces under his influence, and maintain his control of the provinces loyal to him.

The attacks from Echigo and Shimotsuke provinces controlled by Wakatsuki, stopped. These were the latest aggressions taking place against Kozuke province under Kawasomeru. He wasn't standing by while he was having trouble with his provinces to the south. The warlord had his troops flooding to Omi province, and ordered them to create problems for the besieged Wakatsuki staging attacks against the efforts of him to gain control over his warring allies.

The powerful Lord Kawasomeru wasn't without his problems. His wife was overdue with child, and she was becoming hard to be with. Etchu province was reported to be speaking with representatives of Wakatsuki's, and if Fukuyama went to his side, the warlord would be hard pressed to protect his southern flank from attack. He understood if Fukuyama stood with Lord Wakatsuki, he would have no choice but to attack his once ally, and absorb his province in with his province. Etchu province was the only friendly land mass separating Echigo from the southern provinces. This area prevented the south from linking up as one land mass against him.

When the messenger from Shoya Sanuki arrived at Engakuji Castle, he found an unfriendly and uninterested welcome. He was fed and a lesser member of Lord Kawasomeru's war cabinet questioned him, and found his information of a new born child in the ninth village, of no interest to the warlord. His mind was occupied by the upcoming war and threat of war to his southern region, so he didn't bother him with this information of the birth of a child. The messenger was sent away with barely acknowledgment from Lord Kawasomeru and his cabinet.

Lady Mineko had her baby boy and the warlord declared a province holiday for the birth, yet he forced his soldiers to continue their orders to create problems for Lord Wakatsuki. He ignored the uncertainty taking place in Etchu and the outer provinces of Wakatsuki other than allowing his samurai to create covert actions and threats, to keep the unrest in Wakatsuki's provinces growing. The next week in Shinano province was a festive week, and it was brought to a higher crescendo when Lord Ichimatsu Fukuyama rode to Engakuji Castle's gates with his wife and leading samurai protectors, bearing gifts for the new born boy child of the warlord.

At a meeting between him and Fukuyama, an agreement was struck between them where it was decided Fukuyama's Etchu province would defend the outer province of his realm, and Kawasomeru would in return offer the soldiers and military supplies needed to stop Wakatsuki from over running the smaller province of Etchu. This would prevent Echigo, Hida, Kaga, Nito, Mino, Owari, and Mikawa provinces from linking together and surrounding the eight provinces under his influence. Once the deal was set and written in the scrolls and became law, Lord Kawasomeru sent messengers to his other provinces, explaining the new agreement with Fukuyama, and insuring Etchu would stand in the way of Lord Wakatsuki's ambitious.

The warlord barely had time to enjoy his newborn son, when reports surfaced Mino began open warfare with Omi province, but an army from Mino with support from Wakatsuki's army, marched against Echizen province, which showed allegiance to Kawasomeru and his friendly provinces. The warlord of Shinano made good his word, and sent in an army of two thousand samurai via ships which left from Etchu, and sailed around the horn of Nito to the shores of Echizen. The samurai easily beat back the enemy forces invading Echizen from Mino.

The group making up the central provinces erupted in open warfare against each other, which would last for the next fifteen years. Lord Kawasomeru and Wakatsuki took advantage of the fighting, and used this war to eliminate old enemies, and they tried to force the warring provinces to move to their sphere of influence. Kii put tremendous pressure on Yamato province backed by Wakatsuki, by sending in military probes. This forced Wakatsuki to send more soldiers into the region to help defend Yamoto from Kii province, and further separated his armies.

The warlord was enjoying the unrest taking place in the southern provinces. As it stood, three provinces under his influence were involved in fighting, whereas eight provinces of Lord Wakatsuki's realm were at each other's throats. He was pleased he didn't have to pull any troops from Master Trainer Tanizaki. The fighting wasn't that much of a threat, so he allowed their training to continue. He considered sending the master trainer even more troops to train, so he would have an over abundance of trained warriors to defend his realm.

By the time the forces were set in place to carry out the war ahead of Kawasomeru taking command of his troops, he allowed himself a few days to enjoy his newborn son, and catch up on what was occurring in his province. On the third day, he came across the scroll which informed him Tanizaki's wife had a male child. He sat back and was happy for the birth, and thought of what he was going to send to celebrate his son's birth. This was the last day of separation between him and Mineko, and he was looking forward to sharing her bed again.

THE NINTH VILLAGE.

Drips and dabs of information filtered into the ninth village about the wars in the outer provinces. It was the third week of the sixth month of 1339, and life in the ninth village was fine for all. The trainer's separation from his wife was scheduled to end later on this week.

He was sadden when fifty warriors from his village were ordered to report to Engakuji Castle. He was upset for not paying closer attention to their training, and after they were ordered to war, he ordered all male village youths to join his training program. The order for the warriors to report to Engakuji, informed him a war with Lord Wakatsuki was about to break out.

He increased his workload with his training program, preparing the warriors for their time of need which barely left him time to think of his wife and new child. The trainer spent days, stretching into night to train his warriors in the proper way to conduct warfare. Days spanned from sun up to sun down on the makeshift battlefield, and twice a week he called for night attacks to be carried out by the exhausted trainees.

Upon the eleventh week of training, he decided to bring up the practice sessions he was considering employing the week his child was born. He sent out boys not of fighting age to round up as many stray dogs as they could find in the area. The dogs were leashed to trees and fed and cared for until needed. On this day, they would be needed. He had his horse soldiers report to the practice field at first light. He ordered them to mount their horses which they felt the excitement of the instructions. He had the trainees fill their Ebira, open quivers with practice arrows consisting of a shaft with feathers and a blunted end. He ordered the horsemen to place three arrows in their mouths, and prepare one arrow for flight.

The experienced trainer had the warrior's pair off in teams of six warriors. The dog handlers moved eighteen dogs on the training field. Each blunted arrow tips were dipped in different color dyes, so he could tell which samurai hit what dogs, and which horsemen missed their targets. The horsemen received orders not to hit the same dog, or any other dog twice with arrows. He wanted each dog hit only once in this practice session.

He demanded the trainees control their horses with their legs and arm their bows and fire arrows, and hit targets at full gallop. This would enable them to be a harder target while they wreaked havoc and death on their enemies. The time had come and the trainer gave the signal by raising his arm, and dropping it swiftly and the dogs were unleashed and allowed to run across the battlefield. Each dog represented an enemy to the horsemen. His sword and spearmen encircled the horse field to keep the dogs from escaping, and better observe the warriors in action, the other warriors would be the next to mount horses and try their hands at this practice.

It was a fiasco at best, many samurai fell or were thrown from their mounts, while firing arrows and missing many dogs. The first volley was impressive and brought a smile to the trainer. When the trainees tried to reload their bows while fighting to stay in the saddles, and keep an eye on their targets and control their horses. The task proved to be too much, and many warriors went tumbling to the ground in a cloud of dust and bruised egos and sore backs.

The foot soldiers laughed at the spectacle played out before them. Hoots and hollers replaced the familiar war cry from many horse soldiers. It turned out to be such a disaster that many dogs stopped running, and sat to watch as the samurai were dumped from their steeds. Unmounted horses continued to buck across the field as they fled their riders, with some horses dragging warriors who had the misfortune to have their foot trapped in the stirrup.

He shook his head in disgust as he looked to the Heavens for an answer while raising his hand in the air. He seen enough of this debacle and called an end to the exercise. Horse soldiers were limping back to the assembly area. A few warriors needed medical attention, and two foot soldiers were struck by errant arrows, and they wanted to avenge their wounded honor against the horseman who hit them with the feathered missiles.

The day was destroyed and he called an early end to the training, in an attempt to allow the exhausted and battered warriors to regroup and care for their injuries. He ordered their learning to begin anew tomorrow at first light. This decision to put off their training was good for the trainer, because he knew his wife would be allowed out of the birthing house today, and the keeper of births was scheduled to arrive in the village the day after tomorrow, and it would further give him and his wife time to better prepare for their meeting.

He had a lot to do to prepare for the keeper of births, he had to force him to agree with his deception for the master trainer to present his female warrior to Lord Kawasomeru at Gembuku. Gembuku marked the time when a child turned to a man. He was positive once the lord saw how his child was trained in the four disciplines, the lord would not care if the child was part demon. He was certain he would forgive his deception to present such a fine warrior to lead his army in times of battle. The trainer walked from his training area home, surrounded by six samurai. He smiled, for he had sworn allegiance from everyone aware his eighth child was a female. He knew they would go before the blade, rather than risk his wrath, for the blade would be a much easier death for anyone who betrayed him.

It was early, barely after the morning meal and he knew he had most of the day to get acquainted with his child. As he walked through the street, he saw Sanuki putting a distance between him and the trainer, since he became aware of the plot to deceive their master of Shinano province. He didn't care a bit about the distance, he didn't like the old man who only came around when he took control of another batch of his prized sake. The leader of the ninth village was born without a backbone, or the strength to make anyone proud of his actions.

He ignored the bad manners from Sanuki when he saw him walking the street and the fool turned from him. He knew if he wanted, he could be appointed head of the village, and put Sanuki out of office at a snap of his fingers. All he had to do was display an interest in the office before Lord Kawasomeru, and he would be appointed to the position.

The trainer dismissed the idea from his mind as he walked in his front gate, which was opened by one of the samurai protecting his home. He bowed to the warrior as he stopped the shinren cords from moving with his hand. He held up before the porch and stepped on the stone and removed his Getas and slipped into the fresh white socks with the split toes and padded soles, and walked in his home proudly. The first thing he saw was the smiling face of his eldest daughter. She rushed before him and dropped to her knees and bowed, as she informed her father of her mother's condition and where she was.

"Father, mother is out of the birthing building, and is resting in the sun on the back verandah. Our new son is with her, honorable one."

He looked at his daughter and smiled as he touched her on the forehead and said with respect. "Estsuko! You're proving to be an honorable young woman. You'll make a perfect wife for one of our Warriors, but I told you before you don't have to assume the position of respect in our home. I appreciate the honor you offer me, but it's not necessary every time I enter for you to go to your knees. Rise, your mother might need your assistance. How is she feeling? She doesn't tell me much, but I see it in her face this baby hurt her insides when the child was delivered."

"Father, you see with the all seeing eyes of a fearful Kami. Nothing escapes your wisdom. It's as you speak father, I believe the baby has badly damaged mother. I fear she'll no longer be able to carry another baby. I fear it might kill her if she tries again." Estsuko looked into her father's eyes and tried to smile, but a faint lip curl betrayed her.

He displayed one of those rare signs of emotion which robbed a male of face, as he pulled his daughter to him and patted her back. "I'm aware of this, I decided Emiko's days of giving birth ended. I don't know of the ways of women, nor do I intend to explore them. So I order you to find out how the women of the pillow world protect themselves from becoming with child. Then you'll take this information and apply it to your mother. I don't want her to become pregnant. I don't want to lose her until it's time deemed by the ones who control these events, call her." He let his daughter go and found her staring at him in disbelief.

"What have I done wrong now?" He complained at his lovely daughter.

"Father, I was unaware that you or any other Warriors, knew of the many ways we women protect ourselves against becoming with child after pillowing. It was supposed to be a guarded secret, always held from men of Japan."

Her father winked and added. "Daughter, I know it's a Warrior's belief that we, the men of this land control Japan and all that happens in this world. But I'm wise enough to understand everything that happens in Japan, has the hand of a women resting on the deal, the agreement, or planning of the future for the Warrior. I know women hear all of man's valued secrets, and they connive with other women to make her Warrior's dreams or wants come true for the fool. I'm not a stupid old man daughter, I'm well..."

"Father, you're not old, you're merely well seasoned, and most wise and respected by even the mighty Shugo Daimyo, Kawasomeru-sama. Father, to be honored so by such a powerful leader as our Lord, is as good as being honored by Shogun Ashikaga-sama." The trainer's daughter offered with nothing but love and respect for him as she smiled at the old man.

"Ahhh... so this is what the youth of our country are calling the old men of Japan, well seasoned, huh? I'll tell you this, no matter how polite you want to be in dealing with my age, my bones tell me my age every time I awake and leave my bedroll to attack the day's toils."

Estsuko smiled at her father warmly, knowing he was wise beyond his many years.

"Come little flower of the early summer garden, shall we check on your mother's health?" He bumped his daughter with his hip and added. "Estsuko! I'm not a fool, and I know we Warriors are in power because the women of Japan allow us to be so. I promise, for the first time in Japan's history, there'll be a woman in a position where no woman has dared to be before. Your sister will become one of Japan's most powerful Samurai. I further promise it'll be a matter of time before we bring out your supposed brother is your true sister. That day will be the proudest day in Japan's history. A day I look forward to with heart and soul.

"Until that day we'll carry out this deception, and I depend on you and your sisters to help your mother with the upbringing of your sister. It'll fall on your hands to guide her through the times of blood, when her womanhood is trying to rob me of her spirit. You'll have to teach her about the ying and yang, and perils of the weakness of body. I want your sister to be strong in mind, body, spirit, and soul. Everyone from this village will lend a hand in her upbringing. It'll be a chore, but we must fulfill this mission the gods chose to place in our path and your sister's fate."

Estsuko looked to her father and tried to hide the smile. Her heart was pounding, this was the first time her father spoke to her as a woman. She enjoyed when he enlisted her aid in bringing up her sister, who she knew was chosen for greatness by the kami of Japan's faith. She was proud to be part of that greatness, a dream she never allowed herself to believe. "Father! I'll make you proud of my actions."

"Estsuko! I can be no more proud of you then I am already. You're a fine daughter and young woman." He pushed the shoji door aside and stepped on the verandah and smiled when he noticed his wife sitting on a tatami with her legs crossed under her, and the baby held in her arms. The child was suckling nosily at her breast. He glanced around and saw the guards were showing respect for his wife, by not staring at her while she fed the child. He smiled at his wife, relieved she of over fifty years looked so well.

He was scared when his wife told him she was with child. It was believed her age was the time for a woman to consider not allowing herself to be with child. It was not only her age that concerned him, but in the past few years she put on a little extra weight. Though she tried her best to lose or hide it, she was unable to any longer. She was slowing down and he saw she was trying to mask the minor aches and pains which always seemed to plague the aging. He knew it was from the bad times when he and Emiko worked the field. The shortages of food and a frightfully long winter, often took their toll on her health. She had seven children in a short time, and this hurt her health. He cursed for being away ten of the twenty nine years they were married, fighting in the wars raging in Japan, and getting wounded as he mumbled to his wife. "Your child seems to be healthy my lady."

Emiko tried not to stare at her husband, she knew when he drifted off on these short day trips as she called them, and he was always pleasant when he returned to the real world.

Tanizaki shook his head and ordered in a booming voice. "Estsuko! Cha, two cups."

"Hai." She spun around and headed off to make the tea as ordered.

When they were alone, he sat on the step. "Emiko! How is your health?"

"Very well husband. Thank you for worrying about such a worthless old wife as I. A foolish old wife acting worse than a spoiled child. All I done was have a baby. I should be looking after my husband's needs, not sitting on the terrace enjoying the sun like an old woman of the Soft World, after making love to the highest bidder of the day." She cried as she attempted to stand before her husband.

"Emiko! You'll remain where you're resting and allow your body to heal. You're far from being a women of the pillow world, you're my wife. I'll tell you when it's time to abandon the pleasures you're enjoying. You have three daughters capable of taking care of my few worthless needs. It's good for them to assume responsibilities for you. It'll prepare them to become better and attentive wives for their future husbands." He relaxed and asked with concern. "Emiko, how is the child? Has the yellow visitor left the child's body yet?"

"Hai husband of this feeble wife. Here, see, the yellow has left the child's skin and body, and see how her... his skin has the healthy glow of a newborn not suffering from deficiencies of birth. The midwife declared him healthy, and it'll be a long time to wait until we're allowed to name our child. I'll leave the name of the male to you, and I'll name the female part of her we must to keep hidden as long as she's in the service of our Lord.."

"Emiko! I gave the child's name consideration since his birth, and decided to name him after his grandfather Masahiko, who brought honor to his name in the war against the Mongols."

She bowed as she offered. "Husband! It's a proud name which will be sure to bring honor and greatness to her deeds. I agree with your choice. Masahiko Tanizaki-san! It's a proud name."

The trainer bowed. "Have you decided on the secret name known only to you and myself."

"Hai! I decided to name her Yuriko Tanizaki in the privacy of any woman talk we speak of."

"Ahhh so... Your mother's honorable name huh! I agree with your choice. I only wish we could inform your mother of the honor we bestowed on her. But we must refrain from letting her know. Though she's a wise and cunning woman, her mind leaks information as do the clouds when it rains." He was slightly embarrassed he dishonored her mother with his choice of words. But everyone in the fifth village knew Yuriko's mind has been taking day trips, and after each trip her mind took longer to come back to the real world.

"Fear this not my husband, it'll be my duty to inform her on the bed of waiting. I plan to inform my Mother Yuriko of the honor we bestowed on her. Even if I have to wait many sticks of time for her troubled mind to return to the land of reality. I understand my mother is not long for this earth, and her knowledge of the naming of this child after her, will make it easier for her to cross over to the spirit world of wonder and respect. She'll help guide our daughter from the world of beyond, to carry out the quest the gods destined she must travel on." She took in a quick breath as she struggled with another spasm of pain traveling through her body.

"Ahh... Emiko! This is fact, but we have more important issues to face in the future than this minor one. I need not remind you the recorder of births is due in the village the day after tomorrow. We must make sure we're the only ones present when he examines our child. Then we must swear him to silence, or all is lost and I'll be forced to put the child to death."

"Hai, but I have no worry you'll be able to talk the keeper into seeing things our way. You have a persuasive way about you. Beside, he'll be looking after his own skin. All you have to do is point out how displeased Lord Kawasomeru would be to anyone who brought such unpleasant news to his ear. We know the Lord would take his head where he reported from."

"You're wise Emiko and I'll do as you suggested. I fear not this old fool who makes the small chicken marks on the scrolls of recordings, and he..."

The conversation was interrupted by Estsuko carrying a tray with two cups and tea pot.

Emiko made room for the tray and handed the child to her daughter as she served her husband. Death would be the only thing that would stop her from serving him cha.

His chest swelled with pride as he allowed a moment to be pampered by his wife. She turned the pouring of tea for her husband into a form of the respected tea ceremony. She poured from her left side, carefully filling the cup with the brew then she brought the cup to her lips and took a sip. She held the tiny cup at arm's length, and turned the cup in her hand until the spot where she sipped, was facing her husband. Then offered the cup to him with a beautiful smile.

He bowed before taking the cup and took a sip. He again bowed and copied her move by turning the cup in his hand, until the spot they drank from, was facing his wife. She bowed as she took the cup and drained it, she washed it and swirled a bamboo whisk in it, so no one else would be able to share in the honor they just shared together.

Estsuko had to turn her back to hide she was crying. She was so honored by her parents by being allowed to witness such a private display of love between them.

Emiko looked to her daughter and smiled. "Estsuko! I believe your father would like another cup, and so would I. Would you mind pouring cha. Estsuko! I'd be pleased if you'd join us."

"Hai mother." She said as she poured tea from the left side. This was so she wouldn't interfere with a warrior's sword arm. When she offered the first cup to her father, he refused and told her to give it to her mother. Emiko was so honored by the offer, but refused it and offered the cup to her husband. He stared at the cup for a moment then decided to offer it to his daughter. It was an honor to be offered the first cup during any meeting.

She was stunned her father offering her the first cup. Her hands trembled as her mind screamed of the honor being bestowed on her. But tradition ordained she must refuse it. She looked at her father and stammered almost to the point of tears. "Most honorable father, I'm unworthy to accept such a great honor." She bowed as she offered him the tea.

"Nonsense daughter. If anyone is to be honored, it is you. I insist you enjoy the first cup."

Her hands trembled to the point where Emiko feared she might spill the tea as her daughter brought the cup to her lips. "Father, mother. It's as they told me since I was a child. The first cup from the pot is the sweetest. I'll never forget this moment you allowed me to share with you. Domo mother, domo father." She bowed to her parents as she poured their cha. She joined her parents on the terrace, they shared cha and rice biscuits and warming rays of the morning sun.

Emiko allowed her daughter to take the child from her arms and hold her while she enjoyed tea and engaged in talk with her husband. "Tanizaki-san! How did today's training of the Samurai go? You returned home early, I must believe all went well."

He let out with unabashed laughter as he placed his cup on the mat. His eyes welled up over his laughter as he explained the training session to his wife, where his horsemen tried to fire arrows at the dogs while trying to remain in the saddle.

Emiko and Estsuko shared his laughter at the expense of the samurai bucked from their horses. It was bad manners for the women to laugh at the actions of warriors in training. If this insult was discovered, it could cost them their lives. But in the privacy of the home, anything was fair game for their amusement.

The moment was light, everyone in his home was happy and comfortable. The women were enjoying life. The oldest boys made preparations for their journey to Engakuji Castle, to begin their service in Lord Kawasomeru's employ. The youngest was to begin reading and writing training. He was to be trained in the art of poem writing and numbers. He prepared his way to do likewise to be enlisted in the employ of the lord of Shinano province. He was pleased Kawasomeru made it possible for his sons to avoid action on the battlefields. Although they were being trained for battle since they were born, he was happy his sons would be allowed to live at peace for their lives. He wasn't worried about the young men, each was trained in the use of sword and bow so they would be capable of defending themselves.

His youngest daughter wasn't to escape becoming a warrior's wife, thus bound to suffer through the hard life it offered. He had no plans for her future and the lord hadn't opened friendly doors for her. He knew the reason why this was. If he displayed favoritism for his entire family, there would be countless complaints from the other villages in Shinano province. All honored families wanted their sons and daughters to be brought up in the shadow of court lifestyle, and have the honors that would be bestowed on any who shared this way of life.

His heart saddened for the lack of concern his lord shown for his last daughter. He hoped in the future, Lord Kawasomeru would be the one to pick the husband his youngest would marry. It was the only honor the lord could bestow on her now he turned his back on her.

The master trainer's eyes came to rest on his daughter, the new born. A shudder suddenly filled his old bones as he wondered what would happen to this daughter and his family, if the lord were to discover the deceit he was carrying out against him. His mind screamed for him to put this daughter to death, and beg the master to spare his remaining children, even if he had to atone for his terrible deceit with his life. But as his mind screamed for him to dispatch this new female child smiling so pleasing and toothlessly at him as she reached out her hands trying to touch his face and nose. His mind warned this child chosen to be marked by the gods, must be protected at all cost, and be allowed to carry out their bidding on the earth. The thoughts erased all ideas of his destroying this child. He knew he was bound by honor to carry out the gods bidding, even if he didn't believe in gods.

Emiko was studying her husband's face, and knew he was in thought. But she was concerned he was following the steps of her mother, it was taking longer for him to come out of his deep thoughts lately. "Tanizaki-san! Are you all right my husband?"

"Huh? Yes my wife of many years, I'm all right." The trainer replied with a smile.

"I'm sorry husband, but you were deep in thought for such a long time, and I was...." She stopped speaking and stared at her husband, even though it was bad manners.

"And you were worried I was becoming like your honorable mother?"

"Hai! I was in fear of that thought my husband."

"Ha, fear not wife, even though my mind might be getting slow and clouded of late, everything is working fine. Emiko! I was thinking of the deceit I'm carrying out against our Lord. I know honor orders me to destroy this child, but I must carry out the orders of the gods, and protect this child until he's able to fulfill his mission on this earth."

Her smile remained.

"What are you grinning at me like a wanting child for, wife?"

"Tanizaki-san! I worry what the gods think about you. You curse them for any reason that happens. You never honor them, but you're willing to go against Lord Kawasomeru for the sake of the gods. I fear you would've gone against the gods themselves to keep this child alive."

"Huh, do I have a hole in me? Old woman, are you now able to see into my worthless mind? Am I that easy for you to understand? What manner of thought do all women of Japan have over Japan's most fearsome Samurai? I fear nothing man holds scared to himself is safe from the ever prying eyes of the women of Japan, wife of countless years."

"Ieeeee! I thought I was right with my troubling thoughts. When was it you decided you were not going to punish this child for my disgrace of bringing a female child supposed to be a male, to Japan's soil?" She cried as she wiped the corner of her eye as tears threatened.

"Wife! It was the moment I first looked into the child's green eyes, wise woman."

"Huh! You allowed me to believe you were waging a war within yourself. Fighting between duty to Kawasomeru-sama and your heart, to allow this chosen child to live her, err... his life."

He didn't reply, he allowed his smile to be the answer.

"Huh. I cannot believe I was unable to understand this thought. I can't believe I allowed myself to believe you might dare to put this child to death because she was born a female. I must be getting old, or you're becoming better at being able to carry out a deceit against me. Honorable husband, I'd not change one bit of you, you're a fine husband and honorable man. I'm proud to be your wife." She smiled as he reached out and held her hand.

The child fussed and Estsuko took the baby in the house to change her.

The following day went by quickly, with him avoiding having his horsemen try to hit any moving targets from their mounts. Instead, he had them return to shooting at stationary targets from their barely moving horses. Many targets had arrows sticking from them, signs his trainees could fire arrows from slow moving horses and make their mark. He ordered the trainees to aim at the stationary targets while making their horses move more quickly this time. The misses increased, but many arrows found targets.

The master trainer decided to miss tomorrow's training to be with his wife when the keeper of births arrived in the village. There were fifteen births needing to be recorded in the village, He made up his mind he would allow General Kobayashi to conduct tomorrow's training with the warriors. His thoughts went to this afternoon. He was going to order the mounted warriors to charge after stationary targets. Next week, he would reintroduce the dogs to the training field. He assured himself next week would be different.

During next week's sessions, he would not tolerate blunders of this week's failures. Next week, any warrior thrown from his mount would be condemned to the life of a foot soldier, the lower warrior. It would be a disgrace set on the outcast warrior, and he figured the first few would set the example for the remaining to be better than they were. He understood the first warriors dropped from the training program would commit suppuku.

His eyes were focused on what was taking place on the training field, but his mind was with his wife and child, and the thoughts over the keeper of births. He was dying to begin his child's training, he went over in his mind the ways he would train this gifted child. He promised he would make this one Japan's best weapon, its best warrior. His mind was flooded with pleasant thoughts, his plans for this child. He was willing to allow everything in his life to slip while he trained this child. He was going to prove to his lord this female child he took to train, was a better warrior than Samurai Kusunoki ever was.

A shout brought his mind to the training field. A soldier was wounded by an errant arrow. From where the arrow stuck out of the body, he knew it was a fatal wound as he headed for the warrior. Before he reached him, a second samurai unsheathed his sword and the weapon hissed through the air with a chilling whistle as a silver blur. The blade sliced through the neck of the injured soldier as easily as it did the air, and the slivered head rolled to a stop on the ground.

He stopped moving to the soldier when he realized there was nothing he could do for him. The second warrior acted properly. It was an accepted duty if a soldier was downed on the battlefield, and another soldier realized the wounded warrior would die and there was nothing anyone could do for him. It was the hombun, the yoshi-gi, the duty of the second soldier to give the warrior a swift death. On the field of battle it was an insult to the honor of any soldier to allow his foe to suffer needlessly. For a downed enemy becomes a fellow soldier once he's rendered helpless, and should be offered the same honor offered to a soldier. There were no sides in death, death conquered all no matter how large the warrior was in life.

His mind wasn't on the training field, he watched the hinin scurry on field and remove the body and evidence of his death. Once he was removed, the training resumed. Kobayashi moved to the trainer's side and remained there. He allowed his second in command to control the training of the archers until his return. Next week, he was to work with the spearmen. The new general was concerned about the trainer who controlled everything transpiring on the field.

"Tanizaki-san! You carried out your duty well this day. I'd receive it as an honor if you'd allow this worthless trainer to assume the day's instruction, and enable you to be with your honorable wife." He offered to the old master trainer in a concerned tone of voice.

He looked at his old friend, but he didn't reply to his words.

"I'll conduct the training session for the day. Tanizaki-san! If you'll allow me to command the instruction period tomorrow, why can I not begin training this day? I see by your wandering eyes, your minds with your wife and son, and visit of the keeper of births on tomorrow's day."

He drew in a breath and released it slowly, his body weary as he offered. "Thank you for your concern over these minor problems plaguing my mind of late, Kobayashi-san. I believe I'll allow you to do as you offered. This worthless body of mine is beginning to let me down. I can no longer remain standing on my feet the full day. I'm tired and will go home to rest. Work them until late in the day, allow them to eat at seven bells and run a night attack. Use the spear and swordsmen to defend a position from frontal attack by horsemen and archers. Begin the attack at midnight, use the insignificant monk's bell ringing as the time to begin the attack, General."

"Hai! Thank you for allowing this worthless General to lead your trainees in this night attack. I'll bring honor upon the warriors and your training." He bowed to the trainer who was too tired to respond to the bow, as he turned from the battlefield.

By the time he reached home, he realized how exhausted he was. He checked on his wife and the child and spoke briefly with his eldest daughter then went to his room and fell asleep. He slept through the evening meal, his food set aside and kept warm, in case it was demanded later. The women stopped any noise from waking the master.

He was awoken with a start by the monk's bell ringing and he counted the chiming. He was stunned it was time for his trainees to begin their night attack. He couldn't believe he slept until midnight, and now was wide awake and hungry. He got out of his bed roll and headed for the kitchen, smiling when he saw his wife speaking with Estsuko.

When his wife saw her husband she bowed. "Honorable husband! Are you ready to eat?"

"Hai!" He mumbled as he took a seat on the bamboo chest and rested his elbows on the table. His daughter prepared his meal while Emiko fussed around the room. He enjoyed it when his women fussed for him, it made him believe he was in control of his house, even though he knew in his mind, his wife was the leader of the house. He smiled as he remembered how many times she stopped him from beating the children, or how she stopped him from making a fool of himself. He nodded as he resigned himself his wife was the true boss of his house, while allowing him to only believe he was.

A pleasing meal of steamed fish over cooked to perfection rice was placed before him, along with a cup of warm sake. He devoured the meal hungrily, after eating he felt better and invited his wife and daughter to join him while he enjoyed the stars of the night as they traveled through the Heavens. The night was warm and the countless peepers and frogs were out in force, singing their night song of mating, and the fire flies spotted the night air. The incense pots were burning, keeping many mosquitoes from the house. After a half hour of enjoying the night and stars, the three reentered the home, but not before Estsuko pointed out a number of shooting stars. He took them as a good omen, it reminded him of the tiny mark placed on the wrist of his new born daughter by the gods he believed in.

There wasn't much to do in the home so everyone turned in for the night. Estsuko remained with the child in case she woke and needed changing. The daughter realized her father was looking forward to enjoying her mother's pleasures on this night. She was happy she gave her mother the cup of tea with herbs mixed in to prevent her from conceiving.

Estsuko listened to the sounds of her mother making love to her father and smiled. So happy they were still so much in love after many years and children. She prayed to her secret star of the night, hoping she would find such love in her future husband. Her pleasant thoughts were interrupted when her youngest sister stirred and she settled down again.

CHAPTER SEVEN
THE LAST DAY OF THE THIRD WEEK OF THE SIXTH MONTH OF THE YEAR THIRTEEN THIRTY NINE

Everyone in the Tanizaki household woke early, it was the day the keeper of births was to arrive in the ninth village, to record new births of the Shinano province. This was the only method for Kawasomeru to know how many people were living in his province, and who he could draw extra samurai from when he needed them.

By the time the fifth bell chimed, the families who had births in their household, were dressed and waiting for Ogino-san, the keeper of births to make his appearance. All eyes were cast to the main road leading to the village. Shoya Sanuki was waiting by a table assembled on his terrace, which held bottles of warmed sake, along with brush, ink, and sheets of writing paper.

Emiko stood behind her husband holding her child dressed as a male. She used his body as a shield to help hide her from the lie they would tell the old keeper of births to protect their new child. Her two daughters proudly stood by her side and the remaining male children stood by their honorable father's side.

The guard samurai sat in the front garden in formation, prepared to follow the trainer when it was his time to present the child to Ogino. It was a hot day with the sun rising to its highest position. The hum from swarms of mosquitoes faded when he moved out from under the shade of the overhang of his home. He shielded his eyes as he searched the road for first signs of the keeper. Tanizaki and Sanuki had come up with a plan to bring the keeper inside Sanuki's home, so he could examine his child in private. They could also speak to him without other ears overhearing their conversation.

He picked up the lead horse of the caravan. The families with newborn moved to the center of the road and waited. It was hot standing in the road, and the children cried and fussed. As in all ceremonies, the comfort of those to be honored was set aside, and whatever could make them uncomfortable was assaulting them. No shade and nothing to drink, dust blowing, and no place to sit, and nothing they could do to make the newborns comfortable on this day.

The keeper of births took his time entering the village, adding to the discomfort of those gathered. When he past near the people, he ignored them and moved for the shade of Sanuki's porch. He bowed to the Shoya and enjoyed sake and wiped his face with a wet towel. Ogino took his time setting out his book, placing out brushes and anything he needed for the registering of the newborn. He checked the roof, enjoyed a second sake then addressed the families standing in the sun. The keeper bowed from his position. "You will approach when your name is called!" The keeper displayed bad manners by expressing his lack of interest in the people he addressed.

Ogino called out the first child's name in an angry tone. It took twenty minutes for him to register and examine the naked child, and to give his permission for the family to make their preparations for the naming day. The rest of the families with newborns held in their arms, were forced to stand while waiting for their names to be called out by the old keeper.

The Tanizaki family stood in the middle of the road for three hours, until their name was called out. The instant it was, Sanuki leaned forward and whispered in the keeper's ear. Ogino looked puzzled at the Shoya, and he whispered more. In a huff, the keeper got up and announced rudely. "I'm hot and will interview the next family in the Shoya's home, which he has so graciously offered for this use. Tanizaki-san's family, follow me."

Ogino stormed in the building followed by Sanuki and the Tanizaki family. The keeper stopped in the center of the room and crossed his arms as he glared at the Shoya and growled. "Why have you ordered me inside the building? I like to conduct my duty outside in the open air. Why was it necessary for me to interview this family in the confines of your home? Is there something wrong with this child? If there is, the child should be put to the sword, and not be brought before me and waste my time."

Sanuki didn't say a word, instead he looked to Tanizaki and nodded at him.

He stepped forward and bowed to the keeper who didn't return it as he glared at Tanizaki.

"Huh Tanizaki-san! I'm waiting for an explanation to my questions." Ogino spat as he placed his hands on his hips, causing his swords in his sash to rattle slightly.

"Lord Keeper of the records..." The master trainer began his words.

"I am no Lord, I have to work for what little pay is offered me, Tanizaki-san! Continue with the explanation as to why I was ordered in this home to inspect this child of yours please."

He glared as he never glared at another person in his life, without taking his life for his insolence and lack of manners, as he barked. "As you like it! I am Master Trainer Nitaro Tanizaki-san, and I was entrusted with the training of Kawasomeru-sama's army. Our Lord decreed my eighth born is to be trained Samurai who'll replace me when I'm too old to train. I'll be respected or I'll have your faucet as my trophy."

For a long second, the keeper returned the glare and then bowed slightly to him.

"That's better old fool. Now, Ogino-san, as I stated, Kawasomeru-sama ordered my eighth born to be trained as a Samurai elite."

"As it should be decreed Master Trainer Tanizaki-san. Every eighth born child is a lucky one to the realm, and to his Lord. Was not Samurai Warrior Kusunoki-san the eight born of his family and their ancestry?" Ogino asked politely with a smile.

"I care not a grain of worthless rice for Kusunoki-san, his family or if he was the eighth born child or not, foul one. I requested you be brought in the building so I might speak with you in private of a problem we both must put our minds together, and work out carefully..."

"Does this problem have anything to do with your new child?" The keeper barked at him.

"Hai! Indeed Ogino-san." Sanuki replied while trying to keep his tone pleasant.

"Huh, I thought as much. Tanizaki-san! There can be no waving of the rules, if your child is deformed it must be put to the sword. The matter is out of my hands, it's the law no matter how painful this law might be. We cannot allow the crippled to survive and become a burden upon the health of the realm." The keeper moaned as he allowed his impatience to surface again.

"By the gods who inhabit the unknown world of the mist and clouds, must I remove your foul tongue so as to make your worthless mind listen to the words I speak at you, Keeper?" The suddenly fuming master trainer growled at the keeper.

The ferocity and tone of his voice made the keeper pay attention to the trainer's words.

"That's better. As I stated, my child has a slight problem..."

"Does the child have two heads Master Trainer Tanizaki!" The keeper smirked.

He turned red with anger as he allowed the thumb of his left hand to break the brass seal of his katana, and make it easier to be drawn for action if needed. The subtlety move didn't go unnoticed by the keeper, and he backed down and waited for the trainer to speak further.

He focused his eyes on the keeper's throat while his left hand rested threateningly on his sword. The keeper was aware of the trainer's reputation with a sword, or any other killing implement, and he chose the right course of action. Silence.

"My child is not a male child." The master trainer announced to the keeper.

"What? What did you say?" The keeper said, stunned and looked for a place to sit down.

"It's true, the child I bring before you for viewing is of a female child, Keeper Ogino-san."

"What? Why? How come you dare to bring forth a bitch child before me in the guise of a male? It's not a crime to bring forth a bitch child in this world, Trainer Tanizaki-san."

"Huh Keeper! I bring forth this female child before you as that of a male, because it was ordained by our Lord and Master that my eighth child will be trained in the ways of the Warrior. It was ordained by our village seer who stands in the middle of the street, that this child was seen as a male. This is the reason I bring the child before you and proclaim her as a him." He glared threateningly at the keeper of the births.

The keeper looked for something to rest against. Sanuki brought him sake. Everyone waited to speak until the color returned to his face. He was shocked by what the trainer was doing with his child. He looked at the old man and studied the wrinkled but wise face and cried. "Ieeeee! What you're suggesting, goes against every law of Bushido and realm. It's a crime to bring a bitch up in the way of the Warrior. I must not, no, I'll not allow this. There are certain laws we must allow to remain sacred to our Samurai, or all is lost. Ieeeee! The insult you'll deliver to our Warrior Caste. Have your wits taken leave of your foul body, Tanizaki-san?"

"Stop wailing like a wounded hinin, you sound like an old whore who thinks she was cheated with her pay. Ogino-san! You'll go along with this deceit, or it'll cost you your foul head."

The keeper's eyes narrowed and he cocked his head to a side as he stared at Tanizaki for a long moment, waiting for him to explain further the reason for the deceit he wanted to display before their lord. When he refused to speak, Ogino had no choice but to ask. "What do you mean I'll lose my head, Tanizaki-san? I've done nothing wrong here I assure you."

"Huh, you think you done nothing wrong. As we speak, Lord Kawasomeru was informed my eighth child was male. Ogino-san! I bid you to think. Think how our Master would react against the bearer of news that'd change my child from a male to female. You know his rage would be blind, his anger would strike against the person who brought such news to him. But his rage will know no bounds and would not stop at your worthless neck. The Lord would be so enraged his revenge would seek every member of your family, and your family's family. His lust for revenge wouldn't be satisfied until he has erased all trace of your ancestors from our records."

For the first time since they entered Shoya Sanuki's home, a slight protest came from the other families who remained in the sun in the middle of the road, waiting to have their children registered to the keeper of the births.

The keeper looked to Sanuki and announced. "Shoya Sanuki-san! This meeting might last longer than expected. Tell the remaining families I grew sick and will not be able to continue the registration of their children until tomorrow morning. Bid them to go home and care for their children, while I try to work out this most interesting of problems with the Master Trainer."

Everyone in Sanuki's home remained silent as they listened to Sanuki, and then the families protested further until the Shoya turned his request they go home and return tomorrow, into an order. When silence on the street returned, the keeper began again.

"Ieeeee! Master Trainer Tanizaki-san! You seem to be mistaken about a few things and if you would be so kind, I'll be happy to straighten them out for your knowledge."

He bowed slightly to the keeper and stared in his eyes to await his words.

"Tanizaki-san! I'll explain further for you." The keeper decided to remain civil with the trainer, in case he might be correct about Kawasomeru's reaction to his bitch child. It was better to have an ally on his side, if he was forced to break laws of his country or his responsibilities.

"I'm not the one bringing the Lord terrible news. It'll be you. All I'll be doing is writing in my book as I done all my life, the facts as I observed them." The keeper pounded on the dust covered book, and a small cloud rose and he added. "It'll be the one who reads the book to the Lord once a year, who'll suffer his anger. I'm bound by my yoshi gi (duty) to mark all I observed, nothing more nothing less. It'll be you and your family who'll suffer the wrath of Lord Kawasomeru. It wasn't I who informed him this bitch child was male. It wasn't I who gave birth to this lie you're giving our Daimyo. Tanizaki-san! My body shudders to think of the fate that'll befall your family's name, once Lord Kawasomeru becomes aware of this crime you committed."

He fumed as he glared at the smirk on the keeper's face, fighting to control himself he roared. "Ogino-san! Who do you think the Lord would believe, you or me old fool? Do you think the Lord would believe it when I tell him we discussed this possibility, and it was you who suggested I notify him before my eighth child entered this earth that she was a he, old man?"

"You wouldn't dare to say such a thing! It's not true!" He exclaimed as he straightened.

"Ogino-san!   It's about time you come to the understanding with me. I'll do what's necessary to insure this child's survival. She has been chosen by the gods for greatness…"

"She has been chosen, neh? Tanizaki-san! Your wits are scrambled by your age, old Trainer. What do you mean this bitch child has been chosen by the gods?"

At last, he felt he had Ogino where he wanted him.

The wise keeper felt he found a way out of this situation he was trapped in. If it was what he believed then it would be a simple matter for him to go along with what Tanizaki-san wanted him to do. If the female child was truly chosen by the gods, he too was bound by his duty and honor to insure this child's survival, even at the cost of his life.

He pumped up his chest until he looked larger than life. "Ogino-san! My child has the mark of the gods upon her body! Now, what do you have to say about this great deception?"

"Ieeeee! The mark of the Samurai you offer, Tanizaki-san?" The keeper cried.

"Hai! She has the mark of the gods on her body, you old fool."

"Allow me to witness this mark of the Kami upon your newborn, and my opinion might be swayed. I must first see the mark, before I believe such a tail as this, Master Trainer Tanizaki-san!" He ordered, using his position of power to order anything from the feared Tanizaki.

"Lady Emiko! Will you bring our child forward for the keeper's view, and show him where the gods placed their mark upon her body."

Emiko moved to the keeper who bowed, she returned his bow and uncovered the child's wrist.

Upon seeing the tiny red mark shaped in the form of a shooting star, the keeper's knees grew weak. This was the third time he saw such a mark in all his years. His mind raced, yes it was true, and it was as the trainer offered. It was the mark of the samurai, bestowed on few chosen warriors by the gods of the other world. The keeper drew in his breath then offered. "She'll answer to no master on this earth! Which god do you think placed his mark upon this child?"

He searched his mind for the name of a god who marked his child, any god. He cursed for abandoning the gods of his land for so long. The one god who impressed him came to his memory and he recited. "Fujin, the Great God of the Wind!"

"Ieeeee Master Trainer Tanizaki-san! It's one of the strongest gods who placed his mark on this one's arm. If he chose to mark her, so then she must be destined for great deeds in her future. Tanizaki-san! I cannot judge this child, or your effort in protecting her life. The only lord she'll answer to is Kawasomeru-sama. He'll be the only one she'll bow before, you'll not train her in the way of the sword, and this is forbidden by our laws. A female is not allowed to use the weapon of the Samurai Caste under any circumstances. It'd cost the offending family to lose their heads to dishonor the ways of the Samurai as you're suggesting."

"I told you she has the mark of the gods on her body, old fool!" He added again.

"Huh! The mark, this is true. What to do? What do the gods order of me? I'll pray to Lord Buddha for his guidance. Never before in the history of Japan has the mark of the Samurai been bestowed on a female. I pray the gods you haven't insulted them and this is their revenge aimed at you.

To upset the future of Japan by forcing us to teach a bitch the ways of the Warrior."

He let out a disgusted sigh as he snarled. "Ogino-san! I'll do what is necessary to insure her position in Kawasomeru-sama's army! I'll keep the fact she's a woman a secret as long as possible. I don't profess to know the confusing ways of the gods, this feat is for the loathsome priests who confuse our minds further with their words. I only know the way of the Warrior and how to train the soldier. I leave the gods to their duty and I'll remain with mine."

"Iye! Iye! Iye! This is forbidden. I fear what this course might bring down on my house. Don't dare to risk the wrath of Kawasomeru-sama in this way, it's most frightening." Ogino growled as he threw his hands in the air and leaped to his feet and paced the room.

"Ogino-san! All will be forgiven when Lord Kawasomeru witnesses the Warrior that I shall bring forth on the great day of Gembuku, the age of man, so fear not you old fool. This female child will be well taught under the banner of the Claw, my banner. Kawasomeru-sama brought his new vassals to train in the Claw discipline, everyone in Japan knows the Claw fighters make the best Warriors of all armies of Japan."

"Hai Tanizaki-san! All you speak is fact. Your words are free of falsehood. Hmmm... I'll do this much because of your name, I'll check your child. You'll present your child to me for inspection." Ogino demanded as he retook his seat and waited.

He let out his breath in a rush, and gave the signal for Emiko to bring forth his child for examination. For a while the trainer felt he won the keeper to his way of thinking, but now he was unsure and feared all was lost. He understood once the keeper examined the child naked, he would be bound by duty of office to record the child's gender forever in his book.

Emiko moved before the keeper as if she was walking slowly to her death.

"I'm waiting!" He demanded hotly. "I'll view your child. Prepare her, isogi!" (Hurry)

She opened the overcoat and started to unclothe the baby child.

The keeper jumped to his feet and shouted. "Stop! Ieeee! Your child has messed himself. I'll stop the viewing. I have no time to waste on this one child, I cannot wait for you to change and clean him for my viewing." He turned to Tanizaki and bellowed.

"Tanizaki-san! In the interest in saving time, I ask you the sex of your honored child, and I'll record it in this manner." The keeper glared at the master trainer.

He couldn't hide the smile that crossed over his lips, and pleasure he was feeling as he realized the cunning old keeper found a very clever way to clear his intellect of the great deception he planned to carry out against Lord Kawasomeru. The master trainer stepped before his wife and replied to the old man standing before him while glaring. "Keeper of Births Ogino-san, I swear this child brought before you on this day, is that of a male child born to the honorable house of Tanizaki, Master Trainer of the Ninth Village."

"Very well Master Trainer Tanizaki of the Ninth Village, so it shall be marked on my scrolls. I'll so record this birth as a male child, for I was unable to view the child properly. If it comes out you lied over anything about this child. I'll order your death to bring honor back to Lord Kawasomeru and his realm. Is this understood, Master Trainer Tanizaki-san?" Ogino snapped as he openly glared at Tanizaki.

"Hai Ogino-san!"

"Lady Emiko! I must ask the same question of you please. You must swear this child you brought before me on this day is that of a male child." The old man warned her.

"Hai!" She said as she bowed to Ogino and then nodded to him.

"So it is reported and so it is written upon the scroll. Congratulations to the Tanizaki family, you have a healthy male child I see, and you're allowed to name him on the given date. Gyoko, (Luck) Tanizaki-san, I'll pray to the Lord Buddha for his divine guidance of this child born in such confusion. If questioned further in this manner, I'll claim no knowledge of this, if your deception is discovered by our Lord." He said as he bowed to Tanizaki and Lady Emiko.

The keeper looked about and bellowed at the village leader. "Shoya Sanuki-san! This birth has been registered for history, it's time for a celebration I believe. Sake!" He demanded.

The master trainer stepped forward and held up his hand as he offered. "Honorable Keeper of Births Ogino-san! I'd be honored if you'd allow me to supply the sake from my private keep. I assure you there is none finer in all Japan to be drunk by you on this day."

Ogino was stunned by the offer, it was well known he had a certain special way to make his sake the best, and it was sought after by the great daimyos of the land.

"Hai Master Trainer! I'm honored to share a bottle of your sake on this endless day." Ogino bowed, relieved they were able to work out the problem of the newborn between themselves.

"Ieeeee friend, the honor is mine Ogino-san. I'll make sure you have a few extra bottles of my sake for your journey throughout Shinano province. It might make the nights pass more pleasurably, if you share my sake with a female friend, Ogino-san."

"Ieeeee! If it's discovered I'm traveling with five bottles of your finest sake, Tanizaki-san. I'll have every female of the Pillow World following me throughout Shinano, offering me their pleasures for a mere taste of your wine. Domo, (thank you) domo Tanizaki-san! You made my tiring days of endless travel more bearable to endure. Domo!" He bowed graciously to the master trainer who was having little trouble maintaining his temper against the old man.

He was furious because he felt Ogino named his price to bribe his oath of silence. Five bottles of his sake was a ransom he would expect to pay as homage to a lord of the realm, or to the Emperor, not a lowly keeper. As angry as he was, he knew he had no choice but to pay the price. He would give all his worth to have this child trained in the samurai ways. It was a mission for him to prove this female child could be a better warrior than any male.

He swallowed his pride and let out his breath and replied. "Hai Ogino-san! It'd be an honor to supply you with five bottles of my finest sake for your travels of duty." He bowed again to Ogino who returned the honor with one of his own as honorably.

Shoya Sanuki reentered his home at the conclusion of the deal struck between them, when Master Trainer Tanizaki sent his daughter out with instructions to prepare five bottle of sake for travel, and bring two more bottles for consumption by them. His daughter took off without question or hesitation to carry out her father's orders.

Shoya Sanuki was unable to hide he was still upset with them for this terrible deception they were carrying out against their master, but after the third glass of wine, he no longer cared what took place in all of Shinano province, or the realm.

Tanizaki and Emiko left Sanuki's home and as they walked to their shelter. Emiko counted in her mind the days left until they were able to name their child. After counting them off, she turned to her husband and informed him they had nine days before the naming day.

The master trainer used this time to attend to his troop's training, the activity made the nine sticks of time fly by. The naming day was put off until the following Sunday, so the troops in training would have the day off to celebrate the occasion. The Japanese believed from the moment of birth, and for the following thirty days or sticks of time, the soul of the baby wasn't affixed to the body. The greatest of precautions were enforced to assure the wandering soul would remain near the body of the child it was intended for. Rather than becoming confused and losing sight of the baby, and wander for eternity in search of another body to attach itself to. Some Japanese people believed if the wandering soul became to confused, it might attach itself to a body with a soul, thus causing madness to overcome the one infected with two souls.

During time of confinement, neither the mother nor child was allowed to move out of the home, or mingle with others of the village. For thirty sticks of time, the members of the ninth village ignored Emiko or her new son. The only reason he was allowed to walk the village was because he was entrusted with a task of training the warriors which overrode their beliefs. He was treated as if his wife hadn't had the baby and was in time of waiting. Normally, he would be ignored, but Lord Kawasomeru's needs and orders overpowered the beliefs of the village.

He was the first to rise on Sunday, the naming day. All the great and lesser gods of the village was honored for the past few days, and the last with a lamp lit and kept burning during twenty hours before the naming day arrived. It would only be extinguished when the last child of the village was named. Since yesterday, the women, except for those naming their new children worked on the feast. Each house blessed with newborns received a generous portion of this meal, and those fortunate enough to attend the birth of the child, along with intimate friends and relatives, were invited to participate in the feast. This invitation covered about everyone from the village and in some cases, some attendees would be forced to eat two, and even three meals on this day, for they helped with the births.

On this day, all newborn children would be considered to be part of the village, and were now governed by the same laws and beliefs as well as offered the protection of the stable environment of the village. The families assembled in the center of the street before the home of Sanuki. The Shoya remained standing on his porch and asked each family to name their children while holding them up for the gathered to witness. When it came to Tanizaki to name his child, the old man lifted the child overhead and announced to everyone gathered before him. "People of the Ninth Village, I introduce you to my eighth born child and son, Masahiko Tanizaki."

A roar rose from the crowd, each member of the village understood the honor soon to be bestowed on the village by their lord of the realm. The cheering continued until Sanuki raised his hands and bid silence to return. When everyone was quiet, he looked on Tanizaki and his family. "Master Trainer Nitaro Tanizaki-san! You brought great honor to our village, our Lord will have no choice but to elevate our humble village to a higher standing in the realm. Tanizaki-san, I'd like to introduce you to a special envoy sent the distance separating the Ninth Village from the capital of Shinano by our Lord for this occasion. Aritomo Kosai-san." Sanuki bowed to the stranger on the front porch of his home.

Kosai made a deal of unfolding the scroll after breaking the seal containing Kawasomeru's chop and read pompously. "Master Trainer Tanizaki-san! You are elevated to Master Trainer of the Realm, and Kawasomeru-sama elevated your wealth by fifteen hundred koku a year, and move your boundaries from the first bashi (bridge) of the Ninth Village to the third bashi."

There was a murmur that swept throughout the gathered citizens, all were struck with awe at the wealth lavished on one of their own. The speaker from Shinano allowed the whispers to continue, adding to the importance of the gifts for the master trainer. When he spoke again, everyone became quiet.

"Proud people of the Ninth Village! Lord Kawasomeru decreed it's your duty to make certain this child of Master Trainer Tanizaki-san, is trained in every aspect of life. Anyone not showing interest in this child's upbringing, will pay for his disrespect to our Lord's demands with his head. The punishment will not stop there, the criminal's entire bloodline will pay for his indiscretion. This child is marked for greatness in the realm, and it's the village responsibility to insure this child's training. The military training will be carried out by Master Trainer Tanizaki-san. If anything happens to this child, the village will pay with their heads." The master's representative made a big thing out of refolding the scroll, and handing it to Sanuki, who turned red as he received it, which was ordered entered in the village's archive.

Sanuki bowed to the representative from Engakuji Castle, his mind racing. He was worried if he did a wise thing, by allying himself with the deceit carried out by Tanizaki and his family. How could he been so stupid as to allow himself to be talked into hiding this child of Tanizaki's was a bitch child? His mind continued on this path and a sigh escaped his lips as he realized it was the correct course to travel on. He knew if Tanizaki reported this eighth child as a bitch, Lord Kawasomeru would order his village put to the bite of the sword. What they were doing was only putting off this fate. He handed the scroll to his keeper of the records and the little man disappeared with it, locking it away in a vault only he knew the location of.

At the end of the ceremony, the villagers walked before the children placed on display and bowed their welcome to the village. The rest of the day was spent by all in celebration, even the warriors in training were offered some of the feast. The highest honor was paid to Tanizaki by Lord Kawasomeru, sending a representative from his castle to attend the ceremony. It made the naming day special to the village. By the end of the day, Tanizaki, Kobayashi and Sanuki were beyond drunk, with Emiko and her daughter trying to roll him in his bedroll, so he can sleep.

The general was walked home by a guard of three of Tanizaki's samurai ordered to do so by Emiko. It was an honor she paid to Kobayashi for being there when she needed him.

MONDAY, THE FIRST DAY OF THE FOURTH WEEK OF THE

SIXTH MONTH OF THE THIRTEEN THIRTY NINETH YEAR

The trainer woke up feeling ill to his stomach, he was upset he was dressed in the clothes of yesterday's celebration and when he swallowed, he grew more ill. There was a terrible taste in his mouth and his head spun. His irritation rose when he heard the noise from the kitchen, and his mind didn't realize it was time to rise, if he was planning to be with his trainees for the day.

Emiko allowed the children to make noise needed to wake the drunkard so he could eat then prepare to begin the training of the warriors.

He went to get up but was driven back to his bedroll when his eyes registered shooting stars and pain of a severe headache wracking his body. Emiko appeared by the door and offered him herb tea. "Her husband, this will calm that raging thunderstorm taking place in your worthless head. I can't believe Kobayashi-san and you drank so much sake yesterday. Between the two of you, you tried to drink Japan dry in one night's time. Drink my husband, this will help you."

"Why have you allowed the children to wake me!" He growled as he got up on one elbow and sipped the hot brew. Instantly, the searing pain lessened and he looked up at his wife.

"Willow bark." She replied pleasant to her terribly suffering and proud husband.

"Thank the gods for willow." The trainer mumbled more to himself than his wife.

"My foolish husband, I allowed the children to wake you because it nears time to join the Warriors on the field. I know you don't want to miss another day of training. Lord

Kawasomeru might become angry if you lose further time with his soldiers and their work." Emiko bowed to her husband, hoping she hadn't over stepped her bounds by looking after her husband's business.

"Hai, and you call me wise Emiko! If it was not for you and your constant watching over my foolish self. I would've insulted our Lord and Master years past, and would've paid for my crimes with my worthless head many suns ago."

She bowed again, pleased her husband chose to honor her so.

"I'll be ready to leave for the training field soon my wife."

"Do you want food?" She offered to her suffering husband.

"Only if you can figure a way to keep it in my foul stomach. I fear your foolish husband might have drank too much sake yesterday, my Lady."

"A little too much sake you say to me huh?" She lamented with a smile then added. "Ieeeee! Perhaps you're right, foolish husband. If you call what you have drank yesterday too much sake. Then I'm pleased that I control your wealth, or we'd be poor and depending on others to help support us, dear husband." She said as she laughed and rose from her knees and heading for the kitchen and continued. "I'll prepare you something to eat that'll stay in your insulted stomach. I don't want you to leave home without eating. Too much sake you say, neh?" Emiko added as if an afterthought as she left the room.

He walked out of the main door and was further punished by the sun breaking over the mountains. The instant he stepped off the porch, he was surrounded by his samurai, and they walked to the training field. He smiled when he saw General Kobayashi waiting for him. He noticed the general was suffering as greatly as he was.

He walked up to General Kobayashi and dared a slight bow and paid for it, with a new pounding in his head. The general nodded and Tanizaki drew in a breath. "Huh, this is the week the horsemen will hit their targets at full gallop, or the fools will suffer my wrath."

"Hai Tanizaki-san! I'll prepare them for their test." The general offered as he pushed off the tree with his back and headed for the horse field. The master trainer listened as his second in command screamed at the horsemen, ordering them to mount. After drinking from the water barrel, he headed for the field. Three hundred and seventy five warriors were mounted waiting orders. He looked for the dog handlers and gave the head man a nod. Then ordered the handlers to move the first dogs to the center of the field.

He turned to the horsemen and yelled as quietly and painlessly as he could. "You are Samurai, the best in Kawasomeru-sama's realm. Today will be the first day you'll succeed in this area of training in uoimono, the shooting of the hounds. I warn you, any Warrior unsaddled will be classified as enemy, and will be subject to attack by Warriors in their saddles. It'll be up to you if you die on the field of honor, you know the practice arrows will enter your bodies when struck. You die today and you'll disgrace your family's name."

The master trainer said no more to the gathered warriors as he turned his back on the samurai and raised his hand and announced. "First ten riders, prepare for action. Four arrows fired and three targets hit, or you'll be turned over to the hinin class, and no longer allowed to be Samurai. The name Samurai is not a right, it's something you must earn as your right, and you must work hard every day to maintain than right. First ten Samurai out." He lowered his hand and the handlers released the dogs on the field.

The first riders charged on the field, the remaining warriors letting out fearsome war cries as the spear and swordsmen encircled the field, to stop the fleeing dogs from escaping. They must have been practicing, the first volley hit their targets. In less than a heartbeat, the yumi's were reloaded and the second barrage of arrows launched. The arrows hissed as they split the air, each finding a second target. His chest swelled with pride as he watched the horsemen reload bows for a third time and launch arrows. The third volley had two misses, before his mind tallied the hits, the fourth flight of arrows were fired. Each found a new target."

He rushed on the field, forgetting about his headache as he screamed orders for the dog handlers to capture the dogs. He wanted to see if any had two marks from the same archer. Of all the dogs, one was hit twice by the same archer. "Ieeeee! My unworthy Warriors shown me they want to remain Samurai, that their mettle is true. You done well and will return to the rear of the line and wait your second chance at the dogs. Second ten Samurai prepare for attack. Dog handlers, prepare to release the second dogs." He raised his hand and brought it down quickly. The dogs shot on the field and ran in all directions.

The horsemen charged after the dogs, a second war cry was raised by the warriors waiting their turn to attack the dogs. The results was as good with the second set of warriors. For the rest of the day, the success of the first squads was duplicated time and again. Each time the squads were successful in their attack, Tanizaki's chest rose with pride. The horse field wasn't the only place enjoying success on the field. The accuracy of the archers seemed to have gone over to the spearmen consistently hitting their targets also. The swordsmen were also sharing in the spirit of the day and the successes, leaving their trainers with little if anything to scream at them about.

By late afternoon, his headache disappeared, and his enthusiasm returned as he chased after a horsemen who messed up. He adopted the habit of striking the warriors who missed their mark with a bamboo cane to get their attention. It had an effect, no samurai wanted to be struck by the cane, in the places he knew would cause discomfort and pain to the offender. The flourishing day ended with further success on the field. Late in the day, he decided to have the horsemen attack the swordsmen with bamboo swords. He wanted the horsemen to cut the defending army in half, and split them once more, and eliminate the army with a thrust aimed at the heart of the defenders of the attack. The success the horsemen shared was beyond his wildest demands. He returned home, walking proudly surrounded by his samurai guard.

Emiko had supper waiting when her husband entered, it was twilight when he returned. Tonight was going to be a special night, she had the village masseuse scheduled to work on her husband after his bath. She had the bath ready and later, she would try and give pleasure to her husband with her mouth. Her daughter brought news of the novel way the women of the Soft World were pleasing the warriors. She explained it and she felt she could accomplish the act for her his pleasure. She deemed it her duty to please her husband to new heights.

Days blended to weeks and weeks to months, and before she knew it, the honored time of the celebration of Tabezome was approaching. The caring Emiko scheduled the ceremony for Sunday, the day it seemed the easiest for her husband to take off from the training field. Besides she understood he considered Sunday the easiest day for the trainees to rest. She also understood her husband seemed to need at least one day off of training the warriors, and that day was Sunday, and she pampered him all the day long as her gift to him.

CHAPTER EIGHT

THE FIRST DAY OF THE SECOND WEEK OF THE EIGHTH MONTH OF THE THIRTEEN THIRTY NINETH YEAR

TABEZOME:

Tabezome was the ceremony celebrating the newborn child's one hundred and twentieth day of life, it was a great day, and the child enjoyed his first solid food. Everything in the Japanese way of life was celebrated. She made a ceremony of the taking of solid food, she set up a platform in the center of the room of the main house. There she set up a table on which sat a bowl and pair of never used chopsticks The bowl was made of the finest clay died black, to signify the child was a boy. She invited certain members of her family and parents. Even her mother attended the ceremony even though she no longer understood what was happening.   The birthing members, and a few selected friends were also invited to attend.

After she bowed to her guests for attending the ceremony, and their showing interest in the health of her child. She sat on a bamboo chest and placed her child on her knees facing the crowd. Carefully, she lifted one grain of rice on the chopsticks and brought it to her child's mouth. Masahiko Tanizaki ate the grain greedily.

Everyone at the ceremony breathed a sigh of relief and spoke excitedly. All were pleased the child ate solid food, it signified he would live and grow to be healthy. The weaning of the child from the mother's breast was long feared, if the child refused to eat solid food it would surely die. The weaning was put off long as possible by mothers, and she was no different. She believed in the old ways, and this part of the child's development was thought to be one of most danger for the child's health and welfare.

The guests congratulated he and made offerings of handmade gifts to the child for taking solid foods. She knew in the next fifty days, the child would be weaned from her breast all together. In her heart there was sadness, she believed her child died the first life of many he would travel on his march to greatness. She so believed this child was a male, she wouldn't allow her mind to think otherwise. She made Estsuko change the child all the time, so she wouldn't be reminded about the missing stem which separated a male from female child.

The guests began to leave her home, the trainer wasn't present for this ceremony, it wasn't necessary. He was busy working with the training of the soldiers.

As the days went by, she started to feel empty because her child no longer searched out her breast for its life giving food. Masahiko was eating well on her own, better than most children his/her age, using his hands to eat cooled rice, and gnawing her way through the cooked fish after it was deboned. At first she would chew small bits of fish to a mush, and would feed Masahiko by placing the chewed fish on the end of her fingernail for him to eat from.

By the time Masahiko turned six months old, she weighed twelve pounds and was crawling. The child's energy was amazing to the villagers, and the ever present smile, warmed even the most angry old heart of Sanuki.

The eighth child of Tanizaki wasn't the only member of his family receiving attention in the village. Every day, one of the female members of the village appeared at Emiko's home with food or vegetables, offering them to her for the honored child. The fishermen brought the freshest of the catch to his home. Everyone from the village was doing their best to get in good graces of Tanizaki and his chosen child. They knew when the child was inducted into the army of Lord Kawasomeru, everyone in the village would be honored by their master. Tanizaki put on extra weight himself, eating the many dishes cooked for his family.

The dreaded day arrived when Estsuko and the next child were to leave their village for Engakuji Castle, as was decreed on the day when the lord visited the village. This left the youngest female child to help with the raising and education of Masahiko. The boys were still home. Amidst many tears and hugs, Emiko waved good-bye to the girls being escorted by samurai sent to fetch them from their master. This was another thing Tanizaki missed, he was so busy with his trainees he missed saying good-bye to his eldest daughters.

She was lost without her daughters to help with the child whose energy was beyond containment. She spend more time with Masahiko and started to ignore her husband. For the most part he didn't mind, he was eating with the trainees and got in the habit of coming home only to sleep. Their sex life was nonexistent, and she relied on Masahiko for comfort.

One samurai who Lord Kawasomeru ordered to guard the master trainer's life, noticed the unrest in his home, and dared to send a letter by pigeon to his warlord, informing him of the crumbling home life of the master trainer.

THE THIRD DAY OF THE FORTH WEEK OF THE TENTH MONTH OF THE THIRTEEN THIRTY NINETH YEAR.

Without sending foreword, the powerful Lord Kawasomeru suddenly appeared at the beginning of the road leading to the ninth village in the early morning hours of Wednesday. He was an impressive figure to witness dressed in battle armor, his horse was likewise decked out in armor. Amidst the battle cry screamed by his warriors, the lord charged in the village, his horse's hooves raising a dust cloud on the dried ground behind.

The samurai he placed with Tanizaki, ran from the garden to the street. Upon seeing their master they fell to their knees and buried their faces in the dirt, bowing deeply as he rode to them.

His caravan followed him to the village as village members came out to attack them, the men rushed out with unsheathed swords, ready to defend the village against this thought to be attack. They heard the war cry, but had no way of knowing they were under mock attack by their lord. The instant the warriors realized it was Kawasomeru charging them, they dropped and bowed.

Sanuki rushed out of his home without his sword, and Kawasomeru noticed this and was going to make a deal of it when he noticed the trainer standing by his gate with his sword in hand, his stance showed he was ready to defend his family. His aged elbows locked in position, prepared to swing the sword. The point of the blade was held to the ground before him in striking position. His body was turned slightly, giving the attacking warrior the smallest target to strike at.

The lord pulled on the reins of his horse and it changed its direction, he slowed the horse's charge as he rode to the trainer. When he pulled back on the reins, the horse came to a sliding stop. The trainer lifted his sword and dropped to his knees and bowed to Lord Kawasomeru.

He dismounted antagonistically with a deliberate clanging of his armor; each noise had a meaning to it. The feared warlord's feet landing on the ground before the head of Tanizaki which remained on the ground. He couldn't help but believe his deception was discovered, and the lord was here to destroy the village and all who dwelled in it. Why else would he charged the village and startle the people so? He mentally prepared himself for death, sorry he wouldn't live long enough to see his daughter's rise to greatness ordained for her by the gods.

"Get on your feet Master Trainer Tanizaki-san!" The warlord barked down at him.

"Hai my Lord." He replied as he struggled to his feet.

"Tanizaki-san! You look tired, exhausted. Are you not resting well?" The powerful warlord growled as he rested his armor plated hand on Tanizaki's shoulder and looked in his eyes.

"Hai my Lord. I am fine." The trainer offered in his defense.

"Tanizaki-san! You're not allowing the training of my worthless soldiers to endanger your health?" He asked as he led Tanizaki through his gate to the front garden.

"Iye! I been taking good care of myself my Lord."

"How is Lady Emiko?" Kawasomeru asked as he pulled a flower and smelled its fragrance, turning his back to the trainer. Knowing he was giving him time to get his emotions controlled.

"She's doing well my Lord, domo for asking about her health. I fear the birth of my last child has taken its toll on her. I think the days of giving birth ended for my worthless wife."

"Ieeeee! This is bad news indeed to hear for my realm, sad, sad indeed. To think that the great bloodline of Master Trainer and Samurai Nitaro Tanizaki has ended with the luckiest of child born. Karma, Karma." The lord turned to face the trainer and turned serious and offered. "Why it was not you who told me of the pain Lady Emiko is suffering daily, old fool. I would've put off sending for your daughters. The raising of this child is more important to my realm than your daughters serving old men of my Castle. "How does the training of my worthless soldiers go with you old man?" The warlord questioned.

"Well my Lord, they're learning beyond dreams I dare not allow myself to think. They'll be prepared before you need them for battle against Lord Wakatsuki's worthless armies."

"Will they be prepared if I have need of them tomorrow morning, Tanizaki-san?"

"Hai my Lord. They'd serve you well on the battlefield, even as early as today my Lord. Although they wouldn't be as well trained as I'd like them to be..."

"Huh! They're that well along on their training, Tanizaki-san?" He grunted as he removed his helmet and rested it on his knee.

"Hai!

"Tsutomu!" The lord bellowed at someone who they didn't see.

"Hai!" One of Tanizaki's bodyguards said as he popped up and stood by the gate.

"Ieeeee! Release these foolish people from their back breaking bow. Order them to return to their homes and busy themselves. Inform Shoya Sanuki-san I'll be with him shortly."

"Hai." The warrior snapped as he spun and rushed off to carry out his master's bidding.

"Tanizaki-san! Obviously, you've been able to work my soldiers into finely trained Samurai. If their training is so well along then I wish to interfere and suggest you take two sticks of time a week off from their training to rest your body. You can allow General Shimbo-san to run the training for the days you're resting. Old friend, your health is more important to me than the training of these worthless manure eaters I dragged before you."

He bowed to his lord politely as he kept his eyes looking down.

"Estsuko!" Lord Kawasomeru bellowed in a commanding tone.

"Hai." She replied as she appeared before the front gate of Tanizaki's home.

Emiko came out and sat behind Lord Kawasomeru and her husband. Her heart beating faster when she saw her eldest daughter standing outside the front gate of their home. She missed her since she left for the capital and a life at the castle.

"Estsuko! Bring the gift I brought for your honorable father." He snapped at her as he got up with a moan and much effort.

A second later, Estsuko reappeared carrying a long, narrow silk wrapped package. She rushed before her lord and dropped to her knees and bowed, her forehead lightly touching the ground as she raised the gift and offered it to him.

As he took the gift, he turned to Tanizaki. "Not only are you a Master Trainer of my Warriors, you're a master at training your daughters. I brought you a gift to honor your fine work with my Warriors." He offered the silk wrapped gift.

His old hand shook as he took the offering from his proud lord.

"Open it you old fool!"

He slid one hand in the silk tube and held onto the contents and pulled the silk cover from them. He let go of the silk, knowing it would never hit the floor. It didn't, Estsuko took the silk tube before her father let it go from his hands.

"Well trained as I said Tanizaki-san! I admire your teaching abilities." The warlord mumbled, studying his old friend's eyes as he looked over the gift he offered him.

"Ieeeee Kawasomeru-sama! You honor such an old fool far to greatly I fear. This is a gift worthy of an Emperor, not a filthy old useless Warrior who is not smart enough to know when he is too old to properly serve his Lord on the battlefield. Lady Emiko! Come here!"

He handed her the wakizashi while he held the katana in both hands and studied the intricate carvings decorating the length of the polished scabbard. The old man's hands snapped the brass seal of the sword with his thumb, and allowed the exquisite sword to move inches out of its scabbard, to examine the fine steel and edge of the blade. He knew he would dishonor the sword if he removed it out of the scabbard, and the sword wasn't dipped in blood to quench its thirst. It was bad karma to expose the steel of a sword needlessly, for vanity's sake.

"Ieeeee! It's an ancient sword fit to be carried by the greatest of Warriors or Masters, no others." He said as his eyes reflected the glare from the highly polished steel of the blade.

"Huh! You're wise beyond your years old friend. That's the reason I chose to honor you so with this sword made for my grandfather, and was wielded in the victorious wars against the dog eating Mongols. The sword is the fine work of art of the Master Sword Maker of Kamakura, Nakagawa who died three hundred years ago. It's a weapon which must be respected. I give the sword to you for your years of service to my realm. I'll see your newborn child now old one."

He didn't take his eyes off the magnificent blade as he growled over his shoulder. "Lady Emiko! Bring forth Masahiko-san to be viewed by Kawasomeru-sama."

She moved forward, her youngest daughter walking behind her carrying her newborn.

"Ieeeee! He's as big as a standing crane Tanizaki-san. What are you feeding this child to make him grow like the reed? I must have some, and ask Lady Mineko to feed it to my new son." He grunted as he looked over the fine looking young lad.

"He's almost able to stand my Lord."

"Am I a fool to believe such a tall tale." The lord grunted as he touched the child's hand with a finger and the little one locked on it with his hand. "Ieeeee! The strength!"

"If my Lord would allow me to demonstrate for his pleasure. I'll show you how the child tries to stand and walk already." She offered in a most pleasant tone.

"Hai." He snorted with disbelief lacing his concerned tone.

She picked up the child by both hands and allowed the child's legs to lightly touch the ground. Instantly, the child kicked his feet and tried to walk, pulling on Emiko's hands.

"Huh! The child is a gifted one Lady Emiko!" The lord mumbled as he stared at the child trying to walk from his mother's restricting hold.

He watched the scene and offered. "The baby has the mark of the gods upon his body."

Stunned, Lord Kawasomeru turned to the trainer to see if he was playing a joke on him. When he saw the trainer was serious, he said. "The mark old one?"

"Hai my Lord and Master, the child has the mark of the Samurai upon him from the day of birth. The mark has not faded, so he must be chosen by the gods for greatness for your realm, my Lord." He announced as he replaced the sword in its scabbard and held it in one hand, while turning to the lord who couldn't hide the astonishment he was experiencing over being informed the child had the mark of samurai on his body.

"The mark, only once in every century is a child born to the world with the mark of the gods on his body. I must see this mark with my eyes. I never seen one in my life, but I heard about the mark on many occasions. Please Lady Emiko! Will you show me this mark? I must see it, to make certain these stories I heard about this mark is true or not."

She bowed to the trainer, and uncovered the child's wrist, the arm the sword would be carried in, and exposed the birthmark which looked like a shooting star crossing the Heavens.

He leaned forward and studied the mark then grumbled in astonishment. "By the gods locked forever in the Floating World, it's as you spoke. I can't believe my eyes have fallen upon the mark of greatness. Have the priests discovered which of the gods saw fit to mark this child so, Tanizaki-san?" He grumbled as he stared at the tiny mark.

"Fujin, the always angry God of Wind, Lord Kawasomeru-sama." Emiko announced

"The fearsome God of Wind!" He bellowed as he stepped back a few paces, acting almost afraid of the child and what its presence offered to his kingdom.

"Hai!" She said as she bowed again, as if embarrassed over the news.

"Ieeeee! The God of Wind chose to mark this child with his mark. I'll let it be known to the realm the gods chose to mark one of my future Warriors. I'd not be surprised if Ashikaga-sama deems it right, and pays a visit to the Ninth Village to view this mark. The name of Masahiko Tanizaki-san will be feared before the child becomes a man, and steps first foot on the glorious battlefield. This is a great day for Shinano, and for the seven provinces who sworn allegiance to my rule." The lord boasted as he moved to the child and looked at the birthmark once more.

The trainer noticed how the warlord was sweating dressed in the armor and growled at his daughter. "Estsuko! Why do you stand idly while your Lord is so uncomfortable. Have you lost your wits about yourself since leaving my home? Does the comfort of your Lord no longer interest you? Go and make your Master cha. Bring sake also, he may want something other than tea to enjoy on this fine but warm day. Move before I have you stripped and beaten for allowing your mind to wander in the world of daydreams. You dishonored me before our Lord, worthless daughter. Have you forgotten your training you were taught by your mother, young one?"

Estsuko bowed then walked past her father and the lord of the realm as she entered the house.

"Tanizaki-san! Don't be so harsh on your daughter, she must be exhausted from her journey from my Castle. We moved quickly, fast marching all night so we could arrive before sun up arrived on this wonderful day. It's too nice a day for anger to ruin it" The lord barked as he removed the chest plate of his armor and dropped it on the porch. A samurai rushed forward and picked it up and moved off with it. His duty was to place it in its keep chest until needed or requested by his master of the realm.

"Lord Kawasomeru! Why have you chose to burden yourself in your travels, to have my worthless daughter accompany you? Have you decided to honor her by allowing her to serve you alone, great one?" Master Trainer Tanizaki asked seriously of his wise lord.

He leaned back and allowed himself to laugh, daring to risk loss of face to display such emotions in public. But the lord was too tired to hide his emotions behind a false mask of strength, as he grumbled. "Tanizaki-san! I allowed your daughter to accompany me on this travel for a reason. I been thinking of late, and decided Lady Emiko needs the service of her daughters more than Engakuji Castle does. I return your daughters, I'll pay them ten koku a year as long as they serve your wife. I discussed this with them and they agreed to stay with their mother as long as they're needed by her. Once their service is no longer required by your wife, and you feel you don't need them, notify me and I'll send a convoy to fetch them and make sure they arrive at the Castle safely." He returned his weight down on the porch and breathed a sigh of relief.

Tanizaki dared to stare at his lord, as if his wits had left him. His mouth open as he gawked.

"Foolish Tanizaki-san! I'm surprised you'd dare stand before me with your mouth agape thusly. It's insulting me to see your mouth full of rotted teeth." The warlord smiled to show the trainer he was joking as he waited for the reply from the older man.

His mouth snapped shut with a click and he shook his head and offered. "Please excuse this foolish old man's stupidity my Lord. I'm more tired than I realized. My mind's having trouble understanding why it is the Lord of Shinano chose to honor me so. I'm a worthless soldier too old to carry out his duty on the field of battle, and should be allowed to whittle away in the dust from which I was made."

"It's I who'll determine your worth to my realm, not you old man. It's for you to accept this gift I offer you and be done with it. This blade is one of the best ever made for a Samurai to employ against his enemy, I treasured it almost as much as I valued my life, Tanizaki-san. If you allow it, the blade will serve you as well as it served me." He bowed to the old man.

"Hai my Lord, and I'll honor the magnificent sword as you have." Tanizaki again bowed.

"Tanizaki-san! I trust you're aware of the small wars plaguing Japan of late. I tried to enlist the aid of Shogun Ashikaga, but he too is with problems facing his command. There are a number of wars occurring around the capital of Kyoto, and Ashikaga-sama's been forced to commit many Samurai to defend the capital. He reported he had no available Warriors he could send to fight off the problems the dung heap Wakatsuki is causing the lower provinces. I'm hard pressed to supply the Warriors order to defend the lower provinces loyal to me, but I'm doing it.

"It helped when we joined the eight provinces, and had them rely on each other for their province's security. It wearies me to keep my eye on so many wars being fought between these troubled provinces." The lord stopped speaking and took the tea from his daughter. He sipped from the cup after bowing to the young woman who smiled as she bowed and handed her father the second cup. There was no formal offering of cups, Estsuko knew better than to interrupt her father when he was speaking with someone, especially the lord of the realm.

The sake was placed on the porch, and Estsuko disappeared but she stayed near to hear any call, in case she was needed by her father or the lord.

He sipped noisily from his sake and placed the cup on the deck as he offered. "Kawasomeru-sama! You could pull the Samurai I'm training, if they're needed for the defense of the realm."

"Ieeeee! I don't want to interfere or disturb their training? I have enough Warriors to protect the provinces loyal to Ashikaga-sama and myself. I want these Samurai you're in the process of training, to be the best of the best in the art of making war with our enemy. I'll not upset their training except unless the entire realm erupts in war." The lord stopped speaking and drew in a breath, and sighed as he let out his air. "Tanizaki-san! I fear there'll be no Kamikaze, no divine wind come to our aid in this war against the forces under Wakatsuki's command. This time, I can only hope I'm strong enough to stop these wars from expanding to the rest of the realm.

"I fear Japan will not survive the future years of war between our warring provinces as we done in past years. There are too many worthless Samurai who wander Japan without allegiances to no one commander, or to use your word Tanizaki-san, Warlord. If these Ronin filth take to band together and attack the provinces at war, they might take over enough of the provinces to create the unrest that'll destroy Japan. War! What a waste! It must stop, we must learn to work together for the good of Japan's sake. I hope I'm not condemned by the monen, an evil spell to travel the Muryogo-no-michi, the never ending road of war, Tanizaki-san." The lord made a spitting sound as if closing a deal with himself.

The trainer didn't utter a word for fear his lord might turn his wrath on him. He remembered what Kawasomeru warned Wakatsuki when they were speaking of war between their provinces. The master hissed Wakatsuki would wish he were born a dog rather than suffer his wrath.

The warlord rose and bowed to Emiko then to Tanizaki as he mumbled he had to get back to his castle where he could oversee the wars in the lower provinces. "Tanizaki-san! I'll stop by Sanuki's home for a visit then be on my way. Train my soldiers well in your knowledge of war making and I'll be pleased. Luck, I hope to see you soon, if not, I'll look forward to the day of Gembuku when you appear before me with your chosen Warrior. Yoi gyoko (Good luck) Master Trainer, Japan's history will never be allowed to forget your honorable name."

He walked from Tanizaki without further words, the samurai he left behind, dropped and bowed as their lord passed. The trainer held the katana he gave him in his hand as he stared after the leader walking towards Sanuki's house. He didn't dare follow, he wasn't invited.

Emiko moved nearer her husband and moaned quietly. "How come you did not accompany Kawasomeru-sama on his visit to the old fool of the village, husband?"

"Huh! There's a simple answer, I was not invited. I feel our lord is paying a visit to one of the chugen, the people of small account, and didn't want me to waste my time." He said as he turned from the back of Lord Kawasomeru and headed for his house.

Master Trainer Tanizaki's home was the hub of activity, his older daughters were moving their belongings around and chattering like excited sparrows, as they spoke to their younger sister and brother. Emiko smiled, she was happy to have her daughter's home again.

Estsuko rushed to her mother's side and took the child from her and kissed her mother hello. Then cooed with the child laughing with glee at having her older sister playing with her again. The confusion over the child's sex was upsetting to both parents. It was hard for them to constantly call a female child by a male's name of Masahiko.

The master trainer stood staring at his children as they played carefree with Masahiko, when a thought struck him with the force of the blacksmith's hammer laying down on the edge of the sword he was forging. He shifted his weight, drawing his wife's attention. The look in his eyes worried her and she asked. "My noble husband! Are you all right?"

"Hai! I'm fine my Lady, I realized the reason for the master's visit to our worthless village. Kawasomeru-sama traveled all this way, to deliver our daughters to us safe and sound. What an honor our understanding Master has bestowed on us. Everyone who lives in Shinano will be aware the Lord saw it fit to travel to honor the Tanizaki family. Our name will be sung about the camp fires for the life of Japan."

CHAPTER NINE

The days passed and as Lord Kawasomeru feared, the wars in the lower provinces were starting to get out of hand, threatening to drag in the other provinces trying to remain neutral during the conflict, in the wars. He sent five hundred more warriors to be trained by the master trainer, but was forced to pull five hundred of the half trained warriors from his program. These samurai were mostly horse warriors, and the lord sent a scroll apologizing to Tanizaki for the removal of the untrained warriors, he cited the need to protect Echizen from Lord Wakatsuki's forces attacking the province from four sides, Kaga, Hida, Mino and Omi.

Usually, the fourth day of the third lunar month was a festive day in Japan, because it was the start of the celebration of offering prayers and food to the fearsome kami of wind, Fujin-sama. The prayers were to beg the mysterious feared god, to spare the crops during his times of anger, and releasing the winds on Japan. On this special day of happiness, the celebration was over shadowed by the departure of the trainees riding off to join the ongoing war. Kobayashi was standing with Tanizaki when he separated the horse warriors from the samurai ranks, and ordered them to move out for Engakuji Castle. The general was having a discussion with the trainer. "Tanizaki-san! We should make it against the law to war, and remove Wakatsuki from power."

"Huh, what law is stronger than might, neh General Kobayashi-san? Kawasomeru-sama should piss on that maggot eaten fool's face, and be done with it." The master trainer growled as he watched the warrior's line up, salute him and turn and start on their journey for the castle.

Four sticks of time after honoring the god of the wind, the birth of Buddha was celebrated. In the courtyard of the temple of the ninth village, a structure called a hanami-do was erected, and festivity adorned with wreaths of flowers, inside was a statue of Buddha resting in the center of the shallow pool of water. The believers from the village poured water scented with hyacinths from the pool over the statue. After honoring Buddha, they removed a small amount of water for their use. It was believed in Japan the sweet waters had healing properties after washing over the statue. Great bouts of wrestling were organized, and young men of the village showed off their powers before the unmarried women, trying to win their favors and impress their future wives.

More sticks of time passed, word reached the ninth village samurai trained by Tanizaki, engaged in their first battle, and their outstanding deeds on the battlefield were recorded for all to hear. The addition of these warriors was enough to beat back the hard probes into Echizen, by the loathsome forces of Lord Wakatsuki army, and the fighting taking place was forced to stalemate with the added warriors, and neither side able to out power the other.

He pushed the training forward, he eliminated days off ordered by Lord Kawasomeru. He feared he would lose more warriors any day, and didn't want them to leave without being better educated in the art of war. The next day facing the Tanizaki family was celebration of Tanjobi.

THE FIRST DAY OF THE SECOND WEEK OF THE FIFTH MONTH OF THE YEAR THIRTEEN FORTY
TANJOBI:

This was the day the trainer chose to celebrate his son's first tanjobi, his birthday. A day of rejoicing for the child and his family and the village, because this child had the name of Tanizaki and picked by Kawasomeru to lead his future warriors to battle. This added to the celebration. It was the friends of the families chance to honor this child, by showering him with toys, statues, clothes, and kosodes. For two days, the village was the scene of celebration on the scale of honoring Buddha. Men drank and offering ceramic decanters to Tanizaki to add to his cellar.

Generals Kobayashi and Shimbo took turns working with the trainees, allowing Tanizaki to enjoy his child's birthday. Great drums added to the festive mood as Taiko drums beat on well into the night. Sake was sent to the warriors who enjoyed it at the end of their training day.

The master trainer got drunk again, he was pleased because it was the custom of Japan to begin the training of their male child from this day forward. The child was allowed to wear a kosode of moderate colors with a plain sash. He wasn't allowed to play with the wood swords, but was allowed to pick them up and examine them. The trainer had no intentions of waiting until the child's fifth birthday to begin his training. He made plans secretly to teach the child how to place his weight on his feet, so he would be able to spring in action.

He was thinking of different ways to increase the child's strength. He knew this would be a serious problem to work through, never before in Japan's history had a female dared to be trained in the ways of the samurai. He understood this child would have to be stronger than most male warriors, and quicker and have more endurance. She would have to run faster, and be smarter. But the strength was a problem to conquer. He looked at his one year old opening gifts and smiled. The child was as large as most males her age which made it easy to keep his secret. He was happy Emiko fed the child proportions usually served to male children. He forbid the child be made to carry out common chores done by women. The child would be allowed to run around the village and get in trouble the way males did.

He issued orders to the villagers to correct the child if they saw him walking, or other ways of improving his understanding of the ways of life. He gave orders to enlist the child's aid if they need help, everything was geared to keep the child busy with learning. He wanted him to get used to running, he didn't want the child to be lazy or uninterested in anything happening around her. Everything he did was to make the child stronger and smarter than males. The villagers overlooked minor transgressions the child did while growing up.

He spent days on the training field with his warrior then night hours explaining to Masahiko the ways of making war and commanding troops she would be in command of in the future for her lord. The trainer went over different attack strategies and the art of understanding the enemy's thoughts, even before they were developed and employed by them. To understand one's enemy was to conquer that enemy. By the time she was one and a half years old, she was allowed to accompany her father to the training field and observe what was being taught to the trainees. She was smart beyond her age and between priests, Tanizaki, and his wife and older children of the village willing to assist with the training, Masahiko spoke before most children her age. By the time she was three, Masahiko could write sentences and understands and draw characters commonly used in the complicated writing of Japanese words. She could also understand these confusing characters and knew what they meant.

By the time she was four, Masahiko could ride a horse without having a warrior lead it. She could read, speak, think, and care for herself. Tanizaki showed and told her which roots and plants of the forest could be eaten, and which to stay away from, or use as poisons against her enemy. This was in case she was trapped and had to escape in the woods without weapon and food. She would be able to fend and protect herself until she could make it back to her troops, and the safety they offer her.

By her fifth year, Masahiko could outrun most males, and was always challenging the older males to grueling foot races and winning most. Her stamina was untiring and equal to an older male. She carried half her weight in her arms by this age, and Tanizaki pushed her forward, past her limited capabilities and she followed orders without hesitation. He prepared her for the day she would be pitted against the male warriors of Lord Kawasomeru.

The trainer knew the day of Gembuku, the day of the child walking into the adult world would be a trying one. He knew the tests and trials she would be put through before the master, so he could judge her worth not only by the other warriors who would be trying to prove themselves better than the child trained by the master of the ninth village. But the lord would put his ward through a number of tests geared to see how well trained Masahiko was.

During the rare days Tanizaki took off from his training, he would walk with Masahiko in the woods. There he would make her run up hill carrying rocks and heavy branches. Afterwards, he would order her to build a stone wall and support them with branches on the highest peak. He would run alongside his child, yelling at her and making her excel in everything she tried.

By the time she was six, she got involved in her first fight with an older boy known as the village bully. It was reported his child put up a honorable fight against the larger and older boy. But in the end, the weight and strength of the older child ruled out, and he sent her home with her first black eye and split lip.

The trainer was furious with Masahiko for her failure to defeat the older boy, and refused to speak with the child for days. She was crushed by her father's anger and took to moping around until he began speaking with her again. He saw determination etched in his child's eyes as she prepared for the inevitable battle, when she would go against the older boy. From that day forward, she was determined to know the ways of fighting with her hands.

She took to begging her father to show her the arts of Kyushin, combat with the hands. He took up the practice of showing her one hand or foot movement a day, and at the end of the week he would review what he taught her during the week, to make certain she understood each move. Within weeks, she could move the heavier weight of her father aside as she tried to get him off his feet, using the moves he taught her. Each attack was useless, but each time she attacked, he could tell her strength was growing in leaps and bounds. He knew she understood it was easier to use her enemy's power and weight against him, rather than defeat him using her strength. Against his better judgment, he relented and explained the intricate ways of using ones fists to defeat ones enemy without destroying her target.

"Masahiko-san! You think your fists are the only weapons to employ against your enemy? Iye! When I finish with you I'll expose your weapon is here, your mind. Your wits are your true weapon at your command, the sword is an extension of your mind. Your mind controls the weapon, not the other way around. If a Warrior allows his sword to rule his mind, he's defeated before he enters battle." He took time showing the child how to use hands, body, and movements as extensions of her body to defeat her enemy.

By this time she knew more than many adult warriors in the art of hand to hand combat. One day, she went to avenge her loss of face and honor against the older boy. She found him standing with two other boys hanging around the boats, they were fishing and making sordid jokes between them as she approached the three. She walked up to the older boy who beat her and bowed as she announced her name and intent in a commanding voice. "Masao-san! My name is Masahiko Tanizaki-san, son of Master Trainer Tanizaki-san, and I'm here to avenge my honor which you are in possession of. Defend yourself my honorable foe."

The older boy laughed as he lifted his hands, and prepared to beat the younger troublemaker again, he was unprepared for what followed. Forgetting his first law of training of never underestimating his challenger, the boy rushed the smaller one driven by his confidence of the outcome of the previous battle. Masahiko smiled as she side stepped his reckless charge, and she grabbed the sleeve of his kosode and spun him to the ground with it.

"Stand still and fight me like a Samurai." The older one cried as he got up and charged a second time. This time she dipped to her right and spun her leg low, tripping the charging boy, tumbling him to the ground in a heap of dust and bruises. The older child cried out and his friends grabbed Masahiko and began to pound on her with fists, feet, and elbows. It was shameful for all three to attack Masahiko at the same time but their youth erased their honor.

If it wasn't for Sanuki walking his village, the boys might have done serious damage to Tanizaki's child. He saw the three beating the one and yelled, sending them running into the woods, with him calling after them to stop and come back and face him. As children usually do, they ignored the angry Shoya and kept running, laughing as they fled the old man.

Sanuki returned to Masahiko and checked on her health and helped her to her feet, he wanted to carry the bruised child home, but she refused to be carried. Sanuki escorted the bloody and battered Masahiko home, villagers came out and took side long glances at the battered child. It was rude to look directly at any Japanese person, it was considered an invasion of privacy.

Emiko was working in the garden when she saw Masahiko's bloody face and rushed to her side. Sanuki explained what happened, but she ignored him. She was concerned with cleaning Masahiko before Tanizaki returned from the practice fields, and saw she was beaten again. The eight samurai to guard his home surrounded the child and offered assistance. Emiko swore them to secrecy, she didn't want Tanizaki to find out about the beating, she didn't know how he would react to the attack on his child by the three.

The trainer was unaware of the assault on Masahiko, and his wife kept the child out of his sight for the evening. The two were fast becoming inseparable, where any member of the village saw the trainer walking, they knew Masahiko was nearby. Even on the dust covered training fields, Masahiko was becoming part of the landscape, with the samurai trainees stopping and speaking to the child, and answering the countless questions about training they were going through, asked by the inquisitive youngster.

The trainer made a wood sword the weight and feel of a real sword for Masahiko, and she attacked anything in her way. One day he took the child to the fields, he allowed her to play striking the stalks with the wood sword. When the child grew bored with this exercise, she turned to trying to capture frogs, which made their homes along the edge of the paddy. He went to the child and examined the cut stalks and was stunned at what he observed. The ends looked as though they were hacked clean by the sharpest sword, not by a child's play sword. He stared at the back of his child and wondered what game the gods were playing with her. How was she given this power to hack stalks cleanly with a bamboo stick shaped as a sword? He was in awe of this child with the striking smile, and mark of the gods on her body.

He was looking to the day of Kamisogi, where she would receive her first haircut. He knew that would be the day when the child would take her first steps into the world of adult then he would be allowed to begin Masahiko's training in earnest.

Two sticks of time before the celebration was to take place, Masahiko walked with her father as he worked with the trainees on the horse field. One of the horses broke from its master's control, and charged around the field unmounted and terrified. The horse was petrified, and the more it ran free, the more fearful it became, especially when other riders tried to capture it for the owner running behind the horse cursing as it continued to flee from him on the field.

The master trainer stepped on the field and screamed at how the warriors were to capture the horse. A few foot soldiers tried to help by getting in its way and make the animal turn in the direction of the riders. It didn't happen, instead of heading for the mounted soldiers, the horse darted away and Tanizaki found the horse charging straight at him. His mind decided not to allow fear to rule his body and stood his ground and bellowed at the frightened horse, riders, and foot soldiers. He resorted to hand movements in an effort to turn the charging animal.

Masahiko's chest swelled with pride for her father as he stood defiantly before the face of danger, daring the horse to come at him. He placed his hands on his hips and barked orders for the horse to stop creating problems. Her mind screamed the warning her father wasn't going to get out of the way in time, and the horse would trample him to death under its sharp hooves. Without thinking of her well being, she charged at her father, she planned to knock him out of the way of the horse.

Everything happened at the same moment, the horse reached Tanizaki the instant her body crashed into her father. Her fifty one pounds was enough to send him tumbling out of the way. She was stopped in flight in the path of the horse and it trampled her leg, opening a gash above the knee. She was also cut on the back of her right hand, and received a bruise on her right arm from another of the horses flailing hooves.

Every samurai on the field knew of the accident, and the trainer's child was hurt in the incident. They rushed to aid the fallen child. Field doctors wanted to remove the child's clothes and treat the wound on the field, but he wouldn't allow them to work on the child. He ordered Kobayashi to lift the child and carry her to his home. He knew Hachirobe would be at his home, and he could see to the child's wounds. There was no way anyone but the seer would work on the child, this way no one would be aware the supposed male child was that of a female.

The warrior who lost control of his horse rushed before Tanizaki and dropped to the ground, bowing before him. He removed his short sword and offered to commit suppuku to atone for his carelessness with his horse which resulted in the injuries to his child. The warrior had his face buried in the dirt as he bowed to the trainer, offering his life. The trainer didn't acknowledge the warrior, he grunted and turned away. This response informed the warrior he didn't want his life, but was upset over how he controlled his horse.

General Shimbo was at Tanizaki's side and ordered the warrior to his feet, and barked he was no longer to know kyuba no michi. The way of the horse and bow, he was reduced to zusa, the foot soldier and lowest ranking warrior. He further warned him if he caused another problem on the field, he would go to the Shinto priest who would shave his head, and he would forever serve the filthy priest, and would never be allowed to take kishomon, the oath of samurai.

The general relieved the trainer and took command of the training of the samurai while he and General Kobayashi left with the injured child who refused to cry out, even when the field doctor manipulated the injured leg to see if there were bones broken. The child struggled from General Kobayashi's arms and tried to walk. She was unable to support her full weight on the injured leg, and had to allow the concerned general to help support her.

The story of the less than seven year old child saving the trainer's life, and the samurai way the child didn't cry when the doctor examined his wounds, and how he tried to walk on her own, circulated throughout the village. The story changed with each telling of the act of fearlessness and heroism from the child, adding to the esteem of the Tanizaki family.

Shoya Sanuki was informed of the act of heroism by Masahiko, and launched a pigeon to Engakuji Castle, to inform Lord Kawasomeru of the feat by the trainer's youngest child. He was hoping the lord would bestow further gifts upon the ninth village for him to enjoy. Everything that entered the old and crafty Shoya's mind, was for profit, more worth or honor.

It didn't go unnoticed by the trainer how his child reacted when the doctor checked her injuries, and the way she tried to put her weight on the leg. He smiled as he watched her face contort with pain, but refused to utter a cry as the blood continued to flow from the gash on the leg.

He mumbled as he walked with his injured child and general. "If only you were a male child, the honor you would've brought by allowing the doctor to show the wound on your leg to the foolish warriors. By the gods, I see no difference in the way a male and female accepts training and pain, and carries out their yoshi gi, their duty. My uncontrollable warrior, I'll turn you into samurai beyond understanding and belief. The wisdom of the gods who chose you for greatness were wise indeed. I find myself believing in the ways of the gods. To pick you for greatness, shows there are divine forces at play in your fate. You proved to all by this act you displayed before their useless lives. If the fact you're a female comes out, and the naysayers finish wagging their worthless tongues and allow their minds to accept what their eyes see.

"They'll see Japan was robbed years of great warriors, because they were females at birth. What waste to believe such thoughts. Are the minds of Japan so warped they could not allow themselves to thing a female might be warrior? Foolish not to consider this. Foolish we leaders are and this child will prove to all doubters the female can serve more purpose than pillowing."

The trainer was content following behind Kobayashi as he supported his injured child home, the guards fell in step behind him as they headed for his home. A guard from inside the garden hurried and opened the gate as he saw the procession approaching the home.

Emiko heard the commotion as Kobayashi passed through the gate, and the samurai offered their help. She saw her child carried by the samurai and it didn't look like she was moving. She saw blood on her kosode and thought the worse. Estsuko saw the blood and rushed forward and took the child from Kobayashi and went to the house. Tanizaki approached his wife and looped his arm around her shoulder and said. "Emiko, Masahiko-san has proven to these worthless chugen, people of small account of the Ninth Village he's a person of Yukakasa, having high value. Your child was injured in a honorable way, protecting my life from harm. He shown these dung eaters great blood travels through Masahiko-san's veins. The blood of the gods. I'll make a special offering to Fujin-sama tonight."

General Kobayashi took position on the porch, and didn't allow anyone to bother the trainer, or anyone in the home as he attended to his wounded child. Upon entering his home, Tanizaki bellowed in a booming voice. "Hachirobe-san! You're needed, bring tools of healing. Masahiko-san is wounded." It was the height of bad manners for him to yell in his home, but he cared nothing for manners at this time. He was troubled Masahiko's leg might be permanently injured, and he wanted the seer to check the damage and make certain she was alright.

Hachirobe sat in the extension Master Trainer Tanizaki added to his home for the old seer to live in his home. The once filthy animal was clean and scented, he had been eating well and was able to stand and walk pretty much erect. Upon hearing his name bellowed, he feared the chosen child was near death as he got on his deformed feet, and waddled in the house as quickly as his crippled body could move. He examined the child lying on Tanizaki's chodai, the sleeping mattress surrounded by light colored silk curtains.

"How was the child wounded?" He mumbled, his words hampered by the missing tongue.

"Masahiko-san was stepped on by a horse. Is there damage to the child's bones?"

"Tanizaki-san! I'll not know this until I had a chance to examine the child. Estsuko! Remove the child's clothing and wash the wounds, I'll retrieve herbs and bandages. Lady Emiko! A cup of tea and bowl so I can use it to clean the wounds of the child." Hachirobe mumbled, making everyone strain to understand his words.

"Hai Hachirobe-san!" She replied as she hurried off to make the requested tea.

He rushed after the seer and spun him around and growled. "Old fool, if you allow these minor wounds to cripple this child, your eyes will not see another sunrise."

The old seer smiled with a mouth full of rotted teeth and missing end of his tongue, as he replied in broken words. "Master Trainer Tanizaki-san! From what I see of the minor wounds, all Master Masahiko will suffer from this accident is nothing more than a little pain until they heal. I assure you the young master will be fine, the wounds are minor at worst." The seer bowed correctly to the fearsome trainer.

The concerned trainer overlooked the insult by the seer and bowed equally as insultingly at the old man, as he shuffled off to retrieve his healing bag.

The other members of his family who knew Masahiko was a female, called her by her male name, or referred to her as master or he. Each member chose to avoid calling Masahiko as him or her, for fear of making the mistake and arousing suspicions. It was hard for the trainer or his wife to avoid thinking Masahiko as a female. He was training his mind to forget Masahiko was a she, and Emiko and the eldest daughter tried their best to show Masahiko how men walk, spoke, and go to the bathroom, and scratch between their legs for pleasure of the embarrassing action.

Masahiko found it disturbing she had to run her hand between her legs, even though she didn't itch there. As far as she knew, she was a male and he left it up to his wife, where and when she would speak to the child of the deceit they were carrying out against their lord, and explain why this deceit was necessary. Emiko decided she would tell Masahiko on the night of the celebration of Kamisogi, the first haircut. She knew the child would be wise by then to understand why her parents were doing what they were doing in regard to her sex.

The trainer returned to his daughter as everyone waited for Hachirobe to come with his medical bag. Emiko entered with a cup and bowl of tea and placed them on a chest. The youngest daughter was sent away while Estsuko did everything for her sister with the male name's comfort. Emiko never got over the damage the child caused her during birth, she suffered from pain in her belly and was bleeding. It was the cramps which scared her the most.

Estsuko was aware of the pain suffered by her mother, but was helpless to do anything more than look after her the best she could. She was sworn to secrecy by her mother. She gave her word she would not breathe a word of her painful suffering to her father.

The concerned daughter could tell when her mother and father made love, her mother would suffer greatly the next day. Blood would flow, followed by days of cramps and pain. She was worried for her mother and became involved in her life more and more, leaving her no time for the fun of youth. Estsuko wasn't interested in the males of the village, and barely spent time with the other young ladies. Her time was spent by mostly looking after her ailing mother, and their chosen daughter with the male name, Masahiko.

Tanizaki caught the second daughter out of the corner of his eye and barked. "Sake!" He saw her bow and rush off. Seconds later, Enko returned with sake for her father. Hachirobe returned at the same moment and looked to the trainer with his eyes begging him for a taste of sake.

He was flushed with anger he failed to offer the seer sake. He was guilty of bad manners. He bowed as he snarled at his daughter. "Have you forgotten your training? Do you not see we have company, foolish child? Where are your manners? Enko! Get Hachirobe-san sake. Worthless daughter while you are at it, bring sake to General

Kobayashi-san, and see to his comforts before I'm ridiculed as an ill mannered dung heap of a host."

The young girl was crushed by her father's anger, but refused to allow herself to cry before him, she would do that in the privacy of her sleeping quarters she shared with Estsuko. Together, at night they would speak of the perils of growing up in feudal Japan.

Shoya Sanuki came in Tanizaki's home and stood by his side as Estsuko undressed the hurt child. She stopped undressing the child and looked at her father.

He realized her concern and offered in a whisper only she could hear. "Estsuko! It's needless to hide Masahiko-san is a female from him. Shoya Sanuki-san was present when the child was born, and supports my decision to hide this fact from Lord Kawasomeru. Continue, and be finished by the time the seer decides to work on Masahiko's injuries."

"Hai father." She replied politely as she removed Masahiko's silk and cotton pants worn by the male children, so they could rough house without destroying the heavier clothes. Estsuko didn't remove the child's fundeshi which wasn't necessary in this case, the child wasn't injured in that area. If the child was a male, it would have been an honor to remove the child's loincloth, so all could see how endowed the child and future warrior was. Something Tanizaki would not be able to share in, the bragging of the size of his child's golden faucet.

Hachirobe roughly pulled the child's leg straight, cleaned the wound with a swatch of silk dipped in tea. The injured child stiffened as the swatch was pushed in the cut, making it bleed again. Once he was sure the dirt was out of the wound, he wrapped it in silk then tied it off and told Emiko the covering had to be changed twice a day and washed with tea.

Once the seer was certain no bones were broken, he turned his attention to the cut on the back of the hand. It wasn't deep and he could tell no bones were broken, he didn't waste time with the bruises turning purple. He made Masahiko squeeze his fingers to make certain the sword hand was working properly. After he was done examining the hand, he check the rest of Masahiko's body for undetected damage. He was careful with the examination, he knew his life was held in balance if he missed a wound, or damage that might permanently disable the child. Once he was satisfied there was no damage, he ordered Estsuko to help the master dress. He straightened up painfully and stepped away from the child.

The master trainer drew the seer from his daughter's side with the offer of more sake. As they walked to the kitchen, he whispered. "Hachirobe-san! How is Masahiko-san's health? Will there be damage to the body that'll not heal properly?"

He didn't answer until his cup was filled with sake, his mumbling was hard to understand. "Tanizaki-san! Your child will be fine and will suffer no ill effects of the injuries. I must caution the child has to stay off her leg for this day, and must be made to walk and run in three sticks of time. Although there'll be pain, the child must use the leg soon as possible. He can't be allowed to favor the leg, or there could be permanent damage suffered due to the mind saying there's damage when there is none."

He bowed, he knew the energetic child would be looking to walk today, and had no fear the child thinking there was damage when there was none. He looked at the seer and wondered if there was anything to believing in gods. He wondered why Fujin marked his child for greatness. He was thinking why the gods placed this piece of filth in his life, this seer who believes in the gods and their will, and has ways of communicating with the souls in the Floating World.

He made up his mind once Masahiko's training was complete and the child was an adult, he would work this question out if there were gods of help who oversee the ones who need it. Or if the ones who pray to gods are doing nothing more than wasting their time bent in prayer. He reminded himself he intended to make an offering to the fearsome god of wind, for allowing his child not to be killed in the accident. He filled the seer's cup with sake without waiting to be asked. "Hachirobe-san! What is the proper gift to offer to the god protecting one's child?"

He was stunned by the trainer's words, it was known he didn't believe in gods. Yet here he was, thinking of paying homage to one. The seer slurped his sake, and remarked in his muffled voice. "Tanizaki-san! Which god do you intend to respect?"

He was amazed Hachirobe could speak words clearly because of his missing tongue as he replied. "I intend to offer something to Fujin-sama. He's the god watching over this foolish child, and I must keep his protective eye resting on Masahiko's shoulder, or the child will be hurt before he completes his task for the god."

"Ahhh... the fearful god of wind is the one who helps guide your son, Tanizaki-san. So it's only your child who can bring a non-believer to believing in gods. A mere offer to pay homage to the gods is enough to gain their pleasure. It's not necessary to place items of worth in temples. The gods have no solid. Therefore they have no needs for items of solids or wealth. It's the priests who'll benefit from the items left in temples. A simple prayer from one not a believer is more pay than any god could hope to receive. A prayer will forever lock Fujin-sama to your child's ear." The seer stood and complained about his bones hurting him.

He nodded in agreement and added to the old man of mystery. "Hachirobe-san! You gave me more to think about than I planned to contemplate. Your words ring with the sound of truth, these fools who leave their father's worth on the steps of the shrines, give their wealth to priests to enjoy. I believed it was the priests who took the wealth of Japan. This is why we never see a priest or Buddha. I'll pay homage to the god of wind, I gave my word walking with my injured child, but I'll not allow the priests to benefit from my gift. I'll increase the size of the temple I intend to construct for the Shinto priest, who strummed his string to keep the evil ones from entering my child's body. I'll order a section of the temple aside to honor Fujin-sama. In this way I'll fulfill my word to the god, and the priests will not squander the gift I offer him."

"Ahhh... Tanizaki-san! You're wise beyond your years. Remind me never to allow you to become my enemy." The seer said as he began to leave his house for his room.

He watched the old man and thanked the god of wind for sending the seer to him, so he knew which road to guide his daughter on. Emiko's voice caught his ear and he went to his child.

"Emiko! What is happening now? Why are you arguing with the young child like this?"

She bowed to her husband and cried. "Husband! The child will not listen to me or Estsuko. The child has a mind of his own and refuses to listen to wise reason."

"Emiko! What is it the child wants that has you so angry with him?"

"Tanizaki-san! The thick headed child wanted to get up and see what you were doing with the seer who cared for her injuries. He wants to walk and will not rest until tomorrow as ordered by the seer. I don't know what to do with him, I know what is good for the child, but he'll not listen. He only listens to you and will do what he wants. I think you're training Masahiko-san too quickly, and he no longer thinks he's a child, husband. The young one thinks he's an adult, a Samurai who thinks he doesn't have to answer to anyone but himself."

He could see Emiko decided to call the child a he when referring to Masahiko. It was a good idea, one he intended to do. The trainer wanted to scold the child for arguing with his mother, but could not. How could he punish the youth for living up to his training and ideals of what a samurai should be. He looked at his injured child and said. "Masahiko-san! Do you think you can walk on your leg?"

"Hai honorable father, I can." The child replied proudly to her father.

"Huh! If you think you can walk on your injured leg then do so if you dare, Master Masahiko-san! Fate and Karma will teach you the proper ways to think and respect one's wise parents." He offered to his stubborn child with the will of a samurai's heart.

She pushed herself across the mattress and placed both feet on the floor. She pushed off and stood and tried to step. The pain was unexpected as the child lifted her foot and stumbled forward. He went to reach out and assist his stubborn child, but thought better of it and allowed the child to land on the floor in a heap of pain.

After she landed on the floor, she rolled over on her uninjured side, and looked at her father, who smiled as she struggled with her injured body. Then he grumbled at her stubbornness. "You see inflexible one, sometimes your mother is wiser than even I. The next time you'll obey your mother no matter how well honored you become in life. It was decided you'll stay off your injured leg for the rest of today. Tomorrow, I'll expect you to be by my side when I return to the field to work with the worthless Samurai there."

"Hai father." She offered as she smiled at her father.

"You're mistaken Masahiko-san! In this case it is your mother who is the wise one. It was she who told you not to walk, but you were too pigheaded to follow her instructions, little one. The first discipline of a wise Samurai is to honor his mother and father, your sun and moon. It's your youth that saved you from my wrath. Masahiko-san! It's manly for a complete Samurai to apologize to the one he has injured needlessly."

She bowed properly to her father as she struggled onto the sleeping mattress, and then she looked forlorn at her concerned but smiling mother. The child bowed like a tested and in command samurai, greatly as she said. "Most honorable mother of this worthless and thick headed child. Forgive my stupidity and lack of good and wise manners for not listening to the one who is much wiser than I will ever become. I'll never allow my ill mannered mouth to insult you ears ever again mother and teacher of wisdom."

He listened expressionless with trained calmness as his child apologized with humility to her mother. He knew he was correct in choosing to deceive his lord with this child. Every action the child took, showed him she was picked rightly by the gods for greatness. He searched his mind that day, to see if he could discover if any child before the age of seven saved his father from death. Each time he searched his mind, he came up with the same answer. No.

A shadow crossed the window and the trainer realized it was getting late. He decided to release General Kobayashi from his post of guarding his door. He no longer feared anyone would walk in and discover the injured child was a female. He walked out the front Shoji door, and there he found most villagers gathered, patiently waiting for word on the child's condition.

The trainer was embarrassed over the concern they displayed to his child, and bowed to the group and announced. "Masahiko-san is fine, he is slightly injured and will recover properly. Masahiko-san was injured saving this old fool's worthless life. The child showed more intelligence than did his foolish father. General Kobayashi-san will explain to all of you what happened if anyone is interested in learning the facts of the incident."

He turned to Kobayashi and offered. "Thank you for your help with Masahiko-san. I'll be on the field with the trainee's sunrise tomorrow. Masahiko-san will accompany me. The worthless Warriors will be trained as always, General. The day after tomorrow I'll not be attending training for the day. It'll be Masahiko's Kamisogi and I'll attend the ceremony, it's an important time in my child's life, and I'll witness it. You're relieved of duty of protecting my home, General."

"Should I put the soldiers through a complete day of training, or would you like to give the Warriors time off to honor Master Masahiko-san, Tanizaki-san?" The general asked.

"Hmmm... that's a good question. It's an honorable day and should be marked for history and celebrated by everyone living, or visiting the village. I believe the training is going well."

"Hai Tanizaki-san. It's proceeding far better than expected."

"You're correct General. I'll allow the training to end noon on this day. I'll have sake sent to the field and they can celebrate Masahiko's first hair cutting. You'll attend my son's Kamisogi, General?" The trainer ordered more than asked his general standing by his side protecting him.

"Hai Master Trainer, it'll be my honor to attend such a great celebration for your child. That'll make three Kamisogi's I'll be attending on that great day. It's good so many children were born so close together, or I'd never get any work done again, Tanizaki-san. I'd be too involved in attending one ceremony after the other."

"Ieeeee! Three Kamisogi's. Is there word from Kawasomeru-sama of the wars to our south?"

"Hai, the wars continue, word Lord Kawasomeru was going to request more young from your group to fight in the wars." The general grumbled.

"Huh! I don't know what Kawasomeru-sama is waiting for, eh? If I had Wakatsuki's neck in my clutches, his loathsome head would be separated from his shoulders, and his useless spirit would wander the Floating World forever, always awaiting its unworthy rebirth that'd never come to his worthless spirit. I can't believe our Lord's being so patient dealing with the foul troublemaker upsetting the Wa of the realm. Kawasomeru-sama should have dispatched the dog eating fool and his armies long ago. Bad, bad, the matter's of state weight heavy on my mind."

CHAPTER TEN

THE FIFTH DAY OF THE SECOND WEEK OF THE FIFTH MONTH OF THE YEAR THIRTEEN FOURTY FOUR
FRIDAY

KAMISOGI:

It was beautiful and a little warm for the early days in May, the sun was up and shining strong in the cloudless blue sky. The day promised to be warm and maybe even hot, with puffy clouds moving in later in the afternoon, and rain was expected by the middle of the night. Tanizaki was up and about early in the day, and his wife was working in the kitchen. He smiled, for years he offered to hire a cook and a few women to help Emiko with the household chores, but she always refused help saying she wasn't a woman of the Soft World. But he knew the true reason his wife wouldn't allow help in the kitchen, she felt it was her duty to do the cooking for the family. The trainer like to watch as Emiko would display patience as she showed Estsuko and Enko how to prepare meals for their future husbands.

The trainer was pleased with his lifestyle. He felt he couldn't want for anymore than he had from life until Yuriko Tanizaki, known to the world as Masahiko was born. Now, every thought, action and breath he drew, was geared to make the female a warrior that would forever change the shape of Japan's history. Never in his past would he dared to think of trying to deceive the Lord of Shinano. If he entertained such evil thoughts in the past, he would have cut off the useless finger on his hand to atone for such thoughts. But now he was willing to risk his life, as well as the lives of every villager to make this child a warrior in the army of Lord Kawasomeru.

The trainer's concentration was interrupted by his eldest daughter humming as she helped her mother preparing meals. This celebration was more than a hair cutting. After today, Masahiko would no longer wear the clothes of a child, and carry wood swords. The swords of wood would be replaced with real swords. Even though they were shorter than the pair the child would carry for life once she could use the length and weight of the swords.

The women were all over the house, first his wife yelled to get dressed in his best kosode for the celebration. His eldest daughter came in his room and yelled at him for being in the way as she worked on preparing the rice and eel meal. He was yelled at by his middle daughter because he dipped a finger in one of the meals to taste it and she caught him. He gave up and left the kitchen in a huff to pace the room, as his mind searched for the gift he was going to bestow on Masahiko. As he passed, he bumped into his youngest daughter who complained at him for not watching where he was going.

This was the final straw and the trainer knew he had to leave the house to the women, or they would complain all day at him. He went to his living quarters and dressed in his light green kosode with the golden sash, given him as a special gift from Kawasomeru after the war fought against a rival overlord of the Dewa province. Lord Kawasomeru's army was instrumental in conquering the Dewa province claimed in its entirety by the Shogun Ashikaga, three days after the war had ended which was his right to order.

Once the Shogun broken the back of the rebel overlord of Dewa, he turned his attention to the province of Mutsu, and with little fighting the massiveness that made up the two northern provinces, came under control of Ashikaga. The Shogun was now in control of most land that made up Japan. After the fighting in the northern provinces concluded, he was so pleased with Kawasomeru; the Shogun showered him with wonderful gifts for his unwavering support in the wars. Ashikaga bestowed on his head Shinano, the third largest province in northeastern Japan. He also gave him control of the eight provinces and made up the central provinces of Japan.

The Shogun thanked a second overlord for his support in the war against the northern provinces, Lord Motoshige Wakatsuki. He didn't trust this crafty overlord as much as he did Kawasomeru, and gave him control of Echigo province. He thought he had Wakatsuki under control by surrounding his province by his Dewa and Lord Kawasomeru's Shinano provinces, along with overlord Anjoh's Kozuke province, and placing Lord Wakatsuki's back against the sea, surrounding him with his most loyal overlords and the vastness of the ocean.

The powerful Shogun had no idea that the overlord he had appointed to command Shimotsuke province would come under pressure to retire from a few troublemakers. Lord Wakatsuki would come to his aid and after the elderly overlord's death, Wakatsuki took over Shimotsuke and linked it with the province of Echigo. Once he was able to use his newly acquired province, the overlord was let loose and he took over the other provinces unhappy with the current leadership of the Shogun and Lord Kawasomeru's rule.

Lord Wakatsuki's first act was to help Lord Hitachi break away from the Shogun's rule then turned his eye towards Shimosa which bordered Musashi province, under Lord Terukiyo Meguro's command, he was steadfast loyal to Lord Kawasomeru, and by Kazusa to Shimosa provinces south which was under the control of Lord Kawasomeru.

Once the provinces unhappy with Shogun Ashikaga or Lord Kawasomeru saw Wakatsuki offered them another lord to rule them, he gained loyalty from Awa, Mikawa, Owari, Mino, Hida, Kaga and Nito provinces, surrounding the eight provinces loyal to Shogun Ashikaga and putting Lord Kawasomeru and his eight provinces in distress.

He tried to muster the other provinces unhappy with the ruling parties of Japan, to join forces and help him destroy Lord Kawasomeru. Thus making the way clear for him to demand the title of Shogun of the sixteen central provinces. But his plans were placed on hold, for he was soon mired in a number of small wars raging between the provinces allied with him. The wars were in the way of his plan to rule the central provinces. He tried his best to stop the wars, but no sooner was he able to get control of one province and stop the fighting there, than another province under his influence erupted in war with another allied province. It was a vicious circle which he was trapped in, and until he got firm control over the warring provinces, he would not be able to challenge the might of Kawasomeru, and the seven other provinces under his control. If he was unable to defeat Lord Kawasomeru and his armies, he would never become Shogun. He needed the strength of the other provinces to overthrow Kawasomeru.

When the master trainer was dressed properly for the ceremony and pleased with his appearance, he went outside to walk the garden seeking the peace and serenity the garden offered one's mind. He slowly strolled around the sweet smelling flowers and listened to the stream as it peacefully rambled down its pebble strewn path, and he smiled as the song birds called for their mates. The warriors assigned to his personal protection remained at their posts, not moving as the respected master trainer walked around the garden.

Inside the master's home, the sounds of the women preparing the celebration meals could be heard. He cocked his head to the side in an effort to hear the warriors going through their training efforts. He heard a roar and knew the warriors began an attack on one of the training fields. His heart yearned to be on the field directing a charge against stationed enemy. Without knowing it, his body turned to the field and he stared in that direction as if trying to will his mind to see what was occurring on the fields with his samurai.

From in the home, Emiko noticed her husband staring to the field and felt terrible, she knew where his heart lay. She noticed Estsuko and ordered her to tell her father she wanted him to check General Kobayashi, to make certain he was going to attend the kamisogi ceremony.

Estsuko knew what her mother was doing and smiled as she ran to tell her father. When she told the trainer of her mother's words, he looked to his home and saw his wife smiling from inside at him. Without word, he was off like a shot, heading for the practice fields with his guard samurai following behind him. She smiled after her husband, he was a commanding figure dressed in his green kosode.

When the trainer appeared on the training field the instructions came to a stop, and all eyes went to Master trainer Tanizaki who was furious, because the samurai stopped training without being ordered to do so. He bellowed for General Kobayashi, who ran up to him and dropped to his knees and bowed. He didn't return the bow as he growled at the younger general.

"Kobayashi-san! Why have these dung heaps stopped training? Do the fools understand everything there is to be known in the art of making war with one's enemy? It's not time to celebrate my son's Kamisogi, and I have not gave them permission to stop training. Their training is most important. Time is short, each will fight for their lives and honor of their Lord on the field of battle, where I nor anyone else will be able to help them. If they're no longer interested in training, walk them to the filth of a priest and allow him give them the haircut."

"Master Trainer Tanizaki-san. I'm unaware why the Warriors stopped training, I'll go amongst them and find out." The concerned general offered with his head still bowed in respect.

"Hai, and anyone without a good excuse will be marched off to the worthless priest. Ima, (now, at once) isogi (hurry) or none of the manure heaps will have the pleasure of entering the sought after Jade Gate for the rest of their worthless lives, a Buddha is not allowed to pillow." He growled as he crossed his arms, his swords clanking in his golden sash as he shifted his weight and watched his general run from warrior to warrior, asking them questions and bellowing at the warriors and they in return, started to work on their training again.

The general ran to the trainer and dropped to his knees, bowing as he offered. "Master Trainer, the men offer their worthless excuses, they stated it was because of you."

"Me? Iye wakarimasu?" I don't understand, General? How did I stop their training without words?" He hissed as he bulked up and pointed to himself and stared at Kobayashi.

"Hai Master Trainer Tanizaki-san. Please excuse, I'd rather have my tongue cut out and fed to the dogs than to have to tell you what the worthless Warriors had to say about..."

"General Kobayashi-san! Your tongue will remain where it is. I'm interested in hearing what these worthless Warriors told you." He mumbled calmly, and with practiced patience.

The general bowed lower as he offered. "Tanizaki-san, the foolish Warriors say they were stunned by the brilliance of your kosode. They have never seen you so dressed, and it struck them with stupidity. I ordered them back to their training, and I'll settle with them once you left the site." He dared to look up at the master trainer again.

"Ahh... so the foolish Warriors were shocked to see me dressed like a lord are they, General? The worthless things obviously don't know how to act when they're in the presence of royalty I see." He groused as he rubbed his chin. Then he laughed uproariously as he looked over the training field covered by bowing soldiers.

"Get up! Everyone get to your feet! You saved your hair and position this day. I understand what you are feeling. It's like one of you dressing in the robes of our Lord. Hai! It must have been a shock to see me dressed so. Ieeeee! Look at me." He said as he flared the oversized arms of the kosode in the air, and whirled, making the kosode look more like a cape than a robe.

All the while he modeled the magnificent robe before the warriors, he was bellowing with laughter until he actually became light headed. When he stopped his whirling and laughing, he looked at his general staring at the master's feet, not daring to stare at him for fear of insulting him. He also laughed, enjoying the sudden good humor of the trainer and the day soon to be enjoyed by everyone of the ninth village.

"Ahh... my loyal General Kobayashi-san! Why did you not tell me that I looked a fool who should be on the foul Nolt stage, dressed in this robe which should be hanging from a female's body, rather than this Warrior's old bones which know only two things in life, war and art of killing. I fear everyone will have to get used to my wearing these such items of vanity until my honored son completed his first hair cut, and crossed over into the world of the start of adulthood. I beg forgiveness for my ill manners of bellowing as if I was your wife. I'll never allow this to happen again." He bow at the warriors

Battle cries erupted as the warriors banged on their shields or armor, showing their appreciation at the honor the trainer paid them by bowing. The horses whinnied and shook their heads violently over the commotion the soldiers made for the master trainer.

A bell sounded, letting everyone know it was time for noon prayers. The trainer looked to the sky and realized it was close to the time of hair cutting. He looked once more at the soldiers, insulted because he could smell the odor from the latrines, but didn't allow it to upset his mood. He made a mental note to look into the situation and if need be, he would order the loathsome hinin to help with the latrines. It was simple to find more lower than low class, all he had to do was check prisons, and pick the men to be placed in care of the latrines for his samurai.

He held up his hand and silence was restored. "General Kobayashi-san! It's near time to celebrate Kamisogi. It's too late to mount another attack before the time, allow them to wrap up their equipment, look after the horses and clean their armor and have the rest of the day off. You have a lot to prepare for before you arrive at my home." He bowed to the general then turned and headed home with his guards trailing behind him.

When he returned home, Masahiko was the focus of the women's attention. The child had her hair scrubbed clean and checked for lice. Then dressed for the first time in the finest hakama, a oversized set of silk breeches slit at the sides and worn over the kosode, to allow the child free movement for the ceremony. The items were worn by males of Japan until this day.

From this day forward, the life of a child without responsibilities was over. Gone were the carefree days of Masahiko's playing war with fake bows and swords. Gone was the fun loving days of teasing dogs with makeshift weapons of death. Gone were the youth and free loving spirit. He would see to it the weapons his child played with were real. The targets the child would practice against would be the threatening targets the samurai used for training, and dogs would no longer be teased. If a dog drew Masahiko's attention, it could result in the animal's death. Today, the day of Masahiko's first haircut, was the day he longed for since the child was born, and it was discovered the child bore the mark of greatness on her wrist.

The excitement increased as Masahiko dressed and paraded before the family and closest friends. Everyone in his home bowed and applauded as she marched as shown before the guests. Sanuki, marched up to Tanizaki's home, increasing the worth of the celebration and stood on the porch and placed the Go board on the deck. Go was a game consisting of three hundred and sixty one squares representing the battlefield. The object of the Go board was for one player to occupy as many squares as possible, thus destroying his enemy. In war, land was victory, the more land one controlled, less land your enemy had to wage war from.

The guests remained outside waiting at the garden for Masahiko to make his appearance. Shoya Sanuki prepared for the hair cutting, he made certain the tanto blade was razor sharp, and the silver tray on which the cut strands would be placed was ready. He and the child would suffer loss of face if he didn't cut the hair properly.

The time came for Masahiko to make his appearance through the shoji screens. Filled with strutting arrogance and a stiff back, the child took position standing on the Go board. The witnesses bowed to the child who stood proudly on the game board. This was the only time any child was allowed not to return the honor of the bow.

Shoya Sanuki fingered the silk like hair as he pulled it back and formed the honored aquene, the pony tail. Once he had the hair in his hand, he shaved the skull cap clean of hair, with each stroke witness's grunted approval. With educated hands, the Shoya shaved the head in the manner of the samurai caste. Once the skull cap was shaven, the skilled Shoya shaped the rest of the hair properly. When it was shaped perfectly, he added rich whale oil and worked it in the aquene shape which forever would confirm the child's allegiance to Lord Kawasomeru. He doubled over the thick pony tail onto the shaven crown and tied it off so the oiled and hardening pony tail crossed over the center of the child's head.

All the while the child was shaved and hair shaped in the manly aquene pony tail, the child recited prayers to Buddha. She stood rigid as an oak branch while the village headman worked on the hair. When the hair piece was perfect, the child was ordered to rotate while remaining on the Go board. This was to allow the guests to admire the handiwork of the Shoya, and to show all the future warrior, and to share the first steps into adulthood.

The guests bowed with formality to the child now allowed to returned their bows properly. She was invited to step off the Go board and walked among the villagers. Each guest handed small gifts to the child, it was the beginning of building up the child's personal wealth.

By the time the walk was completed, her hands were overflowing with gifts meant for a male. He stared at his youngest child who looked so much like an adult male. His only unhappiness was in the knowledge once her military training for samurai began, she would be forced to give away these fine gifts, for a samurai cared nothing for worldly gifts and wealth. A samurai's only concern was to serve his lord faithfully in life, as well as in death.

His heart pounded in his chest as he saw the pride in his child's eyes when she showed her gifts to her giggling and overjoyed sisters. It was the trainer who held the final gifts. With a grunt he called Masahiko to his side. Once the child stood before him, he offered her a kosode, one without the sash sewn on the robe. From this day forward, she would be expected to tie the sash which would carry the swords properly. It was another step to adulthood for the once child.

Her eyes shined with tears of joy as she stared at the exquisite obviously expensive kosode made of the silk fabric her father's was crafted of. It was the same brilliant green as her father's. She removed the outer kosode worn over the hakama breeches, and struggled into the large over kosode. The crowd mumbled their approval over the fine garment.

He offered the child the golden wide sash she would use to carry her swords of honor in.

She took the sash as if made of gold, Estsuko moved to the child and held the back of the sash in place as she tied the knots in the fabric. This was the only time a female was allowed to touch the sash of a samurai, when he dressed. It was reserved for the wife, but since she wasn't married, it was the eldest daughter allowed to assist a warrior when dressing.

The trainer was proud of Estsuko, as he was of Masahiko. His eldest showed no signs of jealously serving her sister, and her devoted attention was making it simple for him to carry out his deceit. What he might miss in the child's upbringing was covered by her. She was always by Masahiko's side while the child was home. Estsuko informed her of the proper ways a samurai should act. She was trained to serve her future husband and was using this training to educate Masahiko to become a great male warrior in Lord Kawasomeru's army.

His attention was brought to the present when some guests headed for the back of his home to partake in the feast created by his wife. He knew the guests would only sample dishes because many had a second kamisogi to celebrate. It was good manners to sample a taste from all dishes, and not overeat of any. It was good manners not to leave anything on the dish once finished.

He followed the guests he didn't see him, but General Kobayashi stood by him and offered. "Tanizaki-san! It was a great ceremony.   One not topped by other families. Masahiko was proud, perfect, and gave you great face. If the child's past deeds are to be his judgment, the child entered the region of one of the greatest Warriors ever to walk on Japan's soil. To think, a mere child saved a life, especially the life of the Master Trainer, is enough to secure his name in the history of Japan. I can't wait to see what the gods chose to place in the child's path. Ieeee! To see such a child act as a proud Samurai during Kamisogi, proved to all he's marked for greatness. My honor is to be allowed to witness the deeds performed by this, the chosen child."   General Kobayashi bowed to his lifelong friend.

He allowed a smile to cross his weather beaten lips as he bowed. "Kobayashi-san! You'll be more than a witness to my child's deeds of unfolding greatness. I believe the gods chose you to look after him, and guide Masahiko-san if he falls from the path chosen by the gods. Is it not strange you were wounded in such a way so Kawasomeru-sama would allow you to remain and assist training the warriors and my child.   No General Kobayashi-san!   I believe there's something more to this world of the Kami, something I never saw before. I was a stubborn fool to turn my back on the gods. I can't believe the gods of the Floating World honored me in this manner as to mark my child with their mark of honor. I wonder what other honors would be bestowed on the child if I acted properly, and honored the gods over years past."

"Ieeee! It's true Master Trainer Tanizaki-san. The world of the gods are only understood by the filthy priests who serve them. Believe as I do of the gods, I believe your child was chosen because you don't believe in their glory. It was the god's way of bringing you home to their beliefs. Arr... I don't know the ways of the gods. Give me a sword and a worthy enemy and a good piss, what else could a Warrior want or need? I'll leave the gods of the Floating World to the priests, as long as they leave me my enemy on the battlefield."

"General Kobayashi-san! Get something to eat before these worthless dogs finish everything and there is nothing left for my Warrior." He mumbled as he lead Kobayashi to the great feast.

"Ieeeee Master Trainer Tanizaki-san! There's enough food here to feed all the realm."

He paid little attention to General Kobayashi, something caught his eye, it was his wife and she looked different, strange. The trainer realized what he saw in her eyes. Pain. He worked his way to his wife doing her best to serve the horde of guests. His second daughter was by her mother's side trying to help. He looked for his eldest as he moved to Emiko. He spotted her by Masahiko's side, and they were enjoying the gifts given to the young master by guests.

He tried to get his daughter Estsuko's attention, but he was constantly intercepted by guests, offering their phrases for the manners of his child fast becoming an adult. The trainer was polite as he engaged in small talk with the guest then moved on, he was only interested in getting to his ailing wife's side than speak of idle chatter with the guests he had no particular interest in.

He got his daughter's attention, and drew her face to her mother. Estsuko's smile left her lips as she saw her mother's face. It was a mask of pain and effort. She looked to her father and realized he was moving to her mother, she left

Masahiko and headed for her mother. She reached Emiko first and took the serving tools from her hands and started to serve the guests.

Emiko was barely able to offer her daughter a weak smile as she stepped from the table and moved to the background. He caught up to his wife and offered her his hand, he didn't try to pick her up or overly assist her to the house. He didn't want her to lose face before her guests by his making a scene of her illness. She took his arm and placed her hand in it and allowed the trainer to lead her to the house. "Emiko! Are you all right?" He whispered.

She saw the concern in her husband's eyes and offered him a brave and reassuring smile, as she tried to act as if nothing was wrong with her.

He said no more until they were in the home and she rested on the chodai sleeping mattress. "Emiko! What is wrong with you? I knew something was bothering you, you were not there when we made love last night. Are you still suffering from the birth of the child?"

She refused to say anything. Estsuko followed her parents to the room and came to her mother's aid. She rushed to her father and dropped to her knees as she bowed respectfully.

"Estsuko! What is it woman? Can you not see I'm speaking with your mother? It's rude of you to interrupt our conversation. If I wasn't concerned with your mother's health, I'd beat you for your insolence displayed before us. Be off with you and I'll deal with you later." He hissed as he cuffed her on the head. He was surprised when his daughter didn't run off as ordered. Instead, she remained on her knees waiting for permission to speak with her father.

"Huh, this must be important to go against my wishes so. Speak Estsuko, then I'll punish you." He snapped angrily at her as he stepped away from his eldest daughter.

"Hai honorable father. I must speak with you privately. It's about mother."

"Your mother! Huh! I'll listen to your words Estsuko."

She remained on her knees as she looked up at her father. "Father! Mother is suffering the pain from the birth of Yuriko." She used the child's real name, the female name. "When the child came down the birth canal, he did damage to Mother's insides which are unable to be repaired. She's no longer able to have children and has been bleeding of late. More lately than before. I noticed every time mother pillows with you, she suffers for many days afterwards. Lately, the pain remains long after the act of love making."

He looked at his wife, showing he was stunned by this information from his daughter. "Ieeeee my lady of countless years, you're bleeding from within because of the birth of Masahiko-san?"

"Hai!" His wife replied as she looked down, trying bravely to hide she was suffering loss of face having her female problems discussed openly with her husband. Something no Japanese woman would dare. It was insulting to her to discuss female problems in front of her husband.

"Where are you bleeding from?" He demanded to know, allowing his anger to increase.

She refused to reply to his question as she cast her eyes to the floor.

He looked to his daughter and waited for her to answer his question.

"Father! Mother is bleeding from the birth canal."

The trainer reacted as if slapped across the face, he staggered a step back as he stared at his wife. For the first time in his life he was scared. He was afraid he might lose his wife, and to do so further life for him would have no meaning. Once in his life he wondered how life would be without Emiko, after that dream he never wanted to find out.

"How long has this foul bleeding been happening?" He asked almost in a whisper.

"Since the birth."

He moved close to his wife and rested his hand on her head and growled at fate. "What good are the dung eating gods if they honor me by giving me a chosen child. Yet demand the life of my wife. I'll curse the maggot eaten filth that calls themselves gods of both worlds for eternity, if they allow anything to happen to my lady." He ran his hand over Emiko's long black hair.

Emiko wept silently, enjoying the warming and tender touch of her husband's hand.

He turned on his daughter and bellowed. "Estsuko! How come you kept this news from me? I'll have your hair shaven and branded for insolence against me. What you done is more than disobedience, it was deceitful and I'll not stand for it. Tomorrow leave my house and never step foot in it for as long as I live. I'll hate you forever. Leave my sight before I forget I'm a civilized Samurai, and beat you like a wild animal needing slaughter."

The old warrior slapped his daughter. Such a move could cause the one slapped to commit suppuku. There was no greater insult for any Japanese person than to be slapped across the face, or have his face touched by another unless it was in an act of love making.

Estsuko cried as she tried to get up, but her mother left the mattress and came to the floor and wrapped her arms protectively around her daughter, stopping her from leaving. Both women cried as she cuddled Estsuko's head close to her breasts and looked at her husband and cried. "Husband! Don't take your wrath out on your respectful daughter.

Estsuko was carrying out my wishes of not telling you of my problems. Husband! You have enough on your mind to worry about other than wasting your thoughts or time for your undeserving wife, who is allowing minor problems affect her serving of her husband properly. It was my fault your daughter didn't tell you of my suffering. I had her swear to secrecy. If your wrath must fall upon someone's head let it be mine. I'll leave your home sun up tomorrow morning my husband."

Emiko's face contorted in a mask of pain, and she held on to her stomach and groaned. The old war horse turned his head from her suffering before he too cried. He swallowed when he saw fresh blood on the mattress where she sat moments before. His eyes went from the mattress to his wife, and felt bad for causing the women of his home grief and concern. He lifted his daughter's head tenderly by the chin until their eyes met and he offered.

"Daughter! You taught your worthless father a valuable lesson. A day learned from is a day worth living. I see not only the Samurai are ruled by honor and respect. Precious daughter, I made a terrible mistake and in that error I acted a fool against a loving person. I hope in your heart you can find a place where you can forgive this old fool for his stupidity. You'll not leave my house, you'll move to our section of living and look after your mother. I'll send for doctors who know of these problems your mother suffers from. I don't want your mother working, the duties of the house fall upon you and your sister's shoulders. If you need help, hire it! From this day forward you'll be in control of the household monies. The only thing I want your mother to be concerned about, is getting well. Nothing else."

"Hai." Estsuko cried, tears rolling down her cheeks as she looked into her father's eyes.

Emiko protested the best she could. "Ieeeee husband! What about me, am I now a useless piece of furniture to be ignored so by you? Am I to be stopped from doing my wifely duties? If so, I demand the right to commit suppuku, and put an end to my worthless life."

"Enough of this foolish talk." The trainer thundered, never before has he had so many problems with the women of his household. Warriors were easier to control, if they insulted the trainer he could beat them and gain pleasure, dealing with the softer sex there was no pleasure beating them. "Emiko! I forbid you to commit suppuku. If you go against my wishes you'll dishonor yourself and me. I forbid this and will entertain no further words on this subject, the same goes for you Estsuko. I forbid you from the act of suppuku. If you feel you must die then you'll do it in a less honorable way."

He stared at his daughter who moved until it looked like she was protecting her mother. "Estsuko! I need you to take care of your mother. I know of no ways of looking after her. I only know how to handle Samurai and war making, not the women of Japan."

Estsuko gave her father a smile as she sniffled and nodded and mumbled with a sob. "Father! There's nothing you're not able to accomplish. I'll honor your wishes and it'd be my honor to look after mother, because I'm a worthless person unable to look after herself."

He nodded to his daughter and offered. "I'll look after this gaggle of worthless guests outside and send Kobayashi-san to fetch the doctor. I'll have the seer give comfort to your mother until the doctor arrives." He didn't wait for Emiko to reply as he walked out of the room quickly.

General Kobayashi waited on the verandah for Tanizaki to return so he could make his apologies and leave the ceremony. He was surprised at the condition of the trainer as the old man whispered. "Kobayashi-san! Get Hiroyuki Yabuki and have him come quickly."

"Hai Tanizaki-san! You don't feel well Master Trainer?" The general asked of the trainer.

"I'm fine, Emiko's feeling ill. I believe it might be something she ate. I don't like her color and want her checked by the fool of a Doctor. Get on your way and let no one know why you're leaving my home. Have the Doctor come to the front and Estsuko will let him in. Inform the fool I don't want him making a scene about this visit, there's nothing to it General." Tanizaki pushed Kobayashi to hurry him then watched as he left with the spring of youth in his step.

He glanced around for Masahiko and picked up the child showing one of the guests the kosode given her by a visitor. He got the attention of the old Shoya and he noticed his actions and made his way over to the trainer.

"Shoya Sanuki-san! I need your help, I want everyone to leave. I have an emergency I must attend to. Complain you have other Kamisogi's to attend and you must leave. I'm certain everyone will get the message and leave with you. If not, I'll throw them off my land."

Sanuki stared at him and was shocked the trainer would threaten to physically remove someone from his property. In his mind he knew the emergency had to be more than he let on. All Sanuki could do was nod and whispered. "I'll get these clods of humanity to leave your house immediately. I'll be at Matsukawa-san's home in case you need me, Tanizaki-san."

It took an hour for everyone to finally leave his home, the only ones who remained were the closest friends and relatives of the trainer. As in most cases with a Japanese family, the problems remained in the family's nucleus. It didn't take long for the relatives to know something was wrong with someone in the house, and it was easy to discover who was ailing. The only one not helping with the clean up was Emiko, and Estsuko.

Some women believed the daughter might be pregnant, and spread the rumor to other members, but when the doctor entered and asked for Emiko, the snooping ones knew they were wrong. The mood in Tanizaki's home was somber as the doctor disappeared behind the screens. Estsuko wouldn't leave her mother's side and helped the doctor the best she could.

The trainer remained on the other side and acted like nothing of interest was happening. He cursed every god under his breath. He knew he would be at a loss if anything happened to his wife. The relatives tried to engage him in talk, but he paid no attention to them, and when someone got his ear. He replied he was occupied with the problems facing the samurai training.

While he waited for word from the doctor, he stared at the screens as if trying to burn a hole through them with his eyes. It seemed to take hours for the doctor to examine Emiko and when he came from behind the screens he had blood on his hands and on his cotton kosode.

The trainer stared at the doctor as he crossed the room. He was trying to show little concern over his wife's health. The doctor wiped his hands on a piece of clean cloth and grunted. "Ikaga desu ka, Tanizaki-san?" (How are you?)

"How am I you ask? I piss on how I'm feeling, Yabuki! How is Emiko?"

"Tanizaki-san! Your wife is ill. How long has she been suffering in this manner?"

"Huh! How would I know, the women of my home play game of deceit against me. The first time I knew Emiko was ailing was today, when I saw she was having trouble standing and looked white as rice paper." He made a dismissing move with his hands as he flung them at the screens to show his disapproval with his wife and daughter to the doctor.

"Ieeeee Tanizaki-san! I understand your words. The women of Japan move in a world of their own, and will not allow a man to enter that world of secrecy. If only the women were more truthful with me then the better I'd be able to help them." The doctor let out his breath and asked. "Tanizaki-san! What do you think caused this last attack of pain and blood?"

"Huh! According to my worthless daughter it was I who caused her this pain. She said Emiko began bleeding because we did the dance of the serpent last night."

"Ahhh... I see. Perhaps you're too large for your wife's Jade Gate?"

"Old fool, I have been making love to my wife in this manner for countless years. If I didn't hurt her in the past, why would I hurt her now? My serpent is far too old to grow larger. You're displaying foolishness, Doctor. You're a traitor to your intelligence to dare make such a foul statement, great fool." He snarled at the doctor.

"Huh! There has to be a some reason for her to bleed the way she does after making love to you, Master Trainer Tanizaki-san. Perhaps you might be getting too excited without knowing it. Passion is a good thing, but I saw what happens when passion overrules judgment and manners in the act of pillowing. Could this be what is happening to your wife?" The doctor asked while ignoring the terrible way the trainer was speaking to him.

His body shook with rage and he tried to gain control of his temper. What he wanted to do was take this ill mannered doctor outside and lop his head from his shoulders for daring to suggest he willingly hurt his wife. "Huh! Do you think me a dog eater I might bite my wife? Or do anything against her person that might cause her pain when I was pillowing her. Iye! If not for bad manners I'd skin you alive for this insult. I don't know why my wife bleeds so. My daughter said she was damaged inside when she delivered Masahiko. She said Emiko bled since birthing day." He growled hot as he dared the doctor to ask him another foolish question.

"Ahhh... so. Now I'm getting to the reason for Lady Emiko's bleeding. I wish she would've told me this before I was forced to ask you of it. It would've saved us an unpleasant conversation. This world of women will be the death of us men, neh?" The doctor complained.

The master trainer stomped out from the waiting room looking to hit something in his way. He saw Enko sitting in the kitchen and barked viciously at her. "Sake!"

Enko jumped at the force in her father's voice. "Hai father." She replied bowing politely but fearfully towards the trainer as she rushed off and retrieved an unopened bottle of sake and a cup, and offered them to her father who went out on the back porch.

He took the cup and sent it flying across the yard in his fit of rage. The porcelain piece exploded in a hundred pieces as it crashed on the stone pebble walkway. Two guards rushed over and picked out the broken shards of pottery from the pebbles. He plopped down on the step and drank straight from the bottle, displaying terrible manners but he didn't care one bit about what anyone might think of him. Enko disappeared inside the home again.

By the time the trainer finished the sake, the doctor appeared and looked at Tanizaki who barely acknowledged his presence as he offered. "Master Trainer Tanizaki-san! Are you in possession of your wits? I wish to speak with you."

"Speak!" He barked at the doctor who looked like he had something terrible to offer.

"Tanizaki-san!" He started, ignoring the obviously drunken trainer. "Lady Emiko is very ill. You must refrain from pillowing her until I get another Doctor who knows more about this type of situation. I don't know how to help her, this ailment is something I don't know much about. Tanizaki-san! If you insist pillowing your wife, the next time you do might kill her."

He threw the empty bottle on the porch as he growled in a slurred voice. "What do you mean I'll kill Emiko? I'll kill you for daring to suggest this to me."

Again he ignored the drunken trainer as he offered in a calm tone. "Good Tanizaki-san. I'm pleased I have your attention, it's needed. I sent a runner to the second village where a certain Doctor who knows more of this ailment dwells. He'll arrive tomorrow morning. Once he examines Lady Emiko we'll know a lot more of what's affecting her. Master Trainer Tanizaki-san! Once we know what she's suffering from, we'll be able to treat her better."

"Will my wife die?" The trainer mumbled as he looked down at the floor.

"Possibly?"

"Huh! If she dies so do you, fool of a Doctor that you are."

The doctor made Emiko comfortable while waiting for the other doctor to arrive.

The trainer was angry and walked to the garden from the verandah, he stumbled in his Tabi cotton shoes and almost fell before righting himself. He wanted to lose his problems in the masks of fragrances of the flowers, and the songs sung by birds. It was impossible to relieve his mind and in moments he worked his way back home, consumed by worry for his ailing wife.

The second doctor arrived and in minutes determined what was wrong with Emiko. He conferred with the other doctor to compare notes then spoke with Tanizaki. The new doctor bowed perfunctorily to the trainer as he sat on the top step and rested his hands across his lap.

He noticed the hand folding and grunted and stared at the doctor who was unknown.

"Ahhh... Tanizaki-san! I fear your wife is seriously ill, and will need much care in the future. If she's well taken care of, she'll live to see Masahiko-san enter Gembuku..."

"Huh! That ceremony is ten years off. How long will she live after the ceremony has come passed, you old fool? She'll still be a young woman. Can we have another child?"

"Ieeeee Tanizaki-san! I'm trying to keep her alive to participate in the Gembuku ceremony, so she can witness your son enter Lord Kawasomeru's army. So sad, so sad, Lady Emiko is very ill. She's more ill that you thought, Tanizaki-san." He repeated with little emotion in his voice.

"Your unspoken words inform me she'll die?" The trainer asked.

"Yes Master Trainer Tanizaki-san, I'm sorry, she will die! You must accept the inevitable, Karma is Karma and the decisions of Karma must be left to the gods to control the fate of all Japanese peoples. I warn you, if you try and engage in pillowing your wife, you'll kill her by the time you completed your act, Master Trainer. Tanizaki-san, take a consort from the realm to relieve your essence with. There are many beautiful young women in Japan who'd be proud and willing to pillow with the respected Master Trainer of the Ninth Village. It could prove to be interesting to experience." The doctor added cautiously to the staring old man.

"What the devil do I care about any other worthless women of Japan! I only care about Emiko, and if I can't have her to pillow, I'll no longer pillow in this angry world of pain and sorrow. There's no woman in the world other than my wife." He hissed as he searched for a new bottle of sake then bellowed. "Enko, worthless daughter, bring sake!"

Enko rushed out the shoji doors and dropped to her knees as she offered her father the sake and two porcelain cups. The young woman bowed to her father and filled the cups for him and the doctor, and tried to disappear back inside the house quickly.

"Ieeeee worthless little one! How many times do I have to tell you not to wait for me to ask for something I need. You must anticipate my needs, and have what I need waiting. Go, before I have you whipped for your insolence, foolish child." He glared at his daughter.

"Master Trainer! You must think of your words more carefully when addressing your daughter, you're being too harsh with her. She's polite and well mannered, you should be proud to have her serve you." The doctor dared to offer as he tipped the cup and drained it.

"Dung heap of a worthless Doctor! You worry about my wife's health and leave my child's discipline to me. I can order your head removed from your shoulders for daring to intrude in my home's harmony. I run my home the way I see fit, not the way you believe I should control my household, fool." He snarled at the concerned doctor as he glared at him.

The doctor was wise enough not to pay attention to his ranting and threats of death against him. He treated many ailing women, and if he was to suffer the fate Tanizaki threatened every time he delivered bad news to the husbands, he would have lost his head while a young man. It seemed when a husband was concerned with his wife's health, he always resort to threatening the doctor treating her. Nothing he could say would impress him, and his age gave him the daring to place his nose and head where it didn't belong.

The doctor understood he was displaying bad manners, he was also aware he had to have the trainer's attention if he was going to save Emiko's life long as possible, as he grumbled. "Ieeeee Tanizaki-san! For your health you must consider enlisting the services of a consort to relieve your personal needs. I saw men's health dwindle once they no longer used the gifts of the gods. I deem it my duty to inform Lord Kawasomeru of your statements, and make sure he looks after your health, if you refuse to do so." The doctor held out his empty cup for the trainer to refill.

From inside the doorway, Enko appeared and knelt and bowed and refilled the doctor's cup. He bowed to the girl then turned to Tanizaki watching his daughter serve him. "There, you see Master Trainer Tanizaki-san! She's an very obedient and polite daughter, one who honors her father's honorable presence and standing well."

"Huh! You see things the way you want to see them, and I'll see them the way I see them." The master trainer grumbled at the doctor staring at him.

The doctor let out his breath in a sigh, he wasn't sure if he was getting through to the old man, and knew if he would force himself on Emiko, she would surely die at the next pillowing, and he offered the old man. "Tanizaki-san! You're wiser than I, so I must trust you'll do the right thing and enlist the aid of a consort for your health."

His demeanor softened. "Honorable Doctor! You'll keep her alive until the time of Gembuku? It's important she attends this ceremony."

"Hai! I should be able to keep her alive and comfortable until Gembuku as you requested, Tanizaki-san. Only if you and Lady Emiko will listen to my instructions, and follow them as if they were the law to both of you. I'm bound by my responsibility to make a report to Kawasomeru-sama once I'm finished speaking to you, trying to make your beautiful wife as comfortable as possible as long as I'm able to keep her alive." The doctor added to the old man as he smiled at Tanizaki this time.

CHAPTER ELEVEN

The day after the kamisogi ceremony, life changed drastically for Masahiko, along with the trainer and the rest of his family. Master Trainer Tanizaki was more interested in Emiko's health than getting back to training his samurai, even though his daughters were waiting on her hand and foot. Masahiko felt slighted by all the attention offered to her ailing mother, and decided to march around the village alone.

Gone were the carefree days when the future master trainer could parade about the town like a peacock, and invade the villager's privacy as she done before the hair cutting. She dressed in her kosode looked in the first home she passed. The wife came out and swatted at the child and yelled at her for displaying terrible manners for peeking in her home. She rushed off as the woman called her vile names and threatened her. She was confused, before the hair cutting she could look in any window, and if they were eating, the owner would invite her in for food. Now, she wasn't allowed on the porch. The child was bewildered over this change in attitude aimed at her, and walked the street without care. She saw Shoya Sanuki on his front porch, and decided to make her way to the seated old man.

When Sanuki spotted her walking about, he yelled. "Worthless young man! Have you no shame about yourself, how dare you walk about my village as if you have no responsibilities to look after. Straighten your shoulders and walk proud, have you nothing to do? No chores to carry out for the sake of your village? If you're looking for work you come to the right place, I have fields in need of work. Useless child, go home and change from that vain outfit, and dress in the clothes of the village and work for your living. My village's strength depends on the youth. You're no longer a worthless child, you're a man, and as such you have responsibilities." The Shoya glared angrily at Masahiko until she went running home.

Other members of the village came out to see who the Shoya was yelling at, and as she went running passed them, they yelled at her for her insolence to the village.

Masahiko fought back tears, she couldn't understand why the village was so angry with her as if they stopped loving her. She searched her mind to see if she could understand what it was she might have done wrong. She plopped down in the kitchen and stared at the village street.

Estsuko finished giving her mother a bath in bed when she heard Masahiko come in, she went to see what was troubling the child. She explained what happened and Estsuko smiled.

"Masahiko-san! You're no longer a child, you're on your way to becoming a Samurai. The childish pranks you once played on the villagers will not be tolerated any longer. It's the duty of everyone from the village to make sure the children grow up to be proper persons, no matter what paths the gods chose for them to travel upon. You could look into the homes of villagers before, but it's bad manners and as a man, you must understand this. The Shoya will expect you to work in the fields, and you must continue training with your father. Everyone from the village will expect more from you than the other children because of who you are. Masahiko-san! You must remember you're chosen and as such, you must be perfect in everything you do."

Remembering how much this child adored the exquisite kosode she wore, Estsuko added. "Masahiko-san, remember a Samurai will have no need for worldly goods, not because you don't yearn for such things of beauty and vanity. But because of your position as Samurai, makes such wants and needs useless. You must understand this, there's no long life in your future, and you chose the way of the Warrior. Longevity is something that's only dared dreamed about by all Samurai in the employ of his Lord."

"Then I don't want to be the chosen one if I'm forced to give up everything I desire. I want to play like yesterday, Estsuko." She complained bitterly, coming close to tears again.

"Masahiko-san! You have no choice in your fate. The gods chose you for greatness, and greatness is what you'll aspire to. It's the duty of the village under the threat of death, to make sure you ascend to the greatness deemed by the gods for you."

A tear escaped from the corner of her eye and ran down her cheek.

Estsuko captured the tear between her fingers and placed it on the head of the Buddha statue. Then she explained about tears. "Masahiko-san! Tears are the way the body cleanses the soul, and the soul is the being of a Samurai. But a Samurai must never allow a person to witness this cleansing of the soul, or that person will take it as a sign of weakness, and use this as a weapon against your person. Any cleansing of your soul must be carried out in the privacy of your heart. Masahiko-san! You were born with a tender heart, you must guard yourself against this softness from betraying you. You must never cry in the presence of anyone. You must remain strong in every matter you perform. You must be hard, and willing to destroy another soul for the sake of honor and respect for your Lord and for your family as well. I pray to Lord Buddha every night to give you the inner strength that you'll need to carry out the will of the gods, for the good of Japan and for your Lord and Master."

Masahiko fought back tears as she smiled at her beloved sister. Estsuko placed her hand over her sister's shoulder. Neither woman was aware Tanizaki was standing in the doorway listening to them speaking. He cleared his throat then entered the room.

The trainer looked to Estsuko and smiled as he bowed to her, letting her know he approved of her words to her sister. "Estsuko! Your mother has need of you. I sent Enko to retrieve the old seer to help you with her. The doctor must leave today for two days and will return. Emiko's health will be entrusted to you until he does. I'll relieve you of household duties. I informed Sanuki I need two women to come in and look after the home for my wife."

Estsuko returned the bow. "Father, how does mother feel about these strange helpers?"

"Ieeeee my daughter!" He mumbled as he shook his hand. "Emiko was angrier than I ever saw her before. One would think she was stung by an angry Yellow jacket. She wanted me to dispatch her because she tried to convince me she was failing her wifely duties. I laughed at her offer of suppuku and ordered her to rest. I told her it was no insult to be ill and need the help of the villagers, until she was well enough to resume her duties. It took many words, but she relented. I don't believe she was convinced by my foolish words, so I order you to keep an eye on her. I forbidden her to commit suppuku but I don't trust her. I'll be upset if she finds a way to go to the gods before I allow." The trainer gave his daughter a harsh glare.

Estsuko bowed again. "Father, I'll guard against allowing mother the honor of suppuku, until you give her permission to leave this earth."

"Good, attend to your mother. I must go to my troops. Masahiko, accompany me. Get out of that womanly kosode and get in clothes suited to your training. I'll not call you honorable from this day until you earned that right. Is this understood?"

"Hai father." Masahiko bowed. "Don't worry father, I'll earn the san after my name again."

"I worry about your mother's health, but we'll see if you can live up to your boast, young Masahiko. We shall see. Get changed, I want to leave before another cock crows."

She rushed to her living area and changed in the clothes of an adult samurai given her yesterday. In seconds, she stood before her father, waiting with caged up youthful energy, wanting to get out to the fields of man and their training.

He checked his wife before they left, together they walked through the street, followed by the samurai guards. He thought of assigning four guards to Masahiko for her protection. It would give him face to have his guards walking behind him wherever he went. Tanizaki was fearful of treachery played against his child. It would give Lord Wakatsuki great power to destroy the warrior before she could rise to her perch of power. As he walked he agreed to do this, the child reached the first level of becoming an adult and needed more protection now.

They entered the trainer's favorite area, the horse field and he watched as Kobayashi carried out practice with the spearmen trying to dislodge a number of horsemen using blunt ended spears. He watched as the spearmen did everything to gain the upper hand over the horsemen, and they did everything they could to avoid losing control. The combat was fought to a checkmate. Every time it looked like the spearmen would overwhelm the horsemen, they regrouped and charge, and broke up the spearmen's thrust. He smiled, he was proud each of the armies couldn't defeat the other, yet inside he knew these soldiers would have no match on any field of honor. He was certain he done everything to make these, the third group of warriors trained since the day Lord Kawasomeru showed up with the fifteen hundred warriors.

He was winding down the training of the third group and expected to complete it in the next two weeks. He would have two to three weeks before the fourth group of warriors arrived. The master trainer was expecting to use this time to train Masahiko.

When Kobayashi noticed the trainer he moved to him and ordered a second attack by the horsemen, this time against the dug in spearmen. It was an effort to show the trainer how well the warriors were using his methods. The general got to his side the moment the horsemen attacked the spearmen. He bowed to Tanizaki interested in the attack than pleasantries.

The attack worked out well with both sides enjoying success, the horsemen were unable to root out the spearmen, and the spearmen couldn't drive the horsemen off their attack. On the field of battle, wars were won because the attacking side couldn't defeat the defenders. In many battles it was important for an army to fight to a standstill, using many enemy warriors, so a second army might attack the castle and win the war by circumventing the bulk of the enemy forces, and either attacking their rear or avoid them and attack the main nest of enemy.

When the mock battle was fought to a standstill, Tanizaki bowed and said. "General Kobayashi-san! Your troops fought well and accomplished everything expected of them as trained Samurai. Run one more exercise then give them the rest of the day off for their success on the field of battle today. I want to go over the training of Masahiko with you. I believe it's time the foolish child gets serious about the practice session. We have a lot to do with him, and little time to accomplish it. I might lose valuable time with the child looking after Emiko."

"Master Trainer Tanizaki-san! I'd deem it an honor to be chosen to assist in the training of Masahiko-san. I'll make the child the greatest fighter ever to take the field of battle." The general bowed to Tanizaki and then to Masahiko who stood by the side of her father.

He returned the bow with equal respect. "General Kobayashi-san! You'll carry out a part of Masahiko's training. But I insist you omit the "San" from his name until he has proven the child is worthy and earned the right to add the san to his name."

"Hai. When do you want to begin his training?" Kobayashi asked the master trainer.

"Ieeeee! I been training the young pup for months in secret. Now the child's allowed to wear his hair in the manner of Samurai, we can begin his training in the open." He was having no problem referring to Masahiko as a he. In his mind he accepted the child as a male.

The trainer left General Kobayashi with his warriors while he and Masahiko checked on the archers and warriors learning to fight hand to hand employing jujitsu. Small clouds of dust were raised by the warriors as they fought. The soldiers were paired off in groups of twos, and when one defeated the warrior he was fighting, he was allowed to help another soldier. It was the time when warriors would seek revenge against a particular warrior who insulted them.

They laughed as the soldiers attacked each other, using the side of their hands, feet, knees, and hips, and some bled from broken noses or split lips after taking a chop to the face. Trainers walked between the fighters, correcting errors or breaking up a fight getting out of hand and assuming a life or death struggle. On rare occasions, the trainers were drawn in a fight because the warriors hit the trainer which was forbidden.

When they seen enough of the hand to hand fighting, they moved to the archery field. Tanizaki took time to explain to Masahiko the moves the warriors employed against each other. At one point he stopped some warriors from fighting and had one redo an interesting move, so he could explain it better to Masahiko. He had the warrior repeat the move a second, then a third time in slower motions so she could observe the action easier to understand.

Some warriors stopped fighting and took interest in the moves displayed. Then they tried to employ them in their combat maneuvers. This pleased the young warrior and Tanizaki who was so impressed by the warrior he elevated him to trainer second class, which entitled the warrior to remain in the village and help with future training. It also made it possible for the trainee to remain alive, using training to avoid the battlefield as long as he was needed by the master.

By the time they reached the archery field, Masahiko was growing bored with the training. The child still a child, wanted to go to the stream and catch sucker fish with the other children. The fish were from the carp family, boney and hard to eat. But when a child captured one, the parents made a big thing of the capture, and the fish was served as the main meal. Masahiko had no way of knowing she would no longer be allowed to catch fish with the children of the village.

They were bound by honor to bow to Masahiko supporting the manly hairdo of a samurai. They realized they would no longer be allowed to play with the older child as they done in the past while she was growing up.

If she tried to capture a sucker fish, the other children would be honor bound to leave the stream and stand on the bank with their heads bowed to her, and not leave the area until he captured one of the elusive and hard to catch fish.

In the ninth village, life as she once enjoyed, changed drastically and she would be forced to change with it, or suffer greatly. The master trainer observed the boredom in the child's eyes and cuffed her on the back of her head to draw her mind back to the practice field, as the trainer explained why one warrior had three arrows locked in his teeth. While aiming at a pair of fleeing dogs released in front of him twenty five yards away.

The arrow struck the lead dog in the side and the animal yelped and dropped momentarily to the ground and licked the area the arrow struck her in, before getting up and running off with a slight limp. In less than a heart beat the warrior had a second arrow armed in his bow, and the missile struck the second dog in a dead run in the hind end as it ran wild on the training field. The dog went tumbling, but before the dog came to a stop, the warrior had the bow rearmed and sent a third arrow flying at the first dog, hitting it in the neck. The forth arrow struck the second dog as he was just getting up to run.

The trainer whispered to his young trainee. "Ieeeee! See young one, you'll be expected to be better than this foolish Warrior, and I'll make certain of it. But you must forget your childish thoughts and concentrate on becoming the best of the best of Japan's great Warriors. It's your duty to be the best in all Japan, for you are my son."

The trainer's attention was drawn to a dragon fly darting across the field. He drew her eye to the insect and ordered. "Masahiko! Pay attention to how the kachi mushi (victory insect) flies. You can learn from it. There, see how it changes direction when it thinks or feels its way is impeded or threatened. See how the Tombo (dragon fly) never tries to go against the wind or resistance, but allows the resistance to guide its course, thus making it forever able to avoid the wind, yet uses it to give it movement. You must be the same as the Tombo, you must teach your mind to learn how to use your enemy's strengths against him, so he'll expose his weaknesses and you can conquer his fighting spirit. If you master such elusiveness, your enemy will never be able to anticipate from where your attack will begin. Masahiko! Remember how as a child, you and the other boys tried to capture the Tombos? How many times were you successful?"

"Father, I was able to capture two insects in my many tries."

"And how many times have you and the other boys tried to capture one of the proud insects?"

"Honorable father, I attempted to capture a Tombo more times than I can count."

"Then have you learned a valuable lesson today Masahiko? One that'll stay with you for all times to come, little one?" He asked as he looked down at the rapidly growing child.

"Hai father."

"And what is the essence of that lesson you learned on this day, young one?"

"Teacher, I learned a branch that bends in the wind will remain alive, while the branch that offers resistance to the wind, will break off and be drawn from the tree of life and die." She said what she believed her father wanted to hear, even thought she wasn't certain what she was supposed to learn from the lesson he offered her.

"Ieeeee Masahiko! It's the student who becomes the teacher. That's what you were suppose to learned from the lesson. What a day, for me to learn from the student. Come little one, we'll return to the horse field and watch the last of the practices before the Warriors are allowed to end their training." He marched off to the horse field, his shoulders back, a spring in his step and smile on his lips. He was overjoyed at the response from the trainee, and he wanted to show the child off to the other warriors. Masahiko marched as proudly and defiantly two steps behind her father, the six samurai guards a few paces behind her ever on the alert for treachery.

Kobayashi saw the trainer returning and warned his horsemen not to embarrass him on this practice, or he would make them pay for the insult. He had his spearmen set in place, and was going to have the horsemen charge their fortification. He intended to employ a new strategy of allowing two waves of horsemen attack simultaneously from the flanking sides of the defenders. The general would hold a third wave of horsemen in reserve, and employ them when he was sure the defenders were hard pressed holding the first waves of horsemen off. He would send the third wave down their throat in an all out frontal charge at the fortification. He waited for the trainer and his ward to reach his side, before committing the reserve horse soldiers to the attack.

The trainer saw the formation and growled. "General Kobayashi-san! Why have you held back a third army and intend to use the weaker armies to attack with? You go against the normal belief of attacking in force with your main thrust, and allowing your weaker armies to create a sweeping attack from the flanks. Have you lost your mind on this foul exercise?"

He bowed as he offered in his defense. "Master Trainer Tanizaki-san! As you witnessed before, once the spearmen get between those rocks we been unable to move them with three separate assaults, using different modes to attack. I gave this problem much thought of late, and decided to go against the accepted means of attacking a defended fortification, to see if I can catch the defenders off guard. Or confuse them so my horsemen can gain the upper hand against the fools and win this war. I'm employing what you taught, to get your enemy off stride so you can defeat them. If I begin this attack with my weaker forces and hold my main army in reserve until all defenders are unable to defend themselves against a frontal attack, I should win." The general stared at the trainer, hoping he didn't order him to return to the usual means of attacking a fortification with his horse soldiers.

The trainer gave Kobayashi's words thought then a smile spread across his lips as he bowed to his general. "Today is a glorious day indeed, it might turn out to be a day where the teacher becomes the student twice, and learn from my conscript. No greater pleasure could be gained by knowledge, than to have the students become wiser than the teacher. Proceed Kobayashi-san! If you're successful I'll increase your fief by ten hectares from my personal wealth, and I'm certain Kawasomeru-sama will equal my gift, once he realizes the honor I bestowed on you for your military skills and training abilities for his Samurai. If you succeed that is General."

"And if my horsemen fail in defeating the defenders?"

"Then you'll have the knowledge your way was wrong, but it was worthy of a try. It's better to try an experiment on a practice field, rather than employ a guess on a battlefield where your Warrior's lives might be wasted in vain in the attempt. Either way General! You proven to me your understanding the ways of the battle wiser now. You may begin your attack on the defenders with the remaining horse soldiers."

"Hai Tanizaki-san." He lifted his arm and the first and second army of horsemen charged the flanking sides of the defender's position. The spearmen held off the horsemen, but inflicted minor damage to the horsemen staying out of reach of the wood spears, while firing vast volleys of blunted arrows at the dug in defenders. After an hour of probes, the general decided it was time to employ the remaining forces held in check. He made a hooting call, informing the smaller armies to attack in force one last effort against the defenders.

Kobayashi waited until the defenders were engaged against his weaker armies. He raised his arm and the main army charge the front of the defender's position in force. Even though the defenders saw the army and knew what they were attempting against them, they were unable to move enough defending warriors from the flanks to defend against a main frontal charge.

Some defenders shifted position to defend from the main attacking army. The second the warriors moved from the left flank, it crumbled from the attacking horsemen. Now, the defenders were hard pressed to know which area to defend, confusion reigned and the defenders ran in all directions, trying desperately to reestablish defensive lines against the attacking armies. With little effort, the attacking army charged over the defenders, pelting them with gourds, signifying a sword strike. The defenders were dispatched and the war was won by the horsemen. The general's daring tactic proved an equal attacking size army could defeat an entrenched army in short order. It was the first time they defeated the defenders.

"Ieeeee General Kobayashi-san! You prove me wrong. Never, in my thoughts would I attack a fortification with my weaker armies, and hold my strength in reserve. Cunning indeed! The fox has out mastered his pursuers. I'll make sure this tactic is entered in the war scrolls, and employed in the upcoming war against Wakatsuki. I'll enter it as General Kobayashi attack."

The trainer turned to Masahiko. "Hai young one! You see, if the mind is willing it can work its way out of any dilemma. If you allow your mind to remain open it'll not let you down and will see you home safely. The warriors who die in battle are the ones who lose their concentration and defeated by their attacker. Today, General Kobayashi-san proved to you it's better to be on the attack rather than to defend a position, huh?"

"Hai father! General Kobayashi-san is a wise Samurai. Someone I'll pay attention to when he speaks of war, and the ways of waging it." She bowed graciously to the general.

General Kobayashi bowed as politely to Masahiko.

The trainer bowed to his general. "Kobayashi-san! You done yourself honor in this exercise. It's time to allow your Warriors to clean themselves and relax. I'll make sure the Mama-san sends her women, I'll add decanters of sake to help the Warriors celebrate this victory."

By the time he returned home, the seer had his belongings moved to Emiko's room, and he was resting on the floor by her bed. The trainer couldn't help the glare he shot at the seer, but when Emiko spoke in a weak voice, she asked the seer to be near until she was strong enough to get out of bed on her own. His anger subsided, and he bowed friendly to the seer of the future.

He checked on his wife and when he was certain she was feeling as well as she could, he went off to eat. Masahiko was at her father's heels and sat by him while they waited to be served by Estsuko. The trainer waited until a bowl of warm rice was placed before him then asked. "Estsuko! How is your mother feeling on this day?"

"Father! She's doing well today."

"The bleeding?" He grunted. Bleeding in Japan was the most feared affliction to befall a warrior. There was little a soldier could but to place a swift end to the suffering of the downed samurai by taking his life. The sight of Emiko bleeding drew emotions from the old soldier.

"Honorable father, I'm pleased to announce that mother has not bled on this day, and she was able to rest comfortably last night. Mother seems to be drawing strength from the seer's presence in the room. The two spoke most of the morning."

"When does that fool of a Doctor return to check on your mother's health?" He barked, he held doctors in the same light he did the gods and priests. He didn't trust any of them.

"Tomorrow at noon, father."

"He better, I'll have his head for a foot rest if he's late. I want Emiko well, she must be well to witness Masahiko's Gembuku." The trainer looked to his young child and smiled.

"Father, I have no fear mother will be well enough to travel, and will proudly stand beside you at the ceremony, along with the rest of your proud family."

"Huh!" The trainer grunted as he devoured the rice. He stayed home until the doctor returned. He watched as the doctor fed Emiko herbs and potions and placed a pack between her legs. Each medical procedure embarrassed the trainer. Finally, he had to leave the room before he attacked the intruding doctor. All the doctor's actions reinforced the feeling he held for physicians. He felt they did little and served to embarrass the ailing person.

CHAPTER TWELVE

ON THE SECOND DAY OF THE THIRD WEEK OF THE FIFTH MONTH OF THE YEAR THIRTEEN FORTY FOUR

It was a warm May morning when Tanizaki ordered Kobayashi to prepare the troops for the march to Engakuji Castle where they would be absorbed in the first army of Kawasomeru. He gave orders to Kobayashi the night before, and he was allowing the pleasure of taking his time before showing up on the field, to bid his trainees now warriors their final good byes.

His home life changed, he no longer shared a bed with his ailing wife, and decided to allow her time to heal. He didn't look for any consorts to pillow with though, he merely controlled himself and wanted to save himself for his wife's pleasure. The trainer believed in remaining loyal to one woman for life, and that one woman was his wife.

On this day of shameful tardiness, the master trainer heard a commotion outside his gate. He got up and looked out the front shoji screen and saw his guards speaking with a stranger to the village. He picked up his sword, clutched it in his hand and went to see what the matter was. He saw a number of strangers and a set of heimin (commoners) standing by a screened palanquin. The commoners or kagamen were dressed in loincloths.

"Konnicha-wa!" (Good day) Tanizaki grunted as he took position alongside the commanding guardsman challenging the stranger. The stranger dropped to his knees and bowed, and held it until he was given permission to speak from the trainer.

He smirked as he grunted. "Yokoso oide kudasareta!" (Welcome to my house!)

The stranger allowed his head to lift from the ground. "Master Trainer Tanizaki-san, my unworthy name is Nasanori Kataoka, and I been sent by Lord Kawasomeru."

"Are we now reduced to old women we must speak in the middle of the road as if we're discussing gossip? Come Kataoka-san! I'll have you served drink. We'll speak on the porch in the shade it offers." He opened the gate and allowed Kataoka to enter, the strings of the Shinren, the tiny protective cords to ward off evil influences, tapped lightly against the wood of the gate as it opened for the stranger to the master trainer's home.

Kataoka bowed to honor the respect the trainer bestowed on him by adding the san to his name. Once they sat, Estsuko appeared with warm sake and tea and placed it before the men.

He flashed a faint smile at his eldest daughter as he asked the stranger. "Kataoka-san! Would you like cha or sake. Both are of the finest Japan has to offer."

"Ieeeee! You honor me, Master Trainer. I'm but a mere servant sent to honor you by Kawasomeru-sama, to help you in his times of need. My life is in your hands, Master of fate."

"Huh! What makes you believe that I have any interest in your foul life? Why has our Lord and Master sent you and the others of your caravan to me?" He growled as he gave a slight nod to his daughter and she filled the cups with tea.

"You're a graceful and kind Master." Kataoka said in a hurry as he drained the tea.

He nodded again to his daughter who refilled the cup. He waited until the stranger finished before he repeated. "Kataoka! Why has Kawasomeru-sama sent you? I don't understand. I'm certain he has more important things on his mind than to send more people to clutter my village. Are you to be trained in the art of making war? If so, things must be bad in the realm if our Master is sending old men and commoners to train in the ways of the Warrior."

"Ieeeee! You're mistaken Master Trainer Tanizaki-san. I'm of no worth, there for I'm unworthy of daring to dream of being trained in the ways of the Samurai..."

"You great dung heap of a fool then why are you and the rest of the filth eaters wasting my valuable time?" He roared, displaying bad manners but not caring.

Kataoka bowed, striking his head lightly on the tray and holding the position while waiting for the trainer to speak again.

"Kataoka! I'm growing bored with this conversation going nowhere in a hurry, and if you wish to keep your head on your shoulders for a moment longer, tell me why I find you sitting on my porch. I have important things to do than waste time with the likes of you and the other fools with you. Speak or lose your tongue!" He grunted, making sure the stranger was aware he again omitted the san from his name, as his hand tightened on the scabbard of his sword. The trainer allowed his hand to rest on the hilt, displaying he was growing bored with their conversation.

Masahiko grasped the hilt of her sword and dared this stranger to cause her father more grief. If he did, she would hack the unarmed man until he was dead, and seek her father's approval for what she done. Even if he didn't approve, he would be forced by honor to ask her if she felt this man was a threat and she was prepared to answer yes. This response was sure to be enough for her father to agree with her actions of killing the stranger obviously a man of little if any worth.

Kataoka was wise enough to read the threats displayed by the trainer and explained the reason for his appearance. "Tanizaki-sama!" He began and was interrupted by the trainer.

"I'm no Lord, thank the gods for that. I'm a mere Warrior. Speak fool!"

"Hai Master Trainer Tanizaki-san! Lord Kawasomeru was made aware of your wife's ill health, and took it on himself to send you kagamen and screen palanquin for her personal use. The kagamen have orders to carry your honored wife wherever she wants to go in your village. Kawasomeru-sama has sent you servants and cooks from his personal household." Kataoka leaned closer to the trainer, and whisper in the trainer's ear.

"Our honorable Lord and Master is concerned for your personal health, and that's why he chose to included a pair of consorts to look after your personal need. They're well trained in the ways of pleasing an honored and lucky

Warrior. They're young and a pleasure to look upon. I was ordered to inform you they know the ways of pleasing a Warrior with their mouths, Master Tanizaki-san." Kataoka's grin turned into an ugly sneer as he winked at the trainer trying his best to show no interest in anything Kataoka had to say.

His interest was aroused by the stranger. "What do you mean by pleasures of the mouth? What do they do, talk to make a man spread his essence upon the ground, fool?"

"Ieeeee my wise Master. Please allow me to explain of the wonderful pleasures these women possess. The women of the Soft World are schooled in ways not believed before, to give pleasures to their partners. The way of the mouth, they take their partner's faucet in their mouths and using their tongues and teeth, they nip, suck and slide their mouths up and down your weapon until it erupts in waves of pleasure, while spilling your essence in their mouths."

"Ieeeee! And what do they do with my essence once they have it in their mouths?" He asked, getting caught up in the excitement of the words while growing hard in his fundeshi.

"They swallow it my Master." Kataoka offered with another sneer plastered on his lips.

He stared in disbelief at the stranger who brought these foreign women with the strange way of giving sexual gratification to a samurai with him.

"Please Master Trainer. You must experience the delight they offer before you make judgment on the practice and before you die. It's like nothing else you ever witnessed."

The trainer knew he was trapped by his wise lord and was forced by honor to accept the gifts sent by him. It would be the height of bad manners to refuse such gifts and he would likely end up paying for the insult with his life. He realized the consorts were under instructions, and they would report to his lord if he didn't make use of their offerings. Besides, he had to admit he was looking forward to undergoing the pleasures these women had to offer, learned in the city of Engakuji. If these consorts were from Kawasomeru's private stock, they were the best of knowledgeable women in the countless ways of bringing pleasure to their master.

He bowed to Kataoka while having his mind confused by the offerings from his lord. "Kataoka-san! I'm honored by these gifts from Lord Kawasomeru. You must thank him for me when you return to Engakuji Castle."

"Ieeeee Master Trainer Tanizaki-san! I fear that I must be the one who corrects you in this conversation. I'll not be returning to Engakuji Castle, I too am a gift by our wise Lord for your use. I was instructed to inform you that I'm well schooled in the skills of making good sake, but my main responsibility will be to make certain your new unworthy servant's think of your every need and desire. I have two women servants trained in looking after an ailing woman such as your honored wife. I'm positive they'll become a much needed service and close friends to Lady Emiko." The stranger bowed one more time.

The stranger's smile was infectious and his showing of it made Tanizaki smile.

"Master Trainer Tanizaki-san! Shall I show you your new consorts and the other servants sent by Kawasomeru-sama please?"

"Hai." The trainer replied sharply as he went to leave his property.

His lead samurai guard opened the gate to allow them out and then followed them, his hand always resting threateningly on the hilt of his katana. His eyes searching the area, on alert for treachery displayed against his master, and daring anyone to attack and risk his wrath.

There were five palanquins with kagamen in the caravan. Kataoka clapped his hands and the sliding doors of four palanquins slid open and four women stepped out, they were dressed in their best kosode's, and their hair and makeup perfect. Everything about them highlighted their stunning beauty. Each woman stood before her palanquin and waited to be addressed.

He introduced the women he called consorts to Tanizaki. He bowed to her. "Lady Yukie Kidoguchi! Second consort of the First Tea House of Engakuji, this is Master Trainer Nitaro Tanizaki-san. You'll show him tonight how you were trained by your Mama-san to please."

"Hai." She said as she bowed correctly to the elderly Master Trainer Tanizaki.

He went to the second young woman and bowed and announced proudly. "Lady Remi Yamamoto! The first and prized Consort of the First Tea House of Engakuji, this is Master Trainer Nitaro Tanizaki-san. You'll show Master Tanizaki-san of the many ways of pleasure known to the women of the Soft World."

"Hai." Remi replied as she bowed to Tanizaki.

The old man returned her bow just within the limits of politeness, he could tell this woman was older than the first and reasoned this was why she was referred to as First Consort. He stared at her beauty and felt this woman was no older than mid twenties. Her eyes were like liquid pools of brown ink, her skin was so white she looked like the petals of a flower.

"Master Trainer Tanizaki-san! This worthless woman who stands before you is Lady Tomotaka Makiguchi. She and Lady Miho Hamohara will be responsible for the well being and care of the ailing Lady Emiko. They're well trained in the medical ways, and the manners needed to bring comfort to the ailing in their charge."

He glanced at the two older and less pretty women as his attention kept drifting back to the magnificent beauty of the younger one who would soon bring him pleasure during the long lonely night time hours. A thought struck him and he grumbled. "Ieeeee! Where will I shelter all of them? I have no room left in my home for more to move in."

"Master Trainer Tanizaki-san! That's no problem to concern yourself with, Kawasomeru-sama has instructed me to inform Shoya Sanuki-san it's his responsibility to shelter his people. No women will dare to spend the night in your home unless invited by yourself, or Lady Emiko. I believe Shoya Sanuki-san will be moving your neighbors on either side of your home, and we'll assume the buildings until the Lady's health has improved enough for you to release us from responsibility. Then we'll return to Engakuji Castle and make our reports to Lord Kawasomeru." Kataoka bowed to Tanizaki correctly.

"Has our honorable Lord informed you when the next army of worthless Samurai to be trained will arrive in the ninth village?" He barked at Kataoka, trying to take his mind off the stunning beauty of the young consorts standing before him.

"Iye! I don't think he'll be sending you more troops for a number of months."

"Doshite?" Why? The trainer asked the newcomer to his village with concern.

"Because the central provinces are on the verge of erupting into all out war involving eleven of the sixteen provinces that make up the central provinces of our land, Master Trainer Tanizaki-san." Kataoka reported while looking deeply in the eyes of the old trainer.

"Ieeeee! It's becoming that serious for our Lord and his people?"

"More than you could imagine so Tanizaki-san. Lord Wakatsuki is trying everything in his power to prevent this war from taking place. He stopped his minor attacks on Kozuke and Musashi province. At one point he tried to negotiate a peace with himself and Lord Anjoh, to enlist his help putting down the countless battles taking place in the central provinces."

"What about the troops I trained? Any word of their accomplishments in battle?"

"Hai! The first Warriors were sent by water to support Echizen from further attacks by Mino and Hida provinces. Kaga attacked Echizen and your soldiers fought bravely and defeated the forces sent from Kaga in a mere two sticks of time. The Warriors turned to Hida, and drove the invading Warriors from Hida out of Echizen province in seven sticks of time. Now, they're engaging in a defending action against troops mounted on the border between Mino and Echizen.

"The fighting between the provinces slacked because troubles between Mino and Omi province heated up again, with Omi province enlisting the aid of Warriors from Mikawa. When the Warriors from Mikawa joined Omi, Owari attacked Mikawa province. This placed Lord Wakatsuki's provinces in the central provinces at war with each other, eliminating further threats against Kawasomeru-sama. Our Master's content to allow each of these provinces fight among themselves, he's wise enough to know as long as Lord Wakatsuki's allied provinces are fighting each other, they'll not be fighting him."

"Huh! Our Lord and Master is wiser than his years." Master Trainer Tanizaki complained mildly as he noticed a slight commotion occurring in the house next to his. Shoya

Suzuki's family was being moved out of their home by the village samurai under the direction of Sanuki. He watched as the family was lead to the end of the village, and allowed to move into Hachirobe's old and filthy house which he ordered destroyed. He felt terrible for Suzuki's family, he felt the seer's home wasn't fit to be allowed to remain resting on its foundation, let alone lived in by any other civilized family of the village.

More noise to his right and He noticed Hara was escorted from his home with his family. He watched until he saw Hara forced to move in with his in-laws in the middle section of the village. He cursed Japan's intrusive way of life, owning everything yet owning nothing. How easy it was to move two families from their homes with their possessions, and move these strangers to the village in their homes without complaint by either family.

Members of the caravan who invaded the trainer's village, moved in the abandoned homes. The two consorts remained standing before their palanquins waiting for someone to give them orders. They wouldn't move until Tanizaki ordered them to, so they knew where they were going to call home in the new village.

Kataoka saw the confusion in his eyes and whispered. "Master Trainer Tanizaki-san! Your consorts are waiting you to choose one for the night's pleasures I believe."

"Ieeeee! I have to choose one to be with on this night, fool?" The trainer complained bitterly.

"No Master Trainer, you don't have to choose one, you're free to share both or neither in the same bed if you chose. They not only know how to give man pleasure, they know how to give each other pleasures beyond measurement, Tanizaki-san." Kataoka said smugly.

"Iye!" The old man snapped as he looked at the young women again.

"Hai Master. There's no greater pleasure for a man's eyes to enjoy than to witness one woman bringing sexual pleasure to another woman before him."

"Huh! What have you brought me on this foul day. I had no knowledge a woman would dare bring pleasure to another woman. I can see why this act would bring pleasure to a man's eyes observing it, but how does a man compete against another woman's pillowing capabilities? How can a man bring more pleasure to a woman than another woman can? I know the world of women is a world unto themselves, but if this practice becomes widespread, I fear man will never again know of the pleasures of the Jade Gate women once offered them."

"Huh Master, fear not of this worry. No matter how much pleasure a woman can bring to another woman, there'll be the need of a warm yang to finish off the fire another woman started to burn for him." Kataoka grunted with a smirk plastered and wink of the eye.

"I pray to the gods you're correct with your words, Kataoko-san. Lady Remi! I'll expect you to appear in my home when the fifth bell chimes on this night."

"Hai Master Trainer Tanizaki-san." She purred sexily as she bowed then removed something from the palanquin and scurried to the second building which they took for their use. Her private kagamen remained kneeling by the palanquin bowing to Tanizaki.

"Master Trainer. Why not enjoy both women? Allow the worthless ones to display what they been taught in their years of service at the First Tea House living."

"Ieeeee Kataoka-san! I'm of old age, and fear my heart may not be able to live through the experience you speak about. Iye, I'll live by the old ways and enjoy one woman at a time."

All the time they spoke, neither knew or paid attention to Masahiko standing behind Tanizaki. When he followed the stranger he turned and saw her. "Follow Masahiko!"

The master trainer followed Kataoka to the home of his friend displaced. The kagamen known as heimin or commoners and carriers, were placed in the room together. As he entered the home he had a thought. He decided to allow the samurai sent to guard him and his family, share the building. The warriors would keep the heimin in place and make sure they didn't damage the building on the Shoya, and it would save the warriors from sleeping exposed to the weather. Tanizaki didn't like it when bad weather occurred, because his guards were forced to huddle on the rear porch, or move in the birthing building. This was insulting to the warriors, but he had no choice, he knew he couldn't build a home for his guards.

He placed a warning to the hinin he would not tolerate destruction to this home he knew would be returned to his friend when the kagamen returned to their master, and he wanted it in the same condition it was in when they moved in the home.

Masahiko stayed close to her father's side, she had many questions to ask, and this stranger who showed up in the village caused her concern. She never saw her father speak warmly to a filthy man of the lower class. She shadowed her father, matching his every move and happened to accidentally bump into him not watching where she was walking.

He slapped the child on the side of her head for stepping on his foot. The blow was a glancing one, and the trainer saw the stunned look in her sad eyes. She wasn't shocked by the blow, but she made sure she stayed away from the stranger. He bowed to Kataoka and moved away from him with his child and complained at her.

"Masahiko! Why are your wits rolling out of your ear, child?"

"Father! I don't like this ugly stranger, he's a man who I'd rather dispatch with the edge of my blade than have you speak with him so friendly."

"Huh! And what led you not to like this man, little one with the troubled mind?"

"Father, I don't like what he says to you, and don't like the way he speaks to you. He speaks out of the side of his mouth of things I know nothing of, and speaks like he's trying to get you to do something wrong. Then he'll place you on the wrong side of Kawasomeru-sama, father."

He rested his hand on her head as he explained. "Each day you live shows me the gods are wise to have picked you to be a chosen warrior. I'll never understand why the gods do what they do. Masahiko! It's wise to remain silent and listen to conversations spoken about you. You'll learn more by listening rather than speaking. This stranger will never talk me into doing anything to dishonor or shame our Master. Since when can a manure heap as this, talk a samurai into doing something he doesn't truly want to do?"

"Father, he tries to get you to be with another woman other than mother. Why you would want to do this is beyond my limited knowledge. I'm confused why a man and woman would lay together, and what is the difference between the two." She shifted her weight.

"Ahhh... patience my wild kotora (tiger), soon, you'll learn about why a man and woman lay together in the privacy of the night, little one."

"Father! I want to know the reason now, not later. How am I to learn when I'm told in due time, I'll find out the answers to this puzzling question."

"I'm afraid now is not the time to engage in this conversation. I have visitors I'm being impolite to, because you're wasting my time with these foolish questions, which will need much time to explain to one so young. Stand and be silent, and you'll see wisdom will enter your mind without trying to force it. Empty your mind of worthless thoughts, you must learn to eat time with patience, little one." He glared at his child then turned back to his visitor.

Kataoka smiled at the trainer as he spoke with his child, pleased he would take time to explain what was happening to his young samurai. There was no doubt this child was the trainer's child. He was a mirror image of the old man. It was strange the child was so slight, because the trainer was well filled out, wide shoulders and a thick chest. He thought if this child didn't wear the Aquene hairdo of the samurai, he might think it that of the female sex, but this was impossible. Not even the trainer would dare to train a female in the ways of the samurai.

The stranger shook his head to get these thoughts out of his mind as he turned to the others of his caravan, making sure they knew where they would stay and what was expected of them. Lord Kawasomeru had informed Kataoka it was up to the ninth village to feed them and look after their needs. When he entered the village, he followed his instructions and saw Shoya Sanuki before he appeared before the trainer's home. He handed Sanuki scrolls from Kawasomeru, and waited until the Shoya read his instructions. As the Shoya went about his business of removing the neighbors on either side of Tanizaki's home, he went to meet the trainer.

The kagamen parked the palanquin with the pleasant scenes of Japan's cherry trees in full blossom painted on the sides of them, near the front porch of the home and left one kagaman to remain by it. It was his duty to notify the others if Lady Emiko wanted to go somewhere. The trainer sent a guard to fetch the head samurai, once the guard appeared he informed him he and his men would share this home with the hinin. They would be responsible for the condition of the building when this latest group left the village.

The day disappeared and Tanizaki soon found himself getting hungry, he looked out the window and saw it was getting dark. "Masahiko!" He called out, not seeing the child near him.

The child followed the warriors back and forth like a puppy; she would have done anything to get away from the stranger who spoke so secretively to her father. When she heard her name called by her father, she rushed inside the neighbor's home and replied. "Hai father."

"Masahiko! It's time we go home and leave these people to settled in and rest before we need them." He led the way, followed by Masahiko. Once home, they were fed by the eldest daughter already being helped by Tomotaka, an excellent cook and helper for Emiko. When they finished eating, he checked his wife and stayed with her until he was ran out of the room by Miho, when they had to help Emiko relieve herself.

He drifted to the back porch to enjoy sake, and wanted to watch the stars as they traveled across the sky in their never ending search of the vast universe.

"Father." A soft voice called out tenderly.

"Hai Masahiko. Come and enjoy the night. The stars are the souls of the dead as they rush on their way to their resting place with the gods that soar within the heavens."

She went to her father's side and made herself comfortable on the top step. She stared at the flickering stars and when settled, the trainer informed her. "Masahiko! It's time we begin your training in earnest. The day the last Samurai leave our village we'll begin. I have a feeling it'll be some time before our Lord sends more troops to train. By that time I expect you to be better trained than any foul Warrior who shows up at our village. You have the walk, and the stamina and heart of a Warrior. You'll learn quickly."

She remained silent as she stared at the star studded sky. A shooting star shot across the sky and she cried. "Look father, an angry soul is chasing after an evil spirit."

He saw the shooting star and smiled as he offered. "No Masahiko! That's not an angry soul. It's the heart of a Samurai pursuing the evil spirit. That's why you're so marked on your wrist. The gods mark chosen Warriors to carry out their bidding on earth. You bear the mark of the Samurai on your wrist. Here, give me your arm and I'll show it to you, young one."

She placed her arm in her father's hand and stared at him.

"Ahhh... you see this mark my little one. It's the powerful mark of a shooting star, the gods have marked you so as to give you the speed and strength needed to track down any treachery aimed at your Lord and Master, and eliminate it. You're thus marked on the right hand, the sword hand. The gods gave your sword arm the power to wield a tireless hand when fighting against wrong and evil. They'll watch you to make certain your heart remains pure and just at all times. I have no fear the gods will find honor in your soul and actions." He released her arm after tracing the birthmark with his finger.

She stared at the strange mark she so rarely paid attention to then asked her mentor with concern. "Father! May I ask you more questions, please."

"Hai little one. Now we're speaking like adults, ask of me any question that troubles you."

"Father! Why do women lay with men at nighttime?"

"For comfort and warmth little one with so many questions that shall answer themselves."

"Just for comfort and warmth Father?"

"For comfort, and when the time is right, to make a baby to honor their Lord."

"How do you make a baby, father who knows all worldly things?"

"Ieeeee! You're inquisitive tonight. Why is it necessary for you to know of these things on this night. I wish you'd speak to Estsuko about this, she can explain far better than I." He complained as he cast his eyes back to the heavens.

"Father! I thought it wise on my part if I ask the most intelligent of our family of these matters." She used her best smile on her father, knowing she trapped him and he must answer her. If he told her to see Estsuko, he'd be admitting Estsuko was smarter than he.

He stared at his youngest before replying. "Again I see the teacher learns from the student. I'll offer you this, who do you think the gods favor, the spider or the fly trapped in its web? You successfully trapped me in your question. Remind me I must play a game of Go with you. If you're wise enough to trapped your father who has been trapped by generals on the battlefield and remained alive to speak. Then you're old and wise enough to know of the ways of making babies. Masahiko! When the time is right, the male will stick his water making faucet into the great void of the Jade Gate between the woman's legs, and will pump himself until he spills his life giving essences therein. Then, if the gods will it so, the woman will find herself with child. It's a pleasurable act carried out nearly every day by both man and woman at night."

"Does this mean the woman is always with child?"

"Iye! The women of Japan know certain ways how to defeat man's powerful essences. The ways of the woman are far more wondering than the lives of the worthless gods could ever be."

"Is there a difference between a man and woman, my teacher?"

"Ieeeee yes, thank the gods there is young one."

"Father, what are these differences you speak of?"

"Huh! You'll not tire of asking embarrassing questions of me little child older than your years. There's a difference, man has the ying which fits in the waiting yang of woman."

"Do I have a ying in which to make babies, father?"

"Hai, but you'll not notice your ying until you reached the age of adult." He offered, being quick on his feet to explain the void of the Jade Gate between her legs.

"Father, I was concerned over this problem I've been dealing with of late, because I watched Takeji-san do what he called take a piss. He told me there's no greater experience for a man than to take a good piss. He took a finger from his loincloth and used it to spew water from. I stared at it in wonderment because I know Takeji-san is a male, and he had a stalk to piss from. I don't have one of these fine stalks. I must admit it made it easier for him to piss. He invited me to share a piss with him, but I would have to squat to piss, so I didn't join him for I didn't have to pass water. When I become an adult, will I grow one of these useful stalks to piss from, father?"

He turned serious and grunted in a stern, strong voice. "Masahiko! Under no circumstances should you join any male in enjoying a healthy piss. You must piss in privacy until you reach adulthood. When you become an accepted Samurai enlisted in the army of Kawasomeru-sama, then will I explain the answers to your questions you seek here tonight."

"Father, I'm confused over this, the difference between myself and Takeji-san."

"I order you to leave this subject. All will be explained in good time. I told you I'll explain all to you at Gembuku, until that time you'll have to trust me. This is all I'll say on this subject. I order you to inquire no further on this subject of me, or anyone else from the village. You must obey me and pass water in private, and not allow yourself to be talked into sharing a piss with other Samurai. I further order you not to bathe or disrobe while in the presence of another Warrior. Masahiko! You must trust me on this subject, this I order you."

"Hai father. Though I'm still confused by your order it's understood by me, I need not know your reasons for the orders, I'm just bound by my honor to obey them, father." She grunted in her deepest voice, trying to sound manly yet still remaining confused by her father's orders to display false shame over her body.

"Good Masahiko, good. Are there more questions you feel must be answered by me?"

"Iye father, I'm sorry if I displeased you so by asking you of these questions."

"I'm not displeased little one; on the contrary, I'm happy you came to me before you compromised your situation on this matter." He checked on the position of the moon and knew it was late as he added. "Inquisitive one, it's late and I want to get an early start on tomorrow's training. I'll be losing the foolish Warriors, and I want them as sharp as possible before they leave. It's time you go to sleep."

As if to emphasize his point, the Buddha bell chimed, letting all in the village know it was nine o'clock. He watched as his little one got up and bowed then entered the home without further words. He heard a rustling behind him and stared out to his garden, his hand locked on his sword, his nerves on edge and ready for treachery to befall him. "Huh! Anyone there?"

From out of nowhere, four of Tanizaki's samurai stood by his side, forcing him in their circle as they prepared to defend their master from the shape seen moving in the shadows of the garden.

The trainer tried his best to push his way to the front of his guards, but they refused to move as long as this shape headed for them. The shape stopped moving and a soft almost musical voice replied. "Master Trainer Tanizaki-san! It's I, Lady Remi Yamamoto! I'm following orders of appearing before you at the fifth bell sounding." The shape remained standing in the shadows, fearing to move closer before she was ordered to do so by him and allowed by the guards.

The guards relaxed their posture but refused to break ranks, they allow Tanizaki to move to the front and address this beautiful apparition lurking in the shadows of his garden. He had his sword half drawn as he tried to focus his eyes to see in the darkness.

"Lady Remi! You'll come forward so I may see you clearly."

"Hai Master." The sweet voice replied as she came out of the shadows of the night.

"Stop there woman!" The commanding samurai guard barked viciously.

The trainer didn't trust what was happening and decided to allow his commander to take control of the situation. He wasn't pleased to be forced to take this woman, and hoped the guard would find something wrong with the situation, and stop it from taking place. The trainer watched as the guard stomped down the steps and confronted Lady Remi slowly walking at him.

"Do you have weapons hidden upon your person, woman?" The guard demanded.

"Iye! What do you think I am, a dung eating assassin, stupid fool?" She snapped, her words were laced with venom as she glared at the guard blocking her way. She was dressed in a rich dark green kosode of the finest of silk, the outer garment was held together by the softest of golden silk sash. Her hair was perfect, put in a bun on top of her head, and her lovely face a stark white and lips the reddest of red. Her eyes were circled with black carried well past the eyes to make them look longer, and narrow. She stood perfectly erect with her hands lost inside the oversized sleeve of the exquisite silk kosode.

"I'll search your body, witch of the darkness!" The guard growled.

"Am I now a criminal I must be searched as if I were from the lowly eta class, loathsome pig? I told you worthless dog I have no weapons on my person. I'm no threat to my Master Trainer. I'd defend his life at the cost of mine, and would be honored to do so." She snarled at the guard.

The guard ignored her pleas as he repeated his order. "I'll search your body anyway."

She gave in and automatically placed her hands by her side and waited.

The guard leered at her as he ordered. "Remove your sash, woman!"

She did as ordered and the kosode opened, she was naked underneath and the sight of her beauty caused the guards to draw in their breath and stare in awe at her beauty. The commander stepped forward and pulled the kosode from her body, checking to make certain she had no weapons next to her skin, or behind her back. When he was sure there were no weapons on her, he let go of the fine garment and it wrapped around her body as if it were a second skin. The commander bowed to Remi, and turned to the master and offered.

"Master Trainer Tanizaki-san! Lady Remi is without weapons on her body, and is considered no threat to your health. What is it you want me to do with her? Shall I allow her to approach further, or should I send this worthless lazy woman away?"

As old as he was he was no fool. He saw the gift from the gods that stood before him and slurred his words. "You'll allow Lady Remi to approach. Commander, you say this woman is no threat to my health, I hope the gods will give me strength to survive what this woman has in mind to offer me on this night of wonder and fulfillment."

The guards gave a nervous laugh as they watched the beauty move with the grace of a bee hovering over a flower. She flashed a smile exposing her blackened teeth, adding to her beauty as she looped her obi over the guard's shoulder in defiance, and sashayed past him. She was a master on how to drive men wild with pleasure and anticipation, without allowing them to touch her. She allowed the kosode to open as she climbed the steps, with each movement one of the soldiers could see her charms barely hidden by the richness of fine silk fabric of her kosode.

She stopped a few steps before Tanizaki and dropped to her knees with practiced grace. She looked in the eyes of the trainer, and made the most gracious bow he ever witnessed in his life. She rested her forehead on the porch and held it until he addressed her. The guards were stunned by the honor this woman was addressing the trainer with. It had all the extravagance of the distinguished Tea Ceremony which few Japanese males would witness.

She remained kneeling as she continued to look at the trainer, her kosode opened and fell from her shoulders, her breasts exposed to all. She suffered no false shame of body, she used her body for what it was designed and trained to be. Her weapon. She smiled as she remembered the words of the commanding samurai when he announced she was unarmed. She thought the guard a fool if he couldn't see her true weapons.

Although she was well schooled using the wakizashi, she used her body and easily hidden kogai, the skewers carried in the concealed pocket of the scabbard of the katana, as her chosen weapons. When she was sent on a mission by Kawasomeru, she would use her pin point sharp eight inch ivory skewers as a dressing for her hair as a weapon. Five times did Kawasomeru send her to dispatch his enemy. She accomplished this using her body first then a hidden weapon. Once she used a hair comb to defeat one of her master's enemies by stabbing him in the throat.

He stared at this young beauty, getting lost in the pools of her eyes. He saw the reflection of his face in the ink dark eyes. He could do no more than smile at this most beautiful woman.

She knew she had the old master trainer right where she wanted him, and she purred at him in her sexiest voice. "Master Tanizaki-san! I've been sent as a special gift to you from my Lord and Master, to be enjoyed in any manner you choose. It's my honorable duty to bring you to new heights of pleasure of mind and body. I have been well trained in these areas and will fulfill your wildest dreams on this wonderful night, Master Tanizaki-san." Again, she bowed and held the position of respect while resting her forehead softly on the wood deck.

"Get up and cover yourself Lady Remi! These worthless fools don't deserve to witness your stunning beauty for one moment in time. They are here to protect me and every member of my family. They are not here to look upon such beauty and ignore my safety." He grunted as he rudely dismissed his guards with a wave of his hand.

The beautiful young woman allowed her shoulders to relax a little, yet she held her back ridged and straight. Her hair remained perfect with few strands of jet black hair allowed to blow across her left eye, adding beauty to her presence. She pulled the kosode back up on her shoulders and allowed it to cross appealing over her breasts, but she didn't hold the garment closed, and a few movements of her body, she was exposed again to the old man's eyes.

The samurai guards left the porch when they realized what the two were about to do and made their way out in the garden to make sure no one else would approach the master's home, while he was engaged with the woman. Each guard knew the commander would be furious with them for allowing this woman to approach so close to the master's home, and being detected by the master before any of the guards picked up the woman lurking in the garden shadows. The guards had no way of knowing that Lord Kawasomeru had ordered both Remi and Yukie to test his guards at every twist and turn. He wanted to make certain the trainer and his family's life was well protected. Each guard would lose their heads once she made her report to the master.

"Would you like sake or tea?"

"Tea, but only if you'll allow me to serve you properly my Master." Remi purred.

"You have not been in my home long enough to know where I keep it." He laughed while dismissing her offer.

"I beg to differ with you Master trainer Tanizaki-san. Yes I do. It's my duty to know where everything that brings you pleasure and comfort lay within your honorable home. Please relax and allow me serve you. Please Master Trainer Tanizaki-san, allow me to show you the fine pleasures that await you within my spell I shall cast around your sacred Wa." The Lady Remi pleaded as she smiled at the much older man seated before her.

He could do no more than just nod his head lamely while trying to control his breathing, and stare at this beauty as she shuffled off to retrieve the tea for them.

She reappeared at the rear shoji and then knelt then she placed the tray out before them, opened the shoji door from the side and picked up the tray again and moved it out on the porch. Then she stood and crossed the threshold and knelt again as she picked up the tray once more. Always making sure the porcelain cups or bottle didn't make the slightest sound by clinking together as she moved the tray. She picked up the tray and walked with small steps to the trainer seated on a thick straw mat enjoying the night sky.

She bowed with precise formality and elegance at the old trainer then she placed the tray down the proper distance from the master of the house. She carefully poured him the first cup of tea and offered it to him by holding it respectfully between her thumb and slender index finger. Her fingers always kept away from the rim of the cup. Her other fingers of the hand folded behind the cup, with her other hand she allowed the cup to rest comfortably on three of her extended fingers. At no time did the cup ever break contact with either hand or her fingers. This was done to show the trainer her hands were exposed, and she could not possibly be contemplating any form of evil displayed against his person.

He bowed to the offer of the first cup. At this serving, he nor Remi were better than each other. She had the right to pour the cups full and take the first cup if she wanted, and allow him to take his cup if she so pleased. But she chose to serve him in the proper manner of her training and attention. The tea was sweet and warm, and he enjoyed it as he allowed himself to relax. Her soft sweet voice was like a continuing song being sung to him alone and was very pleasing and comforting to him as well.

The old master trainer had no place to bring her for privacy while they shared each other's charms. Japan offered very little personal privacy and she seemed right at home on the verandah. The samurai guards were nowhere to be seen, and he and Remi knew they would display no bad manners by daring to watch them engaging in their private acts of pillowing with each other, if they so chose to do so on this night.

As he sipped his tea, Remi allowed her kosode to sexually slip away from her shoulders, increasing the urgency locked within his old loins. He couldn't remember the last time he made love to Emiko, but he remembered it was a very strained and unfulfilled coupling. At last he could stand no more and struggled out of his loincloth. All thoughts were locked on what Kataoka had told him of the ways the beautiful women of Engakuji brought man to new heights of sexual passions.

She watched as he struggled, and when he was exposed she sat more erect and took his member in her hands and began to gently stroked and rolled it between them. She moved closer to the old man and drew him in her mouth. His mind saw nothing but shooting stars crossing before his eyes as she gave him this great pleasure. With every wonderful thought of pleasure the master trainer was experiencing, his mind's eye showered his inner mind with shooting stars and a spinning head and clouded eyes. As he prepared to explode in ecstasy, he found himself wondering if the gods were enforcing their will on his subconscious by this display, showing him he was correct to deceive Lord Kawasomeru with his daughter. He smiled and finally succumbed to her well educated tongue and maneuvers, and when he exploded, he saw in his spinning mind a comet flashing before his eyes. Now he was positive he done right by sparing his daughter's life, and prepare her for the journey to what the gods chose for her to experience in her offered short lifetime.

He collapsed in a heap of exhaustion and delight on the verandah, panting like a content dog. He looked at Remi smiling at him. She bowed as she asked. "I trust my new Master enjoyed the pleasure I know and brought to him on this wonderful night?"

"Ieeeee Lady Remi! It was like nothing I experienced. It was pleasure beyond any thought and wonder. It's something that I'll beg be repeated many times in my foul future before I go off to live with the foul gods. It suits me fine, I do no work but receive all the pleasure of the act of pillowing. What more can a lazy man want of life other than another cup of fine tea."

"Ieeeee Master Trainer! Please excuse this worthless old woman's lack of good manner and poor efforts of pleasing you. I deserve to be whipped for failing to carry out my duties for my new Master. I'm ashamed that I have failed to refill your Cha. Forgive my unworthy try at pleasing you. I should shave my worthless head and follow the Shinto priests as they wallow in mud and filth of Japan, as punishment for my failures, it was my fault." She was thoroughly embarrassed he had to ask for his cup to be refilled. She quickly refilled it and offered it in the same polite manner as before.

The old and sexually exhausted master trainer smiled, he could do nothing but smile, he was pleased beyond happiness at this new experience he witnessed by this stunning beauty. After letting out a breath held since she first began her to perform her act with him, he finally said. "Lady Remi! If only all who insulted me in my worthless lifetime were able to give me such incredible pleasures. I'd be the happiest man in the world of all gods and their unbelievable myths. You have not insulted me in any fashion, on the contrary Remi, you have honored me more than I ever been honored before in my worthless life, woman."

The proud young woman covered her mouth with an exquisite fan she produced from the over sleeve of her kosode, and fluttered it quickly before her mouth to cover her smile, she was as pleased as the trainer was over this night's experiences. She had succeeded on her lord and master's orders, and gave good health back to one of his trusted wards. She poured herself another cup of tea, and enjoyed it with her new master as they spoke quietly, and shared the wonders of the night sky.

"Lady Remi! I'll have the old seer's room completed within the next week's time, and you'll then move in the room in his place. Hachirobe-san will be moved to the main house in order to enable him to better look after my sickly wife. I'll spend my nights with you until Emiko is well enough to assume her wifely duties for my household."

"Master Trainer Tanizaki-san! You honor me too much by your kind offer to pillow with me every night I'm here to share them with you. I'm unworthy to live under your generous though. That's too much an honor for me to endure."

"Nonsense Lady Remi! You're a most honorable and well behaved woman who would be less honored by living under my worthless roof I fear. Huh! You should be living in a Castle of your own, and you should be surrounded by your own horde of loyal vassals and samurai to serve your every want, needs and protection." The pleased master trainer offered as he bowed to the woman kneeling on the deck by him as he stood, it was late and he was exhausted and all he wanted to do at this time, was to turn in for the night and get rest.

"Master Trainer Tanizaki-san! I shall return to my building until my offered room is finished constructed by your fine workers. The next time that you seek any pleasure of the body and soul, may this unworthy old woman suggest that you try the treasures of the lovely Lady Yukie and her outstanding skills at the art of pillowing with you. She's younger and far less experienced than I, but has her own most unique ways of giving certain pleasure to a man she wishes to please which this useless woman could not possibly master herself to employ. If you'd like Master Trainer, I'd be most pleased to attend your pillowing with Lady Yukie to make certain that the child performs well for your pleasure and entertainment, Master Trainer. I'll even offer to help her give you far more pleasures than just one woman could ever offer one man, Master." She bowed graciously to the trainer as she pulled up her kosode and held it together with her hand before him as she smiled pleasantly.

The old man ignored her words on this wonderful night as he turned from her and entered the door to his home, and pulled the shoji screen closed behind without further words. The old man was tired of the words he heard or spoke, and of the pressures placed on his aching, exhausted shoulders with his wife's illness, and the never ending training of the samurai army sent to him by Lord Kawasomeru. Along with the terrible deceit he was playing out against his powerful Lord Kawasomeru and his realm.

The old master trainer understood well that his life would be over once the great deception he was offering his lord and master was discovered, and he was called before the powerful warlord to explain his deplorable actions played out against him. He was confused by the people who showed up unannounced in his village, invading the privacy of his home and personal business and of the village and people. He was battling the troubling thoughts as to why two such beautiful young women who would normally have the pick of any fine young samurai or person of great worth to pick from to pillow with. Would want to waste their outstanding pillowing abilities on the likes of him.

The wise master trainer did not deceive himself in the least, because he was well aware he was an old man with a extremely short and angry temper, and he was not much to look either, and his days were numbered of him living on the earth. His face was wrinkled and terribly scared by countless years of battles, and his life giving snake came at the drop of a hat now, and was no longer able to bring great satisfaction to a woman before he was done pillowing her. He was also having trouble making his once mighty snake grow to the strength he needed to enter a woman's Jade gate as well. He felt his days were fast coming to an end.

He knew he was no prize to capture for any woman to share her bedroll with. And suddenly he was surrounded by two very beautiful young women, both willing to display before him their outstanding abilities of their act of making love to a foolish old man. Try and he might, he just could not understand why Karma was working out so well in his favor all of a sudden.

CHAPTER THIRTEEN

Master Trainer Tanizaki was up early and was full of a new energy from his sexual experience of the night before. Adding to his energy was the fact that he was anxious to get to the field of training. Today was the day he would release the well trained samurai so they could return to Engakuji Castle, and join Lord Kawasomeru's army. He was relying heavily on Kataoka's words that no new samurai would be showing up at the village for an extended time. He would put this time and energies to good use by starting Masahiko's training.

The noise created by him looking for his katana, and other pieces of his armor and other equipment he brought home, stirred the guards and they were ready to leave by the time he exited his home. He didn't bother wake Masahiko, but when he turned he was surprised to discover the child standing behind him, dressed in her light travel kosode and wide sash. The wakizashi, which she was using for the fighting sword until she could master the heavier weight of the larger katana, was tucked properly in the sash in the correct position. The child crooked her head to her father when she noticed his eyes on her.

"Masahiko! You'll stand by my left and attend me, lazy child. You should've been outside and had my worthless samurai guards prepare to leave before I had to see to it myself , young one. Come, I have Samurai waiting and your laziness is costing me valuable time." He tapped his leg and she scooted to his side, and got in step with her father.

The march to the training field was completed in silence. He smiled when he noticed General Kobayashi was standing at the head of the horse field. He was flanked by General Shimbo, scheduled to march the samurai to Engakuji Castle. General Miyamoto was on his other side, a commander for Lord Anjoh of Kozuke province. General Miyamoto was going to stay on and assist with the fourth group of warriors to be trained.

The trainer stopped just out of sword range of the generals and bowed. The six guards also bowed to the generals. From the corner of his eye, he saw Masahiko bent in a nod. He looked at Kobayashi who stood erect. "Tanizaki-san! Your troops await your presence."

"HAI!" He grunted in his deepest commanding voice, as he marched before the three officers onto the horse training field. It was the only area large enough where all trainees could stand in formation, and wait to be addressed by their trainer, and see what he had to offer.

The trainer marched to the raised sand mound which lifted him over the soldier's height. His guards surrounded the mound, and Masahiko stood by his left. She would stand there until ordered to do otherwise by her father. He looked over the warriors dressed in battle helmets and armor, swords protruding threateningly from their sashes, and a stack of arrows sticking over their shoulders. The seven foot bows held in their hands three inches from the end of the bow to the ground. They were standing at attention before him.

The old trainer's chest swelled with pride as he looked over the young faces of the samurai sure to do him proud on the future battlefield. He knew Lord Kawasomeru would be overjoyed at his army's warring abilities. This group was the best he trained so far. He took a fan from the sleeve and snapped it open with a quick shake while raising his foot high in the same motion as he grunted loudly. "Ooooyyyyaaaa! Ooooyyyyaaaa! Ooooyyyyaaaa!"

A cheer rose from the ranks of samurai as they repeated his call to battle. Many warriors rapped on their shields to add to the fever of the moment.

Villagers who chose to witness the spectacle of releasing the warriors from their training, added voices to those of the warriors caught up in the fever of the moment themselves.

He took an arrow with a Sasa no ha (a bamboo leaf shaped head) tip and held it high and said to the warriors. "This arrow is the symbol of your Master Trainer. It's the weapon that'll bring down all who seek treachery against Kawasomeru-sama. From this day forward, the Master's life is in your hands. A moment of lackadaisical attention might cause the death of Lord Kawasomeru at the hands of those who wish him harm. In your hands lays the future of the realm, you must protect our Lord's life, and his realm with the last breath in your worthless bodies. I sought to train you warriors in the ways of combat and protection of our Master. If anything happens to him while he's under your protection, would mean I failed, and I'd be forced to answer with my life to atone for your failure. I warn you before I go to the world of gods, I'll make sure you, your families and ancestors will precede me to the world of forever floating. I'll not accept failure and neither shall you."

The cheer arose again, louder with the warriors growing fanatical in the response to the trainer's words. To his right was a table with papers. General Kobayashi and General Shimbo worked their way to the table, each holding a tanto blade unsheathed.

The trainer drew the warrior's attention to the generals and said. "I know when each of you march to Engakuji Castle, you'll swear an oath to Kawasomeru-sama. Before I allow you fools to leave my field, I expect each of you to swear kishomon, a written oath to me. It'll be sworn and sealed by Keppan, the blood from the index finger of the sword hand which will be placed on the paper. I'll begin this oath by having my Yabusame, mounted archers, begin the swearing."

Without a word or warning, Masahiko darted from the mound and rushed to the table first, and held out her unwavering finger proudly.

General Kobayashi glanced to the trainer who had a hard time not staring at his child standing before the overpowering general with her hand extended. He fought for control and nodded yes, his chest expanded with pride for the young Masahiko.

The proud General Kobayashi took a second to write down Masahiko Tanizaki's name on the top of the list of samurai. When he finished, he raised the blade and drew it across the index finger of the young child. Not a peep of pain came from the child's lips as she allowed the finger to bleed before pressing it to the paper next to her name. The general announced the warrior's name for all to hear.

"Young Samurai Masahiko Tanizaki, swears blood oath to Lord Kawasomeru's service and protection from treachery."

Massive Taiko drums beat out their praise, as four warriors beat on them. A roar rose from the warriors as they cheered the child's action.

Tanizaki grunted as he held his hand aloft. "Iye! The young Samurai's name is not Masahiko Tanizaki. The Warrior's name is Masahiko-san, proud Warrior of Kawasomeru-sama."

She stared at her father proudly then gave him her most elaborate bow ever.

More war cries joined with the cheering of the warriors as they whipped themselves into a wild frenzy over the honor the child offered her father. The horse warriors dismounted, and spearmen moved forward to maintain control of their horses while they signed the oath. As each warrior was cut, a cheer rose from the other warriors. The excitement grew with each bleeding.

The equally proud young Masahiko rushed back to her father's side on the mound, and resumed her position by his side. It was to the left, the right was the sword side, and no warrior would dare interfere with another warrior's sword hand.

The two remained standing and silent until each warrior affixed their names to the oath to their master trainer, and their names announced by General Kobayashi to the warriors. It took most of the day to complete. When it was done, Tanizaki allowed General Shimbo to assume control over his trainees for the rest of the day.

General Shimbo grunted in a deep, booming voice for the horsemen to assume the lead of the growing column of samurai, they were followed by the spearmen then archers and the rest of the trainees. The warriors lined up in rows of five across, with each field commander separating the different classes of warriors from the others. The lead was covered by the highest ranking officers of the column, and General Shimbo was to assume the head of the massive column of warriors, and the few women who served the warriors while they were being trained.

The himin and lesser support members of the army were to remain in the village, they would clean the mock battlefields and abandoned living quarters, making them ready for the next army of samurai sent from Kawasomeru, to be trained in the ninth village by Master Trainer Tanizaki.

Shimbo remained standing with Tanizaki, Kobayashi and Miyamoto until the warriors were in formation then he snap mounted his war horse. He bowed to the trainer while swinging his arm out then swiftly rode to the head of the column. With a roar from the troops, the column began their long trek to Engakuji Castle. When the last warriors left the field, Tanizaki and Kobayashi allowed themselves to relax. Miyamoto requested and received permission to leave the field. The general found a romantic interest and couldn't get enough of the young woman. It was the reason Tanizaki requested he remain to help with the future training of the next batch of samurai.

The trainer plopped down and sat on the mound, wiping sweat from his eyes with his sleeve. He looked in the eyes of his child and offered. "Masahiko-san! I told you I'd not address you with the honor of 'San' until you earned the right. Today my young pup, you earned this honor. You done the honorable thing by adding your name to the top of the list of Warriors swearing the oath in blood. I know Kawasomeru-sama will be honored when he sees your name topping the list. Word of your deed will precede the column, and Shimbo-san will reinforce your honorable deed with our

Master. He'll be proud you chose to take the oath at such a young age."

"Thank you father! I'm honored by your words. Father, you look tired, exhausted on this wonderful day, would you like me to get you something to drink or eat?"

"Iye! I'm fine little Warrior of future times. I'm looking forward to tomorrow, and tomorrow's tomorrow. I'll begin your training on the field of learning tomorrow. I'll issue you your first katana, little pup. It's time you learn the weight and length of the blade your life will depend on. I'll have General Kobayashi-san cut a horse loose for your needs. It'll be your horse for life, a faithful Samurai will take better care of his horses' needs before his worthless desires. I don't know how long I'll have to donate my time to your training, but I intend to make the most of the days until the next Samurai appear in the Ninth Village for training."

He took a breath, the master's legs were cramping up giving him much pain of late. It was one of the longest times he remained on his feet in a long time. He looked to the sky to determine what time it was, it was overcast so he guessed it was past three.

Kobayashi knew what the trainer was doing and said, "Master Trainer Tanizaki-san! It's nearer to four, heading for five. I suggest we end this day and begin anew tomorrow."

"Hai!" The old man mumbled at his general and long time friend.

"Master Trainer Tanizaki-san! What time do you want to begin the training of your child?"

"Seven in the morning will be early enough to begin the training of the young one I believe."

"Hai! It's supposed to rain heavily later on today according to my wife's mother who claims to be able to tell the weather by the aches and pains that plague her old bones of late." The grinning general announce to the master trainer.

"I believe her General Kobayashi-san, because my old and aching bones are speaking angrily to me. It'll be fine to begin Masahiko-san's training in the rain. A true Warrior can't choose days or whether he's required to fight for his Master's name. A Warrior can and should fight in mud and snow if demanded of him." He placed his hands on his legs and pushed up, helping himself to stand. "It's late and I'm hungry."

The trio headed for home, followed by the six samurai guards.

Tanizaki ate early then rested on the back verandah, watching the sun as it sought its resting place behind the mountains for the night's sleep. The peepers began their usual night cries for their mates. Incense burned, helping to keep the mosquitoes away. The young Masahiko turned in and he checked on his wife showing signs of regaining some strength. Estsuko hovered by her mother's side like a protective mother, and the construction workers stopped work on the extension that would soon house Remi, his consort.

The aged trainer looked to see what the workers accomplished, they had the roof in place and walls closed in. The raised floor was in place and few remaining chores had to be accomplished, before Remi could move in the new room. He saw the room was large enough for Remi's needs, and decided to allow Yukie to also move in with her.

Enko, the master trainer's youngest daughter came outside with a bottle of warm sake and a cup and placed it at her father's side. Then she offered to pour a cup for her father, but he waved her off with a flip of his hand. He was in no mood to start drinking this late, he felt he was drinking too much lately, and decided to lay off the drink. He thanked his daughter for the courtesy, and the child disappeared in the main house.

The trainer daydreamed while looking at the enchanting night sky when he heard the slight rustling of the garden plants. He smiled as he called out. "Lady Remi?"

"Iye Master. It is I, Yukie. Master Trainer Tanizaki-san, Lady Remi instructed me it was my turn to bring pleasure to you on this warm and friendly night. May I approach my Master please?" She asked of her new master politely.

"Hai."

She strolled out from the shadows as if a ghost in search of souls to devour. She moved silently through the garden until she stood by the bottom step of the verandah. The guards paid little attention to the girl as she prepared to be searched as Lady Remi warned her. She untied her sash and allowed it to loop onto one arm. Then she took hold of the two ends of the bright yellow kosode and pulled it apart, exposing her nakedness to the guards. Each man stared with their mouths open, she was a true beauty.

She possessed slightly larger breasts than Remi which gave her greater standing in the world and art of pillowing. Her waist was so narrow it almost didn't exist, and her rearend was small, perfect, her beauty was complimented by long slender legs and small feet. This was evident to all as she turned in her kosode, so the guards could see every inch of her nakedness. Her hair was silken black, worn like the rich women of Japan, long in the back reaching to the bottom of her rearend, and short in the front with the ends barely covering the tips of her breasts, with strands of hair hanging across her face and neck, adding to her outstanding beauty and presence.

A breeze made her hair move, giving an appearance of a living thing, and her hair surrounded her face as if it was a black halo about her. Her face was painted stark white which made her hair look blacker. Her eyes were lined by black thin paint. A hair bun complimented her head. She was tall for any Japanese person, especially a woman, she stood nearly five foot seven.

The trainer grunted a string of unintelligible words at the guards who got the message and filed away from the porch. Then they disappeared in the garden to resume their vigil of guarding him. They were aware of the female's presence and she was checked for weapons by the commander. This is why she was allowed to approach the trainer without challenge.

She saw the bamboo tray and bottle of sake, and bowed as she went to her knees before the tray and began to pour the sake for them. She offered the first cup to Tanizaki who took it and rested it on the deck of the porch. She bowed and chuckled as she sipped her wine. She paid little attention he didn't share his drink with her. Her heart was beating fast, she was scared, and this was the first time she was allowed to pillow with a person of high standing and respect. It was certain to increase her wealth ten times fold to the First Tea House and her Mama-san, she couldn't wait to please her new master on this night.

Remi followed Yukie to the garden, but remained out of sight to observe her ways of giving pleasure to their master. She was acknowledged by the commander of the samurai, and allowed to wait in the garden once she explained why she was there. Her eyes drifted to the extension of the home and smiled, she knew it would be completed by week's end.

He was so exhausted he had little interest in sex, but when she allowed her kosode to fall from her shoulders and rest on her arms, his interest grew. They talked for a while, with the trainer getting lost in the sweet sound of her voice. When the time was right, she invited him to remove his loincloth. The act was repeated with a new sensation, she used her tongue far more and skillfully than Remi. When the act was completed, Lady Yukie remained and spoke with the trainer for hours, both were lost in the pleasantry of the warm night.

Remi watched everything she did to the trainer, judging and rating her every action, and when she felt it was the proper time, she made a sound of a bird calling for its mate. Yukie's young ears picked it up and she stood. She bowed to Tanizaki and made her excuses and shuffled off the porch, barely making a sound as she left the trainer behind.

He fell asleep on the porch, he didn't like the strange women in his home. Masahiko woke, saw her father on the thick straw mat and covered him with a cotton blanket. As warm as it was during the day hours, the night was too cool to sleep outside without a cover.

The trainer paid for sleeping on the wood deck, when he woke he had to roll on his side to get to his feet. Every bone in his aged body ached, and there was a light mist falling, adding to the pain raging in his bones. He entered his home and saw a morning meal laid out for his pleasure. He checked Emiko sleeping peacefully and decided not to wake her before leaving for the field. He went to the kitchen and ate the foods prepared by Tomotaka and his daughter.

Estsuko hovered over her father like a butterfly would a blossom to sip its nectar. He acknowledged her presence with a loud grunted. "Estsuko! It's time you wake that good for nothing Masahiko. I'm ready to go, and the lazy child's tardiness cost the child the right to eat her morning meal. It'll be a good lesson for the child to learn."

Estsuko bowed to her father as she offered. "Father. Masahiko-san has already ate and is waiting outside for you with the Samurai."

He did his best to hide his surprise, and didn't look at his daughter further. Again, he was pleased with Masahiko acting like an adult, a samurai. The trainer got up and wiped his mouth, then bowed to his daughter and left without words. Outside, he barely acknowledged the child as he grunted orders to his guards, and finally turned to Masahiko and ordered her to remove her takaashidas, the higher wood clogs usually worn in bad weather.

Without complaint she removed the shoes and placed them on the standing stone. She was dressed in a yu katabira, a light cotton kosode which offered some warmth when it rained.

The trainer and Masahiko waited for Kobayashi to join them and then they headed for the field with Masahiko following last, trudging through the mud in her bare feet. He began with them gathered at the mound and he explained, a samurai would fight under the most pressing circumstances, such as food deprivation and exposure to the cold and weather conditions. "A worthy Samurai should fight for his Master under the worse of conditions and prevail. Such tests I'll put you through in the next weeks might be considered efficacious tests of endurance. These tests will shape the value of valor in your body for future use." Without another word he turned from Masahiko and spoke with Kobayashi. She remained where she stood, she was afraid to move without being ordered by her father. A clap of thunder sounded and the heavens opened in a deluge, She was unable to see a few feet in front of her as she waited for orders.

He turned back and growled. "Masahiko-san! The code of Samurai is called Bushido. It's the code of collected laws of ideas and manners of ethics and beliefs woven from different threads of ideas and thoughts, with one purpose in mind. To place oneself in harmony with the absolute. Obedience to our Master and his health are our only concern. Our lives mean nothing without our Master's wisdom. Today's training will be short and incomplete, tomorrow I'll take you to witness a public suppuku, the highest honor any Samurai can display for his Master to witness."

Tanizaki waited until the child was soaking wet and weighted down by the soaked kosode, and then made her go through some easy hand to hand combat maneuvers against the wind whipping up with force. Once she accomplished this and without warning, General Kobayashi made a wild charge at her, trying to capture her off balance. It didn't work, she easily picked up the movement and dodged the charge of the general.

The wise general noticed she detected his move and he tried to correct his charge against her in mid motion, so he could complete his quick attack on her. He suddenly slid on the mud and went tumbling in a mess of water, mud and curses.

Masahiko being the child she was, laughed at General Kobayashi covered head to toe with mud. Her laughter brought her a swift slap on the back, and the wetness of her kosode made the blow sting all the more, she dared not rub it as she turned to see why her father struck her so.

"Laughter is the weakness of a foolish child. Masahiko! Are you still a foolish child acting like a Samurai? Laughing at your enemy who failed in his attempt to overtake you, is the height of bad manners and stupidity. It'll never be done again do you understand? Masahiko-san! You must remember to honor your enemy. You're to be proud of your enemy then your success over that enemy is your success to enjoy. The virtues, including valor and honor demand we, the victors, own our enemies in war, so we can prove to ourselves the worth of being friends when the wars ended, and Japan is once again at peace with all her children."

She bowed to her father, her back still stinging from the sharp blow.

"Young child, it's not I you insulted, therefore it is not I you should apologize to."

"Wakarimasu, I understand father." She bowed to General Kobayashi who was struggling to his feet. The child had to order her mind not to laugh as the mud covered warrior shook the mud from his body in much the same manner a dog dries itself.

The trainer was aware it was raining harder than moments before, and in the interest of not having anyone slip and get hurt on the mud, he ended this day's training. On the way home, she bothered him about the suppuku she would witness the following morning. Her father ignored the childish questions by replying. "All your inquisitive interrogations will be answered when you witness the suppuku, foolish pup." The trainer informed he it was an honor bestowed on her by this warrior committing suppuku. He told her it took many talks to get the warrior's permission, for her to be allowed to attend this ceremony of respect.

The night was uneventful, neither consorts were requested by the trainer, and he had his first full night's sleep in days. He was beginning to enjoy sleeping on the verandah, it reminded him of old days when he slept under the stars preparing his mind and soul for battles of tomorrow. He had Estsuko bring two tatami mats and cover them with silk cloth. A silk covered block of wood was used as a pillow. The May nights were warmer than usual, and he enjoyed sleeping away from the women. The roof kept him dry when the night rains came, unless the wind blew from the south. Then he was forced to move in the house or be soaked.

To his surprise, some guards took to sleeping on the verandah with him, adding to the security he enjoyed wrapped around him. It was no secret to anyone in Shinano province, Wakatsuki placed a bounty on his head, and all members of his family. The enemy warlord wanted to cripple Lord Kawasomeru's army in any manner he could, and the best way to attack a strong army, was by attacking the trainers of that army. It was known a snake without a head, was a snake about to die, no matter how much the body wiggled and threatened and tried to survive.

He was woke by the first glimmers of sunlight disturbing his sleep. He moaned as he rolled on his side, and placed his hands on the deck and pushed himself to stand. He was tempted to take a hot bath to soften his aching joints for the day's work ahead, but decided against this pleasure when he noticed Masahiko was moving around the home. With another sigh, he entered the house and sat and waited to be served by Miho preparing morning meal for him and his family.

The trainer growled at Masahiko moving about like a shooting star filled with the energy of anticipation for the sacred of ceremonies. She couldn't sit still until her father yelled at her. She sat and stared at her morning meal, unable to eat.

He smiled as he enjoyed his meal, appreciating what the child must be going through. He remembered the first time he was invited by his father to witness suppuku. It was a sight that never left his mind since. In times of trouble and worry, he would remember the strength displayed by the one about to leave the world on his last voyage to the Floating World by his hand. The memory gave him strength to see him through his problems.

The old man was picking at his food as his mind wandered through the days that occurred, and the lessons he learned from the experiences he lived and fought through. The old master found himself hoping he could make Masahiko learn from his countless past victories and experiences and mistakes. He looked at the child again and realized he better take the child from the table before he ended up insulting Miho, by not eating what she prepared. That would be all he needed, to be forced to calm down a female who didn't want to be at peace. With a groan he pushed from the table and growled. "Come Masahiko-san! It's time we leave, a true Warrior could go days without eating a proper meal and be ready to engage the enemy, and a Samurai must learn to eat food from an empty table to master his hunger."

He gave Miho the excuse for the child not eating before she noticed the insult.

She stopped what she was doing and turned to the master and his ward, and bowed as they left. Both warriors barely took notice of the bow, and it was Masahiko who took a second to return it. The bow was so quick and weak it bordered on politeness or insult.

When the master trainer walked out the door he was surprised to see General Kobayashi kneeling on the ground in front of his home. All seven warriors bowed on seeing the trainer who returned their bow that was more of a nod while standing.

The general grunted from his kneeling position. "Master Trainer Tanizaki-san! Last night it was brought to my attention the suppuku was to be put off until two bells."

He couldn't hide his anger over the change in time the condemned was to kill himself. "Huh! What's wrong with this dung heap? Does he not understand the correct time to commit suppuku is during the first hour of the light of day, if the act is ordered by his Master? Or suppuku is to take place at the last light of day if ordered to be committed because of an infraction that goes against Bushido. I was lead to believe this worthless soul was ordered to commit suppuku by Kawasomeru-sama. What's the excuse for the delay in the act? What does his second have to say of the delay? If it's improper, I'll order the second to commit suppuku for allowing this Warrior to delay the order. The maggot eaten fool has dishonored the sacred act of acts."

The general bowed again to the trainer who, along with Shoya Sanuki was the only two in the village with the power to order a suppuku without argument. He rested his forehead on the ground while formulating his next words he was going to offer to the trainer.

He allowed his temper to rule his mind as he growled. "General Kobayashi-san! I asked you for an explanation for the delay in the act by this dung heap of a criminal! If there's none to be offered by the condemned fool then it's your duty to put the suppuku back on track, and inform the second I ordered him to fall on his sword at the feet of the criminal."

He lifted his head and made his face passive. "Master Trainer! It was ordered by Kawasomeru-sama to delay the act until his representatives arrived in the village to observe it, so he could report to our Lord of the event, and how honorably it was carried out."

"Huh General Kobayashi-san!" He grunted. "You should've added these words in your original report to avoid my getting upset over this matter. Of course, if our Master chose to delay this act, it's within his power to do so. It's only the criminal who is losing face by the delay, General. Where is this representative arriving in our village from?"

"He's coming from the Eleventh Village and should be arriving in two feathers of time."

"Is this worthless soul going to carry out his act at the foot of the Lord Buddha Shrine?"

"Hai Tanizaki-san!" The general replied as he stood up and aligned his back.

"Taihen yoi. Very good I believe we should get there early, I want Masahiko-san to be in a good place to observe the actions of this noble act." He started out, followed by Kobayashi, Masahiko and his guards. Masahiko broke ranks and rushed forward until she walked alongside her father stride for stride. She assumed the pompous stride of all samurai when walking.

The walk was a long one, the ancient Buddha Shrine was at the far end of the village, and the day was showing signs of being warm and humid, with a mist threatening to fall. By the time they reached the shrine, there were a number of villagers assembled. The trainer scanned the faces until he saw Sanuki who nodded at him. He walked until he reached the Shoya who bowed to the group, but ignored Masahiko. He was trying to keep his distance from the child, because he didn't want to be implicated in the deceit the trainer carried out against Lord Kawasomeru.

The trainer noticed the insult, but decided to let it pass without challenge.

"Tanizaki-san! I'd deem it an honor if you'd share my humble position, so you can observe this honorable act." Sanuki offered with a bow of his head, and wave of the hand.

"Hai." Tanizaki allowed himself to be led to his position by the bothersome Shoya. The area was covered by a number thin tatami resting mats for kneeling while the witnesses waited for the condemned one to make his appearance. "Who is the criminal's kaishaku?" He snapped at Sanuki. Kasihahu was the Japanese word which best described the actions of an executioner.

"Ahhh... the worthless one chose Captain Tabata-san as his second! He's assured of having his head separated from his insulting body with one swipe of his sword, many heads have felt the sharpness of his blade. It was a wise pick, for Tabata-san is well noted for his swordsmanship, at least his wits have not fled his foul mind."

The trainer made himself as comfortable as possible under the circumstances then signaled for Masahiko to join him on the next mat. General Kobayashi knelt beside Masahiko. He pointed out the different items set about the raised platform that would be needed by the condemned man. He explained everything in whispers to avoid disturbing the other witnesses.

Sanuki joined the trainer and listened to his words of explanation aimed at Masahiko. The witnesses knelt for an hour before movement began behind the curtains. Many witnesses became edgy over the long delay, but when they noticed the movement they settled down.

The witness sent by Lord Kawasomeru took his place on the platform sitting on a chair with no back. Dressed in armor and helmet, his no tachi hung from his hip and stuck out behind him. The witness sat with his legs apart and hands on his legs, he was hunched forward and looked like he was ready to attack everyone. He was obviously in a foul mood. Sweat rolled down his face, and the other witnesses could tell the warrior was extremely uncomfortable.

Silence was observed by all attending the ceremony from this point forward.

A second samurai walked out from behind the curtains. It was easy to tell the man was a samurai by the way he walked and held himself. No one knew the reason why the condemned one was ordered to commit suppuku, rumor was told the soldier had the misfortune to fall asleep on duty, and was discovered by one of the field lieutenants.

The warrior walked to the military witness and bowed. The witness barely took notice of the bow or the other man, he just continued to stare straight forward as if the condemned soldier wasn't standing before him. It was the height of bad manners for an appointed witness to honor a condemned man by acknowledging his presence before he committed suicide, for fear his soul might be dragged off with the condemned one. The condemned warrior turned from the witness and bowed to his second, Captain Tabata.

Tabata returned the bow graciously then placed his right hand on the hilt of the sword and drew it out slowly. A second warrior washed the blade with pure spring water, allowing the water to run the full length of the blade, and dribble onto the platform from the end of the blade. The captain rolled the blade over to show the condemned one the water washed the blade on both sides. He nodded his approval to the captain. The warrior then turned to the crowd, bowed and held it for a moment. His second followed his every move.

Everyone returned the salutation as ceremoniously as they were saluted by the condemned once samurai and his second. Slowly, and with profuse dignity, the condemned warrior placed his foot on the platform, remembering to keep his back straight and movements short, precise, proud and sharp. As he mounted the platform, all eyes watched his every move. Once he was on the platform, he bowed to the four winds from the north, south, east and west. When this was done, the warrior knelt on the plain white thin tatami mat spreading his legs. He seated himself in the Japanese fashion with his knees and toes touching the platform with the rest of his body resting its weight on his heels. In this position his body would be forced to remain locked in the honored seated position even in death. It was the accepted position of respect and honor to carry out the sacred act properly. The condemned one sat with his back to the south, and looked to his north to Lord Kawasomeru's castle. It was believed if the master decided to stop what he was doing and stared, he would see the warrior's actions.

In front of the condemned warrior rested a single sheet of rice paper, and laid upon that was a short wakizashi stabbing sword. This wakizashi was differently shape than the regular wakizashi blade carried as a second blade by the samurai. This blade came to a sharp point, and measured nine inches of cutting sword. The edge of the sword was as sharp as a razor, and was thoroughly washed in the purest of water from a fast running stream nearby.

The condemned samurai picked up the gleaming blade and held it aloft for all to see, and mumbled words no one heard. Then he tapped the blade to his forehead twice, and returned it to the rice paper mat. He examined the faces staring at him and explained. "I'm an unworthy Samurai, I dishonored my Lord in his time of need. I was foolish enough to fall asleep on guard duty, and placed my Master's life in danger. While I slept peacefully, his enemies would've been able to sneak by me and kill my Liege Lord while he rested for the night.

"Although I'm unworthy to be allowed to die as an honored Samurai, my merciful Master saw fit to allow me this honor. For my crime of placing my Master's life in danger, I disembowel myself before my friends and enemy alike. I beg all assembled to witness my act of obedience offered to my Lord, and hope this will make amends for my lack of attention to his safety."

Bowing to his witnesses, he allowed his kosode to slide down his arms and he pulled his arms out of the sleeves as if he was the center of a blossoming flower and was naked from the waist up. The condemned warrior tucked the sleeves of his kosode under his knees to prevent his body from falling back in death spasms. All this was carried out according to customs, and was to make sure he died a gentleman's death by falling forward.

Deliberately, the samurai picked up the gleaming blade and looked at it almost affectionately for a moment, as he wrapped the second sheet of rice paper carefully around the blade in order to protect his hands from the sharpness of the knife. Then he stopped his movement and it seemed to the witnesses that the warrior might have been collecting his thoughts and summoning up his naijo, his inner help. With a loud grunt, the warrior stabbed himself in the lower left side of his stomach, and slowly drew the blade across his belly towards the right. While he was slicing himself open, he grunted and spittle and blood dribbled from his mouth as he turned the small blade in the wound then gave an upwards cut.

During this procedure, the warrior tried not to move his facial muscles, he had to show the witnesses he was in command of the act. When the dying man withdrew the blade from his guts, he leaned forward as his innards spilled from the gaping wound, and landed on the rice paper mat. In one motion, he stretched his neck as far as he could and for the first time, a sign of pain swept his body as his innards seeped between his fingers, yet still didn't utter a cry.

At this moment, his second, his kaishaku kneeling on a knee watching to make certain the warrior carried out his duties, sprang to his feet and lifted the sword overhead, with his hands wrapped around the hilt of the blade. Then, with a silver flash the sword sliced through the air then flesh and bone and the head of the condemned one rolled free. After a sickening thud, the severed head rolled across the platform for several feet before coming to rest.

A stunned silence gripped the witnesses as they viewed the dying man's death dance, the only sound heard, was the blood pumping through the severed veins of the body moments before was a living, brave and chivalrous samurai.

The dead man's second bowed to the crowd then wiped his blade free of blood with another piece of rice paper. He went to the head and picked it up and brushed the hair in place. He showed the samurai in armor the severed head. The warrior bowed to the head then the second retired carrying the head to the women who would prepare it for private viewing by the master.

The invited warrior got up with a grunt, and purposefully walked to the body and callously shoved it aside with his foot then picked up the blood covered wakizashi and placed it in a silk sleeve to be carried to Kawasomeru to show proof his order was carried out by the warrior.

Tanizaki swallowed and hawked and spat on the ground as if he was angered over the act carried out by the criminal. He leaned close to Masahiko and grumbled at the child.

"He'll be reborn a great and honorable warrior at the time of his rebirth."

All kneeling behind the master trainer heard his words, and grunted their agreement and approval at how honorable the warrior ended his life as ordered.

General Kobayashi rose and ordered the hemin to remove the body quickly, which would be brought to the outskirts of the village and placed on a funeral pyre. Once burned the ashes would be scattered to the four winds. The head of the warrior would be kept until it rotted then placed on a tip of a spear and the birds allowed to pick the bone clean.

The master trainer stretched while Masahiko kind of hid behind him, she was scared to death at what she just witnessed. But something inside her was proud of what the samurai done. She questioned herself, wondering if she would have the strength to follow her master's orders as proudly as this samurai did, if ordered to do so.

He felt the fear in her shaking body, and leaned out his leg so it would give her warmth and security to lean against. He wondered if he done the right thing allowing the child to witness the death of this samurai. He was worried if she might have been too young to witness such an event. He looked at her, she was dressed in her best kosode and wearing the takaashida clogs.

It slipped his mind he wanted the child to go without her clogs on for the next few days to toughen her feet. He looked to the clearing sky and figured it was nearing noon. He was surprised this act took so long to accomplish. The observers disperse with many witnesses commenting on the death of the brave samurai, his crimes were already forgotten by most, and now the dead warrior would be thought of as a hero in the village of his birth. The act of suppuku was carried out so perfectly by the condemned one.

He headed home exhausted and as a second thought, he decided to invite General Kobayashi to join him for a cup of sake. Shoya Sanuki caught up to the trainer, and bowed as he commented on Masahiko's surprising stamina at witnessing the death of the warrior. The trainer was honor bound to invite the disliked Shoya to join them in a bit of sake because of his statement about Masahiko. They would salute the condemned man's departed spirit. For the rest of their lives, this samurai would only be known as the condemned man.

As the group walked from the platform, the young Masahiko kept looking back at the stage. She tried to see what the commoners were doing with the body of the dead warrior. The trainer grew angry at the child's turning and he cuffed her on the back of her head. It was impolite to view the body in this manner. It was the time to give the dead the privacy the spirit needed to circle the platform, and take trips down the path of the three winds until it settled on the fourth, which it would use to travel to the Floating World.

The trainer was home, he was glad this suppuku was over, he wondered if it impressed Masahiko or not, and if the child learned something from the sacred act. The next day he had Masahiko walk to the damp field in her bare feet, it was a cool night and morning for a mid May day, and proved to strengthen her strength. The child was given one of the slightly larger and heavier katanas, which she suffered minor problems mastering. It was hard for her to keep the tip of the blade held at the ready due to the extra weight of the blade. So he was forced to go back to the shorter and lighter wakizashi blade for the time being. Days past quickly in the ninth village, and because there were no other samurai for him to train. He and General Kobayashi spent much of their free time with the rapidly growing and learning Masahiko, whose skills with the katana and bow progressed swiftly for her and her teachers.

CHAPTER FOURTEEN

THE FIRST DAY OF THE SECOND WEEK OF THE FIFTH MONTH OF THE YEAR THIRTEEN FORTY SIX

This day was Masahiko's eighth birthday, and it wasn't only the day to celebrate the family honored time to bless her coming out of babyhood, it was also the time to celebrate word for the first time in many years, the entire realm was at peace.

There was no name for the celebration, but today enabled Masahiko to wear the adult hakama breeches and sash with her first pair of full size swords. From this day forward, the adult was allowed to wear the hitai eboshi, the formal headdress of his master. It was made from a piece of red stiffened cloth tied behind her head, and worn high up on the forehead baring the mark of Lord Kawasomeru placed on the center of the cloth, showing his ownership of the person.

The trainer's control over Masahiko lessened after this day, and the child was allowed to do what she wanted with little supervision for anyone. The young were rarely beaten after this day by anyone in the village. If new adults committed a transgression against village laws, they were reprimanded and sometimes in public depending on the offense. Now she was thought of as an adult, and was looked on almost as a deity by the townspeople of the village.

Although his control over Masahiko lessened, he was still in control of her training, thus forcing her to remain respectful to her father. He chose to bestow on her his first pair of swords given him by Shogun Ashikaga after the battle of Minatogawa. It was a well known sword which the trainer named Kagutsuchi, the ferocious fire god in honor of the sword's will to kill.

She wore the swords proudly for the ceremony. It was alright for the trainer to begin her training as an adult, and as such she would be expected to do all a full grown warrior was expected to do. He allowed her to have this day, but tomorrow, and all tomorrow's thereafter will belong to him and his training. Tanizaki watched from his porch as Masahiko rushed through the cluttered streets, showing the other new adults the swords given her by her father.

The upset master trainer saw enough of his young child's bragging and went to check on his wife growing stronger with each passing day because of the outstanding care she was receiving from the retainers sent to his village by Lord Kawasomeru. The old warrior was able to live with the people added to his household, and nights shared with Remi and Yukie were joy filled times indeed for him. Never did he once think of sending the servants back to Engakuji Castle and their lord and master. Nor did Lord Kawasomeru expect his gifts to be returned.

The next day, the master trainer made certain that he was up well before Masahiko woke for her next day of training. He entered his adult's sleeping quarters and bellowed in a commanding voice at the peaceful sleeping young Masahiko. "Wake up you young worthless good for nothing, the day wastes before you and you still sleep your life away. There's much to accomplish on this day you are wasting." The trainer waited as her to dressed.

"Wear the loincloth and light outer kosode, no clogs or warm cotton under your kosode will be allowed for you on this day of training." He turned on his heels and left the child in a huff as she began to complain at him because she was going to get soaked and cold.

"Father, it's supposed to rain heavily today, and the temperature will not be favorable for such light covering as just the outer kosode to keep me warm." Nevertheless she dressed as ordered.

He totally ignored her complaint and ate and ordered Tomotaka to quickly clear the table before she came out of her room to eat. He smiled as he watched Masahiko look unhappily at the empty table, but didn't complain. He understood she knew she wasn't going to eat much on her first adult training by her father and his general.

"Come with me Masahiko-san! General Kobayashi-san is waiting for us to begin your training. We have a lot to accomplish and little time to do it." He walked out the shoji with Masahiko following. The street was a mud quagmire from yesterday's celebration, and steady rains of the night. As she placed her first foot in the soaked mud, she shivered for it was freezing cold.

The master trainer and General Kobayashi walked fast while Masahiko tried to tip toe through the mud. In moments, she was soaked through. They reached the field and a strong wind added to the unfavorable conditions, she shivered and her teeth chattered. The mound was washed away by winter and rains. Tanizaki motioned for her to stand where the mound was, he carried a bamboo switch and kept tapping his leg with it. He stared at her as if she done something wrong as he slowly circled the shivering girl. He grunted in his deepest voice. "Masahiko-san! I'll go over what you learned and increase your knowledge, informing you of more ways of the Warriors which will, for the rest of your life govern your actions."

She bowed politely to her father, but she was squinting to see him through the teeming rain as she replied. "Hai Master Trainer!"

"Ahhh... so Masahiko-san! You know Bushido is the code that governs all Samurai and his life, but today you'll learn the value of rectitude is the backbone of the wise Samurai. Rectitude represents the time in a Warrior's life, when he must choose the proper time to die, and the proper time to strike out viciously at his enemy, and perhaps even to die on the field of battle. Samurai must know when the time is right to die, a disgrace to all Samurai is to die a worthless dog's death on the battlefield, young one."

She cocked her head to the side in question of her father's words.

"Yes Masahiko-san! You don't know what a dog's death is then I'll explain. But first I order you to pick up those two rocks resting at your feet, and you'll hold them at arm's length while I explain what you must know to survive in the world of the Samurai Caste. This test is to strengthen your arms, and make them ready to wield the weight of the Katana." The trainer waited while she picked up the stones.

"Masahiko-san! A dog's death is the time when a Samurai lays down his life worthlessly for a cause not worthy of a Warrior's death. It's the fool of fools who charges in battle only to be killed uselessly when he's unable to win a victory for his Master. It's a useless death accomplished by even the worthless of Samurai. A Samurai's most important law is to know when to live, and when it's a proper time to die. It's the smarts to know the reason a man should face, and when he should not face fears that'll confront his life while he's allowed to live on this earth. A Warrior must be keen enough to know when it's time to war, and when it's wiser to remain in hiding waiting for a proper time to attack one's enemy on the field of battle.

"Masahiko-san! It's important for a Samurai to know from what failings our virtues are born of. What I'm telling you is, it's your responsibility to know and control your actions at all times, and not allow yourself to be forced into making war at an inopportune time. Losing control of one's destiny is like losing one's water in time of battle. It's a dishonor not only to the Samurai, but it dishonors all Samurai who ever walked this land of Japan since the birth of the worthless gods. War is the foundation of learning of the higher virtues of Samurai. Truth of word is born during these times, and it's through war an honorable peace will be born. A Samurai must be ready for war the instant one breaks out, a Samurai is given life through war, and his strength is diminished by peace, a Samurai is taught by war, and his soul is made weak by peace. A Samurai is trained by acts of war, and his soul is betrayed by the illusion of peace. A true Samurai is born to war, and the only solution to his existence on the earth is to die in peace."

He looked at his child and waited for her response. He smiled as he watched her teeth chatter and her lips turn blue from the mud caked on her bare feet. Although this was ripping his heart from his body, he understood this was something she had to go through, if she hoped to become a samurai in Lord Kawasomeru's armies.

"Hai Master Trainer, I understand it's my duty to know when it's proper time to fight, and not allow myself to be drawn into a worthless squabble unworthy of dying for, or that battle is unable to be won by either side. It's also my responsibility as a trained Warrior to control my actions and thoughts at all times while in the service of my Lord, Master Trainer. It's the height bad manners to display hatred, anger and disrespect in any form to another." She dared a smile through her chattering teeth, seeking her father's approval for her words.

A sharp strike across her thigh was his response to her childish ways of seeking his approval. She cried out in pain as she lifted her leg, yet refused to rub it.

"Ahhh... so, I see the sting of pain gives your tongue movement and noise. I'll address this problem in a few moments little one. You displayed a weakness of your soul, one that's beneath a Samurai. Any actions you do are done with one thought in mind, to display to your Master you're an honorable and wise Warrior who can be trusted with his life. To say words and seek approval is a foolish child's way, this will never happen again before me do you understand?" He smacked her across the thigh with the cane a second time, drawing another cry from her. This time she dropped a rock and rubbed the sting.

He said nothing, he just glared at the rock sitting in the mud.

She knew she made a mistake and picked the rock up and held it out before her.

"I see you have a long way to go before you can call yourself Samurai, Masahiko-san. You dishonored me and your own self by dropping that rock, a symbol of the spine of a Samurai then by your crying in pain, and now by rubbing the minor injury to your worthless leg. I'll not allow your childish ways to change my course of training, Masahiko-san. As I said before, I'll address these childish actions in the manner of my choice. Now, I'll explain the virtue of valor which must rule your every thoughts and actions. The greatness of valor demands a Samurai to die for his convictions. The unworthy valor of the villain is to die for his dishonest cause. One fact for a wise Samurai to understand, is to know the reason he should and should not fear or make war." The old master trainer took a quick breath.

When he began to speak again to the young warrior who was soak and wet he asked more to himself. "Where was I, ahhh... yes, now I remember. I'll explain the virtues of valor young one, and what makes up the strength of valor. In this explanation you'll understand why I was angered by your childish outcries over some minor pain. What's the meaning of valor to you? To know and understand this is to be Samurai. Valor is made up of many smaller virtues of the Samurai belief. Fortitude, of course bravery, but not false bravery, fearlessness, and the last of virtues is courage. This collection of virtues adds up to the makings of the qualities of the pure soul of the Samurai, and his life to the Lord and Master.

"If one of these uprightness is lacking in your soul, the Samurai is less than whole, and could not serve his Master properly, no matter how hard he tried to do so. Masahiko-san! A coward is the worthless Samurai who cries out over minor pain and discomfort to his body as you done."

Again, the trainer struck her leg with the cane and she cried out over its suddenness and stinging pain. He glared at the child as he barked angrily. "Young Child! What did that cry accomplish for your soul? Did it lessen pain you suffer? Did it take the sting out of the strike? Did it make you learn anything about pain you're enduring for the sake of your Master? The only thing it did was to make your enemy know where you're hiding, and you're of weak soul and heart. What would happen? What would you do if you were engaged in battle and lost an arm? Would you stop defending your Master's life, or your own because you lost a worthless limb?

"An honorable Samurai would place his sword in his other hand, and would continue his fight until he lost that arm. Then he'd raise upon his legs and try to defeat his enemy with his legs. If he lost his legs in battle, he'd crawl against his enemy and use his mouth, his water making tool, or any item he could master to destroy or confuse his enemy. Pain, and what's believed pain, is something to be forced out of a Samurai's thought. When the battle is completed, if the Samurai isn't badly injured, he'll be looked after. If he's badly injured, it's the responsibility of a surviving Samurai, enemy or not to dispatch the life of the injured Samurai quickly.

"It goes against the honorable code of the Samurai to allow another Warrior felled on the field of battle in an just cause, to suffer needlessly. A Samurai guilty of such an infraction is doomed to be hunted down like the dog he is by either side, and slaughtered and his worthless body parts scattered to the four winds. Another question young Masahiko-san! How would you cry out, how would you react when the Lord demands the final act of obedience to be carried out by you?

Would you commit suppuku as you witnessed yesterday, or would you roll about on the ground and whimper like a wounded pup, forcing your second to take your worthless head and further dishonoring you and the rest of your family forever."

She stared at her father as she weighed his words carefully. Her being was so captivated by her father's words and explanations that she was no longer aware of the icy cold gripping her soaking wet and shaking body.

"Ahhh...yes, you're beginning to learn young one whether you realize it or not in your mind. You learned to hold your tongue and weigh your words. I see you're beginning to master your body's mind. Good, for Samurai must be totally oblivious to his surroundings, and oblivious to pain and discomfort he's forced to endure in the name of his Lord's sake. Samurai are led down the path of hardship by the gods, or whatever controls his destiny in life, to see how the Samurai performs his purest of tasks. As you're witnessing, starvation and exposure to cold and other disabling conditions are honorable tests, they make the soul of the Samurai strong and pure.

"When a Samurai's stomach is empty by fast or because of battle, he must realize it's a dishonor to feed that hunger. But the true test comes when the loyal Samurai, after suffering for a long period of time, carries out his duties justly for his Lord and Master's cause. In all his training, a Samurai must guard himself from allowing his virtues to change course on him, a Samurai's sternest may turn to cruelty if not locked under his control. He must guard himself against allowing his sternest to turn into madness and ill decision making. He must master his emotion, a brave warrior is forever composed, and a samurai will never allow himself to be surprised by anything. He'll never allow anything to disturb his tranquility, his Wa, his spirit. In the madness of battle, a Samurai must remain in control, in the midst of devastation he must maintain his wits." The trainer stepped back as if he was half his age and drew his sword and made a threatening motion towards the stunned Masahiko.

General Kobayashi, without being told instantly drew his sword and heaved it to the child. She noticed his movement out the side of her eye and dropped the rocks and caught the sword by its hilt in flight. This was made possible by the way he heaved the sword to her. Without giving it a second's thought, she crouched and prepared for the blow from the trainer.

With a bellowing laugh, the proud master trainer relaxed his attack stance and allowed his sword's tip to rest in the mud while he leaned on the hilt, the cane lay in the mud at his feet. He was trying to make her relax her guard so he could swat her with the side of the sword for her lack of attention to a lingering threat. His heart was high, she never let down her guard until he sheathed his sword, and picked up the cane and wiped the mud from it.

Once this happened, Masahiko handed General Kobayashi's katana back to him and bowed gratefully, thanking him for arming her during a sudden threat to her life. She returned the blade because a samurai without a sword, was a useless warrior.

The trainer bowed to his child as he offered. "Masahiko-san! I feel you learned much on this day. You shown the first signs of becoming a worthy Samurai. One I'd be proud to offer to Kawasomeru-sama for one of his Warriors. Young one, you learned to remain on guard and not trust anyone, even me. You're successful in ignoring your surroundings and hardships, and only concentrating on your enemy's moves and threats. The day is late and you learned enough today. We'll go home and you'll take a yu, a hot bath is what you need to take the chill out of your bones. I'll order your sister Enko to prepare your bath while you change. Tomorrow you'll begin your learning again as I go over the virtue of endurance."

The trainer turned to his general and said. "Kobayashi-san! On behalf of Masahiko-san and myself, I thank you for your time and patience. You made Masahiko-san's training easier to endure. Tomorrow, I'll give you the day off, and I'll work with Masahiko-san alone, General."

"Tanizaki-san! I'd be honored if you'd permit me the privilege of allowing me to assist in the continuing training of Masahiko-san." The general bowed to the trainer who nodded yes.

"Masahiko-san and I would be proud to have you assist in Masahiko-san's further training."

"Then I suggest we go home, I'm soaked and feel like a wet rag." Kobayashi complained.

The trio walked the street in the mud and rain to Tanizaki's home. The general broke off and went to his home to enjoy a hot bath, and the young female who he shared pleasure with him. Tanizaki offered him the services of one of his consorts, and the general took advantage of Remi's special ways of giving pleasures. Yesterday he asked if the trainer would allow Remi to show his lady friend the ways of giving pleasure in this manner and he gave his permission. Remi was happy to show the inexperienced girl the ways of this pleasure.

On entering his home, Tanizaki called Enko and ordered her to prepare Masahiko's bath. It was late afternoon, quite early to enjoy a bath. Nevertheless, she did as ordered and had the heimin prepare the fire beneath the tub. In moments, the water gave off a hint of steam and warmth. The trainee entered the bath house thirty feet from the main house dressed in a plain silk bath kosode. She shed the flowing robe and allowed the older child to wash her body with soap, and rinse her off before she climbed in the hot relaxing water. She let out a moan as she relaxed in the tub, sinking until only her mouth and rest of her head stuck out above the water.

The trainer checked on his wife first and found she was resting comfortably. Tomotaka reported Emiko was up for most of the morning, and shared lunch. Then she noticed he was dripping and ordered him to remove his wet kosode while she retrieved dry clothing for him. When she returned she complained about the consorts. "How could those empty headed women allow their Master to walk about in wet clothes? They should be dragged out of their house and stripped and whipped in the middle of the street, to show the villagers how stupid his help is.

"Those worthless women have been living too long in the Soft World, and forgot about manners, and how to serve their Master. They grown too soft over the years, because they had been waited on hand and foot. Once I'm sure of your comfort and warmth, I'll visit those useless women and beat them. Master Tanizaki-san! You should be placed in a hot bath. Estsuko! Come at once and prepare a bath for your father."

He held up his hand, making her silent as he offered in an angry tone. "It's all right Tomotaka! It's my fault. I came in wet to check on my wife. I didn't check with Yukie or Remi. I ordered Masahiko-san to bathe. The child was soaked through and in need of warming his body."

"This is nonsense Master. You're, please forgive me, older than the child and Masahiko-san should've requested you bathe before he, or he should've insisted you share his bath. The child thinks no more than the two worthless women from the soft world."

He held up his hand to silence her again, angry this time. "You who are a guest in my home said enough to upset my harmony! I gave permission for the child to bathe first, and it was I who decided not to bathe with the child. In the light of my decisions, it should be enough to accept it without question." The trainer glared at the woman helper who dropped to the floor and bowed correctly and stretched her neck to receive the blow from his sword as she moaned.

"Master Trainer Tanizaki-san! I dishonored you and I disrupted your Wa, and for that I'm prepared to forfeit my worthless life for my errors."

He stared at the young female, at first he considered taking her life to set an example for his other servants but then he decided against it as he warned her. "Tomotaka! The realm is at peace with itself in countless years. I'll not be the fool who will upset this peace by taking your worthless life. When you're no longer needed by my wife, you'll report to the leper's, there you'll spend your life looking after them people of filth."

She realized she was given a fate worse than death and cried as he bowed against. "Master Trainer Tanizaki-san, please, I request to be allowed to commit suppuku. I couldn't bear to spend my life working with the filthy people."

"Iye! Iye, I'll not allow you to take the easy way out of your responsibilities, woman. I made my decision and you'll live by it, or suffer a greater fate than servicing the rotting people by pillowing with them." He barked as he left his wife's quarters in a huff.

A weak voice beckoned Tomotaka. It was Emiko and she took her hand and offered. "Cry not, I'll speak to my husband and beg him to change his mind of your fate. If he refuses to soften his stance, it'll be I who'll allow you to commit suppuku, before you're to report to the lepers. You served me well, and I'll honor that service by granting your wish of death."

"Lady Emiko! Do you have the power to override such a powerful man?"

"Lady Tomotaka, I have the power to order you to commit suppuku if you insulted me, and my husband will honor that request no matter what he ordered for your fate beforehand." A tear worked its way out of her eye and ran down the side of her cheek.

Tomotaka bowed to the suffering Emiko.

The old master trainer left the home and went to the bathhouse nestled in the garden to check on Masahiko's health, and to see if she was out of the bath, so he could begin to ease the pain he was suffering in his joints. She was out and being dressed by Enko.

He bowed to both females, and stripped down and allow Enko to bath him. Then he lowered himself in the hot waters and let out with a groan of delight.

Masahiko totally ignored her father's presence as she quickly finished dressing, and before she was about to leave the bathhouse, her father called after her. "Masahiko-san! One second if you don't mind. I have further words for you, young warrior."

"Hai father." She cried as she rushed to the side of the bath and bowed and waited to see what her father wanted to say.

"Masahiko-san! You done well on this day of training, excellent in fact. You brought honor and respect not only to yourself, but to me and our family. By the time it's decreed you appear before Kawasomeru-sama at Gembuku, you'll be the best Samurai to have ever walked on the lands of Japan. You may turn in for the night with this thought to ponder. The memory of Japan will honor and admire the Samurai as great, he, who in the face of death, preserves his presence of mind and body. The explanation of valor is offered by composure, calm, serenity and tranquility." He smiled at his daughter as he rested his wet hand lightly on her head.

Through tears clouding her eyes, she returned her father's loving gaze as she replied. "Hai father, I'll ponder these words of wisdom in my sleep."

The trainer was the first up except for Tomotaka preparing morning meal. He said nothing and treated her as if nothing happened. It would be bad manners for either to bring it up. The only way it could be breached was if an intermediate breached the subject with him.

There was a noticeable different in the manner in which he treated and acted with Tomotaka; this was because he omitted Lady from her name when addressing her. This was to show her the order he decreed was still in effect, and he hadn't changed his mind. As far as he was concerned, she no longer existed in his life.

"Tomotaka! Clear the table before the foolish Masahiko-san rises and comes looking for her morning meal." He ordered the young woman.

"Masahiko-san will not be eating morning meal with you today, Master Tanizaki-san?"

"Iye! And the child will not be eating the morning meal until this part of the training is completed. The child must learn to survive on one meal a day as long as possible." He barked at her, showing contempt because he was forced to speak with her as he diverted his eyes out the window to see if it was going to rain.

When the proper amount of time passed, the master trainer went to Masahiko's sleeping quarters. She was still asleep and his heart ached that he was forced to wake the child for another long and hard day of training. He wished he could allow his young child to sleep as long as her body demanded, but life in Japan was harsh and only the strong had the luxury of surviving. Although there was peace in the realm, the trainer suffered no false illusions. He understood it was a matter of time before Lord Wakatsuki began his evil ways and attacked the outer provinces loyal to Lord Kawasomeru. In the recesses of his mind he knew there was a limited time to make Masahiko the greatest samurai to walk the soil of Japan.

With a nasty grunt he barked. "Masahiko-san! Are you so weak of soul and mind that you must be woken every day for training like a lazy woman? Get up, your tardiness cost you morning meal. You have two feathers of time (minutes) to dress, and join me outside, or you'll miss evening meal and starve until tomorrow, that is if you can raise in time to eat the morning meal." He spun around and stormed outside to be with General Kobayashi.

The general was speaking with one of the samurai guards when the trainer came out the door. He bowed with a smile as he asked after Masahiko's health.

"Huh! I was forced to wake the lazy good for nothing child and as a result, he's being punished by missing his morning meal again." A quick flash of a smile crossed the trainer's lips, and it quickly disappeared when a sleepy Masahiko appeared on the front porch while rubbing the sleep from her eyes then she placed her hand to her forehead to protect her eyes against the rising sun, as it peaked over the mountain. The trainer turned to the child and grunted. "Masahiko-san! It's time to begin your training anew. Follow young child!"

Without words of complaint about the missed meal, or she might be hungry, she got in step with her father as they headed for the training field. Kobayashi carried his yumi and an open quiver with a dozen arrows. The group marched through the streets in silence. Many concerned eyes peered at them from the safety of their homes. Only the Shoya stood on the porch and watched them as they walked by. He bowed slightly, and paid little further attention to the three.

A light drizzle was falling and the trainer hadn't checked to see what she was wearing, he felt it was unnecessary to check the child every day. She knew what was expected of her, and was dressed accordingly to honor her father's wishes and training.

As she entered the quagmire of the field, she noticed a horse tied to a post and spears placed in a rack, there were a few warriors standing in a circle talking. When they saw the trainer appear on the field, they dropped to their knees in the mud and bowed.

He returned their bow just within the parameters of politeness, it was slightly more than a nod. It was beginning to rain instead of drizzle and the other samurai were gathered under the tall roof structure constructed to shelter the horses from rain or sun. It was custom for a samurai to look after his horse before himself.

Once again, he pointed to the slightly raised mound that was ordered repaired the night before by one of the warrior's whose job it was to look after the condition of the training fields. She had both her swords mounted properly in her sash and she was ordered to use her swords while training from this day forward. She was ordered to use the katana blade if she must defend herself during any training session. He warned her if she was unable to master the heavier weight of the long killing sword, she would fail her tests and training until she was able to wield the true weight of the sword like it was an extension of her arm. She mounted the sand pile and there she stood at attention staring at her father waiting for his first orders.

The general snorted in a harsh tone. "Masahiko-san!" He threw two stones at her. She caught both stones and held them at arm's length. She assumed her usual position with the stones without changing her facial expression.

He saw how easily she was mastering the weight of the stones and decided he would find heavier stones for tomorrow's training. When he was ready, he grunted at his daughter. "Masahiko-san! Where did I leave off with your training yesterday young one?"

She bowed to her father. "Master Trainer! Your last words were you were going explain the virtue of endurance. I'm waiting to understand this virtue I don't know much about."

"Hai! You're correct child. I'm pleased you paid attention. There's hope for such a worthless child as you. I'll begin, Masahiko-san. Valor is made up of many different virtues, the inner value of valor is endurance. Without endurance, the virtue of valor would be a hollow prudence. Endurance is made complete by mastering composure, calm and self possession. A brave man is comfortable and serene. Let a lesser Daimyo appear over the horizon armed with the knowledge he mastered virtue, and people will gather about him as if he was a wise man. When he chooses to speak, people will listen, and with listening comes obedience. With people flocking about this man will come land, and with land comes wealth for this lesser Daimyo, and with wealth comes power! With wealth and power in this Daimyo's possession, the virtue of just use will arise. This last virtue is the tree of wealth."

He took a quick breath, trying to gather his thoughts then added. "Masahiko-san! I'll explain the working of benevolence. The virtue of benevolence is man and man is benevolence, only if he's whole and at peace with himself in body and soul. When a Daimyo mastered loving what his people love, and hating what his people hate, only then can he claim himself parent and leader of his vassals and retainers. Remember Masahiko-san! Tranquility is courage in peacefulness. Everything I told you for the past few days is a brief explanation of the virtues that dominate a Samurai's soul. It's up to the individual Samurai to discover his own meanings of these virtues to make them complete. I'm only opening your mind's eye to the beginnings of these virtues. Sometimes I remember something I might forgot to speak of when I explained a prior virtue to you, and I'll drop back to it and it'll be up to you to sort everything I speak and set them in their proper order. I'll go back to rectitude or justice for a few moments."

He drew in his breath a second time then continued. "The evil side of rectitude is excess, I'll explain this further. Rectitude carried to extreme hardens to stiffness, with stiffness comes unwillingness to understand and be fair, and with this, the Samurai's judgment becomes impaired and can become guilty of bad judgment and dishonor. Understanding benevolence, if benevolence is allowed to be indulged beyond measurement, it sinks to weakness on the part of the Samurai displaying this virtue. If this weakness is allowed to go unchecked, defeat and collapse of the Warrior's beliefs and dreams comes about, and he'll find himself wandering the world forever making wrong decisions in life, and making himself hated throughout the realm.

"He'll also be the cause of not only his world collapsing, but be the cause of the demise of his Lord. If the masses can no longer trust the Samurai acting in his Master's interests, the masses can no longer trust and believe their Master. And with mistrust comes treachery, and everyone knows treachery will bring down the purest of souls.

"Masahiko-san, I'll venture into another area of the shaping of a Samurai's beliefs and strengths. You must remember the bravest of hearts is the one that'll dare to be tender when needed. Remember this little one, caring is daring. Bushinonaske! The tenderness of the Warrior. Huh, the power of the Samurai lays in his ability of bringing what usurps his power under his control. He must learn to not only use his inner strengths for his best interests, but he must learn to use his inner weaknesses to add to his powers. A Samurai must learn as water masters fire, a Samurai must master his mind in every aspect of life, especially in the way he deals with the people he must rule over every day of his honorable life.

"A wise Samurai is forever mindful of everyone who suffers in the realm of his Lord. He must know who live in distress for a just cause, as Samurai, you must learn three needs that'll forever shape your life and mind. You must learn to forgive the night breeze that musses your hair, and dark cloud that hinders the moon of night from view, and most of all, you must learn to forgive the villain who tries in vain to quarrel with you. You must also learn to guard yourself, and not allow yourself to be drawn in a worthless quarrel neither side can win. Do you have questions little one?" He growled, showing her his displeasure if she dared to interrupt his words.

"Iye Master Trainer." She replied, she was following her father's instructions referring to him as trainer or master trainer while he was on the training field.

"Very well, I'll continue. I'll briefly cover the virtue of politeness. Politeness is a poor and almost useless virtue, if it's allowed to be displayed out of fear of offending good taste, or for the sake of vanity of the samurai. The virtue of politeness should be displayed only as an outward manifestation of a sympathetic reward for the feeling of others who suffer. It's the duty of a wise Samurai to know how to bow correctly when greeting others. He must know how to walk correctly, and sit respectfully, and possess good table manners, and know honorable ways of serving tea, and the art of drinking. Elaborate and strict discipline of politeness, and the knowledge of ceremonies, and this etiquette serve to make the Samurai whole, and being well worthy of serving his Master properly for the rest of his honorable life.

"A well rounded Samurai must experience the pains of his vassals, he must share all, weep with those who weep, rejoice with those overjoyed. Today little one, I'll leave you the unanswerable question on which to ponder your night. One of many you must work out to round yourself, and understand the feelings of others. Which is more important to the Samurai, to tell the truth, or be polite? Remember little one, sincerity is the end and the beginning of all things, without this virtue, there'd be nil. I'll take a break and allow General Kobayashi-san to explain the next virtue. General Kobayashi-san." He grunted as he bowed to his general.

The general wiped rain out of his eyes as he stepped closer to the shivering child. He bowed as he began. "Masahiko-san! I have the honor of explaining a terrible habit. Dishonor! Dishonor is the lowest of low, it's an appalling scar etched forever on the tree of life that nurtures the soul of the Samurai. In time, instead of healing the scar, dishonesty will not allow this scar to heal. On the tree of life, the scar will get larger until at last it kills the tree so horribly scarred. Shame is another dark virtue, it's the other side of virtue, and it's the filth, the cesspit, the void of good manner and morals serving to undermine the upright and honest virtues.

"An honorable Samurai must constantly guard himself from falling prey to these terribly marring and worthless habits. A wise Samurai is whole when he's able to bear what he feels is unbearable in the name of honor. It's in every Samurai's nature to be honorable, but true honor lies in one's inner self, nowhere in the world can this virtue of honor be found but in the soul of the loyal Samurai. The soul of a Samurai must be willing to grow and accept and forever search out wisdom and knowledge where it might seek to hide against him. One can take a wise lesson from the lowly rock. The pebble if allowed, will grow into a mighty rock, a boulder if you will magnificently crowned by flowing robes of thick moss. It's this and the other beliefs that forever shape the life of the always learning Samurai, just as it's the Samurai who shapes and keeps alive his beliefs and loyalty." He bowed again to Masahiko then stepped aside to allow the trainer to takeover and speak once more to his child.

He used the few seconds he had to order the other warriors to saddle the horse and make ready targets. By the time he approached Masahiko, the general finished speaking. He bowed to Masahiko and said. "Little fire, it's my duty to bring that fire to a consuming flame. I'll be responsible for your training in the arts of fencing, archery, jujitsu or yaware which you mastered already. I'll train you in horsemanship, the correct use of spear, and offensive and defensive tactics. Remi and General Kobayashi-san will teach you the finer ways of the Warrior, calligraphy, ethics, literature and history of Japan. I explained the meaning of jujitsu before, but the training laws require me to explain them to a Samurai on the field of training. Jujitsu doesn't require greatness of strength to stop your enemy, nor does it mean every blow is to kill.

"No, it's a weapon to be used against one's enemy until you gain control over the attacker. The art of jujitsu employs no true weapon but the brain and fighting skills of the Samurai. Clutching and striking the enemy's body to make him numb in limbs and mind, and is willing to listen to good reason is the true weapon of jujitsu. As Samurai, you'll learn to hold all earthly wealth in disdain, the making or hoarding of wealth will disgust you. Money and love and greed of it, and the Samurai's steadfast refusal to be mastered by this the weakest of human dignity is a must, a necessity if the wise Samurai's soul is to remain free from the thousand evils roaming the face of earth in their search of unknowing victims to conquer.

"Your loving mother and father are the Heaven and the Earth to your soul. Me, your teacher and your Lord and Master of the realm is the Sun and Moon to the life of a Samurai. We'll serve to make you whole in mind, body and soul. To show no useless outward signs of joy, anger is your true quest. When one speaks all manners of evil things against you, being a wise Samurai you must learn to discipline yourself not to return evil for evil. You must reflect you were more faithful in the discharging of your Master's will and desires. Ambition is another Warrior's virtue, it's the want, greed and need for personal riches that hinders true wisdom to be absorbed by the mind of the wise Samurai."

He stepped away from her. "You're free to release your burden."

She dropped the stones and flexed her hands, she dared not shake her arms to get the circulation moving, for fear of insulting her father and trainer.

"It's time to test your horsemanship. Look to the field, you see eight Samurai in formation. Ride your horse between them, remember not to crash into my Warriors, I need them whole young pup. Ride in half gallop using your arms and legs to control the horse. Begin." He watched as she rushed to the horse and mounted with little trouble or grace. She kicked the horse with both feet to make the horse run, her arms suffering aches from the stones. Her kosode clung to her wet body making it difficult to work the horse properly. The first seven Samurai were passed safely, but as she approached the last Warrior. He suddenly flung his hands and roared like a wild man as he charged her horse, making her animal rear and depositing the child on her back, watching as her horse ran off the training field.

"Ieeeee!" He yelled as he rushed to the child, hoping she wasn't hurt by the fall. He pulled her to her feet and yelled. "Masahiko-san! What kind of useless Samurai are you? It's a fool who rides his horse to battle and isn't prepared for any situation he might face. You can't ride your horse from the ground. What do you do, dream of worthless dreams when riding? You could have hurt your horse, and a Samurai who allows his horse to be wounded, or throw him from his saddle is a shame to his Caste. Get your horse and apologize to him then try again."

He watched as the trembling child ran after a horse that had no want to be captured. General Kobayashi came up to the trainer's side and mumbled. "Tanizaki-san! Do you wish me to capture the horse for Masahiko-san?"

"Iye! It's good exercise for the child to chase after a horse she couldn't capture on her own accord. It'll give her a valuable lesson in endurance and cunning." The two settled down and watched the comedy of the child chasing after the horse. The horse stopping and allowed the child to get just so close to it, before darting away shaking his head as he ran.

After an hour of the amusing and comical scene, he gave the general the nod and he rushed to his horse, and charged after the loose animal. Moments later, he led the horse to the handler who took it to the stables where he cleaned mud from the animal, and wiped it down and cooled it off.

Out of breath, she rushed to her father and dropped to her knees in the mud, bowing as she offered. "Honorable Teacher. I'm but a worthless Samurai who displayed poor efforts in riding and being able to capture my horse. Is it possible for you to find in your heart a place of forgiveness for your unworthy pupil?"

"A lesson learned is a lesson taught, huh young wild fire? Do you think you learned something from your poor workmanship of today's training?"

"Hai Master Trainer! I learned a valuable lesson, not to take anything for granted, my enemy can spring at me from even the safest and protected of areas."

"Ahhh... wild fire, you learn in leaps and bounds. That's what you should've learned from this lesson. Masahiko-san! Since this horse was the object of your learning, I give you the horse to use when it's your time for battle. Don't only learn from your horse, have your horse learn from you. As you learn the horse's moods and reactions, you must teach it of your needs and interests. In this manner if you're unmounted in battle, your horse will know to work its way back to you so you can remount and fight on for your Master's sake. You may stand by my side!"

She looked up and stared at her father. To be given a horse so honorably was a homage paid to her. She stood by her father's left side proudly.

"Masahiko-san! I haven't done you a favor. Owning a horse is a responsibility of weight. It's your duty to feed and water it, clean its stall and make sure it remains in health, so it's ready to serve you in times of need. There'll be times after training or battle you're exhausted, but you must find strength to keep you going until your horse is fed and sheltered. One day when you become wealthy, you'll have vassals who'll share your responsibilities. But your horse must be as respected and taken care of as your sword is. Is this understood?"

"Hai Master Trainer." The child said with pure love in her eyes for her father.

"Good, it's a wise man who knows when it's time to come out of the god cursed rain and warm his body before he catches his death of cold, neh? We trained enough on this dank miserable day. General Kobayashi-san! It's time we put an end to this day's training of the young man. Domo, Kon banwa." Thank you, good evening.

"Do itashimashite, sayanara." You're welcome, good bye. General Kobayashi stayed behind to look after his horse as the trainer, Masahiko and the guards walked off.

They walked home barely speaking. The child was starved and concerned getting something to eat than bathing and changing in dry clothes. Upon entering their home they were warmly met by Emiko sitting at the table. Her smile warmed them. He bowed to his wife as he asked. "Emiko! You look well. How are you feeling?"

"Husband, I'm far from being well but I feel a little better of late. It has been many days since the last time the bleeding visited my body, and I'm able to eat some solid food, and gaining some of my strength and weight at the same time. I long for the day when I can once again care for my honorable husband and his children." His suffering wife let out with a deep sigh and then she slowly lowered her head, sad she was unable to give her husband the proper respect and pleasures he deserved from any loyal wife.

"Emiko! I have no fear it'll only be a matter of time before you'll again run my house. Be patient, Karma is Karma and if it's written on the wind, you'll be fine my lady."

She looked up and exclaimed with surprising strength. "Ieeeee! Look at the both of you. You're soaked to the skin. Enko! Come here at once child."

The young woman rushed in the kitchen and Emiko ordered her to prepare a bath for Masahiko. Tanizaki was surprised his wife considered the welfare of the child over his, and stared at his wife in disbelief. She ignored the stare as she continued. "Lady Tomotaka! Fetch Lady Miho, and go to the market and pick up fresh vegetables for supper meal. Hachirobe-san! Stand by and when Masahiko-san is finished bathing, prepare the bath for Tanizaki-san. He'll require warm sake at his bath to warm his innards." She clapped her hands weakly.

They remained silent until the servants and Masahiko were out of hearing. Once they were alone, he spoke. He made sure he wasn't overly impolite and complained. "Emiko! I know you're ill, but you insulted me before the worthless servants. A wife's duty is to make sure her husband is comfortable and taken care of before the children are cared for. Has sickness affected your wits, or are you suffering from foul manners?"

She couldn't hide the hurt from her husband's words. She knew he was right, but she wanted to speak to him while she had strength to do so. Politely she bowed. "Husband! I beg of you to put up with the whims of an old dying woman. I want to speak to you while I'm able."

His heart was crushed and his stance immediately softened as he moved closer to his wife and rested his hand on her shoulder. "What is this nonsense of you dying old woman? You'll out live this old bag of bones of mine."

She lifted her hand with effort and laid it on his and tapped it with her palm. "Even the Trainer is unable to defeat the will of the gods. I'm no fool and I know the gods are calling me. I remain on earth because of their pleasure. When they tired of my existence and need my space for the young, they'll let me come home and rest."

"Emiko! I'll not allow you to speak of this nonsense. I'm ordering you to put these thoughts out of your mind. I'll not allow anything to happen to you until Masahiko stands before Kawasomeru-sama on Gembuku. Once this is accomplished, the gods can take the both of us home if they want us to bother them in the Floating World. Emiko! We find ourselves alone, what is it you wish to speak to me about? It must be important for you to risk our health in this terrible manner. Speak while we're still alone in the home and can speak openly, woman."

She turned in the chair and gave a poor attempt to smile at her husband as she let out her breath, then spoke with her remaining strength. "Husband, Lady Tomotaka informed me of her insult of yesterday, and has informed me of the punishment you decreed on her head for her to endure. Tanizaki-san! I must beg you to..."

"Huh Emiko! Leave this alone, this does not concern you. I decided and it's useless to negotiate on her behalf. I'm angered she begged your help. I'll order her from my home..."

"Tanizaki-san!" She dared to interrupt her husband.

He took a step back, looking like he was slapped across the face by her.

If his wife saw the look on his face it would have had her cringing in fear, but she knew she was going to die, and this gave her strength to challenge his rule and possible anger. She knew she started this and must continue, she has gone too far to back down now as she offered. "My honorable husband Tanizaki-san! If you'd like, I'll commit suppuku and demand Lady Tomotaka my second. Then I must demand that she be allowed to follow me into the Floating World." She dared to look in her husband's eyes defiantly, summoning up her strength and displaying bad manners towards her husband.

His stance softened further. "Emiko! I order you to put these foul ideas from your mind. You share the life of a crane and live to see Masahiko-san rise to his place in the realm. I'll over look your demands, but I warn you I'll not tolerate another such outburst, woman."

"I'm embarrassed over my terrible behavior, but I have little time and I must intercede on Lady Tomotaka's behalf. My husband, it wasn't she who asked me to burden you with this request. It was a thought of my account. May I continue, or will I be allowed to commit suppuku for insulting my honorable husband of too many years to count in this way?"

He flew in a rage as he heaved his hands in the air and began to pace the room, making Emiko hunch down in fear of being struck. Miho who was near the room, came in to see what the matter was. She never witnessed a male of the house in such a rage.

He looked at Miho and bellowed in his rage. "Be gone with you and allow me to speak privately with my wife, or I'll have your head lopped off its shoulders, and allow the children to use it for a kicking toy. Out! Now foul one!"

Miho's eyebrows lifted in shock as she quickly ducked out of the room and joined Tomotaka heading off for the market for food supplies. She wanted to be out of the home until Tanizaki was able to get his wits about him again.

She decided to allow her husband's rage to travel its course then ebb when he calmed. The old trainer threw a porcelain shaped deity which shattered on the floor. He continued to rave as his steam began to regress some, and his anger began to lessen.

After several minutes of allowing him to let out his steam, Emiko could no longer help herself after she looked at her husband and saw what he looked like in his fit. Although she fought the feeling, her weakened state didn't allow her the strength to fight the feeling off and she smiled. This gave his anger strength and he screamed again.

Now, the more angry he got, the more she laughed. Her soft chuckle weaken his anger and soon he spoke normally. She covered her smile with the back of her hand, but he knew she was laughing at him. The trainer was forced to join his wife in laughter. He sat beside his wife because he was laughing so hard. When he caught his breath he asked. "Emiko! What's so funny? Why are you laughing so at me?"

She knew such a detestable act such as laughing was insulting him. If it was known what she done, no one from the village would blamed him for hacking her body to pieces and scatter them to the four winds. She ordered her mind to stop laughing. "Husband, forgive me." She giggled again then went on. "You looked so funny while in such a rage. Over my many years of living I saw turtles by the pond, but never saw a red faced turtle as I witnessed today. I know it's insulting to laugh at one's husband, but if you saw what your face looked like in your rage, even you would've had no choice but to laugh. Forgive this old woman for my indiscretion, but you were so funny my husband." Again she laughed, causing her husband to join her.

"Ieeeee! I guess it's true the words you speak." He grunted as he wiped at a tear and added. "I've been told many times it's a complete samurai who can laugh at his mistakes. It's strange it took me so long to understand this. I see what it was my father was trying to point out to me over the past years of his honorable life."

She stopped laughing as she turned serious and looked into his tired eyes. The look of begging crossed her pained looking face.

He saw this look many times in his past when she wanted a privilege or special request. The master trainer let out his breath and allowed his shoulders to sag a bit, knowing already he lost this battle with his wife when she looked at him so. When he saw this look, he was powerless to deny his wife any request in his power to grant.

She knew her husband well enough to know when to approach him with a request. She read the looks of her mate. She placed her hands together after straightening out the front of her kosode, her hands didn't move while she spoke. "My understanding Tanizaki-san."

"Ieeeee!" He interrupted. "This will cost me plenty I see. When you address me so elegantly, it makes me go against my better judgment, Emiko!"

"Tanizaki-san! This is what I wanted to speak to you about before. Your usual wise judgment. May I proceed my husband?" She begged softly of him.

His look hardened as he stared at his sickly wife. "Hai Emiko! You made my blood pound in my head already, so you might as well proceed with this torture of yours."

"My honorable husband Tanizaki-san! I beg you to rescind your demand Lady Tomotaka serve the cursed lepers. That's a fate worse than death and shouldn't be leveled against such a loyal vassal. True the useless woman might have insulted your honor and I and she feel she should've been beaten, but forgive her for her error. Husband, if you can't find it in your heart to forgive this unlucky woman, I beg you to allow her to commit suppuku rather than waste away with her body covered with the festering sores of lepers. I can't imagine such a fate suffered by any honorable Japanese person. Why the gods chose to plague our country with such a vile disease I'll never know or understand, husband."

"Emiko! You're entering an area that you shouldn't venture in. I feel you should mind your own business over this matter. I have made my decision on that woman, how'd I look to the household if I changed my mind so freely? They'd think me addle minded and take it on their foolish selves to challenge my decisions in the future. If I were to change it, I'd not blame them for this thinking. Put this insulting woman out of your mind and allow her fate to be decided by Karma." He mumbled, dismissing this subject once and for all.

"Tanizaki-san! I know it's not a wife's place to ask her husband to change his mind and weakening his position in the household. But I don't fear the same apprehensions you concern yourself with, my dear. If you were to change your mind, the others of the household would think you wise, just and a merciful man to rethink a harsh judgment, and show wisdom by changing your order. I believe it's the opposite of the way you read our retainer's minds. They'll think of you a greater man because you displayed a true virtue of a Samurai, that of compassion.

"Husband! I beg you to reconsider, I beg you to revisit the insult and weigh it in your mind to see if it was as serious as you believed. I know you'll see it my way and rescind your order of death without ending. If you can't forgive her, I beg you to allow her to commit suppuku, and end her life honorably. Tanizaki-san! I don't like saying this, I feel responsible for her. If I wasn't so foolish I allowed myself to become ill and unable to care for myself then she wouldn't have been in your house. She wouldn't have insulted you, and her life would be allowed to continue down the path it traveled before she entered our lives." She begged as she refused to leave this subject because she wanted to save the life of who she felt was a loyal retainer.

She took a breath and he observed her hands tremble so he allowed her to continue. She displayed another weak smile. "Tanizaki-san! I trust you can understand why I feel responsible for her life. Dear husband, beat her for her insult yes, shave her hair if this would make you feel better. But I beg you not to allow her to follow your order of her living her life aiding the filthy lepers. I couldn't live with that thought, this is why I beg you to change your mind, or allow her and myself to commit suppuku, and place an honorable end to our foul existence on this earth."

The trainer jumped to his feet and let out his breath, out of the corner of his eye he saw Masahiko and Enko walk past the door to the room. He saw them notice they were speaking and left them alone. He was steaming as he hissed in a low, almost uncontrolled growl. "Emiko! What is this talk about committing suppuku? I'm tired of everyone speaking or offering to commit such a final deed. It's an honorable death yes, but I wish the foolish people of Japan would spend as much energy in living as they do with the want to commit suicide. All this talk of killing one's self no matter how honorable the death, sickens me to my soul. I'm tired of this death and all that has to do with death in our world.

"Ieeeee! I spend weeks teaching young Samurai how to kill or be killed and to die honorably. For the sake of gods and my Master's sake, I now train one of our children in the ways of death and killing. Huh, I'm forced to rob this child of her very sex for fear of what my Lord would feel. At times I wonder if there's a future for Japan. We're supposed to be at peace in the realm, yet I never heard so much talk about suppuku, and spilling of one's innards to nourish the worms of the earth as I heard lately. I grow so tired of this death I find myself questioning the wisdom of our masters who rule the provinces for allowing young Samurai to die for their whims."

He balled up his fists and held himself tight, ready to strike at anything or one who dared to cross his path. He slowly regained his composure when he found himself staring at his dying wife with his fists clenched. He would rather cut his hands off than strike such a defenseless and sickly woman as his ailing wife. The trainer plopped down in the bamboo chair and rested his elbows on the table in exhaustion then ran his fingers through his thinning hair and exhaled in an exhausted sigh. He looked about the room until his eyes fell on his wife trying to smile at him.

She allowed her husband the time he needed to regain his composure before she spoke again to him. "My honorable Tanizaki-san! What you say is true, but your words can cost your family and relatives their lives if word got back to Kawasomeru-sama about Masahiko-san. What you speak you speak as treason against the realm and Master. In our way of life there's no room for question or independent thought. I back your words, and if they cost our lives so be it.

I'll die the happiest woman in the world, proudly by your side." She bowed slightly to her husband, a tear running down her cheek.

"Emiko! This is what I was speaking about. More talk about dying for no good reason. Is there nothing in our future other than death to look forward to? Surely, there has to be something else for our children to look forward to, rather than dying in the mud of the earth. I cry for the proud youth of Japan to be brought up in such a savage world they must look forward to nothing more but dying, than living their lives in peace and enjoyment. Something along the way has gone wrong with us I see." He moaned as he sadly shook his head and stared at his wife.

"Tanizaki-san! You don't intend to stop the training of Masahiko-san or the other Samurai Lord Kawasomeru will be sending to you in the future?" She asked her husband as she stared at him and waited his reply.

"Ieeeee old woman! Yes, it's true I'm upset, but I haven't taken full leave of my wits or responsibilities. I know our children's only hope for survival in this violent world is if I can train them to survive on the field of battle when they're called forth to defend the realm for their Master. No Emiko! My words only served to strengthen my stamina, and want to develop the best of the best Samurai, and the wherewithal to make the Samurai I train, to be the best in all the realm, and an honor for our Master to enlist in his armies." The master trained said to his concerned looking wife this time.

He saw the relief suddenly etched in her eyes as she replied. "Thank you my husband, I'm pleased, I wouldn't want you to insult the Master as Lady Tomotaka done you." She stopped speaking and smiled the smile of one making one's point.

"Ieeeee woman who is smarter than I dare hope to attain! You maybe ailing but your mind is as sharp as ever. You think you won a katsu, a victory over my head? You haven't won this battle, your womanly ways will not intimidate or weaken my resolve." He said as he smiled, proud she was sharp witted and willing to engage him in battle of words.

"Tanizaki-san! I didn't seek to win a victory over you that was the farthest thought from my mind. I was praying I could change your will to allowing Lady Tomotaka to live, or at least leave this world honorably, husband. I want you to consider the thought I beg of you." She stared at her husband with pleading eyes.

"Huh. Do you think this cursed woman is worthy of another thought, more of my time to worry about her fate? I feel we wasted enough time on someone dead in my eyes, and is only waiting for the foolish gods to whisk her away from my sight." The trainer offered in his defense as he continued to argue with his wife.

"But Tanizaki-san..." His wife went to offer but she was cut off by her husband as he began to growl while trying to get her off the subject of this woman.

"But nothing woman! I said we wasted enough time on this insulting women, and speaking of her fate. I should use her body for a target for my trainees to sharpen their skill with, for allowing you to become involved in something that should have not concerned you, my Lady. I simply will not allow you or anyone to continue wasting my time over this foul matter and worthless woman..." He went to say more, but he was cut off by his wife this time.

"But..." She went to offer, but she was cut off again by her husband.

He held up his hand in order to silence his wife as he fired at her, allowing more anger to creep in his voice now.

"Emiko! I heard enough conversation of this most upsetting talk on this cursed day. If I decide to waste time on this foul woman. I'll do it at my leisure, but it'll be of my decision to make and not yours, woman. I'll make up my mind on whether or not to give more consideration to my order aimed against her and then I..."

"But..." She when to offer for a third time, but again she was cut off.

"That is it. Emiko! This conversation is over! I warn you stand on the edge of displeasing me if you insist on carrying this conversation further. I tolerated your terrible manners because of your condition, to continue will be inconsiderate and rude, and it'll cause me to remove this worthless woman now, rather than later if you insist on carrying this insulting conversation further, wife." He pushed his weight from the table then stormed out of the kitchen.

The weaken Emiko remained standing in the kitchen and cried softly when Tomotaka and Miho strolled in the room. Tomotaka had the fear of death in her eyes, and when she saw Emiko weeping she dropped to her knees and sobbed. Miho rested her hand on her head as cooed. "Lady Tomotaka! All is not lost, the Master Trainer might change his mind and at least allow you to die honorably. I'll speak to Lady Remi, and see if I can enlist her aid in this situation. Together maybe we can change what is not meant to be changed."

Emiko turned in her seat and warned her with a trace of anger in her tone. "Lady Miho! That's not a wise thought. The way my husband's feeling, he might order her or anyone else who might try and intercede on Lady Tomotaka's behalf to the same unspeakable fate as he did to her. No Lady Miho, this is my responsibility and I'll shoulder it alone. I'll bring this subject to my husband when I think the time is right. Now, we must learn to allow this to lay at rest. I haven't given up all hope to this problem. I'll have my forgiving husband change his mind over this order, if it's the last thing I do before I reside with the Kami of the Floating World of wonder."

Tomotaka went to speak but the ailing woman held up her hand to silence her, and smiled at the stunned looking woman. She was feeling terrible for Tomotaka because she still believe it was her fault she was placed in the path of Tanizaki. And that feeling was her driving force in her attempt to change her husband's mind over his order to the Tomotaka.

CHAPTER FIFTEEN

Master Trainer Tanizaki rested peacefully in his warm bath, his mind working on formulating different ways to continue the training of Masahiko. He planned to play Go with the child this evening, she would be in training most of the day, stopping only to sleep and eat, until he could plan other ways to continue the training even during those durations. He closed his eyes and enjoyed the peace giving warmth of the tub, his mind listening to the tapping of rain on the roof. Enko sat by the side of the tub.

When Estsuko joined her mother and the others, she noticed she was exhausted and offered to help her mother to bed. Tomotaka forgot her problems and rushed to Emiko's side to help.

He finished his bath and reluctantly climbed out of the warm water and allowed his daughter to dry him. "Where is Yakuta-san hiding at? I think I'll indulge in one of his massages to relieve some cursed pain assaulting my old bones.”

“Father, I’ll retrieve him at once.”

“Hai. Do that daughter.”

She looked for Yakuta, running from place to place in her search for the old man and stopping when informed by a guard who told her he gone to the tenth village to visit his sister. Not knowing what to do, she sat and cried.

Remi saw the young lady crying and went to her and asked. “Enko! Why do you cry so on this day? What upset you so little one?”

She looked at the beautiful woman and said in a shaky voice. “Father has sent me to fetch Yakuta-san. He’s resting in the bath waiting massage. Yakuta-san is away and my father is going to be displeased. He’s not in the best of moods and this will serve to make him angrier at everyone under his roof and protection.”

“Ahhh... child you worry needlessly, I’m well trained in the art of massaging. I’ll replace Yakuta-san for your father. I’ll make sure he is pleased.” Remi offered warmly.

“I’ll return to father and inform him of the change.” The scared Enko offered to her.

“No Enko! That’ll not be necessary. Allow me to surprise him.”

“Hai Lady Remi! That would be wise to surprise father. Maybe it’ll serve to lighten his mood for him and us. He’s extremely upset I fear today Lady Remi.”

Remi purred at the child. “Hmmmmm! That you can be sure of little one.”

She watched as Remi disappeared in the bathhouse. Remi noticed Tanizaki laying on a massage table on his front enjoying the silence. She knew he heard her come in the building, for he began to complain immediately.

"Yakuta-san! Where have you been old fool? It took you long enough to get here, I was about to get up and forget about the massage I need so desperately. Do I have to have you retrained in your duties to me and my household?"

Remi did her best to grunt like a man as she got out of her silk kosode.

"Yakuta-san! You sound like you're coming down with sickness. Are you all right to give me a massage? I need one, but I don't want to come down with sickness. I have too many important things I must accomplish, and too little time to complete my tasks in."

Again Remi tried to grunt like a man.

He was surprised Yakuta didn't reply and he started to get up to confront the old man, but was stopped by Remi who placed her hands on his back after she warmed them in the waters of the tub. She began to knead the muscles of his back between her expert and strong fingers.

The old master trainer gave out with a moan as he griped. "Ieeeee Yakuta-san! You must be sick, your hands are warm so you must be running a fever, neh? Hmmm... you seem to have learned some new ways of massaging. I must admit, they're pleasurable to endure. Continue with the work you're doing to my old bones."

Remi was naked as she ran her fingers over the old man's back. She was surprised to see so much strength in the muscles as she rolled them between her fingers. As she worked, she felt him falling asleep and didn't want that until she finished with him. She worked on his powerful legs next, lifting them and working the muscles carefully, but when she ran her hand between his legs and found his manhood, he jumped awake and turned to strike the old man for this insult. She smiled at the stunned trainer as he realized it was she massaging him.

He smiled as he stared at her beauty then remarked. "leeeee Remi! This is the first time I had a massage by a naked young woman in my old and unending life."

"Tanizaki-san! The massage is only the beginning of the gift I offer you." She smirked as she helped him roll on his back. With both hands she manipulated his manhood until it saluted the stars in the Heavens. When he was of the proper hardness she drew him in her mouth. A moan escaped his lips as he squirmed on the table. He thought she was going to complete her mission with her mouth, but was surprised when she stopped and mounted him. She took his hands and placed them on her breasts and he rubbed them. When he was working them to her delight, she massaged his temples and shoulders.

The more relaxed he got, the more his passion rose until he was pumping like a young samurai. Harder he thrust up with his hips, his breathing increasing as grunts came from his lips. She moaned as well, joining and adding to his passion. In one star filled explosion, he erupted with passions he never reached before. She joined him in his ecstasy and collapsed on his barrel chest and rested until her breathing returned to normal.

"leeeee! Never has this old fool been so aware of what he was missing over all these worthless years, by not taking a consort to bring me extra pleasure and satisfaction. I'll request Kawasomeru-sama allow me to retain your services until I can no longer walk about this world freely." The old man offered to the stunning young woman.

She sat up and placed a finger across his lips. "Master Trainer Tanizaki-san! That request will not be needed, it was given to you. On the day I left Engakuji Castle, Kawasomeru-sama discussed this and in his wisdom he ordered me this. The Lord stated if you accepted my services, I was to consider myself your consort as long as you need me. I'd deem it an honor if you allow me to stay. It'll give me great face and Kawasomeru-sama promised if I could talk you into taking my services, he'd make my brothers Samurai and enlist my Mother in his house. My father passed during the war between Echizen and Mino provinces five years past. My mother is old and we had little reserves to support our family until our Master made this kind offer to me."

"Lady Remi! I'm deeply disturbed at the loss in your realm, I don't understand this at all. If your honorable father was killed in the service of his Lord and Master. Then by kindness his family should have been left sound and taken care of."

"Oh no you must remain lying on your back or all my work will be for naught. Alas, my father wasn't the most wise of Samurai in the Master's employ. He enjoyed gambling and the joys offered at the tea house and it left us little. By the time mother paid his debts we were poor and in debt. I know if it wasn't for the wisdom of our Lord, my family would've been forced to live in the open as do the lepers of the second village."

"Huh! Then it's settled Lady Remi. You'll stay for my remaining days. I'll award your mother five koku of rice a year for her life. This should enable her to live well. I'll speak to Kawasomeru-sama and buy your contract no matter the cost." He said as she got her weight off his chest and stepped from the table. He sat up and swung his legs off the table as he watched her sexually wiggle in her pale blue kosode which hung on the bamboo hook. She didn't pull it closed, she allowed the front to remain open so he could see all she possessed as she allowed a brilliant, room enlightening smile to cross her lips. She threw caution aside as she looped her arms around his neck and kissed him unladylike.

"Ieeeee Master Trainer Tanizaki-san! You're far too generous to this undeserving unworthy woman. There are far more important women in Japan for you to lavish such vast sums of value on. My Lord, I'm forever in your debt and will repay you for the kindness you shown myself and my family. Five koku a year is a Samurai's pay. Thank you my Lord, I'll find ways of repaying your kindness to my family."

"It's a little sum to pay for such beauty and experience, I'm proud to pay it. You may request your mother to join our village, I'll have a house set aside for her."

"Thank you my Lord but that'll be unnecessary, as I told you, my mother is working for the household of Kawasomeru-sama and is comfortable in his employ. The knowledge I have an offer to allow my mother to come and live with me thrills me to all ends, and let me know what value you have placed on my being and services. I'll be forever in your debt my Lord." Remi offered as she bowed to the old man and then smiled pleasantly at him.

"We talked until my exhaustion. I'm tired and hungry and want to play Go with Masahiko-san, to further his education. I chose you to help the child with his writing and reading. For this I'll pay you one koku a year as fee." He grumbled as he pushed off the table and slipped in a clean loincloth and kosode then walked past her as if she wasn't there as she called after him.

"Tanizaki-san! Again you're too generous to this unworthy vassal. Half of what you offered for my services is more than enough for two of me."

He entered the house and sat before the kitchen table which was more a tray, it was set out with a decanter of sake, porcelain cup, and bowl of warm rice and chop sticks.

Tomotaka was serving the hungry master of the house. She came to him carrying his meal over her head so her breath wouldn't soil his food. She had the largest of trout for him. It was his place to receive the best of food, he was the highest ranking member of the household. He grunted with pleasure as she placed it before him, he was so hungry he forgot manners and ate when served.

The fish was cooked to perfection and he was impressed by how she served him. He allowed his mind to wander, he decided she was a good vassal guilty of a moment of stupidity. His wife's words rang in his ears and as he watched the woman serve him respectfully, his anger weakened towards her and he caught himself before he smiled at her.

She wasn't foolish, she noticed the softening in his eyes, and increased her serving abilities by bowing every time she approached him. Her best manners were on display as she offered to pour sake. She poured from the left while making sure not a drop was spilled then she wiped the edge of the bottle with silk and placed the bottle on his tray without a sound. She bowed and held it longer than expected, paying greater honor to the master of the household.

His mind spoke, bragging if General Kobayashi or Shayo Sanuki were here, they would witness how well his vassals behaved when serving. If they observed this grandeur, it would increase his face and they would be jealous at how well his servants and retainers carried out their duties. It would take no time for this to reach every home in the village, and everyone would want to eat at his home to witness this. It would cost him face not to return Tomotaka's bow, and this was the only thing that caused a moment's anger to flash in his mind. He didn't like being forced by anyone to do what was polite. Making it known to her, he begrudgingly gave her a slight bow about bordered on politeness.

She smiled, pleased for what little the old man offered for she knew even the slightest friendliness displayed by him meant there was a possibility of him rescinding his death order on her, or at least allowing her to commit suppuku honorably.

He ripped the baked fish apart with his chopsticks and fingers and savored the pleasing taste of the fresh trout. Tomotaka next came in carrying a bowl of gruel consisting of cooked barley and rice, lightly flavored with a stock she made from the drippings of the fish. Each time she served him, she bowed greatly, and each time he returned the bow. It became easier and more polite until he uttered his first words to her since he doomed her to the service of the lepers.

"Tomotaka! Has Lady Emiko eaten yet?"

"Hai my Lord." She replied pleasantly to the old man who held her fate in his hands.

"Has she taken solid food I dare hope for?" The old man asked her with concern.

"Hai my Lord. I wouldn't leave her side until she ate some trout and soup, Lord. Lady Emiko is getting stronger with each passing day, Master Trainer Tanizaki-san. She'll be strong enough to assume her proper place of serving her honorable husband and children soon. Then my worth will be diminished and I'll be free to carry out my Lord's last bidding."

"Huh foolish woman! It's not my bidding but punishment for your insulting of me. I should have taken your head right there. I could've avoided the problems you now cause me. I guess old age is robbing me of my senses. More sake."

She rushed to his side and poured the wine gracefully. He noticed the hint of shaking in her hands as she served him, and felt he punished her long enough. "Tomotaka! It's good you made Lady Emiko eat some solid food, it's the only way she'll return to health."

"You're too kind to this dumb woman, Master Trainer Tanizaki-san. I'm but a useless fool. I live only to serve Lady Emiko until she returns to health. Then, I'll leave for the leper's pit and my slow death will start. With each passing day I'll offer my suffering to you for the insult I placed on your Karma. If only there was a way for me to erase that blotch, I would've ended my life the next time before my wicked ways were allow to roam freely and insult my Lord." She made certain she addressed the master with his honored and deserved title of master trainer.

"Ieeeee Lady Tomotaka! You should've been a poem writer. Your words are sweet enough to melt the hardest of the hearts." He took a large sip from his rice wine.

Her heart raced, she understood what he just done. By adding Lady back to her name, he confirmed he was rescinding his slow death penalty from her. Now, the only thing left was to see if he lifted the entire death sentence, or if he was going to allow her to end her life honorably. She held her breath waiting for his next words.

He didn't say anything further, he just held out his sake cup before him.

Her stomach turned as bile worked its way in her mouth and she jumped and poured a third cup of sake. He began to feel tipsy from the rice wine, but it gave him a warm and forgiving feeling in his soul. He looked into the tear clouded eyes of Tomotaka and mumbled softly. "Lady Tomotaka! Perhaps your insult wasn't as bad as I believed it to be. Perhaps, I'll give you one more chance to serve me and my family properly. Perhaps, you're worthy of a second chance, you're behaving so well lately, serving and showing proper respect. With peace growing in the realm, who am I to upset this notion by forcing you to commit suppuku, or live with the filthy people. Yes, Yes Lady Tomotaka, there's a new feeling of hope and friendliness blossoming throughout Japan, and it might as well be felt in the Ninth Village. I forgive your disturbing indiscretions and again bid you welcome to my household."

She was so overcome by his words she fell to the ground and banged her forehead on the floor as she thanked the master trainer for changing his mind.

He ignored the woman as she bowed. He finished his meal, enjoying it, sucking the meat from the bones and juices from his fingers. He looked at her. "Lady Tomotaka! You, along with the efforts of Lady Miho are the reason for Emiko getting stronger, and I'll not forget this service to me." The trainer got up and walked out the room.

She fell on her rear and wept, Miho appeared with Estsuko, and both hugged her happily on the floor as they sobbed together, overjoyed she was given new life, rebirth. Estsuko rose and rushed to her mother resting on the bed roll. Estsuko explained Tanizaki rescinded the death sentence ordered on Tomotaka's head, and they shared tears of joy.

He was unaware of the crying or he would have forbade it as he went to find Masahiko resting on her bedroll. "Ieeeee Masahiko-san! Are you too old and useless to weather a day's worth of training? Is your body so weak of strength and mind that you must rest on your sleeping mat? Get up, your training has begun anew. Follow me." He sternly marched out of the room with Masahiko following while trying to tie her kosode's obi.

They went to a sitting room where the trainer moments before set up the Go board. He pointed to the cushions by both ends of the board. "Sit there wild heart." He grunted at Masahiko.

"Father, this is the second time in my short life I saw this game board. I know it's a game, but I don't know how to play it." She cried as she stared at the board.

"Yes Masahiko-san, the first time you set eyes on this board was at your first haircut. What makes you think this board is only a game? I'll explain the object of this exercise, this board is not a game. If you keep your eyes and ears open, this board will teach you military tactics that might be employed by your enemies during time of battle. The object of this game as you call it, is for me to destroy your pieces, thus assuming the space the pieces had. Land, is as important as masses in your army. If my army deprives you of land from which to war, my army will have no choice but to be successful. The green pieces are your horsemen, the black spearmen. These are your useless foot soldiers your lowly Warriors used to slow the attacking army long enough to allow your horse and spearmen to get in position to defend your lands then to reach out and conquer your enemy. If one is good as an advisory, this game could take days to win. We start?"

"Hai father. I understand this well the way you explained it."

"Good! You have first move. This is my Castle and my troops are within as you attack. This is your Castle and your Warriors are inside. How would you begin your attack?"

She cautiously moved her pieces around the board, weighing her moves carefully. He observed every move, smiling as he watched her fall prey to his traps on the board. She allowed his troops trap her horse soldiers who had their backs against the sea with no escape. He smiled when she moved her spearmen down the board to try and stop his foot soldiers from attacking the horsemen's flanks. Instead of doing the wise thing and allowing his foot soldiers to march past the spearmen and attack his foot soldiers from their flanks, using the horsemen as bait for the trap he prepared. He knew she was using her first instincts by trying to save most of her samurai, instead of using the lesser ones to destroy his main body of attacking warriors on the board.

When she realized his next moves would destroy her horsemen, thus allowing her left flank to collapse under his thrust using his spearmen to attack her army, he offered to his daughter. "Masahiko-san, you must learn lessons in way of life and battles. You must understand you can't command respect from your Warriors without giving respect. Just as you can't command honor without giving honor, and you can't win in battle by defending yourself all the time. You must learn to attack when attack is called for. You must reach out and support the Warriors trapped, you must take risks to win the battle and help your Master remain Daimyo of the Eight Provinces. If you fear to attack, to win your battle, this will happen to your Samurai, not only will you lose in battle, you'll lose the realm for the Master."

With this said, he moved his pieces across the board. It didn't take her long to realize the trap her horsemen were in, and how they would be slaughtered by her father's massed warriors attacking her trapped horsemen from two directions.

"There! You're trapped young Warrior with only one move left open to you in your effort to save some of your Samurai. Make the right choice and you'll gain face on the battlefield, chose wrongly and you'll be thought of as the foolish of commanders." He waved his hand over the board with less of her pieces left on it now.

She moved closer to the board as she studied her pieces surrounded on all sides by the sea, her father's pieces as warriors. Her eyes opened wide as she thought she might be able to keep a chunk of horsemen by moving them closer to the sea, and having them break out by the southern end of the board. She didn't catch the fact he had an army of spearmen held in reserve by what was supposed to be a mountain side on the board. Her correct move would have been to charge forward at the small army prepared to defend a narrow pass leading to escape for her trapped warriors. This was the only place he didn't have his reserves held. He knew the young eyes and mind of Masahiko would think this a bad move because of the closeness of the pass she would have to drive her samurai through.

Though the pass was narrow and many lead horsemen were certain to lose their lives, the narrowness made it an impossible position to defend against a strong charge of horsemen. Further, she didn't notice if her horsemen broke out they would end up in his flanks, and there were no more armies left to him to stop their attack against his armies. They would have a clear road to his castle and lord, thus winning the war.

He purposely left his flanks open to her attack, but he was equally aware her young mind would be placed on defense rather than offense. The trainer would never have tried such a daring attack if he was playing General Kobayashi, he would have easily seen his flanks open and taken advantage of the situation, thus defeating him and destroying his castle.

The trainer watched as she studied the board, and the trap she was mired in with her remaining forces. With a shaking hand she slowly moved the three pieces representing her remaining horsemen to the south of the board. He let out his breath and clapped his hands, knowing she committed the fatal mistake of taking the easy way out for her remaining soldiers, and now all was lost to her as the commander of the supposed soldiers left on the game board.

"Ieeeee Masahiko-san! You would've been better served by committing suppuku than have made such an ill thought out move. All is lost for you and your Samurai Warriors." He bragged as he smiled at his young and daring daughter.

"Ieeeee father, I hate to disagree, but my horsemen here will slaughter your foot soldiers, and this defeat will allow them to escape and regroup for further attacks against your armies." She shot back as she moved three pieces forward and took the two pieces representing his foot soldiers from the board. "There, your flank is compromised and I'll be able to escape your trap."

"Huh! You think I so foolish as to leave my rear open to attack, young pup? Watch young fire and you'll see your retreating, your retreating army mind you, be trapped in a snare where none will survive my attack." He moved four pieces from the shadow of the make believe mountain and the warriors cut into her horsemen, splitting her forces in two then two again, and defeated her horsemen on the board as easily as they would have been destroyed on the true battlefield.

She was fighting back tears as she realized she didn't pay attention to all enemy pieces on the board. She was furious for being so easily defeated in her first battle. The unconquerable heart of a warrior was instilled in her body, and refused to allow defeat to overcome her heart. Anger forced her to search the board, to see if she could pull any warriors from other places to help her horsemen out of this new trap. She moved her hand and tapped a pair of spearmen armies.

"Ieeeee Masahiko-san! If you move your troops from that area then my army here will march in, and destroy you from behind from here and here."

"What if I only move one of my spearmen to support my horsemen?"

"You'll compromise both armies. If you leave one spearmen army behind to defend this position against my three armies. They'll be overrun and my spearmen will attack your horsemen from their flanks. Masahiko-san, to move only one of your armies to support your horsemen would make no difference in the outcome of the battle. All it would do is enable my Warriors to destroy more of your soldiers. It was a wise decision though, it was the only door left open to survive the battle. But a wise commander would know when a battle is lost, and his driving force would then be to save as many of his Samurai as he could.

"A successful commander must know when his judgment is wrong, and to attack or fight on would only result in the desolation of his armies. To fight under these overwhelming terms looks more like rage than courage. Courage is displayed only when the commander of the Warriors thinks more of his troops than of a glorious victory which would allow his Samurai to die needlessly in a rout. A wise leader understands his armies will fight on blindly to the last man for him, but it's his duty to know when further fighting is a useless loss of life. Of course, you understand it'd be up to the commander and his officers to apologize to his Master for their failure with their lives. But it's better to lose thirty of your officers rather than one hundred thousand men as you would've done by pressing the battle on the board.

Understand Masahiko-san?" He looked at his child for acknowledgement.

With tears building in her eyes she grunted to her father. "Hai."

His heart was breaking at the sight of the tremendous sadness etched in his daughter's unconquerable eyes. He smiled at the sad face as he offered. "Young Masahiko-san! Please excuse, it's no disgrace to lose your first game of Go. Especially to one who has fought in more battles than you have years in life. I must say Masahiko-san, you did more, and lasted longer than I dared figured. You done no disgrace to yourself, on the contrary you lasted longer than Kobayashi-san did on his first five wars on the board against me. You done well young pup." He bowed and added. "Masahiko-san! Your training lasted longer than I hoped. Turn in for the night, and you'll be allowed to sleep late tomorrow. I don't intend to begin your training until after second bell. It'll be a day of lazy beginnings, I'll meet you on the horse field. Go to sleep, sleep well young Warrior with the unconquerable heart."

"Hai father, I thank you for allowing me the extra sleep." She bowed and shuffled to bed.

He stood and walked to the window and he stared at the star filled night as he raised his hands and groaned. He felt someone come up behind him and cursed for not having his sword within easy reach, thinking he was slowly becoming addle minded. This was the first time in his life he was defenseless in his home. He tightened his muscles, ordering himself to be ready to attack as he turned with a snap in his movements. He instantly relaxed when he noticed Remi locked in a bow, a bottle of sake on a tray and his sword held on her lap.

"Stand woman." The master trainer snorted angrily at her.

She stood, not allowing his sword to touch the floor as she held it at arm's length and said. "Tanizaki-san! I was surprised to see your swords in their stand. I figured you were more interested in the training of your intelligent son than you were with your welfare. So I took it on myself to stand guard over the two of you while you were training your child on the game."

He took the sword and held it in his left hand as he rested his right hand on the hilt. He broke the seal between the sword and scabbard and checked the steel, something time taught him to do when handed a sword, to make sure his sword was whole and ready for action. "Huh Lady Remi! You acted as a true Samurai, you earned my respect, domo."

"Tanizaki-san! There's no need to thank your vassal for carrying out her duties to you and your household. You're too kind and free with your acclamation wasted on my worthless head. It was my duty, nothing more as it is of all loyal vassals' duty to protect your life with their own is the order. You would've expected no less from any of your retainers." Remi bowed to Tanizaki.

"You're correct, nevertheless I thank you for your diligence. I'll be pleased to inform Kawasomeru-sama of your devotion to my welfare. I'm sure he'll increase your wealth."

"It's not necessary to waste your time on my behalf. It's my responsibility to donate my life if need be, to your protection and the protection of every member of your family. It's what I was trained for." She motioned as she bowed again then offered him a cup of sake.

"Hai Lady Remi what you say you speak true as it is as it should be and is commanded by our laws." He grunted, he remained standing while she knelt and poured the sake for them. She held it out to the trainer in both hands. "I heated it warmer than normal on this wonderful night, in hopes it'll help you to relax quicker, and make it easier for you to fall asleep on this exciting night that I planned for you to enjoy, Tanizaki-san."

"Aaaaayyyyoooo! And what makes you think this is an exciting night to enjoy, Lady Remi?" The trainer asked the concerned looking woman standing before him.

"I'm no foolish woman Master. I saw the way your eyes shone as you taught Masahiko-san the art of the Go board. I saw you were impressed by the skills displayed by the young Samurai. I noticed the fire of battle return to your soul, you enjoyed the challenge the child gave. I heard the compliment you offered for his outstanding skills. I understand the charge this placed in your mind, and how hard it is to fall asleep when the mind is occupied by the strains of strategy on the battlefield. In hopes of making it easier to sleep, I offer you the gift of the mouth."

"Hai, I'm pleased by your kind offer, but I fear I'm not of the right frame of mind to enjoy such delights on this unending night. Lady Remi, I'll enjoy the wine and turn in for the night. I have a lot to do to prepare for tomorrow training of the young Masahiko-san. I believe it's wise for me to maintain my strength rather than to give it up for a few moments of pleasure you offered me on this wonderful night, Lady Remi." He sipped his wine again.

"Master Trainer Tanizaki-san! I'm sorry I cannot be of further service to you. I planned to make this night memorable for you to enjoy on this..."

"And why is that?" He interrupted as he asked, showing a little more interest.

"Tanizaki-san! I wanted to make this night special, to show you my thanks for changing your mind ordering Lady Tomotaka to live with the filthy people. It displayed great courage on your part to show you're not such a man, you can't change your mind once made up. This attitude proved to be interesting to this woman. On behalf of Lady Tomotaka I thank you Lord. Kon banwa." Good evening. Lady Remi bowed.

CHAPTER SIXTEEN

The night passed uneventfully, by the time Tanizaki was ready to eat, the table was set by Miho. Birds chirped outside and the sun was high, promising to be a beautiful day. He bowed to Miho in recognition. "Lady Miho! Wake the lazy Masahiko-san. I don't want the foolish child to go to the field without eating, the training will be long and hard on this day."

She stopped what she was doing and bowed as she offered. "Master Trainer Tanizaki-san! I'm most pleased to inform you that the young Masahiko-san has already eaten and is off to the training field without you. The child told me he wanted to feed and walk his horse before his training. It was generous of you to give the child such a gift of the horse. He was concerned over the animal, he's showing signs of becoming a valuable Warrior for his Master, and he'll bring much honor for you and your family."

He didn't say a word, but his eyebrow arched in surprise at the concern Masahiko was displaying for the horse. He was beginning to believe it was a wise move to give the child the animal. This was the first time the child beat him to the field since the training began for her.

There was a commotion at the front door, and General Kobayashi rushed in announcing there was a messenger at the gate, sent by Lord Kawasomeru to visit the ninth village.

He showed little concern for the stranger as he finished eating then casually strolled outside. He remained on the porch and beckoned the messenger. Miho followed and offered the messenger refreshments as was her duty. He offered Tanizaki a scroll with the seal of Kawasomeru intact then accepted Miko's offer of something to drink.

The trainer snapped the seal with his thumb and the scroll unrolled and he pulled it apart and read the message. His eyes narrowed, and a scowl set on his face.

General Kobayashi saw the look and knew right off there was trouble on the horizon for Japan. Mentally, he prepared himself for what fate awaited him.

When he finished reading the scroll, he handed it to General Kobayashi as he turned anew to the messenger. "Takashi-san! When did this come to be known to the realm?"

"Ieeeee Master Trainer Tanizaki-san! Please excuse my stupidity over that subject, I'm ashamed I don't know when. I know there was excitement in the Castle seven sticks of time past, and if I was to place the day this information came to light, I'd be forced to place the timing on that day." Takashi bowed to Tanizaki.

He dismissed Takashi's words with a flick of his hand as he turned to the general. "Kobayashi-san! We have a large task laid out before us. What do you think?"

"About the day this information came to be known, Master Trainer Tanizaki-san?" The confused general asked the master trainer.

"Iye! About what we're going to do about this foul information, General Kobayashi-san."

"Huh! I think we'd be wise to keep the child between us, and prepare for treachery aimed at the child. I think we should also..."

He held up his hand to silence General Kobayashi. He no longer trusted anyone near him when it came to the safety of Masahiko. He looked at the messenger then snapped nastily. "Your mission has been fulfilled. I'm sorry I can't offer you a warm place to spend the night, but alas, my home is overcrowded. You'll return to Engakuji Castle. I'll send a messenger to Kawasomeru-sama once I come up with a plan for the protection of Masahiko-san." He waited for Takashi to bow then move from them before he spoke with his general again.

"Ieeeee General Kobayashi-san! What kind of treachery exists in this Empire when a feared and once respected warlord such as Wakatsuki with mighty armies at his back, threatens a mere child who barely entered adulthood? Eight years old and it comes to my attention the fool placed a bounty on my child's head. We must have spies in our village for the dog eater to know of my child's being. How do I protect a child from such treachery, a child who barely knows the meaning of death, let alone life. I'll summon my friends and together, we'll march to Lord Wakatsuki's filthy provinces and I'll find this worthless dog, and separate his head from his detestable shoulders. The thought of such a powerful man placing a bounty on a child is enough to clear our guts on the floor. The man is without honor." He was raving as he paced.

The villagers came out to see what upset the master trainer so. They were in fear for their lives, worrying if something happened to take him out of the light of their master's eye.

The wise general noticed this and moved to his side to whisper the villagers were watching him. He didn't want any to think he was upset. Shoya Sanuki came out and saw Tanizaki in his fit and rushed to him, adding to the excitement of the villagers thinking the worst.

The general place his hand on Tanizaki's chest to calm him as Sanuki reached his front gate, only to be stopped by an angry guard upset by the fury displayed by his master, and he sharpened his guard against anyone who might approach the home. The samurai didn't know if his master trainer was under threat, and he was prepared to stop anyone from getting near. General Kobayashi pointed out the guard was stopping the old Shoya to Tanizaki who ordered the samurai to allow the Shoya entrance to his property.

Sanuki rushed to his side and bowed. "Master Trainer Tanizaki-san! What happened? I heard your cursing in my home. This is regrettable conduct for such a great man. I insist you stop this raving. You're upsetting the harmony of my village, and this I'll not allow, even by you." The Shoya was worried Kawasomeru might have uncovered the deception he was involved in. He was prepared to further separate himself from the trainer, and try to salvage his life from the bite of the sword, claiming no knowledge of the attempt to deceive the Master of the Eight Provinces.

He glared at him and ordered Kobayashi to show him the note he received from the messenger.

As Sanuki unrolled the scroll, he was certain his worst fears were correct, and prepared to give the order to take the trainer in custody, and hold him until Kawasomeru arrived to take his head, or have him delivered to the castle for punishment. Whatever the master wanted, he would carry out with haste. The Shoya's lips moved as he read, shock replaced his anger as he read where Lord Wakatsuki placed a bounty on the child. He was relieved Lord Kawasomeru hadn't uncovered the ploy. He looked from the scroll to Tanizaki and asked. "Ieeeee! What to do?"

General Kobayashi grabbed the hilt of his sword, causing the guards surrounding Tanizaki to react by encircling the trainer and drawing their swords in preparation to ward off an attack from him. They realized General Kobayashi's wrath was directed at Shoya Sanuki, and being they had no orders to protect the headman of the village, they relaxed and watched to see what the general was going to do to the old man who stood before him without swords or weapons.

The general drew his katana, the sword's steel sung its song of death as it slid from the scabbard then held it above his head as he bellowed in rage. "Shoya Sanuki-san! We'll turn the Ninth Village into an armed encampment with everyone on guard day and night, to protect Masahiko-san from treachery from that dung eating dog in our northern provinces. The women will be ordered to carry weapons, and be ready to strike against assassins sent to destroy Kawasomeru-sama's vassal. To allow this child to be assassinated would bring great disgrace on the Ninth Village. The only way this disgrace could be erased, would be to put everyone to death. It'd be the only way to purge the ugly stain of disgrace in the land. I promise this will be my last duty, if any harm befalls Masahiko-san's head, before I fall on my sword to lift disgrace." He swung his sword, making the steel sing with a whooshing sound, the blade looked like a silver blur as it cut through the air singing its song of death.

The trainer moved to his general's side, causing more distress to his guards who tried to cut him off, but he pushed them aside. He placed his hand on the general's shoulder and warned. "Kobayashi-san! It'll be as you stated. We'll turn the village to an armed camp with one thought in mind, to protect Masahiko-san's life. I'll place six guards in charge of the child's protection. The guards won't leave the child for a moment. They'll sleep outside his room and follow him wherever he goes. I'll hold them and their families and ancestors responsible for Masahiko-san."

The trainer turned to the first warrior guard and hissed. "Commander! You and five Samurai take responsibility for guarding Masahiko-san's life. If anything happens to the child, you'll behead the guards then commit suppuku unattended at the feet of the dead child. You and your family will wish you were born to a dog's life, if you allow anything to happen to my child." He glared at the guard who dropped to his knees still locked in his bow to the trainer.

The commander looked up and then he offered. "Hai Lord! I swear on my kishomon oath, nothing will happen to Masahiko-san on my watch."

"It better not! You're placed in charge of Masahiko-san. Do something about him."

The commander jumped to his feet, called five names out and the samurai rushed to the field.

Sanuki mumbled. "Master Trainer Tanizaki-san! I'll assume the duty of mustering the villagers. Wherever they go they'll be armed and ready to strike to protect Masahiko-san's life. That includes every man, woman and child of the village."

He bowed politely to the old Shoya who he had detested so.

The general added to the words from the Shoya. "Tanizaki-san! I'll send word to the eighth, tenth and eleventh villages, to my friends who owe debt. I'll order them here to protect Masahiko-san from the treacherous Wakatsuki and his henchmen who'll carry out his bidding."

He didn't reply, he just nodded. Every thought was on Masahiko, and the child's safety. He wanted to be with the child, to protect the young one against harm. He knew he couldn't leave now, or it would bring loss of face to the commander, and samurai he sent to protect Masahiko. He found himself cursing Wakatsuki for threatening his child.

For the next five days, life in the ninth village changed drastically for all, every male walked with their swords tucked threateningly in their sashes. They were armed even while tending the fields, taking in fish, or doing chores. The women were armed, though their arms were unseen. Law forbade the women to walk about with a katana on their hip, so the weapons were hid in the folds of their kosode. Children walked with swords. Even the children Masahiko was having trouble with armed and prepared to lay down their lives for the child.

The trainer was proud at the way everyone in the village mustered to his side.

The changes interfered with Masahiko's training. It was harder for her to learn the different ways of riding a horse during times of battle, with five guards riding at her side. Sometimes, their horses bumped into her animal, causing a quick end to part of the training. She became upset at having six samurai in her face. They offered her little privacy, and we're always looking over her shoulder, making suggestions on how to react in a certain battle strategy, and going against the training of Tanizaki. The guards even went in the latrines before she used them, to make certain no one was waiting to do Masahiko harm.

He was upset at the way the training was progressing. The guards were interfering in his thoughts, and causing him to make mistakes and bad judgments. On the first day of the fifth week since the threat was made know, he could take no more and ordered the samurai off the field. He gathered them and ordered them not to follow the child on the field. He was in possession of the knowledge General Kobayashi's men were placed in the forest surrounding the fields and in the village. They were armed with bows, and had orders to kill anyone found lurking in the forest without question.

The trainer knew there were samurai in the homes that bordered his property, and living in the birthing building. Other warriors were taking care of the bath house. He was confident he had warriors protecting every area of attack that might be used by an assassins sent by Wakatsuki.

One thing he found puzzling, was he received no personal message from Kawasomeru. He couldn't help but think by now, the master should have checked on the health of the child by messenger, or at least sent for the child so he could finish his training in the safety of the castle keep. He had no idea Lord Kawasomeru entered into negotiation with Wakatsuki to bring about a lasting peace in the realm. It was the first serious negotiations to take place since the wars that swept the central provinces began.

The warlord was certain he could make Wakatsuki understand how important it was to enhance the peace between the sixteen provinces. The negotiations took place at a neutral place on the border between Shinano and Echigo province. The meeting was carried out in an inn with many samurai in attendance. These warriors were on guard to protect Kawasomeru's life from treachery. Wakatsuki had an equal number of samurai surrounding him. He had no way of knowing Kawasomeru's samurai were better trained and could destroy him before reinforcements arrived in the field to assist his warriors guarding his life. He was also unaware there was one signal Kawasomeru had to utter, and his warriors would swoop down and destroy Wakatsuki and his warriors. He was prepared to give this order if he was unable to talk him into peace.

The warlord was armed with the blessings from the Shogun to destroy Wakatsuki, and his army if their negotiations failed. Ashikaga-sama was busy with his own civil wars to witnessed the negotiations. The Shogun was concerned what took place in the central province, he had most of the other provinces locked up and with Lord Kawasomeru in command of eight of the central provinces, he knew his lack of concern was acceptable to the powerful loyal warlord.

By the tenth week things got back to near normal. Masahiko got used to the samurai around her. General Kobayashi's men found two assassins, but they were unable to get near the village to do harm to the child. The training of the child was going well. The samurai were turning Masahiko into a great horseman, riding with her on the field and engaging in horse races. Showing her other ways they discovered to control the horse by using weight in the saddle, and pressure of her knees and shifting of her position. She understood her horse, and was sure her horse was beginning to anticipate her needs. Her horse became an extension of herself, a weapon in the horses own right. Between the two, they worked together with little control from either. The horse read her lead and by being forced to go through the training with her, the horse was beginning to understand the act of war.

He was pleased with her and her horse's progress, he decided to bestow on them the horse's first armor. He presented it to her in a fine ceremony on the field. She stood at attention in front of the horse, and the horse stood behind her with no control, the reins lying at its feet. The horse tried to hide behind her shoulder, because it understood something special was taking place. He walked up to Masahiko, General Kobayashi followed carrying the armor for the horse.

He bowed as he bellowed. "Masahiko-san! Seeing how well you mastered your horse's spirit, and how each respect the other. Has forced me to pay homage to this joining of souls. It's a great Samurai who can blend his soul to that of his horse, it'll insure the survival of both on the field of battle. To honor this joining I give you your horse's first armor." He bowed to General Kobayashi who stepped forward, and held out the armor.

Proudly, Masahiko moved forward and uncovered the armor, the first thing she saw was the neck covering with the rich silver inlays that went all the way from the horses ears down to the saddle. There was a highly decorated silver muzzle, and a pair of iron stirrups with the same silver inlay decorations. A straw blanket which was to protect the horse from sword strike was included, but the most striking item was the armor neck protector. She pulled it from him and held it out for the horse to see. The horse sniffed the metal ribbing. She looped it over the neck, and the added weight made the horse skittish for a moment, until it got used to the new weight.

She examined the intricate carvings on the highly decorated neck guard, and looked to her father to see if he would explain the fine carvings to her.

"Huh Masahiko-san! I see in your eyes they're as sharp as your wits. Yes that's my horse's armor, given to me by Shogun Ashikaga, to honor my actions in the battle of Minatogawa years past. If you look closely, you'll see the relief depicting the death of the greatest warrior to walk on the soil of Japan, Samurai Warrior Kusunoki Masashige-san. It was his most admirable day in life and after his death, you'll see the death blow to Samurai Kusunoki-san's army.

"We took five thousand heads on that great day of days, until the river flowed red and Shogun Ashikaga's Warriors grew tired of killings. It took the greatest carvers two months to place the reliefs in the silver on the horse neck shield. The Shogun gave me this neck protector on the day I retired to the Ninth Village to await my death. It was Lord Kawasomeru who breathed new life in my old soul by offering me the privilege to train his future Samurai. Along with this privilege came the honor of a Warrior and Kawasomeru-sama's generous gifts and lands." He took a quick breath, allowing Masahiko to say something if she wanted.

"Ieeeee father! But this gift is beyond anything I earned. It's too valuable to be given to an unworthy person as I. One who has yet to prove he's able to ride a horse without falling off. No father, as much of an honor as this gift might be, I'm bound by honor to refuse it." She bowed to her father, who accepted the bow with all the dignity it was offered.

He returned her gracious bow with an equal bow. "Masahiko-san! I don't remember giving you permission to refuse such a fine gift. No Masahiko-san! The gift is yours to enjoy and protect you horse's life on the field of battle in the future, although you're correct saying you're not worthy of this gift, because you're untested on the field of battle. But I know the god's will show you the way to greatness, and you'll be proven in battle. A gift such as this is wasted hanging on a wall as a decoration to be gawked at by visitors to my house.

"No Masahiko-san! To give honor to such a prize, it must be hanging from its horse's neck, stained red in battle for one's Master. I'm too old to ride in another battle for our Master and live. I fear my next battle will be with the worthless gods of the wonder world, and where they intend to place me in their world of myth. Be prepared Masahiko-san, all I have will soon be yours, and I'll not tolerate argument over the matter. You're the one picked to replace me as the next Master Trainer for our Master's sake" He gave his daughter a slight wink of his eye.

All she could do was stared dumbly at her father with her mouth hanging open, she couldn't believe her father was honoring her so with such fine gifts.

He saw the look of awe and smiled as he continued. "Masahiko-san! The gifting has not finished. I have another to give you, and today is as good a time as any to receive them. Saburo-san! Bring Masahiko-san's next gift."

A samurai broke ranks to chase a few children from the field, Tanizaki didn't want any village children playing on the field digging it up, or disturbing the grounds. The worse thing to have happen was for a child to dig a hole in the dirt, and have a warrior's horse step in it, breaking its leg and possibly hurting the warrior in the tumble he was sure to experience in the accident.

The called warrior rushed to his side and bowed. On his back was an open ebira, the quiver had a dozen arrows in it, they were tied to the quiver by a red silk thread. The samurai remained bowed as he removed an arrow with a decorative hirane ne or flat arrowhead. The center of the brass head was hollowed out, and a web like weave of polished brass formed a sculpture of its own. In the center of the webbing were two Japanese symbols representing Masahiko Tanizaki's initials. It was an honored, and a proud gift he had to offer to his child.

She stared at the handiwork of the arrowhead with her initials carved in it, she fingered the sharp edges. The tip of the arrow looked as if it could pierce the most worthy of armor. She looked to her father and cried. "Father, what have I done to deserve such valuable gifts as these. I'm unworthy to receive such wonderful items. Surely, one of your other sons is more worthy to receive them. I'm embarrassed to be forced to accept such wonderful things for no good reason."

"Masahiko-san! Of all my worthy sons, you're the only one most worthy of my weapons and armor. Although you're yet too small to wear my armor, I'll order it altered when time is ready for you to wear it. I took care of my other sons in my will, so they're not to be worried about. I order you to take what I offer in the manner it's offered. As far as not being worthy to posses them, your honest refusal of the gifts make you the most worthy. Masahiko-san! I give you time to dress your horse for war before I begin your training anew. Be prepared, you have twenty feathers of time to prepare the animal, and yourself for the new training."

The general moved nearer the child, and offered to help her dress her horse, the guards also offered to assist her as did the other samurai whose duty it was to protect the field from vandalism. Her horse was loving the attention the warriors were lavishing on it as they helped dressed it for battle. It seemed as though the horse knew it looked proud in its armor, and was glad for being dressed so, the horse began to prance around once she wore the armor properly.

Masahiko and Kobayashi watched as the horse danced egotistically, proudly showing off before them. "Ieeeee Masahiko-san! Even your horse is proud beyond vanity. You should be self-satisfied, by having such a fine steed beneath your fine rump in times of battle."

Tanizaki returned to the field, and the festive mood of dressing the stamping horse ended as the samurai lined up on either side of Masahiko, preparing to assist the trainer while she grabbed the reins, and led the horse to her father. Kobayashi was on the other side of the horse, adding to the majestic scene unfolding. He was proud to stand with her growing in skills and intelligence. The general smiled with the knowledge a child mastered the spirit of her horse. It was impressive, and showed the child was gifted, and picked correctly by the gods for greatness.

The trainer inspected the horses' armor, everything was proper as he figured it would be. He circled the steed, tugging on its tail to see if it would rear or kick at him, it didn't. This was another sign she had control of the animal. As he got in front of the horse, joining Masahiko and General Kobayashi he grunted. "Your mount is perfect, well trained and mannered. You brought honor to yourself. I'm proud of you and your efforts with your horse." He knew the horse was well trained, and he wanted to see if the horse would accept the child as her new master. It was plain to see the child and horse had come to an understanding. The trainer turned to Kobayashi and growled. "General Kobayashi-san! Why do you stand there so with this foolish young Samurai not yet proven to be a fit to be called a Warrior?"

"Tanizaki-san! I wish to sponsor this child to Warriorhood if you'll allow me that honor and privilege. I'll be responsible for the training of the child to make him whole, a great

Warrior to be respected by all." The general bowed proudly to the trainer.

The remaining samurai started beating on their shields with the hilts of their katanas, cheering the honor General Kobayashi offered, displaying their approval.

He glared at the samurai to silence them, once quiet returned to the ranks, he set his attention to Kobayashi and grunted as he bowed to the grinning general. "General Kobayashi-san! Why have you decided to offer such an honor to a mere child?"

"Because Master Trainer! I believe there's something great in the soul of this child, and I wish to be part of it." He replied as he stood at attention and stared at the trainer.

"Ahhh... So it's a matter of vanity you offer such a fine honor to this young child?"

"Iye... Master Trainer Tanizaki-san. You misunderstand my intention. That's the furthest thing from my worthless mind. I want to sponsor this child, because I believe he's the salvation and future of Japan, and I wish to offer the child my services to make certain what the gods chose for this one to accomplish in his life, he'll deliver." Again, he bowed to Tanizaki.

This offer came as no surprise, both warriors discussed this as they walked to the field that day. It was the only way he could get such a powerful warrior to guard his child closely, to have the warrior sponsor the child in the training time. He understood with Kobayashi standing by her side, no assassin's attempt would be successful. After a few moments pretending to think, he snarled. "General Kobayashi-san! You bestowed a powerful honor on this worthless child's foolish head. With your backing, Masahiko-san is considered a Samurai trainee and with your guidance, the foolish child will become a great Samurai when the time arises for him to do so. Thank you for taking interest in the making of this Samurai's future. The gods will repay you."

The training and days passed during the span of time covering the next three years, with the child absorbing everything offered before her. She displayed great knowledge in the inner working of the samurai world, she showed a fine ability to understand the strategy of making and winning war. She learned how best to use her troops, and the way to attack her enemy when they were dug in, and defending an encampment from attack. Or how to defend her dug in position if they came under attack by a superior attacking enemy force.

The master trainer had found his match when playing Go also. Try as he might, he could no longer easily defeat her in board battles. Twice in seventy games, she boxed him in an inescapable corner, and once the child even defeated his troops before he could retreat from the battle she engaged him in. He gained much comfort knowing he didn't allow the child to beat him, she had done it on her on abilities at waging war.

When he was unable to challenge the young mind further until he had time to recoup, the general stepped in and challenged the child in new tactics and methods of war making. In no time, the child understood the way he thought and reacted, and how he used his troops and what advantages he sought and in a few attempts, she soon defended herself against his style of waging war. In a few days, she placed General Kobayashi on the defensive and fought him to a standstill and finally, she defeated him on the game board.

Kobayashi was so frustrated in his many battles on the Go board and in the training field that he was at a loss as to discover new ways to trap and defeat the surprisingly intelligent child.

The trainer had trouble trying to think of ways to attack Masahiko, and on her eleventh birthday he sent a message to Kawasomeru, to see if he could borrow General Shimbo to help with the further training of his child warrior. He wanted to send a message to his lord and master to inform him of how Masahiko was doing on the training fields and understanding the art of waging war with her enemy. He was hoping the warlord would inform him of what was happening with Lord Wakatsuki.

It was two years since the warlords set brush to paper, and work out a lasting peace between them and their provinces. Even though there was no official word from Engakuji Castle on the manner, it was understood the bounty on Masahiko-san's head was rescinded, and the death penalty was lifted. Tanizaki had General Kobayashi send out his spies to make sure the bounty was truly lifted, and to see if he could find out if any assassins were still hunting his daughter's life. Every time the spies reported in, they confirmed there was no bounty on the child.

Days passed and no word came from Engakuji Castle. On a particular day in the middle of the afternoon, a lone samurai horseman defiantly rode into the ninth village and dismounted noisily from his steed in front of Tanizaki's home, and there he waited in the center of the road. The most impressive samurai was dressed in armor, and looked like he was daring to challenge the old master trainer to mortal combat.

ON THE FORTH DAY OF THE FIRST WEEK OF THE SEVENTH MONTH OF THE THIRTEEN FORTY FIFTH YEAR

The eight warriors assigned to guard Tanizaki's life and his family, rushed to the gate and started to threaten the ominous figure standing so proudly before them, obviously unimpressed by their threats and actions aimed at him. The trainer was in his home resting from the morning's training with his child.

With a resounding grumble, the impressive figure silenced the angry acting samurai. They were threatening the stranger to their village with angry words and violent motions by grabbing the hilt of their blades, and acting like they were going to unsheathe them and attack this samurai. No warriors went too far with their threatening by drawing their swords, or they would have been bound by respect to fight this fearsome looking warrior to the death. The warrior took one step forward to Tanizaki's gate, then stopped and waited for the trainer to appear on the porch.

After hearing the commotion outside, he stormed out the shoji screen in a huff. Still dressed in his training kosode he stared defiantly at the strange warrior standing before him. The stranger looked like he was challenging the trainer to a fight to the death. Tanizaki reached inside and picked up his sword and walked towards the threatening stranger without fear.

From out of nowhere, Masahiko appeared with her bodyguard warriors standing protectively behind her. She was likewise dressed in her dirt covered training kosode as she stepped before her father, impeding his way as she drew her blade and challenged the strange and extremely large samurai warrior to battle.

Her guards tried to stop the child from going too far in her challenging such an obviously well seasoned and ready to fight samurai, but they were rendered silent when the samurai issued a grunt then she took a step forward. The samurai dressed in black armor smiled, he did what he had set to do. To draw this young and supposed well trained samurai out and force the foolish child to a sword fight. He was surprised it was so easy to accomplish, he knew of the trainer and his established ways of training, and figured this child would be more disciplined than it seemed. To throw caution to the wind such as the warrior done, and challenge a much larger and wiser warrior than he, was sheer folly. But the samurai wasn't going to allow the child to get out of the situation he placed himself in easily.

Masahiko's samurai reluctantly relented and stepped aside and allowed the child to move forward. General Kobayashi rushed up behind the threatening warrior and called after him, challenging him to battle with the general instead of the child. He was prepared and stood with blade in a threatening stance.

The action took place in less than a heartbeat. General Kobayashi was exhausted from the long day's training with the child, and was caught off guard by the blinding speed this unknown samurai attacked with. Barely giving him the time to react to the fierce assault against his body, although he was prepared he was defeated swiftly before he could mount his attack against the strange warrior. In a blinding movement the black samurai's sword was out and in two lightening strikes, the general found himself on the ground bleeding from a head wound. The first strike from the black warrior shattered his katana midway down the shaft. The second blow was delivered by the blunt end of the warrior's sword to the head, it sent the general to the ground with a nasty gash over his eye, extending down his cheek. The samurai was skilled enough to make certain there was no serious damage done to his eye, he was only interested in sending a message to the warrior, not to serve as his death angel. Villagers moved out and dragged him to safety and looked to his wound.

By the black warrior's swift moves, Tanizaki realized who it was dressed in the armor and though he couldn't see the samurai's face because he wore the brass sneering face cover, he relaxed his stance against the warrior. It would be a lesson for Masahiko to experience crossing swords with the greatest swordsman in the Empire. He smiled as he realized the Samurai Masahiko Nishihara was standing before him, preparing to do battle with his daughter.

Two of Masahiko's guards shot forward to take up the challenge by this fearsome samurai, they were called back by Tanizaki who waved them to the side. Then he ordered them to remain out of the battle. The guards stared in disbelief at the trainer, unable to understand why he would allow such a young child to wage battle with so obviously seasoned and battle tested warrior.

Sweat broke out on her forehead as she realized her father was going to allow her to do battle with this threatening stranger to their village who so easily defeated Kobayashi. Scared to death at the thought of dying, she stepped forward knowing she went too far to back down from her challenge to this threatening warrior now, and went outside the gate. The samurai in black armor back stepped to allow the child warrior room to defend herself properly in battle.

Samurai Nishihara was more than impressed at the stamina, guts, valor, and way the child was prepared to defend herself and her father's honor. The challenging samurai had no idea the child was eleven years old, and was able to see the training in the child's steps instilled by the old trainer. The threatening samurai knew he should have thought no less of one of his pupils.

She was tall and deceiving for her age, and in better shape than most children her age because she had the best food to eat, and carrying weights long before any other child of the village would have been expected to. When Nishihara was certain the child was ready for battle he grinned then bowed. He adopted a threatening stance waiting for the child to respond.

She stared at this imposing figure before bowing to him, knowing she was trapped in the fight of her life. She stepped towards the huge warrior then made her first thrust which was easily brushed aside by the sheer strength of the black warrior, but he didn't press his attack against the suddenly out of position child. Instead, he waited for her to reset and defend herself again. With a loud clanking of swords she attacked furiously at the evil looking stranger. The first of her blows came from overhead, and she immediately spun on her left heel and came back at the powerful warrior from his left side, actually forcing the large warrior to move off to his right side to fend off the second attack against him.

She allowed the force of the defending blow to spin her around, and came back at the intruder with a blow at chest height from his right side. The child let out a mighty roar from deep in her bowels that took the black samurai off guard momentarily, and allowed this thrust to get through his defenses. Her blade nicked his chest plate and his chin, and drove him back a step before he was ready for her next wild blow. The black warrior was surprised at the ferocity and manliness of this child's calculated attack against him. He was impressed by Tanizaki's child and her outstanding training. She was fearless and building honor in her first battle.

The visiting Samurai Nishihara prepared for her next attack, and her thrust came from low beneath his knees with the speed of wind. The blow worked its way up between his legs, seeking the lesser protected crotch of the black warrior's armor. It was only many years of experience in fighting that saved his manhood from being split as the child's sword bounced off the side of his mantel plate, and deflected in the air.

She almost lost her grip on the hilt of her sword as it flew over her head from the force of her attack on the invader. She had to regrasp the weight of the sword a second time, as she came down in a defending position against the large warrior who charged into her sleepy village.

Again, the large warrior did not press attack against the momentarily disadvantaged and out of position child warrior. Instead he allowed the child to reset herself then prepared for her next attack against his body.

It was strange for her to understand, she knew twice if this warrior chose, could have defeated her, and she would have been walking with her ancient ancestors by now. She was confused by the actions of this samurai who stood before her grinning like a fool without a care in the world, and his katana blade held high and ready to strike her without striking. Her first thrust knocked the brass face cover from his face.

Samurai Nishihara unexpectedly bowed at the attacking child, displaying awe in his eyes at the skills the child warrior with the blade locked in her hands, was displaying against him. But his bow didn't impress his attacker as she came back at him with a thrust at neck height. Again, the black samurai was forced to react to fend off the lethal blow aimed at his body, and to make certain he ended up in a good position to fend off what he believed to be the next blow from the child samurai. But it didn't come from the direction that logic would have deem proper.

Instead of her attacking him from the left where his force would have dictated the blow to come from, Tanizaki's child stopped her momentum in mid-stream and changed the course of her blade in strike. The attack came at him from his right side, catching him off guard. The blow was stinging and if it was delivered by a full grown strong warrior, his head would surely have been rolling down the street, and the child would be hacking the rest of his body to pieces in her victory rage. Then Masahiko's sword would have been lifted high in victory over him.

Nishihara rolled with the blow in an attempt to lessen the effectiveness of the strike, and removed his helmet in one motion as he ended up sitting on his rump in the middle of the road. His sword ended up resting across his legs and he bellowed and rubbed the nick on his neck. Even in his laughter he held his sword in a position to place it at the ready, to defend himself from further blows from the warrior child standing before him in a threatening manner.

She didn't allow the laughter of this huge samurai warrior to sway her attack in any manner, nor her preparedness as she moved in for the killing blow. She moved with the swiftness of a cat, an attacking tigress as she raised her blade and charged at the sitting samurai, roaring with power over the downed and dominated warrior.

The standing on guard master trainer bellowed in such a commanding tone which instantly gained her attention, he screamed out. "IYE!"

The sheer force of the word from her father made her turn in fright that something might be happening to her father. She was bewildered to see him smiling not at her, but at the samurai sitting on the ground. Never lowing her sword nor relaxing her stance, she stared at her father before turning back to the samurai on his rump, to continue her attack against him. Suddenly, she held back her thrust, now assuming the stance of defense rather than one of offense, and waited for her father to join her.

The trainer, laughing rested his hand on her sword, forcing the point of the weapon down as he ordered her to relax. His laughing informed the child obviously the samurai on his rump in the dirt, was a warrior sent to test her maturing skills with the blade by their master. He had to admire her strength by holding the weight of the blade out before her for so long a time.

He left Masahiko and went to Nishihara and offered his hand to help him on his feet. "leeeee Master Warrior Nishihara-san! The ground is no place for such a great Warrior. By the Kami who stalk the afterworld of wonder, I swear your sword was moving slow, or was it my child's sword moving with the speed of the Floating World?" He chuckled as he slammed his hand on the back of his old friend. The trainer turned to his guards and announced for all to hear.

"All you dung eating fools of the Ninth Village, allow me to introduce you to this great Warrior who wasted his time standing here and allowing me to address him. He's the greatest swordsman in all the realm. This Samurai is Masahiko Nishihara-sama of the First Village!"

There was a murmur from the samurai as they dropped to the ground and bowed.

He grunted approvingly at the reaction from the guards as he hissed this time. "Yes, all of you better shake in your worthless loincloths before the great Samurai Nishihara-san takes a notion, and separates your foul heads from your worthless shoulders for your lack of manners and respect, for not recognizing him right away as I have done."

As the warrior continued to laugh and Nishihara wiped at a tear and said to the trainer. "Ieeeee Tanizaki-san! What type of devil child did you spawn from your foul loins? I can't live with the shame of having a mere child best me in battle before these fools. By the worthless Kami I must be getting old and feeble by age. I can't force my mind to believe this young one is so able to understand my attacks, and the art of defending one's self so early in his life. Huh Tanizaki-san! You outdone yourself with this devil's born. I pity the poor fools who dare to cross swords with this one when he's no longer a child, and walks proudly on the battlefields for his Master. I hope I live long enough to fight by your child's side. It'll be an experience of my life to see Masahiko-san locked in battle against all of Kawasomeru-sama's enemy." Nishihara bowed first to Tanizaki then to Masahiko who stared intensely at the warrior while still keeping her guard up and slightly warning the warrior she was prepared to continue her attack against him.

Masahiko was still extremely worked up from her battle with the samurai who invaded her village, and held her blade at the ready, but not in an attacking position. She didn't return the bow offered her from the fearful warrior.

Tanizaki was angered by her childish response to Nishihara's offering of the bow and barked. "Masahiko-san! Have I so ill trained you that you forgot good manners when dealing with another Samurai of great respect? Samurai Nishihara-san should demand honor from you, you insulted me and yourself by not returning the esteem he displayed to you. Your actions are detestable for a true Warrior trained by my hand and mind, foolish child."

She was at a loss of what to do next. All she knew was moments before this samurai dressed in black armor tried to kill her and her father, and now her father was treating this hated invading warrior as if he was a long lost uncle. She wondered if her father's mind took leave of his senses. But she understood the harsh glare her father leveled at her, and knew she had to do something before risking his further wrath. Slowly, and with care and respect, Masahiko bowed first to her father then to the samurai standing alongside her father with his arm looped over her his back. Her bow wasn't great but was within the boundaries of politeness and proper respect.

Her bow didn't calm her father who remained glaring at her. He was unhappy with the weakness displayed by her bow, and was ready to yell at the child until Nishihara cut him off.

"Ieeeee Tanizaki-san! What unseen power do you have over this child who is no child? You spawned a youth able to defeat a man Warrior in battle. You have the child ready to fight, to climb in the region of the mind which erases all thought but the thoughts of defending one's self against his honored enemy. Then you're able to pull this child's mind out of that world of madness, and bring him back to the civilized world as easily as I pass wind after eating supper. This one will be a fitting part of Kawasomeru-sama's army, Tanizaki-san." Again, Nishihara bowed towards the child warrior barely breathing heavily.

This time, without thought or hesitation she returned the fine bow equally as polite. This removed her father's angry stare from on her shoulders.

"How old is this young master swordsman you have spawned from your old body, Master Tanizaki-san?" Samurai Nishihara grunted with a grin, not daring to taking his eyes from the child, fearing another attack from the child warrior.

"Eleven years and fifteen days of age, Nishihara-san." He bragged to the stunned samurai, not losing the fact his child did good battle with an experienced warrior as Samurai Nishihara was.

"By the gods who made me addled and filled my mind with dung and a pounding headache. Do my ears play tricks on my old mind? Do you want me to believe this child is merely eleven rings of the willow? Ieeeee Tanizaki-san! You must think me a fool who allowed his mind to wander in a state of awe and wonderment. How can a child of eleven hold the weight of the katana, let alone swing the blade with enough force to place me on my boils in the middle of the road as he has done? At the risk of insulting my old friend of too many years to count, I want to know what type of joke you're trying to play against me, old man." He stared at his friend as if waiting for him to say the child was older than eleven.

Tanizaki bellowed with laughter as he announced to the samurai staring at his child with awe in his eyes. "May my painful boils bleed and cause me ten times trouble if I'm trying to deceive my old friend. The child Masahiko-san is only eleven years of age, Nishihara-san. By the great gods, just eleven rings of the willow is his true age, my old friend."

"By the flies that drive my horse mad on his journeys, the realm is not ready for a child of eleven to take the field of battle with them against his Master's enemy. The fools who can write will be crafting ballads to the child Warrior who placed Nishihara on his rump during battle with me. I can hear Kawasomeru-sama roaring with laughter at my expense, Tanizaki-san. I'll be forced to shave my head and follow the teaching of Buddha, and have to expose my boils for the pleasure of the priests to enjoy. Ieeeee, the life I'll endure for my failure against this child in sword battle, old man. What have you done to me, Tanizaki-san? The shame of it all." Nishihara bellowed with equal laughter as they walked to Tanizaki's house.

As the samurai laughingly entered the front gate to his home, Tanizaki dared to ask the feared warrior of countless battles. "Nishihara-san! Why have you decided to pay my village a visit?"

"Huh Tanizaki-san, I see you're still trying to play games on my head! As if you don't know why I'm here, old man. It's your fault I was ordered to your village. Kawasomeru-sama read your letter requesting General Shimbo-san to come to the Ninth Village and challenge this young pup of yours in battle tactics and skills. But General Shimbo-san is otherwise employed with moving of troops to Kozuke province to help defend the province against a possible sneak attack by Lord Wakatsuki. It seems Kawasomeru-sama's enemy is once again threatening to set the sixteen provinces on fire."

The trainer stopped walking and grumbled in anger. "Ieeeee! Is this not going against the peace treaty signed by Kawasomeru-sama, and that worthless dung heap Wakatsuki?"

"Yes my friend, but Lord Kawasomeru doesn't trust the fool as far as he can see him. Lord Kawasomeru is in possession of certain documents which inform him Wakatsuki-sama is secretly ferrying troops to positions of attack in Echigo and Shimotsuke provinces. It's further believed he's moving troops around in Awa and Shimosa, and placing his province of Kazusa at peril from these foul troops about to invade the provinces."

"Ieeeee Nishihara-san! Then this worthless peace in the realm is only a low time in which our Master is taking advantage, by moving his troops around the province to positions of defense against what Wakatsuki plans to do against him?" He moaned as the two started walking.

"And what makes you believe our wise Master has intentions of being on the defensive in the upcoming wars, Master Tanizaki-san?" Nishihara hissed, not looking at his friend.

"Ahhh... yes, it was foolish on my part to assume anything my Master decides to do or not do."

"Hai Tanizaki-san! Yes, it's believed we'll be at war encompassing the central provinces along with the eight provinces under control of our Lord soon. We'll destroy Lord Wakatsuki's influences and free the provinces under his control at long last. It's believed the freed provinces will join Kawasomeru-sama and this joining will end the bickering of the provinces of the central region. I know if the provinces don't stop their constant warring, Kawasomeru-sama will destroy their provinces and absorb what's left to his supporting provinces. Kawasomeru-sama is growing impatient with the stresses these provinces are placing on the entire realm. It'll give me pleasure to go after these troublesome Daimyos who cause unrest for my Master. Great pleasure."

"I agree Nishihara-san. I believe these provinces created enough problems than Wakatsuki and his attitude and desires to become Shogun of Central Japan." He added as an afterthought as they came to his porch and sat on cushions. His household understood these old warriors would speak outside. Most of their lives was spent lying under the stars warring in the mud.

When the two battle tested warriors were comfortably resting on the cushions, Tomotaka and Miho appeared. Tomotaka carried a tray with a bottle of warmed sake and two porcelain cups. Miho carried a tray covered with rice and dried fish as a light snack for the warriors to pick on.

Nishihara held his helmet in one hand and opened his armor to allow him to sit comfortably as she poured sake. Tanizaki made a motion and Tomotaka offered the first cup to Nishihara.

"Ieeee! I'm unworthy to receive such an honor. I insist you receive the first Tanizaki-san."

"No Samurai Nishihara-san! I insist you take the first cup. Take it as an honor for teaching my worthless child how to defend himself with the sword. I couldn't offer you enough worth for such a valuable lesson, so I insist you enjoy the honor of the first cup."

"Tanizaki-san! You're wise in your old years I see. You're correct and I'll enjoy the first cup of sake, and the honor that goes with it." Nishihara added as he took the cup and bowed.

When the shock of the swordsman's manners wore off, Tanizaki relaxed and sipped his wine. Politeness would have dictated the warrior insisted he should enjoy the first cup. After all, it was his sake, his village the samurai was visiting. The warriors ate and enjoyed talk, but when he asked Nishihara how long he was going to remain in the village, the conversation turned serious.

"Tanizaki-san! I'm ordered to remain in your village for seven sticks of time, to test this child you gave birth to. I'm allowed to leave earlier if the child proves to be as you bragged to our Lord in your many letters." Nishihara turned to the child standing in the garden staring at him angrily, which was her right to do after the minor victory she held over him. He tried to figure out what the child was thinking, but he was unable to be certain of his thoughts. He shook his head as he grumbled. "Tanizaki-san! I'm pleased to announce I intend to inform Kawasomeru-sama every word you sent him was truth, and the child is wise like his honorable father."

He turned to the child resting with her sword in her hands, glaring at him and grunted. "Masahiko-san! Put away that blade before I grow angry and teach you a real lesson in the art of defending yourself with the blade, foolish one. One you'll not forget I warn you child."

Tanizaki had all he could do to stop himself from smiling over how easily his daughter was able to get the wise warrior off step and allow his anger to rule his mind, in his aged eyes he felt his daughter was able to fight him to a standstill. Maybe enjoy a second victory over the fighter of so many battles he fought against for the master, Nishihara from the First Village of the Moss.

Samurai Nishihara felt he was laughing at him and ignored the feeling growing in his barrel chest, as he continued with the trainer's child. "I'll wait until you sheathed your sword."

She defiantly sheathed her sword as ordered before the fearsome samurai warrior.

The wise Samurai Nishihara leaned close to Tanizaki and whispered so only he could hear his words. "Huh Tanizaki-san, it's plain to see this child is of your always angry seed of life, old man. The young one is brazen enough to display your insolence I witnessed over the many years I've known you, and did honorable battle with you against our common enemy. Is there anything else you have not seen fit to teach this inconsiderate child? I fear if Masahiko-san dares to display such frightful lack of manners before Kawasomeru-sama, he might in his great wisdom, order the child's head separated from his foolish shoulders, old man."

"Samurai Nishihara-san. There's nothing I dared not train this child. Masahiko-san must be whole in spirit and mind, and with every thought he shares for the protection of his Master and for his realm. Even if that spirit is reckless and challenging at times against anyone he's involved with. Is it not better to enjoy a horse that bucks, than share a ride with a horse with no spirit, and a soft gait to rattle your old bones?"

"Huh Tanizaki-san! If there's one thing to be relied on, this young stallion will buck many a foolish Samurai to their boils during times of battle. You were wise to instill your unconquerable spirit in the young Warrior's body and mind." He boasted as he stared at Masahiko who sheathed her sword, but still stood as if she was challenging the swordsman to do battle again.

His anger got the best of him and barked at the child standing before him. "Dare not challenge me so foolishly young Warrior, if I'm angered properly, not even your father would stop me from dispatching you, for this insult you're delivering against me." When his words were blurted out, he was instantly ashamed over what he uttered against this young samurai, he realized he fell victim of a trap, by allowing himself to be mastered by this young dangerous child's strong and commanding will, she was aiming at him, causing his discomfort and anger.

The seasoned samurai was embarrassed at his loss of face. His first instinct was to order the child to his knees then lop off his insulting head for his display of insolence aimed against him. But the fact he knew he would be forced to apologize to Kawasomeru-sama with his life if he was to dispatch this child, made him control his anger as he spoke. "Masahiko-san! Take the evil spirit from your eyes, and the salty vinegar from your face and approach me."

She failed to move, but when Tanizaki gave her a harsh glare, she moved forward with her hand resting on the hilt of her sword. When she reached the porch she dropped to her knees and bowed correctly, resting her forehead in the sand. The bow was delivered with such grace and respect it made Nishihara relax and smile at the respectful child.

"Huh Tanizaki-san! You trained this child of fiery spirit in many ways I see. I was unaware you were so well versed on such good manners. I thought you only understood one kind manner of life, of not allowing your defeated enemy to suffer beyond what is deemed necessary for a victory over the fools." He didn't wait for Tanizaki to reply to his stinging words as he snapped.

"Masahiko-san! Approach further with your sword. I have something I offer for allowing me to cross swords with you, and to be deposited on my boils in the middle of the road."

She rose to her feet and climbed the steps separating her from Nishihara and her father, but she remained well out of the killing range of Nishihara's sword arm.

A sneer more than a smile spread across his lips as he grumbled at the old man. "Yes Tanizaki-san! Your child is well trained and bright enough to stay outside of my sword zone. It took me three scars and a lost finger to understand this on my own. Masahiko-san! Approach, I have something I want to give you to honor your fine skills with the sword."

She entered the dying zone of the samurai's sword strike and cautiously put out her hand. Nishihara allowed a solid gold tsuba sword guard fall in her hands as he remarked with respect. "Huh young Warrior Masahiko-san! That tsuba was given me by my great grandfather who was given it by his great grandfather who fought at the side of Yoshitsume Minamoto-sama during the Gempei war of Japan's past. It's been in my family since the god himself came out of the clouds and gave birth to the eight islands of Japan. I don't have children to leave such a valuable prize to, I planned to drop it in the sea for the serpents to enjoy before my death. I believed in all Japan, there was no one Samurai born worthy enough to own such a prize. That was until I laid eyes on your brave fighting soul and spirit. If there's anyone alive to give pride to such a worthy tsuba, it's surely you young one who'll share many a fine victory on the battlefield."

She couldn't hide the pleasure in her eyes as they went from the gold guard to Nishihara's weather beaten face. The child's chest filled with pride as she allowed the fingers of her sword hand to trace the exquisite intricate deep carvings decorating the shining gold sword guard. Her hand closed around the prized then she bowed with reverence to the warrior. "Lord Nishihara! I'll bring nothing but honor and respect on this magnificent tsuba in your name and memory."

"Hai! I know you'll do as you boast, Warrior of the future. That's why I chose to give it to you, young one. You're a proud young Samurai well trained in the art of war making abilities in deed. I have one other gift for you to enjoy. Something also in my family for countless centuries past, Masahiko-san." He held out his hand with a small tanto scabbard stuck out of it.

She took the blade and checked the sharpness of the edge, satisfied it was top quality she tucked it in her sash then bowed appreciatively to the warrior sitting next to her father. When everyone was satisfied with the gifts to the child, and respect offered to everyone involved in the testing of the child, the warriors ate then Tanizaki offered to show Nishihara the fields he set up for the training of the samurai of their master. On the trip to the fields, Nishihara took time to inform Tanizaki that Kawasomeru-sama planned to send another army of over twelve hundred samurai for training, beginning on the first month of the fiftieth year of the thirteenth century.

This information allowed him to realize the words Nishihara spoke were true, and the realm was about to erupt in war between the sixteen provinces that made up the central region of Japan. Hopefully, the last war the realm will battle in this region. For the rest of the week, the crafty Nishihara went through a number of long training sessions, checking out the child's reflexes, strategy and outstanding skills with all weapons of the samurai caste, and her understanding of the actions she would have to carry out on the future battlefields. The child was surprisingly adapted to all arts of war abilities, and how to wage it properly against their honorable enemy.

On the seventh day he left to head to Engakuji Castle. He was confident he witnessed a future great samurai, and was prepared to inform his lord that Tanizaki's son was indeed everything he bragged to him he was. A great warrior of the future.

CHAPTER SEVENTEEN

ON THE FORTH DAY OF THE FIRST WEEK OF THE
FIRST MONTH OF THE YEAR THIRTEEN FIFTY

This was the year that the young Masahiko was to turn twelve. Not only was she old enough to engage in any training Master Trainer Tanizaki saw fit to teach her, but she was taller than most samurai and strong beyond any woman's normal abilities. She was nearly five feet tall and able to hold her katana sword at arm's length for hours, and use it without rest. She wasn't only skilled at swordsmanship, but she was adapted at the art of archery, spear and warfare. Although she was still learning hand to hand combat, she rarely lost a fight no matter who she engaged in this respect. Her mind was swift and her wits ample enough for her to win, or to at least come out even with any of her adversaries.

She rarely lost a battle, fight, or strategy, few warriors wanted to engage the child in a game of Go for they all lost now. Few villagers or samurai could give her a good battle on the game board. Even the trainer had trouble surviving the game, and was unable to trap her in a position where he would come out on top against her.

Early on this fine day, an army of samurai appeared on the outskirts of the expanded ninth village. General Kobayashi, who healed from the minor wound inflected on him by Nishihara, rushed to inform Tanizaki the new warriors arrived in the village from Engakuji Castle.

He took time preparing to go to the field with Masahiko. He no longer thought of her as a child because of her height, weight, knowledge, and growing military skills. He greeted the general who brought the samurai in from Shinano province. The excited general appeared with a scroll from Lord Kawasomeru for the trainer, and introduced himself to the old warrior.

"Master Trainer Tanizaki-san! My name is General Yasuhiro Sakurabayashi-san, of Kawasomeru-sama's second army. I been ordered to the Ninth Village to assist the training of these worthless Warriors. The men are so inept in learning the ways of waging warfare and protecting their Master, Kawasomeru-sama gave up on them and their training. Our Master ordered me to inform you if you're unable to turn these dung heaps into Warriors, they're to be used as targets for the next trainees arriving. Their arrival will be rushed if you're unable to work with these combatants. They're foot soldiers who showed a desire to learn the Warrior ways. I have a scroll from our Master that'll explain this better." Again, General Sakurabayashi bowed to Tanizaki as he took the offered scroll.

"How many Samurai dung heaps have you brought to my village, General?" He asked as he snapped the small wax seal with his thumb and read the text.

"Master Trainer Tanizaki-san! I brought one thousand, two hundred and fifty four trainees. Included, but not counted, are three hundred himin shit movers, and two hundred cooks, and one hundred cleaners responsible for washing the Warrior's cloths, and see to their creature comforts. I have fifty women from the pillow world that'll make our Warriors whole, and look after their health." Sakurabayashi offered to the top of Tanizaki's head as he continued to read the scroll.

"Hai! Hai." He mumbled without looking up at the samurai officer as he read the words from Lord Kawasomeru then grumbled. "How many officers do you have in your caravan, General?"

"Master Trainer Tanizaki-san! I have two well seasoned field Generals, ten competent Commanders, fifteen wise Lieutenants, and a number of lead Samurai and minor Commanders. That number includes myself in the count."

"Good, I have my own General who'll be in command of the Samurai you dragged to my village. You met him, General Yoshio Kobayashi-san, and is the Samurai standing on your sword side." He waited until the general bowed to General Kobayashi before continuing. "Any problems, insubordination or requests will be turned over to him to be dealt with. I have a second General I depend on, General Tadayoshi Miyamoto-san. He's not here, but I'll introduce you when he appears. I'll rely on you and the others when you proved you're worthy of being an officer in Kawasomeru-sama's army. General Sakurabayashi-san, you have not enough himin to deal with such a large army, so I'll look through the ranks of this worthless Samurai to break down to himin class. Is this understood? No Samurai will be allowed to heal his mistake by committing suppuku until I have enough himin to look after this army you brought before me. Where is this army stationed?" He asked as he looked at the general.

"Master Trainer Tanizaki-san! I've been ordered to assemble my army on the training field waiting your inspection. I hope their positioning in the field is correct, it was my judgment to make." Sakurabayashi announced confidently to the old samurai.

"Who is the one who issued these orders to you General Sakurabayashi-san?" The3 suddenly concerned master trainer asked the military officer.

"Lord Kawasomeru gave me these instructions before I set out for the Ninth Village, Master Trainer. He ordered me to appear before him for private audience, so he could explain what he wanted done with these useless Samurai I brought for training, and how they were to conduct themselves while visiting the Ninth Village. Our Lord and Master has informed me about placing some Warriors in the ranks of the himin for the smallest of infractions, until the worthless ones ranks swollen to the numbers needed to properly look after these Samurai."

"Hai General Sakurabayashi-san then we understand each other and I wasted my breath explaining what I intended to do until the himin ranks were filled. Now you know what's expected of these dung heaps you brought for my training program, General."

"Hai Master Trainer Tanizaki-san, hai."

"Shall we view your worthless Samurai, General Sakurabayashi-san?" He snapped as he stepped next to the general. Masahiko-san was working with her horse on the field when the new batch of warriors marched in like a wave of water lapping at the shore. She saw one officer break off and head for the ninth village, while a second officer took command of the warriors, barking orders at them. She mingled in with the newly arrived samurai, already trading stories with them as they showed off their swords and fighting stance. She was easily accepted by the new warriors, especially when they found out she was the supposed son of the master trainer. Each trainee treated her with the greatest of respect and honor as they spoke to her.

Generals Sakurabayashi, Kobayashi, and Tanizaki took to the training field and watched the samurai rush to assemble in formation to be addressed by him. A warrior approached the three officers, he was a field lieutenant and spoke to Tanizaki as if he known him all his life.

"Ahhh... Master Trainer Tanizaki-san! It's good to meet you, I have the Warriors assembled for your viewing. I think it'd be good to put off their training until tomorrow morning, to give the fools time to settle down and rest and prepare for the practice fields and training. I'll be willing to see to this before you add..."

The trainer glared at the officer, his look was enough to silence him. Once the officer was quiet, he addressed the general. "Huh General Sakurabayashi-san. Who is this vile, uncouth fool without proper manners, and dares to speak to me as if I needed his worthless council?"

"Master Trainer Tanizaki-san! This is Lieutenant Michiya Kunihiro-san who worked himself up from foot soldier to his present position. He's an able Samurai capable of controlling and make his Warriors follow orders faithfully, Master Trainer."

"General Sakurabayashi-san!" The trainer grunted as he studied the lieutenant who stood as defiant as a whelp panting like he was given a bone to gnaw on. "That might be so, now your Lieutenant is an officer in the ranks of the himin. You'll have this worthless person of no account removed from my sight, before I end his miserable existence with the bit of my sword."

With a unexpected flash of motion, Kunihiro threw himself at the feet of the trainer and bowed. At the same moment the lieutenant moved threateningly at him, Sakurabayashi motioned his samurai to remove the officer from their presence, and when Kunihiro moved, General Sakurabayashi instantly drew his katana to defend the trainer's life.

He held up his hand to stop Sakurabayashi's death thrust, he realized the lieutenant was no threat. All he wanted was to plead his case as was the right of any samurai thusly condemned. Once Sakurabayashi relaxed his stance but didn't sheath his sword, Tanizaki growled at the shaking officer. "Huh Kunihiro, you're still without manners, foul one. I'll allow you to address me before I have you removed from my sight forever, fool who has insulted me unwisely."

"Domo Master Trainer Tanizaki-san! Domo. I beg of you to be allowed to commit the honorable act of suppuku rather than be moved to the ranks of himin. It's my right as a once officer of Samurai to demand this right which I now do, Master Trainer Tanizaki-san." Antagonistically, the warrior dared to glare at the trainer.

Sakurabayashi noticed the insulting stare and lifted his sword, again he stopped him from reacting by raising his hand and ordering. "Sakurabayashi-san! If you strike this dung eater, you'll be no better than he. Can you not see what he's attempting before you? He's trying to get you to lop off his worthless head so he's not forced to join the himin. He's trying to manipulate you into sinking to his cursed depths. If only this worthless warrior placed as much effort in being the best he could be, as he does trying to force anyone into joining him in his low class, he'd never have been forced to join the himin. To punish him the right way will be to allow him to live a crane's life as himin, which he'll do." Tanizaki barely notice the lieutenant anymore.

"Kunihiro, you received the right due Samurai for Lord Kawasomeru, and I refused your request to commit suppuku. A proper Samurai must be respected to be allowed an honorable death which you are not, fool." He growled as he refused to address the warrior by his officer's rank, and looked to the samurai gathered before him and announced. "This worthless Samurai is no longer of Samurai class. He's himin, to be scorned as an outcast of the lowest class, any Samurai who dares speaks with him, will receive the same fate. Remove this person from us."

Two warriors stepped forward and waited for Kunihiro to join their ranks. Instead, the once officer rushed into the ranks of samurai, bumping into many and begging them to take his head. When no samurai broke ranks and did his bidding, the lieutenant dared and spat at the warriors. Even this act did not bring the angry warrior what he wanted, a quick death.

Exhausted, Kunihiro stopped running and dropped to a knee as he searched his mind what to do next. He was forbidden to take his life, so he had to force someone to take his head. He knew he wasn't going to join the himin. He wouldn't dishonor himself or his family by doing this. He looked at the impassive faces. He begged them to help, but the faces just stared at him as though they didn't see him, as if he no longer existed.

He searched until he found his closest friends and fellow warriors, but they stared at him as if his soul were made of glass. Finally, the warrior charged his once friend and slapped him across the face. This was the largest of insults that could be delivered to any samurai. The red faced samurai glared at Kunihiro who continued to slap him. Then he looked at Tanizaki who nodded.

In less than a heartbeat, the insulted samurai roared a cry not many heard before. He drew his katana and held it high with both hands and charged the condemned samurai who moved from him. He crashed into Kunihiro, roughly knocking him to the ground. The samurai in ranks howled with the warrior defending his injured honor. With one blow the head went ten feet in the air before coming back to earth. While continuing to roar, the insulted samurai hacked at the arms then chopped the legs from the dead samurai's torso. After hacking at his shoulders and waist, he continued slashing and chopping and roaring at the body until there wasn't enough left of the warrior, to identify the remains as human. Exhausted, the insulted warrior stopped, he bent down and picked up a piece of the dead samurai's kosode and wiped his blade clean. He returned to the ranks of the samurai with warriors nodding their approval over his actions.

When the exonerated warrior was with his comrades, Tanizaki growled at the himin assembled at the far end of the formation. "Filthy people, clean the remains of this dishonorable Warrior from the field. Every trace of this man must be erased from this field of honor. Feed the remains to the dogs, they'll serve an honorable end by making the dogs strong for their cause."

The warriors nearest to the dead samurai, moved from the pile of death as himin moved in and picked up the scattered pieces of the body and placed them in baskets. After they were carried off, other himin moved in and raked the sand until there was not the slightest trace of the dead warrior to be seen anywhere on the field. Seconds later, everyone heard the dogs barking. The himin picked up the smallest pieces of the body and carted them away. When they were done, they disappeared from view or the warriors.

The trainer viewed the new warriors, he was surprised when he came to the end of the second line of warriors, and noticed Masahiko standing with them. He walked by her as if he didn't notice her, but she saw the slight smile on his lips and slighter nod, and knew she done right.

When he was satisfied with the samurai's formation, he ordered them to prepare their toozamurai, the building that would house the foot soldiers, until they proved to be more than foot soldiers. They would then be moved in the better constructed and larger shoinzukuri, samurai houses. A number of warriors were directed to the umaya to attend to the horses they would soon use in their training. There was only one kami he allowed to be honored on the practice field, that of Hachiman, the kami of warfare.

The old trainer decided to begin and end each day with a run of five ken in armor, this exercise was to make the samurai ashigaru, fleet of foot. He was upset at the scroll sent by Kawasomeru. It complained a few samurai trained by him were unable to run distance in armor. The scroll was short and impolite, and he took it as a warning his master was unpleased by his past trainees. He vowed he would make the next batch trained in every aspect of warfare and endurance.

He got Masahiko's attention and motioned her to join him. He was lucky to locate the child, she was drifting away with the other samurai as they broke ranks. She rushed to his side and stood while he addressed her. "Masahiko-san! It was proper to join the trainees, I was going to suggest that. But I insist you don't share their unworthy quarters, nor bathe with the fools."

She stared at her father with questioning eyes as she cried. "Please father I want to be Samurai in every way, and in all ways. To be held sequestered from the others you'll soon train I believe is wrong. If I'm to be accepted by them then I must prove I'm acceptable to them. For is it not as you stated. I cannot master respect unless I'm at peace with respect. How could I demand respect from these Warriors if I don't respect them, by sharing every hardship they must endure during their training time? Father, I don't mean to question your wisdom, I don't understand why you wish to keep me from them. Am I to be trained differently? Will I not spill my blood on the same battlefield as they? If this is not true then why in your wisdom, do you wish to keep me apart from the other Samurai?"

His irritation rose as he fought to control his temper. He was not used to having his words questioned, especially before the samurai. But he knew he was training this child to be self sufficient and being with independent thinking, and he must refrain from punishing the child when she displayed this spirit before him. He thought of the day he would offer her to Lord Kawasomeru, and this made it possible for him to control himself as he nodded and offered.

"Masahiko-san! It's not your position in life to figure my reasoning for your training, it's your duty to carry out my bidding. Hai! You'll remain home and not bathe with these filth eaters until they prove they're worthy of being Samurai, and being in your presence." With these words, he turned his back and spoke with Sakurabayashi and Kobayashi, dismissing her rudely.

She didn't know what to do now, so she headed off in a huff to be with her horse.

He spoke with the generals, he was aware where his child was going. He was pleased she gained the trust of her horse, the more time spent with the animal, the closer the bond.

Most of this day was spent settling the warriors in their quarters. He was pleased with the energy displayed by Sakurabayashi as he looked after his samurai and his enthusiasm became contagious, and it showed up in General Kobayashi, General Miyamoto and finally him. Everyone rushed around the quarters, barking orders and having the warriors learn their places.

Masahiko used the mass confusion with the other warriors to her benefit. She saddled her horse and rode off in the woods at full gallop, parting branches and bushes alike. Her ever present guards formed a protective screen around her as she rode to her favorite place, the running stream. She went across it and into the boundaries of the tenth village.

Quickly, samurai from the tenth village showed up to see who these strange samurai were that invaded their village. When it was discovered the main rider was the gifted Masahiko, these samurai joined her warriors, adding to her protective shell.

The trainer was unaware Masahiko went riding or he would have been furious with her. Armed with information of a pending war between the provinces, he was sure Wakatsuki ordered the bounty reinstated on her head, if not, it would not be long before he reinstated the order of death. Her life would again be in danger. It was lucky for her that Tanizaki never found out she went riding, or she would have been punished for her lapse in good judgment, probably by being forced to watch as the old master trainer slaughtered her steed.

When she finished her ride, instead of returning to the umaya, the stable to tend her horse, she rode home. She allowed the guards to tend to her horse while she rushed to bathe. Something was wrong with her physically, she showed a slight bleed from between her legs, and was frightened. She changed to a bathing kosode and rushed to the bath house. She washed then lowered herself in the steaming hot water and fought off tears of fear. She was worried she might have caught the disease that inflicted her mother. She laid in the hot water staring at the thatch ceiling, scared to death at what might be happening to her.

Emiko, feeling a bit stronger and hadn't bled for over a year, saw Masahiko rush to the house and change and fled to the bathhouse. It was a mother's instinct and she felt she knew what was upsetting her. She called Estsuko to her side, and sent her to look after her younger sister. Once Estsuko was gone, Emiko called Tomotaka, she ordered her to assemble her kagamen, and have them prepare her traveling palanquin for a journey to the training field.

Tomotaka rushed to carry out her orders. Once on the porch she barked orders at the kagaman, telling him Emiko wanted to visit the trainer. She watched as the kagaman ran to the building to get the others, they came back and aired out the palanquin, and took it off the porch and waited kneeling by the litter until Emiko came out of the home.

She moved carefully with Tomotaka and Miho on either side for support. Once she was in the carrier, the kagamen hoisted it on their shoulders, and walked at a comfortable pace for the field. The kagamen were well trained and didn't allow the litter to swing from side to side, knowing if she was upset in any manner, it would cost them their heads.

Estsuko went in the bathhouse and sat alongside Masahiko in the bath and softly stroked her forehead and hair, as she told the child she was experiencing a slight bleed from riding her horse much and long. She was trying to make Masahiko believe the bleeding was from the saddle of the horse, and was nothing serious to worry about

She asked her sister with pleading eyes. "Are you certain what's affecting me is not what is effecting Mother, Estsuko?"

Estsuko let out a laugh as she offered. "Ohhh... Masahiko-san! How anything could only affect a lowly woman, ever possibly affect a Samurai such as you? What you're suffering from is nothing, so don't worry. In two or three days the bleeding will stop, and you'll feel fine, Masahiko-san."

"Perhaps so Estsuko. But I feel no ill effects from this bleeding except for some mild stomach cramping, and I also have a feeling of having had too much water to drink. I was worried I might have eaten bad fish."

Estsuko turned serious as she explained further to her sister. "Masahiko-san! You must be prepared for this bleeding at least once a month. It happens to all Samurai until their innards become used to riding a horse they must do for their Master's benefit. Masahiko-san! I have a special loincloth I know many wise Samurai wear when this happens. It must be changed and discarded often, and it must be done in secrecy I warn you. If the other Samurai who conquered this inconvenience see you bleed, they'll be cruel and make mockery over you."

Estsuko knew she was lying, but she was sworn by her father to hide Masahiko was a female at all costs, even from the child. Estsuko hoped she didn't know she was going through the beginning of womanhood, and know she was lying. She hated using the samurai in this fashion, but she would do anything to force her to hide the womanly things a female must do at this special time of the month of the bleeding dragon. Again, Estsuko stroked the forehead of her younger sister and said in a soft voice. "Masahiko-san! I'll get some special loincloths I prepared for you for you to use during these times of bleeding."

"Please my wise sister. I thank the good Kami I have you to look so well after my foolishness, and stop me before I make a complete fool of myself in front of the other Samurai. I swear by Lord Buddha, if I'm aware of another Samurai bleeding from his ride, I'll not engage in mockery on his person, and I'll be more tolerant of his discomfort."

"Masahiko-san! You're wise beyond your young years I see. I'll get the special loincloth for you to wear at these times of bleeding." Estsuko smiled tenderly at her younger sister then left the bath house in a rush. Everyone in the household was under strict orders never to interrupt Masahiko while she was enjoying herself in the bathhouse, or when she was with her older sister Estsuko. This was to insure the secret of the child being that of a female from the others of Tanizaki's household.

The trainer stood with General Kobayashi as they kept an eye on the samurai straightening out their quarters, and they didn't see Emiko's palanquin turn the corner. By the time he was aware of his wife's presence, they were preparing to help her out of the portable shelter.

Tomotaka walked alongside the litter protectively, she held up her hand and the kagamen stopped and made certain they held the litter level as they slowly lowered it to the ground. She and Miho rushed to the side and opened the door and then helped Emiko out. She straightened up and ran her hands over her kosode, smoothing it then stood erect as her body would allow while waiting for her husband.

General Kobayashi was the first to spot Emiko and brought the fact to Tanizaki's attention.

He couldn't fight the feeling of doom about to strike his home, as he rushed to his wife's side. With each step he took he looked for Masahiko, she was nowhere on the field. The trainer bowed elaborately before his frail wife who returned the bow with as much honor and respect.

"Emiko! Is this wise for you to be up and about? It's a cold day and I'm certain your bones must be aching and complaining and causing you grief." Suddenly, the trainer glared harshly at Tomotaka and growled savagely. "It was unwise to allow my ailing wife to stress herself so, foolish woman. If anything happens to her, I'll have your head for being so uncaring and inattentive to my wife's health, Tomotaka!"

Emiko took hold of her husband's hand as she pleaded. "Tanizaki-san! It wasn't Lady Tomotaka's fault. She did her best to stop me from coming here, but I have something I must speak to you about. It's imperative I speak with you my husband."

His anger subsided as he looked in his wife's sad eyes and said, "Emiko! What happened that forced you out of the house on such a cold day?"

"Tanizaki-san! Walk with me please. We must talk."

Without word, they walked to the stream separating the ninth from the tenth village. Ice was already forming on the edges of the rapid moving water and his eyes saw where a number of horses recently rode through the water breaking up the ice. When they were far enough from listening ears, Emiko stopped walking and turned to her husband and smiled tenderly then said. "Tanizaki-san! What we feared for so long has taken place. The blood of womanhood has visited Masahiko on this day, and the child was scared to death by the visit of the blood dragon."

"Ieeeee Emiko! What did you do about it?" He snapped at her as he stopped walking and shifted his weight on each foot, to keep them warm from the biting cold.

"I sent Estsuko to the bathhouse to speak with the child. We rehearsed what she'd say to the child when the visits started beforehand, husband."

"Did the child believe what Estsuko told her?"

"I don't know because I left before Estsuko returned to speak with me. I don't fear the child wouldn't believe anything she told her. You know how close they are to each other. I believe if Estsuko told Masahiko she was the one true Kami. Masahiko would believe her until the day she died." Emiko said as she blew on her freezing hands.

"Huh Emiko! The words you speak are true, the two are close. Lord Buddha, how long I dreaded this day arriving. I don't know what I'll do if the child doesn't believe her sister."

"Tanizaki-san! I must go, I fear this cold is numbing my old bones beyond endurance."

"Come my foolish wife. You must be exhausted, I'll walk you back to your palanquin then escort you home to see if Masahiko-san is still sound of mind and body."

He walked alongside his wife, allowing her to rest her hand on his arm, making sure she didn't slip on the ice covered ground. When they were near the palanquin, Tomotaka and Miho took over. They helped her to the litter and in moments, she was on her way home.

The trainer was the first one to enter the home and checked on the small stove he placed near Emiko's sleeping quarters. He was furious the stove was allowed to cool and bellowed for the servant responsible for the maintenance of the stove, and ordered him to make it glow red with heat. He didn't want his wife to catch a chill. He turned to Enko and ordered her to prepare a hot cup of cha laced with sake for her mother as Emiko came in the home, being escorted by her ever present helpers to her bedroll and covers.

When he was sure his wife's comforts were cared for, he called his eldest daughter. "Estsuko!" There was no reply so he called again with the same results. The trainer stood by as Tomotaka helped Emiko to her bed, the room was warm and getting warmer. He smiled when he noticed her place a heavier cotton blanket over his wife, and saw how Emiko thanked the attentive servant not only with words, but with her eyes and a slight bow.

When he was certain his wife was settled in and comfortable, he headed to the bathhouse. Outside, he heard Estsuko speaking with Masahiko and called. "Estsuko!"

"Hai father. I'm with Masahiko-san, he's in the bath, father."

"May I enter to be with you my daughter?"

"Hai." Both women replied as one as they looked at each other then giggled.

He entered and saw Masahiko in the water. He saw the special wearing items most women wore at time of bleeding, and knew she believed every word her sister told her. He regrouped and snapped at his child. "What is the meaning of this laziness? Why have you taken to the warmth of the bath so early in the day? Are you growing weak of body because cold of winter setting in? A Samurai knows he must stand the cold and be ready to fight at a moment's..."

Estsuko interrupted her angry acting father by bowing then waited for him to acknowledge her request to speak. He was waiting for Estsuko to interrupt him, because he didn't want to yell at Masahiko at this special time. The ways of women embarrassed him, and speaking of the bleeding time was not one of his greatest subjects. He looked at his daughter then grunted. "Estsuko! It's the height of bad manners and is rude to interrupt me when I'm speaking to someone. But I'll overlook this minor infraction because you done it with honor and respect. What is it you wish to speak to me about, foolish daughter?"

"Father," Estsuko began while remaining kneeling and looking up at him. "Masahiko-san has been attacked with a severe case of saddle sores that opened and bled. Since this was the first time Masahiko-san experienced such a thing, he was unsure as how to react to the situation. Masahiko-san was scared he was being plagued by the infliction which has stricken mother. After I explained to Masahiko-san why he was bleeding, he relaxed and allowed me to assist him with this problem. I offered the young Samurai the special loincloth worn by all new horsemen." Again, she bowed low to her father.

"Ieeeee! Boils Masahiko-san? Terrible. Terrible." He laughed, giving another explanation to her bleeding. "Boils, the curse of the horsemen, Masahiko-san. Did your sister warn you not to allow the other foolish Samurai know you're forced to wear the cushioning of the padded loincloth while riding your horse, little one?"

"Hai father, Estsuko was informative on the warning. I'll not be the fool to allow myself to be the center of jokes. I'll not dishonor my father or his family by allowing anyone to laugh at me and live." She snapped from the bath defiantly.

"Ieeeee Masahiko-san! It's so good you have such an intelligent sister to guide you wisely during the growing years, and all the trials you'll be forced to wander through during these troubling times for our realm. We'll eat together then I'll challenge you to a game of Go to use up the long hours of night. Huh! It might be good if you'd allow this old man to win a game once in a while, Masahiko-san. Always losing to you is most embarrassing and bruising my ego, huh the teacher beaten by the student." He complained with a half smile as he bellowed with laughter, relieved at how well his daughter handled this latest dilemma to effect Masahiko's life, and he was proud of Estsuko's diligence to her younger sister. The trainer started out of the bathhouse laughing with Masahiko calling after him.

"It's not I who must allow you to win a game father. It's you who must not allow me to win so many games from the Master Trainer of the Ninth Village, who forgot more about the art of waging war and the field of battle than I'll ever know."

"Ahhh... Masahiko-san! You're to wise and too kind to such an old man. I'll wait for you in the game area." He called over his shoulder as he left the warm bathhouse.

Estsuko held out her hand and Masahiko took it and allowed her sister to help her out of the bath. She realized this deceit was going to be over with, and there would be no more need to lie to the young warrior. She saw the first signs of the budding breasts on her sister's chest as she dried her off then offered in a loving tone to her sister acting like a male. "Masahiko-san! Father really loves you you know."

"Estsuko! Father loves everyone in his household equally, even the servants. He's a wise and honorable man. One who'll never be able to be replaced. I hope when time comes for him to cross to the void of the Floating World, the worthless gods will know of his deeds on earth, and afford him a position of proper respect. I know it'd not be long before father takes over the Floating World, and begins his training of the foolish Kami to make them as wise as he. Father is an honorable Samurai with yukakasa for the gods." She boasted proudly of her father.

"Ieeeee Masahiko-san! It's not wise to speak ill of the gods, you sound like father. Their ears are always listening to our words. I beg you respect them for your own sake."

"Huh Estsuko!" She grunted loudly as she climbed out of the tub and then slipped into her warmer heavier cotton kosode after being dried off by her older sister as she replied to her. "I'll respect the gods when father does."

"Masahiko-san! I beg a favor, don't tempt the fearsome wrath of gods. Father is strong enough to pit his will and fighting spirit against the consuming will of the gods and win. You're not as strong yet, I beg you to take care in choosing your words when speaking of, or to the gods, young one. You never know how their wrath will strike back at you."

The trainer ate and engaged his daughter in two games of Go, one he won and knew she was toying with him, and allowed him to win to keep his interest in the game. The second game lasted long into the night, and again he knew she was toying with him, she allowed him to box her in twice, and when he felt he had her blocked and ripe for slaughter, she escaped with little loss to her army. At one point, he knew if Masahiko attacked his position, she and her force would have overran his position, but she refrained from attacking. It took him a long time before he realized what she was doing. She was controlling his army on the board, and allowing them to move around, but not allowing them to get in a position to threaten her castle and master.

The trainer stared at his daughter with respect, it took a samurai in command of knowledge and skill of warfare, to allow an army to expend their energies in attempting to engage an invisible army, until the soul and spirit of the attacking army no longer existed. He looked at Masahiko, armed with this knowledge he said. "Masahiko-san! My army is exhausted, what will you do to my Warriors, young one?"

"Father, I'll seek to negotiate with you. I'll allow your army to join forces with mine and together, I'll take over the opposing Castle without further bloodshed to either army."

"Ieeeee! And what would you do with my worthless life, young tiger of the wind?"

"Simple father, I'll take your head and force your Samurai to sign an oath of allegiance to me, using the blood from your body. In this manner, if they deceive me, they'll be turning against you, their original General. Every Warrior who walked the earth, knows they'd be hunted down by the dead spirit of all Samurai who fell in battle, if they were to play treachery against two Generals on the same battlefield. There'll be no place for them to hide, even after the battle been decided, these Warriors would be hunted down by both sides. There's no dishonor in changing sides in the battle, only dishonor to disrespect a sworn oath of blood."

"Ieeeee Masahiko-san! You're too wise for life on this rock. It's a judicious offering you made. One I must be bound by honor to accept in the interest of saving some of my Warriors from death. To know I trained you well gives me happiness, and makes me believe you'll never die on the field of battle. For there has not been a Warrior born to this earth who'll master such a strong spirit as yours. Masahiko-san! You won this game in an honorable way, I bow to your superior ways of making war with your enemy. I'm tired and will go to sleep, I'll sleep well, and comforted by the knowledge you'll bring great honor to the name of Tanizaki." The trainer stood and bowed to his daughter then headed for his quarters built on the rear porch.

Remi was waiting in his room with warm sake. He plopped on the sleeping roll, and Remi began to massage his aching muscles. She was amazed the muscles in the old body held so much strength. The small stove had the room heated to the desired temperature and in moments, he was snoring on his bedroll. She wiggled under the cotton cover, absorbing heat from his aged body, as she snuggled in with him for the night.

CHAPTER EIGHTEEN

For the next two years, the master trainer worked hard and long with the armies sent by Lord Kawasomeru. Masahiko turned fourteen and went through both training sessions with the new armies, and everything occurring in the realm kept it in a stable and peaceful state. There was increasing probes carried out against Kozuke from the provinces under control of Lord Wakatsuki. The probes were more annoying than destructive, with little damage to the villages invaded on the border of the warring provinces.

Many of the last armies he trained were sent to defend Kozuke province from further attacks once their training was completed. Master Trainer Tanizaki was under strict orders to expect a third army of warriors reaching his village by the end of the third month for his special training. Masahiko was growing every day in strength and height, and the child was as tall as any male samurai, and at least five inches taller than most women of the village. Her intelligence at warfare couldn't be mastered by any samurai Tanizaki pitted against Masahiko. The trainer was out of samurai he could call on to test his daughter further.

With each passing year, and each report sent to Lord Kawasomeru on how well the samurai child was doing learning and training in the ninth village. The feared lord would send many gifts as tribute to the child's development. She was now the proud owner of fifteen horses and forty sets of armor, including armor for forty horses, with twenty personal samurai, and enough small arms to equip an army of five hundred fine samurai for battle.

In one message sent to Tanizaki, Lord Kawasomeru apologized he was sorry he was going to be unable to visit the ninth village before his gifted child was to be presented to him at Gembuku. He folded the scroll but never destroyed it.

ON THE FIFTH DAY OF THE THIRD WEEK OF THE EIGHTH MONTH OF THE YEAR THIRTEEN FIFTY TWO

A swift hard hitting action carried out by Wakatsuki's armies, invaded Kazusa, Kawasomeru's personal province. One invading army attacked from Awa province on Kazusa's south, while the second enemy army launched from Shimosa on the north side of Kazusa. The suddenness and size of the invasion force so surprised the defending armies of Lord Haruo Tamaki that they were swiftly overwhelmed, and the fate of Kazusa hung precariously in balance. The collapse of Kazusa would lay open the provinces of Izu, Sagami, and Musashi for invasion by Wakatsuki. Lord Kawasomeru was concerned and sent a massive army of a hundred thousand samurai to bolster Tamaki's failing army.

The army fought to Kazusa by ripping a path of destruction from Musashi through Shimosa province under Lord Wakatsuki's influence.

The armies of Shimosa was hard pressed to stop such a large invading army, and the added armies Lord Mitsugu Aokawa sent to destroy or slow down the crawling army sent to defend Kazusa by Lord Kawasomeru's armies, were easily destroyed. Most warriors Lord Aokawa sent to engage Kawasomeru's army were his reserve samurai. Now Aokawa was unable to support his army operating in Kazusa, or stop the army marching across his province to support the enemy soldiers. Lord Aokawa sent a carrier pigeon message to Wakatsuki, informing him of the enemy army sent by Lord Kawasomeru, were entering Kazusa from the north of his land.

Lord Wakatsuki was furious the crafty Lord Kawasomeru assembled and sent in action such a powerful force of samurai in so short a time, and march them where they could support his enemy, Lord Tamaki of Kazusa. Wakatsuki realized his move was going to cost him over one hundred and fifty thousand samurai, if Kawasomeru's army was able to defeat his army in Kazusa. He was at a lost as to how to take the pressure off his trapped army so he could get them out of Kazusa, before they were cut off and destroyed by Lord Kawasomeru's army.

CHIYODA CASTLE

The fuming Lord Wakatsuki assembled his generals and together, they decided on their next course of action in their attempt to stop the powerful army sent to Kazusa province by Lord Kawasomeru. Wakatsuki was informed Tanizaki was to receive another army of samurai, and understood if he kept training Lord Kawasomeru's warriors to a finer art or warfare, there would be no hope of winning the war with his counterpart. Although he didn't want to kill the child of the old Master Trainer Tanizaki, because it went against his beliefs to declare war on children. Nevertheless he was forced and reinstated the bounty on Tanizaki's child, hoping to cause the trainer enough grief where he might take his own life. Or at least be so consumed by grief where he could no longer be capable of training further warriors.

Lord Wakatsuki heard stories of this gifted child born to the trainer, and how the child bore the mark of the gods on his body. That was all he needed, to go against a child thought to be protected by the gods, and the armies operating under Lord Kawasomeru's command. It was not easy to order the death of the child, but he would do anything to create problems for Lord Kawasomeru, before his armies attacked Kozuke in force, so he could link Echigo and his other province together, and become strong enough to ward off any attacks from the armies supporting Lord Kawasomeru against him.   The two provinces were separated by a land bridge of fifteen miles connecting Kozuke to Dewa province, and it kept the provinces separated forever. That was his driving force, to smash Kozuke, and deal a lethal blow to Kawasomeru's defenses, thus making his two provinces ripe for invasion and destruction.

Lord Wakatsuki was aware of the reputation of the greatest Samurai to walked the soil of Japan, Samurai Kusunoki Masashige-san. The warlord didn't want such a reputation to be labeled on the trainer's child in training. He understood with just the reputation of Masashige-san, gave the warriors under his control more power in their arms, and these soldiers fought with the strength of the Kami and defeated all enemy. He could ill afford such reputation being attached to the old trainer's foolish child, for fear of what that reputation might give strength to the samurai surrounding this supposed gifted child trained by Tanizaki for Kawasomeru's armies.

He ordered his most powerful general to attend a meeting, so they could discuss what moves they should adopt to stop Lord Kawasomeru's armies. When General Masahatsu Motoshima entered the room, Lord Wakatsuki spoke. "General Motoshima-san, we have to stop the child of Tanizaki from becoming a feared Samurai in command of his own army. Though I hate to stoop so low as to make war on a mere child, I have to do something to break down the successes Kawasomeru is enjoying. I fear the only way I can disrupt his success is by killing this child, and placing the Trainer in the mood to take his foul life and stop training further armies for Lord Kawasomeru. General Motoshima-san, I must rely on your wisdom on how you accomplish the child's death." He stopped speaking and stared at the feared general waiting his reply.

Motoshima went in thought as he contemplated and rubbed his chin. Drawing in a breath then letting it out slowly, he offered. "Lord Wakatsuki, I'll sent fifteen of our best assassins from the Ninja Snake Head clan, to destroy this god spawned child of the old Trainer of the Ninth Village. With the death of this child is sure to weaken the steadfast resolve of Tanizaki's training program for Kawasomeru's Samurai. I'll order these assassins to leave immediately, Lord Wakatsuki."

"This is why I sent for you, General Motoshima-san. To hear what you had to offer about my plans to destroy this child of Tanizaki. I agree with what you offered as a solution to this problem facing me, I order you to head out and set the wheels in motion to destroy this hated child. What have I come to, declaring a death order on a child. Karma." He stared at the general until he rose, bowed then left the room to carry out his orders.

Outside General Motoshima mounted his horse and galloped off for the Ninja stronghold, once there he spoke to the commander of the Ninja assassins, and ordered him to send his assassins to destroy the child. The general remained standing as the commander of the Ninja assassins called the names of the ones he wanted to destroy this child. As the assassins assembled before their commander and received orders, they acknowledged them and prepared to leave on their mission.

The general followed the assassins as they left. He followed them until they dispersed at the point of Shinano which protruded into Echigo province. Some assassins remained alone, while others paired up, and some prepared to join the warriors to be sent to Tanizaki for training.

THE NINTH VILLAGE

The arrival of the third army of samurai sent from Lord Kawasomeru was held up for a short while, and didn't appear on the field of training until the fifth month of the year 1352. Tanizaki was in his second month of training the latest group of samurai when he received word two assassins were captured in the fifth village heading for his village. Under torture, they admitted there were more assassins with orders to kill the gifted and feared Masahiko for Wakatsuki.

He allowed Masahiko to take up living quarters with three samurai who shared a structure in the center of the village. The building was small and easily defended, and made smaller by the twenty samurai guarding her life wherever she went in the village, or training fields. The wise trainer decided to inform the young samurai that her life was in danger and he set off for the building she shared with the other samurai of the village.

The trainer took to riding horseback where he went, because he was getting old and it was hard to walk in pain. He rode to the home with two guards and dismounted and stomped his way to the front gate of the building, nodding his head to the guard then entered the house without knocking. Along with age, bad manners prevailed most of the time, made worse by pain he suffered from years of warring and beating his body warring for his master.

To his surprise, he was informed Masahiko was upset by something and the warrior rushed to the woods, striking saplings with his sword as he ran. The trainer didn't know what to make of the childish outburst, nor was he concerned by it. He was upset about the whereabouts of the child, and the protective shield he must weave about her, to guard her against assassin's attack. He ordered one trainee to fetch Generals Kobayashi and Sakurabayashi. He was pleased Lord Kawasomeru allowed Sakurabayashi to remain in the village, his energy kept him alive. He went out and ordered the guards to assemble then indicate which direction Masahiko ran off in. Once the guards pointed in the direction, his anger took over questioning why they didn't accompany Masahiko when she rushed off for the woods.

The commander stepped forward and bowed as he announced they were ordered to remain behind, against his better judgment he was forced to obey the order from Masahiko.

He glared at the commander as he snarled. "Commander, there's a new death threat leveled against Masahiko-san by that dog eater Wakatsuki. I warn you Commander, if that child is hunted down and destroyed by these disgusting assassins, I'll expect you to make amends for your failure with your life. You were ordered to guard my child every second of the day with no exceptions, and yet you failed to carry out my orders faithfully, fool."

The commander bowed lower as he replied in an excited voice to the angry trainer. "Hai my Lord, without hesitation I'll make amends for my failures." The commander was pleased he was offered an honorable way to end his life if harm had befallen the child.

His anger was interrupted by General Kobayashi and General Sakurabayashi. The master trainer went over what transpired and informed the generals of the new death threat leveled against Masahiko's life. They lined up and charged in the woods where she was reported gone. The trainer and his samurai guards headed out in a wide arch to try and capture any assassins found lurking in the woods. It didn't take long for the samurai to locate Masahiko standing by the stream skipping stones and pacing angrily. She would not allow herself to cry, but her mind was spinning with questions and accusations against her family.

The deeply concerned General Kobayashi was the first one to come across the young Masahiko, he let out his breath when he noticed the child was smart enough to take her swords along with her when she ran off in the woods. The general said he wouldn't want to cross swords with the child because she was that good with the weapons. Slowly he and General Sakurabayashi walked to the troubled child. He approached the last feet alone and growled. "Masahiko-san! What is the meaning of this? Are you all right?"

She glared at her long time friend and refused to speak. She found herself blaming the general for her problems. She stopped pacing but remained with her back to him.

He approached further until he stood by the side of the child and looked at the fast running water. He waited a few seconds before addressing her. General Sakurabayashi closed in but was more concerned with security than what was bothering the irritated child. He stood with his back to the warriors and his eyes searched for treachery, or movement in the woods.

The general moved closer until his hip touched the child's. He didn't want to interrupt her concentration with words and felt a friendly, warm touch would bring the child back to the rationality of the real world. The general was surprised and even shocked by the harsh reaction from Masahiko, instead of responding to his intentions in a friendly manner, she moved from him without acknowledging his presence. He knew something serious was upsetting the child now, and his first thought was maybe something happened to Emiko. Again, the concerned general approached and lightly bumped her.

She didn't look to General Kobayashi, instead her hand went to the hilt of her sword.

He grew angry at this threatening move and growled at her. "What is this you offer me young pup? You dare to threaten your old friend of so many years in this foul manner? Terrible, terrible, you're guilty of the most foul of manners I ever witnessed in my life, little one. You make me ashamed of the claim to call you my friend, little one."

With the swiftness of a dolphin roaming the sea, she spun around, her hand still threateningly on the hilt of her katana, but her mind displayed the best of decisions by not drawing the sword against him. She screamed wildly at the stunned military officer. "How dare you accuse me of being guilty of foul manners, General? It is you who betrayed my trust in you, and everything I believed in, General Kobayashi-san.

Your secret is out and it cost the life of a Samurai as your lies were exposed. It's I who am ashamed to call you my Tomo, my friend. It's I who am ashamed to be a Tanizaki. I should commit suppuku, it's the only way I know I can erase this terrible stain which mars my very being."

From behind Kobayashi a familiar voice growled in a booming tone. "Masahiko-san! What is this filth you spit from out of your vile mouth? Has someone pissed in your ears to scramble your brains, and make you threaten Kobayashi-san in this fashion? I order you to take your insulting hand from the hilt of your sword and bow forgiveness from my General. Then I order you to explain what the reason for this childish outbursts is about!" Tanizaki stepped up to General Kobayashi and ordered the samurai to take a protective position far enough away so they could not hear what was said. The only samurai allowed to remain was General Sakurabayashi.

When Masahiko didn't respond to his orders as quickly as he felt she should have reacted, the angry trainer bellowed again as he rushed in on his upset daughter. "Masahiko-san! You embarrass me beyond foul manners. Did I not order you to apologize to General Kobayashi-san, foolish child? Your Tomo of as many years as you breathed on this foul earth."

She ignore her father's angry words as she suddenly ripped the front of her kosode open to expose two perfectly formed breasts. Tears streaming down her face, she cried in frustration. "Father! What is the meaning of this evil? What happened to my person? What kind of joke are the filthy gods we pray to, playing against me? To turn me into a weak willed useless woman of the realm. I'll tell you what kind of joke the Kami play, and who is playing it against my person. It's you who lied to me for so many years of my worthless life. All the time you made me believe I was some great

Samurai, a male with no equal in all Japan. You made me act like a male, train like a male, I lived like a male and eat like a male, and I believed I was a male! Now I can't belong to either sex. I can't call myself a female, nor male. What have you done father!"

He stepped closer to Masahiko and slapped the child across the face to clear her senses. The move was a terrible insult and it made her automatically reach for the hilt of the blade, but she caught herself before her fingers wrapped around the hilt of the katana blade.

The trainer saw the move and correction her. "Huh! At least all your senses have not taken leave of your scrambled mind. How dare you question anything I done in life! You're too young to question me in any manner, and it's only your youth that's saving you from my wrath. Who has told you about your sex and how did it come about?"

"It was poor Aritomo-san. We were resting in the building and he was enjoying sake..."

"Where did he get the sake from? Sake is forbidden to the worthless trainee unless it's offered by me for their accomplishments on the training field, or by one of the generals responsible for the training of these fools. Or they have earned the right to have some."

"I don't know where he got sake nor do I care, father." Masahiko snapped.

"You're correct, the sake is a minor infraction in this case. Continue your words."

"Aritomo-san was getting drunker and in his drunken state he offered to show me a wonderful experience. He called it satisfying the lowly ground gods. He told me it was an honor to spread one's seed on the ground when there was no whore about to rob a Warrior of his strength. After telling me of this he hitched his loincloth to the side and removed a long snake from behind it. I was shocked he had such an ugly thing growing between his legs, and when I questioned him over the snake he laughed. Aritomo-san told me all males have such a powerful snake, it was the way they give pleasure to a snake submissive woman. He thought me addled of mind not to know of this. I told him I didn't possess such a foul snake and he ordered me to prove it. When I hitched over my loincloth he called me a worthless whore and offered to stick his snake in my void. He wanted me to handle it, he accused me of living a lie.

"He told me every one in the realm thought me a male and great Samurai, and they would shame me by making me pillow with filthy lepers as punishment for living a lie against Kawasomeru-sama. He dared to push his hand in my kosode and played with these foul things on my chest." She grabbed her breasts and tried to rip them from her body.

His face remained impassive as he growled. "What happened next young one?"

"Aritomo-san hurt me by grabbing my arm and twisting it behind my back, he wanted me on my knees and take his filthy growing snake in my mouth. It was here I resisted and broke free and lopped his head from his body in a fit of rage. I ran away, my mind screaming whore in my ears over and over. How could you do this to me? I trusted you with my life. I'm disgraced and must take my life for deceiving my Liege Lord so terribly, father." She cried as she closed the front of her kosode and stared at her father.

Kobayashi looked around to make certain no samurai saw what was happening. His eyes stopped when he noticed Sakurabayashi staring at them in disbelief and disgust. He bowed to Sakurabayashi and tried to explain why it was necessary to play this dangerous deceit against

Kawasomeru. His words were echoed by Tanizaki as he explained the same to Masahiko.

The angry General Sakurabayashi wouldn't or didn't want to understand his words, all he knew was this child lied to his master, and betrayed her oath to Lord Kawasomeru, and for this she must pay with her life. The fuming general tried to push his way around General Kobayashi as he drew his sword in the same motion, wanting to kill the liar where she stood. He allowed himself to be shoved aside so he could draw his sword and defend the child's fate. He called Sakurabayashi's name and as he turned, Kobayashi lifted his sword at him. He waited to allow him to defend himself then charged. Back and forth the generals struck, both trying to kill the other. Tanizaki tried to stop the combatants, but the two were so locked in their battle to the death words from Lord Kawasomeru, would not have stopped the life and death struggle.

The angry General Kobayashi hit the sword arm of Sakurabayashi with his blade, nearly severing it from his body, forcing him to drop his sword to grab at the terrible wound. Being samurai of the upper caste, the wounded general didn't attend his wound, instead he lifted the sword with his left hand then pressed the battle further. Left handed, he was no match for Kobayashi, and he easily had him defenseless lying on the dirt waiting for the death blow in two quick moves. He didn't want to kill the general and looked to Tanizaki for the final word.

The trainer didn't speak, instead he turned his back on the downed general. Kobayashi knew this was his death sentence and with one thrust, Sakurabayashi's head was separated from his body. Tanizaki turned and ordered Kobayashi to give him a samurai's burial, and have his ashes sent to Engakuji Castle with the report he would write once he finished with Masahiko. He turned to his daughter and ordered her to accompany him as they walked the bank of the stream.

Masahiko was still extremely upset, confused, and angry at everyone in her family, especially her sister Estsuko for lying to her so long. She was unaffected by the savage death of General Sakurabayashi as her mind worker overtime on the terrible situation she was facing. She figured if Estsuko explained this nightmare to her long before she found out herself, she might have understood why her father wanted to use her as a pawn in this subterfuge played out against their lord and master, and place her life in jeopardy. For the first hundred feet, father and daughter walked in silence along the swift running stream, formulating their thoughts and enjoying the soothing water. The elderly Tanizaki patiently tried his best to explain to Masahiko why it was necessary for everyone around her to be part of this deception.

"Little wild one, if I were to tell you that you were born a female to the world, you would've believed as all females of the realm do. The you were placed here to serve and give pleasure to man. How would I have been able to shape you into the greatest Warrior Japan has ever witnessed on her soil? How would you have possessed the fortitude needed to follow my training? How would you have been able to force your mind to correctly concentrate and remember all I trained you for, little one? How would you had the strength to wield the Katana, better than any male in Japan? How would you mastered your female traits, and placed them aside until you became a feared Samurai in your own rights?

"You see little one, it was impossible for me to tell you were born female. It tore me apart keeping this secret from you. Forcing the others of our family to do likewise, making

General Kobayashi-san who is your greatest ally, refrain from telling you of my secret. No Masahiko-san, what I done was for your good, and if you can't understand this, you have my permission to commit suppuku, and I'll second you in death as well as in life." He puffed up his chest and stared at the child with the tears in her eyes.

She exhaled then looked deeply in her father's eyes, seeing nothing but honesty in them, she knew he was right and bowed graciously. They turned and he explained his reasoning for the lie. By the time they walked to the first bridge, she understood what the lie was about. By the time they returned to where General Sakurabayashi met his death, she understood enough to lose her anger and open her mind to her father's words. A light rain began to fall and Master Trainer Tanizaki lead her to the field stable, was closer than the building she lived in.

She headed for the stables to check her horse. The horse was comfortable resting in the stall, there was fresh hay before her and the horse was eating peacefully. Upon hearing her voice, the horse neighed and shook her head happily.

The trainer remained outside the barn under the shelter, the smell of horse waste made his sinuses pound. He listened as she cried and explained her new problems she faced with the animal who continued to eat and more or less ignored her words. He had the samurai leave the area so Masahiko could have privacy with the animal. He knew she needed to speak with the animal to work things out in her mind. He hoped she didn't demand to commit suppuku, he knew he would be forced by honor and respect to allow her this privilege.

The rain ended and the sky showed signs of the sun trying to burn through the clouds and overcast. She came out of the stable and walked to her father and dropped to her knees and bowed in the mud. Then she looked up, a touch of mud rested on the tip of her nose as she offered. "Father. It's beyond my limited knowledge how you're able to put up with this troublesome daughter. I should not have been allowed to live. I understand what you and mother done, and the sacrifice you both suffered for my sake, and I'm sorry and embarrassed to have been the cause of such grief, and the burden I placed on your and mother's shoulders.

"I'm embarrassed at the appalling thoughts and words I insulted your presence with moment ago, father. I should be stripped and whipped like a dog in the center of the streets, and allowed to remain there for the children to throw mud at me, for the insults I hurled on you and everyone important to me. I beg my father's forgiveness for my shortfalls, and I'll do anything in my power to make these insults right." Again she bowed elaborately to her father.

The old trainer breathed as he returned the bow then offered his daughter his hand and helped her to her feet. She leaned against her father for warmth, closeness and comfort. It was the closest thing both could do to resemble a hug. After a few moments they walked home. As they walked they passed the building she shared with the samurai. Chugen, people of small account, removed the body of Aritomo from the building. A second samurai pointed to her in haste, he stood with Shoya Sanuki overseeing the removal of the body. He looked in the direction the samurai pointed then rushed to the pair. He looked her in the eye and asked. "Masahiko-san! There's a Samurai trainee found dead in that building. The Samurai say it was you who killed the Warrior in a fit of rage. I hope you had just cause to kill this Warrior."

She moved from her father and took a step to Sanuki and bowed. "Hai Shoya Sanuki-san! I had just cause to kill the lowly one. The Samurai insulted me and I demanded satisfaction. When he went for his sword I reacted. It's only by the grace of Buddha, and the better training of Tanizaki-san I was more skilled than he, or it would've been I lying in a pool of blood."

"This is the way it happened, young Samurai Masahiko-san?"

"Hai Shoya Sanuki-san. This is the way it happened." The child had replied.

"Very well Samurai Masahiko-san. I'll so mark it so on the records for all to witness to show all you were in your right to seek honor from the criminal. Do you want me to have the head cleaned and dressed for your viewing, after all it's your privilege and right, Samurai. Or do you not wish to honor the fallen Warrior in this manner?" Shoya Sanuki asked Masahiko.

"Where would you display the head?" Masahiko asked, knowing it was her duty to inquire.

"Hmmm..., I'll order the foul thing to be displayed on the archery field for your viewing if you desire. It'll have to remain there for one stick of time (a day) if you so choose to honor the fool in this way." Sanuki allowed a slight smile to cross over his lips as he waited for her reply.

"Hai Shoya Sanuki-san. I'd like to view the head and honor his spirit for the day. Mark the ear, he's the first of many worthless Warriors who'll fall before my blade for insulting me or my family, or for being an enemy to my Liege Lord or the realm." She replied and bowed.

A slight bow was returned as Sanuki offered. "Shall I have the head perfumed, and sent on to Kawasomeru-sama as tribute of your first known kill offered to him, Samurai Masahiko-san?"

"Hai Shoya Sanuki-san! I thank you for the trouble I caused you and you're going through to honor me in this manner. I'm appreciative by your kind consideration displayed to this worthless Warrior." Again, she bowed to the old Shoya.

Once the proper questions were asked and answers received by the Shoya, the trainer lead her home. As they walked the last few feet to the front gate, she announced to the trainer. "Father! I had enough living with the trainees from my true home. I believe my place is at home with my family until Gembuku. I'm sorry for the trouble I've been to you and my family lately."

"Masahiko-san! If all my troubles were as small as what you gave me over the years of your life. I'd die a happy man. Indeed, a most happy man. I'm hungry, shall we eat?"

"Hai father." She didn't move right away and he had to stop to wait for her. She caught up to her father and asked. "Father! How am I suppose to act in our home?"

"Huh foolish one. You'll act as you always acted in our home, as a respected Samurai in the future employ of Kawasomeru-sama's army, neh? How else would you or should you act in my worthless home, foolish one? Nothing has changed except for you having gained knowledge. You're still the same person as before, just a bit wiser now Masahiko-san."

"But how am I to act father? As female Warrior or a male Samurai?"

"Huh! In my eye you're a proud male Samurai, and you'll act like one as long as there's breath dwelling in your body. I'm sorry you were forced to live such a lie for life, but we have gone too far to change things now." He warned his child.

"Hai father, but what about Estsuko! I can't possibly order her as before, she's my equal, better, and she's older and wiser than I."

He turned to his daughter and offered in a proud voice. "Masahiko-san! You're Samurai! Whether you be female or male, you're Samurai. You have the power to order, request, or demand a female do your every menial bidding, and you have the power to order punishment of a female even to her death. Until the day the gods deem you served them long enough and they call you home, you'll be Samurai. Enough of this foolishness of indecision and ill thought and words. I'm hungry and nothing changed. You're still Masahiko Tanizaki-san, Samurai." The master trainer walked through the front gate as a second shower hit.

She joined her father on the step where she removed her clogs and followed him in the home with him bellowing at Miho. After the meal, she headed for the bath, she wanted to soothe the pounding in her head. She was unaware Estsuko followed her. The sister wanted to speak to her. She was informed Masahiko discovered she was a woman. Estsuko was shocked and wanted to make sure she didn't blame her, she would die if her sister was angry at her.

Masahiko entered the bathhouse and was pleased to discover the water was warm and waiting her enjoyment. She pounded on the side of the building, and the vassal in charge of the bath placed more wood on the fire to heat the water further. She smelt the wood as it burned and the odor relaxed her more. She opened her kosode with her back to the door and flipped it off her muscular shoulders, something didn't allow the kosode to fall to the ground. Instead, it slid off her as though someone helped remove it.

Her training took over her instincts and she spun around, prepared to attack the one who come up behind her so silently. Her mind cursing for not being aware someone was there. Her stance softened when she realized it was her older sister standing and shocked before her.

Estsuko dropped to her knees and bowed to her sister, but to her surprise she pulled her to her feet. She looked in the sad eyes of the older sister and smiled as she lightly ran a finger down the side of her cheek. Without words, both sisters hugged, crying in each other's arms. The words didn't have to be spoken by either to be understood by them. They shared a good cry while Estsuko softly stroked her shoulders and fine jet black hair. When the two were cried out they separated and Masahiko caught a shiver and crossed her arms over her chest and hugged herself.

"Masahiko-san please sit and allow me to bathe you so you can get in the warm water. You'll catch your death of cold if you don't heat your body. It was foolish on my part to allow you to stand for so long without clothes. I'll never forgive myself if you become ill."

She sank in the water and let out a groan as the waters engulfed her taught body, her toes sticking out of the water as she stared at the ceiling and her sister ran a cloth over her face, wiping sweat. Estsuko allow her time to relax and mill over what happened. When she felt Masahiko was ready to speak, she asked. "Masahiko-san! Do you have questions about today? Or maybe questions about what to expect from your body now I no longer have to be dishonest to my sister. Masahiko-san! I'm so ashamed at my behavior, I found it hard to sleep because of my dishonesty to you. I hope you can forgive my disloyal ways, Masahiko-san."

She turned a dreamy eye to her loving sister and mumbled. "Estsuko! There's nothing to forgive you for. I come to peace with what my family has done for me. I'm at peace with the knowledge that I'm a female Warrior. Estsuko! I swear by the oath to Lord Buddha, I'll be the best Warrior to ever walk the land of Japan. I'll be better than any Samurai at horsemanship, spearmanship, and my skills with the yumi will not be matched by any Samurai, or any other Samurai who'll be born in the future to Japan.

"I don't know Estsuko, maybe this is for the best. Maybe if I'm able to prove to Kawasomeru-sama I, a lowly woman can be an important addition to his Samurai ranks. Maybe, if I'm good enough, our Lord will see the error in his ways of thoughts and will allow women of Japan to be more than vassals for child production, and comforts of man. Yes Estsuko! It's time for the women of Japan to show the foolish Samurai Caste, we women are as good as any male Warriors on the field of honor. Huh! I'll be that good! I'll be better than any man warrior! I'm pleased for the opportunity my father set before me, and will make the best of it to honor his efforts."

"Masahiko-san! You'll be better than any male who ever lived, or who'll ever live in Japan. You're far better than any Samurai you crossed swords with. But I can't shake the feelings I betrayed you, lied to you and started you down the road of destruction. I'm sorry for what I done to you." She lowered her head and sobbed.

The female samurai reached out and ran her hand through the silken hair of her sister as she offered. "Estsuko! You done nothing to be sorry for. If anyone owes anyone, it's I who owe you an unpayable debt. I thank you for my foolish life, if it wasn't for you, mother and father's wise guidance, I'd been put to death with my first breath. Instead of killing me, my family dared the wrath of our Master by allowing me to live. My family risked the lives of our relatives by concealing

I was a female from Kawasomeru-sama. You all placed yourselves at risk by training me in the many ways of the Samurai. I'm the only female in Japan allowed to handle the katana, and go to battle with the sword. No Estsuko! It's I who owes my life to my family."

Estsuko smiled at her sister as she bowed and thanked her for the honor she offered her. She knew she had many things to tell her about the problems she would face in the future as a woman. The items she would need to look after her health, and time and need to couple with a man in private. Together, the women talked for hours, giggling and getting embarrassed over some of the subjects they covered with each other.

It wasn't until it began to get dark the trainer had to go to the bathhouse to see what was happening between the two women, and to tell them of the time, or how cool the water of the tub had become. Before he entered the bathhouse, he listened to his daughters speaking. He smiled when he heard them giggle and got embarrassed listening to Estsuko's rendition of her belief of how a man felt, when his sperm spilled forth to create birth within a woman's body. He wondered how she knew so much about the pillowing world and men. He had no way of knowing women knew more than man would know of the art of pillowing. Rather than walk in on them, he respected his daughters by tapping on the side of the building, and waited until they bid him entrance. He entered as Estsuko wrapped the kosode around Masahiko's body.

Masahiko turned and smiled at her father. "Father! May I ask you an important question?"

"Hai. You may ask of me anything you chose, daughter."

"Father! What is my woman name please?" She asked with concern in her tone.

He turned red as he cast his eyes to the floor because he was embarrassed by her question. He wasn't only embarrassed by the question, but he forgot her female name. It's been so long since he heard it whispered by Emiko in her dream state while sleeping.

Estsuko saw her father's dilemma and knew he forgot her name, so she offered politely. "Masahiko-san! Father's being respectful by not using your woman name, for fear of insulting your Samurai ways. Masahiko-san, your female name is Yuriko."

"Yuriko Tanizaki! It's a proud and just name. Thank you father for giving me such a proud name to bare for life." She bowed deeply to her pleased father.

The night passed uneventfully and at first light, the trainer with Masahiko and Kobayashi, showed up at the training field. Work there was hard, with the trainer coming up with different ways of challenging the wit and intelligence of his trainees. They grasped the ways he was training quickly, and by the second week he had most warriors riding horses, something they never done. Masahiko was so well at her training he was using her more as a trainer than a pupil.

They had no idea six assassins were going through the program with the trainees, so they could get at his child. They were diligent at their work, waiting for time to strike out against Masahiko.

Day after day did the assassins waited their time, getting closer to their target all the time. Two tried to gain her trust. The assassins knew who each were, and during the tenth week of training, they pooled their energies and work together to improve their chances of accomplishing their task of killing the child. One stormy night, the assassins met in the stable. They devised a plan for them to trap Masahiko in the shoinzukuri while the remaining samurai stayed outside, stopping anyone from entering the building. The outside samurai would inform any samurai an insult was passed, and the parties were working out their differences in the building. This would be enough for the trainees to remain outside until satisfaction was accomplished, and the fighting finished. The assassins weren't going to tell the others it was Masahiko doing the fighting in the building, nor would they tell them she was fighting four assassins. They didn't care for pride and honor, they were concerned about killing their target, and getting out of the village alive.

Two sticks of time passed since the death of Sakurabayashi, and Tanizaki sent a runner to inform Lord Kawasomeru of the general's death, and continued with the training of the samurai. The runner was expected to arrive in Engakuji tomorrow. On this day, he relaxed his guard, for no assassins were uncovered and he felt maybe they been discovered and stopped before they entered the village. The security was so tight around his daughter he had little fear of assassins not being discovered. He never considered the possibility of assassins in the ranks of the trainees. Today's training was going to be with the horses, and the first round of dog targets.

The day was warm, the trainees were eager to try their hand hitting the dogs. To his surprise, these trainees were the best at hitting dogs on the run from horseback. By the end of the day, every warrior to be trained had at least one chance at the dogs. Even Masahiko had a go at them on the field, she hit all three dogs with one arrow, and two dogs a second time with the two remaining arrows she held in her mouth, before firing them at the swift moving dogs.

The out of breath runner reached the castle before sunset, and was given an audience with Lord Kawasomeru, to inform the master about the death of General

Sakurabayashi. He wasn't surprised over the general's death, given the fact he was so high strung and hard to work with. The lord didn't bother asking the runner why or how his general died. He took it for granted he died in a fight with a samurai being trained in the ninth village. The lord was certain if the fight wasn't honorable, the old man would have the warrior who killed Sakurabayashi put to death.

The runner informed Lord Kawasomeru he carried the ashes of the general, and was instructed by the master trainer to give the ashes to the captain of the guard for their proper storage and future honoring. He thanked the runner and ordered him to be fed and given a bedroll, while he wrote a message to Tanizaki. The realm was being drawn in a war involving the eight provinces under his control, going against the eight provinces under Lord Wakatsuki's control.

The warlord was waiting for the invasion of Kozuke to begin the war. He was prepared to send warriors to beat back any invasion force sent in by Lord Wakatsuki. But this support left his province open to invasion from his flanks through Hida, Mino, Owari and Mikawa provinces. He decided to ask Tanizaki if he could push the training of these samurai up.

The trainer stood on a dais twelve feet above the ground, this gave him the capability to oversee the practice fields with a turn of his head. He stood like a god on the dais with his arms folded across his chest, as he watched the trainees wrapping up their equipment, and the stable hands taking control of the exhausted horses. The warriors headed for the shoinzukuri buildings to prepare to receive the retiring samurai. The twenty guards of Masahiko stood behind the dais out of the way of the scrambling trainees. They weren't allowed on the field while she worked.

General Kobayashi was with Tanizaki standing one pace behind and to the left. The trainer never thanked him for dispatching Sakurabayashi, nor did he feel he had to. It was expected.

The trainer searched for Masahiko, he wanted to know where she was, and didn't want her to get lost in the crush of samurai completing their duties. He became concerned until he saw her walking with two samurai. He relaxed knowing she was in the presence of trusted samurai.

Masahiko was led to the quarters by a trainee who offered to give her a new bridal for her horse. She was promised the bridal in return for training by her with the sword to this interested warrior. It was a fair trade, and she was without fear following the samurai to the building. It was late, twilight, and the shadows made it possible for the crafty assassins to be hidden about the interior of the building without discovery. The samurai told her the bridal was on the tenth bedroll on the left side of the building. He stopped short of entering the building, stating it was against his belief to enter the sleeping area without the intent of sleeping. She had no problem with this explanation, she was ordered by Tanizaki not to enter the quarters unless she intended to sleep. It was a standing order, the exception being to fetch something needed for training. Tanizaki didn't want his warriors resting while there was still day light left in which to train.

She entered the building and waited for her eyes to adjust to the darkness. The samurai who led her was joined by a second samurai and they assumed a guard stance outside the door.

As she moved deeper in the interior of the dark building she suddenly heard a slight shuffling sound in the consuming darkness. Instantly, her senses were alive and prepared to defend herself against any threat leveled against her inside the building. Silently she withdrew her blade, the only sound came from the blade as it whispered its stinging song of death, as the steel was dragged along the wood of the scabbard. She held it before her, her arms at her waist and the blade coming up before her face stretching outward. She knew someone was in the building, but she didn't know if he was a threat against her. She understood it was in her best interest to disappear in the shadows to force her enemy to show himself in his search for her. She back stepped in the dimness and stared in the darkness, forcing her eyes to see in the pitch. She wasn't only using her eyes to see, she was using her ears also.

There was a second shuffle to her right nowhere near the first sound. Now she knew there was more than one person in the building, and was certain they were a threat. She knew if there were two then there were probably more. She lowered herself to the ground and prepared to attack. Out of the corner of her eye she picked up a movement. She reached in the sleeve of her kosode and removed a skewer and shifted it around in her hand until she had the weight just right. A seven point fighting star whistled through the air and stuck in a support beam inches from her head at eye level. A second star landed in the bedroll by her feet. She never took her eyes off the area where she saw the first movement, she noticed it again and sent the skewer flying. She heard the thump as the weapon entered the body of her would be executioner, and heard air escape from the punctured lung and heard the blade fall from the hidden one's hands.

The assassin knew he was dealt a death blow from the skewer which did damage to his body, as it worked up his damaged chest to his lung. With a last gust of strength, the dying slayer launched himself in the direction from where he was certain the skewer came from. She was quick enough to pick up his awkward move and stepped back a pace and swung her sword at the same time the body charged by her, chopping his head and part of his shoulder from him while in flight. The assassin's form tumbled recklessly across the floor, and ended up in a heap of death resting at the feet of a second killer cautiously working his way behind her back in the darkness, using the battle to cover his moves against her.

She watched silently as the body flew by her, and noticed the second assassin sneaking up against her. Now she knew of three assassins in the building, one was out of the equation. She lowered her blade and flipped it over in her hands to enable her first thrust to come at this butcher from the side. She hoped to rip his guts with such an attack, rendering him helpless as he went in shock and bled to death. She didn't want to be drawn into a prolonged sword fight with this one; she knew the other murderer would use this attack to work himself in the shadows, so he could come at her from behind. She understood she was fighting at least three assassins without honor, to attack her in the darkness like the lowly dog packs that attack deer at night.

She dared not move or breathe properly, for fear of giving away her position to the searching killers as she sensed, more than saw the assassin working his way at her in the darkness of the building. She closed her eyes, forcing her mind to see the shape of the warrior in the pitch in her mind's eye. When she sensed he was in sword range, she swung the blade in what she believed was his direction. The strike hit something solid and she felt the blade rip through flesh and bone as she heard the warrior cry in pain, as the blade ripped him in half near the waist. He fell to the floor, dead before his body came to rest on the ground.

The insignificance of her second move drew the attention of the remaining assassins, they moved to get in better position against their target. Their movement wasn't stealthy enough, and drew her attention to them. She had them zeroed in and was prepared for their combined attack against her. She saw one assassin moving quicker than the second, she decided to take him on first then change position to intercept the remaining assassin and defeat him next.

Outside, trainees gathered near the structure, wanting to get in and rest. Some warriors heard the commotion and demanded to know what was happening in there quarters, and why the samurai outside were blocking their entrance.

The samurai who talked Masahiko into entering the building held up his hand, and defiantly announced a battle of honor was taking place in the shoinzukuri building, and the samurai would have to remain outside until the insulted one's honor was satisfied. He went on to state a foolish samurai insulted Masao then compounded his insult by challenging Masao to a fight to the death. The challenge was delivered in the building, so the insult had to be unstained inside. The samurai's words were enough to make the warriors understand the battle raging in the building. All were happy to sit on the ground to wait the outcome of the struggle waging within. Muffled sounds of the fighting drifted from inside. Each samurai tried to hear what was taking place.

General Kobayashi noticed the actions by building three, and pointed out samurai sitting on the ground outside the quarters to the trainer. He leaned close to his general and asked. "General Kobayashi-san! What do you think is happening? Do you think one of our Samurai has taken it on himself to explain one of our exercises to these foolish Warriors?"

"Iye Tanizaki-san! These dung heaps don't possess that burning desire to understand the true ways of the Warrior. No, I believe a battle of honor is taking place in the quarters of the third building, and the Samurai are waiting for the outcome." He bowed to the old master trainer.

"Where is Masahiko at?" He suddenly barked at his general.

Both warriors looked to the building again and the general announced excitedly. "Assassins!" They rushed down the shaky dais and headed to building three with speed.

Inside, the executioner was clumsy at best, and his actions noisy and showing lack of experience as he worked at Masahiko. This third assassin was foolish enough to walk in the only light entering the building to make his travel in the darkness easier to accomplish. It was plain to understand this one couldn't master the stealth to survive in the world of darkness and assassins.

She allowed a quick smile as she heard him trip over something lying on the floor. Then continue as if he wasn't afraid of what was waiting him a few steps beyond sight. She moved silently at the executioner to intercept him in motion. The warrior was sure she was adding distance between herself and the last assassin.

She got in the proper position to attack the third assassin then disappeared in the shadows of the interior. She couldn't be seen by either remaining assassins as she waited for the clumsy one to get in her sword striking distance. The female warrior controlled her breathing and body and at the appropriate time, she held her breath. Her eyes opened wide when she saw the butcher almost walk past her position in the shadows. She zeroed in on his exposed neck and with one swift swing of her sword, the assassin's head tumbled to the floor. A long pair of streams of blood splattered her face and chest as the headless form turned and sank to the floor, pumping blood was sprayed everywhere as the assassin's dead hands dropped the sword to the floor. Then tried to claw at the air for a handhold and life.

She tasted the saltiness of the killer's blood as it sprayed on her face and across her mouth. She heard and felt the warmth of blood as it covered her body from head to toe. Without regard to the soaking of her body with blood, she moved silently, preparing herself to receive the last assassin's attack. She didn't have the exact position of the last assassin in her mind's eye yet.

The young trainee turned assassin was Masao. He was the best experienced of the latest class of trainees sent to the ninth village for the lord's special training programs, and was nearly as skilled as Masahiko. He was smart enough to lurk in the shadows of the interior and wait for his target to give away its hiding place. He allowed the three killers to be slaughtered to draw out his target, so he could appraise the fighting skills of his adversary. He was likewise trained by the wise Tanizaki, and was able to see the flight of the blade in the darkness, no matter how dark it was in the building. The shine from the blade cut a fine line of light through the dark, on its way at the throat of the third would be murderer. He smiled as he used the commotion of the death of the third assassin, to cover his moves as he rushed from his hiding place in silence then charged at his located antagonist in the darkness.

He fought with cunning as he stopped short of her sword strike, and swung his blade back and forth as he charged forward. He slashed at where he was positive she would be hiding. His blade striking nothing but the side of the building, air, and a support post.

The clanging of the sword on the side of the building made the samurai gathered outside grunt with delight, they were sure one of the combatants had been struck by a sword.

The last assassin knew he missed his opponent, and she moved in anticipation of his attack. He was now scared of the darkness and the spirit waiting in the shadows, as he slashed out again at the unseen figure. But she wasn't in his sword striking zone, he allowed the momentum of his strike to carry his thrust around him. He threw himself in the direction he last felt rather than saw the figure of his enemy standing. His sword was held at the ready to deliver the death blow, but his enemy moved in anticipation, and with agility and speed and using the stealth of a kotora, a tiger, used to making his kills in darkness. His reckless thrusts forced her from her hiding place and react to his foolish attack. Her movement caught his attention and he roared in rage as he charged at her again in the darkness. His blade whispering as it sliced through the air.

With a swift move his enemy struck out with her foot which found its mark true in his guts. The heel digging deep in the soft folds of his belly. Seething pain exploded in his body almost to the point of paralyzing him. Showers of blinding lights flashed in his eyes as he fought to remain conscious and in control of his actions. The force of the blow sent him tumbling back a few steps. His once sacrifice, his soon to be victim was now his master, and she was in complete control of the fight of life and death now.

The assassin was successful in using the blow to help him roll over until he was crouched low, but standing and balanced on the balls of his feet. He bounced up and down a few times to give him power to spring at his antagonist, if she decided to press her attack against him. His bouncing also served to help absorb some of the pain he was working through from the kick. His bouncing and movement gave away his position, and she moved in with the speed of a cat, silently, stealthily towards him. She moved in rapidly for the kill.

With one swing of her razor sharp katana, the sword a whirling blur of silver in the dark, striking him across the throat. The last executioner's head tumbled through the air like a straw basket caught in the wind. The head hit the floor of the shoinzukuri with a sickening thud some ten feet from the body, and rolled a few feet hair over chin, thumping the floor as it tumbled forward, and only stopping because it came to rest against a trainee's bedroll.

General Kobayashi, the younger of the two warriors reached the shoinzukuri first, just steps ahead of the elderly Tanizaki. Both had their swords drawn with the general rushing to the door only to find his way impeded by the two on guard assassins.

The one who walked with Masahiko spoke to the angry general. He tried precariously to explain that a battle of honor between two of the trainees was raging inside the building. But the general was having none of it as he ordered him out of the way so he could enter the building, and place a stop to the fight raging between the trainees. Some warriors balked at his insult at the threat of interfering with the fighting samurai, but a commanding grunt from Tanizaki silenced any objections from the trainees.

The assassins knew their time was up and one challenged Kobayashi to a fight by aiming his sword and holding it before him in a threatening position. Instantly, the trainees knew something was wrong and scrambled out of the way of the swordsmen about to do battle to the death.

With little regard to the scrambling trainees, Kobayashi answered the butcher's challenge with a charge and thrust. The point of his blade dug deep in the assassin's belly and with one swift movement to the side, his blade disemboweled the samurai, his innards spilled forth and fell to the ground. Slowly, his body lowered to the ground when he pulled his blade from his body. The second murderer tried to strike the engaged general from behind, but Tanizaki's blade cut his arms off before the elbows with one quick blow. Then he whirled around and brought his sword up at the same time, and lopped the surviving slayers head from his shoulders, sending the headless body hurtling back, coming to rest in a heap on the ground. A dust cloud enveloped the assassin's body as it twitched wilding on the ground, while life drained from his mangled body.

The general didn't waste time as he hurtled his body against the door of the structure, sending it flying from its rope hinges, and plunged in the darkness of the building. He blinked his eyes in an attempt to make them accustomed to the murkiness in the structure. When his eyes focused in the darkness, they beheld a forbidding figure standing in the middle of the walkway a few feet from him. The demon like figure was covered from head to toe with raw blood with drops dripping from its outstretched arms and chin, and from the katana held tightly in the right hand. In the left hand of this abhorrent creature was held the head of the assassin, Masao. It was likewise covered with blood, and held by the warrior aquene knot, dangling from the creature's hand. The lifeless eyes of Masao staring at the stunned general.

He was forced to draw in his breath to help control his rattled nerves, he was uncertain whether or not he should challenge then charge this chilling apparition walking ahead of him, before he was attacked by the fearsome creature covered in death. He was uncertain if this person was human, or if it was an evil god sent from the depths of the red hell, to destroy him and steal his soul. The confused general took a chance and he slowly lowered his sword, and the creature did the same and lowered her weapon.

Teeth suddenly shined through the blood covered face, and the head nodded to the general in a weak but polite bow. By habit, General Kobayashi returned the bow without thinking.

The creature walked quicker towards the general and from behind him, Tanizaki rushed to his side, ready to defend himself from the evil lurking in the dark interior. The trainer stopped in his tracks when he saw this person walking at Kobayashi. He had to fight the feeling of pushing his general aside, and striking at this threatening specter as it neared his officer. He stopped these troubling thoughts when the spirit smiled and bowed at Kobayashi. Something about the smile was familiar then he realized it was his daughter. He called out her name. "Masahiko-san?"

"Hai father." The creature called back as she lifted high the hand with the head of her would be executioner locked in it in the air and offered it to her father as a gift of honor.

"Ieeeee Masahiko-san! What evil born to the realm caused this attack against your person for no reason but you're my child? Come out of this loathsome building! This place turns my stomach ill with its being in my village, young one." He ordered as he and General Kobayashi back stepped out of the structure, followed by Masahiko, guarding against further surprise attacks from other possible assassins still lurking inside the long building.

When she came out of the building holding the head of the almost assassin Masao in her hand. The samurai trainees cheered and stomped their feet in the dust of the field. Although they were shocked by the chilling vision and condition Masahiko was in. Nevertheless the warriors paid homage to her for her deeds in the battle of honor they realized was a bloody fight indeed. They were in awe of the powers of warfare held in the body of the young warrior walking before them with her father and training general.

The trainer glared at the blood covered face of the assassin's head in his daughter's hand, as he looked in the closed eyes of the failed assassin. The trainer recognized Masao as the older child from the village beating his daughter during her growing stage, until she was finally able to defeat him at his own game. He decided to place the assassin's entire bloodline to death by the call of the sword for this treacherous deed committed against his daughter, as he and General Kobayashi stepped aside and allowed Masahiko to walk past them proudly.

He was aware Masao moved from the village when his daughter bested him in hand to hand combat, and knew he went to the training of Ninja by the warring Sohei monks. He was so angry over this assassination attempt against his daughter, he ordered a torch brought to him, and he reentered the building to see if he could determine what took place in the structure. He counted the slaughtered bodies of the four dead assassins on the floor of the long building, killed in a bloody and horrible way by his daughter inside the structure. From where the bodies laid, he tried to figure out the attack angle they employed to attack his daughter.

The concerned trainer leaned forward and studied the slaughtered bodies of the assassins, trying to discover the path taken by each in their attempt to kill his daughter. He located where she defended herself against a force of accomplished, paid slayers. The old warrior noticed the throwing stars meant to kill his daughter, one was stuck in the support beam, the other lying harmlessly on the floor by his feet. He swallowed his bile with effort, proud his daughter was able to kill four well trained murderers on her terms in the building. He smiled as he spat on the bodies lying at his feet, proud of Masahiko's outstanding abilities with the blade and her defense.

Surely, it was a matter of time before Lord Kawasomeru was informed of the feat performed by his daughter on this remarkable day, and he would make certain it was sooner than later the master was made aware of this fact, and great battle won by his daughter against four assassins. When he had his fill of viewing the ugly carnage created inside the building, he walked out of the structure in disgust. He stopped just outside and threw the torch inside the structure to burn the building to the ground. He ordered a number of samurai to stand guard over the fire and not allow it to spread to other buildings of the encampment, or escape into the woods. None of the trainees complained about their belongings being burned in the building. They understood the trainer would make sure they received replacements for the items lost to the fire.

Then, the trainer and General Kobayashi walked to either side of Masahiko, and escorted her to his home. He allowed his daughter to carry the severed head of the loathsome assassin in her hand, all the while they walked through the streets of the village.

She was enjoying displaying for the townspeople of the prize, and to show them what a true samurai looked like after doing honorable battle for life and death with their enemy.

Everyone in the ninth village came out of their homes to view the fearsome spectacle walking down the middle of the street. Many staring and stunned women placed hands to mouths out of fear of the blood drying on Masahiko's body. The men of the village nodding in approval of the warrior proudly, showing their teeth and bowing because of the obviously fierce battle she been successful in victory. As she walked through the streets past them with great strides, and a youthful spring in her steps as she marched with her father and general to her sides.

The master trainer and general mostly ignored her as she stomped to his home, allowing her to bathe in the glory of her feat of destroying four assassins ordered by the dog eating Wakatsuki to destroy her. He knew he was going to seek revenge on the head of Wakatsuki for his attempt to take his daughter's life so early in life. As proud as he was over her victory, he was fuming at Lord Wakatsuki for his want to kill his child.

The master trainer couldn't believe so powerful a warrior as Lord Wakatsuki was in life, would stoop so low as to order the death of so young a samurai. He believed the warlord was only acting out in desperation to order the death of his child. Smiling from ear to ear, he enjoyed the victory she won over the once respected warlord.

CHAPTER NINETEEN

Master Trainer Tanizaki escorted his daughter covered and still dripping fresh blood in the house, her samurai guards walked behind her and stopped and waited outside the garden area. They dropped to their knees and stayed until she came out and acknowledged the honor they displayed to her for winning her battle with the assassin.

Emiko cried when she saw the heartbreaking condition of her young daughter, but she was stopped in her tracks by Tanizaki from rushing to comfort the child. Estsuko bowed to her sister, understanding the battle for life she endured. Enko cried and ran from the fearsome sight of her sister. Tomotaka bowed and approached while carrying a wood platter. She held it out and waited until she rested the severed head on it.

When she laid the head on the plank, Tomotaka announced. "I'll clean the head and fix its hair, and will shower it with perfume and herbs so it'll not offend. I'll then place it on the spiked gunyoki and wait your bidding for the head. You're an honorable Warrior, Masahiko-san!" She bowed as she would if she stood before the master of the realm, displaying honor to Masahiko.

He nodded at Tomotaka approvingly, proud of her display of respect. Then he looked to Estsuko and barked. "Estsuko. You have the honor of bathing this young Warrior. Clean Masahiko-san, bath him in the hot waters and attend him until the Samurai is clean of body as he is of soul. Masahiko-san! Samurai! Best in all Japan."

Everyone bowed to the blood covered samurai, smiling from ear to ear over the honor they were showering her with. Even her aged father bent his knees to her, something he only did when standing before Lord Kawasomeru. All in his house were happy and a great meal was prepared by Miho and Tomotaka, and even Sanuki came in and displayed his happiness with Masahiko. Slowly, the Shoya came around showing more interest in the female child being passed off as a male child to everyone in the realm.

The trainer allow Masahiko to take as much time as she wanted to rest in the soothing waters, with Estsuko attending her every need. But as time passed, he decided to check on his daughter, to make certain she suffered no ill effects from her battle for life with Masao. Before he left he went to Emiko's quarters and retrieved what she was working on for the past few days.

He motioned to his wife he had the item and let her know he was going to give it to her. The trainer walked out the shoji and noticed the guards surrounding the bathhouse. He was pleased at their tenacity protecting his daughter. He was informed by the commander from this day forward, they would be on the fields with Masahiko. He was told the commander was embarrassed by the attempt on her life by the assassins, and was going to review his samurai, and he felt sure one or two would lose their heads over the loathsome incident.

The trainer wasn't interested in this as he passed the commander. He entered the bathhouse without knocking and bowed to Estsuko on the floor with her hands in the water. Masahiko was undisturbed in the water, her head back and eyes closed, enjoying the warmth of the hot water.

He scanned the interior of the tub and noticed the blood covered kosode. It looked like it was used to wipe the blood from a thousand dead after battle. He saw a number of silk pieces stained crimson, and knew Estsuko used them to wash her body, before she entered the tub. The puddles on the floor were stained reddish by blood washed from her body. He moved closer to the tub and leaned over her, looking for signs of life. He had to clear his throat to get her attention.

Her eyes flew open and she smiled her father when she saw his face.

He nodded then held out his hands, offering her the silk breast band Emiko made for her to use when she was out of the home. With questioning eyes, she looked at her father as she unfolded the fabric and tried to figure out what it was. He was embarrassed having to explain to her what the gift was, he stuttered trying to sound positive with his daughter. "Masahiko-san! Perhaps you can understand why I was forced to forbid you from bathing with the trainees?"

"Hai father, you're wise in your precautions for me." She said as she sat up, allowing her breasts to rise above the warm water.

He was surprised to see how larger her breasts were than most women of Japan, and she displayed no false modesty before him. He shifted his glaze as he said in a guarded tone. "Your mother made this for your need, it'll hold your breasts close to your body so no one will know the secret you hold in your soul. I'm distressed you're forced to wear such a cursed thing, but it's necessary. Estsuko will show you how to wear it, never leave your living area without it. I don't believe it'll hinder your sword arm, but if it does you'll have to work around it. It's important you keep the fact you're female a secret, until the time is right to announce you're otherwise to our Master and the world." He walked out as quickly as he had entered the bathhouse.

Estsuko took the garment and straightened it for Masahiko as she got out of the bath. She laid the garment on a bench and dried her sister. Then helped her struggle in the tight fitting chest band, forcing her breasts in the tight fitting band. Both women laughed hysterically at how funny she looked with her breasts flattened against her chest, until they no longer seemed to be on her. As much as she was ashamed to admit it she liked her breasts, it made her feel she belonged to one sex. And the fact her breasts were larger than usual filled her with pride. She was proud not only was she samurai, but if she had to live the style of a woman later in life, she would have the shape to make the men follow her like puppies in heat.

Estsuko had to stick her hand down the front of the band to move one of her breasts to a more comfortable position. This caused them to laugh again. She was sorry Masahiko had to say everything in such a manly voice, it removed her femininity. But she understood why her father made her grunt like a man, she was supposed to be one. Next, she held the manly loincloth, and Masahiko struggled in it, she looked ridiculous, and they laughed anew. Estsuko held her kosode and she slipped in it. She fixed Masahiko's hair, reshaped the aquene pony tail perfectly, shaved the center cap of her skull then tied down the aquene, making her look more samurai than the samurai visiting for added training. When she was ready, Masahiko walked in her home.

The celebration honoring his daughter for destroying four assassins was going well and when Masahiko walked in the home, everyone bowed to the warrior. The cleaned head of Masao was drained of blood displayed on the gunyoki, the spiked board made for special viewing of a severed head. Offerings of food were placed before the head in mockery, showing the spirit of the assassin he was no longer able to eat. A wood skewer was placed through each eye, this was the only way to stop the spirit of this assassin from being reborn in the forty days.

The trainer made up his mind he would do anything to defeat the evil spirit of the assassin in life. Once the celebration was over, he was going to order the mouth of Masao be filled with stones then carried off the coast of Japan. There, it would be dropped in the ocean so crabs and other water scavengers could pick it clean of flesh, so not enough of his spirit would remain to collect itself, and reform in forty days for rebirth. He decided he would give the trainees the next day off, so he allowed them to celebrate her victory over Wakatsuki's assassins with sake.

The sun shining through the window woke the trainer at sunrise and he tried his best to remain in bed, but once his mind started to work, it was useless to sleep further. He rose and noticed the guards wasn't standing at their post, and grew concerned. He called to his guard and demanded to know where the other protectors were. He was informed Masahiko woke early and went to the stable to check on her mount and take the horse for a ride. He sprang from his room, cursing the endless energy of this child, and her growing love of the horse as he bellowed. "Get my mount! I'll ride to meet Masahiko-san, I require four guards to accompany me on my journey."

The guard bowed then took off to ready his horse. He rode to the stream, it was her favorite area for seeking peace, and he knew he would find his daughter there. He found her walking her horse through the cool water of the stream. It was hot and the horse seemed to be enjoying the water running around its hooves. The guards were positioned surrounding his daughter. Nothing short of a small army would pierce the tight ring of security they formed around her.

He rode up to her in a gallop and she bowed to her father as his horse slowed and got in step with hers. "Masahiko-san! Have you given thought to the name of your horse?"

"Ieeeee, I searched my mind for hours, and as yet unable to come up with a suitable name for her. I don't wish to name her foolishly father. Her name should fit her moods."

"Masahiko-san! It's not necessary to name the horse now. There's plenty of time before you witness Gembuku for that honor to be bestowed on your steed. It'll be necessary to have a name for your horse if it's with you when you go before Kawasomeru-sama, and only if he asks her name, which he rarely does. He's one leader more interested in his Warriors than their horses."

They followed the stream, and he went over her training, comparing it to the signs of nature he was drawing her attention to. "Masahiko-san! Your yoshi gi, your duty to our Lord is like the wandering water of this stream. It continues on its way, overcoming obstacles fate placed in its path. A cunning Warrior can take a valuable lesson from the waters of the stream. What the water cannot overpower with force, it allows water to build up behind these obstacles until it has mass to overpower and push the obstacle out of its way. The waters are patient, see how the water builds up behind that rock? It can't move it out of its way, so the waters can continue fate's mission. So the water allows its force to be diverted until it's able to bypass the stronger obstacle, thus continuing on its goal of reaching the Ocean.

"A smart Samurai who wishes to be successful, must learn this lesson from the stream. A Samurai must know when it's his preference to stand and fight, committing his army in battle, as well as when it's prudent to allow the enemy to remain where they are unmolested. And bypass those entrenched troops in search of an army easier for him to conquer with his troops."

He stopped speaking to take a breath, the bouncing on the horse was giving him pain in his kidneys, and he was in need to relieve his bladder. The trainer continued riding but not speaking until he could no longer take it, and offered to his attentive daughter with a commanding voice. "Masahiko-san! Forgive me but I must relieve myself."

He jumped from his horse and moved from the stream's water to urinate. He was upstream of the village and therefore he wouldn't piss in the stream, because villagers took drinking water from it. He hoisted his kosode then moved aside his fundoshi loincloth. A healthy stream was shot in the bushes. Relieved, he gave a hardy laugh as he boasted. "Ieeeee Masahiko-san! There's nothing more pleasing to the spirit of a Warrior than a healthy stream from a full bladder, to bring one back to good health and fine feeling in his soul and mind."

He shook himself vigorously to shake off the last few drops of urine then stuffed himself back in his cotton loincloth. A smile replaced the once look of pain. He pulled himself on his horse and they continued on, crossing over the first bridge heading for the second.

She began to laugh as her mind through.

"Masahiko-san! Has something flown in your kosode, and is that thing's buzzing giving you pleasure you're not supposed to be enjoying, young one?" He joined her in laughter. It was the first time he laughed with her since she discovered she was a woman.

His words made her laugh all the more until she stopped and between her chuckling and trying to breath, she informed her father of what she thought funny. "Father! I was thinking, the only thing I miss at not being a male, is the capability of making a healthy stream with the snake like yours. All I have I'd trade for one of those small things to make water with. It's such a troublesome chore for a foolish woman to make a healthy stream, father." Again she laughed, it was a healthy laugh which lifted her and her father's spirit.

Her laughter caused the trainer to join her again as he tried to pretend he was insulted by her calling his snake a small thing. "Masahiko-san! You must learn an important lesson when dealing with man's vanity. You must never call his mighty serpent a small thing. Man thinks his serpent is strong enough to conquer all women. That when the snake rises to its power, its full length and strength that it's mightier than his Katana, and with it he can slay more Warriors than he can with his sword. A man's yang is the most powerful thing a man or woman can handle."

They laughed as they rode on. It was a good ride, and they were closely bonding with each other. It was Masahiko who forced the conversation back to serious talk when she asked him. "Father! Why have you referred to your mighty snake as a yang?"

"Ieeeee Masahiko-san! Has your worthless sister not explain the ying and yang to you?"

"Iye!" Masahiko replied as she stared at her father.

"Huh! I'll try my best to explain the difference between them. The yang is the most powerful weapon given to man by the gods. It's his mighty tool used for reproducing his image to a new generation of young for Japan's future."

"Father! I thought it was the woman who reproduced children."

"That's true Masahiko-san! But a woman's well would remain dry and arid if it wasn't for the male's snake. The yang which penetrates the ying, the void, the Jade Gate. A woman's sex has more names than do the foul gods who created us, child."

Again, she interrupted. "Father! I fear I was mistaken when I offered I didn't know the difference between the ying and yang. Estsuko did explain the art of pillowing of a man and a woman. She used different words than you employed. I apologize for making you waste your time explaining further to this worthless woman what I already know." She bowed to her father, adding as much grace as she could from the saddle of her horse.

He let out a sigh, he was pleased he wasn't forced to get deeply involved trying to explain the difference between the ying and yang to the child staring deeply into his tired and burning eyes.

She had her yumi, her bow looped over her back, and her swords tucked in their proper place hanging from her hip. The trainer was the first to notice the rabbit rushing from one bush to the other, rousted by their horses. He pointed and she did the rest without being order by the trainer.

With the speed of the wind not blocked by mountains on a clear summer's night, she flipped the bow from her shoulder and whipped a sasa no ha arrow from her quiver, armed her bow and let the arrow fly. It struck the rabbit in the chest and the animal tumbled head over heels to a stop but it was still slightly moving.

"A second arrow quick!"

Almost as quick as the words were spoken, a second arrow was sent through the air straight and sure, and struck the hare before it stopped its crashing death tumble.

"Ieeeee Masahiko-san! You have the eye and speed of a Falcon soaring in the Heavens in search of a meal. There's none in Japan who could best you with bow and arrow, daughter." He raised his hand over his head and from out of nowhere, a warrior charged for the rabbit, he dismounted and retrieved the arrows and as quick he remounted his horse and disappeared.

She bowed, proud her father thought so highly of her skills, this was why she always tried to hone her skills to a finer perfection. She didn't realize, but she was trying to be the best to prove to the Empire and Shogun, a woman was every bit as good as any male was, and in this case she was better than any male could hope to become. Most warriors didn't have the luxury of almost twenty four hour training a day from the greatest trainer in Japan.

A sudden roll of crashing thunder in the distant west, warned the pair they better start thinking about getting back to the stables before the rain started to fall.

TANIZAKI'S HOME

While he and his daughter were enjoying their ride to the stables, his house was left defended by four samurai guards, and a pair of crafty assassins moved in for the kill. They were looking for Masahiko in the home. They had no idea the samurai wasn't in the home. The executioners scouted out the house cautiously. There were two guards stationed in the front of the home, with the other two warriors guarding the rear of the structure, they didn't look alert.

Using the silence of sign language, the lead invader pointed to one guard. Silently, like a snake working its way through grass to its unsuspecting meal, the butcher worked through the plants and bushes of the rear garden. He crouched and used the shadows from the bushes to cover his moves. The freshly watered garden made his moves silent. When the assassin worked his way to position to attack, he stopped movement, then checked the unsuspecting guards again and reached in the sleeve of his black, short, tight fitting kosode. His legs were covered by black long, tight fitting pants, and his feet covered with black tabis with the split toe.

He removed a seven pointed throwing star with razor sharp edges which identified him as a monk assassin for hire from the illegal Sohei warring monk's Ninja sect from Mount Hiei. The stealthy killer checked his line of sight and sent the star flying as if propelled by an unseen force at the warrior guarding the home. The star hissed through the air silently as it hit the guard across the throat, ripping it open and making it impossible for him to utter a warning of alarm. Without a sound of protest, the body sank to the ground.

The second slayer was to take out the remaining guard. He took out a uchine, a short throwing arrow and heaved it striking the guard in the ear, the point came out the other side of his head. Then, silently the murderers made their way to the front of the building and dispatched the guards outside. They dragged the bodies in the underbrush and returned to the rear of the building.

One killer moved to the rear and took his katana and slashed the shoji savagely in two. He moved in the building, followed by the second assassin. It was early afternoon as they checked the interior of the home for Masahiko, or the master trainer.

Tomotaka, attending to Emiko's needs, heard the commotion caused by the violent destruction of the shoji door, and knew their lives were in danger. She moved to the wall and removed a katakama yari, a long single bladed spear, and moved out to intercept the invader to the home. She moved to the main room, silently looking for the one who dared to enter Tanizaki's home violently. She wasn't an accomplished warrior so she was easily detected by the stalking silent assassin, who put up his hand and stopped the trailing slayer behind from moving further in the home. The leader waited for the next sound, so he could tell where this threat was coming from. He was worried the skilled master trainer was somewhere in the house, and he heard them enter and was stalking them trying to protect his samurai child.

The lead assassin stopped moving and with a few swift hand signals, he allowed the trailing killer to take the lead. The second murderer was armed with a heavy hachiwara, a paring weapon six foot long, armed with a hook shaped razor sharp projection on the end of the weapon. It was the weapon commonly used to rip open the body of one's enemy. The second slayer took the lead, moved in the room and saw the female staring at him. She was armed with the katakama yari spear. At the same instant they saw each other they charged, neither making a sound of alarm as they clashed together in the center of the room.

The opening thrust by Tomotaka was able to be fended off by the more powerful and skilled assassin. In the motion of defending himself, he tried to bring the end of his hachiwara weapon up in hopes of catching the weak female off guard, and rip her belly opened. His thrust missed her body, but succeed in catching her thigh, ripping open a five inch gash which bled profusely.

She stepped back and covered the gaping wound for a brief moment as she assessed the injury, and thought out her next move of defense.

This was all the time the stealthy assassin needed to press his attack further. The alert assassin dropped to a knee and swung the hachiwara weapon by the end, using the hook as the main weapon during this attack. As she turned to the killer, the hook found the softness of her belly. The weapon grabbed in, forcing her to drop her katakama yari and grip the end of the hachiwara in an effort to stop it from doing more damage to her body then already done, and ripping her wide open in the same motion.

The assassin was too strong for her to fend off his attack, and with one mighty pull up on the end of the hachiwara. The hook cut upwards through her rib cage, allowing some organs to spill forward from the gaping wound in her chest. She fell to the floor, her breath now coming out of the gash in her lungs. She died a terrible death, choking to death on her blood as it filled her lungs, and her body trashed about on the floor as it struggled to continue life in her body.

The hard breathing assassin gave one more powerful tug up on the handle of his hachiwara hook, it moved and almost splitting her upper body in half as the end of the razor sharp hook ripped out of her body by the throat. The slayer wiped the blood on his weapon on her torn opened kosode then went back on the offensive again.

The trailing assassin heard a slight shuffle and moved to check out the noise. With one slash, his katana blade easily split in half the fragile shoji door separating the kitchen area from the rest of the building. His eyes opened wide when he felt he found Masahiko as he stared at her youngest daughter Enko, frightened to death by the sudden appearance of this threatening invader, she was cowering in the corner in the kitchen.

Enko was so scared she froze where she hid. Not even when the sneering killer lifted his sword did she move. The blade whistled through the air and the sickening thud came as the blade split the child's head in half, and continued down the body until the sword's edge was stopped by the breast bone. The sword stuck in the body, the weight of the child pulling the blade momentarily out of the hands of the executioner. When he went to retrieve the sword, he was forced to place his foot on the child's chest to free the blade of the body. But the murderer wasn't prepared for what happened next.

Estsuko heard the commotion and entered the building from the outside. She was cleaning her father's room on the porch when the assassin's attacked. She found one of her father's katanas and unsheathed the weapon and went to confront the killers. She came up behind the trailing invader as he placed his foot against Enko's chest, and tried to pull his sword free of her body.

With rage locked in her heart she struck out, almost severing the invader's head from his shoulders, she didn't possess the power in her arms to complete the task.

The injured assassin's hands dropped the sword, and they went to his neck to try and stop the terrible damage from continuing to his body. It was all for naught, for life as he enjoyed ended when she struck again from the other side of his neck. His head popped a feet inches in the air before falling to the floor. She jumped over the flailing body of the murderer, and checked on her sister's condition. One look told her all she needed to know. Enko died in a savage and deplorable way. She couldn't control herself and cried as she tried to move the two halves of her sister's head together. One eye wasn't to be seen. Sobbing, she gave her sister dignity in death by trying to reassemble her body the best she could.

The lead assassin continued working his way deeper in the house, until he came across Emiko lying helplessly on her bedroll. One look at her and the killer for hire knew she wasn't well, he decided to allow her to live out the remainder of her years in peace. His face, mostly covered by a black silk mask only allowing his eyes to be seen, bowed slightly before the prone Emiko, never once taking his weary eyes from her form.

The second she saw the bowing assassin she tried to roll on her side and reach her tanto blade, in hopes of defending herself against this invader.

The assassin laughed as he stepped further in her quarters and tapped her hand with the point of his blood red hachiwara as he mocked her. "No, no, foolish old woman. As long as you remain unarmed you're no threat, and I'll allow you to live. Go back to sleep old one, this nightmare will end before you open your eyes again." The assassin tapped her on the head with the side of his hachiwara, not hard enough to kill, just to render her unconscious long enough for him to complete his assignment then flee. He checked the room to make certain the child warrior wasn't hiding in it, then left. He checked the rest of the house and found no one, he headed to where the trailing killer went. He saw the split shoji and shook his head, disgusted the fool would destroy so much of the home. Their orders were to kill the chosen child, nothing more.

As the killer closed in on the kitchen, he noticed his partner's body on the floor in a heap motionless. Then noticed the back of a woman as she looked after what was obviously a child's body. The surviving assassin smiled, overjoyed with the knowledge his partner was successful in his task of killing the so called chosen child. He didn't want to kill the woman attending the body, killing for the sake of killing went against the code of the assassin. So he worked his way at her silently. When he was in striking distance of the unsuspecting woman, he smashed her on the head with his weapon, knocking her senseless. Blood came from the wound the hachiwara made on the top of her head as she fell forward and covered the small body beneath her.

The killer took time to check his partner's condition, when he saw his head lying a few feet from his body, he knew there was nothing he could do for him. He bowed to his accomplice then disappeared from the house as silently as he entered it.

They made it to the stable just as the heavens opened up, and released their life giving waters in a heavy and steady rain. Fierce lightening struck the ground near the dais, the crack of thunder made the horses jumpy and neighed in fear. The old master trainer looked to the west and could tell this rain wasn't going to last long, he noticed the sun already shining in the distance. He pointed this out to his daughter and they decided to wait out the ending storm in the stable. In less than an hour the rain stopped, and they walked home. He was the first to see his wife standing weakly on the front porch, and noticed she was crying.

"Trouble!" The trainer bellowed at his daughter as he rushed to his home.

She drew her sword as she rushed after her father. The guard samurai ran after them. He crashed through the gate, almost ripping it from its hinges. He jumped up the steps and grabbed his wife just as she fainted in his arms.

Miho was coming back from shopping carrying fruit when she noticed the commotion, and dropped the basket as she ran to help the trainer with his wife. She took over attending to her needs as the trainer, Masahiko, and the guards cautiously entered the home, not knowing what they might find waiting within. Other samurai rushed around to the back of the home, and entered from there. All entered the home prepared to defend against assassins.

His lip jumped when he saw what the invaders done to Tomotaka, her body was left in a mangled heap in the center of the room. He leaned to Masahiko and growled as he pointed to her body. "Who else was in the god cursed house today?"

"Four guard samurai, Estsuko, and Enko was home, father." She replied as her eyes searched for the other members of her family. She was the one to see the body of the assassin on the kitchen floor. She pointed it out to her father and they worked their way to the kitchen. She was in the lead and it was she who saw Estsuko on the floor lying over something. She dropped her katana and rushed to her sister's side, fearing she was dead like Tomotaka. She rolled Estsuko over and saw she was still breathing. She wiped blood from her mouth and brushed hair from her face. She paid no attention to what Estsuko was lying on in the kitchen.

Estsuko coughed and her eyes flew open and her hands started beating at the face looking over her. Masahiko had to slap her across the face to bring her back to her senses. When she saw it was her sister attending her she cried. She pulled Estsuko to her and as her hair came off the small body underneath her, her heart jumped in her throat. She saw the butchered body of Enko lying under her sister. She pulled her from Enko's body as tears filled her eyes. It was easy to tell she was dead, almost split in half to the waist. A roar of hate came from deep in her shaking body, as she hugged Estsuko close to her body and wailed for her sister. No one had to tell her Enko was dead, because the murderers took her for Masahiko in the home.

Over and over she allowed the frighteningly, terrified wail to come deep from her soul. When she could finally speak words again, the young warrior cursed the gods dwelling in the Floating World, for allowing this terrible act to happen to so innocent a young child. She was so caught up in her grief, she cursed her father, Lord Kawasomeru, the realm and Empire and the soil of Japan. So deep and overwhelming was her grief it robbed her of her breath, and she was forced to stop her cursing in order to breathe properly.

Estsuko was covered with the blood of the assassin and it mingled with that of her sister. Though she joined her sister in her wail, her grief wasn't as deep. She regained her wits and pushed Masahiko to her feet. She led the furious and trembling warrior from the kitchen. When her wits returned, she growled. "How long ago did this attack occurred, Estsuko?"

She looked at the blood on her hands, it was wet and dripping as she replied. "Masahiko-san! The attack could not have happened less than ten minutes ago."

Without word, she stood and ran through the house, picking up her killing sword as she rushed from the building and out into the woods. Her samurai guards charged after her without hesitation. Once in the woods they quickly fanned out and headed in the direction they felt the assassin might be heading off in. Running faster, she rapidly closed the gap between her and the murderer moving fast before her, but nowhere near as fast as she and her warriors charged after him. It took them half an hour of hard running, before the first warrior gave out the alarm, letting the others know he spotted the killer in the woods.

It didn't take long for the guards to form a circle around the assassin. The commander moved forward as Masahiko entered the glade where the slayer was trapped, ready to defend himself. Realizing he was trapped, the assassin tried to kill himself, but the commander smashed the arm holding the knife with the back of his katana, shattering the bone to the wrist. The assassin dropped to his knees supporting his arm and waited for fate to befall him. His wait wasn't long, she charged through the guards roaring savagely at the assassin, her sword held over head.

The first blow was dealt against the assassin with sufficient force to kill him outright, but she kept chopping at the downed body wildly in a rage. Ten chops, twenty, thirty, she kept hacking away and cursing the body of the assassin, until there wasn't enough left of the body to cut with another blow from her sword. All the while she attacked the body, she roared with hatred, hatred at the savagery that made Japan great. She roared for her sister, for the countless samurai who died before her on the battlefields. She roared for the future samurai of Japan. What she didn't understand was, in her mind she roared for her death she didn't realize was so near in her future.

Exhausted from her overwhelming grief and draining attack on the assassin, she collapsed, kneeling right on the scattered remains of the kaishaku, the executioner. The point of her blood coated blade dug deeply in the soft earth. Covered with blood and flecks of flesh and bone, she looked to the Heavens then lifted her sword with superhuman effort, and with one last roar from deep in her soul. She gave a final salute to her sister Enko, by holding the blood covered sword up and calling out her sister's name. "ENKO!" Knowing as long as she lived, she would never mention her sister's name again in her life.

She had to stick the end of her sword in the ground, to use it as sort of a crutch in an effort to help her exhausted body stand. With one final act of anger and revenge, she kicked at a chunk of the assassin's body with her foot then spat at it. Slowly, her breathing came under her control.

The commander of the warriors moved close to the honored warrior and asked. "Masahiko-san! What do you suggest we do with the remains of the filthy killer?"

She looked at the captain of her samurai guard for a moment with unseeing eyes, and he was forced to repeat the question a second time. Her anger took over her thoughts and she searched her mind for the most insulting thing she could possibly think to do to the remains of the butcher. A thought struck her and she ordered the commander to order his warriors to step up and have them piss on the remains of the assassin.

The captain dared to grin at her as he gave the order to his warriors, and one by one his samurai stepped up and urinated on a chosen part of the dismembered body of the assassin. She waited until the captain moved up next then hitched his loincloth to the side standing before her, and removed himself and pissed on the part of the assassin's head lying at the blood soaked feet of Masahiko. When everyone pissed she ordered them to head back to the home, while she decided to remain standing in the small glade still trying to get her breathing under control.

The grinning captain balked at the samurai's order, informing her his duty given to him by Lord Kawasomeru, was to protect her life at all cost. He was instructed by their master never to leave her side for a moment, or risk losing his head for disobedience.

She held up her hand in order to silence the concerned captain's complaint then in no short terms she ordered the captain to take the rest of his men, and leave the area without further complaint or hesitation. When she was sure no one was in sight of her, she moved her loincloth to the side and squatted over the remains of the head of the dead executioner, and relieved herself on it. What she didn't know, was her father watched as she defiled the assassin's soul in a terribly disgusting and insulting way. Silently, he nodded approval of her action then waited for her to come out of the glade to join him.

She noticed her father standing on the rim of the shallow glade watching her actions, and went to him. He looped his arm protectively over her shoulder, and together they walked home in silence. He pulled her close to him and said. "Today Masahiko-san you learned the taste of another virtue of life, the virtue of revenge. A complete Samurai must know of this virtue to make him whole, he must understand when the proper time to display this virtue is. When it's proper to show mercy and forgiveness to one's once loathsome enemy.

"Masahiko-san, your actions were correct and honorable, and served to make you a whole Samurai on this day of disaster. I'm proud of you young one. You learned well, I fear there's nothing more I can teach you, Masahiko-san. Huh! I believe it's I who can learn from your vast knowledge of worldly things. There are nine months left before you reach the age of Gembuku then I can present you before Kawasomeru-sama. Today Masahiko-san, you're Samurai!"

She looked to her father then smiled weakly as they continued to walk home.

"Yes Masahiko-san! You're Samurai of the highest Caste, the First Caste. But there's still one more decision you must make to seal you soul to the Samurai world forever. What do you wish done with the assassins' contaminated remains?"

She turned to look back to the small glade for a few seconds as she thought of what to do then she snapped angrily. "Father! I made my decision on the lowly dog, I decree from this moment on, the body of the filthy attacker should remain where it lies, to feed the half man, half bird Tengu wood goblins and the rest of the scavengers of the woods. I'll pray to Lord Buddha to allow the forest animals to spread the foul remains near and far, so the foul gods will be unable to find enough of the assassin's soul to allow him to be reborn Samurai."

"Ieeeee young Warrior of vast knowledge! Wise, most wise indeed daughter. For the foul soul of that piece of dung would never come back to this world as a loyal Warrior to serve his Master.   It'll return as a worthless Ronin, and the gods know we have enough of them pieces of filth walking the lands of Japan." He offered to his daughter.

The rest of the night was spent with little sleep for the trainer, he consumed the hours of night formulating the course of the next day's training. He was the first up in his household, and sent a samurai to fetch General Kobayashi then he waited for Masahiko to wake. General Kobayashi rushed in his home ready to defend himself against any attacker. He had his swords tucked in his sash and carried a two handed long tachi blade threateningly in one hand. The trainer ordered him to the training field, he wanted the trainees to be ready, standing in formation by the time he arrived at the field. The general rushed off to carry out the master's orders.

When the child woke and came in the kitchen, he stood and ordered her to follow him without word, not giving her a chance to eat her morning meal. She did as ordered without complaint and followed her father out the home. It didn't take long to figure out where they were heading. She was surprised to see the samurai trainees standing in formation, their weapons collected resting on the only grass section of the training field. She looked to her father for explanation, but he ignored her as he stormed to the front of the formation of samurai. His mind working on what he was going to order from them.

Generals Kobayashi and Miyamoto stood behind a table with Shoya Sanuki. All three well seasoned warriors were armed and wearing terrible scrawls, and seemed ready to hack anyone to pieces for the smallest infraction, or insult against them or the trainer. Her guard samurai joined forces with General Kobayashi and the other warriors, and they took up a protective stance threatening to all gathered on the training field.

The trainer stepped closer to the warriors, not bothering to climb the stand to address them. He stared angrily at the samurai, showing all he was upset by what transpired last night and the death of his daughter, and in his deepest commanding voice he bellowed as he scolded the warriors. Ordering ten of them to step forward and commit suppuku while he continued to yell at the other warriors. Without reason, he picked another samurai and ordered him to commit suicide before him. When it was done, he continued his angry words to the trainees.

"As Samurai, each of you worthless fools was forced to swear a blood oath for your Master. I decided to force you fools to take yet another oath. I demand each one of you trainees to swear an oath to me, personally. And in that oath you'll denounce Lord Wakatsuki and all he stands for, and you'll further swear none of you are assassins waiting in hiding to bring more death to my family. I'll return your swords when you proved you are faithful Samurai for Kawasomeru-sama, and without an agenda in your foul hearts and souls. Each Samurai will step up to the table and make your oath loud and clear. I'll not accept any excuses from you fools. You refuse my order or hesitate for any reason, you die. Begin! And be quick about it I warn you dung heaps. My patience is wearing thin standing here being forced to stare at the lot of you fools."

The upset trainer demanded of the trainees as he folded his arms and watched the first line of samurai stepped up to the table. He knew a samurai, especially an assassin would never allow himself to swear a second blood oath if it went against the first one he sworn to. As bad as the Ninja monk assassins were, they would never swear a second oath to another, once they sworn an oath to kill the child warrior for the one paying him.

The first warrior to move forward allowed the finger on his sword hand be sliced on a razor sharp wakizashi blade then placed the bloody fingerprint on the scroll next to his printed name. Then, and only then did Kobayashi handed the warrior back his fighting swords. Everything was going well with the swearing of the oath. It moved along with surprising speed and without problems, until one samurai stepped up before the table, thought about allowing his finger to be sliced by the blade of truth then pulled it from the blade. There was no explanation offered by the hesitant warrior, nor was one requested as the guards of Masahiko charged as one at the samurai, drawing their swords at the same time. Unarmed as he was, the warrior was unable to do anything about the dominating warriors who had their swords out swinging them at him with revenge in their hearts and actions aimed against him.

The assassin once hiding in the group of trainees, was besieged by the small army of guard samurai ordered to protect the trainer's life, and the lives of the rest of his family, as they violently hacked the would be assassin's body to pieces. Within mere seconds the assassin's form looked like a pile of manure lying on the bloody training field. He died a quick and honorable death for his chosen profession.

A rag of cotton was passed around, and the warriors who dispatched the killer in hiding, wiped their blades clean then the last one threw the rag on the pile of death lying before his feet. From out of nowhere, three hinin moved in and cleaned up every piece of the slaughtered assassin's body, until there was no trace of him lying on the soil of the training field.

Again, he spoke in an extremely threatening and angry voice to the trainees under his direction. "Ieeeee! This is the fate that'll be suffered by all who plan treachery aimed against our Lord Kawasomeru, his realm, or against me and mine! Continue with the oath before I have all you worthless fools slaughtered, merely because I can order this to take place!"

After the oath was completed, the warriors were ordered to take the rest of the day off, and reflect on what transpired before them. The following month of waiting was used for a time of healing and burying of Enko and Tomotaka, and to allow the trainees to prepare for the long trek to Engakuji Castle, to be greeted by their lord. So he could witness their fine training abilities at waging war then assigned them to their respective units and new duties.

CHAPTER TWENTY
THE YEAR THIRTEEN FIFTY FOUR. THE YEAR OF GEMBUKU

The first three weeks of June were spent preparing to leave for Engakuji Castle by the his clan. The trainer was slowing giving in to the calling of age, and want to end training of samurai for Kawasomeru. Emiko was again bleeding and losing weight and strength. He made sure he finished the training of the next batch of trainees on the same week he was to leave for the castle, assuring there company with his trained samurai. The entire ninth village sworn an oath against Wakatsuki for allowing assassins to enter their village to kill a child. Every man of the village joined the samurai to be trained. The wars between the provinces were heating up, and there was word Wakatsuki was preparing to invade Kozuke in force. Totomi and Suruga provinces were coming under pressure from Mino, Owari and Mikawa provinces loyal to Lord Wakatsuki.

He placed a small shrine honoring Tomotaka who gave up her life so honorably to protect his family, when the filthy one entered his home and killed his youngest daughter so savagely. Miho mourned the death of Tomotaka and Enko, she blamed herself for not being there when the murderers came to hunt.

No one from the ninth village knew Lord Kawasomeru planned to allow the last samurai trainee group to join forces with the armies from Musashi and Kozuke province. The master was going to invade Echigo and Shimotsuke to hunt Wakatsuki down and kill him for allowing the murder of Tanizuki's daughter. The warlord swore an oath of death against the powerful warlord of Echigo province, for daring to kill a child of his province. He took a chance turning his back on Kazusa, the army he sent in to defeat Lord Wakatsuki's done its job, but he was forced to pull them out of Kazusa, so those samurai could linkup with his army ready to invade Echigo and Shimotsuke. He decided it was time to end the small wars by plunging the eastern sixteen provinces in total war. It was a gamble to allow Kazusa to fall under the combined weight of Awa and Shimosa provinces, two of Lord Wakatsuki's allies.

The warlord knew if Kazusa fell to his enemy, his entire southern flank would be open for invasion, but it was a chance he had to take to get the jump on Lord Wakatsuki and his massed armies. He discovered a plot that showed Wakatsuki planned to invade Kozuke in force on the twelfth month. Armed with this latest information, he pushed his provinces to prepare to attack Lord Wakatsuki's army, to cut off his invasion force. He banked everything once Echigo and Shimotsuke collapsed, the rest of the warring provinces under Wakatsuki's influence would sue for peace. Thus ending the wars soon to be ripping the many provinces apart.

The master trainer was acting like an angry bear that got stung by a swarm of bees for destroying the hive in search of honey. But everyone knew he was pushing them beyond endurance, because he had to have Masahiko, and the trainees ready to report to Engakuji Castle two weeks before Gembuku. The ceremony was to be held on the same day of the year, and children who would become adults in that year, were scheduled to arrive at the castle. He made certain Masahiko had her best kosodes packed, he wanted her to make a good impression on the powerful liege lord.

Today was Saturday, and everyone who intended to witness Gembuku from the ninth village, was ready to move out on Monday at sunrise. The trainer had Miho keeping an eye on his wife, in his mind he knew she was never to return from the ceremony. The reason he wanted to get to Engakuji Castle two weeks before the ceremony was to be, because it was a time for the samurai to get to know one another. Their time would be spent engaging in mock games designed to test skills with horseback, spear, and sword.

Even though he would never admit it, his heart pounded for having the honor to attend the ceremony. He looked forward to hearing stories by samurai no longer able to fight in war. He knew he would relive past battles, and come home with new memories of battles he never fought in. There was a chance he might pick up new tactics developed by other soldiers, which he could employ in his future training. He was aware to be samurai, he must be open to new ways of waging war, if he was to keep on the field of battle. He polished his swords and lightly taped rice power on them then placed them in the scabbard. He made sure his armor was polished and in proper order, he planned to march to the castle in armor in much the same way Lord Kawasomeru rode to his village the first day he brought samurai to be trained. He ordered his vassals to place a few of his finest bottles of sake in the caravan to be given to Lord Kawasomeru and his generals as gifts that couldn't be out done by the recipients.

Saturday flew by and before he knew it, it was late. He ordered Yukie Kidoguchi to remain home and care for his buildings, and make sure the other servants didn't take advantage of his absence. He decided to allow Remi to accompany them to Engakuji, so she might visit her aging mother. It was getting so he didn't want to spend a night without her by his side. He knew once Emiko entered the Floating World, he was going to ask her to marry and spend life with him.

As he prepared for sleep, a thought struck him. He knew his wife wasn't coming home from the ceremony, and he wanted to share her bed one last time out of respect. He went to the kitchen and heated sake and carried them to his room and the company of Emiko.

Miho was asleep at the foot of Emiko's bedroll, when the trainer entered the room she knew what was on his mind and left without a sound. Before she left she bowed to him to assure him she approved of his actions, she too knew Emiko's days were coming to a fast end.

He waited until Miho was out of the quarters then moved to the head of the bed and lightly tapped her awake and grinned at her. Her eyes opened and he offered her sake with his smile. His wife struggled to sit up and sipped it noisily, bowing with effort. She laid back and threw the covers off her body. She was wearing a light sleeping kosode with five simple ties.

With patience and tenderness, he opened the ties. She allowed the fine silk to fall from her body. Each move made her wince with pain, something that didn't go unnoticed by the old man. He felt her stiffen as he prepared to mount her, the desire to pillow her left, not out of anything but respect for his ailing wife. His mind screamed she was ready to endure great pain to share one last night with him. His conscious warned him if he was to part her thighs, she would be robbed of the pleasure of witnessing Masahiko becoming a samurai for Lord Kawasomeru.

Instead of pillowing his wife of countless years, He pulled her body close, and she slept comfortably wrapped in his protective strong arms all night. At times, he heard her sobbing softly and felt the wetness running down his chest. He had no idea how much it meant to her for him to want to share her bed before she died, if not to pillow her, to be with her. She knew she was dying, she felt it in her body and felt the pain spread, taking over her whole being. Her tears flowed, but not for her, they were being shed for the husband she would leave behind, and for her daughters and sons. But mostly for Enko who wouldn't be there to share her sister's honor at being enlisted into the caste of samurai, a man's world that finally ran its course in Japan.

The trainer was the first up on Sunday morning. He was awakened by the thrill of what he was to do on that day. Word of the master spending the night with his wife, spread throughout the house then the village. Everyone respected him for giving his wife a special night. His clumsiness woke everyone in his home, and Miho came in the kitchen complaining he was making a mess of her room. He smiled, pleased she was there to look after his wife. A number of times the trainer offered to bring another housekeeper in, so the burden of the house would be lifted from Miho's shoulders. But she refused to hear anything about replacing Tomotaka, she went so far as to threaten suppuku, if he dared to bring another woman in his home on her.

He was pleased Miho thought of his house as her turf, her property. He allowed her to force him to leave the cooking and take a seat so she could serve him. He was all smiles, and she was worried maybe age robbed him of what wits he had left. She heard stories about a man's wits leaving them when they reached a certain age, leaving them like a child who needed more care than a newborn ever did, but she never witnessed this story taking place.

At one point, he reached out and rudely rubbed her rearend. She pushed his hand and turned around and placed her hands on her hips, but it did nothing to take the spirit burning within his soul. Miho finally yelled at him to leave the kitchen so she could finish cooking for the rest of the household. He grinned at her.

She spotted the tubular silk scarf leaning against the corner and knew what the old man was up to, and why he was in such a good mood as she offered. "Tanizaki-san! Shall I wake the lazy Masahiko-san, so you'll leave me alone?"

"Iye! Let the child sleep, he'll be losing sleep when we get to Engakuji, and he's with the other Samurai. I lived through it, but I don't yet know how. I'll be patient and wait the child to awake so I can give him my greatest gift."

"Suit yourself Tanizaki-san, but it'll give me peace of mind if you'd turn this attention to Masahiko-san, rather than wasting it on me."

"Nonsense Lady Miho! You're a fine woman pleasing to the eyes, and the touch of this old man's weathered hands." He retorted as he grabbed her breasts, displaying the worse of manners against her person as he rolled her breast and smiled at her.

"Ieeeee! The temper of the Devil Kami is in your soul on this day, Tanizaki-san. I better get you something to eat, maybe that'll force you to give me peace of mind today, Master Trainer."

He turned serious as he asked about his wife's health of Miho.

She allowed her shoulders to sag a bit as she replied. "Huh! Lady Emiko spent a peaceful night's sleep. But today she woke weaker than when she went to sleep. I fear for her health and the time she has left in the land of the living."

"Lady Miho! I'm pleased at your ways of taking care of my wife. I feel you'll not have a job to occupy yourself with when we leave for Engakuji Castle."

A shocked looked clouded her gaze, as a tear was forced from her eye. She drew in a breath in a sigh to not cry, but it did no good and tears flowed. "Huh! You have the sharp eyes of an eagle to know Lady Emiko is about to die. I hope the endless trip to Engakuji doesn't kill her outright. I pray to the Kami she lives long enough to see Masahiko-san be accepted by Kawasomeru-sama to his army. Master Trainer! I'm puzzled by your words. If the gods deem it right to allow Lady Emiko to walk in their world of wonder, why does that mean I'll no longer have responsibilities to the Tanizaki family and residence? Who'll take care of you and your children, old fool?"

"I'll be asking Lady Remi to become my wife after waiting the proper amount of time."

"That doesn't mean you'll not be needing my services further, Master Trainer." She replied to the bothersome master trainer.

"Huh, you wouldn't mind staying on with my house if the worse happens at Engakuji?" The master trainer asked with concern lacing his tone.

"Ieeeee! How could a man with such wits and wisdom on the battlefield, have no wits about him when it comes to dealing with his household, and his worthy vassals? It's my duty to remain in the Tanizaki clan until the gods deem it fit to allow me to cross over to their Floating World." She complained as she turned to attend to the rice cooking on the stove.

"Lady Miho! I'd take it as an honor if you'd stay on with my family until it's your time to leave this world." He offered, knowing in his heart he would die long before she would cross over.

"Domo." Miho said over her shoulder as she placed the rice back on the burner again.

"Thank you for what, Lady Miho?" Masahiko asked as she came to the table. Her words made the old man jump, she was so light on her feet his ears didn't hear her coming.

"My words don't concern you young one. Huh little fire, do you think everything said in this world is about you? Vanity! I must warn you Masahiko-san. Self-adulation is the least valuable virtue for a Samurai. It's beneath a Warrior's worth to be conceited, for what does he own? Nothing! Everything in his world orbits his Lord. His wife is the wealthy one, she's the one who handles money, buys food, pays bills the Samurai accumulates, and if she chooses, she could ruin him by wasting their worth. So you see, a Samurai has nothing to be conceited about."

"Hai father." She replied, not knowing if her father was in a foul mood or not. She had no idea how good a mood he was in. After all these years she was still unable to read her father's many moods, they changed from one to another without much warning.

"Eat young Warrior, we have a lot to accomplish before we head for Engakuji Castle."

She spoke no more as she followed her father's orders; it was rare when she had some time to eat a meal at her leisure. She wrote it off to her training. When she finished eating her father stood and picked up the silk wrapping and walked out of the kitchen. He looked over his shoulder and grunted. "Masahiko-san! Follow!"

She pushed her food aside and followed her father to the porch, there he dropped to his knees and placed the silk tube across his legs as he waved for her to join him. Her father's lips moved as if engaging in silent prayer. She bowed to give him privacy and waited until he addressed her. She didn't know her father was waiting for Kobayashi before he offered her the gifts for her.

The general appeared as ordered, and allowed entry by the guards. Their number was cut to fifteen, because he had five guards commit suppuku for allowing the assassins to get close to his daughter. The general sat on the top step of the porch and waited in silence.

He lifted the long red silk tube and touched it lightly to his forehead and blessed Lord Kawasomeru and his realm then handed it to Masahiko.

She took the silk tube looking at her father.

"Huh! What do you look at Warrior? What I offer you is something you earned by past deeds and efforts. You merit the blades by doing deeds of honor." He held his hand out and waited.

Remi appeared with a second silk tube and the trainer took it and tapped it to his forehead, again blessing Lord Kawasomeru. He handed the second tube to the general as he said. "General Kobayashi-san! Wise Commanders know well they're great because of their lesser officers who look after them, and stop them before they make a mistake and lose their head for the infraction. It's a rare moment when a General is so honored. Take these swords as reward for your devotion, and to the Samurai whose education you were instrumental in. For that, I'm in your debt, a debt I couldn't possibly repay in two lifetimes." He bowed to General Kobayashi and to his surprise he noticed Masahiko joined him in honoring the general.

He returned the bow and slid the ancient swords free of their wrapping. Not only did they look old, they smelt and felt old. He turned and offered. "Master Trainer! These swords are beyond worldly worth. I couldn't take them in good manners. A true Samurai would be willing to die just to touch the fine steel of these swords."

"Huh! Have you forgot your manners? It's impolite, insulting to refuse a gift from someone who appreciates your diligence to duty, General Kobayashi-san? Take the swords, my arms are too old to swing them in justice any longer." He rejected the swords with a wave of the hand.

The general took the swords then with his thumb placed against the tsuba sword guard, and his other hand holding the scabbard, he broke the seal. More ancientness greeted his senses as he pulled the sword half out to check its sharpness and steel. It was perfect. He slammed the blade in the scabbard and bowed. "It's a great sword. I'll honor it with every breath in my worthless body. It'll shed the blood of all who wager treachery against our Lord and Master or his realm."

The trainer bowed and turned to Masahiko and grunted. "Young Warrior! Your manners impress me. Anyone not in control of his emotions, such as a child who wouldn't know better, or a self-admiring Samurai would've opened his gift before Kobayashi-san, the older being honored first. I thank you for your respect to my General and your friend. Now child, I'm interested in seeing what you think of your gift. You may open it now Masahiko-san."

Her shaking hands quickly untied the silk strings with childish speed and allowed the ancient swords to glide in her hands. A gasp from Kobayashi when he saw the blade, he recognized it. The handle of the sword was encompassed with kinran and ginran, gold and silver brocade, and five gold crests which held the brocade in place, left no mistake what the swords were made for. She looked from the swords to her father in stunned disbelief, her mouth open like a child unsure of what she was witnessing.

"Yes Masahiko-san! They're the swords personally given me by Lord Kawasomeru's hand, as a special gift of honor for past service to him and his realm. They were made especially for our Master by the greatest swordsmith ever to do his craft in Japan, Sugahara-sama. It was the last swords made by the Master, before he started his journey with the gods of the Floating World. They were given to me with respect for my accomplishments and loyalty to Kawasomeru-sama. Now, I give the greatest gifts of my life to you, to honor you in the same way. Masahiko-san! No, forgive me. Yuriko Tanizaki! You're the greatest swordsman in Japan, and to complement your outstanding abilities you need swords of equal greatness. Swords such as these." He bowed until his forehead actually touched the deck.

Her mouth snapped shut as she fought tears. She was happy her father used her female name in front of General

Kobayashi, it gave her honor and face. She bowed equally to her father. The child in her couldn't wait to see the steel of the sword. As General Kobayashi done, she broke the seal of the sword with her thumb. But she didn't respect the sword as he had, she removed the blade from the scabbard. She turned the blade in her hand, examining both sides and tested the sharpness with her thumb which was a mistake learned. She received a minor gash for touching the edge of the sword. She ignored the trickle of blood, making sure none of it got on the face of the sword, she touched the tip and shook the sword in her arm to get the feel of the weight. It was perfectly balanced and the blade felt as if it could swing itself.

She placed the wakizashi blade along with the gold inlayed katana zutsu, the tubular wood scabbard on the mat by her knees, not allowing them to touch the floor or each other. Then she practiced several swift moves used in a sword fight with an invisible adversary. With each thrust and swing, she beamed with delight. The sword fit her hands as if it had been made especially for her use. The guards moved closer to see the blade as it sliced the air as easily as it would slice through the strongest back of the most worthy enemy she'd do battle with.

When she tired of her practice swings with the ancient sword, she picked up the scabbard and wakizashi blade, she knelt on the tatami mat and laid the wakizashi sword across her legs as she slid the long katana in its scabbard. The sword clicked home with a distinguishable snap. Again, she bowed to her father.

He took a breath, deciding if he should scold her for taking the sword from the scabbard. The only time a samurai was to remove his blade from its resting place, was to fight or test the sharpness of the blade hacking through a criminal's body, or when he used it for education or celebration. To remove the sword for play as if it were the toy sword she used in the growing years, was insulting to the blade. As he thought, he decided against ruining the moment of the gift. He shrugged, knowing he should say something to her, but he was at a loss at what to offer her. It was General Kobayashi who opened the door for him.

"Masahiko-san! Your gift is still a virgin weapon. Untested to the taste of blood."

She turned to the general and asked simply with concern. "Huh?"

The trainer picked up the conversation, relieved he had something of worth to offer the child. "Ahhh... General Kobayashi-san. You're correct and wise. Masahiko-san! General Kobayashi-san has so rightly pointed out your sword never split the skin of your enemy. It has never tasted blood of a criminal. To open communication needed between your ears and that of your sword's soul, it must be by your hand the sword gets its first blessing and taste of blood."

"Ieeeee father! How would this be possible? Must I wait until my first battle of honor to open this relationship with my sword?"

"No young and impatient Warrior. Your sword must and will taste blood today, it was your stupidity that makes this a must. You forgot your first law of the sword. A knowing Samurai must never remove his blade for show. For vanity reasons. Masahiko-san! Kobayashi-san will take you to the jail compound, and there you'll get a chance to test your blade's strength and sharpness. I'll pack for our trip. You'll take both swords to Engakuji, and only wear the Sugahara swords when you're presented to our Master. Is this understood impatient one?"

"Hai father." The child offered as she looked at her father.

"Very well. General Kobayashi-san! Accompany Masahiko-san to the penitentiary compound, and order the keeper to setup a test of the blade for the child to experience?"

"Hai Tanizaki-san." He rose and waited for Masahiko to join him.

She placed the swords in her sash and got in step with the general as he led the way to the stockade at the far end of the village. The criminal compound was a mile from the village and took minutes to arrive. Her guards formed a screen around her and the general. They stormed in the jail as if gods. The keeper rushed up and dropped and placed his head on the ground.

The general barely took notice of the lowly hinin bowing before him, as he grunted in a snarling tone. "Foul one, we're here to perform a sword test. Prepare it lowly dog!"

"My Lord, I'm so sorry but we had no executions for the past few sticks of time. Alas, I have no new corpse to try your blade upon, my Lord."

"Huh filth of the mud! I can't believe there's not one worthless dog that doesn't deserve killing in this compound. I don't believe this, fool. Huh! If you have no one worth killing, I demand you take position on the do dan, and we'll try the blade upon your foul body." He didn't take notice of the man still bowing before him. A do dan was a mound of sand used to support a body of the criminal executed, so a warrior might used it to check the sharpness of his sword on.

Sweat ran down the hinin's grime covered face as he searched his mind for which criminal he was going to kill for the demanded test. No way was he going to crawl on the mound and loop his arms and legs around the pegs then wait to be hacked to pieces by a conceited warrior who though he was better than everyone else.

Without getting up from his kneeling position, the hinin clad in a torn colorless filthy cotton kosode, called to one of his helpers. "Yakuta, bring the criminal Sumiyoshi and prepare the fool for a sword test." The hinin weren't allowed to place the san after their names, they lost that respect when they joined the ranks of hinin. Preparing the criminal for a do dan meant the criminal would be strangled moments before carried out to the do dan.

They waited for the second hinin to carry out the criminal as ordered. The hinin had the dead, or supposed dead criminal looped over his back, with the man's arms looped over his shoulders, they were held in place by the hinin's hands. The body was dropped unceremoniously on the slightly raised mound. There were four stakes driven deep in the sand, and the limp body was placed with two stakes coming out between the arms. His arms were tied to the stakes. The other stakes were by the dead man's feet, his ankles were tied to them. The body was usually dressed in a filthy torn loincloth, and sometimes he was naked as this one was. The mound was constructed in such a way as to force the chest and midsection of the corpse upwards, the arms were forced from the body so they didn't interfere with the test.

He leaned to her and mumbled so only she could hear his words of advice. "Masahiko-san! When you're ready for the test of your great sword, you're to unsheathe your katana and strike the body across the chest or belly, whichever you chose with all the might in your arms. To prove your sword worthy, it must cut the body in half with one blow. Take proper time to prepare your soul and mind for the strike. Remember, you're not only proving your sword's worth, but your sword's proving its worth to you. One swipe and there'll be two halves of the worthless one's body resting on the mound."

"Hai General Kobayashi-san. I understand your words and know what I have to do."

"Good. I'll wait by your side until you're ready to strike the worthless one. Don't look at the filthy ones, their time doesn't matter Samurai. They'll stand all day if you so wish it to be so, Masahiko-san. Gyoko!" Luck!

She felt him take a step back, this was done to allow her space to swing the blade. She looked at the criminal, it was easy to see the chest raise and falling in the course of breathing. She, as well as everyone in the compound knew the criminal was stunned by a blow to the head. As she examined the filthy body, she could see a steady flow of blood from the slight head wound.

The general moved to her and offered. "Alive or dead his life doesn't matter one grain of rice. You're giving the criminal a slight honor in a swift death, to allow him to give up his life for the test of your blade. The criminal will be given a commoner's burial, not of the hinin filth."

She knew once a hinin died his body was usually thrown to the dogs. The knowledge this criminal would receive the burial of a commoner, gave her strength to carry out the test on his body. With the grace of a samurai, she broke the brass seal of the sword with her thumb then moved her legs slightly apart and set them. Then she drew the remaining length of the sword out of the scabbard with the speed of an arrow launched in flight. In one continuous motion she raised the blade over her head and with a practiced battle cry, she brought the sword down swiftly, splitting the body in half, cutting into the sand mound also.

The hinin bowed until his face touched the soil over the power possessed by her sword and arm, cheers from the other criminals and jailers were raised, paying homage to such a fine weapon and young warrior. Although they were all criminals, many were once proud and respected samurai, and they still respected the caste and would do so until they too were picked for the honored sword test.

The general stepped to her side and bowed as he took the bloody sword and held it out to the hinin standing to her left. The outcast wiped the blade clean on his torn and soiled kosode, making certain none of his skin touched the steel of the sword. He wiped off the stench of the hinin, before handing the sword to her. He waited until she placed the sword in its scabbard.

Once her sword was in its scabbard, he rested his hand on her shoulder and reminded her. "Masahiko-san! Your father is waiting us. Shall we go?"

She turned to General Kobayashi and asked. "General Kobayashi-san! What about your sword? Are you not going to test the power of your sword today?"

"Testing my sword is not necessary nor required, Masahiko-san. The ancestors of your father's clan spoke to me through the steel. It's been well tested on more battlefields than I can count. I bonded with the sword, thank you for your consideration though young Warrior Masahiko-san. It shows me you're a wise Samurai. Shall we go?"

"Hai General! The smell of this foul place turns my stomach to water and ill."

"Hai Masahiko-san! As it should turn the stomach of all worthy Samurai to water. This is a deplorable place for one to visit and inhale the odor from these filthy people. A place no respected Warrior would want to live his remaining sticks of time. Let us leave this filthy place before we become contaminated by its evil."

"Hai General, at once if you don't mind." She said as she followed him.

They left the jail proudly as they arrived. They walked the main street followed by the guards. As they neared the home, Masahiko asked General Kobayashi a question.

"General Kobayashi-san! Will my sword speak to me as does yours to you?"

"Hai little worried one. It'll speak when it has something to tell, or warn you of, Masahiko-san. But it's the Samurai's ear that must hear the words of his sword."

"General Kobayashi-san! When and how will I know my sword is speaking to me? How will I understand the words it tries to speak, or what it may want of me in my future?" She cried and stopped walking and turned to see the general better to wait his reply.

"Ahhh... little one. Your sword has spoke to you loud and clear, evidently you have wax in your ears and were unable to hear its words." The general mocked her lightly in a kind voice.

She stared dumbly at the grinning general. "Were you able to hear the words offered by my sword with it spoke, General Kobayashi-san?"

"Hai! The words were clear to my ears, little Warrior of greatness."

"What did they say General?"

"Your sword echoed with words in its whisper, respect and honor me young Warrior, and I'll forever protect and serve your honorable life on any battlefield you venture on."

"Ieeeee! I fear you must think me addle of mind to believe such a tall tale as this you spoke, as if I didn't know better of life, General Kobayashi-san."

"Huh! I don't make light of the virtues of honor and respect inquisitive one, and if you don't believe in the words of your mighty sword. Then how was it able to slice clean through the worthless body of that lowly criminal, and yet not displace one organ? Do you think the weakness of your arm has given the power needed to your sword to complete such a great act? No little Warrior, it was the power of the sword speaking clearly to you, giving the strength to your arms to prove to the world that you're a fearsome and honorable Samurai. To be honored, respected, and above all, feared by all honorable Samurai."

She stared at him, weighing the general's words carefully.

"Huh! You seem not to believe my words Masahiko-san. If you listen with your ears you'll still hear your sword singing the adulation of your past and future feats. Listen with your heart as well as your ears, and you'll hear the words spoken clearly to you."

She stopped breathing as she concentrated her thoughts to her sword's soul. A breeze gusted and blew through the kinran and ginran of the sword with the five gold crests, making a slight whistling sound as it passed through it. Although it was a common occurrence, in her mind she believed she heard the spirit of her sword speaking. From that moment on, she respected the sword with a new reverence and honor.

When they made it home, it was a beehive of activity and confusion, with Miho, Remi and Yukie making certain the lesser retainers, packed Tanizaki's equipment properly. It was uncontrolled mayhem at best, with everyone speaking and yelling at the same time, ordering and counter ordering anyone in eye sight. And vassals running off in all directions following orders.

She looked for her father and saw him sitting on the porch out of harm's way, while the women ran around as if they had a wasp in their kosodes. She walked to her father and bowed and informed him how well the sword test went.

He was pleased the sword had performed so well then he looked at her guard samurai and noticed they stood waiting further orders from their ward. He looked at his daughter and snapped. "Masahiko-san! Do you think it a good idea for you to order your samurai guards to pack for their trip to Engakuji Castle? I'm certain they have personal things they have to look after, before they leave on this journey. Relationships to end, or beg you to allow them to take the women they found to the Castle with them."

"Hai father, that's why I can never hope to be as wise as you. I fear you forgot more than I'll ever learn. You see with an all seeing eye, and realize what I have not paid attention to. How stupid of me to overlook my Samurai. It's a wonder they serve me. I'll give them the day to prepare to leave." She moaned as she stood and her father stopped her with words.

"Little Samurai, you have too much on your mind to worry about everything for yourself and your Samurai. That's why a wise Warrior must learn to rely on others to make him whole and at peace with himself, and his Master. Why do you think I rely so much on General Kobayashi-san for? Because he sees what I foolishly overlooked. As for allowing the Samurai the day to prepare for their trip, again you forget training. A Samurai must be ready to leave for battle instantly. All they should need is one feather of time (hour) to prepare. If a Samurai asks to bring women, you must not allow it. It's a wise Master who forces a Samurai to leave something of worth to return to. It helps cement their loyalty to their Master. If you make it too comfortable for them on the road, why should they think of returning to the village, neh?"

"Once more father your wisdom shows me how much more there is to learn."

"Huh Masahiko-san! The only time a Warrior stops learning, is when he no longer exists in this world. Then he must begin anew to learn the troublesome ways of the foul gods and their Floating World of wonderment. So he can better prepare himself for the forty day wait to be reborn Samurai better than he was when he died in his Master's service. Learning is a never ending road we must travel upon, young Warrior." He was interrupted in his conversation by Remi, who asked if he wanted to take his tachi, the slung sword to the castle.

"Ieeeee Lady Remi! How many swords do you think one Samurai can carry before he becomes a lowly kagaman, rather than an honored Warrior, woman?"

"Huh! You're getting so I don't know what has the worse temper. You, or the angry yellow jacket. All you had to say was no, and I'd not bothered you further."

"No!" The old trainer snapped then smiled at her.

"I'll return it to your worthless trunk. You would've been twice angry if I didn't ask if you wanted to take the sword." She walked away in a huff without bowing to the old man.

She laughed as she asked her ill tempered father if he wanted her to find a younger woman to boss around. Her father ignored his daughter's biting words as he looked off in space in silence. She bowed and headed out for her samurai and found the captain and ordered him to send the warriors off to prepare for their journey to Engakuji Castle.

The captain didn't move, forcing her to add. "Are your feet stuck in unforeseen mud I'm not aware of? Is there something else you have on your mind, Captain?"

"Hai Master Masahiko-san! Some wondered and wanted me to ask if it'd be alright for them to take ladies to the Castle. Some grown close to certain ladies of the Ninth Village and I was..."

"Captain! The needs of pillowing don't concern me. Since when does a Warrior need a soft woman to lay his head near? A Samurai will sleep with his sword and find the happiness he seeks for his soul in the bite of the blade. He should be concerned about my safety and the good of the realm, and security of Kawasomeru-sama, than pillowing with a female. This was a childish request, one I'll remember for many sticks of time, Captain. The Warriors will have to wait until they return to the Ninth Village to enjoy their ladies again!"

"Hai Master Masahiko-san, I'm terribly embarrassed I was the cause of distress to your Wa. I'll tell the Warriors of your just decision. The Samurai's only thoughts should be over the realm, their Lord and Master and yourself. I'm sorry for wasting your time with squandering matters of no concern, Masahiko-san." The captain bowed politely.

She waved it off with a simple rapid movement of the hand.

The rest of the day was spent stacking the countless packed items, leaving them lying on the street for pickup the following morning by their carriers. The night passed and Tanizaki woke by the crowing of the cock. When he arrived at the morning table, Miho had food on the table to enjoy, and Emiko was dressed and picking at her cooling meal. She looked so thin and frail it broke the trainer's heart. He was worried she might not live through the trip to the castle. Everyone was dressed in their travel kosodes except Yukie, who was to remain in the village so she could to look after Tanizaki's house and his belongings.

General Kobayashi ordered the stable samurai to bring their horses to the front of Tanizaki's home. They were saddled and waiting for their owners.

After they ate, Tanizaki, his daughters, Emiko and his consort Remi stood. Miho helped Emiko up and she walked her outside and helped her get inside the palanquin. When she was sure Emiko was comfortable, she stood and the kagamen lifted the palanquin level and slowly. Then she entered the second palanquin and they lined up behind Masahiko and Tanizaki, mounted on their horses. The samurai trainees ventured in the village carrying nothing but their okashi katanas, the swords of the lesser ranking samurai. Those swords were replaced with the katanas given them on the last day of training by the master trainer. It made them honorable samurai soon to be part of Lord Kawasomeru's armies.

Since the samurai came with nothing, they were put to use carrying Tanizaki's equipment and needs. It took an hour before the endless caravan was ready to begin their journey to Engakuji Castle. Masahiko-san's samurai were allowed to ride horses, and were on orders to ride ahead and to the flanks of the caravan, to keep their eyes open for assassins looking to attack them.

The trainer was concerned about the roving bands of unorganized Ronin, who made their living preying on the caravan's criss-crossing Shinano province for their wealth. With a wave of his hand, he started the caravan in motion, the mounted samurai rode ahead. There was an army of three hundred samurai who rode the rear of the caravan. It was General Kobayashi's last minute suggestion they take the horses, so the few stable samurai would only have to look after twenty horses of Masahiko's, and fifty horses of the trainer.

The master trainer was pleased with Kobayashi's suggestion, it gave them a mobile army ready to charge after any assassin, or band of Ronin filth who might dare to attack his caravan. The day's travel went swiftly, and his caravan reached the fifth village as the sun began to disappeared behind the mountain range, and became too dark to travel further safely. The fifth village leader allowed the caravan to use a harvested barley field as a camp ground for the night.

The Shoya of the fifth village had the field ringed with torches, and an honor guard to make certain no unwanted visitors gained entry to the camp. The Shoya invited Tanizaki, Masahiko, Emiko and Kobayashi to his home for a hot meal. After sake and food, he turned in for the night. At first light he was up and ordered the caravan to assemble. The Shoya, with his wife and children were the only ones of the village to see Tanizaki and his caravan off.

By the third hour of travel, the long caravan made it past the forth village. General Kobayashi guided his horse closer to the trainer and asked when he caught up to him. "Master trainer Tanizaki-san! When do you think we'll enter Engakuji?"

"Asatte!" Day after tomorrow he barked at his concerned general.

"Tanizaki-san! When do you plan on entering the Castle?" He asked while fighting to keep his horse in step with Tanizaki's. The general's horse gave him trouble because it wasn't used to walking so close to another horse, and his tried to kick Tanizaki's horse in defense of its rider and master a few times.

"Huh General Kobayashi-san! I planned to enter the Castle at the first morning light. You, Masahiko-san, General Miyamoto, and myself and our Samurai guards will ride in first in full armor and in a tight formation. The rest of the fools will follow after a feather of time has passed. That'll give us the time we'll need to get settled in, and view our party as they enter the Castle before their Lord and Master and ourselves."

"That's a wise plan indeed. I agree with you Master Trainer Tanizaki-san."

He ignored his general's words as he watched where his horse was going. He knew where he wanted to spend the night before they entered the village. There was a cut field outside the fifth bridge. They could bathe the dirt from their bodies in the stream, and rest for their grand entrance the following morning to the lord's castle. The good thoughts made the day go by quickly, but he miscalculated and found his caravan caught between the third and second village as the sun was turning in. He sent two riders forward to look for a suitable field or clearing, on which to set up camp and spend the night. He cursed for not pushing hard enough to make the security area of the second village, before night fall set in on him.

It took the riders fifteen minutes to find a clearing large enough to allow his caravan room to settle for the night. He decided he wasn't going to set up tents. Everyone was ordered to spend the night under the stars. He looked to the sky, it was dark and he saw the abundance of stars filling the sky, and knew there wasn't much of a chance for rain. Yet he felt the pain in his bones and knew rain wasn't far off. He understood tomorrow's ride was to be an unpleasant one to endure. He hated to travel in the rain, it made travel so miserable for him and the others.

The trainer was right, it rained by the second hour of traveling. It continued to rain for the day's progress, and ended when his caravan reached the bridge. After the rain ended, the temperature lowered and made it comfortable for sleeping. He was the first to wake and woke Masahiko, they bathed. This was so her secret would remain as such. Just as they dried off and got in their kosodes, General Kobayashi and General Miyamoto charged wildly down the sloping embankment, and stripped as they ran and dove in the freezing water, as if children. They hollowed because of the cold water then they splashed around like children done for years past time. More samurai followed the two officers into the water.

"Huh Masahiko-san! Maybe you should thank the gods you were not born a male, as you can see, males never grow to adults fully." They shared a laugh and as they reached the top of the knoll, just as other samurai charged by them, stripping as they ran for the cold water. As each man dove in they came up yelling at the coldness of the water, and the fun they were enjoying.

The trainer rested his hand on her shoulder. "As I stated, the male animal never grows up, they only appear to be adults, but in their heart they're nothing more than children."

As they returned to the encampment, they were surprised to see everyone up. The master trainer checked on his wife and when certain she was all right, he dressed. It was easy to understand why everyone was awake. The clamor the samurai raised bathing was enough to wake the long dead ancestors of Japan's past.

Miho helped Tanizaki dress and when he was done, she helped Masahiko, once they were dressed, and the pair looked like an extremely threatening couple. Masahiko appeared slightly more threatening than Tanizaki, because of the Sugahara swords tucked in her armor. He noticed this and ordered her to remove the Sugahara swords and replace them with the older swords he gave her when she began training. Although she was upset, she did as ordered by her father.

Even their horses were decked out in their finest armor. All the silver, gold and brass was polished so they shone in the pale light of the early morning haze. They mounted their steeds then went on to the road and waited for the others to assemble with them. The generals and samurai gathered and took positions of honor. Once everyone was ready, he held his hand up, holding everyone in position until the proper time to make their appearance at the castle.

CHAPTER TWENTY ONE
THE FIRST DAY OF THE SECOND WEEK OF THE SEVENTH MONTH OF THE YEAR THIRTEEN FIFTY FOUR.

THE YEAR OF GEMBUKU.

Just as the sun's glaring eye began to peek over the far off mountain range, Master Trainer Tanizaki brought his hand forward and his party wildly charged into the sleepy capital city. Over the seven bridges they charged forward, their horse's hooves pounding heavy on the wood of the bridge. The samurai rode on raising a cloud of dust. The further they rode, the more people they came across. First they past crowds of commoners then commoners mixed with samurai then samurai then the samurai mixed in with the upper class of the capital. Everyone he past bowed politely and roared their approval of the way the master trainer and his generals rode in the capital city like a conquering small army.

The trainer was leading the charge, his armor making a racket as he rode on. He was the first to see the greeting party waiting for their arrival at the main gate to Engakuji Castle. His chest swelled with pride at the thought Kawasomeru standing at the main gate waiting to greet him. There was nothing more he could hoped for than this great an honor. He saw one warrior dressed in his best armor, and figured it was Kawasomeru and rode at him at full gallop. The old man dug his spurs in the flanks of his horse, trying to get that last bit of speed out of the animal.

Hundreds then thousands of citizens lined the road leading to the main gate of the castle. As the charging group neared the dirt road turned to one of set stones, making a hard surface. His horse's hooves thundered on the surface. Not until the samurai in armor raised his hand did he pull back on his reins. The horse slowed as he pulled the leather straps harder, stopping fifteen feet from the great samurai, but not before his trusted steed reared on his hind legs, and moved its legs like it was trying to run in the air. The horse's front legs came back to the earth.

Without flinching the samurai stood near the ranting and heavy breathing horse. He stared uninterested at the perched on top of his mount. Two warriors rushing from behind the samurai, grabbed the horse's reins and helped steady the steed, while Tanizaki ceremoniously dismounted the horse. He waited until his daughter, Generals Kobayashi and Miyamoto dismounted then they walked up by his side and waited, as he approached the grand looking warrior alone. The samurai guards stood by their horses and knelt and bowed to the earth at who they thought was Lord Kawasomeru. They never lifted their eyes until ordered to by Tanizaki or the master himself. He stomped up to the magnificent decked out samurai, his armor making enough noise to upset the horses. The trainer stomped his feet on the ground to add to the noise he raised as he approached the warrior waiting to greet him. Not until the master stood before the warrior did he remove his brass hoate mask and fukigayeshi helmet.

To his displeasure, he noticed it was General Shimbo-san standing before him. He was with the first batch of the trainees sent him by the liege lord for his training. He gone too far to stop now, making like he knew the samurai was General Shimbo all along, he bowed to the general. His party did likewise and not one made like they were disappointed it was a general, and not Lord Kawasomeru welcoming them to the castle keep.

General Shimbo returned the bow as elaborately then he stood erect and offered Tanizaki his arm. He took hold of it and used it to help him to his feet and they shook.

The general laughed as he offered the exhausted trainer. "Master Trainer Tanizaki-san! It's good to lay eyes upon you again, old friend of countless battles and years of life. I admit you worn my arse down by the inch, and turned it into one huge hemorrhoid you'll be happy to know, is stopping me from resting my arse on the ground comfortably. You said I sat too much, so you found a way to stop me from sitting, neh. Never before or since have I rode so much as when I was in your honorable presence."

He couldn't hide the disappointment of not being greeted by Kawasomeru and Shimbo read the sadness and offered apologetically. "Master Trainer Tanizaki-san, I'm terribly embarrassed to inform you Lord Kawasomeru decided it wouldn't be proper for him to greet you when you arrived at his Castle. Although he wanted to more than anything else, he reasoned if he was to greet your party then by the show of good manners, he'd be forced to greet the other bands bringing their children to celebrate Gembuku. He's aware your child is the most important visitor to his Castle, but as I stated, old friend.

"To greet you then our Master would've been forced to greet all others coming to his Castle. As you can tell, there wouldn't be enough sticks of time between now and the great celebration for Kawasomeru-sama to waste on the countless visitors, and do all of what is necessary to prepare himself, and his Castle for the observance. I'm embarrassed by your disappointment, but I can tell you Kawasomeru-sama is prepared to pay you a private visit tonight. He doesn't want to greet Masahiko-san until Gembuku as is right. He wants to be surprised by the child and his outstanding reported skills, when the Lord first lays eyes upon him." General Shimbo bowed.

He barely returned the bow which precariously bordered on an insult to the general, as a commotion was raised and he looked to the road. His party entered the capital and General Shimbo moved to him and offered. "Master Trainer Tanizaki-san! Your people will be well looked after, how is your wife's health, old friend?"

"She is weak and I don't think she'll live long past Gembuku I'm afraid."

"Ieeeee! Why are the best of Japan chosen so young in life by the foolish gods. Huh! I know Lady Mineko plans to visit your Lady in private, Tanizaki-san. She's to greet her later today, and take her to the Castle where she'll be more comfortable, and better cared for."

"General Shimbo-san! You must thank Lady Mineko personal for me for her display of kindness to my ailing wife. It's kind for her to take such an interest in my wife's failing health. I'm certain she has more important things to look after than to concern herself with my worthless wife's condition.   Kawasomeru-sama picked himself a most understanding and wise lady for his honorable wife." He bowed to General Shimbo.

"Huh Tanizaki-san! As First Lady to our Master, it's her yoshi gi (duty) which she carries out efficiently. I'll inform her you were pleased by her concern over Lady Emiko's health."

The pair stopped speaking as the rest of his party came up and stopped behind his horses. Masahiko-san was by her mother's side looking after her.

Again, General Shimbo offered. "Master Trainer! You outdone your training of this Warrior I see. I find it interesting a great Samurai such as he would display affection in public view. The child is confident of his being, because the Samurai doesn't fear this display of affection to his mother might be misconstrued as weakness. This display makes me believe this Warrior is complete in body and soul. To my eyes, you done well and your child honors you greatly."

"Domo, thank you General Shimbo-san.   I must know where my people will be housed."

"Master Trainer, Kawasomeru-sama set aside the best of the best area in the protection of the Castle for your group to enjoy. It's in the shade of the wall and there's always a cool breeze, and plenty of fresh water to drink and bathe in at this spot. It's the eastern section next to the great yagura, the defense tower will also add greatly to the security of your party. Although Engakuji Castle is guarded at all times, it's not without its share of predators. Lord Kawasomeru is aware of the failed attempt on Masahiko-san's life, and is saddened by your daughter Enko's savage death at the hands of the assassins. He plans to honor her at the ceremony. I ordered tents erected for your party to shelter under. Of course, Lady Emiko and yourself will be housed on the third floor of the Castle. Kawasomeru-sama won't allow anything to happen to you or your Lady. The Samurai you trained won't be allowed in the Castle, they'll join the other Samurai gathered outside the Keep. The twenty Samurai guards you enjoy..."

"There are fifteen." He growled at the concerned general.

"Huh! Am I to believe these are the Warriors of great worth and skills to you?"

"Hai." The trainer replied without thought to the general's question.

"Good, they'll be allowed to stay and enjoy your encampment, but my Samurai will be solely responsible for your party's security and protection while you're visiting the Castle. They'll have little to do, so you may use them accordingly. Masahiko-san will be expected to join the ranks of Samurai to be honored. You'll not be allowed to communicate in any fashion with the child Warrior, until after the ceremony has been completed."

"Hai General Shimbo-san. I know of the laws covering the ceremony." He grumbled, upset she would be separated from his influence. He hoped she would hide she was a female from the others long enough for the fact, once discovered, not to mean much.

General Shimbo egotistically turned and gave a number of quick hand signals, and three samurai broke rank and rushed to his party. One spoke to the general directly then walked to the eastern wall. The rest of his party followed the warrior. The general turned to the trainer and offered. "Master Trainer Tanizaki-san! You and your Lady will have the run of the Keep. No place will be off limits to you except for the assembly area where the Samurai celebrating Gembuku will be housed. To enter this area will cost the one in error his head. The Master's sleeping and private quarters are also off limits to all, but I'm certain I didn't have to inform you of this restriction. Do you understand my warnings Master Trainer Tanizaki-san?"

"Hai." The trainer replied to the general's words as he turned to him.

"Good, now that foolish unpleasantness was concluded, welcome Master Trainer Tanizaki-san and your party of Warriors to Engakuji Castle. Your presence is pleasing to enjoy, I'm honored to be the one elected to greet your arrival to our Master's home." General Shimbo bowed then turned and left him standing by the gate, free to roam the compound at will.

For the next two weeks, everything in Engakuji Castle was fun, pleasant, and enjoyable. Masahiko and other samurai enjoyed many sticks of time filled with games of Go, tests of strength, agility, and skills covering every aspect of a samurai's life. Food and sake flowed for everyone gathered to celebrate the ceremony. The new samurai, being so close in age, formed selected bonds, some swearing allegiances for life with each other. She formed three such pacts with others of the new samurai caste. Never once had she picked up the resentment building between her, and a few jealous and weaker trained warriors over the attention she was receiving from many samurai there to be chosen by their Lord as samurai in his armies. They chose never to bring their displeasures to the surface to be confronted by her. Instead, the few allowed this festering resentment and displeasure of her actions to turn into hatred of the samurai, who had bested them in countless games or tests of skill.

The night before the great celebration was scheduled to begin, the young samurai were allowed a taste of sake. Many youthful warriors headed for the waters of the stream, stripped and dove in the chilly water. Each young warrior shared their sake with the others, and splashed about like children. All except for Masahiko, she remained in her tent working out more strategies for the battlefield and her understanding.

The resentment against her festered as certain samurai began to complain they noticed Masahiko wasn't bathing with them, or taking baths when no one was around. This behavior led to theories as to why she was acting like this. Every warrior knew from birth the importance of baths, and how dangerous it was to remain with dirt of the day on them. Quickly, stories of her not bathing with the others spread through the ranks of warriors. The stories were varied, and some so outlandish they got the attention of the Captain of Guard, who ordered the ones spreading the stories about Masahiko, to a private audience.

The captain intended to punish the samurai with the poisonous tongues, there was no greater crime for any samurai to commit, than spread false rumors about another warrior. It showed the ones with the wagging tongues that they weren't to be trusted in the ranks of the samurai caste, and to their obedience to their master.

The captain assembled the trouble making samurai and listened in awe of their complaints. The samurai explained how Masahiko was suffering from the filthy habits of the hated eta class, because she had not bathed since arriving in the encampment two weeks past.

The captain was shocked by Masahiko's disturbing behavior, he realized he had to do something about Masahiko, in case these puzzling stories were with truth. He made the complaining samurai swear they would not speak another word about this behavior until he addressed it firsthand. He made them return to their housing then headed for his commander's quarters. He recapped what was told him by the samurai. As the captain was shocked by Masahiko's behavior, the general was equally surprised. He told the captain to watch the habits of Masahiko and he would inform General Yoshinobu Shimbo about them, to see what he wanted done with them. He assured the captain the general would know what to do about the filthy habits of Masahiko.

The general in command of the samurai, reported to General Shimbo who wasn't the least bit amused by the wild stories. He noticed the omission of the san after Masahiko's name by the general, but overlooked it. He knew Tanizaki for a long time and respected him, his habits of cleanliness were impeccable. The general knew the child since five and never seen him dirty. He dismissed the general for daring to repeat words spoken by obviously jealous samurai over the skills and habits of Masahiko. He scolded the general as he admitted he heard rumors, and found them without foundation. He warned the other general for allowing himself to be persuaded into repeating the stories about a warrior to his commander.

The general cleared his throat and repeated the last story, the one that made it imperative he breach this subject with General Shimbo. He waited to speak further with him.

General Shimbo saw the field general wouldn't leave his sight and growled. "Ieeeee General! You have been dismissed. If you value your head, I suggest you leave my side, unless you have something of untruth to add to this unflattering story you offer me. I warn you General, speak further of these lies against Masahiko-san, and it might well cost you your foolish head."

The general bowed then rushed his words, afraid he would be cut off by the general of higher rank. "General Shimbo-san! I must report it's been suggested Masahiko-san might be suffering from the ailment of leprosy, or maybe worse. Many new Samurai are fearful he's a filthy leper. General Shimbo-san, what possible reason would there be for Masahiko-san not to enjoy a hot bath with the other young Samurai, or enjoy a jump in the river and share fun with Warriors he might one day command, or die with? Ieeeee General! It was reported Masahiko-san only goes to the water when he's certain there's no one around to see him, and the confused Warrior would never be out of his clothes entirely.

"It was uttered to my worthless ears Masahiko-san would bath dressed in a loincloth, and a strange looking top that covered his upper chest. I must report General Shimbo-sama, these complaints continue for fourteen sticks of time, since he showed up in the Castle, and they merit to the complaints I offer. Ieeee! Think how filthy the child must be if he only bathed twice since anyone noticed, and always half dressed in a chest protector and the loincloth, General."

As much as General Shimbo hated to admit it, the field general got his attention over this disturbing matter they were discussing. It was his duty to make certain all his soon to be accepted samurai were in top notch health, a dirty samurai could not be a healthy one, and his habits of body could affect the other samurai. He stared at the officer letting out his breath as he barked. "General! You raised my concern. I'll beg an audience before Lord Kawasomeru. He's the one with the power to demand this child bathe. I dare not challenge the child for fear of Master Trainer Tanizaki's noted wrath. I'd rather be reborn a dog than risk his anger. Leave, and don't utter another word of this disaster until I get back to you on the outcome of my meeting with our Lord. If he orders me to commit suppuku, my last order to you will be for you to do the same. Get out and don't let me see you again on this cursed day."

The commander waited until the general left his presence then he headed for the castle to speak with Lord Kawasomeru. He stood before the commander of the mononobe, the hereditary palace guard, and informed him he had important matters to speak with the master of the realm. The general was forced to wait in the hallway for half an hour before he was sent for by the busy Lord Kawasomeru, to see what was troubling his wise commander.

The general entered the viewing room as if he had the weight of the world on his shoulders. He saw the master sitting on a low dais, being attended by two of his favorite consorts, and three military officers sat to the side, as well as six palace guards. The worried general removed his swords and left them standing in the rack by the door, as he bowed to his master. This move showed the master he wished words in private with him.

The warlord looked at his consorts and with a wave of his hand, dismissed them rudely. The female consorts scurried out of the room in haste. He looked at the three officers in the room, without a word passing between them, they stood and bowed and left the room.

The master barked at his general loudly. "You may approach General Shimbo-san. This must be an important matter troubling your mind, for you to dare interrupt my consequential meeting with my other officers, General Shimbo-san."

"Kawasomeru-sama! It's enough to request the guards to leave so we may speak in private. No one but you must hear the words I'm forced to speak, Kawasomeru-sama." General Shimbo bowed and held it until he dismissed the guards. The last guard to leave the room, stopped long enough to pick up Shimbo's swords. No one was allowed to be with the master with weapons.

The powerful warlord was weary and placed his katana across his lap, ready to repel any signs of treachery from his upset military officer. General Shimbo stopped well out of attacking range and seated himself on the floor before his master.

"Huh General!   You have my undivided attention. What has your piles in such an uproar?"

He explained what was told about Tanizaki's child. The master was unable to hide the heated look glued to his face. Anger replaced the stunned look as he accused the general of poor judgment for choosing to bother him over such a weak and meaningless problem.

When the general suggested it was believed Masahiko might be a filthy leper, the warlord knew he had to do something about the matter. Before the stories got out of hand, and he grunted angrily. "The worthless Warriors feel there's a problem with Masahiko-san's health?"

"Iye my Lord! It's only the ones who haven't formed a relationship with Masahiko-san, doing most complaining about the young Warrior."

"Ieeee! It's these few who speak evil of Masahiko-san. Who are the ones doing the speaking against Masahiko-san?" He demanded harshly as he shifted his weight.

"My Lord of the Heavens and Earth! It's only the ones who been defeated one time or another by this Samurai on one of the fields of skill, doing most complaining against him my Lord."

"General Shimbo-san! Were there many fools beaten by this Samurai of Tanizaki-san's?" He asked interested, allowing a smile to cross his lips as he waited for the answer from his general. He wanted to know if this warrior was that good in the skills of war making.

"Ieeeee my Lord! Everyone who faced this Warrior spawn from Tanizaki-san one time or another, suffered pains of defeat at his skilled and honored hands, Kawasomeru-sama."

"Huh! Your eyes are covered by foolishness and deceit of the jealous. It's simple General. This disgusting evil is a shameful story dreamed up by weak Samurai fools defeated by this Warrior in the games of skill and battle they engage in, until the ceremony begins for the fools. Shameful, shameful, the fools should be stripped and beaten for their weakness of soul and mind." He growled, angry over the matter. "Is this Warrior that good?"

"Masahiko-san is the best Warrior of all by far that I have witnessed, my Lord and Master."

"Better than any other Warrior before that arrival to my Castle, General Shimbo-san?"

"Kawasomeru-sama! Far better than any Warrior of the future I believe. There'll never be a more skilled Warrior to walk the lands of Japan. There's something special about this one's outstanding fighting spirit and skills with any weapon he picks up, my Lord. Something great shines from within the Warriors eyes."

"Then I'll not be part of this insult against a fine Warrior. General Shimbo-san! I order you to punish the foolish Samurai who suffer from a poisonous tongue and evil mind and foul manners." He looked from the general, coldly dismissing him without further word.

General Shimbo didn't move after being dismissed so rudely by his master.

"Is there more to be added to this unpleasant tale you bring before me, General Shimbo?" He thundered while omitting the san from the officer's name, rising to his feet and glaring at his general. His shout brought his guards rushing back in the room. The warlord took his wrath out on them as he snarled. "Get out before I have you beheaded for your stupidity. I'll punish each of you after this meeting has concluded with my General." He turned his glare on General Shimbo's face, as he hissed in an extremely angry voice. "Well General Shimbo?"

"Kawasomeru-sama! I hate to be the source of disruption to your Wa, but many new Samurai suggested they would somehow stop Masahiko-san from being part of Gembuku. If I don't do something about his hygiene, and make certain he isn't inflected with the disease of leprosy, my Lord." The general bowed low before his master, waiting for his sword to fall and lop his head off. It never happened, instead he grunted nastily. "General Shimbo! What do you have me do to Masahiko-san, have the Warrior stripped bare and displayed like some common whore for the satisfaction of these few unworthy Samurai, who act like I have some responsibility of proving anything to their ego? How dare they expect anything from me, their Lord and Master. They're here to serve me, not to threaten to make a problem at Gembuku. I have a mind not to allow any of them attend the ceremony or be in my armies." He roared at his officer.

General Shimbo didn't reply, he cast his eyes to the ground and remained silent.

The powerful warlord added. "Ieeeee General Shimbo-san! You want me to have the Warrior stripped, and forced to stand before his worthless accusers like a commoner accused of a crime?" He began to pace on the narrow dais.

"Hai my Lord!" General Shimbo replied in a trembling tone, knowing he gone too far to stop before the problem was rightly solved. He knew his neck was on the line, and if he was going to lose his head, he would get everything on this subject in the open and finalized before his death. He hated to admit it, but he agreed with the concerned samurai. If Masahiko was impure of body then the child should not be allowed to join the samurai caste.

He stopped his pacing and roared. "Impossible. Impossible, General Shimbo-san. What the devil happened to these Samurai to dare risk my wrath? I should have them put to death, and allow Masahiko-san to remain alive in spite of them. This Samurai is the only one not giving me problems." He threw his hands in the air and paced again, allowing his anger to rule his mind.

"But Kawasomeru-sama! The Warrior is thought of a filthy leper. If this has truth, it's our duty to find out. How can we allow a Samurai with filthy leprosy, no matter how great a Warrior he might be on the field of honor, to be elevated to the rank of Samurai in your army? It'll be a terrible insult to the other Samurai, past, present and future. Our ancestors will come back and wage war against us, over this insult we offer, in their memory of past deeds on the battlefield."

"Ieeee! I can't possibly order Masahiko-san to strip naked before these troublemakers as a filthy eta. The insult would be too much for the Warrior to bear. I fear Masahiko-san would demand to be allowed to commit suppuku, and I'd be forced to honor the untested Warrior's request. I'd demand the same right if I was forced to undergo such a terrible insult to my person, to be forced to prove to these fools I was of pure body and soul to the lowly fools.

"Ieeeee! Think of Tanizaki-san. He'd lose his temper and hack the lot of the fools to pieces, and I'd help him. No General Shimbo-san, this request is impossible, I can't allow it to be ordered, and I must not allow it, and I'll not order it to be carried out. It'll destroy Gembuku, and I'll lose face over the matter. Huh! Think of what Wakatsuki would have to say over the evil matter. He'd use it as another weapon in his foul arsenal against me, and weaken our alliance with the other houses of the eastern provinces under my command." He began to pace again.

An idea crossed General Shimbo's mind and he offered. "Lord Kawasomeru! Why not have the chosen Samurai tattooed. This would be an easy solution to invoke the age old honored custom of tattooing the Warriors under your command."

He stopped pacing and stared at Shimbo as he mumbled. "Tattooed General Shimbo-san?"

"Yes my Lord!" The crafty general replied as he looked to the ground at his feet.

"Yes, a simple but smart solution to our problem, General Shimbo-san. Order it done, starting with Masahiko-san when he's brought before me at the ceremony of Gembuku."

"Hai. It'll be as you ordered, Kawasomeru-sama." General Shimbo offered as he rose and left the room, pleased he retained his head on his shoulders.

CHAPTER TWENTY TWO

GEMBUKU:

The day of ceremony arrived and the birth of the day was announced by the pounding thunder of the mighty drums of Taiko, as the sun ate a hole through the overcast mist of night. Everyone in the castle and surrounding area was called by the massive drums.

Excitement filled the air as children rushed out of their homes to the call of the drums. To the rear of the castle, seven hundred and three young samurai were assembled for Gembuku. They knelt before a raised dais covered by a tent on poles opened on all four sides. The samurai were assembled since before daylight, and began to heat the earth under them. At the sound of massive drums everyone bowed, their heads touching the earth. They held this position until Lord Kawasomeru finally appeared on the dais, and sat on the only chair resting on the platform. He was dressed in his finest battle armor, the heavy helmet making him sweat. When he was seated he grunted and every new samurai went to a sitting position, their feet crossed under them, their hands held open resting palms up on their legs, to show the powerful warlord they had no evil intents harbored against him.

The thunder from the drums was deafening, and no one spoke until they finished their endless beat. It took several seconds for the resounding echo to subside before he addressed the warriors. The liege lord rose solemnly and took several steps forward then removed his blessing fan from beneath his armor, and snapped it opened as if a weapon. He raised his foot then brought it down heavily on the platform, making it resound like the drums echoing in the morning air.

A roar came from the gathered ones who hoped to be inducted into the ranks of samurai and Lord Kawasomeru's armies. Their roar was joined by all who witnessed the birth of the samurai.

His heart was heavy as he searched the crowd for Tanizaki. His battle mask hiding the unnerving pain locked in his soul, for what he was going to do to his proud son. He was scared at what this child of the trainer might be hiding. Was the child's body covered with sores of the curse of leprosy? Had the gods been so cruel as to make the child marked for greatness, to be cursed by the body eating disease of the gods? How inhuman it would be to bless a child with such great skills, only to punish him for life with the slow death of rotting alive. He found himself cursing the gods much in the same way Tanizaki done in the past.

He retook his seat and allowed the Shinto monks to begin their endless prayers and opening ceremonies, boring him and the others gathered to death waiting to see him bestow on the children the rank of samurai. After two hours of prayers the priests handed the ceremony to the samurai generals. Their orders were as painful as the priests to bare. Then it happened, the samurai and trainees were turned over to Lord Kawasomeru's command.

The samurai were to be honored in the order of their greatness. Masahiko led the group, the warrior's past feats were listed and bellowed aloud by General Shimbo. Everyone in the castle was informed at how at the age of five, the young warrior saved his father's life, and of his outstanding skills with the bow, spear, horse and hand. How the young warrior defeated four assassins sent to kill him, and gained revenge on two assassins who savagely slaughtered his sister in the home of Tanizaki, Master Trainer of Shinano province. General Shimbo went on and on until the people gathered groaned when he took a breath then continued on.

Masahiko, and three other samurai were the only ones being elevated to the ranks of samurai first class. The rest were to be elevated to rank of samurai trainee, and scheduled to follow Master Trainer Tanizaki back to the ninth village for further training.

He looked once more at the old master trainer in the crowd, and didn't like what he witnessed. His wife was being supported by two women on either side of her, and looked like she was waiting death to visit her at any second. The trainer seemed to have aged years in just days, and he too looked like he was waiting death to claim his abused body. He was bent by age and pain, and his movements slow, painful to witness. He knew Master Trainer Tanizaki wasn't long for this earth, and was suffering in silence as it should be. He felt bad he was unable to relieve the terrible pain suffered by his loyal subjects. Again the master cursed the gods for their cruelty. His attention was drawn to the ceremony by General Shimbo, as he ordered the young samurai to bow to their master as he introduced them to the lord.

He stepped to the front as he called out the first name to be honored. He opened the scroll and bellowed. "Masahiko Tanizaki-san. Proud son of Master Trainer of Samurai, Nitaro Tanizaki, son of Lady Emiko, brother to Estsuko, and the slaughtered Enko. Stand before me."

Masahiko broke ranks and stomped before the raised dais and her liege lord.

A thundering roar broke out from the crowd and ranks of warriors. It seemed every warrior was proud f the accomplishments of this young warrior.

She stood before the lord defiantly and offered him the scroll detailing her feats of strength and honor, accomplished in her short life. He was stunned to see the great blades made especially for him he honored Tanizaki with, hanging from this arrogant pup's hip. He remembered how he presented the pair of swords to Masahiko's father for his countless years of devoted service. He remembered the look of pleasure which lit his weather beaten eyes as he took the two swords as if they were made of the finest porcelain, and cradled them protectively in his arms as if his own breath might shatter them to a million pieces. They were a great gift offered to the master trainer for his diligence in training the thousands of the lord's retainers he worked with over the years, teaching them the honor of sword, archery, and hand to hand combat.

The warlord knew if this warrior before him, armed with the scroll of acceptance written by Tanizaki, had to be respected and treated well, or he would lose face before the realm. He realized the training of this samurai was bound to be perfection, because he was the son of the proud trainer. This child had to be better trained, and possess the best of weapons, and command the greatest loyalty and respect, and should be considered to be a leader, a soon to be a general in his army. He stared at the swords hanging from her hip, and remembered the honor he gave the trainer and realized he thought enough of Masahiko's skills to give him the swords.

"Give me the scroll of your father, young Warrior of the future!" He growled loudly, barely recognizing the young swordsman standing so defiantly before him. He crushed the wax seal on the delicate paper with his thumb and unfolded the tri folded paper and read it from right to left. He read the words explaining how the master trainer begged him to allow his young son and samurai, to serve him for life on the future fields of battle. He vowed for his son, and honoring his liege lord for life by swearing a special oath of unwavering loyalty to him again. The powerful warlord grunted, pleased with the words from his master trainer as he refolded the paper and handed it to a servant hovering by his side. The servant walked to the torches and allowed the rice paper to burst into flames, to show all this samurai was accepted to his army.

Another roar from the crowd and samurai as they beat on shields to honor the moment.

The warlord allowed the cheer to last just so long then moved an arm and the crowd quieted. He glared at the young warrior while trying to shake Masahiko's confidence as he barked loud enough to be heard by most. "Masahiko-san! You come before me highly regarded by your Master Trainer and wise father, the great Tanizaki-san. Never before have I read such outstanding praise from so powerful a man for so young a Samurai. You must have impressed him, for Tanizaki-san to put words to paper as he has done for your sake. Huh! I'll witness these abilities he boasts of your abilities. Yes, an exhibition of your swordsmanship is in order, but you'll not dishonor such a great sword, by fighting it in a bloodless war. You're forbidden to use the katana hung on your hip for anything but dealing honor and death in my name. You'll use the training blade for this exhibition. Bring this Samurai's training blade at once!"

While they waited, he lowered his voice until only Masahiko could hear his words. He leaned forward to keep his words secret as he hissed in his lowest and commanding voice. "Masahiko-san! Don't be ashamed, is there anything wrong with your health, young one?"

"Iye my Liege Lord." The proud warrior replied without hesitation.

"Don't be ashamed to tell me child, are you healthy of body? I must know of your health."

"Hai my Lord, I'm perfect of body and soul to serve you my Master."

The sword arrived and the servant waited out of ear shot until the lord finished speaking to the young warrior in private.

"Very well then young Warrior, the test shall begin. Give Masahiko-san the sword." Lord Kawasomeru roared at the other samurai holding the sword.

The instant he stopped speaking, four samurai quickly move forward and formed a loose circle around the young samurai to be tested. All were out of range of Masahiko's sword strike, and each was holding an apple, waiting for the signal to begin this test.

"What is the name of your sword young Samurai?" He asked before he allowed the test.

"Ieeeee my Liege Lord, I have not yet considered a name for my honorable sword." She moaned, sorry she didn't have the wherewithal to remember to name her great blade.

"Huh Masahiko-san! Then perhaps you'd allow me the honor of naming your blade, if you're able to pass the test I devised for you, young Warrior."

"Kawasomeru-sama! It'd be a great honor you'd bestow on this worthless vassal, if you'd name my sword. Then I'll know forever, it'll serve you and you alone."

"Ahhh... spoken like a true Samurai of great age. Allow your blade to breathe warrior."

She did as ordered and broke the seal of the blade with her thumb then moved the shaft out about three inches from her sheath, so her master could see the shine from her training katana.

"You take good care of your weapons, the sign of a well trained Samurai." Then, with a nod, the samurai tossed the apples in the air at the same moment at Masahiko. The warrior knew what was coming and stood with her eyes cast down, using her mind's eye to see the flight of the apples. In one fluent motion, she finished unsheathing her sword and caught the first apple with little effort in the air, slicing it in half. She spun on her heel to her right and caught the second apple while it was still over her head, slicing it a little off center. She spun further to her left and swung her katana where she felt more than saw the third apple in flight. She easily intercepted it at breast height, slicing it perfectly in half then spun behind and dropped the sword tip down while flipping it over in her hands, and swinging upwards with the blade catching the fourth apple in air at knee height, splitting it off center before it hit the ground.

There was a gasp from the gathered warriors, there were only two others in all Japan's history able to cut four apples while in flight before they hit the ground. The great Shogun himself, and the master trainer of the ninth village, who was thought to be the greatest swordsman ever, and now this young pup. Masahiko Tanizaki.

He had to fight to hide the surprise and amazement in his eyes over Masahiko's outstanding abilities with the sword as he said in a passive tone to the young and out of breath warrior. "Ahhh... you have done well with the first test, Samurai Masahiko-san. But you're not done with the test period just yet. I'm not such an unwise fool as to be tricked so easily by your skills with the sword. I know the wise Master Trainer would know of this test, and who knows how long he might have had you practicing for it, Masahiko-san." The liege lord looked to Tanizaki and smiled, showing him he wasn't questioning his creditability, but wanted to test this young samurai further before he finally enlisted him into the ranks of his army.

The warlord looked to General Shimbo and ordered. "Bring me three well trained Warriors from your ranks. They'll test this pup with the blade. Every blow will be delivered with the back of the sword, the first one who brings blood to the surface will lose his head. If any samurai defeats this Warrior. I'll increase his fief by twenty koku a year as a reward. But lose to this Warrior and you'll be dropped to the rank of foot soldier, the lowest rank in the Samurai Caste. Bring your chosen Warriors forward for me to witness, General Shimbo-san."

He picked out three of his best men and they circled the young samurai.

"All three of you will attack at the same time but properly I warn you." He snapped, meaning they could attack, but one at a time to not allow the child to rest for a second during the test. The largest one moved forward first, but made the foolish move of lifting his sword over his head before striking at the warrior. She reacted swiftly, too swiftly for the larger samurai to counter her attack. She smashed the flat end of the blade into the bone of his hip, forcing him to drop his sword and roll on the ground in agony. She smacked him on the forehead, showing she split his head in two if it was a fight to the death. Allowing her momentum to carry her through the blow, she attacked the second warrior before he could react to her attack. It was the furthest thing from his mind that she would dare attack two warriors nearly at the same time.

Her first blow struck the unsuspecting second warrior on the point of his shoulder, causing him to drop to a knee, but he wasn't rendered defenseless and out of the fight that easily. He fought off her second blow from his knee, and their swords ringing anger at clashing together so violently. She spun on her heels and lowered her next strike. The blow would have sliced the samurai open at the waist if delivered by the blade's edge. The samurai tried to continue, but Lord Kawasomeru held up his hand, stopping the fighting momentarily. He looked at the second warrior and bellowed. "You were defeated, fool. Out of the fight!"

Once he was out of the way, Lord Kawasomeru hissed. "Resume the exercise."

Both samurai bowed to the master, the third hoping to catch the less experienced Masahiko off guard by attacking her from the bowing position, but she was waiting, anticipating the blow as if reading his mind. She fended off the blow delivered at chest height, the power of the swords coming together made her arms ache from the vibration. Around and around the two combatants went, each trying to gain the upper hand against the other. One second it looked as if she was going to defeat the third samurai, but he got out of the trap while almost trapping her in one of his own. It wasn't until the third attacking samurai committed his first and fatal mistake during the test, did she finally win the fight over him.

The fuming samurai tried to leap at her in an attempt to deliver a side kick to her exposed solar-plexus, but she easily intercepted the blow using the hilt of her blade, and shoved the attack to the side with it. This caused the samurai to stumble and fall to the ground. She was on him like a cat moving in for the kill, running the flat of the blade over his exposed neck. It was a death blow delivered, and the samurai straightened up and bowed respectfully towards the younger and far better fighter and warrior.

A roar rose from all in the courtyard. Samurai stomping their feet on the ground.

The warlord held up his fan and everyone quieted. The master looked at the heavily breathing young samurai resting on a knee, who just best three of his greatest swordsmen. He grinned when he noticed General Shimbo picked out three of the best of his samurai to cross swords with what he believed was the best swordsman in his army. Again, the respectful liege lord was forced to hide his amazement behind a mask of indifference, as he offered to the young warrior. "Masahiko-san! You have proved yourself a great Warrior with the sword. I would've thought no less of your skills. Samurai, you'll drink from the same cup of brotherhood, from this moment on, all gathered Samurai will be of the same mind, body, and blood."

The lord waited until the servants rushed in the huge formation of samurai, and refilled the flask over and over until every samurai, even Masahiko drank from the one cup. The warlord moved to the edge of the platform and held out his hand, and the vassal placed the cup in his hand and filled it for the last time. He lifted it overhead and announced proudly. "I'll drink from the same cup as my loyal vassals, to bind us as one forever. Then everyone will follow by swearing this allegiance to me and my Realm. My Katana will rest edge up, and your thumbs will be pressed on the razor edge to draw blood, and your blood will be stamped on this ledger of fate, alongside your honorable name or mark, this will seal your pact with my spirit."

Just as he issued the orders, he stood with an open black fan with an orange sun rising on it in his hand. He waved it with speed before his face as each new warrior stepped forward and sliced the thumbs of their right hand, and placed the blood impressions on the roster containing the samurai's names. It took three hours to complete this ritual, and once it was done, Kawasomeru-sama turned to Masahiko and grumbled. "Masahiko-san! I order you to name the fighting sword crafted by the master sword maker Sugahara, Wind! For I see even your training sword moves with the swiftness, and the biting of the untamed wind of our lands, Samurai Warrior."

He stopped speaking to draw in a breath before bellowing. "All Samurai standing before me will bare your chests for tattooing." It was his way of branding his samurai, and assuring him of their undying allegiance to his honor for life.

She was rocked to her soul by this stunning order from her master. She wasn't prepared to strip and allow them to tattoo her chest. How could she allow them to tattoo her, they would discover her secret? She remained at attention, staring at the liege lord in disbelief. She was trying to will him to resend his order of tattooing her, to seal her oath to his honor.

He noticed the hesitation in the warrior's eyes and barked. "Masahiko-san! Are you hard of hearing? Is there dung trapped in your ears it blocked my command? I issued an order for you to strip to waist and prepare for tattooing of your discipline."

She looked for her father in the crowd. She found him and he turn his face from her. His silent words told her she had no choice but to obey her master's order and remove her top.

With shaking hands she slowly undid her armor breast plating, another samurai from the ranks swiftly moved up and took the discarded armor, not allowing it to touch the ground for an instant. She next removed the arm covers, her helmet and fearsome brass face mask, and handed them over to a second waiting warrior. Then she undid her obi after handing the training sword to a third samurai. She quickly wiggled out of the top of the kosode and allowed it to drape loosely over the heavy leg protection of her remaining armor.

Everyone in the crowd stared at the strange looking chest wrapping she wore tightly around the upper part of her body. The suddenly concerned Lord Kawasomeru stepped forward and tried to discover what the need for such a piece of equipment might be for this young samurai. He tried to understand if it was some kind of added protection from the bite of the blade or arrow. He felt the thin fabric in his fingers. It was nothing more than a mere silk item worn tight around her upper body. The powerful warlord wondered if this young warrior was having some trouble breathing, and this helped him somehow. He shrugged, thinking it was something this warrior wanted to wear out of some kind of idiosyncrasy. Nothing the samurai did surprised him any longer. All he wanted to do was get this one tattooed then get on with the endless ceremony, so he could get out of his heavy armor and relax and enjoy the rest of the day.

The liege lord stared at Masahiko, his temper coming to an eruption point and he roared angrily at her. "Samurai Masahiko-san! You're wasting my time needlessly with this display of hesitation you are offering me. Let's get on with the tattooing so I can piss on this day, and bring it to a final conclusion. There are hundreds of other Samurai waiting for you to be finished. I thank the gods that be I only have to ink four of you young Warriors on this unending day, or we'd find ourselves standing under this sun forever."

Not knowing what to do next, she slowly wiggled out of the tight fitting silk band.

He took a few stunned steps back, reacting as though he received a hard blow to the face, as he stared at the pair of well formed breasts resting on Masahiko-san's chest and snapped at the warrior. "What is the meaning of this insult?" He bellowed as he looked for Tanizaki in the crowd and added. "What manner of treachery is this? Who is to blame for this terrible crime?"

The samurai near enough to realize what happened, grunted and cursed the deceiving female obviously trying to pass herself off as a male to their master. There were calls for the samurai's head to be taken, other warriors called her a whore from the pillow world. Other soldiers called out phrases too derogatory to be given thought or consideration to.

He recovered his composure and stepped closer to the female samurai. He whispered as if he didn't want anyone to hear his words. "Masahiko-san! What is the meaning of this deceit? Are you really from the blood of the great Tanizaki-san lineage?"

"Hai Lord." She cried as she dropped to her knees, overwhelmed by grief she was suffering by hurting her lord before the samurai. With every fiber of her body, she wished she was dead.

"Why did you not tell me you were woman before I embarrassed you so, Masahiko-san?"

"My Lord! Because I wouldn't have been allowed to be trained Samurai."

"Huh! That's not true young one. It's in my power to appoint anyone I chose to the rank of Samurai. Especially one who displayed such fine abilities with the sword, spear, and horse." The master took a second to think. His mind raced and his heart pounded in his chest. He knew he was going to cause displeasure and grief to his other warriors and officers, when he announced he planned to appoint this woman to the ranks of the samurai caste, and give her a position of general in his army. He also understood he would have samurai falling on their swords, feeling they were dishonored by the induction of this woman in their sacred and guarded ranks. He again looked for Tanizaki, he saw he was taking care of his wife. The decision on him was decided. He owed it to the trainer to induct his child to the ranks of samurai.

The wise Lord Kawasomeru understood he probably would have inducted Masahiko even if what was believed of her was true, that she was suffering from the dreaded leper's curse. Now he knew why the young child would not bathe with the other samurai. He was hurt that Master Trainer Tanizaki didn't come to him with the problem first. If he had, this terrible embarrassment would never have taken place in public against his daughter.

He grunted and held up his hand as he announced. "Masahiko-san! Masahiko-san who was once a man now woman. Everyone in my Realm, be it known Masahiko-san is woman Samurai. I bestow on her the guarded right to use the Katana, and all weapons to defend herself with the sword and to defend my honor with sword, spear, and bow on any battlefield she treads on in my sake for my honor. I order every Warrior under my command to greet this new woman Samurai with honor and respect. Masahiko-san! I know this isn't your given name. What is the name your honored family called you in the privacy of your home from birth?"

She looked up and whispered softly. "Yuriko Tanizaki my Lord and Master."

"Yuriko. It's a proud name indeed I offer you young Masahiko-san. It'll be spoke with pride and respect from this day forward. Yuriko! You'll be branded with the sign of your discipline. What is the sign of your father's training?"

"Kawasomeru-sama! It's the sign of the claw, the same as my honorable father."

"Then that'll be your given sign to honor me with." The warlord offered.

There was an angry uproar in the ranks of the samurai gathered before him. One warrior broke ranks and rushed forward and dropped to his knees, and begged to speak.

Against his better judgment, the warlord allowed this brazen young warrior to speak as he hissed. "You think you have something to say to me that I might be the least bit interested in hearing from your foul lips to my ears, young fool?"

"Hai my Lord and Master of life." The samurai offered from his kneeling position.

"Very well, allow me hear these great words of wisdom you have to offer me."

The samurai who came forward rose, fighting desperately to regain control of his breathing and raging anger. Once he was able speak, he began. "Lord Kawasomeru! Look upon this filthy woman who dares to wear the sacred aquene knot of the respected Samurai Caste. Thousands of Samurai died honorably to make their Caste great, and now it's being invaded by an unworthy woman. She shouldn't be standing before our Master with Samurai of true men.

"This foul woman should be forced to the service of a Tea House rather than insult the honored Samurai Caste like she's doing before you, my Lord. She should be learning the ways of women servicing male Samurai where she'd be useful to real Samurai, instead of trying to lie her way into becoming a respected Samurai in your Army. I don't care one grain of rice how skilled she is at handling a sword, spear, or bow which she has no right to use, my Liege Lord. Ieeeee my Lord! She must be punished before all for this insult she leveled on this loyal Samurai Caste. She lived out a detestable lie before our Lord and Master and your armies.

"Then this deceitful one should be made to understand she's nothing more than a lowly woman, not man Samurai of the upper class. She has to be shown she doesn't possess the manly faucet, or the powerful stream which marks the Samurai a true man. She has to be beaten back to the world of women, a woman whose duty is to serve Samurai, and I'll be the first who'll teach this evil one the road she should be traveling upon. This unholy Warrior's sword should be snapped in half before her, and buried in a manure heap. This he that is a she should be buried alive in an eta village with her head sticking out of the ground, for the hated eta's to relieve themselves upon. This unworthy and dishonorable person's family should suffer the same foul fate, until they drown in the vile urine of the lowly filthy eta class.

"Once she's dead, her head should be separated from her body, and placed upon a spike and dishonorably displayed upside down for all to curse for her deception played out against you, my Lord and Master and the Realm. An ear tag should be placed in her right ear, explaining to all who'll take time to read it, of her crimes committed against my Liege Lord. It should read, 'Here is a female who faked being male to try and become Samurai. You are ordered to erase her cursed memory and worthless deeds from your mind forever. Her name should never cross an honorable Warrior's lips again.'" As the warrior spoke his terribly upsetting words, his anger kept growing until it ebbed, and he jumped into action against Masahiko.

Without words, the angry samurai roughly shifted his fundoshi to the side and exposed himself to Masahiko. Then he tried to stuff his stiffening member in her mouth. There was a gasp from the crowd as warriors shouted their agreement with the samurai's brash actions aimed at the woman dressed in samurai armor.

The warlord didn't stop this insulting action, because he believed it was up to her to work out of this dilemma on her own. To prove her worthy to him, and to the others she was deserving of becoming samurai. But he did look to Tanizaki to see how he was reacting to these insulting and vile actions carried out against his daughter by this angry warrior. His heart saddened when he noticed Emiko fainted, and the trainer trying his best to carry her from the stirring mob surrounding him, shouting curses at his daughter. The warlord turned his attention to Masahiko being manhandled by the fuming warrior.

As the samurai held her head roughly in his hand by her samurai knot, he nastily dragged his member back and forth across her clamped lips, and she reacted rightly against this assault of her body and honor. In less than a heartbeat, she exploded and unsheathed her close in fighting sword, and in one swift motion, she grabbed hold of the offending member and cut it from the brazen samurai's body. The cut samurai let go of her head let out with a roar, a mixture of pain and rage as he stared in disbelief at the bloody end of the severed stalk still held in his hand. The wounded warrior dropped to his knees trying desperately to try and stop the bleeding with his hands. He looked to the formation of warriors, begging for help from someone in the group. He knew he was going to die if help wasn't administered immediately.

One samurai who formed a friendly relationship with Masahiko stepped forward and unsheathed his katana as he walked forward. In one swift action he raised the blade and brought it crashing down on the exposed and shaking neck of the insulting and dying samurai. His body dropped to the ground, with streams of blood shooting three feet as his life's blood drained in the dry ground. The slaughtered samurai's feet kicking at the air in defiance of his violent death.

The samurai who killed the offending warrior dropped to his knees by Masahiko's side as she fixed her kosode and bowed to his lord who nodded to the young man, approving of his actions. He wondered what powers this child of Tanizaki possessed, to force a samurai who she barely knew, to come to her aid as this one did. The powerful lord understood this was the mark of a true leader, adding to the worth of this warrior he waited years to arrive.

A grumble of protest rose anew from the ranks of the samurai as many of the warriors reached for the hilts of their swords, and surged slightly forward a little in the ranks at the two samurai kneeling before their lord and master.

The warlord held up his fan before his face as he barked at the soldiers. "Iye!"

All forward movement stopped instantly.

The confused Lord Kawasomeru drew in a huge gulp of air then roared at the gathered warriors. "This Samurai who kneels in humbleness before me is merely guilty of avenging a terrible insult forced upon her person by this detestable inconsiderate Warrior. This foul Samurai received what he deserved, and Masahiko-san is guilty of reacting in a manner I myself would have, if such a fool hearted abominable act was carried out against my person. I'd expect each of you my Samurai, to react in the same manner. I decided to allow this female who'll keep the name Masahiko-san on the battlefield, to join the ranks of the Samurai Caste. She has proved herself worthy on the battlefield and on the field of honor, and her steadfast loyalty to me, demands I accept her in the ranks of Samurai Caste. If any of you fools have a problem accepting my decision over her fate, step forward and commit suppuku before my feet."

Fifteen warriors stepped forward, knelt and opened their armor then kosodes and drew their small swords and opened their entrails to the air and ground.

He didn't speak and waited until the bodies stopped moving then with a flick of his hand, an army of hinin moved out and removed the dead. A second army of hinin appeared and removed all signs of blood. When everything was back to normal, he looked at Masahiko and ordered. "Masahiko-san! You'll remain kneeling at the base of this dais until every one of the Samurai has been accepted into the ranks of Samurai and my army. Then we'll talk further?"

"Hai my Lord and Master." The child warrior replied from her kneeling position.

"Good, cover yourself properly then move by my left." He pointed to the east side of the platform then added to his angry words aimed at the female warrior. "Masahiko-san!

You'll remain until I send for you. Be patient little one, all is well and will be as it shall be."

The warlord rushed the rest of the ceremony along as fast as honor would allow. The three samurai to be tattooed were marked with his mark of the Hawk, after she was marked with the symbol of the Claw. The other samurai were ordered to report to the twentieth village for training. His words struck her as if she been hit with the back of an armored protected hand by her master. She realized he wasn't going to allow her father to train the next group of trainees. It was a terrible insult, one she would not be able to live with. She decided she was going to beg her lord to be allowed to commit suppuku at the end of the ceremony. Then she spent the rest of her time preparing her mind for the death that was the answer to her problems.

As the sun went beyond the mountain for its long awaited sleep for the pending night, did the ceremony come to a grueling completion. The lord walked away from the platform in a slow walk as if he had the weight of the world on his exhausted shoulders, without addressing her further. Leaving her to contemplate her fate. It was a further insult leveled against her from her lord and master. The dispersing samurai and villagers realized this insult, and sneered their disgust at her for daring to deceive the warlord.

The sun slowly dipped behind the mountain tops and she feared even the sun was abandoning her to her fate. She felt the sun was angry at her and was hiding its warmth giving rays by disappearing behind the mountains. When the sun disappeared, the mosquitoes attacked her with a fever for a taste of her blood. A heavy swarm of the blood sucking things buzzed around her head, drawn by the odor of her sweat, and the heat from her exhausted body. They bit her face and neck and any other part of her exposed body they could get at, but she dared not to swat at the evil things for fear of further insulting her lord and master.

Her stomach growled from the lack of food, demanding food or water she hadn't tasted since early the night before. It was late and her mind questioned if her lord forgot, or if he was refusing to see her. In her mind she knew that was impossible. She held the kneeling position as was ordered by her angry master, every muscle and joint of her body ached, and cried out with pain at being forced to remain locked in one position for so long a period of time.

Finally, an angry palace guard marched out, stopping just inches before her face nearly resting on the ground, and grunted in a harsh tone at her. "Get on your worthless feet, filthy fabricator to the Realm and my Lord. Your honorable Master demands your worthless presence before him. I don't understand why, nor do I think he should see your lying face and give you audience. He should allow you to be given to us, the true Samurai you have insulted by your presence for proper dealing with. But I'm not the one to question Kawasomeru-sama's wisdom and decision, he's far more wiser than I can ever become in a hundred lifetimes. Follow me in silence, I don't wish to hear any further fabrications from your detestable lying lips and dog wagging tongue, housed within your god cursed being."

The guard stomped away, forcing her to struggle to her feet and rush to follow him. She got up painfully and limped and dragged her legs behind her, her knees screaming with pain, her back ached and refused to move properly as she tried to straighten it. The guard knew she was in stress and hurried himself, forcing her to rush faster.

The young and beautiful female warrior was led into a private room just off the main hallway, and formal meeting room of the third floor of the castle. She was rudely pushed in the room where General Shimbo waited in a kneeling position on a thin tatami mat. There was no mat for her so she knelt on the hardwood floor and waited. Her eyes met the respected general and he angrily turned his head from her eyes in disgust over her deceit. Then she bowed until the tip of her nose actually touched the floor.

Stealthily, from her bowing position, her eyes searched the room. There were three officers present who she didn't recognize. The outer wall was lined with guards, all staring at her with hatred in their eyes. The lord was nowhere to be seen. She bowed to the dais, resting her forehead on the cool, polished floor to wait Lord Kawasomeru, and her fate at his judgment.

After some minutes the shoji door open swiftly and the upset warlord, without his armor and obviously bathed, stormed in as if angry at the world. He took his position on the platform, sitting on a pillow to ease the pain from his piles. Once seated, he turned to General Shimbo and asked. "General Shimbo-san! Have you been able to come to terms with this female warrior I intend to allow to join the ranks of the Samurai Caste?"

He bowed politely and replied in one phrase to his master. "Hai my Lord!" Then he bowed to his lord and master and took a calm seated position.

"Fine, then your death sentence has been lifted from your shoulders. Ieeeee! If I knew the wise Master Trainer was going to play such a game of wits on me. I would've been better prepared. I was expecting greatness from his child, but I was expecting a child with a golden faucet to appear before me, not a woman Warrior with a great void that could be wrapped around another Samurai's faucet. None of my foolish vassals will ever surprise me any longer I fear."

His words made a number of the officers in the room give out with a nervous chuckle.

The still angry Lord Kawasomeru drew in a breath and looked at the female samurai with her forehead resting on the floor and snapped. "Now for you Masahiko-san! Lift your foolish head from the floor so that I might speak with you eye to eye, young one."

She lifted her head and blinked her eyes she had shut while locked in the bowing position, after she checked out the people in an effort to block out what might happen to her next.

"Well Warrior, what do you have to say for yourself?"

"Kawasomeru-sama! I brought great displeasure to the shoulders and Wa of my Liege Lord. For this terrible insult against your person, I beg to be allowed to commit suppuku and put an end to my worthless existence." She bowed then reached for her wakizashi blade and unsheathed her short knife and laid it out before her face.

Her unsheathing of the blade so near Lord Kawasomeru's person brought an instant reaction from the special castle guards. No one was allowed to be armed within striking distance of the lord, in case there was an assassination attempt played out against him. The samurai guards rushed forward and formed a tight protective screen around the lord of the castle. The officers also unsheathed their sword and took threatening positions facing Masahiko while standing between her and Lord Kawasomeru, all wanting the excuse to dispatch this dangerous fabricator kneeling before them and their master.

He pushed the guards out of his way so he could see the child he knew was no threat to his life then roared. "Guards! Back to your positions! Officers! Back to your tatamis. I wish to speak further with this Warrior. She's no threat to my being. Relax, it's by my order. SIT!"

It took a few seconds for the samurai to return to their positions. When everyone was comfortable, he began. "Masahiko-san! You committed the first mistake in your life. It's not you who'll decide if you brought me displeasure. It's I who'll decide who has, and who has not brought me displeasure. Sheathe your sword Samurai. The mistake you were offered to me as male is not of your doing. You were too young to make any difference in that decision when first cast upon the wings of fate, so rest your mind at easy."

She sheathed her short sword as ordered. She was stunned he addressed her with the honorable san at the end of her name. She couldn't believe her ears, the powerful liege lord told her he wasn't going to allow her the honor of killing herself. Why? She asked herself in silence.

"Huh! Young one, it must have been difficult, the training I mean, living like a male, the questions you must have asked and battled with. The battle which must have waged within your honorable being. I know your father and he must have pushed you beyond all endurance with his training of you. Your abilities prove my thinking correct. If only your wise father came to me first, all this unpleasantness could have been avoided. I would've worked out accommodations for you. Masahiko-san! The eighth child born of the great Tanizaki-san, a child chosen and so marked by the gods for greatness. Yes indeed, I would've worked out something, anything to please the god who chose to mark you so.

"If the gods chose to mark you, a female born for greatness then it's my duty to carry out their confusing wishes and demands. Your father is a great and wise man, Masahiko-san! I gave your situation consideration and come to the conclusion I'll place you in command of my Fifth unit horsemen. I'll have a special Shoinzukuri building set aside for your use and comfort. I don't know what a female Samurai needs in the ways of comfort and needs. I'm certain you'll inform me of your needs as they arrive. What's your preference for pillowing? A male, a female?" He grunted, surprised he was being so nasty towards the respectful child.

"Kawasomeru-sama! I don't know, I have not been with either I fear to offer you."

"Ieeeee! You have not looked after your inner health, foolish one."

"Iye!" She replied to her lord and master's question.

"Then I order you to attend to this need of your body. I'll have a male and female vassal, whichever is your preference placed at your disposal. They'll be educated in this area, and will teach you the difference between the ying and yang, and the joy this mating brings the soul of a Warrior. How could one who has been trained so well in so many different ways, have not been trained in the ways of the world? I'll speak to your honorable father over this mistake on his part. In your Shoinzukuri you'll be the only one who'll inhabit the building. You'll be allowed to invite your officers in to discuss strategies and habits, and issue orders for the day.

"There are countless bad times about to be unleashed upon every corner of the Realm, and I fear I'll need every able bodied well trained officer I have at my command, to beat the hatful Wakatsuki at his own game, and come out of this war as the victor. You're elevated to field commander of my horsemen. A Captain until I see how well you control your Samurai, and how well you handle yourself on the battlefield. If I approve of your actions, I'll then elevate you to the rank of General. Huh! You're dismissed young Warrior. Follow this samurai guard to your living quarters in the Castle walls. Masahiko-san! You're at liberty to handle any treachery displayed against you in the manner of the Samurai code of justice. Report any treacheries to the Dokoro, the office of the Samurai immediately.

"Samurai Captain Masahiko-san. If there's ever a display of treachery leveled against your person, you're at liberty to handle it as you deem fit, when you see fit to respond to any indignity aimed at you. I'll accepted you as Samurai, and that means my Warriors, no matter who they are, or how high an officer rank they control, must accept you in the same manner. Or I'll take many heads I assure you. Leave me at once my new Samurai Masahiko-san!"

She struggled to her feet and bowed then followed a samurai to her quarters. It was a small shoinzukuri, a samurai house constructed for officers, and was meant to house up to fifteen to twenty warriors. Her sleeping roll was the only other item resting inside the long building.

The lord finished with his officers then sent them away. When he was alone except for his guard, he whispered to an unforeseen force standing behind the curtain covering the back wall of the room. "Lady Yuko?" His beautiful and young consort came out of the shadows, and moved to the powerful warlord as smiled at him over his decisions covering Masahiko and the way he handled the situation with his officers over her being offered a place in his army.

"Well what do you think of my decisions on this most confusing of days, my little cherry blossom?" The master asked of his favorite and wise consort with concern in his tone.

"My Lord, you made a wise and just decision on this wonderful day I offer. It's about time a female Warrior was allowed to join the ranks of the stuffy Samurai Caste."

"Yes Lady Yuko, you're correct with these words and ideas. It was your tongue that had persuaded me to allow this young child to live, and to join the ranks of the Samurai Caste, young lady. You always guided me wisely in the past, and all your decisions were correct and wise, and brought me wealth, happiness and pleasure. Some of your guidance I employed on the battlefield. Please Lady Yuko, bring paper and ink. I wish to send a message to Tanizaki-san."

"Hai my Lord. At once." The lovely Lady Yuko replied to her lord and master.

INSIDE ENGAKUJI CASTLE

The old master trainer struggled desperately trying to carry Emiko's limp body to their quarters in the castle. The doctor was standing at her side as Remi and Miho were doing their best to make the dying Emiko as comfortable as possible under the present circumstances. Blood was freely dripping from between her legs, and her strength was ebbing rapidly. Miho looked to him with tears in her eyes, knowing his wife was going to suffer mightily until the end of her honorable life. The doctor placed his hand on his elbow and applied pressure, trying to lead him from her bedside. He looked in the trainer's eyes and said with compassion.

"Master Trainer Tanizaki-san! I must report to you that Lady Emiko is dying, she might last three, maybe even four days but she will die soon. You must prepare yourself for a period of great suffering from her before she is finally allowed into the world of the Floating. Her insides have been eaten away by this terrible disease my modest skills are not able to defeat. I'm sorry for my failure to your Lady, Master Trainer Tanizaki-san." He bowed politely then left so he could report Emiko's poor condition to Lord Kawasomeru.

A courier appeared outside his temporary quarters in the castle, and waited to be invited in the room by the respected man. When he called out to allow him entrance, the messenger dropped to his knees and offered the folded scroll to the master trainer. Then he turned and disappeared as quickly as he appeared before the trainer's room. He broke the seal then unfolded the scroll and read it. The letter was from Lord Kawasomeru.

CHAPTER TWENTY THREE

After the master trainer read the scroll from Lord Kawasomeru, he followed instructions swiftly. He made sure his wife was comfortable then checked on her health before leaving to visit with his master. He spoke with Miho and Remi to make certain they knew what was expected, and how they were to care for his wife while he spoke with his lord. He left the room and headed for his room where he cleaned the day's grime and dressed in a fine kosode.

He prepared for this meeting with his master since the birth of his daughter. He allowed his mind to wander, concerned over her health and wellbeing. He wondered what his lord decided was the fate of the child. He hadn't received word on her fate whether she was alive or not. He breathed a sigh as he closed his kosode, and wrapped an obi around him and tucked his swords in the sash properly. He checked himself, satisfied he looked his best he sat on the floor and waited for time to pass so he could meet with his master of the realm.

The lord spent the remaining hours of night of Gembuku in a tossing and turning fashion. He couldn't get the hurt look etched in Masahiko's eyes out of his mind, when he ordered her not to wear the aquene knot of samurai. It was an order he didn't deliver easily, he knew what the knot meant to a samurai. But the wise lord had another need for her not to wear the knot and tail of hair. He wanted her hair long, cut in the manner of the normal women of Japan. In the accepted fashion of kami no sagariba, the hair on the back of the head long, reaching below the curve of her back. The hair in front of her head worn shorter, hanging just below the nipple of the breast.

He felt this, his first female samurai might be more valuable looking like a woman than a man. Besides, now he knew she was a woman and would look ridiculous with the crown of her head shaven. In his tossing he decided to allow her to continue using the name of Masahiko. He didn't understand why this was to be, but he felt the gods who control worldly things wanted this so, and he wasn't about to go against the gods.

There was a tapping on the floor by the shoji door, and his eyes flew open as he stared in the darkness of the room and growled deeply. "Hai?"

The shoji moved to the left and Yuko knelt in the hall. She bowed and offered in a sweet tone of voice. "Please forgive this worthless woman for interrupting your sleep my Lord. You requested this foolish woman to wake you an hour before sunrise. Please forgive me, but it's time for you to wake, though I rather you sleep more for your health. I'm aware of the terrible night sleep you suffered, Kawasomeru-sama. The decisions you have to make concerning Master

Trainer Tanizaki-san and his daughter, along with the pressures of Wakatsuki weighing heavy on you. Ieeeee! I don't know how you sleep at all and yet remain in health. I thank the gods of the Floating World for looking after you my Lord."

He smiled, surprised at how long winded she was this early in the morning. "Lady Yuko! It's not the gods who look after my health. It's your pillowing that has me in such good health. I'm up and will meet Tanizaki-san on the fifth level of the Castle."

She covered her mouth with the flowing sleeve of her exquisite yellow kosode, to cover her chuckle as she laughed over the compliment the master offered. "My Lord, you're most kind to this worthless old woman whose pillowing abilities are below standard."

He stood naked and unashamed as he retorted to the stunningly beautiful woman. "Lady Yuko! I'm in no mood to lock horns with you over compliments on this morning. Take what I give and leave me, I have to get ready to greet Master Trainer Tanizaki-san."

She bowed and backed silently out of the room. She moved with the grace and elegance of a soft breeze on a warm summer night.

The lord dressed even though he was exhausted, he wanted to be in position when Tanizaki arrived for their meeting. When he was dressed he headed up the stone steps for the fifth floor of the castle, and went to the open section of the courtyard. It offered him a spectacular view of the sunrise. When he reached his favorite position, he smiled when he noticed the pot of steaming Cha resting on the table with two cups. He was going to pour the tea for this meeting.

Time passed slowly and he enjoyed the way off lightening of the night sky, as the sun made its appearance for a new day's travels through the Heavens. A guard came up behind him and waited to be spoken to. The guard knew his master was aware of his presence, and it was only a matter of time before he acknowledged him. The master trainer stood behind the concerned samurai guard, worried what the lord had on his mind.

At the first cry of a seagull, he grunted. "Ahhh... good morning Master Trainer Tanizaki-san! Please honor me by sharing this glorious sunrise."

He moved up to his lord and was motioned to sit on his left hand side.

Seagulls cried in angry protest as they launched into the brightening skies. Noises of his awakening town filled the air, and the world as he knew it was bathed in a comforting blanket of warm sunlight, as the golden sphere rose at a leisurely pace in the sky. The sun's warmth filled the secluded area of his palace, and his bones with life giving heat. The air was fresh and clean and alive, as a strong breeze carrying the sweet smell of salt water on it. As the sun gave birth to new day light, he understood it was going to be a beautiful day, as he offered to his long time trainer. "Nitaro-san! Thank you for sharing such a beautiful sunrise with me."

"It was my pleasure my Lord and Master, and I thank you for inviting such an unworthy subject as myself to share such a breathtaking view privately with you. It'll fill my remaining days with its beauty and memory." He bowed, overwhelmed with pride the master would request to share a favor with someone who should have his head lobbed off for his deception. He waited in silence for his lord to speak further.

After a few moments of strained silence and enjoying the sun as it followed its prescribed path through the Heavens, he finally growled. "Cha Master Trainer Tanizaki-san?"

"Hai." The master trainer stared in awe as he poured the tea, and even offered him the first cup. The way the warlord offered it, he knew he was in no mood for the polite game of refusing the first cup. He took the tea and slurped it loudly.

"Thank you for sparing me the boring game of bantering over the first cup offered to the one to be honored on this day. Master Trainer Tanizaki-san! What I have to speak to you about leaves no room for politeness and good manners on this upsetting day to experience. Excuse my rude forwardness my old friend of countless years past."

After a few moments of tea drinking, he began again, but he removed the title of Master Trainer from the old man's name this time. "Tanizaki-san! I have invited you here to share this beautiful sunrise so that we may speak in private, free of prying ears of the Castle fools who listen to everything said within these walls. I decided to accept your daughter to the ranks of the Samurai Caste. I have appointed her Captain of my horsemen, her outstanding skills with the blade justifies this order. When Masahiko-san proves to me that she's a worthy subject, I'll elevate her to rank of General of all horsemen of my Realm. I know she'll earn the right, I see nothing but greatness in her future."

Stunned over what he was hearing, he dropped his cup as he stared at his master. All this time he feared the worse for his daughter. He was worried the warlord would tell him he had her put to death, and he was banished from the castle. In his mind, he never dared to think the lord would honor him so for his sinful deceit.

The powerful warlord asked if he would like another cup of tea after observing him drop the first cup, the master was pleased his words caused the old man confusion, but he refused and the lord went on with his words. "Tanizaki-san! I allowed your daughter to maintain her manly name, to avoid any further problems for her or my samurai to accept her into their ranks. That was the good part of this conversation. Now for you. Master Trainer Tanizaki-san! I have to deal with you, punish you. I lost much sleep over this and believe I have come up with a fitting punishment for you, and a solution to my problem. One that'll leave you with honor and face even in death. Tanizaki-san! I witnessed the suffering your honorable wife is living through in silence as it should be, acting like she was in no pain, and I honor her for her bravery.

"Tanizaki-san! I instruct you to put her out of her misery, it's not right for one so loyal to you and my realm to be allowed to suffer like she is obviously doing. You'll accomplish this order in a most compassionate way. Go speak to the Mama-san of the Fifth Tea House on the other side of the capital. From what I was told about this experienced old woman, she's advised in the elixirs that'll make a person fall asleep and never wake up. I'm assured the death is painless and peaceful. It bothers me to order this of my old friend of many battles, I feel it's better to stop her suffering now, rather than allow her to continue living in pain." He stopped speaking and looked into the eyes of his friend. For a second he swore he saw a tear in the old man's eyes.

"Ieeeee! You're a wise and just leader, for I decided today was her last day on this earth. I can't bear to see her suffer so." He offered.

"I'm pleased you obviously agreed with my decision about your honorable wife, but I'm not through with you yet. Once Lady Emiko is dead and her fine spirit sent on its journey to the Floating World. I order you to leave your finger on the table in your room and have General Kobayashi-san bring it to me. You'll then scale Mount Fuji and slice your belly. Of this order you'll give me the finger you once used when your swore blood allegiance to my father countless years ago, when you first appeared before him.

"In this manner your commitment to my family will be completed, and your sprit will be free to leave this world in peace. Tanizaki-san, allow your essences to flow in the crater that feeds the fire gods of the mountain. There, your unconquerable spirit will mingle with Mount Fugi's many ghosts and gods, and there they'll intermingle with the metals from which we make our swords. In this way you'll be instrumental in defeating our enemy, even in your death old friend." He raised his hand to silence the excited trainer before he interrupted his words.

"Before you speak, allow me to continue. I'm not without seeing eyes or listening ears. I have noticed the pain in your back and slowness of your walk. It's honorable to be allowed to commit suppuku in the service of your Lord and Master, than be allowed to waste until you're too weak to take your life properly. I'll look after Masahiko-san as if the child was of my blood. I'll take the surviving members of your family, and offer them positions in my government.

"Your vassals will be looked after with many joining my vassals. I'll place your land, home and worth in escrow to be held for your daughter, when she retires from my service. I'll make certain your children are rich beyond dreams. If Masahiko-san is felled in battle, your worth will be divided equally among the remaining children. But what happens to Masahiko-san, what the future and gods holds in store for the young child, this I promise you! Her name will be sung in songs, her accomplishments made into a Nolt play and acted on the stage, making all aware of her great feats and her honor will also be sung in ballads in Kyoto. You may speak if you have something of worth to say to me, old friend."

"Hai, I thank you for allowing me an honorable end to my worthless life, my Lord and Master. I thank you for looking after my worthless children and accepting Masahiko-san into the Caste of Samurai. I'll honor you in your orders. I'll carry them out beginning today." He didn't offer the fact he was also having trouble pissing.

"Delay your journey to Mount Fugi and Floating World, until your virtuous wife has been awarded by a noble burial. Once she's burned to ash and her spirit lead to where the spirits go for their long sleep, scoop some ashes up and carry them to the base of Mount Fugi with you. There, you'll add them to the strength you'll mix to the steel of our swords. Master Trainer Tanizaki-san, you'll wait for the proper time before you leave the capital."

"Hai my Lord, I'll do as ordered." The shaking old man replied to his master.

"Good, is there anything else we have to cover on this day, Tanizaki-san?"

"Hai, I'd like to see my daughter before I leave this earth forever, my Lord."

"Master Trainer Tanizaki-san! This is allowed with great pleasure, but refrain from informing her of your pending death. I'm certain she expects the death of her mother, it's written in her eyes. Handle this problem your own way. The young warrior will be going through enough troubling times without her believing that she might be responsible for your death. I know she'll not blame herself for her mother's honorable death. Once you left the capital, I'll inform Captain Masahiko-san I sent you to the Fifteenth Village, to defend that section of the Realm against a possible invasion by Owari province.

"Your daughter will understand I sent you to the least likely section of the Realm to see any fighting. I hope she believes this was to save your life. Later in the future of time, I'll inform her that you lost your honorable life in battle. That way you'll be bigger than life in her eyes. Order General Kobayashi-san to stand as your second, he'll assist you in your final honor to be displayed before me. I'll place him in command of my spearmen for his unending loyalty to you and myself. Forgive me for this small lie my friend, I believe it's the only way I can protect the good health and spirit of Captain Masahiko-san."

Every samurai of Japan knew it was customary for a warrior about to commit suppuku to have a second stand by his side in order to assist him during this time of honor. The second would stand behind and to the left side of the honored one kneeling. It was the second's duty to make certain the death of the honored one was swift, by decapitating him with one swift strike of his sword. It was an insult to the honored one and his second if the samurai's suffering became so unbearable and unduly long. The honor of having a second was necessary, demanded for the actor's accomplishments during life. It was to die in shame if a samurai died with his head intact after performing suppuku. It proved to the world that he died friendless, who with no one attending him mourning his spirit in the afterworld.

The stunned master trainer bowed to his liege lord, pleased he was being allowed a samurai's death more than he dared to expect, more than he had the right to deserve for daring to deceive his lord and master in the manner he did.

His lord smiled, he didn't inform Tanizaki the doctor had reported on Emiko's rapidly failing condition to him. Remi also reported, informing him the trainer was having trouble performing his duty, and she noticed a trace of blood in his urine, and his wife was alive because of her will to see Masahiko-san be accepted to the ranks of the samurai in his service.

The crafty liege lord knew with satisfaction he was right to order the death of Emiko and of the trainer, but he was going to make the name of Nitaro Tanizaki-san, Master Trainer of the Ninth Village, live in honor for Japan's history. He understood there were some samurai who would remain upset over the fact he allowed a female to join the ranks of samurai. More would join the ranks of the angered when it became known he was going to allow Tanizaki's family to live, honor them by placing them in choice positions in his city and government. In addition to this anger, he knew they would get used to his decision, or would die by his order.

The leader of Shinano province looked at his old friend one last time, before he would allow him to begin his journey to the afterworld of myth and wonder. He put on an angry a face he could muster then growled. "I have finished speaking with you and I'll not see you again in my lifetime, old friend. If I ever see you again, I might change my mind and put you to the proper death you so richly deserve. Leave my side, I'll never speak of your name again." He turned and looked at the sun drenched mountains, dismissing him rudely.

The aged trainer stood, bowed as best as his old bones would allow then he followed the guard who led him to Lord Kawasomeru's side. The lord waved his hand and a second samurai rushed to his side. "Meet the Master Trainer at the entrance to Engakuji Castle, escort him to visit his daughter. Assure them privacy in their conversation."

"Hai my Lord." The guard ran after Tanizaki.

The warlord looked to the heavens and smiled, pleased he wisely handled the fate of such a loyal vassal as the old man walking from his sight. He lifted his chin to allow the warming rays of the sun to bathe him and mumbled. "Piss on this worthless day."

Word a female samurai was allowed to join the samurai elite, caused many samurai to bet amongst themselves, wagering money on who would be the first to pillow with the female samurai. Something that never took place in the history of Japan.

The master trainer was lead out of the castle to prepare the funeral pyre for his wife, when another samurai walked up to him and bowed. He informed him of his orders, and the old man followed him in silence inside the castle.

The female warrior was meditating outside her private quarters when she saw her father walking towards her. She bowed to the gods and stood and bowed to her father who weakly returned the honor. He waved his hand at the ground, and she returned to her position of meditation. He joined her in silence.

She reached out a hand and covered her father's with it. The move was soothing to both, adding to their health. At last, he sighed and she knew bad news was coming. She braced herself for what was burdening her father so heavily.

He stared in the sad eyes of his daughter. "Masahiko-san! You see in my mind. You know me too well, I can't hide anything from your will. Yes Masahiko-san! I have bad news. It's your mother. She's suffering and I pleaded on behalf of her to our Lord, begging permission to end her unending suffering. In his wisdom, our Master agreed and ordered me to visit a tea house, and get the poison that'll make your mother go to sleep forever." He paused to allow what he said to enter her mind. To his surprise, she seemed relieved than upset.

"Father! This news I have longed to hear from your honored lips. Mother is suffering terribly, and the feelings she was no longer a woman and of service to you, has disabled her mind vastly on her. I'm of the knowledge that every night mother prayed to the gods for death to end her long and unbearable suffering. Father! I too have begged the gods to take mother's life. I'm sorry for these evil thoughts, father." She had to fight not to cry. It seemed since she discovered she was a woman, tears wanted to flow easily.

"Don't fret so little wild fire. To be honest Masahiko-san, I prayed to the worthless gods for my wife's death to come swiftly and painlessly. But I feared the loathsome gods ignored my requests because of the curses I offered them, instead of prayers in the past."

She leaned forward and rested her forehead lightly against her father's. She no longer cared for the display of strength as tears dripped on his prized kosode. With tenderness, he raised his hand and gently stroked her hair. He was proud she was a woman, and he was no longer afraid to display the feelings usually shared between a father and his daughter, as he cooed. "It'll be alright wild fire. Everything worked out for the best. I couldn't have wanted it to work out any better. Fate! Karma! You, daughter are Samurai, and you'll live and be allowed to fight for your Lord and Master on the battlefields. Remember little wild fire, your sword is the door to Heaven or hell. What else is there in a Samurai's life but obedience?

"You done well all your life, and you'll survive on any road you choose to travel upon, you may boast being the Master Trainer's child. Keep your eyes open or you may end up dying like an old woman on the battlefield. To avenge a Master's wrongs is the Samurai's revenge, his duty, his way of life, his beliefs and his privilege."

Fear suddenly took over her mind as it screamed, her father's words sounded as if he was preparing her for his death. One word ripped through the depths of her mind until it was overwhelmingly echoing in her ears. "Nooooooooo!" It screamed as she looked to her father, raising her head from his, tears streaming down her face she asked.

"Father! What about you my honorable guide in life? What is your fate to be? Have you been ordered to kill yourself by our Master? Am I going to be alone on this earth, to be damned to walk aimlessly without family to guide my foolish foot falls along the path of life? Please father! If you must go, allow me the honor to come with you, a world without your loving face to brighten up the sad days ahead, is not worth living in."

He pulled his daughter close and said. "No foolish child. For some reason our Lord honored me. Although he'll no longer allow me to train his future Warriors, he ordered me to the Fifteenth Village where I'll be allowed to assist in the village training. I fear there'll never be battles there, the only province near that would invade is Owari, and that province is too weak to attack any village in Kawasomeru-sama's control. I feel our Lord ordered me to the village so I can live my life in peace. He's a wise and just leader who must be obeyed in all decisions."

She let out her breath in a rush as she replied. "Father, how will you live in a new village? You're so established and honored in the Ninth Village. It'll be like starting over again, without mother by your side. I fear for your health father, I wish I'd be allowed to attend you until the faithful time visits you." She cried as she buried her head in her father's chest.

"I'll not be alone in my worthless life little one, so trouble yourself not on this day."

She pulled from her father and stared at him like she didn't understand.

"Masahiko-san! Fear not for me nor my worthless health and life, I'm wise and well taken care of. Lord Kawasomeru allowed me the privilege to take my wealth with me to the new village. Our Master ordered me a new and larger home to be constructed to live my worthless life in, and I'll be allowed to take my vassals with me. As far as my being alone for the rest of my worthless life, have you forgotten about Lady Remi?" He smiled at her.

Her eyes searched her troubled mind then joined her father in sharing his smile as she replied with vigor. "Oh yes father! It's not wise to want to live alone. You brought comfort to my inner being with these wonderful words. Of course father, you'll remember mother in your mind?"

"Huh! I gave Lady Remi orders to construct a shrine to your mother's memory. We'll support two priests so they'll spend the rest of their worthless Shinto lives praying for your mother's soul and life." He brushed a few strands of hair from Masahiko's face.

"Ieeeee father! You gave me the strength to carry on with my life in peace. I swear by the spirits which give my sword breath and guide me through life. I'll forever bring great honor and respect to the Tanizaki name and memory." She pulled away from her father and stood proudly, displaying her wild spirit. She smiled at her father and assumed a warriors stance, and stiffened her back at the same time

"Huh little wild one. You're so slight of frame, light, therefore you must put your entire soul and body into your blows of truth for your Master's sake. Sheathe your sword, it's not good to draw your Katana without forcing the flow of blood from your enemy. I have no doubt in my mind you'll bring honor and respect to your name in your life." Tanizaki stood.

"Father! When will you end mother's suffering?" The child asked her father.

"Sadly tonight daughter. I'll share your mother's bed one last time then wait for her spirit to leave on its journey to the Floating World. Then I'll have her body brought to the pyre fire tomorrow morning at dawn. You know how your mother liked the dawn. I'll free her soul at that time then leave, but not before I take some of your mother's ashes with me, to share my fire when the time comes for me to return to her side."

She rested her hand lightly on her father's arm and asked him with humility. "Father! Will I be allowed to attend the funeral of my beloved mother, please?"

"Huh! I'm sorry daughter, but your duty is to your Lord now. If he doesn't allow it, you'll not attend." He leaned closer to his daughter and added. "If you're not allowed to attend your mother's funeral, look to the south and witness the smoke, it'll be your mother's spirit departing this earth. I'm sorry I'll never see you again in this world, but I'll be waiting for you in the next world." He smiled to his daughter, bowed, turned and headed off, knowing she would never be allowed to attend her mother's funeral, her lord had to show he was punishing her.

She watched as her father disappeared behind the stone wall and ran in the building, dropping on her bedroll and cried for her mother. She cried for most the day, worrying about her mother and father's fates. She was angry at Lord Kawasomeru, but knew better than to ask permission to attend the funeral. She didn't want to appear to be self centered to the master. She convinced herself she should be happy he allowed her and her father to live their lives in peace. She decided to repay the master for allowing her father to live out his years by becoming the most feared and respected warrior of Japan, and bring great victories in the wars with the lowly dog Wakatsuki. She unsheathed her sword and held it high overhead as she took an oath to herself, not to stop fighting until her sword ran red with the very blood of Wakatsuki's soul.

She spent a fitful sleep and was up before dawn arose, she stood staring to the south and as the sun peeked over the mountains, a plume of smoke appeared. She stared at the smoke and at one point, she swore she saw her mother's face drifting in it. It was smiling at her as it lifted to the Heavens. She bowed to the cloud as she whispered to her mother's spirit. "Honorable mother! I'll miss you dearly. I'll see your spirit in everything I see and touch from this moment on. I'll remember and respect you for giving life to my worthless being. I know of the hardship I put you through on earth. Forgive me mother. I'll remember you. Good-bye mother. I'll be with you in the Floating World, and together with father, we'll begin a new life together." Again, she bowed to the bellowing plume now turning light, clean, pure, and knew her mother gone from her side.

The master trainer knelt to the bellowing fire the body of Emiko was placed in, so the four winds could sweep through the covering housing the pyre. This was to give the spirit of Emiko a choice of which path she wished to travel on, for her forty day stay in the Floating World awaiting her rebirth. He recited many prayers he didn't know he remembered, hoping her spirit would chose the right path in which to travel. So she could return to the world of the living in a new body, and live a better life than she did in the previous one with him.

As the trainer continued to pray for his wife's departed spirit, he was flanked by General Kobayashi, General Miyamoto and many samurai he trained throughout his years. Remi, Miho and his daughter Estsuko attended the funeral pyre, along with his sons and close relatives who lived in the capital and surrounding area. What he didn't realize was Kawasomeru, Mineko and his first consort, Yuko knelt on the third floor verandah in prayer offered to his wife's spirit. It was an honor for the master to bend a knee to honor someone who died in his capital. But she was a well respected and honored vassal, and it was his duty to pay homage to her memory.

When the fire ran its course and ashes cooled, he went to where the head of his wife was placed, and scooped up ashes and placed them in a small silk sack. He tied off the sack and placed it in a small wood box and sealed it. One of his vassals rushed up and took charge of the box and disappeared. He was forced to remain in the capital for three days before he would cut the finger from his hand, and leave it wrapped in a silk cloth in his quarters, and begin his long trek to Mount Fugi to carry out his bargain with his lord.

His daughter was kept busy for the remainder of the day meeting with officers in the lord's army. She was brought up to speed on the small wars taking place in other provinces of the realm. She was informed the master planned to invade Echigo in the next twenty months, once he was sure the forces he needed for an invasion were set in position. She went over the map of the future battlefield, reading where the lord's forces were stationed, and studying the forces from Wakatsuki's armies positioned, in their attempt to defend against Kawasomeru's armies.

It seemed to her the first battle between Kozuke, Lord Kawasomeru's ally, and Echigo and Shimotsuke province under control of Lord Wakatsuki, was going to take place at the Agano River separating the provinces of Echigo and Kozuke. As she studied the map, a skill taught to her by General Kobayashi, she saw the dangers they would face during the upcoming battles. There were a number of narrow valleys where an army could easily be cut off from support and supplies, and if this army found itself with its back pinned against the Agano River, it would easily be slaughtered by the enemy armies.

She studied the maps, determining in the mind the correct routes she would likely take in this region. As she scanned the map, the words of training her father taught her, entered her mind. 'Remember Masahiko-san, your troops are your strength. They're your master's strength as well. It's his way to put forth his wishes for the other lands to follow. You must take care of your Samurai. Reward them as your Master rewards you with land and weapons and personal wealth. Give your Samurai who served you, conquered women to soothe and look after their exhausted bodies, as their reward for their valor on the battlefield. Plunder fertile lands taken in war to supply your Samurai with provisions for their hunger. Pay attention to nourishing your Samurai.

'A well fed Warrior fights with uncommon valor on the field of battle. Never tire your Warriors by foolish exploits and battles not able to be won. You must unite your Samurai in spirit, mind, and body. You must be willing to throw your Warriors in a position from which there is no escape, so they'll fight to the death proudly, and your Samurai must be willing to carry out your orders, and when faced with death, not flee and accept their fate. Prepare them well for death and there'll be nothing they can't achieve for your honor'.

She smiled, she realized as she scanned the map, her warriors were well treated by the traveling women of the willow looking after the needs of their bodies. She understood her samurai would follow her to the fires of Mount Fuji, if she commanded without thought or hesitation. Her samurai trusted her without question. She never heard them grumble disconcerting about her leadership or orders. A samurai upset, would not fight the battle as well as a contented and trusting samurai would. She lived up to her father's warning of being the best general in the master's army.

Turning her attention to the map again, she understood if Lord Wakatsuki controlled Kozuke, he would reinforce his troops invading Kozuke province at his leisure. Then Lord Kawasomeru's armies would be hard pressed and powerless to stop him. The Agano River region was the most strategic sector in this area of the battleground. To control it meant victory over their enemy. Once she worked out her path of attack, she informed the other officers and they stared as she traced her proposed route out on the map laid out before them.

Captain Okita pointed out if her horsemen were trapped in the narrow valley she planned to use, in her attempt to take the high ground on Lord Wakatsuki's warriors. It would mean the slaughter of her horsemen, she would be committing a serious mistake in judgment. By allowing her army to be trapped in a narrow three prong valley with the running waters of the Agano River at her back, thus cutting off any escape for her warriors. If Lord Wakatsuki's army realized this, they would trap her army in the valley, by merely placing armies at the head of each valley's fingers, and allow her to enter his waiting trap then attack her warriors in force.

The young and concerned captain further pointed out to the young female warrior, the valley they were considering to employ for her horse soldiers, was nothing more than a mere narrow passageway through the mountain ridge that made up the banks of the Agano River. It would be foolishness for anyone to allow one's self, or her army to be trapped so hopelessly in the tangle of the earth, he warned Captain Masahiko of.

She smiled at the captain's warning then sneered as she offered if she was successful in her attempt to take the high ground over the warlord and his army. It would give the archers control of the Kii road, while employing the minimum of warriors needed to cut off Lord Wakatsuki's main supply line to his troops warring in Kozuke. She hinted if her army made it through the valley before being cut off. They could come from behind Wakatsuki's army which would likely be poised at the main road leading to Echigo. Once there, her horse soldiers would catch Lord Wakatsuki's forces trapped between General Shimbo's army, and the spearmen of Lieutenant Aoki and Captain Okita archers and foot soldiers and her horsemen. She showed it would be Wakatsuki's army who would find themselves cut off with no hope of escape or survival.

The captain leaned over the map and carefully studied her offered plan of attack and smiled, knowing if her plan was successful. They would own the northeastern part of Echigo province, and would spearhead a path of destruction right through the very center of the province, splitting Lord Wakatsuki's forces in half. Her army would then take their time with destroying what was left of the enemy armies. The captain stared at her while forming his words then offered. "Ieeeee Captain Masahiko-san. If you win the high grounds and trap Lord Wakatsuki's worthless army before you, you'll end the war in six months, bringing great honor to your name and those of your horsemen. If you're brave enough to risk this foolish attempt, I'll vote for it." He announced then looked at Aoki and asked. "Lieutenant Aoki-san! What do you think of Captain Masahiko-san's plan as it was laid out before your foul eyes?"

"Ieeeee Captain Okita-san! It's a wise plan of attack, if our army isn't trapped by Lord Wakatsuki. But what happens to our army if they're trapped by the enemy troops? Captain Masahiko-san, have you given consideration to that happening against your horse soldiers? You know Kawasomeru-sama would never commit more Warriors to come to your aid if you find yourself cut off from our other troops. He would use the course of your losing as a deception then order us to attack the enemy forces from a different position. Thus leaving you and your horse warriors to the terrible fate of annihilation on the battlefield. Think of the appalling disgrace you'll earn for your name, Captain Masahiko-san."

"Ieeeee Lieutenant! I care not one grain of worthless rice for personal gains and respect in this battle. If I did, I'd want to stay behind and be one of a few of Kawasomeru-sama's Warriors who'd remain alive after the battle ran its course. Lieutenant Aoki-san! If Lord Wakatsuki is successful getting his troops in position before us, he'll own most of the upper eastern section of Kozuke. That'll leave us in the same position I want to trap Lord Wakatsuki Warriors in.

"I'm surprised the crafty warlord hasn't yet realized the significance of this region to his evil aims, and captured it before he went after the capital of Kozuke. It was very foolish on his part to allow his northern flanks to remain jeopardized in this fashion by my horsemen. The warlord's foolish generals already accept they'll defeat our armies on the battlefield, and I'll prove that way of thinking wrong to the great fools. I'll be successful in my attack against Wakatsuki's flanks, and destroy his worthless army in the process, or I and my Warriors will die in the attempt." She turned her glaze from the lieutenant and cast it on Captain Okita's face.

The young captain understood he was expected to respond to Captain Masahiko's war plan put forth, deep in his heart he understood she was correct to use this dangerous avenue to begin her attack against their enemy troops. He had to admit that he was pleased she planned to use this dangerous attack, so it would not occur to Lord Kawasomeru, and he might end up being forced to attack from this general region himself. The captain bowed as he offered to the female captain. "Hai Captain Masahiko-san! You must be shinigurai (being crazy to die) to think of attacking an enemy from this foul position. But I admit you're wise to plan to attack Lord Wakatsuki's army from this area. It's a risk all situation you offer, and if successful you'll be remembered as well as we remember the great Samurai Masashige Kusunoki-sama, and your horsemen will win the war for our Lord.

"But if you fail on your quest to destroy our enemy's army, you and your horsemen will be remembered as an army of fools who died a dog's death on the battlefield, for a no good cause on a foolhardy attempt to gain personal honor and respect, at the cost of your Warriors and their horses. Captain Masahiko-san! I'll back you when we bring up this plan to Kawasomeru-sama's attention for his final judgment. I wish you the gyoko of the Kami. I believe you'll need all the luck you can assemble about yourself, if you're to be successful in defeating our teki, our enemy on the field of battle, Captain. I pray to Buddha to ask the gods who wander the world of respect, to smile on this plan, Captain Masahiko-san.

"You're a toda chu, and I'm certain Lord Kawasomeru will repay your loyalty displayed before him on this battle many times over in the future, if you and your Warriors are successful with this supposed attack of yours against our enemy forces." Captain Okita bowed to Captain Masahiko while thinking how she would be in the art of pillowing. He wanted to win the vast bet and prove to the other foolish warriors he was the best pillowing warrior in their ranks.

She returned his bow then asked Lieutenant Aoki when they would be brought before the master of the realm, so they could explain their plan of attack in person.

"Asatte, day after tomorrow will be the earliest Kawasomeru-sama would see anyone presenting their plans for attack to him. I believe our Master was to send a messenger to Chiyoda Castle. In an attempt to see if our Lord could talk the foolish Lord Wakatsuki into stopping this war before it got out of hand, and the entire realm erupted in war. He fears the Shogun might step in and take a hand in this war." Lieutenant Aoki moaned.

"Ieeeee! And I might grow wings from my arse and fly with the gods if that happens, fool. The great Shogun has his own problems that he must contend with, so he will ignore the problems of the sixteen provinces of Central Japan until he can no longer turn his back on this ongoing situation." Captain Okita griped as he suddenly flung his hand in the air, dismissing Lieutenant Aoki's thoughts of an end to the wars.

"Huh! I agree with Captain Okita-san's assumption over this present situation. The only solution to this war between the two houses of Central Japan, is the total destruction of the foolish Lord Wakatsuki's evil influence over the eight other provinces of the region. It's been many years and every time we think the realm is going to experience years without war, Lord Wakatsuki comes out of his forests and does something new to upset the Wa of peace threatening to overtake the region. We suffered through countless years of wars in this region, and the only way to end them is to end Wakatsuki-sama's existence. It's been taught throughout life, to kill a snake one must cut off the head of the serpent, not the tail. I believe the only way to stop Lord Wakatsuki's wild ambitions, is you must destroy him. Then his unworthy ambitions will die with his cursed spirit."

The officers agreed with Captain Masahiko's assumption for the upcoming battle against Lord Wakatsuki's troops. The officers swore an oath they would spend their breath to destroy Lord Wakatsuki, and his aims and armies. Then rid the realm of his leadership over his eight provinces of central Japan.

CHAPTER TWENTY FOUR

Master Trainer Tanizaki waited the mandatory three days for mourning his wife. On the morning of the forth day he woke early. He carefully wrapped a silk cloth around the thumb of his right hand below the knuckle and pulled it tight. He then went to the drawer and removed a tanto knife with a razor edge. He was cutting off his thumb as instructed by Lord Kawasomeru, because this was the finger he allowed to be sliced on the first sword he used in the defense of Lord Kawasomeru's father, Magosaburo-sama and his heirs. He used the bloody finger to place his mark next to his name on the scrolls as he took the oath of obedience, and the samurai code to fight with his heart and soul for Magosaburo-sama. He extended his finger with courage and placed it under the edge of the blade. Then, with super human strength, he brought the knife down, severing it below the knuckle.

The trainer's general scooped up the thumb using a piece of silk cloth, and wrapped it up and placed it in a lacquered box. He was ordered to bring the thumb to Kawasomeru as proof he did as ordered. The general was with the trainer's wife when she died, and saw the look in her eyes, they seemed to know Tanizaki was poisoning her, and believed she welcomed the quick death he was offering her. The general remembered how peacefully her eyes closed for the last time, with a slight trace of a smile across her lips. He was crushed over the lady's honorable death.

He rushed off to bring the severed thumb to his master. The trainer spent the remainder of time stopping the bleeding of his hand, and preparing for his death to befall him. He placed tags with name of persons he selected to possess certain items of his, and made sure he left enough wealth and rewards to Remi, so she would be a free woman who could look after herself.

When he was certain he looked after everything needing to be looked after, he plopped down on the top of the chest which served as a chair, and waited for his general's return. He looked at his hand, the blood stopped flowing. He released the pressure from the silk cord and blood seeped again, but it no longer flowed. He decided to allow it to bleed, at least with the pressure off it, it no longer throbbed as bad.

The general returned to the trainer's room in the castle as quickly as he could, he was carrying a tanto blade wrapped in silk cloth, and offered it to the old master trainer.

"What is this?" The old man asked of his old friend and general.

"It's a gift offered you from Kawasomeru-sama. He said it'd be an honor if you use his blade to commit suppuku. He wants you to take it into the fires of Mount Fuji with you. Our Master wish me to inform you it was with immense sorrow he made the decision to cast you in the void of the fiery mountain. But he feels you'll find Lady Emiko waiting for you there in, and together you can train the gods of the Floating World on how to behave properly, Tanizaki-san."

Master Trainer Tanizaki gave out with an agreeing grunt as he took possession of the small knife and offered. "What do you think torturer of the truth? Is the wise Kawasomeru-sama punishing, or is he honoring my old bones, General Kobayashi-san?"

"Ieeeee great one! Our Lord is paying you great homage, I see nothing malicious hidden in either his aim or thoughts over this matter. He's wise beyond thought, and is concerned with your honorable death, Tanizaki-san." Kobayashi offered to the old man standing before him.

"I agree, General Kobayashi-san. I believe we wasted enough time over this subject. Shall we go my old friend? I grown tired of this foul world we dwell in. I find myself looking forward to seeing what awaits me in the next world I'll soon visit." The trainer turned serious as he added to his words to his military officer. "General Kobayashi-san! You been a loyal and true friend who looked after me, and stopped me on numerous occasions from making mistakes, many that would have cost me my head. For this I thank you, but I must beg another favor of you I fear."

"Hai?" The general asked when Tanizaki took a second to take a quick breath.

"General Kobayashi-san! Look after Masahiko-san well for me. She's strong headed and rash and wild at times I worry. She has something to prove to the foolish world with every breath she inhales. Look after her as you looked after this old fool and she'll be safe, and live a long and honorable and successful life, General Kobayashi-san."

"Master Trainer Tanizaki-san! It'd be a honorable duty of which I'll accept proudly to look after the young Warrior, even though she needs no looking after."

He bowed as he stood and placed the tanto blade in his silk sash and headed for the shoji. Together, the respected warriors walked out the front gate and headed down road towards the foot of Mount Fuji. Two horses were waiting for them at the seventh bridge.

Ever since she woke, she was plagued by a feeling of pending disaster. Though she didn't feel threatened personally, something about the day bothered her and she placed her swords in her sash, even while she was safe in her building. The female warrior made herself inconspicuous. She felt the less the samurai saw her, the more they would accept her presence in their caste. She had trouble concentrating on anything, and the next day she was to meet with Kawasomeru. The warlord put off the meeting for the past two days.

An owl hooted ominously in the early afternoon, adding to her feelings of doom. It was a sign someone close to her was about to die. She couldn't get her mind off her sister Estsuko, she was happy when she learned she was enlisted by Lord Kawasomeru for his personal staff, because she was able to read and write the characters of language. But the feeling she had, warned she might be in danger. She never dared to think it might be her father whose life was about to end.

MOUNT FUJI

At exactly sunset, Master Trainer Tanizaki and General Kobayashi reached the first vent of Mount Fuji. Steam and hot ash rose angrily out of the aperture, but it saved him from having to climb to the very top of the mountain, which could have taken him two days to accomplish. Without words, the general handed the old trainer the box containing ashes of his wife. He watched as he dipped a finger in the ash then smeared it across his forehead. He then poured the remaining ash in the boiling smoke hole of the angry mountain.

Captain Masahiko was so drained by the consuming feeling of pending disaster, she gave in to the weariness and laid down on her bedroll to rest. But sleep would not come to her.

The already exhausted master trainer knelt before the vent then took the small blade from his sash and opened the front of his kosode and then prepared himself for the final obedience to his lord and master. He turned to General Kobayashi and bowed and offered to him. "General Kobayashi-san! Thank you for being my friend and honorable retainer, you made my life worthy." The old man folded the rice paper around the handle of the blade.

The general moved nearer to the old man, and after showing him he bathed his katana sword clean in the pure water, he allowed him to see the blade.

The master trainer nodded slightly in approval then plunged the knife in his stomach. His innards seeped out of the gash he made across his belly.

At the same instant he sliced himself open the general swung his blade, instantly chopping the old man's head from his shoulders. Thus, making it possible for his death to be swift and painless as possible. When he was certain the old man was dead, he carefully pushed his body into the boiling vent. He then picked up and cleaned off the head of dirt respectfully with his hands, and looked into the unseeing eyes of the old man and ceremoniously dropped the head in the vent. He picked up the tanto blade and heaved it in the vent along with the trainer's body. He cursed then offered a short prayer for his old friend and then went back to the horses. He mounted his and held the other horse's reins and rode off to return to the castle and report to his lord and master of Tanizaki's deed.

LORD KAWASOMERU'S ENCAMPMENT

Locked in the darkness of her private building, Captain Masahiko's eyes suddenly flew open as she sat up with a start. One word crossed her trembling lips. "FATHER!" She cried as tears flowed freely, and her heart was crushed. A terrible feeling of being all alone on the earth completely engulfed her being. She rolled over and cried like a child, unashamed. Her mind understood a great light in her life was just snuffed out forever. Her father was dead, she knew it, she had no way of knowing for certain, but her inner self understood her father was moving among the non living world of her dead ancestors. Outside the building, the captain of her personal guard heard her crying and tapped lightly on the shoji door of her quarters to see if there was something he might be able to do for her suffering.

She barked out as angrily as she could at the voice. "What!"

"Captain Masahiko-san! May I be of any help to you? I have a good ear for listening, and a trusted mouth that'll not speak of troubles shared with me. I know what you're going through, and I respect your courage and honor, Captain Masahiko-san."

Her head spun, her soul cried in agony for another soul to be with on this long, terribly lonely night. "Hai Captain Katsunoke Seisakajo-san! You may enter."

The young good looking captain entered and saw her lying on the bedroll, her kosode opened exposing her breasts. He walked over and knelt and in a soft voice asked what was troubling her.

"My father has just left this earth, Captain." She cried, tears flowing again.

The young Captain Seisakajo smiled as he pulled her close, and allowed her to cry against his chest. This was what she needed more than anything in the world, she really began to cry as she buried her head deep in the captain's chest.

"How do you know of this death of your father, Captain Masahiko-san?" He asked with concern lacing his tone.

"I heard his mind silently bidding me good-bye forever." She wailed at him.

"You heard this in your mind? Is this normal for a Warrior to hear voices in one's mind." The captain tried to make light of her misery, but his attempt failed. But what happened next he wasn't expecting. When she looked up then kissed him, he didn't know how to respond.

Passion overruled their better sense as she pulled desperately on the captain's kosode with a need, a passion. Kissing his chest and neck with abandonment, with a passion she never realized existed. He was caught up in the same emotion as he pulled on her kosode, pawing at her breasts, kissing and sucking on the hardening nipples, and reaching between her legs. She reached between his legs, finding the rock hard finger as she called the male member.

She pulled the captain to her bedroll with what was left of his kosode with surprising strength, and joined her and with patience and tenderness, entering her slowly. He knew she was a virgin, so he took care to give her as much pleasure as he could with her first coupling. A cry escaped her lips, her teeth held tight together, but her need to be with someone at this time in her life overrode the slight discomfort she was experiencing with what he was doing to her body. Soon, she was moving with rhythm and passion that guided her through life since birth. The deeply concerned young Captain Seisakajo didn't want to make her pregnant so he pulled out, coming on her flat tight stomach.

She was so caught up in her wild passions, she didn't know he had withdrawn from her, but when the warmth landed on her stomach she opened her eyes. She touched the milky white liquid on her belly then ran it between her fingers while studying it closely. She looked at the captain with questioning eyes.

"Huh! You're truly without experience, that's the sacred fluid of life Masahiko-san." The smiling young military officer remarked.

She stared at it confused, smelt it, and tasted it. "Does this mean I'm with child."

"No my brave one, I wouldn't allow that to happen on our first pillowing."

"Good, I'm very pleased Captain Seisakajo-san. Ieeeee! I was unaware of what pleasures I was missing all these wasted years of my worthless life. That was wonderful, is it always as pleasurable to enjoy Captain? Can we do it again please Captain Seisakajo-san? This time making it last longer, something wonderful happened to me at the end of our pillowing. My body felt as if it was floating in the afterworld, and I was suffering no ill will, Captain Seisakajo-san." She moaned as she stretched with her hands over her head and crossed her kegs, allowing the captain to see all of her nakedness.

"By the gods who no longer enjoy a woman's pleasure, you're a beautiful woman, Captain Masahiko-san! Someone I'd be pleased to spend the rest of my life with, to honor if you'd allow, to have this worthless fool standing by your side for life." He tenderly cupped her breast again.

She purred sexily, forgetting all about the despair she suffered just moments ago, happy a man, any man found her desirable and wanted her. But her mind entered her thoughts and it put an instant end to this wonderful feeling. She stiffened then snapped at the captain. "That's impossible, we must never do this foul act of pillowing again as long as we live. I'm totally embarrassed over my weakness of body and mind. I'm ashamed at myself and you must forgive a weak woman's unworthiness. Leave at once Captain, I'm aware of the wagers made at my cost. You should feel proud, you're a rich man now." She hissed as she wrapped her torn kosode around her and turned her back on the stunned warrior.

"Ieeeee Captain Masahiko-san you accuse me falsely I assure you. I'm a Samurai with honor, and not part of that childish wager. I made love to you because I felt you needed someone to be with, you had a special need and I was proud to be there for your need. No word of this coupling will ever cross my worthless lips, no matter how much money the fools offer. I coupled with you with my heart, nothing else, there was no ill in my heart. If you want me to leave, I'll go. But I feel deeply for you, and will protect and respect you with every drop of my blood." The captain stood and bowed to her then turned to leave.

"Wait a moment Captain Seisakajo-san! I believe I want further words with you before you leave my side." She barked at him.

He turned and stared in her lovely eyes.

"Will we do this pillowing again, Captain Seisakajo-san? When I have need of someone to be with in my times of urgency for the pleasures of the pillow?" She asked cautiously.

"Hai! Whenever you want company let me know. I'll be pleased to help you live through any time of need, Masahiko-san. I'll do anything to make you happy." He offered to her tenderly.

"Hmmmm! I believe I'll call on you when the feeling of wanting comes over me again Captain Seisakajo-san. It was a most enjoyable experience to share, one I'd like to live over in my future, Captain." She said with enthusiasm as she turned her back on the captain, pulling her kosode close to her body. Enjoying the warmth of her arms wrapped around her nakedness.

He took this to be his dismissal and resumed his position as guard of the door. All his senses were on alert for treachery.

A second guard who saw the young captain enter the building and spend time with the wonder samurai, moved to him and offered with a sneer. "Ieeeee Captain Seisakajo-san. How was the male female Warrior in the act of pillowing?"

He glared as he hissed with contempt at the nosy warrior taunting him. "Huh! I should tell Captain Masahiko-san that you think she coupled with me, fool. I'm certain she'd be most pleased to seek revenge on your evil tongue for its useless wagging, fool. I didn't couple with the female Samurai, though I would've been honored to do so. If I hear of word to the contrary from any other Samurai, I'll lop off your head then use it for a piss pot. Get back to your guard position or I'll report your failure to duty to Lord Kawasomeru." He glared a second time at the young guard until he moved off.

The guard was confused on whether or not he coupled with Masahiko. Finally, he shrugged, not caring if he did or not. It meant nothing because it wasn't he who coupled with her, so it wasn't he eligible for the cash prize offered for the pleasure of pillowing such the female prize. He smiled as he thought of the face he would have earned, if he was the one to pillow with Captain Masahiko, the daughter of the famed and feared master trainer.

She was awake when the samurai guard tapped on the door. She was informed Lord Kawasomeru sent him to fetch her for an audience. He was interested in her plans of war and wanted her to explain them further. She dressed in her best kosode, tied the obi sash around her waist and placed the Sugahara swords in the obi. She fixed her hair which looked strange because she allowed the skull cap to grow in. Then she pushed her shoulders back and marched behind the samurai, her guards following silently in step after her.

The palace guards stopped the guards of hers from entering the castle, and ordered them to stand in the lower garden to await their captain's return. She was led up the three flights of teak stairs to the room where her father shared the magnificent sunrise with Lord Kawasomeru, on the day he ordered his death.

The powerful warlord sat before a long low table resting on an overstuffed pillow. To his left sat First General Satauki Okumura, General Shimbo, and to his left, General Kobayashi. Sitting off the platform were Generals Miyamoto, Kometani, and Yoshizawa. Captain Okita and Field Captain Tachibana stared at her who was said to be the saving warrior going to be the one to turn the tide of the war for her master against Lord Wakatsuki.

She dropped to her knees and touched her forehead to the floor waiting for the warlord to allow her to speak. He cleared his throat then hawked and spat while scratching himself between the legs as he grumbled. "Captain

Masahiko-san! I was informed by my Generals you worked out a plan of attack to win this troubling war. Enlighten this fool on how you plan to accomplish this feat, Samurai." He spread his arms apart in a gesture for her to begin her explanation.

She stood and moved to the maps on the table, and began to read to get the feel of the maps.

General Shimbo suddenly jumped to his feet and warned in an angry voice. "Leave your worthless swords by the door of this room, Captain Masahiko-san."

The warlord glared angrily at his upsetting general as he snapped at him in a commanding and strong voice. "Captain Masahiko-san is one of my most trusted and respected military officers, this fact alone entitles this young Samurai to remain armed in my presence. It's her duty to be armed, General Shimbo-san."

"Hai." The general said as he bowed to Lord Kawasomeru, his face red with anger and embarrassment from being yelled at by the master over this deceitful child, who stood so defiantly before him and the rest of the officers.

She ignored the anger in the general's eyes as she looked over the map, it took her ten minutes to explain her plan to the officers, and lord of the realm. The generals, Shimbo included, refused to give the plan credence, citing she would lead five hundred horsemen to their slaughter over a fool hearted chance to get in Lord Wakatsuki's flanks. General Kometani pointed out that Lord Wakatsuki would not be so stupid as to leave his southern flanks open to attack, so a young pup of a captain could march an army in his ranks and rip apart his army from within.

Being a wise commander, the warlord allowed his generals to do his talking, while he weighed their worries offered against Masahiko's attack plan. When he heard enough he stood and started to pace behind his pillow. He stopped pacing and looked at Tanizaki's child, and said with a snort. "Hai Captain Masahiko-san! Do you feel you and your horse soldiers will be able to drive this wedge into the heart of Lord Wakatsuki's worthless flanks?"

"Hai my wise Lord and Master of life. Easily I offer to my Liege Lord. I don't expect the evil Lord Wakatsuki would ever consider such an attack to occur in his flanks by my horse soldiers." The proud warrior offered to her master.

"Ieeeee Captain Masahiko-san! If you're able to do this attack successfully, you'll shorten the war by years, saving many proud Warriors in turn, and you'll be instrumental in destroying my teki, my enemy for all times. It's a gamble, but a gamble worth taking. I give permission to move your horsemen in position of attack. When do you think you'll be prepared to attack?"

"Lord Kawasomeru, I believe it'll take me few sticks of time to get used to the horsemen you offer, and fourteen sticks of time to ride to the position of attack. I could be prepared to begin my attack in twenty one sticks of time." She offered as she shifted her eyes to General Shimbo.

The warlord rubbed his chin as he thought over her boastful words and attack plan. He checked the day, it was the seventh day of the second week of the ninth month of the one thousand, three hundred and fifty second year and remarked. "Captain Masahiko-san! I expect you to begin your attack on the seventh day of the first week of the tenth month. Have your forces in position by that time, all depends on your horsemen, I'll commit my spearmen and archers on this day if you begin your attack or not, Captain. I'll fight even if you're cut off and slaughtered to the last in your army. In case you don't realize it, I'll use your Samurai to begin my attack against Wakatsuki's forces, you'll be on your own and I'll not aid you. You chose an impossible task. Don't waste my Warriors foolishly, Captain Masahiko-san." He warned.

"Hai my Lord, I'll succeed and not seek support from you. I understand this battle is mine to win. I'll not lose my Lord." She bowed to Lord Kawasomeru then to the generals and officers. Only a few returned her courtesy. Many were still upset a woman was leading samurai in battle.

"Huh, I assure you you will, young and foolish Samurai. You started down the long muryogo no michi, the never ending road carved out by war and despair for Japan, Captain Masahiko-san. I hope you're the Warrior ancient myth speaks of, the Samurai who'll deliver us from the very teeth of war and the uncountable death that war brings to the children of Japan. You're dismissed so go and find your destiny, Captain Masahiko-san!" Lord Kawasomeru growled as he turned to First General Satauki Okumura and spoke with him now.

Two palace guards moved then marched her out of the room in silence.

She rushed to her quarters and grabbed everything of what she believed she would need to lead the battle then headed to the stable. Before she entered the structure, she ordered the young Captain Seisakajo to have her horsemen assemble at the umaya. The warrior rushed from the building carrying her armor and bow. The stables were constructed in the northern part of the Keep, constructed downwind of the castle, and the main area of the capital. It took her ten minutes to rush the distance, her arms aching due to the weight of her pieces of armor, and other equipment and weapons. She was surprised to see General Kobayashi with the horsemen. She bowed as her guards fanned out protectively behind her.

General Kobayashi returned the bow as politely to the young female warrior child.

She handed her armor to Captain Seisakajo, who she found herself leaning on for more than pillowing and closeness. When he took the armor from her, she walked to General Kobayashi and took his arm and led him from the others under her orders. She said low to him as she looked the general in the eyes. "General Kobayashi-san! I wish to have private words with you."

He nodded and followed her in silence.

When they were far from listening ears, she whispered. "General Kobayashi-san! My father is dead! Were you with him at the time of his passing?"

He stared at her with disbelieving eyes, stunned to his soul over she was somehow aware of her father's death. His mind cursed as it searched for the name of the one who betrayed a trust over her father's death to the warrior. The general knew Kawasomeru was going to be roaring mad over the fact she knew of her father's death. He didn't respond, nor did he deny her words.

It was all the proof she needed to assure her father was dead. She saw the look in his eyes and understood the meaning of what she was reading in them. "General Kobayashi-san! No one told me my father died, I felt it here." She tapped her heart then added. "I felt the pain of his death here, and in my mind. His mind spoke his last words with mine. Were you with him when he died, General? I come to an understanding with his honored death."

He was suddenly in fear of this mystical young woman standing before him waiting his reply. Were her words true, could she actually communicate with her father at his death, and if so, what were the words spoken between them? Should he kill this child of the gods with such an understanding of life and death? Was she controlled by the kami from the underworld. Is she evil, what to do, what to do? His mind screamed.

"General! I'm waiting words to come forth. I repeat with impatience, were you with my father at his death!" She demanded for the first time from the stunned general, harshly.

"Hai! I was with him Masahiko-san" He replied with hesitation in his voice.

"Did my father die by his hands my old friend? Did he commit suppuku, General?"

"Hai! He committed suppuku proudly, Masahiko-san."

"Did you second his death? He died an honorable death? He didn't die alone did he?"

"Hai Captain Masahiko-san! I seconded his death. He died an honorable death, young one. A death to be proud of, as proud as the way the great Samurai lived his life." He replied as he continued to stare at the child with all seeing eyes.

"Thank you General! I'll speak no more of this tragedy to my heart and mind. To know my honorable father died a true Samurai's death is comforting to my Wa and mind, General." She bowed greatly to the confused general. She dared not ask who ordered her father's death, for fear of how she might react against the knowledge. She turned back to the horsemen.

For the next three sticks of time, she rode hard and ran countless war games, and gave the horsemen exercises to accomplish. She tested skills and their ability to work with each other, and see how smart they were, and what they knew of the art of waging war. She was pleased by the testing, and picked out the better trained samurai who would lead the other warriors to battle, and singled out the few she wouldn't trust to be part of her army. She sent them packing to the ranks of the hinin class.

General Kobayashi stayed with her, carrying out his oath given to her father, but his duty of working with an army of spearmen was taking up most of his time lately. By the third day of her working with her horsemen, the general was forced to leave the area with his spearmen. Because it was going to take them longer to get in position, as they would be traveling the long distance to the battlefield by foot.

The days of her working with the horsemen were exhausting and long, at night instead of sleeping she went over strategies, preparing her mind for battle. Every conceivable way of her army being cut off by Lord Wakatsuki armies was discussed and went over time and again. She didn't want to leave a chance of defeat unexamined, she wanted to be prepared to react to his possible moves against her horsemen. Any attempt of his armies to cut off her retreat had to be examined, and prevented while leaving her army intact to fight the main engagement.

On the day before her horsemen were scheduled to leave the Castle Keep, she was suddenly summoned to a private audience by her lord and master. She was surprised it was a singular meeting between just her and the master of the realm. The powerful Daimyo offered her some cha and then went over the reason he sent for her.

"Captain Masahiko-san! Out of my most loyal Officers and Warriors, none have dared to challenge Wakatsuki's forces in this manner you chose to attack him. It pleases me you were so well trained in the art of war by your father over the years past. It's a shame your first battle for me will be your last on this earth."

She bowed as she dared to interrupt her master. "At the risk of displaying foul manners to my Liege Lord. I find myself forced to disagree with your assumption of my plan, my Lord. This is not to be my last battle on earth, it'll be the first of a long list of battles in which I'll be successful for my Liege Lord. I don't intend to lose any battles my Lord of the earth and sky."

"Ieeeee Captain Masahiko-san! I see your honorable father has instilled his unconquerable spirit and will in your body. To hear of your so proud but rather foolish boast, makes me believe that you have half a chance to succeed in this unwise attack against Lord Wakatsuki's worthless army." He grunted as he poured a second cup of tea.

"I'll succeed in battle my Lord. I know of no other thought to believe my Lord and Master." The female captain responded to her liege lord.

"Huh foolish Captain Masahiko-san! Not with the worthless Warriors that I gave to you to attack our enemy with, Captain Masahiko-san. They're not enough in number or in training to go against Wakatsuki's well trained armies and survive the engagement for long. This is why I called you here before me. Tomorrow morning, you'll start on your long journey to the Kii pass, to prepare your trap for Lord Wakatsuki's god cursed army. I decided to increase your army to five thousand Warriors. This way, maybe you'll have the strength in numbers to cut a swath through my enemy, and gain entrance to their flanks. If you can force them to turn their defenses to face and defend against your attack, I'll cut them into dung heaps with my attack against the fools." The liege lord boasted and raised his hand over his head and clenched his fist.

"I shall succeed in my quest my Lord, and the blood of your enemies will stain the ground red I walk upon. Or I'll take my life for my failure, my Lord." She growled as she bowed.

"You'll go with the gods protecting you and your fine Warriors, Captain Masahiko-san! I'll not see you until after your great victory over our enemy has come to past, and we celebrate the demise of the rebel dog eating Wakatsuki, and his armies of evil."

She stood and left the room without further word, pumped up by his words, along with the knowledge she had more warriors to work with now.

That night went quickly and the next morning, she headed for the stables ready to ride to battle. She smiled when she noticed her horse warriors were mounted and waiting her to arrive, and lead them to victory on the battlefield promised them by her. Five thousand of her lord's finest horse warriors were stationed in tight formation, the first five hundred ill trained soldiers were nowhere to be seen. Captain Seisakajo rode alongside and gave her a quick nod.

"Captain Masahiko-san! These five thousand horse Warriors are many Samurai trained by your honorable father's hand. They're used to his way of thinking and fighting, Lord Kawasomeru felt this would make it simpler for you to work with them. They're a fraction of our Master's horsemen. It's believed his army of horsemen count over one hundred and twenty five thousand Warriors. Our Master pays you homage to be given such a powerful army as these fearless soldiers. I'm proud to be part of your army, Captain Masahiko-san."

She bowed to her lover Captain Seisakajo for sharing this information with her, as they rode up to the other officers at the head of the warrior formation. Captain Toshihiro Tachibana sat mounted with Lieutenant Takao Kiribuchi and Lieutenant Yasuyuki Kusado. Captain Tachibana who she recognized from her meeting with Lord Kawasomeru, introduced the other officers. She bowed to each and fell in formation with them. Proudly, she waved her arm and the column of horsemen moved out as one. There was little speaking, and the sounds of the horse's hooves beating on the ground filled the air.

Captain Tachibana dared to ride up alongside her right side, the sword side, the forbidden side. Seisakajo rode to her left. She didn't mind the intrusion of her space, she felt this officer wasn't a threat against her person. She acknowledged his presence with a slight nod and he spoke.

"Captain Masahiko-san! I'm hoping to reach the Village of Snakes on this day which is a fifth of the way to the Shinano, Echigo and Kozuke borders. This will put our warriors five sticks of time from the border, and another ten sticks of time from the Kii pass where we'll attack the warriors under Lord Wakatsuki's command."

"Hai! This is a good strategy to employ, but I'm concerned about the feeding and looking after the minor comforts of an army this size. While we march on Kozuke and Echigo to attack Wakatsuki, Captain Tachibana-san." She offered with concern as she stared at the captain.

"Huh Captain Masahiko-san! Were you not informed by Captain Okita-san that there were many worthless villages we'll be staying at along the way at night, under direct orders from Kawasomeru-sama to shelter and feed and make latrines accessible to our warrior's needs, for our trek for battle? We went over this situation with our Lord and Master, and he picked this path to travel, because of these villages scheduled to support our Warriors as we marched for battle, Captain." Captain Tachibana grunted in an angry tone.

"Iye! All we went over at the meeting were plans for my attack against our enemy troops." She replied, relieved the welfare of her warriors were taken in consideration by their master.

"Huh! I'll speak to the worthless fool when next we meet. He should've taken this minor worry off your mind, the manure heap he is, Captain Masahiko-san." The upset Captain Tachihiro growled as he looked ahead and placed an ugly scowl on his face.

She didn't reply as her warriors reached their destination of the Village of Snakes, just as the sun was preparing to go behind the mountains for its night's rest. The samurai were starved and the villagers took good care of them. She spoke with her officers as they ate, she went over their plan of attack carefully, so she was certain the warriors knew what was expected of them in this upcoming battle. She felt the other officers couldn't hear the attack plan enough to understand it completely. When they finished eating, they bedded down in the field where a number of smudge pots burned to keep the swarms of mosquitoes from the warrior, and every fifty feet stood a guard. Her warriors were fanned out in a protective circle around her, with Captain Seisakajo sleeping closest to her. The morning could not come soon enough for all concerned, the horses even seemed eager to set out to do battle.

The massive column of warriors moved off at a slow pace to start as not to raise a dust cloud, and alert Lord Wakatsuki's warriors. She was trying to keep their position a secret for as long as possible from their enemy. She had no idea Lord Wakatsuki was in possession of her planned attack against him and his warriors, and the warlord was taking steps to put a quick end to this so called chosen samurai and her efforts to destroy his army.

She stared in awe over the wonderful sights she witnessed for the first time in life, as her army rode to their destiny. The different villages they rode through, and strange new lifestyles of the villagers interested her. Nowhere she traveled before this, did she feel threatened.

Her liege lord was commanding an army of ten thousand horse warriors, fifteen thousand spear samurai and twenty five thousand foot soldiers and follow on forces. General Shimbo was in command of a force of warriors as large as Lord Kawasomeru's. First Field General Okumura was in command of the largest army of the three. His responsibility was to place Wakatsuki's Chiyoda Castle under siege by his army if Lord Kawasomeru and his armies were able to engage Lord Wakatsuki's army, and keep them occupied until Lord Wakatsuki's castle fell to General Okumura's forces. Lord Kawasomeru's attack was massive and a good one which fell in place when she came up with the missing part of the plan he already knew of, and was planning for. The powerful warlord didn't know who to order to make the fool hearted attack from that position until the female warrior offered to.

Deep in his heart he felt Masahiko's army was going to be slaughtered to the last, but she and her army will not have died in vain for his cause. If he was able to attack Lord Wakatsuki while he was engaging her army attacking his flanks, there was a chance of his army splitting Lord Wakatsuki's army in a number of smaller, and easier defeatable fragments. If this occurred, he would eliminate each of the fragmented armies, providing Captain Masahiko's army held out long enough for his attack to succeed on the field of battle against the enemy warlord.

The hard march by Lord Kawasomeru's massive armies was taking a terrible toll on his warriors and equipment.

Some warriors died from sheer exhaustion, others were killed in different accidents, and a few horse warriors were injured when their horses threw them or stumbled. Food and water were at times, very scarce to find and in one village, his army had to hack the village population to death, because they refused to offer any food and shelter to the samurai, claiming there wasn't enough food for them and the samurai to eat.

Her horse army fared the best on their trek, making good time on their march. Her warriors past clean streams coming from the distant mountains, because she headed in a northeasterly direction towards the mountain range to the far north, which housed the almost impassable Kii valley, referred to as the great Kii pass. The villages in this region of the realm were among the richest and largest in Shinano province, and this fact made them more than willing to share their food and supplies with the countless samurai. Many villagers were friendly to Captain Masahiko and her army and in some instances, they went out of their way to make certain the samurai had food and drink needed to sustain them.

One village her army past through, the people offered food, sake and even some women to share the night, usually the women went to the officers and samurai of higher positions. The villagers were unaware that the commander was a female, and they offered her a women to spend the night with. The same experience happened to her on their way to Kii valley.

She was pleased on how well her warriors were holding up on their march to battle. Their youth and strength made it possible for her to increase their pace, and enabling the samurai to pick up a full day and a half traveling in under a week and four days of time. General Shimbo was sharing the same kind of luck on his journey towards the future battlefield, and this enabled him and his warriors to progress further than expected of his army of samurai. Even the weather was working out well with the armies.

General Okumura shared the luxury of being able to increase his army's pace, and found himself and his massive army entering Echigo from Dewa province on a section that Lord Kawasomeru was aware Wakatsuki would not think one of his enemy's armies would dare employ against the warlord. Dewa was Shogun Ashikaga's province, and so far the Shogun was staying out of the wars plaguing the central provinces.

The section of province General Okumura's army was going to employ was the roughest area to traverse on the future battlefield in their quest to sneak up on Lord Wakatsuki's army, and attack them from an area least expected.

CHAPTER TWENTY FIVE
ON THE SEVENTH DAY OF THE FIRST WEEK OF THE TENTH MONTH OF THE YEAR THIRTEEN FIFTY TWO

On the seventh day on march, Captain Masahiko's army of horse warriors finally reached their assigned position. It was the height of the bad season, but the eastern and lower northern provinces were spared many of the powerful storms raging around the capital of Kyoto. For the past five days the capital and lower western provinces were being ripped apart by the feared and powerful typhoons, and a third was expected following the next day. Fighting in this region stopped as the warring provinces found they needed the help from their neighboring provinces. Shogun Ashikaga was certain once these storms passed, the civil wars would never start again. This was the worse typhoon season Japan suffered. The devastation was horrendous, with many smaller provinces were sure to be absorbed by the stronger ones, adding to the growing possibility of lasting peace in the lower provinces of Japan.

She felt the pressures changing in the weather, and knew the lower provinces was taking a pounding by the angry gods who sent the foul weather to assault Japan. There was nothing she could do about the weather, her concern was to enter Kii pass the next morning at daybreak. Then attack the enemy armies of Wakatsuki wherever she found them. When her army entered the region, she sent scouts out to locate Wakatsuki's armies. She wanted to make certain her army wasn't riding into a trap. The spies rode off while she ordered her warriors from their horses to rest them and their horses for the next day's engagement. When she was certain her samurai were taken care of, she sent her personal samurai guards out, to fetch her military officers for their last meeting before they opened their attack against Lord Wakatsuki's armies.

LORD WAKATSUKI'S ENCAMPMENT

Lord Wakatsuki's scouts returned to their encampment and reported to their master when Captain Masahiko's warriors stopped, and pitched tents for the night. They reported of her army's strength, and where they would enter the narrow Kii pass. Armed with this information, he checked his war map. He surveyed the area until he found the region he wanted to spring his trap against this child warrior of the gods. He pointed to a three prong fork where he could place three separate armies, he would commit against this supposed god picked warrior. He realized he wouldn't need many warriors in one pass, because it was too narrow for this young pup to use for an escape route, or to attack from.

His first general, Masakatsu Motoshima explained how a mere three hundred archers and spearmen, would be able to hold the pass and stop Masahiko from breaking out in their flanks. The feared General Motoshima offered they could pull a number of the samurai from the army committed to defend the second finger leading out of the narrow valley, to booster the other army's positions that would bear the brunt of Captain Masahiko's attack. Satisfied with this plan or defense from his general, he gave his officer permission to commit the samurai needed to destroy this enemy warrior, and the army that followed her to battle against him.

Neither Lord Wakatsuki or General Motoshima gave consideration to what would happen if Captain Masahiko's army charged down the narrowest finger pass, to escape their trap against her troops. The wise general didn't pick up if Captain Masahiko's army was able to overwhelm the archers in this pass, they would break out in their flanks and wreak havoc, and forcing Lord Wakatsuki to turn his army. To deal with the invading horse warriors about to deal a lethal blow to his plans of destroying Lord Kawasomeru on the great plain.

The general left the tent and walked to the five thousand horse samurai, and gave the order to take up positions to defend against Captain Masahiko's pending attack. They were to allow their enemies warriors to pass their positions unmolested then permit Captain Masahiko's army to enter the three finger pass. Once the enemy captain's forces were in the pass, the horse samurai were to move out and seal the pass from escape from the enemy warriors. General Motoshima heard the unbelievable stories of this captain Masahiko's bravery on the field of honor, he was not going to give this warrior the possibility of adding to her name at his expense. He smirked over the unbelievable stories he heard about this warrior spawn by the gods. The one he liked best was the one that said this warrior was a female.

"Huh!" The first general grunted. "As if a lowly woman would ever be allowed to enter the guarded Samurai Caste, let alone make such a name for herself on the field of battle was a tall tale not to be believed." He scoffed at Lord Kawasomeru who he felt was behind this tall tale. He figured it was a rumor started by the wise warlord, to increase the wealth of this samurai's name. General Motoshima raised his sword to the Heavens as he barked. "I'll split this chosen Warrior up the middle to prove he's a he and human. Follow me, our Master's enemy is waiting on the other side of these mountains."

Five thousand horsemen moved out, followed by ten thousand spearmen and foot soldiers. It was a great army to send to do battle against five thousand horse soldiers, but these warriors were trained by the respected Tanizaki, if he trained them then they were an army to be respected and feared. And to be led by the eighth son of Master Trainer Tanizaki, made it all the more important to savagely attack this small army as if it was ten times its size.

Lord Wakatsuki's second army moved out as well, as did the three hundred archers chosen to defend the narrow finger pass, leading out of the trap he was setting for this warrior child.

CAPTAIN MASAHIKO'S ENCAMPMENT

Captain Masahiko's scouts reported they found no trace of the enemy. The spies were yet to be heard from, they were to report by carrier pigeons to their commander. This was the reason why Wakatsuki held back his armies until the last moment, knowing the Tanizaki child would send out scouts to check the surrounding area of the narrow pass. He sent a number of his spies out to intercept Captain Masahiko's spies and destroy them.

It was late and she ordered her warriors to sleep, or rest the best they could for their upcoming battle. The night passed quickly, and at last it was time to attack their enemy. She dressed in her armor then mounted her horse and waited for her samurai to follow her lead. Before they mounted the warriors called out a new war cry for their commander. "Shi to all of Kawasomeru-sama's hated Teki!!! Death to all of Kawasomeru-sama's enemy!"

The cry of the warriors raised the crows and sent the foraging rabbits scurrying for cover, as it echoed throughout the land. At the last cry, the samurai bowed to Masahiko and her officers as one then she began their charge. She returned their bow sitting on her horse, her fifteen guards surrounding her. Captain Seisakajo was riding by her side as always.

"Captain Seisakajo-san! Has there been any word sent from our dung eating spies?" She asked her captain as she looked at him while guiding her horse.

"All but one has reported no sign of our enemy discovered. Ieeee Captain Masahiko-san! Can the hated warlord be so foolish as to have left this flank area unprotected to attack?" The young Captain Seisakajo growled as he struggled to steady his horse.

"No Captain Seisakajo-san! Lord Wakatsuki is far from foolish. You can rest assured the wise warlord will be waiting for us somewhere along the way Captain, and I hope he setup in the wrong position against our attack." She hissed angrily, certain she would never hear from the one missing spy again, knowing he was probably killed on his mission.

The sun came over the mountain, shining in all its anger and she gave the signal to move out to begin their attack against their enemy. In formation, the samurai headed for the Kii valley. Cautiously they entered the valley with mountains rising on both sides of their army. A quarter of a mile, half a mile, one mile into the narrow valley.

A rear samurai charged up to Masahiko, and reported an army of enemy horse soldiers circled behind them, and sealed off the entrance to the pass. She and Captain Seisakajo's eyes went to the mountain tops. Nothing. Three miles into the pass, her army was by the finger pass leading out of Kii pass to Lord Wakatsuki's flanks. The female warrior held up her hand and stopped her column's advance. She was going to rest her horses, she was aware a unit of horse warriors split off of her column, and rode ahead to scout out the pass before her.

Forty of her warriors rode to the mouth of the Kii pass and Echigo province that lay just beyond the mouth of that pass. The warriors rode around a large boulder that fell into the pass, then went around a sharp bend. There, they were facing a mounted and prepared Lord Wakatsuki army, commanded by Field General Takeshi Kumagai waiting for them to arrive.

The instant the enemy general saw the mounted horsemen from Captain Masahiko's army, he waved his arm in the air, and three hundred horse soldiers gave chase after the fleeing warriors. Her men armed their bows and sent a volley of arrows ripping into the charging enemy samurai, without dismounting their horses to attack the other army.

This new tactic stunned the crafty General Kumagai, who saw the first thirty five of the forty arrows hit their marks, sending that many of his samurai tumbling from their horses. He cursed aloud at the enemy attacking his warriors. "What evil manner of warring is this? How can the enemy warriors be so accurate with their arrows riding at full gallop? What unforeseen Kami cursed force guides their arrows to my warriors so true?"

A second volley of arrows were let loose in less than a heartbeat, taking out as many of his warriors. This was followed by a third then a forth volley of the arrows.

The fuming General Kumagai had no other choice open to him and he gave the signal that stopped the pursuing soldiers. By the time they returned to their ranks, they were a hundred men light in numbers. A hundred samurai lay scattered about on the ground dead or wounded, other warriors called for a fast death delivered by another hand. The general granted their wishes, a number of samurai headed forward in order to dispatch the badly wounded warriors, and help the ones who might live through their wounds. Each warrior knew if the belly of a fallen warrior wasn't slit open, the soldier's spirit would not escape the body and in return. The chest would swell and the spirit of the warrior would be devoured by the filth trapped within the fallen body with the soul, and the dead samurai would not be allowed the privilege of being reborn as all Japanese warriors believed.

The suddenly confused General Kumagai pondered what to do next. Should he continue his charge after the fleeing enemy horsemen? Suppose they can launch arrows without having to use their hands to guide their horses? What manner of devil's work is this that allows their horses to know where to go, while permitting their samurai to launch arrows faster than his archers can standing on foot? He questioned his mind, he knew he had to charge after Captain Masahiko's army, or Lord Wakatsuki's rear army would be caught in their own trap. He raised his arm and lowered it and his army charged wildly forward after the fleeing enemy horse warriors.

Captain Masahiko's scouts raced back to the main formation of warriors and the leader told of the enemy army laying ahead of them. She realized she was trapped between two enemy armies, one to her lead and one to her rear. She assumed a third army lay in wait in the finger valley. Her instinct was to fight in the widest area of the pass, to stand her ground and make her enemy come to her, and pay dearly for any victory they might claim over her army. Just then a second scout reported the lead army separated into three columns, two lagging behind the first.

The female warrior called out the lead army would attack in waves of three to weaken their enemy's resolve. Once weakened, the army trailing behind would charge in and finish their enemy off. She ordered her warriors to prepare for battle and decided the first engagement would be fought in the widest part of the pass. Then she would see where fate would push her and her samurai army next to attack. The first sign of the enemy appeared before her, it numbered two thousand samurai strong, all mounted and charging wildly at her. Without thinking or hesitating she charged forward, her five hundred horsemen followed, her guard samurai riding close to her side. Her warriors fired arrows as they charged forward, rapidly whittling down the main forces of the attacking enemy army. By the time they clashed together, her samurai emptied their quivers, and nearly a thousand enemy warriors lay dead or badly wounded on the ground.

With a thunder of hooves so deafening it echoed through the valley, and the air filled with angry shouts, horses neighing and mass confusion A cloud of dust raised by the countless charging horses as the two armies locked together in their battle to the death. With a resounding clash of steel and armor, the opposing armies clashed in the middle of the pass. She had her sword out striking any enemy warrior she encountered during her attack. The sound of swords ricocheting off swords, and howling cries of pain from horses and men alike, echoed as warrior's heads and arms were lopped from their conquered and destroyed bodies.

The swordsmanship of the enemy left a lot to be desired, and they became easy prey against the better skilled and disciplined Captain Masahiko warriors. Horses fell and were trampled in the earth by the beating hooves of other charging horses. She used her legs to stay on her horse and control it, while she swung her sword at the heads of her enemy. One, two, three, ten, fifteen, and then eighteen fell before her sword. Her legs and chest were covered by blood, and her face and hair sprayed with the warm liquid of the slaughtered. The sickening smell of fresh blood filled her nostrils and added to her killing spirit.

As swiftly as the battle began it was over, with over one thousand eight hundred enemy dead or wounded. Her forces lost less than a hundred dead, and or wounded.

General Kumagai watched in awe as Masahiko chopped and slashed his warriors to death before his eyes, sending all who came against the youthful warrior's arm, to their departed ancestors. Angered by the slaughter of his samurai, and loss of face he suffered at the hands of this child samurai he heard so much about, he allowed his emotions to rule his mind and better judgment. The fuming general ordered his second army to engage the staggered enemy army.

As the next five thousand Kumagai warriors charged forward, they were met by a devastating volley of shaft death. They were stopped with over two thousand warriors falling, arrows sticking out of their bodies in a grotesque manner. The general cursed as he waved his fist in the air at the enemy captain controlling the attacking warriors pitted against his samurai. He cursed his enemy's ability to launch arrows so accurately from their wildly charging horses. This kept his warriors off balance and unable to press the attack further on the enemy. Now, he was forced to wait for his archers to catch up to his main body of soldiers, so he could fight arrow for arrow. General Kumagai had to admire the young Captain Masahiko's army eliminated the need for their usual foot archers, by giving the horse soldiers the ability to use their arrows first. Then resort to their swords when their arrows were spent, along with great numbers of his warriors.

She had her samurai rearmed with arrows before she was attacked by the second army and realized the enemy general wasn't pressing the attack further against her samurai, she knew the enemy commander was waiting for his archers to arrive. She also knew she had to act and act swiftly if she wished to be successful and survive this attack, she wasn't going to allow her army to be slaughtered in this narrow valley. She heard screaming from her rear, and understood the trailing enemy were beginning to probe her flanks. Time was up for her and her army, she didn't expect the second enemy army to go in action so quickly against her forces, and thought she would have some more time to decide her next course of action in battle. She was trapped and it was up to her to get most of her army out alive, or she was going to be sung as a fool in many plays and ballets to amuse the old.

Something about the battlefield seemed vaguely familiar to her sharp mind. She couldn't help but feel she fought this very battle somewhere in her past. She took a second to allow her mind to search her memory then it came to her like a lightning bolt. Her father and their first game of Go. He trapped her army in a valley much like this one on the game board. What did she do to escape his trap on the board game. Then she remembered she did not escape, and her father destroyed her army. She searched her mind as to what her father told her was the proper course of action she should have employed, to save the bulk of her samurai. She cursed herself for not remembering the lesson, it was a block until one horsemen made a dash in the narrow valley, and cried when arrows crashed in his body.

"How stupid of me not to remember my father's training of the past." She screamed as she raised her sword then pointed to the narrow valley mouth. Without question, her remaining warriors charged in the pass, horses crashed into each other, sending their riders tumbling under their hooves, as they madly charged forward. Horses whinnied, warriors screamed their war cry, as large choking clouds of dust were raised, engulfing the wildly charging samurai army.

She had not a second of doubt in her mind her warriors would follow her to their death without hesitation. Her father's words echoed reassuringly in her ears loud and clear. 'When prepared to die, your samurai will set forward their ultimate exertion, in a frantic situation your warriors will fear not the enemy warriors. With no way out open to them, they'll stand together and fight as one, as if the demons themselves were guiding their honorable thrusts with their killing swords. Remember Masahiko, when there's no alternative left opened to life, your samurai will engage the enemy on foot if need be, fighting hand to hand and win the battle for you and your Master'.

Her chest swelled with pride as she glanced behind her and witnessed her samurai following her without hesitation, and realized her samurai would engage the gods themselves if she led the way for them. More words of her father flooded in her mind. 'A desperate warrior needs no prodding from their Generals, to display his worth on the field of battle. Without imploring their support, you'll be showered with it. Without attempting to invite their devotion, you'll receive it most willingly. Without demanding their unwavering discipline, you'll enjoy it even in the face of their pending death. Be a good and sure leader, and your samurai will follow you anywhere'.

Lord Wakatsuki's archers didn't know what was charging down the pass at them, but they launched their arrows at the all consuming cloud of boiling dust coming at them. When the first flight of arrow found its mark, she bellowed and her warriors responded with a sun blotting flood of arrows of their own. In the volley all but thirty enemy warriors were killed or wounded. The survivors allowed the charging enemy warriors to pass and get a few shots off at their flanks as they sped by their position.

The dust stuck to the drying blood covering the warrior's bodies as they broke out of the tight passageway, and were met with minor resistance from the fleeing enemy warriors.

Wakatsuki's General Motoshima's army charged in the valley and came up against General Kumagai's army rushing at the cloud of dust being raised by General Motoshima's army. Thinking it was Captain Masahiko's soldiers trying to flee their trap. There was a minor engagement before the two attacking armies realized they were fighting each other. Kumagai found Motoshima and complained bitterly at the commander. "Ieeee General Motoshima! Who is with this child born of the Devil Kami? Does Masahiko control the ability to make his army disappear then reappear before us at will where we least expected them to attack from?"

"Don't be such a fool! This worthless warrior is smart and cunning and more daring than I gave him credit for. The samurai led his fearless army in the gorge, and by now our archers are picking them apart at will. Come General Kumagai-san! We must relieve the archers before they fall under the weight of Captain Masahiko's worthless army."

The two armies turned as one and charged forward towards the narrow gorge. General Motoshima kept looking for any signs of a battle raging within, he was growing concerned with the lack of dead enemy they came across in the gorge, and no sign of fighting continuing. He came across the position where his archers were believed to be stationed, and found only dead samurai waiting to greet his charging army.

"Ieeeee General Kumagai-san! The worthless warriors of Lord Kawasomeru have broken through our trap! We have to cut them off before they get in the flanks of Lord Wakatsuki's army and rip us apart at will." General Motoshima bellowed as he urged his troops forward with his sword and bellowing voice. They were greeted by a cloud of arrows when they reached the mouth of the gorge. Hundreds then thousands of General Motoshima's men fell before his horses. The bodies piling up so deep it was nearly impossible for their horses to get over the wall of death closing off the mouth of the narrow gorge. The fuming general had no choice but to pull his samurai back, or to make it possible for the pile of dead to increase, by continuing to allow his warriors to die in a battle they had no chance to win.

The angry general gave the order, and his badly mauled army pulled back into the safety of the gorge for cover and protection. He decided to try and make it around the mountain then come at Captain Masahiko's attacking army from the other side of the wide gorge. He was going to be too late in any event to the outcome of the battle.

Just as Captain Masahiko destroyed General Motoshima's army, Lord Kawasomeru's armies engaged the main forces of Wakatsuki's army in the Yukata plain, which extended all the way back to his capital city of Chiyoda, waiting for the outcome of the battle within the vast valley.

More of her honorable father's words rang true in her ears as she pressed forward her attack at Wakatsuki's rear. "Seek the flanks of your worthless enemy, and you'll win all your battles honorably. No army could possibly withstand an attack from a powerful army from their flanks, while trying to defend their army from a frontal charge."

Lord Kawasomeru led the charge on the plain, and was shocked to see a second army that seemed to be hitting the flank of Lord Wakatsuki's army, at the same time as he attack the same enemy warriors from the point of the enemy formation. The warlord didn't know which army it was. For a moment he thought it was reinforcements for Lord Wakatsuki's aide. When the second attacking army sliced in the enemy flanks, and slaughtered them with lust, he knew he had allies working the unprotected rear of his enemy warriors.

General Kobayashi riding hard to the left of the charging Kawasomeru-sama called in an excited tone so he could be heard over the fighting. "Lord Kawasomeru, it's Captain Masahiko-san and her army!" He pointed to the army attacking Lord Wakatsuki from the left.

He pulled back on the reins of his animal, forcing his horse slid to a stop on the blood soaked battlefield, when he realized it was indeed Captain Masahiko's army attacking his enemy from the rear. He lagged behind so he could observe the charge led by Captain Masahiko's vastly outnumbered army. He yelled at the back of General Kobayashi as he rode past his general. "Tanizaki-san's child has more guts than the sea has fish. I'll make her a Lord in this world, and a god in the next! We'll win this worthless war with her warrior's addition. Thank the gods for her birth." The liege lord waved his sword overhead and spurred his horse onward.

Lord Wakatsuki's warriors were an impenetrable wall of swirling blades and fired arrows, but when Captain Masahiko's warriors emerged from the narrow passage, and commenced their attack against Lord Wakatsuki's warriors from their rear position. The besieged warlord was quickly forced to weaken his wall of death and defense to reinforce his crumbling flank section. Since the enemy warlord was ill prepared to defend himself from a two front war, his plight was doomed at this point. It didn't take long for the once organized defense from Lord Wakatsuki's powerful forces to break down, and when chaos replaced once well disciplined warriors. It gave Lord Kawasomeru and Captain Masahiko's forces the opportunity to pick apart Lord Wakatsuki's forces at will from the front and rear of his now trapped forces.

Lord Wakatsuki planned to get through the Kii plains where he would place archers among the many boulders at the mouth of the plain, before he pressed his attack on what he believed was Lord Kawasomeru's main force of warriors. But Kawasomeru's warriors were already in position on the plain. With this attack in his rear, the enemy warlord was forced to change his strategy, and retreat before his army was annihilated by this second army attacking him.

Archers fired at wild horse warriors, and the horse samurai rode over archers and spearmen alike. Spearmen stabbed at the horses to try and tumble the riders. The slaughter was on in all its madding fury and mayhem. Hundreds then thousands of samurai from both sides dropped in battle.

The war of death lasted for over three hours, horses had to be abandoned because they could no longer be used because of the countless bodies littering the vast battlefield.

Lord Kawasomeru worked his way to where he last witnessed Captain Masahiko fighting the enemy warriors. He climbed on top of a knoll and stood on a taller rock and horse, and scanned the vast battlefield. He located the female warrior standing on top of her dead horse wildly swinging her blade at all who charged her body. At one point she grabbed a samurai and pulled him forward, impaling him on his brother's swords then she lopped the head off the second samurai who stabbed his comrade. She stood in the midst of her enemies, swinging her katana like an evil angry Kami. Filled with hatred and rage of life, while standing in a wheat field laying his blade to the wheat stalks of human warriors, as did the farmer to his crops.

Within the madding melee of death and disorder, she held in her other hand the shorter stabbing sword, and sliced the throats of wounded enemy lying at her feet. The powerful and proud warlord stared at his female fighter in awe and admiration. She was covered from head to toe with blood dripping from her arms and armor. A pile of enemy lay dead at her feet, and her attackers were forced to climb over the dead to try and get at her body, and this made them easy fodder for her slicing blades. Flicks of skin were glued by drying blood to her armor, and arrows stuck out of her armor, three from her heavy chest plate, and two in each leg, and one from her left arm armor. One of the fukigayeshi, the great turn backs of her helmet was sliced off, and two arrows stuck out of her armor from the back. None of the arrows forced their way through the thick armor protection to find her skin, and do harm to her body. The yoroi hitatare, the heavy armor robe stopped them all from injuring his warrior.

The liege lord, stared in astonishment of Captain Masahiko's unconquerable fighting abilities, as his and her enemies crumbled before her feet. As she wildly continued to slash and hack at the mounted enemy foolish enough and came within her sword range. The swarm of dead and slowly dying continued to grow in large numbers until the enemy warriors could no longer get anywhere near her body to harm or stop her.

The respected warlord looked over her body, there was a chunk of her breast plate armor missing, and many protective silver and gold kasazuri plates were no longer attached to her armor robe, obviously hacked away by her enemy's blades. He figured she should have been killed at least fifteen times on the battlefield, judging by the condition of her armor. Yet she continued to stand tall and kill his enemy on a vast scale. Proudly, he sprang from the knoll he was perched on, and headed for the child warrior in an attempt to lend aide to her battle. It seemed many enemy turned their attention against her, and singled her out and were trying to kill her. The liege lord figured Lord Wakatsuki issued orders to kill the chosen one to his warriors. He couldn't wait to reach her and fight at her side, never had he seen any one warrior fight so bravely as this one was doing before his stunned eyes.

By the time the warlord reached Captain Masahiko's side, most fighting was mostly over and only a mop up operation was placed in motion. Lord Kawasomeru walked up to the exhausted female warrior as she dispatched a wounded enemy before his eyes. He drew in his breath when he laid close eyes on this fearsome apparition, so covered with blood and the innards of her enemy. Stuck on her remaining breast plate was an ear and part of a face of a dead warrior. He struck her katana with his as he bellowed.

"Captain Masahiko-san! You killed enough of my cursed enemy on this glorious of days. I order your mind to come back to the world of the civilized people, and leave the madness of the black world of the murdering kingdom for another day's visit. Leave what killing is left to the hinin and foot soldiers to carry out. They'll put the wounded Samurai out of their suffering. You done your duty for this battle, Captain. You served me well on the battlefield on this day, and brought great face to your honorable family's name forever."

She allowed Kawasomeru's sword to force the tip of her blade to the ground. She drew in an exhausted breath then let out a deep sigh as she collapsed to her knees in a heap, drawing in deep breaths as she came to rest sitting on the body of one of her countless dead enemy warriors.

"Bring me mizu! Water! Now!" The warlord bellowed to no one in particular, as he stabbed his sword in a body of an enemy soldier lying dead at his feet. Then he helped her suffering from exhaustion and struggling to breathe properly. Her once beautiful face was so covered with drying blood and dust, he had to actually pick the clotted blood from her nostrils, so she could breath correctly again in the living world.

A samurai carrying water rushed up to the side of his lord and master.

She was so exhausted she was unable to drink for herself, so he ordered the samurai to wash her face. General Kobayashi, wounded in his left arm came rushing up to Lord Kawasomeru's side carrying a flask of sake and offered. "Here my Lord, you seem like you could use something a little stronger than mere water to drink."

He smiled at his general as he took the flask, but instead of drinking he held her head in hand, and placed the flask to her lips and poured the warmth giving liquid in her gasping for air mouth.

She gagged on the harsh liquid and turned her head to avoid more of the burning taste.

Kobayashi grunted at his master with amazement. "Tanizaki-san Warrior will live my Lord."

"Hai! For a long time to come and so will you. Get over to the herbal physicians and allow them to look after your wound, before it gives you trouble General Kobayashi-san. I'll handle Masahiko-san." He scanned the battlefield until he saw kagamen standing by a litter. The warlord saw a samurai doing nothing and ordered him near then ordered him to fetch the kagamen. He had a driving force making him want to get Masahiko off the littered with dead battlefield. In his mind he looked at her as a female, and a battlefield was no place for a woman.

LORD WAKATSUKI'S RETREATING ARMY

Wakatsuki realized further fighting on his part would be useless, and a waste of his warrior's lives, so he regrouped and pulled back as many of his samurai he could save. It was better to retreat and live to fight another day, than waste more samurai for a battle unable to be won.

General Motoshima's armies successfully worked their way around the mountain from the pass separating Kii valley from the great plain, but by the time his army reached the massive battlefield. The war was over and there was no use committing his men to useless slaughter. The general located Wakatsuki, rapidly working his way from the battlefield with a large section of his army intact, and moved his men out to linkup with their soundly defeated lord and master.

Out of the nearly seven hundred thousand samurai of Lord Wakatsuki's army who took part in the battle, there were less than four hundred and fifty thousand retreated with their warlord.

Other problems plaguing his army were many samurai sized up the situation, and decided it was in the best interest to change sides and swear allegiance to Lord Kawasomeru's victorious army. Hundreds, followed by thousands of once enemy warriors, turned on Lord Wakatsuki. With the massive numbers of deserters fleeing his army, he found himself unable to protect his flank, and was forced to break off further contact with his enemy. At the first opportunity he took his anger for the desertions out on the depleted soldiers, by ordering the slaughter of warriors who remained loyal to him. Blind rage blocked good sense from the fuming warlord as he watched the murder of countless hundreds of his soldiers.

LORD KAWASOMERU'S VICTORIOUS ARMY

Lord Kawasomeru gave the order for a section of the battlefield to be cleared of human carnage and death, and for his army to pitch a permanent headquarters from which they would continue their war. He was to keep pursuing Lord Wakatsuki's army on the run from his. The sun began to set and the exhausted, loyal warriors settled down and slept in the open on the battle scared field. Dead horses were cut up and their cooked meat added to the depleted food stocks of the warriors. Even samurai who never ate meat, ate greedily of animal flesh, forsaking their religious beliefs. The warlord didn't care a piss about religion or personal beliefs or fears, he wanted to have his samurai rested, fed and ready for the next encounter of Wakatsuki's warriors.

He sent a number of his warriors to surrounding villages, drafting inhabitants and forcing them on the battlefield, to help clear away the dead and to look after his exhausted warriors and their spent horses. Water was diverted from a nearby canal, so his warriors had fresh drinking water and water to bathe, and clean their wounds and battle equipment. A small army of hinin took the discarded armor to the stream and washed the blood and grime from it then returned the items of war back to the proper warriors. Their battle clothes was likewise washed, and repaired if needed and returned to the rightful warriors dried.

The warlord planned to give his loyal samurai the next two days to rest and rebuild their strength, before pressing his attack against the fleeing enemy army. He knew a halt in the battle would give Wakatsuki time to regroup and make his army stronger, but understood he couldn't push his warriors harder without rest. Tomorrow he decided he would make the warriors bathe in the stream and relax. By the time the sun sank below the mountains, every samurai who took part in the battle were asleep. Only the guards remained awake to safeguard the samurai from surprise attacks. The odor of death was growing less offensive to the warlord and his warriors.

The next morning was pleasant with a hint of light rain in the air. The hinin worked the night, and had most of the battlefield cleared of death, and huge pyres burning, freeing the dead samurai's souls of their earthly bonds. Clean dirt was spread over the countless pools of blood and small body parts which were easier to bury than pick up. The warlord was one of the few who had a proper tent to sleep, so he had a great night sleep. When he woke, he issued orders, food was on the way along with drums of sake. Clean clothes and replacement armor was arriving to the massive encampment. Tents were erected and an army of villagers were constructing a small dais. Commoners raked around the dais and battlefield.

He smiled when he came from the tent, he saw many samurai making use of the diverted waters of the canal by bathing and cleaning themselves along with their clothing. The concerned warlord looked for his officers, spotting Shimbo with Kobayashi standing together, he bellowed in a commanding voice. "General Shimbo-san! General Kobayashi-san! I need to speak with you." The warlord went to sit where there was no folding chair, and one instantly appeared by a guard ever watching over the warlord, before he lowered himself on it. The officers rushed to the warlord and dropped their knees and bowed then waited to see what he wanted of them.

He shook his fist and bragged to his officers. "Ieeeee, by the gods that was a battle to enjoy! With the help of Kami of the underworld small and large, we have Lord Wakatsuki reeling on this battle. We taught those manure heaps not to cross swords with the Warriors from Shinano province. I decided to award fighters for their courage during this battle. I'll start with Captain Masahiko-san." He stared at both officers, waiting for complaints, none came.

"General Shimbo-san?" The warlord asked of his general as he stared at him.

"I have no complaints, no gripes to offer to my Lord. I witnessed the young Warrior in action on the battlefield, and I'd not choose to cross swords, or even words with her foolishly."

"Hai!" General Kobayashi added with a grin and pumped up his chest.

"I'm pleased my Generals agree with my decision to allow her to become Samurai in my army. I'll lift her to the rank of General on this glorious day, and give her her own fief to live her remaining years, once this cursed war has ran its course. My officers will be likewise rewarded for their service to my cause. General Shimbo-san! For your many years of service to my Realm, I give you all of Echigo province. General Kobayashi-san! I'll give you Shimotsuke province. Lord Wakatsuki forfeited his claim on these provinces for forcing us to this endless war. The rest of my officers I'll see and reward them for their service at the ceremony where I'll honor Captain Masahiko-san. General Kobayashi-san! Inform the young Samurai she'll be expected to appear before me at the last flicker of light from the sun."

"Hai my Lord." The general and lifelong friend of the young female warrior replied happily.

The day passed slowly, with everyone of his samurai preparing for the night's ceremony. The surviving fine clothes were aired and pressed, and the samurai dressed properly to appear before their master. Captain Masahiko was one of the luckier ones, she had a trunk full with many changes of clothes stored in it. She was allowed the trunk because her lord felt like all women, she would prefer to change her clothes more frequently.

The camp was a beehive of activity, and the massive Taiko drums were carried over and setup on crossed Leggett stands and every once in a while, one of the drummers would try out a huge drum, making certain the ground the samurai walked upon vibrate under their feet.

LORD WAKATSUKI'S RETREATING ARMY

Wakatsuki was surprised no follow on enemy forces were sent to harass his retreating army in disarray about him. If he were Kawasomeru, he would have all available warriors mounted on horseback, and attack the flanks of his warriors as they tried to escape his army. Killing as many of his enemy as possibly before being forced to engage the main body of his army a second time.

He not only cursed Lord Kawasomeru for his overwhelming victory over his warriors, he laughed for his lack of victory over his retreating forces. He couldn't help but feel Kawasomeru committed his entire army against his forces, and if that was all the damage they could inflict on his army, he was confident he would be able to regroup and enlarge his devastated army, even if he had to employ villagers and farmers to booster his depleted troop's ranks. Once his army was of proper size, he would again attack Lord Kawasomeru and destroy him by sheer numbers.

GENERAL OKUMURA'S ARMY READY TO LAY SIEGE TO CHIYODA CASTLE

General Okumura attacked Lord Wakatsuki's capital of Chiyoda, and was surprised at the lack of resistance he encountered from worthless and ill trained defenders. Many defenders were ill prepared for an attack against the castle, and were caught off step. Lord Wakatsuki's samurai seemed the least interested in battle, and gave up when they realized they were surrounded, and under seize by a large force of samurai. In many cases, General Okumura offered Lord Wakatsuki's warriors the chance to change allegiance to Lord Kawasomeru's side. Many did, the others lost their heads in blind obedience to their defeated master. It helped General Okumura's samurai marched confidently into Lord

Wakatsuki's capital in the same type formation once employed by the enemy army. Before the defenders were able to realize General Okumura's army was from Lord Kawasomeru, it was too late for them to react against them.

General Okumura's less than savage war against the defenders of the castle lasted but a few hours, before his forces were able to breach the lightly defended walls, and his warriors forced their way in the fortification. Floor by floor General Okumura's samurai defeated the hapless enemy defenders and by the time night set in, heads were taken. The general ordered the death of all samurai refusing to change alliance to his master, and any castle consorts and villager who dared to look at his warriors the wrong way, suffered the same fate, swift death.

By the time the general was in control of the capital, castle and surrounding lands of the enemy warlord, over four thousand heads lay scattered about on the ground. Huge Pyre fires were hastily constructed, and bodies of Lord Kawasomeru's enemies were set ablaze and turned to ash. General Okumura following orders of his master, made the castle and city his military encampment, constructing long hataito fences, tsuiji, the great walls of lath and earth, and the high yaguras, the defense towers to better defend what he won from the enemy defenders of the castle and surrounding area, from being taken from him by the enemy warlord's army, if they returned to the castle for rest, refitting and food.

Everything the general did in the enemy capital and castle was done to defend it from Lord Wakatsuki's retreating army, which he was certain was marching for the safety of the castle. General Okumura laughed as he thought of the look that would be plastered on the once feared, and now less powerful Lord Wakatsuki's face. When he realized he was in control of his capital, and now Lord Wakatsuki had no safe haven to return to and lick his wounds of battle.

LORD WAKATSUKI'S RETREATING ARMY

The all but defeated enemy warlord Wakatsuki and his retreating army, tried in vain to keep his army together, and have the warrior's minds set in a fighting mode for tomorrow's war against Lord Kawasomeru's army. The fuming warlord was forced to put to death a number of officers for failing to maintain control over their samurai, and allowing desertions to take place against him. The retreating army marched deeper in the vastness of Echigo province, they were destroying all villages they passed on their unorganized retreat. The warlord was determined to leave nothing of worth standing for Lord Kawasomeru's army to make use of.

He ordered all bridges burned, or otherwise destroyed or blocked, trees were chopped down and piled across roadways, and huge boulders were rolled in the roads, all fields of crops were burned to their stalks, after his retreating warriors ate their fill of the crops, and took what they wanted or needed to sustain them on their forced retreat. Any drinking water was contaminated by human waste and slaughtered bodies of deserters or villagers, were left rotting in the once clean drinking waters and wells of the region. Game was killed when Lord Wakatsuki's samurai came across them, and all eatable roots and other means of food an d substance were eaten or soiled or burned where it grew.

His samurai killed every occupant in some villages then left the bodies lying in the roads, in hopes their rotting corpse would so sicken the pursuing army of Kawasomeru. The invaders would leave his province in haste and disgust. In some areas such as the narrow passes, tight valleys, marshes and tall grass fields along with strategic cross and main roads. Wakatsuki left a number of archers and spearmen to fight a delaying action, harassing and slowing the pursuing Kawasomeru army long enough for him to replenish his army from villages he traveled through. And to create a distance between his retreating army and Lord Kawasomeru's perusing army.

Everything possibility any retreating army could do, to slow their pursuers was carried out by the enemy samurai. The all but defeated warlord was livid and took out his unfettered anger on his battered samurai and commoners alike. His wrath knew no bounds as he ordered the death of anyone he was angered by or against. Food found in villages he crossed was confiscated by his soldiers, with no regard to the villagers of the area needs. All huts and buildings were collapsed in on themselves, or burned to the ground. No comforts were left standing intact for Lord Kawasomeru's samurai to make use of against him or his retreating army.

The fleeing warlord had no feeling of respect or honor or care for his samurai's health, as he pushed the warriors beyond endurance throughout the day's forced march. He didn't allow them to rest even at night, always forcing his samurai onward, or standing guard to defend against attack by Lord Kawasomeru's massive army. He pushed his samurai as the sun rose in the sky, and was lucky at finding numbers of warriors to strengthen his depleted army with. In many instances, the craft warlord drafted men from hundreds of villages, and when there weren't enough males to add to his growing army.

He started to take women and armed them then ordered them to kill any of Lord Kawasomeru's samurai. In some instances, the once feared warlord had the women left in the villages swear an oath of death, that they would carry knives and attack the enemy soldiers in suicide fashion, because he wanted to whittle down Lord Kawasomeru's army by any means opened. He made certain he left no stone unturned in the construction of his weakened army, while also delaying Lord Kawasomeru's pursuing warriors.

To add to his growing woes a heavy rain was falling, and carried with it a cold breeze. All roads he used to escape the battle and Lord Kawasomeru army, turned to mud. He welcomed the rain, he knew it would aid in slowing the progress of his trailing enemy warriors. The rain lightened his spirits until they came across the runner dispatched from Chiyoda Castle, to find and report to him of the city and castle's collapse to Lord Kawasomeru's warriors.

The exhausted runner was brought before the fuming warlord, and when he informed the warlord a large army of Lord Kawasomeru's warriors had successfully attacked his capital, and they had taken and were using Chiyoda Castle as their encampment. The runner was immediately put to death because of the terrible information he brought before the angry warlord. Lord Wakatsuki didn't know where to turn next, until General Motoshima offered they head for the second largest city of Echigo province. Where he might find many samurai waiting to get back at Lord Kawasomeru, and his army of warriors.

The warlord smiled at his general as he gave the order for his army to head for Hokke and help the larger village could offer him and his depleted army. The warlord's army turned as one, and the remaining samurai headed for the city of Hokke, and any safety it afforded them from attack from Lord Kawasomeru's army, he was certain was in pursuit of him.

CHAPTER TWENTY SIX

ON THE NIGHT OF THE FIRST DAY OF THE SECOND WEEK OF THE TENTH MONTH OF THE YEAR THIRTEEN FIFTY TWO

The great warlord Kawasomeru waited resting on a cross legged chair as Captain Masahiko was marched before him. Massive Taiko drums beat their phrase of the female warrior, as the sun sank behind the distant mountains. A cheer from the samurai rose as the drums pounded away, and Captain Masahiko marched proudly forward. She was dressed in armor, what was destroyed in the battle was replaced by new by her master. Her Kabuto helmet with the fukigayeshi, helmet turn backs was repaired, and the missing kuwagata horn was replaced.

She wore the fearsome brass hoate face mask with a grotesque sneer embedded on it, with the connected shikoro throat guard decorated with silver inlays. Kasazuri plates hung from her armor for added protection against the sword's biting edge, where the armor was least protected. Kote sleeve armor adorned her slender arms, and were richly decorated with heavy silver and gold inlay. Her suneate leg armor was equally decorated, and a yoroi hitatare armor robe completed her body protection. Over her right arm was slung a agemaki, the ornamental bow, and on her back rested the open quiver with six arrows tucked in it. Two sashimono banners rose over her armor proclaiming her abilities in the Claw discipline on one, and the name of Tanizaki written in below that of Lord Kawasomeru's on the other. Her deadly Sugahara katana blades were tucked in the sash around her waist. She came forward and dropped to her knees and bowed as best she could in her armor.

"Captain Masahiko-san! Your presence is appreciated to witness before me, as it was a surprise when you first appeared before me on the battlefield against our enemy of the Realm. I expected your attack to come from elsewhere, Captain Masahiko-san." He grunted almost in condemnation of her attack against the dog eating Wakatsuki's forces.

"Ieeeee my Lord! I failed you on the battlefield, and was unable to contain my wanton fighting spirit, and foolishly attacked in the wrong area, allowing your enemy to escape our trap. As punishment for my poor efforts, I don't deserve to live. I'll commit suppuku before you my Lord." She announced, ashamed she attacked the center of the enemy instead of the rear.

"Huh Captain Masahiko-san! On the battlefield there is none other greater than your unconquerable fighting spirit. As for your failing me in this battle, true you have failed me, but you'll fail me again in the future on the battlefield. I hope all your mistakes in the future will work out as well as your failure on this battlefield has done for me. You served me well yesterday, and you deserve homage. If you'd allow me, I'll honor you in the way you earned. As of today you're elevated to the rank of General of horse warriors."

A cheer rose from the warriors as the drummers pounded away on their drums, and the warriors banged wildly on their wood shields with armor covered hands.

The warlord ignored the racket as he continued with his words. "As further reward for your bravery on the battlefield, I'll give you as your personal fief, all lands that run from the Seventh to the Eleventh Village, plus an annual fee of three hundred koku a year in rice, one hundred kiki in silk, one hundred horses, and two thousand sets of armor, and three thousand sets of Katana blades. I'll include an army of five thousand samurai horsemen, General Masahiko-san."

She was stunned at what she was hearing from her lord and master. What he spoke was a fee worthy of a mighty daimyo, not a lowly samurai.

"General Masahiko-san! I was the one who chose to name your sword, as of today I order you to change the name I had bestowed upon your weapon. From this day forward you're no longer a person. You are Wind, my Wind, and my Divine Wind. I chose this name for you because your sword is as swift as the wind, and no force on this earth can possibly contain it, or your fighting spirit. You'll rename your sword, ahh... let me see, yes, this will do fine I believe, young Samurai. In keeping with your honorable name I just bestowed upon you, I order you to name your mighty Katana sword Wind's Breath, for the way it easily slices through the wind and bodies of my enemy alike, General Masahiko-san.

"Your great sword is as fearsome as the dragon's breath that warms the earth, but it's your warrior spirit that has conquered your mighty Katana blade's will, therefore it's just a mere extension of your honorable name and unbeatable spirit, young warrior. I know my place in this universe has been set in place by Karma, but you my Wind. You're much like the winds of your name that sweep across Japan from the sea, on its never-ending journey to seek the forever peace. I fear you'll never know your true calling in the universe, Samurai. Your world lays spread out before you, so go forth and seek out your Karma in this world, but in my name only. Your exploits upon the battlefield have earned you this position and right I offer. I heard the name my foolish Warriors have bestowed upon your presence, 'Warrior of the Willow', because you allow yourself to bend but never break, but I'll stay with my choice.

"Wind. We have one more battle to win for peace to be installed throughout my Realm, once the miserable Wakatsuki and his dung heap followers are dead, you'll be free to carve out your own niche in this world, until the next time I have need you and your services. You'll reside at the Ninth Village as your honorable father has done all his life. You'll train my future Warriors to your warring skills, they'll be as great as your father's Samurai."

He suddenly stomped his foot on the wood dais without warning. It was as loud as one of the massive drums. "Ooooyyyyaaaa!" The master growled and waved the victory fan before his face, which he produced from the wide sleeve of his kosode towards General Masahiko.

She bowed to her lord as the warriors picked up the cry from Lord Kawasomeru, and repeated it over and over as the drummers pounded away on their huge drums. It was a maddening and confusing scene at worst, with hundreds of torches lighting up the night, and the great funeral pyre fires continued to burn the enemy bodies to ash, and cook horse meat for the exhausted Samurai to eat. The drums made the air around the platform reverberate, and an army of samurai called out Lord Kawasomeru and General Masahiko's name. The fever pitch increased when the warriors shouted Wind as her new name as proclaimed by their lord and master.

When he spoke again, every samurai immediately quieted in order to hear his words. "General Masahiko-san! Wind! Tomorrow we'll give pursuit to our hated enemies, we'll whittle the worthless fools down until we come across Lord Wakatsuki's main forces of dog eating warriors. I have reports which state there are many small pockets of enemy left behind, with orders to hinder our forward progress in pursuit of the lowly dog eater himself. I'll send your honored horse warriors to destroy this minor resistance, so we can march right into Lord Wakatsuki's foul Castle. General Okumura has already taken command of Chiyoda Castle and Lord Wakatsuki's capital city, and his spies reported the great fool Wakatsuki's retreating army has turned towards the vile Village of Hokke, where he's assured of finding many able bodied Samurai to help replenish his weakened army so they can defend themselves against our army.

"We'll look to engage his army of worthless dogs in the vast Kugyo plain, which lies between his cursed capital city and the Village of Hokke, and is the only wise place for us to do honorable battle in this region on a grand scale against our enemy. It'll be our last chance to destroy this maggot eaten mongrel's god cursed army. Once this battle is over, his loathsome army will be so dispersed, we'll never be able to hunt them all down and end his threat to my Realm once and for all, so he must die in this upcoming battle." Lord Kawasomeru warned as a cup of sake was placed in his hand. He walked over to General Masahiko and offered her the cup.

Another roar rose from the formation over the honor their lord was bestowing upon Wind.

She struggled to her feet, her armor restricting her movement, and accepted the cup offered by her liege lord. She brought the cup to her forehead and touched it while holding the porcelain bowl with both hands. Then sipped from the rim, slurping the warm wine noisily.

The honored warlord bowed to the young samurai and this brought a new roar from his warriors as they called his name frantically. He smiled, knowing he whipped his samurai into the killing state needed to make them as savage as needed to destroy Lord Wakatsuki's army.

"General Masahiko-san! Wind! You need not my permission to hunt down our enemies no matter where they might hide from your unfettered wrath and killing sword. You're free to pick out the Samurai you want for support, and attack the vile nests of filth where you find them hiding throughout the sixteen provinces of Central Japan. You, Wind, are as free as your name suggests, to do what you choose, and go where you want and destroy my hated teki throughout my Realm. I want this war finished by month's end. Go Wind and seek out and destroy my Teki and find your destiny. My enemy await their fate."

She proudly drew her katana and held it high over her head, as she grunted in her deepest and most masculine voice. "My Lord and Master's enemies are my enemy for all eternity to come, Kawasomeru-sama. I'll never rest at peace until the worthless enemy are walking with their foul ancestors within the Floating World of forever. My task will not end until all your enemy in Japan are nothing but a bad memory, my Lord."

Another roar came from the ranks of samurai, as Wind noisily left Lord Kawasomeru's side, and took her position at the head of the horsemen formation. A second warrior marched up to his lord's side to be likewise honored by him.

The ceremony stretched well into the morning hours and before sunrise, the warriors were allowed to sleep. Wind slept not a second, she was too worked up over being allowed to hunt down her enemy at will, and use the troops she wanted to accomplish this feat. She was up as the sun broke over the mountains and she walked out of her tent, and was instantly surprised to see her horsemen already assembled by their horses dressed in their armor, ready to begin their hunt with her. A horse was dressed in her dead horse's armor, and stood peacefully unattended at the head of the formation. Captain Seisakajo stood by her side and grunted with pleasure to see her samurai honoring the female general so.

She walked over to the waiting horse and took the reins once she inspected the animal, and approved of her warrior's pick for her. She pointed to the first unit of samurai, and they swiftly mounted and rode off to pursue Lord Wakatsuki's fleeing troops. As Wind's army entered the first valley after the enemy troops, a spray of arrows greeted them as they approached a clump of boulders blocking the road. Forty of the enemy archers were trying to keep Wind and her warriors from pursuing their master further. They were no match for her five hundred horse samurai who rode over the rear guard, dispatching them without losing one warrior to their misguided arrows. Throughout the rest of the day, her army came across three other pockets of slight resistance, they met the same fate as the first. The last group had success with her forces, killing ten before their slaughter was complete.

It was getting late in the day and she was exhausted from the long ceremony and minor battles of this day, and called an end to their march. She ordered tents pitched in a wide clearing. Then appointed twenty samurai to stand guard for the night as the rest slept.

One hundred of Lord Wakatsuki's samurai were scattered about in the crevasses that made up the structure of the valley, and they waited as Wind's army settled down for their night's sleep. Runners were sent out to assemble more of Lord Wakatsuki's warriors for a night attack. The enemy recognized Wind by her armor, and word went out that the feared Captain Masahiko was trapped. By midnight the enemy's ranks had increased to five hundred warriors, and they prepared to attack their unsuspecting enemy. It was a dark night with many clouds blocking out what light was emitted by the moon and stars. Lord Wakatsuki's warriors moved out from their hiding places as silently as the night's breeze, and moved in on their sleeping enemy targets.

A young and aggressive Warrior, Tetsuo Hatanaka watched as his samurai dispatched the few night guards protecting Wind's warriors. When the guards were dead his samurai move closer to the sleeping warriors of Lord Kawasomeru. When they were as close as they dared go without detection, Hatanaka raised his hand and his warriors let out a war cry as they charged the sleeping enemy samurai, their blades slicing many who didn't react quick enough to fend off the charge.

Wind ordered her samurai to sleep with their swords lying across their legs at night. When they heard the war cry from their attacking enemy warriors, her well trained samurai leaped up with their katana swords in their hands, as they prepared for battle. She was unaware a hundred of her fighters were already slaughtered, before they had a chance to defend themselves. She saw enemy samurai rapidly working their way towards her, and charged at them without hesitation. She was amazed at how easy it was to fight without the heavy armor impeding her sword's movement as she attacked the foolish warriors who thought they were going to kill her.

Three of Lord Wakatsuki's samurai closed in and attacked her together, going against the beliefs of the code of the warrior. She displayed the motion of sword swings, kicks, thrusts, and punches. She caught the first enemy warrior off guard with a heel kick to the solar-plexus and when he folded over and grabbed his stomach, she lopped his head from his shoulders with one swing of her sword. She had to bring her sword up quickly in order to fend off a thrust from the second attacker, who used her involvement with the other samurai against her. Their swords ricocheted off each other, and she used the momentum to block the third warrior's attack against her. She brought down a blow against his sword in hopes of freeing it from his hands, but the sword stayed lock in them but was knocked away from her body momentarily.

She had to parry a second blow off by the other attacking samurai. Another enemy warrior joined the other two, forcing her to back step some to keep them in her sword's killing range. She slashed at the newcomer, catching him off guard and delivering a terrible gash to his sword hand and left leg in the same motion. He bellowed in pain bringing shame to himself, but the cry was cut off by her sword as it found his throat.

She caught the movement of the other attacker and was forced to ignore the other aggressor for a moment, this one attacking her was a more immediate threat against her life. She did the unexpected and charged at her antagonist, whirling her katana at his chest as she came at him. The tip of her blade found the attackers chest bone and cracked it with a violent blow. The invader dropped his sword and with his hands and last breath, he tried desperately to hold the bones together. She brought down a cruel blow on his head, splitting it in two. She didn't have a chance to enjoy the kill, or take in any life giving air before the remaining enemy warrior charged her, screaming as he hurled himself wildly at her body.

In one hand he held the katana blade, and in the other he held the shorter stabbing blade. She easily fended off the blow from the attacker's katana, but the wakizashi blade caught her high on the shoulder, opening a slight gash on her body. The last enemy warrior stopped his attack and hissed with a sneer on his lips, thinking he had her at his mercy. "Huh great one! If you lay down your sword we can speak of the terms of your surrender to me and my Warriors."

"Ieeeee foolish one who spits filth from his worthless mouth at me! I don't speak useless words, I speak only with sword, and my sword is speaking to me now. It's telling me it wants to drink the impure blood of mine and my Lord and Master's enemies, thus it's speaking loudly." She hissed at the sneering attacker, blood running down her arm and seeing her blood for the first time in life, gave her super human strength as she let out a roar and swung her blade wildly at the last attacker. They locked swords with a thundering clash of metal and tumbled to the ground. She kicked out violently, bringing her knee up and using her elbow to beat her attacker by striking him in the face with the point of her elbow. The only way she broke his hold on her was when she brought up the hilt of her sword and caught him on the chin as she seethed at the enemy samurai as her sword dispatched his life. "Such is the fate shared by all who plot treachery against my Lord and Master and his realm."

The last invader lay helpless on the ground out cold, but what she didn't know was lying at her feet was one of the warrior leaders of Lord Wakatsuki's army, General Tetsuo Hatanaka. Nor was she aware that just moments before she engaged this warrior in mortal combat, he was able to dispatched her lover, Captain Seisakajo by sneaking up on him as he slept and he slit his throat. She rested her foot heavily on the chest of the fallen fighter, the tip of her blood drenched katana lightly touching the body of the downed samurai. After a laugh and grunt, she violently got down to hacking the fallen body to pieces. Then she scattered the pieces apart to destroy the soul of the dead enemy fighter.

Another enemy samurai charged at Wind as she finished with the leader of the group of assassins, she had to dip down to the side to avoid this one's wild charge at her. She spun on her heel and struck the charging warrior on his back with her blade, slicing through his rib cage and backbone, and sending him tumbling to the ground to die painfully. Once the battle died down some, she surveyed the fighting arena, and observed where most of the fighting was still taking place. Then she charged into the swirling melee of swinging katanas and screaming warriors, taking on two enemy warriors as they pressed their attack against some of her horse warriors trying to defend their position against the attackers.

Some of her samurai broke off their attack and got to their bows, arming them and stared picking off the remaining enemy attackers as they now tried to flee from their new attack against the assassins. Swiftly, the fighting ended when what was left of Lord Wakatsuki's fighters broke off their attack, and quickly disappeared back in the crevasses and pitch of night. A light rain started to fall, and her first order was to trap some water so they could wash the blood of their enemy from their exhausted and battered bodies and weapons.

She turned and was surprised not to see Captain Seisakajo standing by her side as always. Over the year she had become accustom to his being there for her. Fear overtook her as she realized she hadn't seen her warrior and sometimes lover since the battle began. She rushed to check on her samurai lover, looking for the only man who ever pillowed her, and gave her pleasures beyond thought and needs. She saw he wasn't with the unharmed samurai, and quickly checked on the wounded warriors, not daring to accept the thought that he might possibly be wandering among the dead. Again, she didn't find her captain or his body. Finally, she called out his name in hopes of him calling back to her.

A warrior heard her calling the captain's name and called back to her. Hearing this warrior she headed for the voice, it was one of her personal guards, and he pointed to the ground where the hacked apart body of Captain Seisakajo lay, among the other bodies of fallen warriors from her army. She slowly knelt by Captain Seisakajo's severed head and respectfully cleaned a clump of dirt from his eye socket. Then she looked up at her guard and ordered a special fire to be prepared. She told him she wanted to take the captain's ashes with them, to give the fallen warrior a proper samurai burial later on when they returned to the safety of her master's lands.

As the samurai cleared the battlefield the best they could being they had no himin to assist them, she took to walking around as if locked in a stupor. She tried to hide the overwhelming pain and longing ripping apart her heart, but it betrayed her. She was constantly on the verge of tears and soon became extremely irritable and lethargic, dragging her feet on the ground as she walked aimlessly about, snapping at some warriors, and dispatching enemy warriors thought to be saved. Her warriors paid no attention to her black mood, but the few who wished her ill, observed her actions and talked behind her back. Trying to weaken her standing among the other samurai. The back stabbing ended when one of Wind's loyal samurai heard the evil tongue wagging, and lopped the head of the offender off.

The night was over by the time she finally returned to her bedroll, and the light drizzle came to an end, but she didn't sleep a wink for the night. She cried for her fallen lover and warrior, it was a new emotion she was suffering through, one she didn't know how to deal with properly, or conquer with her will. With the vast training to become a samurai, her father never thought to teach her how to deal with this disabling grief of a fallen lover.

Daylight came and she was up and mounted without looking at the horse warriors, and rode well ahead of them as if still asleep. The remaining army mounted and followed her without word. Rumors Captain Seisakajo was sleeping with the female warrior Wind, floated around the samurai ranks, and this was accepted as the reason for her suffering her black mood. The warriors gave her the respect and time to heal her loss.

Lieutenant Matsushita took it upon himself and rode up to her left side, the side once shared by Captain Seisakajo, and paced his horse with hers. He didn't want her to feel alone at this time of mourning. He understood what she was going through, he lost his wife in one of Lord Wakatsuki's raids in Kozuke province where they lived.

She barely glanced at the lieutenant and smiled slightly, she was glad to have someone riding in Captain Seisakajo's position. After a few silent miles, she felt a little better about herself, and leaned in her saddle and spoke calmly to her officer. "Lieutenant Matsushita-san, am I right?"

"Hai Wind." The lieutenant replied to her.

"It's no longer Lieutenant Matsushita-san. From this day forward you're elevated to the rank of Captain Matsushita-san. You're now in command of my personal Samurai guards. How many of our Warriors survived the sneak attack leveled against us by Lord Wakatsuki's lowly dog eating warriors, Captain Matsushita-san?"

"Ten in battle and one hundred and three in their opening sneak attack against our forces my Lord." The lieutenant said as he watched his horse walking beneath him.

"I'm not a Lord fool, I'm Wind, Samurai! When we get back to Lord Kawasomeru's encampment, I want you to pick out another ten Samurai to join my personal guard. I want twenty protective Samurai around me at all times, to help guard against any evil treachery aimed against my person. I can't possibly allow myself to be killed before I'm able to carry out Lord Kawasomeru's orders of killing the dog eating Wakatsuki."

"Hai. You honor me greatly with such a raise in rank to Captain, General Masahiko-san. I'll prove my worth to you with every action and breath of my being." The new captain offered with a bow as they continued to ride.

"I have no doubt in my mind of you proving your yukakasa, your value to me and my plans, Captain. You proved I can't get along without you already, Captain. Along with your raise in rank comes the wealth Captain Seisakajo-san had enjoyed. He has no one to honor him, so you'll take his fief as part of your reward for service to me, Captain Matsushita-san." She returned to her silent world as they trailed Lord Wakatsuki's fleeing army, coming across two more pockets of enemy and dispatching them without mercy.

LORD KAWASOMERU'S ENCAMPMENT

The respected warlord made his encampment right in the heart of his enemy lands into a permanent one. The smell of cooking horse meat sickened him to all ends, because he never ate meat. But his concern was for the health and well being of his samurai overrode this unpleasant situation. He knew a starving warrior was of no use to him or his army, he was also aware it would take three sticks of time before his supply lines were firmly established, and his food supplies and needed equipment were finally able to catch up with his rapidly advancing army. Until the supplies arrived, he would force his warriors to eat whatever they had to remain alive, and in fit condition to continue to wage war against his enemy. In the back of his mind he was worried if Lord Wakatsuki was smart enough, he would double back and attack him when he was the most vulnerable. The warlord sent runners out to the villages in Kozuke, ordering all able bodied samurai to join his forces. So he could start replenishing his slightly depleted armies for their final push against Lord Wakatsuki and his army of fools.

The well respected warlord needed warriors and he would get them any where he could find them. He spared nine thousand of Lord Wakatsuki's samurai captured alive during their fighting, when they offered to change allegiance from Lord Wakatsuki to his rule to his command. Once a samurai gave his word to fight for one warlord, he would never do anything to harm him. But if he was captured and given the choice of suppuku or switching sides, it was considered an honorable act for the captured warrior to switch allegiances, for either his death or switching sides completed his duty to the original warlord. The samurai who refused to join forces with Lord Kawasomeru's ranks, met a slow and extremely painful death, many of the prisoners were tortured for countless hours and even days before finally being allowed to die. The lowest ranking soldiers were impaled on stakes or roasted alive over open fires, or were slowly boiled to death in great metal vats, while other enemy were sliced and hacked to death or crucified on a cross on the open plain and left to rot in place.

On the fourth day since her horse soldiers departed Lord Kawasomeru's camp, the food arrived, along with another army of over ninety five thousand samurai from all regions of Lord Kawasomeru's vast realm and the other provinces under his command. With his army fully replenished and well fed, the warlord set off for what he believed would be the final battle against his enemy warlord, but it didn't come that easy for the warlord. For the next year, he was led on one false chase after another, in his never-ending search for Lord Wakatsuki and his army. Hundreds of minor engagements occurred throughout the year, leaving countless villages in Echigo province destroyed, and the slaughter of tens of thousands of civilians caught up in the fighting between the two warlords and their armies.

The powerful Lord Kawasomeru sent out many different groups of spies to search for the hiding place of the elusive Wakatsuki and his ever growing army. The wise master knew what the enemy warlord was doing, every time he thought Lord Wakatsuki was caught in an inescapable trap. The crafty enemy warlord would order his samurai to put down the uniform of the warrior and ordered them dressed in the clothes of commoners and villagers and farmers. Lord Kawasomeru knew he couldn't put to death men without arms, or a threat against him and his army, so he was forced to overlook these commoners in his ongoing search for Wakatsuki.

Word of Wind's exploits were reported to Kawasomeru, but for the last forty five days no engagement took place between his and Wakatsuki's warriors. Twice in the past year, messages were sent to Lord Kawasomeru by Shogun Ashikaga, demanding he report to Kyoto city. Once there, the Shogun wanted an explanation of what was taking place in Echigo. The Shogun couldn't understand why it was taking his superior forces so long to destroy Wakatsuki's army.

The angry warlord Kawasomeru realized Shogun Ashikaga was growing extremely impatient over the amount of time he was taking to end the fighting in the eastern provinces. The powerful warlord also understood it wouldn't be long before the Shogun finally took an active hand in the war, and forcing its final outcome. He was aware the only door open to the Shogun was to end the fighting through negotiations, and that meant Wakatsuki would be allowed to survive and continue making further problems for him and his vassals and provinces in the long future ahead.

By the end of the year, Lord Kawasomeru was putting heavy pressure on his spies and Wind to locate Wakatsuki and his army in hiding. He was mainly interested in the man himself now, he cared little for his army, if they were destroyed in their search for the enemy warlord, it would be all the better for him and his provinces. He was aware if he killed Lord Wakatsuki before being forced to negotiate with him. What's left of Wakatsuki's army would be more than willing to join his forces, thus joining the warring lands together, and putting a conclusion to the long years of war. He was thankful the other provinces that made up his and Lord Wakatsuki's domain, hadn't conspired to go at each other while the warlords were locked in their personal war against each other. It was making it easier for him to draft the needed warriors from villages spread throughout his realm, to help hunt down the elusive warlord, Lord Wakatsuki.

The extremely upset Lord Kawasomeru had no way of knowing that Lord Wakatsuki was sending a constant stream of envoys to Kyoto, and the personal headquarters of Shogun Ashikaga, begging him to intercede in the unending war. By demanding Lord Kawasomeru stop hunting him and his warriors, and the two warlords be forced to talk peace, so the war could come to a end and bring peace back to the realm.

The crafty Lord Kawasomeru moved his massive army onto the vast Kugyo plain for the second time this year, in hopes of drawing the sneaky Wakatsuki and his army out in the open. The warlord left his rear flanks open to attack, or he at least made it look that way to his enemy. Even this enticing a target couldn't bring Lord Wakatsuki out from his mountain hideouts.

Time was quickly running out on the warlord, forcing Lord Kawasomeru to take more daring and reckless chances, to try and force the final confrontation with Lord Wakatsuki and his wandering army. He ordered Wind to take her army out and work over the mountain range to the northeastern of Echigo province in a widening search of his constantly hiding enemy. It took her thirty five sticks of time to flood the mountain area with her warriors, but aside from locating just a few small pockets of enemy warriors she dispatched quickly. She never found any sign of Lord Wakatsuki's main army, or the warlord himself.

A year later the wise Lord Kawasomeru moved his massive encampment from the vast Kii plain to the much larger

Kugyo plain, right in the very heart of Echigo province, in the face of Wakatsuki realm. He smirked, knowing the great loss of face of the hiding warlord suffered to have the invading army of his enemy, make an encampment in the middle of the heart of his land. Even this powerful insult wasn't enough to force Lord Wakatsuki's hand and him out of hiding.

Instead out coming out of his hiding and attacking the insulting Lord Kawasomeru's army begging to be attack by Lord Wakatsuki and his army.   He countered Lord Kawasomeru's strategy by sending another envoy to Kyoto, to beg the Shogun to take a more active hand in bringing the unending war to a forced conclusion. This last envoy was the one who caused the Shogun to finally react and he sent an envoy of his own to Lord Kawasomeru's encampment, informing him he had thirty sticks of time to find and destroy Lord Wakatsuki and his army, or he was going to intercede and force an end to the conflict.

Lord Kawasomeru was fuming as he ordered his spies to locate Lord Wakatsuki or his military officers and if they failed to locate his enemy, the spies were to fall on their swords.   The fuming warlord warned the spies in no uncertain terms that they had only one week to find Lord Wakatsuki and his army, and at the end of that week if they failed in their duty to find the warlord, they were to commit suppuku with no second to die a dog's death. To have it witnessed by a second and send word they carried out his orders.

The female warrior Wind looked after her horsemen, making certain they had enough to eat and seeing the horses were looked after and fed properly. Her hair had grown in and was beautiful, and she shaped it in the way of kami no sagariba. She had the loveliest face, her beauty matched her battle skills, but her armor hid most of her beauty from the world that she was a woman.

LORD WAKATSUKI'S ENCAMPMENT IN THE NORTHERN MOUNTAINS

Lord Kawasomeru wasn't the only warlord suffering from frustration and exhaustion over this never ending war, and his search for the missing enemy leader. Lord Wakatsuki's time was spent pleading to the Shogun to force an honorable end to the fighting, sending his spies to assassinate General Masahiko Tanizaki, the so called chosen warrior. He knew if he could dispatch such an important warrior then Lord Kawasomeru would be more willing to seek a peaceful and swift end to this exhausting war. The only thing that continued to be reported to the angry enemy warlord, was word stating General Masahiko was a female samurai.

He scoffed at what he thought was false information being purposely spread by the crafty Lord Kawasomeru. He believed it was just another way his enemy warlord was trying to insult his intelligence, and make him lose even more face among his samurai, by offering a lowly woman warrior was killing so many of his well trained samurai warriors. To try and make him believe that a mere woman would dare go up against a male warrior, let alone be as successful as this warrior appeared to be, was nonsense and hard to believe the fable. As Lord Kawasomeru continued to send his spies out to locate him, Lord Wakatsuki sent his assassins out to kill the son of the Master Trainer Tanizaki.

LORD KAWASOMERU'S MASSIVE ENCAMPMENT

The powerful and well respected Lord Kawasomeru was awaiting word of Wakatsuki's whereabouts, was busy sharing a light moment with some of his military officers. Wind was with General Kobayashi, and General Shimbo was with Lord Kawasomeru. They were discussed marching into Hokke, the Village of Lotus, but the main topic was the new kosode named kimono, which was the new hit among the Japanese women being worn by court women of the capital city of Kyoto. The warriors laughed about the rich colors adorning the new kimonos, when one of his spies entered the camp. The spy was immediately brought before Lord Kawasomeru, and he reported that Lord Wakatsuki's First General, the long feared and well respected General Motoshima. Was going to move his warrior army from the Village of Hokke, and make his way to the Village of Nagashino in preparations for an all out attack to the south by means of the Kai pass through the Kai Mountains. The Kai pass was carved out of the earth long ago by the mighty Kai River, which still ran along the path of the narrow pass.

Believing he finally had a way to get at Lord Wakatsuki, Lord Kawasomeru suddenly shook his fist in the air, pleased he had the one whose death or capture, would completely cripple Lord Wakatsuki's warring abilities, and it could actually force the crafty enemy warlord out of hiding. He looked at each officer while he worked out his plan on how to attack the famous general in his mind. He studied General Shimbo's face for a moment as he thought, searching his mind for a workable plan to capture or kill his enemy warlord. It came to him like a lightning bolt as he shifted his stare from General Shimbo and rested it on Wind's lovely face. He turned his back on his general and growled at the gathered officers. "All will leave my presence except for General Wind-san. I have some special services needed and she is the only officer I have at my disposal that can see them to their final conclusion. She's the only warrior who can possibly get near enough General Motoshima-san, to dispatch him."

The warlord waited until his generals were out of his tent then he went to his cushion and plopped down on it, his piles driving him crazy lately. He glared at Wind for a moment and then he began to explain what he wanted from the female warrior. "Wind-san! As it was reported, a river runs along the Kai pass that General Motoshima and his army of dogs will use for his travel to the Village of Nagashino. He'll be in the presence of a large army of personal warrior guards, and his well trained Samurai, but I know of this foolish General's only weakness of body and mind. A weakness that'll surely lead to his long awaited demise if you're able to carry out my plans, Wind-san. General Motoshima-san has a feebleness for beautiful women and a healthy sex drive, and this you can employ as your weapon against the great fool of a cursed General who'll betray his duty to his Lord and Master just to lay with a women for a few moments. I have witnessed him on numerous occasions order his samurai guards to leave him when he came across a woman he was interested in pillowing with. You're of twenty years plus two, so it's time you put to use the other weapons that you have at your disposal, Wind-san."

"Ieeeee! How will I properly use this information as my weapon against this so powerful and well feared enemy General, my Lord and Master?"

"Ieeeee Wind! You're without education in the world of pleasures. You're a woman, neh?" The smirking warlord asked of his female general.

"Hai my Lord." She replied as she blushed red over the words of her lord and master.

"That fact alone is your undefeatable weapon to be employed against this foul but great enemy General and warrior. Wind, you must use your body in order to gain his worthless attention slaved to your body and the upper hand over his foolish spirit. Then once you have captured the fool's attention, you'll simply dispatch the great fool while he's drooling all over your exquisite body. Once you have destroyed the great fool, you'll bring me the proof of his demanded death, I order this Wind-san." The concerned warlord snapped as he leaned to his left to get some weight off his piles and legs.

"Wakarimasu, I understand what it is you are ordering me to carry out, but my Lord, what proof can I possibly bring back to you that'll make you rest peacefully in the assurance that I have successfully accomplished my mission as ordered by you, Kawasomeru-sama?"

"Huh! This is the easiest part of the problem that you'll be facing in order to accomplish the mission I have set forth for you successfully I believe, Wind-san. General Motoshima-san has been well noted for an extremely strange and very interesting tattoo printed on his worthless body. It's been tattooed on his mighty peerless pestle, his probing shaft, his Chin Chin. It's a tattoo of a mighty dragon which wraps itself completely around and down to the golden globes that hang below his woman enslaving unconquerable shaft. The dragon's body wraps completely around his foul shaft, and it's said that the head of his mighty shaft is the head of the dragon. Ieeee... The terrible pain that the great fool must have endured for this prized vanity, neh? And when the eye of his great shaft comes out of the hanging skin, it's said it looks like the dragon is actually opening his angry mouth, in order to completely devour the waiting Jade Gate of the woman he's enjoying pleasure with.

"It's been further mouthed that when the foolish General explodes his life giving force within a woman's gate, his mighty serpent spits fire and heat in this force, and it adds greatly to the vast pleasures he offers to his female partner. The proof I seek will be this great tattooed shaft and his great dragon tattoo which I'll proudly use for my trophy. Is there any question about your orders I have placed out before you, Wind-san?" The warlord wanted this prize as his proof of the first general's death. If this fact was true, he would display the severed shaft for all his samurai to view, to show them the well feared General Motoshima-san, was not as immortal as he acted throughout his worthless life as the warlord added to his orders for his female general. "The sought after trophy you'll return with after the General's death, would serve as a further warning for all who dared to go against me and any of my desires on the field of honor that before they lost their lives to me, they'll also lose their woman pleasing worthless shafts. Thus, my hated enemies would not come back to the living world at the time of their supposed rebirth, because the great fools were not whole at time of their worthless deaths."

"Iye my Lord! If this pleases you I'll carry out my mission as ordered. Everything you spoke is clear in my worthless mind, my Lord. When am I to set off to destroy this enemy General to your Realm? I take it you're not considering taking the General prisoner to be bargained with, my Master of time and earth?" She asked as she shifted her light weight on her crossed legs.

"Ieeeee! You're correct in your way of thinking, Wind-san. I have no interest in keeping this extremely dangerous enemy General alive for another moment, longer than I'm forced to endure his worthless presence on Japan's soil. He has used up his time allotted by the Kami gods on the earth.

He's cunning and extremely wise and dangerous, and it's more prudent for you to regard him in this manner. If I took him prisoner, I'm confident that he'd find some way to escape my prison, and I'd again be forced to fight him in the future of time on the battlefield. Something I'd not look forward to I warn you. Iye Wind-san, once you have him in your power, you're to dispatch the fool without thought or mercy, as quickly as you can possibly kill him.

"I want, no correct that, I demand this enemy general dead, Wind-san. I want and demand Wakatsuki dead, and I want this unending war to be over, and I want to be able to return to my Castle and live the life I deserve with my wife and children to enjoy. I'm no longer made for these endless campaigns of war, living in the open like I'm forced to in my search for Lord Wakatsuki's foul head. Ieeeee, my old bones scream at me, and cause me great pain and terrible suffering, when I force them to live as I had when I was of your younger age, Wind-san." The warlord took a breath then called out. "Cha!" to an unseen person.

Yuko appeared from behind her master carrying a tray, and placed it at the feet of her lord and poured the requested tea. Then offered them to Lord Kawasomeru and Wind. No longer was the game of first cup played by either of the warriors. She was unaware Lady Yuko had arrived at the encampment as she nodded politely to Yuko then offered kindly. "Domo Lady Yuko! I trust your travel was of a most pleasant one for you to endure?"

"Hai Wind-san! It was a most enjoyable journey at that I offer you. It gave me the opportunity to check on my mother's failing health. I'm sorry to say, I fear she's near death. Life and death, air and water are but the same, Wind-san. You need all to find inner peace within yourself, neh? My honorable mother lives on the route I traveled, and I fear this is the last time I'll see her alive. You're kind to inquire of my journeys and mother's health, Wind-san. Domo Wind-san, domo."

The conversation would have lasted longer if it wasn't for the harsh glare that the slightly upset warlord shot at Yuko. Instantly informing her that he wanted to speak further with this warrior privately, and she was stopping the conversation from taking place by her babble to Wind. She picked up the silent warning and bowed to Wind, and stood and left her master to speak privately with Wind again.

Once she was gone, the warlord began his words anew for his general. "Wind-san, my spies have reported that the loathsome First General Motoshima-san was scheduled to leave for the worthless Village of Nagashino asatte, the day after tomorrow. That'll give you the time you need for you to get set in position, leave immediately when we finished this long winded conversation between us. If you're not successful on your quest to destroy this General, your brothers and sisters will pay for your failure to my orders and myself. It's your mission to have the General leave his worthless Samurai guards to join you and your pleasures of the body. It's the only way you'll succeed against this wise and extremely dangerous General Motoshima-san. You must dispatch him quickly, and if you're successful in destroying this one powerful General, you'll be the reason for an end to this war raging between the sixteen provinces for past years, General.." Lord Kawasomeru so respected this enemy general he added the san at the end of his name, when he spoke of the respected general.

"Lord Wakatsuki can't possibly continue his war against my armies without the fearsome First General Motoshima-san guiding his worthless army against my army. It's a simple solution to a complex problem we're faced with, Wind-san.

I'll not accept anything but complete success by your efforts on this order, Samurai. I'm with information First General Motoshima-san travels with an honor guard of one hundred well trained and highly disciplined Samurai Warriors. You, will be allowed to travel with an equal amount of Samurai guards to assist you on this mission, but you'll be forced to leave your Warriors behind before you come across the foul General. If you're smarter than he is, you'll have no problem with forcing him to leave the protection of his foolish Samurai guards. Once you're alone with the great fool, you must kill him and make haste or his Warrior guards will take you prisoner or kill you.

"The reason I want you to leave immediately on this mission, is because I want you to have time to locate the position that you'll need to employ for your ambush against First General Motoshima-san. Be wise and succeed, be foolish and you'll be cursed for eternity by all living in my Realm." Lord Kawasomeru saw the disappointment etched in Wind's eyes and knew she was having a problem with this order.

"If it pleases you my Lord, I'll follow my instructions as received."

The powerful warlord smiled then offered his female warrior in a polite voice. "It pleases me greatly, but of course Wind-san, because of your honored and highly respected family's name, and your rightful position in my army. I'll allow you a second option to ponder for a moment over this mission I ordered you on. Your lineage is old and as ancient as time itself, and highly honored throughout Japan's fiery past. So I'm bound by honor to say you don't have to endure the unendurable for my sake and for the sake of Japan's future. You don't have to betray your inner self for my Realm and my needs and desires, Wind-san. If you feel you can't conquer First General Motoshima-san that your wits and skills are no match for his. Or because being forced to use your body as a weapon against this worthless General. Then you have my permission to commit suppuku. But if you chose this honorable course of action, it'll be unattended, and your body will be left to rot in the dust of disgrace and dishonor."

She stared at her master then bowed. "My duty, my life is to serve my Master."

"Very well Wind-san, I'm finished speaking with you at this time. If you have nothing else to add to this conversation then you're free to leave my presence and get on with your mission for my sake and honor. I have other pressing matters that I must attend to I'm afraid, Wind-san." Her lord and master stood to get the pressure off his backside as he shook his leg, to get the circulation moving again in it, because it had fallen asleep on him.

She bowed to her master then stood and turned to leave and begin her mission.

The warlord watched his female general start to leave and snapped one word at her back as she left their meeting. "Gyoko!" Luck!

"Domo my Lord." She hesitated for a moment and replied as she left the warlord's tent. She rushed to the stables and found Captain Matsushita looking after his horse, and ordered him to have one hundred of her personal horse warriors prepare to leave on a special mission at once.

General Matsushita bowed to his commander then rushed off to carry out his orders as she pulled her horse from the stall, threw the blanket over her back and then placed the wood saddle on its back. She strapped it in place and slipped the bridal over the horses head, and set it in place in her mouth. She refrained from placing the heavy armor on its back, she felt if she wasn't going to wear her armor for this mission then there was no reason for the horse to be forced to labor under the weight wearing her armor. When she had her horse prepared to ride, the hundred samurai shown up and they went about quickly saddling their horses. She spotted the captain and ordered him in no uncertain terms.

"Captain Matsushita-san! Have our worthless carriers take enough food and water with them to cover for a ten stick of time of engagement in the field. It shouldn't take us this long in order to accomplish what has to been set out before us to accomplish for our Lord and Master's will. But I want to be well stocked with provisions in case we're forced to hunt down our target, if he finds a way to escape the trap I intended for his worthless self. Swords and bows will be carried by all Warriors for this engagement. You'll remain behind to make certain that my orders are followed properly by the worthless carriers of our caravan. Once this is completed, you're ordered to ride hard so you can catch up with our column of Warriors and myself before we engage the enemy we are going to be searching for, Captain Matsushita-san."

Without further word she jumped up on her horse and pulled on the reins, tugging her horse's head to the left, then she was off on her mission for her master. The mounted column of warriors took after her, and fell in tight formation behind her lead, as the rest of the column caught up to their general.

CHAPTER TWENTY SEVEN
THE FORTH DAY OF THE THIRD WEEK OF THE SEVENTH MONTH OF THE YEAR THIRTEEN FIFTY FIVE

The young female warrior's army rode hard for many hours to get set in a position where she could leave her warriors behind. She feared her samurai might be discovered by First General Motoshima's warriors if they went further together on her mission. She left her samurai in a secluded position and rode on three hours until she slowed so she could look for the proper position of advantage to employ against the feared enemy general. She already carefully worked out most of the plan in her mind, what she needed was to find a place from which to attack the enemy officer. She rode on until she came across the first signs of the narrow Kai pass. She knew she reached it when she found the swiftly traveling waters of the river running by her side. She dismounted her horse and brought her down to the water to allow her to drink. She even joined the horse, the water was cool but not cold. The river had its birth high in the Kai mountains from the snows of winter, and she half expected the water to be freezing. The fact the water was warmer was going to make her plan easier to carry off against the dangerous general.

When the horse drank her fill, she mounted knowing the horse had to move to cool off and not become crippled by the cold water she just drank. She started the horse up the dirt road running along the side of the swift moving stream, in search for the spot she hoped to find. Yard by yard the horse walked the pass until she finally found the exact spot she was looking for, a shallow in the midst of the deeper water of the stream. She dismounted again and dropped the reins at the horses' feet, knowing her horse would stay put until she returned. She stared in the water and saw it dropped off deeper quickly. She stripped her clothes and then lowered herself in the river which felt freezing to her then she swam out to the shallow area in the bend of the river.

Only once did her feet not touch the bottom of the muddy riverbed, finding the shallow area that was only covered by less than a foot of water slightly warmer than the faster running water of the deeper river. With her hands she searched the bottom and found a number of places where she could easily hide weapons under the water. When she was pleased with the location, she dove back in the water and swam to her horse. She took three small tanto blades and a number of sharp skewers, and four kogai's, the razor sharp implement carried in a pocket of the katana.

She also took a few protective plates from her armor, sharpened to a fine cutting edge on one side, if she was forced to use the plates as a weapon in order to defend herself against the imposing enemy general and the attack on her body she was certain coming for her. She picked up a number of throwing stars in case she had to fight off any of First General Motoshima-san's guards. As Lord Kawasomeru done earlier in their conversation, she displayed respect for this enemy general by adding the san to his name when she thought or spoke of him. The powerful general's past deeds earned him this much and more respect from her.

The last items she took were a few karimata, the forked broad arrowheads she removed from the shafts of their arrows. They were sharp and could easily be used as knives, or for the removal of First General Motoshima's famed dragon tattooed shaft. When she accumulated the weapons she felt she needed to accomplish her orders for her master, she wrapped them carefully in silk cloth and then paddled back out in the stream which felt colder than moments before. When she reached the small island again she quickly salted it with her cache of weapons, hiding a tanto blade here and an arrowhead there, and a metal plate elsewhere.

When she was done, she carefully studied the hiding places of the small catch of weapons, and when she felt she had a weapon hidden in every position possible at easy hand's reach, she smiled over her efforts. Her attention went back to a small stand of trees and a group of branches and thick bushes dotting the small island she was going to employ in her attack against the powerful general. After studying them she was struck with an idea and dove in the frigid waters, and swam back to her horse. She removed two battered katana swords, leaving her Sugahara blade resting in the strap. She also took a pair of worn out wakizashi blades, and dove in the water and swam to her small island again. She wisely hid the battered blades against certain small trees and branches, these weapons were her only protection if the fearsome general ordered his samurai guards to stay near him.

The cunning female samurai understood the crafty enemy general would call out to his warrior guards when he came under attack by her. When she was satisfied the hidden blades couldn't be seen easily by anyone who didn't know they were there, she dove in the water for a third time. She came out on the river bank and removed her long bow and grabbed as many arrows as she could carry, and dove in the swift running water and returned to the tiny island. She searched around and planted the arrows behind some other branches and trees, placing the long bow by the largest tree on the tiny, just below the water level island. She would refer to these weapons if she came under attack by either the general or any of his samurai guards. If she was going to die on this mission, she was more than prepared to take the general and as many of his samurai guards with her before she was finally killed by the enemy from the bank.

Once she had all her chosen weapons place properly on the raised clump of earth in the middle of the stream, she allowed herself to relax for a moment, and gave the island another quick look over, to make certain that she couldn't see any of the hidden weapons. She picked up an arrow which she hid better, and one of the hilts of the katana she rearranged until the blade disappeared completely in the background of the bushes of the island. She took a breath, pleased with her handiwork and a shiver made her body shake, and she dove in the water one last time. She came up on the bank and wiggled into a warm cotton kosode for warmth, wishing she had the pleasure of trying on one of the new silk kimonos Lord Kawasomeru spoke of the other day.

Many times lately she found herself wanting what the other women of Japan shared, the finer clothes. The rich lifestyles, and having their hair fussed over by their lowly vassals, and sharing in the gossip of the realm and most of all, pillowing with one's lover in the safety of a home. She breathed a shivering sigh as another shiver from a chill wracked her taught and exquisite body. Finally, when warmth returned to her body, she mounted her horse and walked her further up the narrow pass.

She went about three miles further up the narrow pass until she heard her target coming down the valley before her. She guided her horse up a side path that went over a knoll to a high advantage point overlooking the unending pass for miles in either direction. The female warrior had to adjust her eyes against the sun's harsh glare. After shading them she easily picked up the long column of enemy samurai casually walking their horses and talking amongst themselves. It seemed as if they had nothing on their minds as they looked at some of the wildlife their presence rustled up of the area, and the warriors seemed to be enjoying the different shades of the mountains and the smaller animals that rushed from their hiding places as the warriors slowly approached them. The enemy warriors were so relaxed that they were looking in the water to see if they could spot any fish swimming around.

She surveyed the column of enemy warriors, counting them until she finally picked out the dangerous general riding in the center of the large group of guard warriors. A frontal attack against him would be totally useless for her to attempt, before the general would make good his escape and his guard warriors ended the threat against their general. He was too well protected riding in the center of this large formation of warriors from the front and rear of the column, a wise move on his part she thought. When she seen enough of her enemy she turned her horse and charged down the path and onto the pass and swiftly raced back to her tiny island.

She rode until she came across the hiding place she picked out for the animal. She tied the horse's reins to a tree and kicked a bundle of grass and plants near her horse, she also placed water in her helmet for her horse to drink then she left to wait for her target to arrive at her position. She ran up the steep pass until she was equal with the island, stripped her warm kosode and neatly folded it and left it resting on the top of a rock on the river bank as she swam to her island. Once there she prepared for the attack against the enemy military officer.

It took the leading elements of the column of enemy samurai a feather of time to travel the short distance separating her from the long column of samurai. Advanced scouts were the first to come across the exquisite kosode folded neatly resting on a rock by the river's edge. They scanned the area looking for the owner of the fine garment. Their senses on alert for a possible ambush to be carried out against their general and commander. The first scout pointed to the beautiful woman he spotted sitting on a rock which barely poked its face out of the water. The beauty was washing her long jet black hair in the cool water. The sun was shining off her wet skin mingling with the shadows of the leaves and trees, making it look as if her body was shrouded by a fine coating of light flames.

Adding to her stunning beauty, were the many shadows criss crossing her form as she continued to wash, making her look like a goddess bathing in the swift running waters. From her posture and the length and her silk like black hair, the gawking samurai knew she was a woman of honored bloodline and great worth. The grinning warriors stared at her as they saw her breasts with the erect nipples pointing upwards with no sign of sag to them. The soldiers gawked in admiration at her narrow waist, and hard muscles they could see rippling under the taught and flawless golden skin of her beautiful body.

In the manner which she sat on the rock and washed herself, the warriors could see her rearend was small and perfect. Her long legs were stretched out before her body and she pointed her toes that showed just above the shallow waterline, enabling the scouts to see they were perfect in shape and size. Never before in their lives had the warriors seen such a beautiful woman washing her gorgeous hair in the running waters some fifteen yards from the river's bank.

She actually smirked as she forced herself to act like she didn't notice the foolish samurai gathered on the river's bank staring at her so foolishly, as she continued to seductively wash her hair, and when her hair was wet she suddenly snapped her head back, sending a fine mist of shower of tiny drops flying through the shaded bushes. She found herself fighting a strange and wonderful feeling assaulting her body of having these foolish warriors staring at her in this manner of lust and wanting. Even with the freezing water she still felt warmth growing between her legs, and this feeling made her shiver not over cold, but of desire.

To the group of scouts gathered on the bank delight it looked as if a deity descended from the Heavens, and had just thrown a hand full of shinning pearls throughout the forest bushes, the way the small drops of water glistened in the sunlight and splashed between the leaves.

She again smiled to herself, exhilarated that she could so easily conquered the male's life and ego by merely exposing her exquisite body to their drooling view. Now she understood what Lord Kawasomeru meant during their conversation, explaining she was a female and would know what to do when the time came for her to act. She decided to add to her strength over these foolish warriors by running her hands slowly over her breasts, rubbing the nipples and pouring water over them then cupping her breasts and lifting them gently.

When she ran a hand between her legs she felt the foolish samurai were going to dive in the water, and rush her in wild frenzy of desire and lust. She found herself wanting this, demanding this from the fools, fighting as she was she couldn't get the wanting of a man out of her mind any longer since finding out she was a woman, and shared what women do with their male counterparts. Her thoughts rushed to the fond memory of her young Captain Seisakajo, and the wonderful joys he introduced her to in the art of pillowing with a man. She fought a tear, knowing now wasn't the time to travel down this road of the past, and relive what was not livable. She forced the pleasing thoughts of the only lover she ever experienced out of her mind, vowing she would relieve them, once her duty to her master was done.

The enemy samurai dropped behind some stones to try and avoid being discovered by the stunning beauty and losing this beautiful view forever. The warriors watched as she continued to bathe as if they were not there for as long as they dared, before slowly moving away and continuing on with their security duty for their general's trailing column of warriors. The scout ordered to report back to the general, spoke in a whisper to one of the other samurai. "Ieeeee! Have you ever witnessed such a rare beauty being displayed before our worthless eyes like this? I wonder why this woman chose this spot to bathe her body, I thank the gods for?"

"Hai, I'm certain this woman was more used to the cursed and foul gardens of the capital of Kyoto, only to be displayed for the worthless eyes of the Shogun and his chosen leaders and politicians and foolish artists. We're lucky beyond dreams to be allowed by the foolish gods to witness such beauty as she washes in the waters of this filthy river. As long as I live I'll never forget this wonderful vision and this bitch. Oh, to pillow with such beauty I'd die a happy Warrior indeed. I'll never be able to pillow my wife again in the same manner, after witnessing this vision from the gods. This lowly woman must be of the highest value to the realm, and would only spread her foul legs for the greatest of worth fools of Japan."

"Hai! I agree with everything you uttered from your foul mouth, fool." The other scouts replied as one as they took one last long look at the stunningly young female sitting in the cold waters washing herself, as if she hadn't a care in the world.

"Huh! I wonder what dung eating heap owns her worthless contract." One guard asked the others as he continued to stare at the beauty of the river.

"Ieeeee! What makes you think a beautiful woman like that one, is owned by any one fool? I say she's a private consort of a powerful Daimyo, and will only respond to a Samurai of equal wealth, respect and class. We poor manure heaps will have to be satisfied with mere glimpses of such beauty reserved for the ones who own us. May the worthless gods take their hatred out on the foul heads of the wealthy, making it impossible for them to enter such a beauty, by striking their worthless dragons dead. For keeping the vast wealth and beauty of Japan to themselves, and forbidding us poor Samurai to own anything of wealth and beauty for ourselves to enjoy. There is nothing in our future but war and death."

As the samurai scouts talked between themselves, each one offered to swim out and pillow with the stunning beauty of the river water. But each warrior knew the feared general would have their heads, if they forsook their security duty of his personal safety for a few brief moments of pleasure with the woman of the river. The excited warriors understood it would be the general who would try this beauty's pleasures, and they would lose their heads for defiling such a prize meant for the general's pleasure if they forced themselves on her.

The scouts reluctantly split up with four warriors continuing down the long pass to make certain there were no possible ambushes setup against their commander, while the fifth scout returned to the large column of warriors so he could report of the beautiful woman's presence washing herself in the river to his commanding officer. It wasn't too uncommon to find someone bathing in the clear waters of one of many of Japan's rivers. So this didn't cause any urgent alarm when the scouts came across Wind bathing in the fast moving waters of the river.

The lone scout rode swiftly back to the general's side, and explained what they found washing down river of their present position. First General Motoshima interest was aroused and asked the samurai a number of questions about the naked woman bathing in the river, as he looked down river in an attempt to try and see the naked woman for himself. At first there were questions regarding his security, and the possibility of this strange but beautiful woman being a plant to cover a possible ambush aimed at destroying the famed general.

The fearful scout reported that they carefully searched the entire area surrounding where they discovered the beauty washing herself, and found no sign of any possible ambush that would prove successful, to have planted this woman as a diversion for their evil actions. Once the general was sure this wasn't an ambush setup against him, his questions quickly turned more racy. Asking the scout to describe in much better detail this beauty's body, starting with her breasts and going to her rearend and then legs. The general's guards closed ranks so they could also listen to the description from the excited young scout, and when he assured the powerful general this beautiful woman was one of fine wealth and position, his interest peaked, and he worked his way up towards the front of the long column of warriors.

As the column neared the spot where the beautiful woman was reported bathing in the river, the lead horsemen picked up the beauty still washing her body. One turned to another warrior and announced sarcastically as he strained his eyes in order to see what the scout reported on. "This woman must be whore of the lowest class to be so dirty as to be still bathing in the foul waters of this filthy river. I feared that we might have missed this sight, but alas she is still there and still washing her foul body. I thank the gods for sharing this vision with me."

"Ieeeee! Dirt or no dirt, I'd give any of my worthless consorts and a year's pay, for the pleasure of pillowing her for one night of pleasure. Look at the beauty possessed by this foul one who has nothing more to do with her worthless life than to be enjoying her bath before us as if she doesn't know we're here watching what she is doing. I believe she is washing just to give us a show of what we'll never be allowed to enjoy for ourselves."

The female samurai's senses were on full alert and she heard the hooves of the approaching horses beating on the hand ground, and had no choice but to acknowledge the enemy warrior's presence. By slowly turning her back from the gawking, gathering samurai staring at her from the bank of the river. She crossed her arms over her ample chest and smirked at the fools staring at her as if they had nothing better to do with their worthless lives.

The many lines of shade criss crossing her back and slender but powerful shoulders, added greatly to her stunning beauty, and took the breath from the horse warriors as they slowly filed passed her. The samurai noticed her exquisite kosode resting on the rock, and understood she was trapped on the tiny island until they all had a good look at her wonderful nakedness. Some of the grinning warriors called out nasty remarks at the beauty caught in the water, while other warriors made obscene noises and cat calls at her. Some of the foolish warriors even tried ordering her to turn around and move her arms from her body so they could see more of her naked form in the waters of the river.

The female warrior known as Wind could not help herself and smiled as she tried her best to ignore the rude remarks being called out to her from the foolish warriors as they stared at her as they rode by her. It took over ten minutes for the column of samurai to ride past her. The excited general finally caught up to where she was reported bathing and picked up the naked young woman in the water of the river. He dismounted and his second in command did likewise, and held the reins of the general's horse while he took in the lovely sight of the naked young woman. Together, they stared at her until the well feared First General Motoshima announced cantankerously to his second commander. "Huh Captain Sannomiya-san! I think it's time that I have a bath for myself.   I fear that I'm more dirty that I believed on this foul day."

"It's been a time since you last pillowed with a young woman if I remember right, First General Motoshima-san." Captain Sannomiya offered with a smirk and quick head movement towards the naked woman washing in the water.

"Ieeeee!   You know me all too well I see, Captain Sannomiya-san. You, woman sitting on the foul rock out there in the filthy water, turn and move your worthless hands from your cursed body, so that I may visit upon your beauty, and judge it for myself, foolish woman! I warn you woman of the water, I'm not with unlimited patience."

She totally ignored the barking and commanding order from the bellowing general as she smiled to herself, knowing she had him right where she wanted him now.

"Woman on the Rock, this is First General Masahatsu Motoshima-san from the Village of Dogs under the command of Lord Wakatsuki who owns the very ground that rests under the fine rump of your. I have just ordered you to do something for me, neh woman? Do as I ordered or I'll placed an arrow in that finely crafted backside of yours to make you carry out my orders more swiftly, foolish woman." With that said the powerful general removed his long bow from his horse and then armed it with an arrow and aimed it right at her exquisite body and waited for her to carry out his orders.

From the corner of her eye, she was able to see the angry general truly armed and aimed the arrow at her back and knew she had to do something, or she was going to die for no good reason before she even had a chance to carry out her orders from her lord and master. She called back over her shoulder to the officer in her sweetest but teasing voice. "My Lord who is in possession of the big mouth and a loud voice, how am I to know you are who you say you are? Am I a mere common whore of the lower class eta, that I'd dare expose my body to any lowly commoner in the possession of a great mouth, and a deep and commanding voice. I think not my lord and master of the strong tongue and loud voice." She gave one of her most seductive chuckles and a slight wiggle of her shoulders at the general.

"Ieeeee! A commoner you dare call me, neh foolish witch of the polluted waters of this filthy river! I have all of the proof you need to know woman with a sharp tongue and terrible manners. But first you'll have to turn to witness the proof that I shall offer for your information and knowledge, and I see your foul beauty with my eyes at the same time." The grinning general announced proudly, while he waited for her to do as she was ordered by him.

She turned slowly and faced the powerful general defiantly but refused to remove her arms from her body.

"Now drop your foul arms from that body so I might see the beauty you possess as I ordered you to do before I lose my patience with you and end your worthless life with this arrow, Goddess of the River." First General Motoshima growled from deep in his stomach at her.

"Only if you show me the proof you are who you bellow you are, Lord of the loud mouth." Wind purred sexily at the interested enemy officer.

"Foolish woman of the cold running waters, it is not very wise to tease me so, it could cost you your worthless life for the insult. Now Witch of the water, if you know anything about me and my reputation then you're well aware of my mighty Chin Chin (Penis) tattoo." With this said, First General Motoshima hitched his fundoshi aside then exposed his hardening member to her view. He was actually holding himself in his hand and shaking his member until it stiffened to its full length and strength.

She witnessed the great dragon growing within his foul hands and smiled to herself. She had to admit she was wanting to see his mighty member.

"Does this answer your worthless question, Witch? Young Goddess of the cold River Waters who dared to call me a commoner and still breaths. Me, First General Motoshima, General in Lord Wakatsuki's great army a god cursed commoner. I should plant an arrow in that fine rump of yours for daring to insult me in such a foul manner, evil woman."

"Hai First General Motoshima with the swaying mighty dragon locked in your foul hands. I do know of your outstanding reputation and you truly are who you say you are to me. I have heard many stories of your famous woman pleasing dragon, and his exceptional ability to make a woman cry out in wild passion and lust at their coupling. I see from where I am washing that many of those stories I heard seem to be true, General Motoshima-san." She purred again at the enemy general as she continued to smile at the military officer.

"Huh! Now you know who I am woman of the river, allow me see what you truly look like so I can judge if I want to waste my time with pillowing you in the waters you wash in. Remove your foolish arms away from your body, so that I may drink upon your unlimited beauty that's being hidden from my view with your arms." The general demanded angrily.

She slowly lowered her arms by her sides, and stood straight in the eight inches of water.

"Ieeeee will you look at her Captain Sannomiya-san! The fool of a worthless scout was correct indeed, she's a true goddess of the rapid running waters of the river. Foolish woman of the cold water! Turn sideways so that I may see all of your stunning profile. At once, my patience is growing thin with you I warn." The general growled loudly then waited for her to do as ordered.

The continuing line of passing young samurai warriors took in the lovely sight of her nakedness, as they slowly rode by their general in silence.

She did as ordered by her intended target, but she carried out her orders slowly, defiantly, taking her time to comply with the general's angry orders. She continued to smile over what she was doing to this loud mouth but powerful and extremely dangerous enemy general.

The angry general drew in his breath and grumbled at his military officer a second time. "By the worthless god who pollute the dreams of the foolish Captain Sannomiya-san! Have you ever seen such fine breasts on a lowly woman in all your foul life? This one must be of private stock for the god's own worthless pleasure. I'll truly enjoy her fine skills in the art of pillowing, and then I'll kill her for daring to waste my time as I'm doing with her arrogance she is displaying before me. Have the foolish Samurai continue on with their foul march and orders. I'll catch up with you and the rest of the column after I have had my full of this worthless woman. And I had successfully dispatched her so no other fool can enjoy what was offered to me." First General Motoshima started to crawl out of his heavy armor.

"First General Motoshima-sama! I'm not very pleased with this situation as it's being played out before me. By good judgment and safety I have to go against your wishes to enjoy this foul woman's pillowing abilities. I have orders from Lord Wakatsuki to protect your life at all costs. I'd be failing my duties to our Lord and Master and yourself, if I leave you behind with this foul woman of the river. I'll lose my head even if nothing happens to you, except for your enjoyment with this evil black haired witch. Wakatsuki-sama has little patience when it comes to one failing his duty and orders." Captain Sannomiya offered in his defense as he actually took hold of the general's arm in order to stop him from undressing further.

The instantly fuming General Motoshima stopped undressing and glared angrily at his captain for daring to lay hand on his person, as he growled savagely at the concerned officer. "Captain Sannomiya-san! How would you like to lose your worthless head for failing to carry out my orders, fool? I know of Lord Wakatsuki's foolish orders, so your breath is wasted on my foul ears needlessly repeating them to me. I have just decided to take some time to enjoy myself, and that's exactly what I intend to do with this fine looking witch of the river. Since I don't like an audience when I conquer a woman's sexual spirit, and make her squeal like a seagull begging fish. I suggest you carry out my orders as I said them to you, and leave me alone while I taste this woman's fine treasures." The general continued to glare at his lesser officer.

Captain Sannomiya gave a sigh of displeasure then he nodded in compliance with the general's orders and he let go of his arm, and offered in a much calmer tone to his commander. "First General Motoshima-san! I hope this foul witch of the forest is as good with giving pleasures on a rock as she appears to be on an overstuffed pillow. First General Motoshima-san, I'll hold the column of Warriors up at the next turn in the unending road we travel on and then we'll wait you there until you have finished conquering this Witch of the water."

"Huh! I believe I just told you that I didn't like an audience when I'm pillowing a woman, any woman, Captain. So that'll not do good enough for my likes, Captain Sannomiya-san. I have just order you to keep the Samurai moving forward all the time. We have to make up time and reach the worthless Village of Nagashino by tomorrow morning at the latest, Captain. If we're to be successful with our planned attack against our worthless enemy. I'll ride hard down river to catch up with the column once I'm finished with this evil one in the river. I have spoken and the matter is closed to further conversation as far as I'm concerned, Captain Sannomiya-san." The general glared hotly at his young captain, while placing his hands on his hips and waiting for the officer to finally do as he was just ordered by him.

The concerned captain finally relented and he bowed at the still fuming commander. Then he turned and relayed the powerful general's orders to the other warriors who were kind of bunching up by them in their attempt to see the beauty of the river. The samurai instantly increased their pace after the order, passing by the quickly stripping general who once naked, stomped off in the swift running cold waters of the river as if he was angry with the water. The general was unable to swim, but his head stayed above the water by his tip toeing, he was three inches taller than Wind. A few times he lost his footing and his head dunked below the water momentarily, but he retained his composure and continued until he came across the shallower water of her small island. By the time he reached her island, his entire column of warriors had passed by them, and were moving off and slowly out of sight.

First General Motoshima because of his position and nature was a bore, and displayed this terrible fact as he rapidly moved in on Wind like a wild animal in heat, and he roughly shoved her back like the brute he was, as he physically manhandled her breasts. Painfully pinching the nipples and hurting her as his fingernails dug deep in the soft, perfect flesh. Although she was looking forward to another coupling with a different man, she came to resent this inhuman animal violently assaulting her body as if she was a common whore of the lower class. The overexcited general sucked on her nipples, biting and nipping at them as he enjoyed himself at her expense and pain, everything he did to her body, caused her pain and terrible embarrassment and anger and he didn't care a lick for her pleasures as long as he enjoyed himself with her body.

She forgot how pleasant the art of coupling with her lover Captain Seisakajo was, as she found herself fighting off the savage attack of this inhuman pig. The general wouldn't budge an inch as he continued to pinch then bite and nipped at her breasts. He ran his hand roughly between her legs, forcing them apart and stuffing his stubby fat fingers inside her, causing her to cry out in pain momentarily which the crazed general took for a pleasure moan, as he grumbled at her in an angry tone. "Ahhh... Lowly Goddess of the Swift Running Waters, I see you like it rough, neh? This is good to know worthless woman, that's the way I like to share a pillow with a witch such as yourself." The general hissed as he forced a second finger in her. He roughly bit the nap of her neck, actually drawing a trace of blood as he forced her deeper in the shallow water so he could mount her, and begin his final assault and insult against her exquisite body. Not caring a bit if she was enjoying what he was doing to her, the angry general was only interested in fulfilling his own lust and desires.

Everything was happening too quickly, and she was rapidly losing control of the situation with the overbearing general's attack against her body. She found herself desperately trying to regain control over the wild acting general's harsh movements, by placing her hands against his barreled chest, and her pushing hard against him by it.

"What is the matter with you now Whore of the Seaweed and smelling fish? I don't pillow you like you're accustomed to by the ones you service with your loathsome body? I pillow like a true Samurai Warrior, rough! Like I lived my life all these foul years. I don't pillow like the cursed politicians whose lives have become so soft and wasted by their foul years of good living and growing fat and lazy on the backs of us Samurai. Get down on your worthless back and spread your filthy legs and make room for the mighty dragon to enter your endless void, evil woman who insults me further by hesitating in doing what I demand of you. You're about to ride my mighty dragon to heights you have never achieved before in your worthless life."

The general looked so foolish to her, standing before her with his member stiff as a dragon's tooth, while swaying back and forth as he moved in with his hands reaching for her body. But she had to admit the sight of the awesome dragon which appeared to continue to grow in length and width, made a most interesting vision in her eyes.

The general kept grabbing and pinching at her exquisite body, displaying the most putrid of manners leveled against her being, by not giving the slightest concern to her pleasure nor enjoyment, as he tried to mount her body again.

She pushed on his thick chest again, but the general wasn't to be denied this time as he roughly shoved her back on the ground, and her head dipped beneath the water momentarily as he used his weight to keep her pinned to the ground. She ended up lying in six inches of water when the overweight and excited general plopped heavily down on top of her, and forced himself in her as if she were a mere whore who worked the back streets of Kyoto for mere copper coins. Grunting like a deer in heat, the fearsome general kept pushing on her body, hurting her and forcing her head under the water more than once while he continued his attack of her. At one point she was actually forced to roll out from under his heavy weight so she could get her head out of the water and breathe. She came up gasping and fighting for air while trying to get his weight off her body. The self centered general slid out of her and tried to force himself back in her roughly, as she rolled on her side on him while still gasping for air.

She struggled to her knees, forcing the still excited general to get to his knees, so he could try and force enter her while kneeling before him. One hand of the general tried to force himself roughly back in her, while his other hand continued to pinch and hurt and paw at her bruised and battered breasts.

"Please First General Motoshima-san! You're working way too hard at this wonderful experience of pillowing with me which is to be enjoyed by both of us. Please relax First General, and allow me to bring you some special pleasures that I'm capable of exposing to your interest." She purred as sexily as she could at the excited officer, as she kept moving one hand under the water, inching ever so closer to the place where she hidden one of the small razor sharp tanto blades. While her other hand kept pushing on the powerful general's chest in an effort to try and keep him off her body so she could kill him.

Lord Wakatsuki's well respected and feared general thought she was speaking of giving him pleasure with her mouth, and grunted in anticipated delight as he suddenly arched his back and placed a heavy hand on her head. Then he tried to force her head down to greet his swaying dragon before her face. He growled powerfully at the beautiful woman as he continued to try and guide her head towards his waiting shaft. "That's it worthless woman of the filthy river, lift my Kin Tama (Golden balls) and roll them gently in your worthless hands. Then take my mighty Dragon in your mouth and show me this great pleasure you offer to me, worthless woman."

She resisted the heavy pressure the excited general was placing on her head, as she replied in a calming tone. "Please First General Motoshima-san! You're still working way too hard in your search of pleasure with me, please my Lord, relax and allow me to bring you such pleasures that you have only dared to dream existed in your many years of honorable life." She suddenly shoved him roughly back and the general landed placing all his weight down on his knees and ankles, using his arms behind his body to stop himself from tumbling backwards. She heard many stories of how the women of the Tea House pleased their samurai, and she tried to remember the ways to keep the foul general's attention glued to her, as her hand cautiously felt below the water in her search of the tanto blade she hid earlier. She took his stiff member in her hand and slid it up and down on his shaft, as she cried at the powerful military officer.

"Ieeeee First General Motoshima-san! Your mighty dragon is greater than any spoken about in all Japan. You're a powerful Warrior with enough of a joy stick to bring great pleasure to many women on one night I fear." She offered as her hand quickly brought him up to steel like hardness. She slowly ran her hand up and down the shaft of the general, and every once in a while she would pinch the very tip of it, making the general squirm in pain and delight.

At last, her fingers finally touched her very edge of the small blade. She grasped and moved the blade stealthily around under the water in her hand, until she had the proper grasp on the handle of the weapon. Then, with her left hand she ran her fingernails on the bottom of his shaft, making the enemy general close his eyes in expected ecstasy. He was so lost in his anticipated pleasure of her mouth that he didn't realize when it was she replaced her fingernails with the biting edge of the razor sharp tanto blade at the base of his shaft. Then, with her other hand she worked the shaft making it as hard as ever. When she felt the time arrived, with a swift movement she cut his offending member with one swift swipe. Then she held a death grip on it as she brought the hand with the knife swiftly up and out of the water.

The stunned general didn't even realize he was just deprived of his tattooed manhood, and by the time reality set in, she moved the blade up against his gasping throat. In a chilling tone she hissed right in the once powerful general's face, showing absolutely no fear of his greatness. "Evil and loathsome First General Motoshima-san who is under the command of my Lord and Master's hated enemy! This is the foul fate suffered by all who wage war against my Lord and Master, Kawasomeru-sama!" She slit the general's throat.

Blood splattered on her face and bare chest, but it was quickly dissolved by her soak and wet body.   Lord Wakatsuki's foolish general didn't utter a word, as blood surged from his mouth and nose. Choking on his blood, his eyes stared the look of death as he desperately grabbed at her body with both hands. He couldn't speak because her cut was so deep in his throat, the slash severed the general's vocal cords. While his life was rapidly draining from his bloated body, his grasp on her body lessened until he finally let go of her all together. His body slowly sank into the swift running waters of the river, as the general's hands continued grasping at the air for a handhold and the little life still left in his body. She had to shove the overweight general's body away from hers, and it was instantly swept away by the strong current of the water.

She threw the razor sharp small knife in the water, and placed the severed member of the general in her mouth, and dove in the chilling waters and quickly swam for the river bank for the last time. She slipped in the dry kosode and ran for her horse as fast as she could run. After mounting she rode over the same path she used to get to the river's edge. As she rode off she opened up an ever increasing gap between herself, and the enemy general's samurai army.

The concerned Captain Sannomiya disobeyed his commander's orders and ordered a showering of the pace of his column despite the warning from the angry general. This strange woman washing in the river didn't set very well with him, and he fought the ill feeling of doom hanging heavily over his head. The column of warriors continued on for another fifteen minutes before the captain finally called for a break, so the exhausted warriors could water their horses and relax their legs and enjoy a quick rest. The samurai shared a light moment, they cursed and told stories of their exploits in some of the shadier Tea Houses of the realm under Lord Wakatsuki's control. The break lasted longer than Captain Sannomiya intended because he was subconsciously waiting for his general to catch up with the column, and he was just about ready to order the warriors to remount their horses and ride on, when a samurai suddenly spotted a body floating by in the water and called out to the captain the alarm.

At first, the captain thought it was the body of the woman killed by his general, after he had his way with her body. As he studied the body closely as it floated by him, he suddenly realized the hair was cut in the way of the samurai, and the stunned captain called out to the samurai who spotted the body in the water as he pointed at it. "Get the foul body before it passes us, fools!"

Fifteen young samurai immediately dove in the water without hesitation and struggling mightily to hold on the wet, slippery and overweight naked body of their once feared general. The warriors roughly dragged the body of First General Motoshima back to shore by means of his well oiled aquene knot and slack heavy arms. Captain Sannomiya's heart was caught in his throat as he looked disbelieving at the terribly butchered body of his famed general. He snapped out of it and snarled angrily at one of his officers from the column. "Samurai Toshikazu-san! Take fifty Warriors and ride out and bring that witch of the river back to me! I want her captured alive so Wakatsuki-sama can melt out her foul fate. Don't come back to me without her, or her cursed body at least. I'll apologize to our Lord and Master for our failure of protecting our General. Wrap his body in a kosode then we'll return to our stronghold on Mount Miochin."

The samurai carefully and respectfully placed the general's body across the saddle on his horse then they rode off to Lord Wakatsuki's main encampment stationed at Mount Miochin, where they left with the general to reach the Village of Nagashino.

Meanwhile, Wind rode like a crazy person, trying to put as much distance as possible between herself and First General Motoshima's samurai army, she was certain would be perusing her once they discovered the general's body floating in the water. She knew it was a short distance separating her and her samurai waiting her return and once she was with them, she would ready them to engage the enemy soldiers in pursuit of her.

First General Motoshima's samurai reached the place where they left the general with the woman bathing in the river, and they easily picked up her tracks in the mud and her horses', and in no time they were riding hard the same pass to try and catch up to her.

The female samurai almost rode right past her waiting samurai as she charged down the pass at breakneck speed, causing her horse to actually skid on the ground trying to stop at her command. As soon as they saw her the waiting samurai mounted then quickly assembled and waited further orders from their female commander.

"Isogi! Hurry, I'm certain to be trailed by First General Motoshima-san's worthless Warriors. I don't want to engage the fools trapped in this narrow valley. Once we break free of the foul pass, we'll then take up position of defense at the very mouth of the valley, and then we'll allow the foolish enemy Samurai to ride right into our trap, and we'll spring on and slaughter them to the last worthless warrior." After giving her samurai their new orders, she rode off with her samurai charging right behind her.

By the time the samurai under Captain Sannomiya's command went by the path Wind used to escape once she slaughtered their general, she had her samurai set in position for attack. Lieutenant Toshikazu's men broken out of the valley and ran head long right into Wind's entrenched samurai. In a brief but extremely costly battle, Lieutenant Toshikazu's warriors were slaughtered to the last samurai, with only twelve of her warriors falling to the battle. Most of the enemy warriors were brought down by a cloud of arrows before they could even get set to defend themselves against the attack. Once the enemy samurai were dealt with, she then ordered her samurai to mount up and then head back for Lord Kawasomeru's encampment.

It was getting late by the time Captain Sannomiya and his column of warriors finally arrived near Lord Wakatsuki's massive encampment. He moved his samurai as quickly as he dared in the twilight, and only increased his pace when he picked up the harsh glow from the cooking fires of the vast camp. His warriors slowly rode into the encampment in a very solemn mood. He spotted Lord Wakatsuki standing with a number of his advisors who were already informed of the captain's arrival in the camp, and he came forward to greet him. The fuming warlord stormed up to the concerned captain and growled. "What is the meaning of this foolishness, Captain? Your army was ordered to escort First General Motoshima-san to the Village of Nagashino. Where the devil is the General? Get off of your horse, because I don't like looking up to anyone I'm speaking with, Captain Sannomiya."

Captain Sannomiya dismounted as ordered by his extremely upset lord and master, and called Samurai Nozoe forward, who brought up the horse with the general's body draped over the saddle. Lord Wakatsuki couldn't hide his anger as he moved closer to the body and lifted the head of his general by the top knot, and stared into the lifeless eyes of his dead first general. Spitting fire and seething with anger, the wild acting warlord turned back to Captain Sannomiya and demanded angrily of him. "What the devil happened to my god cursed General, kisama!" (lord of the donkeys)

Captain Sannomiya immediately dropped to his knees and bowed as he quickly explained what happened and how First

General Motoshima had ordered him to leave him behind over his strong objections with the strange and beautiful woman bathing in the river water. He ended his words with the offer to commit suppuku for his failure to stop or protect the general from the harm that had befallen him and cost the general his life.

Lord Wakatsuki was unable to control himself, he was crazed with anger as he stormed around the horse and nastily pulled the body of his general off the horse, and he allowed it to fall unceremoniously to the ground before his feet. The upset warlord kicked at the twisted body of his general then stormed up to Captain Sannomiya and kicked at him as well. When the captain informed Lord Wakatsuki of the indignity that the general suffered at the hands of his female assassin, by having his mighty ChinChin cut off by this female beauty, he went absolutely wild with rage. He demanded to have the missing member found at all cost, and have the head of the loathsome female executioner brought before him, so he could shit in her face before he killed the female assassin, once he had enough of abusing her body for what she had done to his once feared and powerful general.

Captain Sannomiya further informed Lord Wakatsuki he dispatched fifty warriors in pursuit, in an attempt to hunt down the bitch assassin, and they hadn't been heard from since he ordered them out to capture the assassin. The angry warlord drew his sword and out of sheer rage he lopped the captain's head from his shoulders without word, while he knelt before him. He then ordered the general's personal samurai guards to dismount and commit suppuku before his feet one after the other. As each warrior carried out his order without complaint or hesitation, Lord Wakatsuki quickly walked down the line of self slaughtering samurai, and he angrily hacked their heads from their shoulders in a wild rage.

LORD KAWASOMERU'S ENCAMPMENT ON THE VAST KUGYO PLAIN

The powerful and well respected Lord Kawasomeru was enjoying a cup of cha and sharing some pleasing conversation with a few of his military advisors and officers when the first riders from Wind's warriors rode in the massive encampment site. The warlord threw the small porcelain cup aside, and instantly stood and went out to greet the returning exhausted warriors. His female warrior was the twentieth rider to enter his camp, something she had picked up from the late and once well feared enemy First General Motoshima, to ride in the center of the column of warriors instead of riding at the lead as she was accustomed doing. So she could be better prepared to defend herself if her column came under attack by enemy warriors. She proudly rode up to Lord Kawasomeru and jumped down from her horse and instantly dropped to her knees and bowed greatly to her lord and master.

Along the way riding to Lord Kawasomeru's encampment, she ordered a break in order to rest the horses for a while, and she took the time to dress in more appropriate garments, and had her swords tucked properly in her wide sash.

"Ahhhh, Wind-san! Tell me you brought me my sought after prize for that lowly General fool, Samurai?" Lord Kawasomeru snapped in a deep and threatening but commanding voice. Forgetting about good manners as he waited her reply.

"Hai, I have what you desired with me, my Lord." She replied as she held out her hand and offered the severed shaft wrapped in a clean silk cloth to him.

"Ieeeee, not out here foolish Samurai! Carry the foul Chin Chin to my tent for my private viewing, General Wind-san." The grinning and proud warlord barked as he turned his back and stormed off with his female samurai following behind him. Once they were in the tent, the lord sat before a lacquered table and snapped at her. "Cha!" He motioned for her to sit by his side while he prepared to view his prize.

"Huh, allow me to see his foul member. Is the unbelievable rumor true, he had dared to have his shaft painfully tattooed, Warrior?"

"Hai, it's as you have stated to me my Lord. It is indeed tattooed with the great dragon." She announced as she placed the cut shaft on the small table and unwrapped it carefully.

"Hieeeee Samurai! I bet that must have hurt the great fool when they tattooed the shaft in that manner. Look Wind-san, look at the rich colors and how the wise craftsman carried the dragon's form all the way around the thick shaft of the worthless and arrogant fool. Huh! Where is the tail of the great dragon tattoo, Wind-san?" The pleased lord suddenly growled as he carefully rolled the shaft over using the very tip of a small tanto blade, fearing to dare touch the slivered shaft with his bare hands.

"My Lord, I fear to explain that the tail of the mighty serpent was entangled within the bag that hung from his mighty shaft. I didn't take that prize for fear of the amount of damage my removal would have caused the hanging sack." She offered as she lowered her head in a weak bow, fearing that she might have let her lord and master down by not taking the rest of the dragon tattoo from the hated general's body.

"Hieeeee! The great fool had dared to even have the tender sack and rounds tattooed as well as his mighty shaft! I'd like to have been there when they tattooed that area on the great fool, consumed with vanity and self-indulgent to dare order this done to himself. I bet the worthless General had a lot to say to the skilled craftsmen and gods, when they began working their magic there in that area. Huh Wind-san! You have done well, very well indeed and I believe that you have single handedly broken the back of the lowly mongrel Wakatsuki at long last. Wind-san, while you were gone I had luck with locating where the foul Lord Wakatsuki and his dog eating Warriors hide. They have a camp stationed in the mountains at Miochin. I have my officers preparing to march off to begin their hopefully final attack against him and his worthless army tomorrow morning. This will give you time to rest before you march by my side. We'll not be forced to engage his loathsome army, where he hides is easy enough for us to just lay siege to the fools once we have successfully trapped the worthless dog eaters there. We'll just starve them out of their shelters then we'll slaughter them to the last as they come out of the mountains in search of food and water."

The smiling lord continued to stare at the severed member of the general's tattooed member then he dismissed Wind by offering her in a calming tone of voice. "Huh, you seem weary my young Warrior. Make use of my personal hot tub, have something to eat then sleep until we're ready to march off to our final victory over this great dung eater and his foul army. Domo Wind-san domo, you are as your father had warned me, Warrior. I had something delivered from Kyoto for your pleasure and enjoyment. I hope you'll enjoy the fine present I have for you for accomplishing the impossible what I sent you out to accomplish."

"Hai, domo Kawasomeru-sama. I'm certain whatever the gift is, it will please me as all your wonderful gift have done, my lord and master." She bowed as she took the gift from her lord.

"Wind-san! I can't wait and hold my tongue. It's one of the new kimonos worn by the honored women of the capital of sin and pleasures, Kyoto. Enjoy the gift I offer you, it's a token of my pleasure and honor at the work you have done for my cause." He returned her bow.

The female general left the warlord's side and went to her tent set up for her by the warriors of the encampment and once she was inside the tent, she opened the rice paper wrapping carefully. It was a beautiful kimono made from rich silk in vibrant colors, and more elegant and far better than used in the older kosode garment. She allowed the fine silk to unfold in her hands, it was longer than most kosodes she worn before. Flowing, softer and felt so soothing and cool against her skin. The colors were the most striking of the beautiful garment, the yellow looked like the sun at its full glory, and the blue looked like the water of the ocean.

"Oyasumi nasai!" Good night! Lord Kawasomeru replied as he followed her to her tent and waited until she opened the gift so he could see her reaction.

"Oyasumi nasai my Lord."

The warlord smiled and then turned and left her alone in her tent.

When her lord and master was gone from her tent she quickly stripped of her traveling kosode and took advantage of the warlord's hot tub. She bathed, the water soothing the many small nicks, bites, and scratches she suffered at the hands of the ugly First General Motoshima. Once she completed her soak, she slipped into the new kimono and it felt so wonderful against her bare skin. Awakening feelings she didn't know were in her body. The exquisite garment made her feel more like a woman than a man for the first time in her short life, except for when she pillowed with her only love, Captain Seisakajo. She rushed back to her tent and fixed up her hair, creating a small bun on the top of her head, allowing the longer strands of hair to flow freely over her chest and back.

She held the bun in place with a pair of finely crafted Ivory skewers, she next covered her face with the stark white rice powder, and making sure every pore on her face was covered with powder. She then applied the brilliant red given her by her wise and caring sister Estsuko, to her lips with a brush. She dipped a fine brush in the black and carefully encircled her beautiful eyes, carrying the tail out from the corners of her eyes, to make them look longer and narrower than they were. Then she added the dot of black high on her cheek as she seen countless fine women of Japan do in the past. The female warrior used the reflecting metal disk given her by her master, to make the finishing touches on her makeup. She stared at the face in the reflecting disk used as a mirror, and smiled at herself. She knew her body looked the same as most females of Japan, but seeing her face made up as a true Japanese woman of worth, was stunning for her to witness.

She realized that she looked better than most women she envied and saw in her life, when she went to Lord Kawasomeru's courts and the many gatherings he ordered. She wanted to run outside and allow all the samurai under her lord and master's control to see her in this manner, but her mind stopped her from moving out to do so. She lit a few candles and some sticks of incense then had a little warm rice and some dried fish and turned in for the night, proud of the way she looked as a woman.

But she didn't fall asleep right off, instead feeling like the woman she was lead her to explore her body in ways she never dared before. Exploring her inner self in search of what General Motoshima and the men of Japan searched for from a woman for those times of pillowing. She found it when by self manipulation, she experienced what she did on the night, wrapped securely in the arms of her only lover in life, Captain Katsunoke Seisakajo.

LORD WAKATSUKI'S SAMURAI ENCAMPMENT

The still fuming and wild acting warlord Wakatsuki ordered three envoys to meet him at his tent once he killed all the samurai he had assigned to protect his general's life. He rushed to the tent, not bothering to wash the blood from his hands, as he sat and composed another letter to the Shogun. When he finished the letter he gave a copy to each of the waiting envoys, in case one was captured by Lord Kawasomeru's ever searching samurai. The envoy was to kill himself to avoid captured, after he had completely destroyed the message written by him for the eyes of the Shogun alone.

He was leaving nothing to fate. Once his envoys were gone from his encampment, he sent for four assassins he had obtained from the sect of the Talon Ninja at great cost. When the assassins assembled, he ordered them to kill the famed son of Master Trainer Tanizaki. The leader of the assassins was the only one who motioned, the others stood as if it would cost them their lives to dare move a muscle or speak one word. The hired executioner nodded in agreement and then he turned and quickly left the master's tent with the other assassins following in silence. The supposed son of the master trainer was well known by all who had meaning in the realm.

The suddenly exhausted warlord finally allowed himself to relax for a few minutes and enjoyed a quick breath before sending for his next in command. General Sadeyuki Okamatsu marched in his tent with all the arrogance and a terrible sneer mounted on his face that he could muster. The still upset warlord motioned this general to a tatami resting on the floor five feet from where he sat, and when the general was comfortable, Lord Wakatsuki began his words on what he wanted his general to accomplish for him.

"General Okamatsu-san! You're now elevated to the prized position of First General of my Warriors and officers. If you want to keep this position as well as your foul head resting on your shoulders for a day longer. I command you to prepare our worthless Warriors to march out against the capital city of Kyoto at once. Notify all our allies immediately to be ready to march side by side with us, as we pass through their foul territory for the capital of Japan, Kyoto." The warlord shifted his weight and then waited for his general's reply to his new orders.

"Ieeeee my Lord and Master! Kyoto! The capital city of Japan you wish to lay attack against, my Lord? Why are we going to dare cross swords with the powerful Shogun and his massive armies to our south in his city of sin? Why awake such a sleeping dragon, my Lord? It's foolhardy to dare to attack so powerful an army, especially on their own turf, my Lord. Think of the armies the powerful Shogun could command to his aid if we dared such a fool hearted move as this." The surprised military officer cried as he stared in the eyes of his commander.

"Because for your worthless information General Okamatsu-san not that I owe you any explanation of my plans! If I owe you an explanation, this is the only way we'll force the foolish lazy and ever growing fat Shogun to finally take an active hand in this unending war with that lowly dog Kawasomeru. Right now the foolish Shogun backs Lord Kawasomeru's crazed ambitions more than he favors my desires, because the Shogun's precious capital city is free of attack. The great fool spends great sums of worth constantly building and extending his dung heap of a capital into a grander city of sin and laziness every day. The Shogun would be sick with worry that my army would destroy his priceless city, if we dared threaten attack against him in his capital. He'd do everything in his worthless power to stop this threatened war, before we reach his city and bring it down upon his foul ears.

"Thus General Okamatsu-san, I'm banking everything I hold dear to myself on the worthless Shogun ordering the hated and worthless Lord Kawasomeru to make peace, before we reach his precious city and attack it. It's a gamble, a daring gamble true, but one I must take if I'm to end up with my province and wealth still intact, fool. I curse the hated spirit that successfully killed my foolish First General who was weak of skin and mind, without him leading my foul army I find myself forced to resort to such dangerous tactics of threatening to attack Japan's capital city and our worthless Shogun. One way or the other, I'll have the loathsome head of the lowly assassin who has killed my First General if it's the last head I take, before entering the Floating World myself. Assemble my army and send messengers out to have the other provinces loyal to me, to assemble their worthless armies to support my last orders, General. I hope a mere strong show of force will be more than enough for that worthless dung heap living in his city of sin Kyoto to react in the manner I'm demanding of him." The warlord gave his general a quick wave of his hand, dismissing him crudely. The general didn't move.

Drawing in a huge gulp of air, the extremely angry warlord snapped hotly at his concerned general. "Yes General Okamatsu-san? You seem to have something else that you wish to add to this discussion?"

"Hai my Lord and Master, I'd like to speak further with you, Lord Wakatsuki." General Okamatsu bowed in fear of his life.

"Enlighten me with your words of wisdom even though I don't seek the words you believe would change my mind at what I have just ordered, General." Lord Wakatsuki ordered nastily.

The overly concerned military officer bowed a second time to his lord and master as he offered with caution lacing his voice. "Wakatsuki-sama! What happens if the mighty Shogun takes excepting to your threat and he assembles his great armies, and they then engage us for daring to threaten the capital city of Japan and our Shogun? There is always that one possibility where the Shogun might combine his vast armies under his command with those of Lord Kawasomeru's armies, and then that one massive army would attack us. We'll be trampled to dust under just the mere size and weight of those powerful and overwhelming armies, Wakatsuki-sama. There'd be no possible hope for us to survive if the Shogun takes to attacking us with his massive armies, let alone if he combines his armies with those of Lord Kawasomeru's armies. We'll lose everything we have if we dare to challenge the Shogun and his Realm so."

"Ieeeee First General Okamatsu-san!   Look around yourself now you great fool." The angry warlord ordered as he brought his hand from his chest and waved it out before him angrily, as he added to his angry words as his new first general.   "In case you haven't noticed as yet General Okamatsu-san, we have already lost everything but our worthless necks in this never-ending war. I'm daring this extremely bold and dangerous move, in an all out attempt to try and hold on to my two worthless provinces, so that I can again rise up another army powerful enough to finally dislodge the worthless Lord Kawasomeru from his branch and two worthless provinces.

"Then we can take over the eight central provinces one after the other, so I can elevate myself to the order of Shogun of the Central Provinces, and later in life, challenge the worthless Shogun Ashikaga-sama himself wasting his foolish life in his sinful capital of Kyoto, for dominance over the entire Empire of Japan. The loathsome Kawasomeru holds me by my foul piles, and I need time so that I can regroup and grow my army, before I can march out against him again.

"I find myself locked in the terrible position of being forced to sue for a temporary peace with the hated Lord Kawasomeru and his worthless supporting provinces, and allow myself to keep as much of my power as I can intact, and the only way to accomplish this great feat. Is by making Shogun Ashikaga-sama's water run with fear of my ambitions aimed at his worthless city and Realm. By the lowly gods I'd dare to challenge the Divine Son himself to mortal combat, if I thought it'd save my provinces. First General Okamatsu-san! I have just issued you a number of orders to carry out, and if you don't possess the mettle in your foolish body and back to carry those orders out, I'll find another General from my ranks who does. You will lose your head for failing to support me and any orders I aim at you." Lord Wakatsuki turned from the general, showing him he was rudely dismissed.

The only thing General Okamatsu could possibly think of doing in a response to the angry warlord was to bow to the back of Lord Wakatsuki and then quickly leave his tent while his head was still rested on his shoulders.

LORD KAWASOMERU'S VAST SAMURAI ENCAMPMENT

Lord Kawasomeru who was in an extremely great mood stood on the slightly raised platform, and watched and waited as his massive samurai army quickly assembled before him, for their final engagement planned against Lord Wakatsuki's army. The powerful warlord understood it would take at least fourteen sticks of time in order to get his great army in position in the mountains, so they could surround Lord Wakatsuki and his army hiding on Mount Miochin. All the while he waited for his warriors to be ready to march off, more warriors were coming into the vast encampment, and joining the ranks of his ever swelling army. The proud warlord looked for his female warrior, but didn't see her anywhere in the melay of moving samurai and horses.

The still exhausted young female warrior heard all the commotion taking place just outside her tent, but she decided to rest a while longer before investigating why the commotion. She was enjoying the outstanding feeling of the exquisite kimono and makeup on her body. She was really tempted to walk outside her tent in the makeup, but knew she would lose great face among her warriors for daring to do so. She was crushed by the knowledge that the only time she could ever really look and feel like a real woman of Japan, was in the privacy of her tent. She felt sad she might never have another man to pillow with for the rest of her life. With a deep sigh of despair, she rose from the bedroll and washed her face, and then she changed from her beautiful kimono into her fighting kosode.

As many times as she washed the well used garment, the battle kosode still smelt of dried blood and stale sweat and horse odor, and it always felt dirty against her clean skin. She tied the obi around her waist and then she slid her pair of fighting swords between the strapping. She then fixed her hair in the style she wore it in times of battle, and then slipped into her sandals and left the tent to see what was happening outside. It was good she came out just when she did, because when she stepped foot outside her tent, she bumped right into the concerned Lord Kawasomeru, who was coming to her tent to check on her condition. He smiled at her as he followed her back inside her tent for a moment.

The worried warlord stared hard at her face for a moment to make sure she was all right, there was some of the white powder still remaining on her face, and the observant Lord Kawasomeru took notice of it. He knew what she had done and was sorry for her, he made a mental note to pick a few of his best and more handsome young warriors, and order them to seriously court his female warrior for her sexual attention. He cursed himself for not looking better after her inner spirit and health. He bowed as he spoke softly to her as he held her in his gaze. "Ohayo gozaimasu Wind-san!" Good Morning.

"Ohayo gozaimasu Kawasomeru-sama! Anata wa yoku nemutta ku?" Did you sleep well? She asked as she politely smiled at her lord and master.

"Hai, Domo, thank you for asking Warrior. Did you sleep well also Wind?" The powerful warlord replied as he returned her smile with one of his own.

"Hai my Lord. Very well thank you." She replied with a smile.

"Wind-san! We're about ready to march out against the great dung eating Wakatsuki and his foul army we'll soon have trapped in the mountains where they hide. I heard nothing from his camp, I dared hope he'd do the wise thing and surrender to us to avoid the bloodshed about to take place between our two armies, now that the great fool has lost his fearsome First General to command his worthless troops in battle. You did your duty for me, and I'll reward you properly for your faithful service when we finally return to Engakuji Castle and my realm, after our great victory over this lowly mongrel has been accomplished. Are you in good health on this great day, my Warrior?" Lord Kawasomeru asked with concern in his tone of voice.

"Kawasomeru-sama! It's not necessary to be rewarded by you all the time for my merely doing my duty for you and your Realm. You embarrass me greatly with the overly generous offer you keep heaping upon my worthless shoulders. And yes my Lord and Master, I'm in good health and I thank you for asking, Kawasomeru-sama." She was actually shocked by his impolite directness aimed at her person during this disturbing conversation.

"Huh! I'll reward you for your fine efforts the way I see fit Samurai, and that will be that. Enough said on this subject of gifts, Wind-san. So, you're in good health you offer my worthless ears to hear? This is good to hear and enjoy, Samurai! Does this mean you have pillowed with one of my lucky Samurai fools, Wind-san?" The powerful warlord displayed terrible manners by daring to ask such a personal question of her, but he wasn't known for his tact or good manners.

She felt her cheeks redden as she replied, totally embarrassed by his question. "Hai my Lord. I'm in good health and feel well my Liege Lord." It was her duty to answer any question put forth to her by her master honestly.

 "Ieeeee my Warrior! Who was my lucky Samurai who you shared your pleasures with, Wind-san?" The master of the realm bellowed with mirth as he openly grinned at his female warrior while waiting her reply. Then he added while increasing the insult he was aiming at her person. "Is the great fool still with life remaining in his poor body, General Wind-san? If you pillow in the same manner that you fight in battle, I fear for the life of any of my worthless warriors who have the good fortune to pillow with you."

She hesitated for a brief moment before answering the impolite question, again totally embarrassed by her liege lord's directness in the questions he was asking of her as she replied while trying to keep the sadness from her voice and eyes at the same time. "I shared a pillow with Captain Seisakajo-san, my Lord and Master."

Now it was the powerful warlord's turn to be embarrassed by his words as he mumbled. "Huh! It was a shame to lose such a fine young officer as Captain Seisakajo-san was. Karma is Karma and death is but a short sleep, until we're reborn by Lord Buddha to a new Samurai life. Captain Seisakajo-san will be reborn a great Samurai in a few week's time with much wealth in his possession I assure you, Wind-san."

"Hai my Lord, I pray to Lord Buddha every day for that to be true." She replied, speaking barely over a whisper and her unending pain.

"Wind-san! Did the foul General Motoshima-san hurt you in any manner, before you were able to dispatch the great fool to the land of the Floating World of wonder and myth? I understand it was a terrible mission I had sent you out on, but I hope you understand you were the only warrior that I had that could possibly accomplish what I needed and demanded done." He asked concern, as he stared in the beautiful eyes of his young female warrior.

"I understand why I was picked for that certain mission my Lord and Master. And all I received from the foul General was just a few minor nicks and bruises I fear, nothing serious though I offer my Lord." She replied politely to Lord Kawasomeru's question.

"Good. Good. I guess it's time for you to join your Warriors then, Wind-san." The respected warlord watched as she bowed politely then rushed off. As he watched her, he found himself wishing he had an army of Winds under his command, if he did then there would be no military or army he couldn't conquer in all Japan. Again he reminded himself to order a few of his better young officers to court her hand.

The massive encampment was sheer madness at best, with hundreds of horses angrily neighing as they were hurriedly saddled, along with samurai screaming at one another and running all over the camp and officers giving out orders to the rapidly moving samurai. A horde of hinin was rapidly packing up the samurai's equipment then carrying it off and armor of the excited samurai clanging. The mayhem made the warlord want to cover his ears.

General Shimbo slowly walked his horse up before his lord and master with the warlord's horses reins locked in his hands. The general stopped and waited for Lord Kawasomeru to mount his steed, and together they rode off to the head of the rapidly forming column of warriors. The warlord was the first to speak between the two warriors and he offered in a matter of fact tone of voice to his military officer. "General Shimbo-san! I wish a favor of you, I want you to order a few of your better disciplined and kinder officers to court my young female Samurai's pleasures. I want her spirit and health well looked after properly by the fools picked by you to do so. It's not wise for her to be so unpleased all the time, General. That General I have to look after more than all my other officers. She asks for nothing from me but give her all."

"Hai, Kawasomeru-sama, I understand this. Any particular officers you have in mind you want courting the female Warrior, my Lord?" The general asked as he struggled with the reins of his horse and replied in a non-interested tone of voice.

"Iye! No! I'll leave that up to your decision, General. You pick out the foolish warriors you trust the most because you know the fools much better than I. You will warn the great fools if they hurt her in any way, their worthless dragons will join that of General Motoshima-san's, hanging from my war banner behind me, General Shimbo-san."

The general's eyes drifted up the pole of the war banner waving gently behind his master's head, and was able to just make out the shriveled and drying tattooed shaft of the dead enemy general, hanging so ominously from the tip of the flag. That was enough said on this subject of courting then the warlord rode off in silence, leaving his general lagging slightly behind while pondering his last orders of him.

LORD WAKATSUKI'S SAMURAI ENCAMPMENT

A carrier pigeon suddenly appeared flying over Lord Wakatsuki's massive camp. It was quickly caught and the contents of the message reported to the concerned warlord. The contents of the report informed him that Lord Kawasomeru's entire camp had just pulled up stakes and was now on the move, and it seemed the enemy army was heading directly for the Kai mountains through the narrow Kai pass heading north directly towards his camp. He was ill prepared to get involved in a full engagement with his enemy at this point, so he was forced to change his plans.

The extremely concerned enemy warlord ordered many of his warriors to move to their secondary hiding places spread throughout the vast mountain range, and they were to employ these positions in which to attack the massive enemy army reported marching at them. Each warrior was ordered to engage any parts of Lord Kawasomeru's army, only if they could inflict heavy injuries and death on their enemy. Then the attacking warriors were ordered to break off their engagement of the enemy forces and escape in order to fight again. He intended to fight a war of attrition against his hated enemy of Lord Kawasomeru. He understood Kawasomeru's army was further away from his own lands, which meant his supplied were forced to be moved greater distances to catch up to his mighty army, and this could cause his army to break off their attack until their supplied reached them.

CHAPTER TWENTY EIGHT
KYOTO CASTLE, THE CAPITAL CITY, KYOTO, JAPAN

The special envoy sent out by Lord Wakatsuki, made it safely to the capital city of Kyoto. He was given an audience with Shogun Ashikaga-sama. The fearful envoy handed the Shogun the scroll with Lord Wakatsuki's chop resting on it. Then waited for the powerful Shogun to read it and give him a reply he could return to Lord Wakatsuki with.

Shogun Ashikaga snapped the wax seal with his thumb with little interest in the message. Then he unfolded the three fold paper and read words of Lord Wakatsuki, as if he was bored to death over the entire matter. As he read, he slowly stood and began to pace his platform, he was furious that Lord Wakatsuki was daring to threaten an attack on the capital. His mind raced, he could ill afford an all out war right in the very heart of the capital city of Kyoto. It would make him lose great face among his people, he promised them as long as he lived, Kyoto would never come under direct assault from any invaders to the lands of Japan.

The suddenly fuming Shogun's first instinct was to organize his vast army's then attack this foolish brazen daimyo for daring to threaten his court and capital. The Shogun fixed his glare on the face of the envoys from Lord Wakatsuki. He stopped his pacing and bellowed at the man. "How dare you bring me this foul warning from the worthless fool you serve. Go to the courtyard and commit suppuku at once. These foul words of your Lord and Master has disgusted me to my soul, and you fools shall pay for this insult with your worthless lives."

The fuming Shogun Ashikaga waited for the envoys to leave his presence then spoke with his First General who escorted the envoys to his presence and asked the officer. "General Mitsuyoshi Morimoto-san! What's your opinion of this threatening and disrespectful scroll, sent to me from the dog eating Wakatsuki?" He handed the paper for the general to read.

General Morimoto quickly read the paper then barked angrily. "I'll gather my army and ride off and find this fool and hack off his worthless head. Then his hands for daring to threaten my Liege Lord in such a foul manner, Ashikaga-sama."

"Yes General Morimoto-san! That was my first thought as well, but then I reconsidered my angry thoughts with a clearer mind. I think we should step in and order Kawasomeru-sama and Wakatsuki to make peace between themselves. I can ill afford to have an army of Lord Wakatsuki's marching against my city threatening to destroy it and myself. Ieeee General Morimoto-san! Here's what I'll order you to do in this rapidly unfolding drama. I order you to take a full detachment of Samurai to Lord

Kawasomeru's massive encampment I know is stationed at the Kugyo Pass in Echigo province. It should take you a little over twenty sticks of time to find the Master and his encampment of Warriors.

"General Morimoto-san, you'll deliver my scroll personally to Lord Kawasomeru. Then you're instructed to find where the foul Wakatsuki's worthless encampment is located, and you'll send a rider out and deliver him a second scroll in my name. I order you to stay in position in Kawasomeru's encampment and oversee the peace negotiations you'll instigate under my name. You'll not leave Lord Kawasomeru's encampment until you have a signed agreement in your hands from both these warring fools. General Morimoto-san! You have the power to take the heads of either or both of these fools, if they're too stubborn and foolish to make peace with each other, whether it be Lord Kawasomeru or Lord Wakatsuki that pays the price for this continuing foolishness with their worthless lives. I have had it with this warring raging on in the eastern provinces upsetting the entire of Japan and my Wa.

"It's beginning to give the rest of the foolish Daimyos some bad inclinations if the war is allowed to continue unchecked, and all Japan might find itself in the handhold of war. It's time this war is finished with. General Morimoto-san, pick the Samurai you need and want to escort you, a force of fifty warriors should be more than enough to stop any god cursed Ronin from disturbing or attacking you on your travels. Yet your detachment will be small enough not to impede you speed. General! Order Samurai from any province to join your ranks if something happens to your men and they are somehow depleted. I'll send pigeons out to Dewa to place the armies in the lowland on full alert. If this fool dares to mount an army and aim it at my city of Kyoto, I'll have my armies swoop down from my province of Dewa and slaughter the maggot eaten fool and his worthless followers. Make haste General Morimoto-san."

"Hai my Lord and Master. I'll be leaving at once Ashikaga-sama." The excited general replied as he left the Shogun's side.

As Shogun Ashikaga watched his general rush off to carry out his orders, he decided to send a pigeon out to Lord Kawasomeru's encampment. Ordering him and his Samurai to remain where they were stationed, until his personal envoy arrived under his name and banner.

LORD KAWASOMERU'S SAMURAI WARRIOR ENCAMPMENT

Although most of the samurai left Lord Kawasomeru's encampment, a small unit of samurai were left behind to guard the camp against invasion from Lord Wakatsuki's armies. Samurai Keijiro Ota was in command of the camp, making certain the hinin packed up Kawasomeru's needed provisions, when the pigeon flew low over the camp. The handler brought it down by means of chucking a dropper, a pigeon that had its wings clipped so it couldn't fly well. When the dropper landed on top of its coop, it caused the other pigeon to land on the coop next to the other. The handler easily caught the pigeon and removed the note and rushed it to the lead Samurai Ota. His eyes were unable to hide the shock at reading it, the message came from the Shogun, and when he announced it, the samurai near him dropped to their knees and bowed.

Samurai Ota knew he had to catch up with Lord Kawasomeru and his slow moving columns of warriors, and inform the powerful warlord that the Shogun ordered him not to attack Lord Wakatsuki, and he was to remain stationed at his encampment until a special envoy arrived with word from Shogun Ashikaga from Kyoto. The samurai mounted and rode hard, it was fifteen feathers of time since Lord Kawasomeru's army marched off to engage the enemy forces under Lord Wakatsuki's command. He rode at dangerous speed throughout the night until he finally caught up with his master's army. He rode along the column until he caught up with Lord Kawasomeru, he jumped off the horse and knelt before the warlord and bid his attention.

The powerful and exhausted warlord held up his hand and the column of warriors came to an immediate stop. The warlord dismounted and walked over to the worried samurai, the sun was just rising in the overcast sky as he asked. "Samurai Ota-san! Why have you chose to leave my encampment I ordered you to remain at and protect against any possible attack from our enemy forces? Has the dog eating Wakatsuki circled around my flank and attacked the camp and defeated the remaining samurai left in the camp with you?"

"Iye my Lord! You're encampment has not come under attack from Lord Wakatsuki's forces. I left the campsite and came after you because I have a message from the Shogun. It arrived by carrier pigeon two feathers of time ago."

The suddenly concerned Lord Kawasomeru grunted as he took the slip of paper and read it, a samurai had to run with a torch so the warlord could make out the words printed on the paper. Without a change of expression, he barked at the samurai. "You done correct to bring this note to me immediately, Samurai Ota-san. We'll wait until the sun is high, before we turn and head back to the encampment. General Shimbo-san, General Kobayashi-san and Wind-san, prepare your forces to return to our campsite. We're ordered to wait there by the Shogun, for the arrival of his special envoy from his command. Give the orders to the other Samurai."

The fearsome warlord knew what this paper and order meant, it informed him that he finally ran out of time, and the interceding Shogun was going to force him to make peace with Lord Wakatsuki. He cursed the karma that made the world work for his ill luck at hunting down the worthless enemy warlord, before this note reached him and ordered him back to his camp.

The army of the warlord turned and headed for Kugyo Plain, it took lord Kawasomeru's army a stick of time to reach it. He wasn't pushing his samurai, his thoughts were troubled with the knowledge he was being forced to make peace with Wakatsuki, and this was eating at him. He ordered his assassins and spies out in hopes they might be lucky enough to end Lord Wakatsuki's life, before the envoy arrived from Kyoto. He held little hope of the assassin's success, and soon he turned his mind to working out terms to peace he would accept with the foul one.

The angry Lord Kawasomeru knew he was in a far better position than his enemy Lord Wakatsuki was, and this would enable him to demand better terms in dealing with the loathsome Lord Wakatsuki. The warlord was in low spirits and nothing got him out of his black mood. He understood he had to watch his back, because Lord Wakatsuki's assassins were sure to be thick as head lice on an eta's head, and they were most likely hunting him.

LORD WAKATSUKI'S SAMURAI ARMY

Word quickly got back to Lord Wakatsuki that Lord Kawasomeru's massive army suddenly turned, and was heading back to their original campsite stationed on vast Kugyo Plain. The enemy warlord was stunned over the troublesome news, and he was at a loss as to why Lord Kawasomeru would dare turn his mighty army from the conflict he was mired in. He called his generals together to work out the reason why. One general offered the only reason was if something dreadful must have happened to Lord Kawasomeru, while marching with his army.

"Like what!" Lord Wakatsuki bellowed at his officer as he glared harshly at him.

"Maybe Lord Kawasomeru died, or was suddenly struck ill of health my Lord. Maybe one of our assassins was successful in hunting him down and killing or severely injuring him."

Lord Wakatsuki jumped to his feet and began to pace as he milled over his general's words. He stopped pacing and grumbled at his military officers gathered before him. "Ieeeee! Do we dare desire for the unattainable to have happen? Could the gods in their infinite wisdom, removed the only obstacle blocking my way for dominance over the sixteen central provinces of Japan? Have my prayers to the lowly gods been answered by the fools? Have they chosen me to lead the central provinces to greatness that has eluded them for countless years? If they have I'll build many great shrines of homage in every conquered province under my command, to each god for their support of my ambitions. None in Japan will be more magnificent than the ones I'll construct, if the gods removed Lord Kawasomeru from this equation. Send out more of our spies and see if what you have suggested took place. If it has, you'll be one of my most important Generals in my armies, if not you'll be boiled alive General."

LORD KAWASOMERU'S ARMY MARCHING BACK TO THEIR ENCAMPMENT

By the time Lord Kawasomeru and his army returned to his campsite, the remaining samurai left to protect the area had it ready to accept the influx of countless samurai and their lord and master. It was expected the special envoy from the Shogun to arrive the next day. The still fuming warlord's black mood continued as he snapped at anyone who dared cross his path. He ordered the massive camp prepared to receive the Shogun's envoy, though he didn't know who Shogun Ashikaga sent to organize the upcoming forced peace talks. It didn't take long to find out, for the Shogun's general made great time on his travels, and arrived in the camp that night.

The camp was well lit by many torches and countless campfires, when one of the samurai guards spotted the special convoy and his entourage coming towards the camp, gave out the alarm. By the time Lord Kawasomeru was dressed, the envoy and his following had entered his camp. The warlord rushed to the horse warriors and examined the faces, he was stunned to see Shogun Ashikaga's First General, Mitsuyoshi Morimoto-san sitting on the horse peering down at him with an angrily scowl plastered on his grime covered face. The surprised warlord bowed with precise formality towards the well known general.

General Morimoto's horse was lathered and rode hard near death, and shifted the general's weight on his back as the tired animal tried to rest on its legs. The general dismounted and bowed curtly to the warlord then demanded a tent where he could change, and a bath and new kosode. Lord Kawasomeru's samurai dropped to their knees and bowed to the angry acting general, as the liege lord lead him to his requested tent. Once inside, the exhausted military officer breathed a huge sigh of relief, but didn't relax completely. He was well noted for his brass rudeness, ruthlessness, and ill manners displayed against all who had contact with him. The general's eyes burned from dust and dirt of the road, and the lack of rest added to his foul temper and mannerism. The general's kosode was stained and filthy from sweat and grime from the hard ride to the encampment, and didn't do anything to help calm his boiling rage, so he didn't mince words when he began to speak to the warlord.

"Kawasomeru! Shogun Ashikaga-sama is extremely upset at your failure to end this foolish war with the dog Wakatsuki with haste. He has ordered me to intercede on his behalf between the two of you foul fools. The Shogun's extremely worried the entire Realm might erupt in flames, if this cursed war between you and Wakatsuki is allowed to continue unchecked. The Shogun has deemed it fit to bestow upon my shoulders, the power to force peace between you two fools. Or I'm to order both lords to commit suppuku, and then I'm to take your worthless heads back to Kyoto, for the Shogun's private viewing and pleasure.

"Lord Kawasomeru, I bound by my honor to inform you that I have sent a special messenger to Mount Miochin to order Lord Wakatsuki to come to your encampment. If he doesn't appear by tomorrow's sunset, I was instructed to order the southern armies of Shogun Ashikaga-sama from Dewa province, to march against his armies of dog eaters. I'm to combine their strength to that of yours armies, and together we'll hunt down and slaughter this lice infected army of Lord Wakatsuki's. My messenger should be arriving at his worthless encampment as we speak, Lord

Kawasomeru. I want food to enjoy and meet this General Masahiko of yours I have heard so much about, and am unable to believe half of those foul lies you have spread about this young warrior, my Lord. I heard too many stories of this Samurai to believe them all true. You, Lord Kawasomeru have great rumor spreaders I admit." General Morimoto complained as he plopped down on the pillow then removed his swords while preparing to eat.

Lord Kawasomeru had ordered food and sake prepared long before the honorable general arrived at his camp and had it brought in abundance to the tent, as he offered to the Shogun's officer. "General Morimoto-san, the glorious stories you have heard about Master Trainer Tanizaki's child are true. She's the most valued Samurai I have in my armies."

"Ieeeee Lord Kawasomeru! I fear that you might have been in the field for too long a time. Now you can no longer tell the difference between male Warriors and a worthless female. You have just erred calling this General Masahiko a she. Have your wits eluded your mind and will, Lord Kawasomeru?" The now grinning General Morimoto replied with a smirk as he sipped sake then scratched himself proudly in front of the warlord.

"Iye!" The liege lord snapped loudly at the angry acting general from Kyoto.

The general stood while angrily throwing his cup aside, as he glared harshly at the warlord and growled. "Kawasomeru! Don't dare inform me that you had the piles to enlisted the services of a lowly woman into the Samurai Caste. I can only hope that you're using this woman as a pillowing service for your honored Samurai to enjoy when they return from battle."

The instantly angered warlord overlooked the obvious insult leveled against him by General Morimoto, when he had omitted the 'Sama' from his name for the second time since arriving, as he spat at the officer. "This fearsome Warrior who I named personally, will defeat even the mighty General himself in war. Wind-san is the best ever with sword, spear, and is deadly with the bow. She can out ride most my male Samurai, and can fight them to a draw with her hands. She's the chosen child by the Kami, and this fact has made me overlook the one mistake that the foolish gods had committed, when forming her being in her mother's womb. Allowing her to enter this world as a lowly woman. Even so, I'd pit her against your best of Warriors, and she'll defeat them with haste I assure you, General Morimoto-san."

"Hai Kawasomeru-sama! If all of what you offer is true, I'll see what I can do about setting up a worthy match of skills for your fearsome female Warrior, when you're ordered to the capital to make this peace official before the Shogun. I'm certain that Shogun Ashikaga-sama would be extremely interested in witnessing a female Warrior who can defeat his best Samurai. Hai Lord Kawasomeru! It should be an interesting match indeed to witness." The general sneered as he scooped up a fist full of rice with his hand then shoved it in his mouth. This general was known to be a pig when he ate, and he was proving the rumor wasn't unfounded at this meal.

LORD WAKATSUKI'S SAMURAI ARMY

The messenger General Morimoto had dispatched, was successful in tracking down Wakatsuki and his wandering army.   When the warlord's scouts came across the exhausted messenger, he showed them the Shogun's chop, and was immediately taken to the waiting Lord Wakatsuki.

The interested enemy warlord eagerly open the scroll hoping it was the answer to his many problems and after reading the words he raged at the Heavens. "By the worthless Kami who slither their loathsome way in the darkness of the underworld! I have done it, I have brought the great Lord Kawasomeru down to his worthless knees if he lives. The Shogun has issued an order for peace be restored between our four warring provinces. I'm ordered to Lord Kawasomeru's encampment for peace talks with the fool, and the special envoy sent from our Shogun. I'm under the protection of the flag of Shogun Ashikaga-sama. I have been ordered to take two hundred and fifty of my best Samurai to accompany me to the dung heap's worthless camp. This many Samurai will be more than enough to protect me from any possible assassins roaming the field sent against me, and my interests in the central provinces.

"But I'm only allowed to enter the dog eaters' encampment with just one hundred of my best Samurai guards in tow. General Okamatsu-san! You'll pick out the Samurai who'll accompany me on this great quest. Give our envoy all the food and drink he wants to consume, and make a consort available to attend his personal needs if he desires one. He's to be shown every courtesy we have at our disposal, and he will remain in my encampment until I have returned with the peace paper in my hand, signed by the great dung heap that has wasted his time hunting us for so many months now. By the sacred jewels of the Emperor himself, we have done it; we have brought the great Lord Kawasomeru down from his foul perch above us."

The envoy made like he was going to complain at the warlord, but Lord Wakatsuki cut him off before he was able to speak. "He'll have all the sake he can possibly drink and if he wants more than one foul consort to enjoy while he awaits my return, he may have two, three, ten, as many as he wants. His personal health is all I'm concerned with."

These words made the envoy happy to wait for the warlord's return to his camp.

Lord Wakatsuki watched intensely as a mass of his warriors ran off in all directions, the ones ordered to accompany him to Lord Kawasomeru's encampment immediately headed for their horses. The other warriors who were to remain behind moved in to help the ones chosen. Horses were packed with provisions for the dangerous trek.

General Okamatsu leaned forward and whispered to Lord Wakatsuki, so the envoy standing a few feet away from them might not overhear his words. "My Lord, what about the assassins we have dispatched to kill this child god Samurai Warrior we have heard so much about?"

The warlord Wakatsuki turned, a surprised look plastered on his face as he moaned at his general. "Ieeeee! I forgot about those worthless fools. Send Samurai out to hunt them down and take their lives. I don't want any word getting out that I have released assassins for any reason. It might upset the Shogun and my plans. I'm working against time here, General Okamarsu-san. I have orders to appear in Lord Kawasomeru's encampment by no later than sundown tomorrow night, or risk suffering the wrath of the Shogun and his mighty armies."

"My Lord, what happens if Lord Kawasomeru is dead as we suspect? Who do you think you might be forced to deal with if he's truly dead, my Lord and Master."

"Then it'll be I who'll hold the fate of the Realm within my fist. And I'll deal with whoever has replaced the great fool, and I'll deal with the fool on my terms and my terms alone, not his General Okamarsu-san." Lord Wakatsuki emitted a chilling laugh as his horse was brought up before him, saddled and ready for travel.

"Iye, not yet shall I leave for that dung heap's worthless encampment! I have to properly prepare and pack first, General Okamarsu-san. I have to look like the next ruler of the sixteen provinces of the Central Realm." The overexcited Lord Wakatsuki disappeared back inside his tent, he opened his chests and pulled the entire contents out. Flinging them about as he looked for his finest yellow kosode with the crane hand painted on the back of it, as it stood in the water looking at a brightly colored fish. Yellow was the sign of victory over one's enemy, and the crane standing on one foot signified the power that Wakatsuki believed he held over his eight provinces. He believed the fish painted on the kosode about to fall victim to the strength of the crane, represented Lord Kawasomeru, or his eight provinces if he was dead, which he prayed for with his heart and soul. The warlord knew the yellow kosode would be a powerful insult aimed at Kawasomeru, if he was still alive and attend the ordered meeting with him and the envoy.

When he found the kosode he was searching for, the pleased warlord wrapped it between two sheets of rice paper then he handed it to a waiting consort for careful packing. Other vassals located the warlord's tongs and obi, and other compliments he needed to be a most imposing figure, when he arrived in his enemy's camp. When everything was packed to his approval, the grinning warlord rushed from the tent and mounted his horse, stood in the stirrups and overlooked the samurai ranks in proper formation behind him and his mount. He was pleased by his general's choices of warriors to accompany him to his enemy. He turned to General Okamatsu mounted at the place of honor at his left side and grunted. "General Okamatsu-san. You were most wise in your picks for our foolish guards, shall we ride to our fate?"

"Hai my Lord." The general replied as he prepared himself for the long ride.

Lord Wakatsuki angrily sank his spurs deep in the flanks of his horse, drawing blood and making the horse rear and scream out with pain, before lunging forward at a dead run. His samurai were ill prepared for such a quick start, and they had to kick their horses before they were moving nearly as quickly as their lord. A few riders were thrown from their horses and ended up trampled under the beating hooves of the trailing horses. General Okamatsu took these few deaths in consideration, and had other samurai standing by along the road to replace warriors unable to keep up with them. The general wanted his master to ride in Lord Kawasomeru's camp with the right amount of allotted samurai in his attendance protecting the powerful warlord.

The general took nothing for granted as he had other samurai ride off before Wakatsuki's column started out for Kawasomeru's encampment. These chosen samurai were to be at the general's disposal, in case something happen to a few samurai during their hard ride. They were under strict orders if they weren't needed before Lord Wakatsuki's column reached the vast Kugyo Plain, they were to turn back and return to their camp and wait their further orders.

The hard riding warlord nor his generals feared any possible treachery from Kawasomeru, because his warriors were traveling under the protection of the Shogun's banner. Any assassins seeing this flag of the Shogun flying behind them, would immediately back off or fear the Shogun's unfettered wrath falling down on their worthless shoulders.

The warlord carefully guided his horse along the narrow road that his First General Motoshima was killed on by the female warrior. He was a master rider in his own rights and he charged his mount down the narrow Kai pass heading for the Kugyo Plain at breakneck speeds for his horse and samurai alike. As he raced on, two more horses lost their footing, one stumbled but caught his balance before tumbling under the flesh cutting hooves of the trailing horses. The second horse went flying in the swift running river waters with his rider holding on for dear life.

A few guards called out and laughed at their comrade who went for a unscheduled bath along with his horse. A cloud of dust rose high in the air behind the wildly charging horses, with many samurai screaming out their battle charge as they rode on, trying to urge even more speed from their mounts. The faster the horses galloped down the hill, another one suddenly lost his way, and both the horse and rider tumbled into the waters of the river. The horse's neck broken and the hapless samurai ending up trapped under the horse and drown under its weight before any of the other warriors were able to get to him and free him from the horse's weight.

No samurai called out this time, because they realized the seriousness of the fall. Besides, they were traveling so quickly that none of them wanted to take their eyes from the road, or their horse for fear of ending up being trampled to death under the trailing horses' hooves.

On and on they charged wildly forward with Lord Wakatsuki leading the way while kicking his horse harder, blood freely flowing down the flanks of the injured animal as it raced onwards. The first sharp turn in the pass witnessed a terrible accident, with fifteen horses crashing into the stone wall of the mountain, throwing their mounts right in the path of the oncoming horses behind them. Bodies of samurai tripped a number of trailing horses, adding to the mounting death and carnage of the accident. By the time the warriors slowed down their pace to safely navigate the sharp turn in the road, and avoid most of the downed and injured samurai and horses. Twenty five horses and their riders were sprawled out on the road, suffering broken bones and necks. Animals died, or were quickly put to death so they didn't suffer. The severely injured warriors suffered the same fate as their dead mounts.

Other riders descended from their hiding places along the pass and filled in the ranks of Lord Wakatsuki's shrinking column of samurai. As pleased as the warlord was, he was still punishing his samurai for no reason by having them ride in such a reckless manner, killing thirty warriors and their mounts. In the back of his mind he was fuming that he was still unable to defeat Lord Kawasomeru on the field of battle, without having to drag the feared and powerful Shogun into the picture. No matter how well he would work out in the upcoming negotiations with the hated Kawasomeru, or the filthy one who replaced his hopefully rotting body. He understood he was going to lose some position due to the Shogun stepping in and forcing an end to their warring. He couldn't take out his anger on the Shogun, so subconsciously he was beating on his samurai, by having them take such wild chances by riding so quickly on the narrow and winding road.

Once the road straightened a little better for the riders, the samurai picked up their scream and yelled out their famed war cry again. This added to the uplifting and exhilarating thrill of the breakneck ride. It made the warlord proud of his loyal fighters.

LORD KAWASOMERU'S MASSIVE SAMURAI ENCAMPMENT

Once the general had his fill of food and sake, he looked around Lord Kawasomeru and growled as he continued searching behind him. "What is this foolishness, I don't see this chosen female Warrior you spoke so highly about before me, Kawasomeru-sama. Did you not tell this lazy female Warrior that I demanded to see her when I finished eating my fill? By the worthless Kami both great and small, a lowly whore in the famed Samurai Caste, I fear for your once great mind and future, Kawasomeru-sama!"

"Fear not for my mind General Morimoto-san, I assure you that it's sound as ever, your worries and concerns will be laid to rest once you have witnessed her outstanding skills with the blade. General Shimbo-san, tell the warrior General Wind-san that I'll see her at once, and make certain that she's with blade and prepared for an exhibition before us."

"In your presence my Lord?" His general replied with surprise in his tone.

"General Shimbo-san! If Wind-san wanted to take my worthless life, she had countless opportunities to have my worthless head many times in the past as her memorial to her victory over my foul carcass. Yes she is to appear before me with her blades, General Shimbo-san."

General Morimoto leaned a little closer to Lord Kawasomeru and grumbled in a mocking tone. "Ahhh my powerful Liege Lord, speaking of memorials to past victory. I was lead to believe that you're in certain possession of the famed tattooed dragon shaft of General Motoshima-sama.

Ieeeee my Lord! I can't believe one of your skillful Warriors was enough to go up against such a prize well tested Warrior on the field of battle, and lived to breathe another day's breath in his foul body. Once I finish with this Wind Samurai that you named, and you boasted so proudly over, my Lord Kawasomeru. I'd like to share a cup of sake with this other great Warrior of yours if you don't mind, my Lord."

The proudly smirking Lord Kawasomeru didn't reply to the words from the rude acting general, instead he smiled at the grinning general for a moment.

Cautiously, Wind slowly entered the tent and instantly dropped to her knees, bowing until her forehead touched the ground before both General Morimoto and her Lord Kawasomeru.

"Ahhh.. come in, you may approach us, General Wind-san." The smug warlord offered upon seeing her enter his tent, and using Samurai to further insult the general by using that word and honoring a female of the realm.

Again, General Morimoto leaned nearer the warlord and grumbled at him. "Ieeee...I believe you have more piles than brains my Lord. You offer that you appointed this female warrior a General in your Armies. I hope for your sake she is as great as you offer."

When she was within sword range of the general and himself, Lord Kawasomeru stopped Wind's approach by offering. "That's close enough, General Wind-san. To my left sits First General Mitsuyoshi Morimoto-sama of Shogun Takauji Ashikaga-sama's honorable palace army. He's reported to be one of the greatest swordsman to have ever lived in all the Realm. That's until you were given birth by the gods. I have requested your presence before me so that you may give both I and the General a quick exhibition of your sword abilities."

The warlord's words brought a harsh glare from the seated and angry general. He picked up the insult the warlord aimed at him and he resented it and it showed in his face.

The smug acting Lord Kawasomeru totally ignored the ugly glare from the general as he continued speaking to the female warrior. "I have ordered you before me armed, so that you might give the General and myself a demonstration of your outstanding abilities with the blade, General Wind-san. The demonstration begins now." Without further words, Lord Kawasomeru suddenly threw three buns in the air.

Wind's crafted Sugahara katana was out in a flash, the sword sang its song of death as it hissed through the air like a silver striking cobra, as it sliced through the three buns with little effort in flight. Lord Kawasomeru threw three more buns in the air and before she sliced these three in half with her sword, the warlord threw two more buns with speed right at her body chest high. She got the first one easy enough, but it was impossible for anyone human to have sliced the two buns thrown directly at her with such speed. In less than a heartbeat, Lord Kawasomeru picked up his stabbing blade from the stand, and threw his wakizashi directly at her face, with a sincere attempt to try and kill her with the smaller blade. The suddenness and speed of the move took General Morimoto completely by surprise, and he jumped because of this action and immediately grabbed the hilt of his sword in order to defend himself against a sudden attack.

With the speed born to the despised Devil Kami of the underworld, she easily caught the blade in flight just inches from her face. Then Lord Kawasomeru suddenly called out to her in a commanding voice. "General Wind-san! The General's great chin whiskers are too thick and insult me with their presence, and I believe they could use a small space at the very tip of his foul chin to please my likes a lot better."

She let out a chilling roar from deep within her body, as she dropped the small blade and spun her killing blade right at the concerned general's face. Even before the general had a chance to react against the blow, the razor sharp blade passed close by his face, with her spinning around and ending up resting on one knee, with her katana blade snapped back in its scabbard, and her rear to the general in a kneeling position with her head bowed, while struggling to control her breathing and uncontrolled fighting spirit.

Feeling the slight breeze created by her blade which he saw pass so near his face, the surprised general cautiously ran his callused hand along his chin whiskers as he had done for so many years and to his surprise, he found his beard was cut in two on each side of his chin. He checked his hand for any trace of blood as he glared at the back of this heavily breathing female samurai with her back exposed to him, there was no blood on his hand.

"Ieeeee! What evil Kami that floats in the underworld beyond sight, vision and understanding, guides this one's hand and skills with the sword. Huh Lord Kawasomeru! If I was to draw swords with this young Warrior pup of yours, I'd be committed to fight to the death against her proud spirit from the beginning. I have never saw such fascinating skills displayed with the katana, my Lord. Are all her other skills with weapons of the Samurai as equal skilled as this one is with the sword, Lord Kawasomeru?"

"Hai! If her skills are not better I assure you General Morimoto-san. This Samurai was trained since the age of five in the fine arts of war making abilities by Master Trainer Tanizaki of the Ninth Village himself. There's nothing

General Wind-san can't do with a weapon, or skills with any other implements of warfare. She was even able to master the confusing Go board during her early learning years with the Master Trainer, General Morimoto-san." Lord Kawasomeru proudly bragged about the female samurai knelling before them.

"Impossible! You're boastful words are too hard to believe true. I believe I saw the best of Samurai and their abilities with all weapons in Kyoto, but since witnessing this young Warrior abilities, makes me realize how slack and lazy we truly become in our foul ways of living in the capital. When I get back to the capital city of Kyoto, you can take my words for it heads will roll. My Samurai will be every bit as an equal to this young Warrior of yours, or I'll have no Warriors left to command in times of battle by the time I'm done with the fools. Huh Lord Kawasomeru! What you have mentioned about the Go board interests me I admit. Though it's been countless years since I last played the child's game, I used to do quite well at it I offer you. I'd be most honored if your young female Samurai would indulge me in a simple game of Go, before I return to the capital either with an agreement to end this unending war, or the heads of you and Lord Wakatsuki." General Morimoto announced with an amount of pride.

The powerful warlord Kawasomeru grunted. "General Morimoto-san! That decision would be up to my Warrior if she would care to indulge you in a game of
Go. But I'm certain she'd be pleased to indulge your interest in a simple game of Go. Why not ask her yourself for she's within earshot of you, General Morimoto-san."

"Huh!" General Morimoto growled as he shifted his eyes from Lord Kawasomeru, and leveled them on Wind as he snarled at her. "Samurai! Would you indulging a feckless old man in a game of Go? Mind you Samurai, I'm known a sore loser at anything I attempt to do for your information." For the first time, something resembling a smile crossed the old fighter's crusted and yellowed lips, as he slightly bowed to Wind.

"I'd be honored to play a game of Go with one much wiser and skilled a Warrior than I will even hope to attain. I'd deem it a wise learning experience to endure at your skilled hands of making war, General Morimoto-san. I'm certain the General can give me countless new ideas to ponder, which I'd never dreamed to employ by my worthless self on the field of battle, General Morimoto-san." She bowed to the old but proud warrior.

"Huh! If her manners are anything like her skills on the great board of chance. I'm fearful I might've overstepped the limits of my poor knowledge and skills with this young one. I must admit Kawasomeru-sama! She's well trained as Samurai, and her manners are exceedingly well displayed. This young female Samurai is an excellent addition to your army I believe, Lord Kawasomeru." The Shogun's General Morimoto snapped without taking his eyes off the female with the killing swords hanging so threateningly from her narrow hip.

The liege lord rumbled in his deepest voice at the officer. "General Morimoto-san! Need I remind you that you're speaking of my female Samurai as if she was a great male Samurai. Do you now deem her sword skills are equal to that of any golden faucet supporting male Samurai in the entire Realm, General Morimoto-san?" He suddenly smiled at the old warrior as he waited for his reply, feeling he just boxed him in a corner

"Huh Lord Kawasomeru! She far surpassed many well trained Samurai I know in her brief exhibition before my unbelieving eyes. In all of my days I have lived on the soil of Japan, I have never witnessed a Warrior pass the four apples test. By what she displayed, I'm positive she'd be the one to pass such a hard test to master. You're wise to have enlisted this female Warrior in the ranks of your honorable army, Lord Kawasomeru. She'll serve you well for many years of service to come. I would've enlisted her in my army I believe, even if she suffered two heads, and her skin had the many colors of a worthless Nolt actor's kosode on her body. Kawasomeru-sama, you were wise, most wise indeed.

"General Wind-san! I can understand why your wise Liege Lord has bestowed this name upon your great fighting spirit, your killing blade performs like the wind itself, young Warrior. You have pleased me beyond endurance with your outstanding exhibition you have just displayed before me, General Wind-san. It's an experience I shall relive many times over in my foul life. Have you had the intelligence to name your great Katana blade as well, young female Samurai? Surely a mighty blade such as yours that can slice through the bodies of one's enemies so swiftly, deserves a great name for it to own to be honored." The Shogun's general asked of Wind as he held her locked in his harsh gaze.

"Hai General Morimoto-san, but it wasn't I who named my sword, it was my wise Lord and master who was thoughtful enough to honor me so, by naming my Katana blade for me." She bowed politely to the general again.

"Hai. It's a wise Lord and Master who blesses one of his Samurai by naming anything for the fool." The general mumbled as he rubbed his missing chin whiskers a second time. Then turned to the warlord grinning as if he had a woman's hand inside his kosode.

"General Wind-san is most correct indeed, General Morimoto-san. I took the liberty of naming her uncontrollable killing sword. I ordered her to name it Wind's Breath, for her Katana is a killing extension of her arm. In all my days I wandered the soil of Japan, I never saw a Warrior especially so young, so one with her swords will and mastery over her enemy's souls. Every move from her sword compliments her body and war making skills, and every action from her body so compliments her sword in return. They're truly like one with each other and honoring one with each other, General Morimoto-san."

"Huh! It's an honorable name, a good pick and a good Samurai Warrior stands before me. Kawasomeru-sama, you're a wise and most daring leader who employs new ideas and Warriors within his countless armies. Who else would've been brave enough to dare allow a lowly woman to join the ranks of the famed Samurai Caste, just you, and I, I believe my Lord." The general turned to Wind again as he continued his words aimed at her this time. "Leave my sight so that I may speak with the Samurai Warrior that Lord Kawasomeru honors so. The one who was able to defeat the undefeatable General Motoshima-san, and returned to his master's side with such a fine trophy for his private viewing." General Morimoto turned from Wind back to Kawasomeru, slightly stunned at what he witnessed by the female warrior, trying not to allow his amazement to show before the warlord and his female samurai warrior.

When the general noticed she hadn't moved off as ordered, he snapped angrily at her. "Samurai Wind-san! Clear the filth from your foul and clogged ears and listen before I order you to commit suppuku for displaying such insolence aimed at my being. Leave and send in the other Warrior who defeated General Motoshima-san in battle!"

Again she didn't move, she dared to barely breathe as General Morimoto suddenly stood and glared angrily at the her, but his anger and unwise action was cut off by Lord Kawasomeru's biting words growled at him. "Don't be angry with my Warrior, General Morimoto-san. The reason she had not moved off as you ordered, is because she's the Warrior responsible for dispatching the powerful General Motoshima-sama."

The stunned general was unable to control his awe of this young female warrior, as his mouth hung agape and he stared at this woman warrior with disbelief etching his eyes, as he grumbled at the lord in amazement. "Ieeeee Lord Kawasomeru! You mean to offer me that this lowly woman Warrior of yours was the one who successfully defeated the great General Motoshima-san, slayer of countless hundreds of well trained male Samurai on the field of battle in his crane's life? By the Karma that controls our destiny and holds the world together. She's truly a great Warrior I laid eyes upon, Lord Kawasomeru. I can't wait until I return to the capital, and inform Shogun Ashikaga-sama of her stunning feats upon the battlefield. Kawasomeru-sama! Don't be surprised if the Shogun doesn't claim this young female Warrior for his army. I'll surely suggest he do just that, for the Shogun's army should have only the very best Warriors employed in his army." General Morimoto bowed towards Lord Kawasomeru.

The wise and cunning Lord Kawasomeru knew there was no way the Shogun was going to steal Wind from him as he nodded slightly to her, dismissing her while he spoke further with the general. Morimoto and the warlord shared much sake, and spoke of many past war stories, and enjoyed farting and pissing long into the night, and didn't finish speaking until the first cock crowed the waking of the dawn of this day.

The general was so drunk by the time they finally finished their exhausting conversations that he fell asleep lying on his pillow after loosening his obi for easier breathing, and placing his swords at his feet. Lord Kawasomeru also fell asleep in the tent, but he had the best of pillows to make his sleep more restful.

The warlord's number one First Consort, the Lady Yuko Takenaka came in the tent to check on her master's condition, and had to wave her hand before her face because of the smell from stale sake and bad air. She carefully covered her warlord and general with blankets then she took position and stood at the tent entrance and stopped anyone from entering and interrupting their sleep for the rest of the night. Yuko knew the two men shared a good time last night, she heard their many laughs and curses, and long winded stories of personal conquests upon the battlefield, and with the art of pillowing women.

The warlord's female samurai spent most of her night collecting her thoughts and preparing her finest armor, polishing the gold and silver inlays, and making certain that the armor was clean and free of any dried blood, or old skin flecks and mud from the inlays carved deeply in the metal. She knew tomorrow would be a great day that would be written about in Japan's history books. It would be the fine day that the two powerful warlords of the sixteen provinces of central Japan met face to face, to discuss peace terms between them for peace to return to the realm. She worked long in the night on her armor and weapons, she wanted to look her very best when she came before the despised enemy Lord Wakatsuki, so she might spit in his worthless face. Then challenge him to a battle to the death with sword, and her skills with the weapon if the foul warlord was willing to stand before her with his sword.

The massive encampment remained silent during the first hours of day, mainly because Lady Yuko warned the officers that Lord Kawasomeru was drunk and still asleep. Many warriors were put to work cleaning up the camp for the visit of Lord Wakatsuki and his honored guards. A horde of hinin packed supplies and removed debris. Rakes came out next, and sand was smoothed over, rocks were set in positions, and bushes and branches were removed from the area. The hearths were cleaned of ash and new fires set in them. All traces of cooked horse meat, or bones of the animals were buried deep, to keep them from Lord Wakatsuki's ever prying eyes. It would be terribly insulting to their lord, if it was discovered that he ordered his warriors to eat the flesh of the horse, something forbidden by many faithful Buddhist followers.

The horses were moved from the security of the center of camp out to the far end, and stalls erected for the animal's protection from the elements or injury. The samurai were ordered to clean and appear before Lord Kawasomeru dressed in their finest kosodes or armor.

The female warrior was extremely upset her horses were treated as if they were a problem. She had a number of her warriors go with the horses to make certain they were properly cared for, which meant they would miss the peace ceremony. Wind was hoping Lord Kawasomeru would not entertain Wakatsuki, instead she hoped when her master set eyes on the great dung heap, he would draw his sword and lop his head for his shoulders.

Within her heart, she blamed Lord Wakatsuki for her father's death. She also blamed the many problems caused by him, for the reason her father was forced to deceive Lord

Kawasomeru she was a she child. She wondered how life would have been for her, if the war wasn't in the wings of the Eight Provinces. How life would have been to live, as the gods chose her to live as a woman. With a deep sigh, she cursed karma and the gods and Lord Wakatsuki. She missed her father dearly, he was with her, training her, forcing her to be the greatest samurai to ever walk the lands of Japan. She knew if her father had not taken time with her training, she would have been put to death when the great warlord found out she was a female being passed off as a male child to him. Everything she was, everything she would ever amount to be in her life, she owed to her honorable father's training and guidance.

On one of those rare occasions, she would allow her mind to travel to the past, to think of her loving mother. She was never close to her that was because of the vast amount of time she spent with her father on the training field. She remembered the first day she was allowed on the training field with the other samurai trainees. How well she was accepted by the trainees, with each warrior taking time to explain anything she wasn't certain of. She remembered how the trainees watched their colorful stories whenever she approached their gatherings, and how they tried to protect her from all harm. She smiled while remembering how the samurai to the man on the field, volunteered to go after the assassin Masao Okazaki when he beat her in her first test with fists in the village. Her mood darkened when she remembered the assassin trained by Ninja monks in the shoinzukuri, and how she killed Masao in the darkness when he came at her from the shadows inside the samurai living quarters by the training field like a dog.

She grew upset as she thought of how the despised Masao held a long time grudge against her for so many years, for the beating she delivered against him after their forth hand to hand fight in the street of the village of her birth. This occurred after her father shown her some of the ways to use her hands as weapons, not to kill but to immobilize her enemy. Again she cursed the blacken disgusting spirit of Masao for his daring to attack her like a thief in the middle of the night, dressed in the black cloth of the loathsome Ninja.

She knew she had to force the black thoughts from her mind, as she fondly remembered the constant smiling face of her older sister Estsuko. Who taught her so much about the countless ways of a female, and how she was supposed to act when in the presence of someone important for the good of Japan. She wondered what Estsuko was doing in Engakuji Castle under Lord Kawasomeru's care. She missed her sister the most of all her family, outside of her father. She smiled over these pleasing thoughts in her mind.

The endless day dragged on slowly as the massive encampment made ready for Wakatsuki and his samurai guard's arrival. Every warrior in the encampment, understood why the enemy warlord was riding to their camp and they were not allowed to attack him or the warriors riding with him. They all wanted the war to end, so they could return to their loved ones and homes and their own lives, so the warriors were calm and looking forward to the peace talks to begin. Lord Kawasomeru and General Morimoto finally woke and had something to eat. Then they came out of the tent after sharing more laugh at the remembrance of the night before memories, and its pleasantries that passed between them. The warlord let go of his gas and the two laughed again.

The First Lady Yuko chased after the two powerful warriors around with hot cups of cha to drink to help clear their throbbing heads, and stopped when her lord and master threatened to kiss her in public. As he and the officer stood, General Morimoto informed the liege lord that the Shogun gave him strict orders to allow the warlord to have one hundred of his samurai remaining in the encampment when Wakatsuki rode in with his once hundred samurai in tow.

Lord Kawasomeru turned serious as he complained bitterly at the Shogun's General. "What type of foolishness is this that I'm forced endure for the sake of this dog coming to my encampment so peace might return to the Realm? How come it is up to me to have to drive off seven hundred and fifty thousand of my loyal Warriors, and have them retreat in the woods like common Ronin criminals and filth? Then I'm forced to allow the largest of criminals to be born and walked on the soil of Japan, to march in my camp like he was a conquering hero to the Realm, who'll be surrounded by hundreds of his samurai dogs. Has our great Shogun been lavishing in the capital for so long to dare place me at such disadvantage with this man despised by any civilized person?

"Ieeeee! I find this order extremely hard for me to follow General Morimoto-san. Surely, there has to be another way around this drama, I'd be most pleased to meet the filthy mongrel on a one to one basis. But I'll not allow myself to be placed at such a disadvantage, as is offered me by you and our Shogun, not after fighting against this dog for so long."

The wise and understanding General Morimoto allowed Lord Kawasomeru to vent his anger, before adding in an angry tone. The general was not used to his words being questioned by anyone but the Shogun himself. "Lord Kawasomeru! Although Lord Wakatsuki is traveling with two hundred and fifty Samurai as his personal escort guards, to make certain he arrives alive to this encampment. He was instructed to enter with the same number of Warriors as you have remaining in your encampment. This is why I ordered you to have a guard of only one hundred Samurai to greet his caravan. It's my Lord's wish Lord Wakatsuki doesn't feel threatened in your camp, this way, serious words of peace can be spoken and this unending war will finally be allowed to come to a conclusion on this foul day."

The Shogun's general noticed the harsh expression etched on the Lord Kawasomeru's weather beaten face, and read his inner thoughts. Then added as a further warning against him, and his warriors still gathered in the encampment. "Kawasomeru-sama! Lord Wakatsuki is traveling under the personal protective banner of Shogun Ashikaga-sama. Any foolish attempt on his or his Samurai guard's worthless lives, will be dealt with in the most vicious and harsh ways by me I assure you. It'd be the fool of fools who'd dare to attack Lord Wakatsuki, while the great fool is riding under the protection of this banner of his Shogun, Kawasomeru-sama.

"Even if a horde of assassins were given certain orders by a powerful Daimyo such as yourself I add cautiously to your person Lord Kawasomeru. They'd have committed suppuku by honor by now if they saw the Shogun's personal banners flying over this fool's foul head. If any possible assassins saw Shogun Ashikaga-sama's banner flying over the worthless head of Lord Wakatsuki. They'd know instantly they couldn't attack him or his caravan without suffering our shogun's mighty wrath, thus failing their duty to their Master. Thus suppuku, neh Kawasomeru-sama?" The crafty general cast a sideways glance at the warlord.

The fuming inside warlord let out his breath in a rush and then agreed with the general, because he was forced to agree with his words and warnings as he offered in return to the Shogun's envoy. "Hai General Morimoto-san, any worthless assassins would surely be dead by now as you have suggested." Under his breath, the angry warlord cursed karma. Then, in a commanding voice he suddenly bellowed for his officers and personal guards to remain in the camp, while the other warriors not needed for the peace talks were ordered to the surrounding hills. Before he finished speaking to his soldiers, he gave orders to his warriors. If they came across Lord Wakatsuki's dog eating warriors hiding in ambush. They had his permission to engage any lowly assassins if discovered, and destroy them before they could carry out their orders against him or any of his troops.

General Morimoto and Lord Kawasomeru understood that Lord Wakatsuki ordered many of his warriors out in the hills surrounding his massive camp for his protection, in case the enemy warlord was riding into a trap heading for his camp. He watched as his warriors mounted, or walked out of his camp as if they were insulted by him, and the Shogun's general, and he shook his head over these orders issued them.

CHAPTER TWENTY NINE
THE THIRD DAY OF THE FORTH WEEK OF THE SEVENTH MONTH IN THE YEAR OF THIRTEEN FIFTY FIVE, THE ALARM WAS RAISED

A horde of Lord Kawasomeru's samurai scouts were spread out in the area surrounding the massive encampment, and when one of them picked up the cloud of dust being raised by the hundred and one horses of Lord Wakatsuki's army, he gave out the alarm to the other warriors that the enemy warlord was approaching their encampment. The warrior had no idea the enemy warlord ordered his other one hundred and fifty samurai to wait well out of sight the Lord Kawasomeru's encampment. He furthered ordered them to be on the alert and to rush to his aid if he came under attack by his enemy's lowly warriors.

It was none too soon the last samurai were about to leave Lord Kawasomeru's encampment from the north section, because Lord Wakatsuki and his warriors were riding in from the south. As Lord Wakatsuki and his warriors broke out from the confining Kai Pass, and had a clear view of the Kugyo Plain and Lord Kawasomeru's vast encampment. He ordered his warriors to halt while he cautiously surveyed the camp and surrounding area. Only when he was confident there was no traps lying in wait against him, did he order the wild charge of his chosen warriors from his new position. At breakneck speed, again he bolted from the pass and charged directly for Lord Kawasomeru's camp as if attacking it in force.

Lord Kawasomeru stood with General Morimoto by his side, they were flanked by his female warrior, General Shimbo, General Kobayashi and General Miyamoto, and some of his lesser officers of his army. Angrily they watched the ugly insulting spectacle their enemy Lord Wakatsuki made as he entered the camp in the wild charge.

General Shimbo was so angered and insulted by the foul display he barked and his armed samurai standing in a neat formation, snapped to attention then waited Lord Wakatsuki's arrival and possible orders to attack his caravan. Wind's hand went to the kashira, the pommel of her sword. She wanted to be ready to strike in case Lord Wakatsuki wasn't to be trusted.

Just before Wakatsuki's warriors rode in the campsite proper, his protective guards separated, with the warriors breaking off and instantly surrounding Lord Kawasomeru's samurai on foot, while Lord Wakatsuki and his officers charged right at the fuming and insulted Lord Kawasomeru. At the last second, Wakatsuki pulled back mightily on the reins and made his horse come to a sliding halt just yards from the very feet of Lord Kawasomeru. Continuing his motion and wild charge, Lord Wakatsuki leaped from his horse and stomped his way up to the waiting enemy delegation, followed by his chosen officers.

Without orders to do so, Lord Kawasomeru's loyal samurai turned to Wakatsuki's samurai on horseback and prepared to fight against the gathered enemy troops. The enemy warlord stomped up to Kawasomeru and bowed to General Morimoto who returned his bow weakly. Then he bowed to Generals Kobayashi, Miyamoto then Shimbo. He then turned and bowed to the one enemy officer he didn't recognize in the group, and took a few seconds to study the young warrior's face. At first he thought the warrior to be a female, but he knew better than to believe that foolish thought. He slightly bowed again to this unrecognized samurai general then he finally turned to Lord Kawasomeru and bowed just within the limits of politeness towards his enemy warlord, but he refused to look him directly in the eyes.

Kawasomeru's samurai grumbled their displeasure at the terrible insult just leveled against their lord and master. The respected warlord ignored the grumbling from his warriors as he returned the weak bow with one of his own. This time causing Wakatsuki's samurai to grumble their displeasure over the insult the other warlord just leveled against their lord and master.

Stepping between the two angry warlords and their warrior protectors, to stop them from coming to blows or allowing the anger of their warriors to reach the point they attacked each other. General Morimoto asked in not a very friendly tone of voice if he had a safe ride to Lord Kawasomeru's encampment to calm everyone down.

"Hai General Morimoto-san! It was a safe trip I offer for your interest." Was all he barked, not daring to take his eyes off Lord Kawasomeru's form, who openly glared at him while daring him to make a move for his sword.

"Huh! Are we now no better than lowly dogs that we're content to stand under this miserable sun, and speak words of peace? When one wants peace to come, he must be comfortable so he can think of peace better." General Morimoto barked at the two warlords as he turned and headed for Lord Kawasomeru's tent. The powerful warlord waved his arm out before him and motioned for Wakatsuki to follow the general. Then he followed the leader of his eight provinces to his tent. The officers from both sides moved behind their chosen warlord.

The important general sent by the Shogun entered the tent first, then Lords Kawasomeru and Wakatsuki entered almost side by side, each warlord moved to opposite sides of the tent, and sat on the laid out pillows. The warlord's officers had to be content to sit crossed legged on thin uncomfortable tatami mats placed about the large tent.

Wind couldn't take her eyes off her master's hated enemy for a second who she wanted so desperately to kill nearly from birth. The angry female samurai tried to force her mind to will Lord Wakatsuki into making a foolish move for his sword inside the overcrowded tent. So she could have at him, and put a quick end to his worthless vile life, and the problems he was the cause of and rid Japan of his stench forever.

The concerned Lord Wakatsuki caught the unknown young general staring at him with a chilling harsh glare, and wondered if he somehow had insulted this obviously dangerous warrior some time in his life, and he didn't remember the insult or the warrior. He stared intensely at this strange looking samurai who looked more like a woman than a man. He broke his stare off when the Shogun's general suddenly cleared his throat, and remarked in an angry voice.

"Wakatsuki-sama! I'd really appreciate your undivided attention before me over this serious matter, while we try and discuss peace terms between you two fools. We have pressing matters to straighten out between us three. Before we start I must warn the both of you fools, the Shogun gave me the power to put to death either foolish or stubborn warlord, who doesn't want to make peace with each other at this foul meeting. Shogun Ashikaga-sama is extremely upset about this worthless war being waged between two of his powerful warlords in his Realm, and he demands a quick end to it on this day. Therefore, no one will leave this worthless tent until we have worked out lasting peace terms between the two of you, or one or both of you are dead." General Morimoto glared at the warlords for several seconds to set his words in their minds.

Lord Kawasomeru bowed to the angry general, but Lord Wakatsuki growled at the two, displaying terrible manners before them as he growled at the powerful general. "This war you complain about was started all because of Kawasomeru-sama's loathsome greed, and his foul attempt to stifle my province's progress. For years he has placed himself in the way of my joining my two provinces together, and giving Echigo province more access to the sea from my south region. Many times over the countless years I have tried to make peace with the stubborn leader, and to work out a much more suitable solution to my problems, but year after year he had ignored my kind offerings I made in the name of peace between the two of us and our Houses and provinces, General Morimoto-san."

The Shogun's general looked cautiously at Lord Kawasomeru, and he nodded then spoke in his defense. "It's true that Lord Wakatsuki tried to speak of solutions to the countless problems facing his two provinces, but all his solutions consisted of his invading Kozuke, or slicing up the province for his liking, and giving no regard what Nobuhiko Anjoh-sama, or his people what they felt about his worthless offers. I pointed out on numerous time to the thick headed Wakatsuki-sama, Kozuke wasn't my province to give away or to slice up for his foul greed.

"I further warned him that any invasion of Kozuke province would risk the wrath of my army, which I'd sent out in force in order to defend Kozuke under my command. Nevertheless Wakatsuki-sama invaded after my countless warning to him not to attempt any invasion, therefore my army rushed to the aide of Anjoh-sama's province as was promised him personally by me. There is no question, if an end to the war is demanded by our great Shogun in Kyoto then I demand Wakatsuki-sama's army move to his original borders, and he no longer threatens any provinces under my influence or protection. Or there simply will be no peace between the two of us ever, General Morimoto-san."

Lord Wakatsuki angrily threw his hands in the air and grumbled at the Shogun's envoy. "There General Morimoto-san, this is what I've been fighting all these years. General Morimoto-san! You can see for yourself that Kawasomeru has no interest in bringing peace to this part of the realm, unless it's under his conditions, and his conditions alone."

Even before Lord Kawasomeru could raise a complaint over the insult of Lord Wakatsuki omitting the sama or lord from his name, General Morimoto intervened on his behalf and warned Wakatsuki in no uncertain terms to keep a civil tongue in his mouth, and refer to Kawasomeru-sama by his well earned title. The angry general further warned the shameful warlord that the Shogun's massive army was massed in the lowlands of Dewa province, and it would only take a lone carrier pigeon to start his great army on the march against him and his invading army if he so ordered. The Shogun general looked at Lord Wakatsuki with the threat locked in his eyes, erasing all question as to where his beliefs lay.

Lord Wakatsuki's angry outburst made his samurai guards flinch. General Wind and Lord Kawasomeru's officers moved their hands to their swords, daring the warlord Wakatsuki or his warriors to make a fatal move before them.

The fuming Lord Wakatsuki being an extremely wise politician, knew that he had to dance extremely careful and bowed to Lord Kawasomeru as he begged again. "Please forgive my terrible lack of manners, I was a fool of fools to allow my passion to rule over my better judgment in this conversation, Kawasomeru-sama, General Morimoto."

Lord Kawasomeru didn't respond to the angry warlord's contrite words, he merely nodded in acknowledgment of Lord Wakatsuki's poorly spoken apology, and accepted it graciously.

General Morimoto started his words again for the feuding warlords. "Kawasomeru-sama, Wakatsuki-sama! It doesn't appear to me that we're too far from finding an agreeable solution for this most foul of unending wars. Wakatsuki-sama! All you want from Lord Kawasomeru is a wide enough passageway between Kozuke and Dewa provinces, to allow you free access to the sea to our south, neh?"

"Hai that among other demands that need to be addressed if peace is to return to the realm, General Morimoto-san." Lord Wakatsuki snapped back instantly.

"Wakatsuki-sama! We'll not get anywhere with this meeting, if we start out our conversations with demands and lack of respect for each other. We're speaking, let us continue in that manner, speaking and not making demands of each other." General Morimoto growled at the obviously upset warlord, as he let out his breath in a disgusted sigh.

Lord Wakatsuki drew in a huge gulp of air then bowed to the general sent from the Shogun. He was trying to get his rage under control, while doing his best to force Lord Kawasomeru to lose his temper before the angry acting Shogun's envoy.

"That's better Wakatsuki-sama, in the spirit of communicating and making peace between you two, I'd like all outside parties to leave this foul tent immediately. I don't like having all these armed and angry looking and acting Warriors sitting so close to my piles. We'd be able to speak on much better terms if we spoke in private without so many ears listening in on our conversation." General Morimoto offered then looked at each of the warlords.

Lord Kawasomeru spoke over his shoulder and each of his military advisors instantly rose and bowed first to General Morimoto then to Lord Wakatsuki before turning as one, and marched out of the tent. General Morimoto's attention turned to Lord Wakatsuki and the warlord snapped at his officers. "First General Sadeyuki Okamatsu-san! I'm safe here, take the officers outside, but secure the perimeter and wait for my presence before you. Make certain there's no treachery aimed at my person here, General Okamatsu-san."

All Lord Wakatsuki's officers stood as one and bowed to General Morimoto then to Lord Kawasomeru and quickly filed out of the tent. Lord Wakatsuki smiled to himself at the way his warriors marched out of the tent.

"Ahhh... now that we have rid ourselves of those troublemaking officers, we can speak much more freely." General Morimoto grumbled as he pulled his swords from his obi, and laid them out by his side within easy reach. Then he untied his sash, farted and scratched between his legs as he shifted his weight on the pillow, and mumbled at the warlords. "My foul bladder is full, I want a peace agreement between the two of you fools before I have to piss, or I'm going to take a few heads around here I assure you." With a smile the general looked at the two warlords and added. "We'll place all formalities in the piss pot and speak freely. Wakatsuki! What are these other demands you seek from Kawasomeru?"

"General Morimoto-san..." Wakatsuki offered to the envoy general first, as he puffed up his chest and prepared to bellow his words.

"Morimoto will do fine for this foul meeting right now. I'm more interested in a peace agreement between you two fools, than any pleasantries between us. We're Warriors, so I piss on pleasantries and other foolishness." The general interrupted him curtly.

"Hai Morimoto! I deman... err, I request that Kawasomeru pull his horde of Warriors out of my provinces and others under my influence at once, and he stops invading my lands in the future. I further request more access to the steel that he controls so we can make our own swords, and other weapons and farming implements needed by my people. I also request the flatlands of Kozuke for planting to feed my people, and want my surrounded province of Kai by the provinces under Kawasomeru's control, to be given a direct and secured corridor to the sea between Suruge and Sagami provinces. Under the present conditions, my province of Kai has her provisions reaching the province by means of traveling through Kawasomeru's lands. Thus they're charged ridiculously high tariffs and other fees we're forced to endure for the mere privilege of traveling through

Kawasomeru's lands. I want no revenge taken against any of my Samurai, and my lands are not to be taxed, and I'm left in command of Echigo and Shimotsuke provinces. This is all I request to place a halt to this unending war we're locked in, Morimoto."

General Morimoto turned to second warlord and asked. "Kawasomeru! What do you have in the way of any requests, and what do you say to Wakatsuki's many offers and needs? I refuse to recognize these requests as demands, in the name of peace."

The powerful Lord Kawasomeru looked in the eyes of Wakatsuki then complained. "Why is it always the worthless aggressor who demands no retaliation be taken against him, or his foul followers of his crimes committed against the realm and her people? As in any past wars, the losers always paid with their worthless heads. That is how I feel but I'll say no more on this subject, as far as my slicing up Kozuke province for Wakatsuki's likes and needs, as I stated before in this conversation. Kozuke is not mine to slice up for anyone. Wakatsuki wants to transport merchandise through other provinces, yet he doesn't want to pay the proper going taxes and tariffs on his needed goods. Yet he charges the same taxes and tariffs for anything transported through the provinces under his worthless command. Even the Shogun is not free of the burdensome taxes and tariffs that plague all that live on the sacred soil of Japan.

"As far as my giving Wakatsuki access to more raw steel to make his swords and farming implements and other weapons of warfare. I have no problem with this request in the least, as long as he pays the going price for the stock in cash or trade. Wakatsuki! I'd like nothing better than to get my loyal Samurai out of your foul land, but in order to accomplish this feat, there has to be peace between our two houses first. One thing I must demand without argument, is for you to forfeit one of your foul provinces as punishment for starting this unending war, and as payment for the great sums of money, and lives it cost me and my people to battle your evil ambitions. I have no problem in not taking revenge against your honorable Samurai. I feel we had enough killing to last us for the rest of our foul lives. To make the forfeit of one of your provinces palatable for you to accept this punishment. I offer you a safe corridor of free tax to Kai. The path will be thirty Ri wide, and will allow Kai province to build a seaport on the shore, to accept merchant ships and their trade stuffs you require for your people's needs."

"Ieeeee Kawasomeru-sama! Give up one of my provinces to appease the likes of you! That's totally out of the question, that's impossible for me to endure. I'd rather fight you to the death, before I give up either of my two provinces. Iye! This will not happen I assure you Kawasomeru." Wakatsuki barked as he suddenly jumped to his feet.

General Morimoto glared angrily at the liege lord over his rash and threatening move of jumping to his feet and snarled. "Wakatsuki! If you want to retain control of even one of your foul provinces, I suggest you sit that pile riddled arse of yours down, so we can continue to work out this problem between us three with this boring conversation. I'm certain we can come to a settlement that'd soothe the wounded ego of each warlord seated before me." The general waited for Wakatsuki to sit himself, the moment he did he continued. "I have listened to both sides on this matter of unending war, and I decided in the interest of time to intercede justly. Since both sides are so close to a fair settlement, I'll make the final decisions for both, which will bind each of you fools and the provinces under your influence, to this agreement for the rest of your days on this earth, or you can takes your lives and I'll take your worthless heads.

"One: I have decided that Wakatsuki to lose one province is completely out of the question for this settlement. But Kawasomeru is correct in demanding some form of payment for the vast expenses that was placed on him and his people, to defend his eight provinces from the invading forces under your influence and dependency, Wakatsuki. Here is my decision on this matter, Shimotsuke province will be split in half, with the southern section going over to Kozuke. To help with this great loss, I'm prepared to give Wakatsuki two thousand Ri of the horn on Dewa province, to open a path between Echigo and his lower provinces. There'll be no revenge sought against either honorable Samurai army in this matter of war. I'm pleased that Kawasomeru saw the need for this corridor for Kai to exist, because I was going to order this corridor in either case. The raw steel to make your swords will be made accessible to Wakatsuki, at the going price as was suggested by Kawasomeru. I cannot possibly order Lord Kawasomeru to offer his raw metal to you at a better price than he offers to the leaders of the other provinces. Even the Shogun pays the going price for this metal so that ends that problem.

"I'll levy a special tax of fifty thousand koku of rice, ten thousand kiki in silk, and five thousand horses to be paid to Kawasomeru, to help him absorb the vast sums of worth he was forced to invest in this dishonored and unending war. Wakatsuki will have no access to the low lands of Kozuke province, and Kawasomeru will be given thirty sticks of time to remove his massive army from Wakatsuki's provinces. Wakatsuki, you'll be given seven sticks of time to remove your Warriors from all Kawasomeru's provinces. All agreements here are nonnegotiable and binding under our

Shogun's command and chop, and any interruptions to this agreement, the punishment is death to the offender. Any province, any warlord who dares to go against these agreements, their provinces will feel the unfettered wrath of Shogun Takauji Ashikaga-sama's mighty armies." The general looked at each warlord while waiting their response.

Kawasomeru proudly announced to the military officer. "General Morimoto-san! It's plain to see why the wise Shogun Ashikaga-sama chose to send you to negotiate this agreement between us. You are most wise and just. I agree with all the decisions you have put forth before we two warlords, General. I shall do everything in my power to stay within the guidelines you set forth." Kawasomeru hawked then spat on the floor to seal his part of the deal.

Wakatsuki was angry yet relieved, he was walking away with more than he had dared to think possible in this forced agreement. He glared at Kawasomeru then offered hotly. "Of course Kawasomeru would be in complete compliance with your wise decisions General Morimoto-san, because they all favor him and his eight foul provinces. The only reason I'll agree with these foul decisions, is solely because I want to put an end to this unending war of the central provinces under both our influences. But I demand one further request be fulfilled, if the Shogun wants this war to end honorably." Wakatsuki looked from the angry general to Kawasomeru.

General Morimoto let out a disgusted sigh, knowing he was well within his right to make one final demand over this situation, before agreeing with the decisions of this meeting he was forcing on the two warlords. The general was surprised Wakatsuki agreed so easily with his decree, without trying to get more as he snapped at the warlord. "What is this last demand that you request of my and Lord

Kawasomeru, Wakatsuki? If it's in my power to offer you, I'll grant it, just to place an end to this war that refused to end before I die of old age, Wakatsuki."

A smile of victory slowly spread across the face of Wakatsuki as he replied to the special representative sent from the Shogun. "General Morimoto-san! I demand the head of the lowly Warrior, who assassinated General Motoshima-sama. Normally, I'd not demand the head of a victor of any battle of honor. But in this case, my General was killed in a most savage and very despicable way, and I was forced to bury him not whole of body. Every Warrior worth his salt, knows if the body isn't whole when buried, the soul of the Samurai can never come back to visit this earth, and his body can never be reborn Samurai. If the General was killed on the field of honor in a fair fight to the death properly, I'd demand to pay great homage to this Warrior of Kawasomeru-sama's. But since this worthless Warrior attacked my General under the guise of a female ready to pillow him, is insulting to General Motoshima's honor.

"General Morimoto-san, since when has there ever been a female assassin employed by any warring faction in the history of Japan to get the upper hands for any enemy? I'm within my right to demand the head of this vile uncouth, detestable assassins to be sent to destroy such a great General of respect and honor." Wakatsuki stared angrily at Kawasomeru all the while he spoke his words of anger at him and the Shogun's general.

The stunned Kawasomeru couldn't hide the rage and anger clouding his face, as he openly glared at Wakatsuki. The hated warlord saw the anger etched in Kawasomeru's face, and knew he just enjoyed the final victory over Kawasomeru, and decided to push the point home as he hissed at the envoy. "General Morimoto-san! You know worthless assassins are the lowliest of the low, and they don't deserve the protection of the honorable Samurai Caste and code of honor. Throughout their worthless lives they operate detestably and on the outside of the honored laws that govern Samurai actions. Bushido means absolutely nothing to these lowly etas, allowed to wipe their foul feet on our beliefs and respects. Again, I demand the head of this unholy Warrior if you truly want peace to be returned to the realm." Lord Wakatsuki defiantly folded his hands across his belly and smirked, further driving the insult at Lord Kawasomeru.

General Morimoto sadly shook his head as he turned wearily to Kawasomeru and replied in a shadowy tone, even though he fully understood that the crafty Wakatsuki was demanding the head of the female warrior who was just in his presence before the meeting between the two warlords and himself and grumbled. "Kawasomeru-sama, Wakatsuki-sama is well within his rights to demand the head of this worthless assassin as he calls this honorable Warrior. I'm inclined to agree on this belief, and the way that he feels about assassins used in times of war and peace as well. I'm prone to grant his request unless you can convince me otherwise as not to allow what he requests of me, Lord Kawasomeru."

Lord Kawasomeru was fuming over the demand of Wakatsuki and was doing his best to try and control his rage mounting in his chest. Nevertheless, it surfaced and cost him loss of face before the general and Wakatsuki, when he snapped savagely more at the other warlord. "This request is totally impossible for me to accept! I'll not give up the life of this one honorable Warrior, just to appease the worthless Wakatsuki and his foul wants, desires and demands of me. He has received enough from me in these binding agreements that both me and he accepted to end this war he started in the first place, General Morimoto-san."

"Kawasomeru-sama! Let us not upset the progress that we have accomplished so far in our search for a conclusion to this endless god cursed war. What's the worth of one lowly assassin in the best interests of all provinces of Japan? Surely this lone assassin is not worth the price of peace." The general snarled at the stunned warlord.

"The loyal Samurai you're calling an assassin, is not an assassin but an extremely loyal and honorable Warrior held in the highest regard by me and rank in my army. Therefore, Wakatsuki isn't standing within his worthless rights to demand the head of this loyal Warrior. He's in no position to demand anything further from me or my provinces. It should be I demanding his foul head be brought before me resting on a gunyoki spike, for my viewing pleasure."

"Huh, just because the great Lord Kawasomeru has declared a worthless and detestable assassin an honorable and highly respected Warrior of the Samurai Caste, doesn't make the executioner a Warrior of great respect and honor. His believed power and word isn't that great in the pulse of Japan, even though he might believe his power is total and to be obeyed by all living on Japan's soil. A true and honorable Warrior would never stoop to the foul depths, as to allow himself to become a dog eating hated assassin. But, if a Warrior has allowed this then he's lower than all cursed assassins of the past and present times of Japan, for forsaking his Samurai respects and beliefs. Now, armed with this new information, more than ever this gives me the right to demand the worthless head of this murderer of the great Kawasomeru. General Morimoto-san! I'll not agree to any decisions agreed to here today, unless this cursed assassin's worthless head is brought before me for viewing, dressed on an honored gunyoki, the wood plate and spike for head displaying before the victor of the war."

Lord Kawasomeru was unable to control his raging temper and again he displayed bad manners before the two by growling angrily at the other warlord. "Wakatsuki! Didn't your wise father ever explain to you that your worthless mouth is not used for breaking wind? Did he not further explain to you that your foul mouth is used for seeking honorable solutions to bad situations? Seeking revenge on a highly honored Warrior because this Samurai was only guilty of following his master's bidding is bad Karma, and to this is a terrible lack of good manners and honor, from such an honorable man as you profess to be, Wakatsuki-sama."

The upset warlord Wakatsuki completely ignored Lord Kawasomeru's angry words as he smiled triumphantly over his demand of the assassin's head, realizing how much this one warrior obviously meant to his rival. He was pleased with knowing General Morimoto was bound by honor to agree with his demand. Especially since Kawasomeru admitted it was a samurai of great respect, who acted as a lowly assassin who killed his well feared First General, and the Shogun's general wanted peace no matter what the cost to either warlord at the meeting.

General Morimoto realized the crafty Lord Wakatsuki had successfully trapped him in this agreement, and he despised the hated warlord for it as he also lost control of his temper, and snapped at the outraged warlord. "Wakatsuki! I know well what the devil an honored gunyoki spike is, without you wasting your and my time by explaining one to me, you horses ass. I warn you fool, don't dare to try insult my intelligence, nor my endurance at this worthless meeting between you two foul fools. I warn you in the grave of manners that I'll not stand for it for one moment longer.

You'll not enjoy my wrath if you're able to find my boiling point and force that wrath to be unleashed against your pile ridden arse, Wakatsuki." The extremely upset Shogun representative turned to Lord Kawasomeru and added.

"Kawasomeru-sama! I'm deeply distressed over this terrible matter that was just brought up to my attention, and the god cursed demands and counter demands being tossed about at this foul meeting between us as if those words and demands carried no consequences with them. I find myself being forced to agree with Wakatsuki worthless demands over this manner of the assassin's head, and I have decided in Wakatsuki's favor. Even though I had the pleasure to meet this honorable Samurai Warrior, who is the point of this contention and Wakatsuki's unchangeable anger. But only because the death of this one Warrior, will bring a lasting peace to the realm. But I'll do this much for this respected Warrior, Kawasomeru-sama.

"Once her head had been brought before Lord Wakatsuki for his private viewing, the head will then be returned to the body, and you'll give this Warrior a proper burial according to the laws of the samurai. This believed to be assassin will be allowed to commit suppuku, and you have the pleasure of picking her second to witness her honorable death. Even though I'm well aware of the Samurai we speak of at this meeting, and I'm deeply sadden she'll lose her life over my order. This matter is closed according to my decree, and I have nothing further to add to this most unpleasant conversation." The general clapped his hands to signify the conversation was over, but Wakatsuki wasn't done yet, and dared to speak further.

"General Morimoto-san! When will the head of the assassin be taken from the foul thing?" The once enemy warlord was overjoyed by the victory he was enjoying over

Lord Kawasomeru. He never dreamed his demand of the head of the assassin who killed his general, would affect the other warlord, and he was surely going to make the best of his power over Kawasomeru. He was also banking on possible offering not to go through with his demand of the assassin's head, if they could work out something more palatable for him to bear.

"Ieeeee Wakatsuki-sama! You're truly without good manners to ask me such a troublesome question. Lord Kawasomeru! I order you to take the head of this Warrior tomorrow at sunrise as is the right time for any honorable Samurai to obey the final order of his Lord and Master." The general spoke no more as he rose and walked angrily from the two warlords, knowing who Lord Wakatsuki wanted dead to answer his want for revenge.

Warlord Wakatsuki dared to smile dominantly at Lord Kawasomeru, as he fluffed up his insulting yellow kosode, representing total victory over his enemy and offered. "Now that peace has again come to both our lands, Kawasomeru-sama. We must try to become friends, and even work together for the betterment of the realm and our provinces. Since we're alone and can speak privately without unwanted ears sharing in what I plan to discuss over with you. Kawasomeru-sama, I'm prepared to offer you a further bargain to consider. One that I'm quite certain will be much more palatable for your enjoyment than the one we had agreed to with that foolish General sent to force us to speak of peace terms between us. I'll become your willing and most loyal vassal, and serve you honorably for the rest of my life. If I'm allowed to retain both my provinces whole and completely intact, Kawasomeru-sama."

"Huh! How dare you speak to me in this detestable manner! Fool, don't be so foolish as to attempt to bargain with me as if you were a lowly trader, a dung eating merchant! Only your position is saving your worthless head, keeping it resting on your loathsome shoulders, that and the protection of the Shogun's banner and my goodness, you still find yourself breathing. Don't push me further in this terrible matter, lowly dog eater. You lost the war and it's only your cunning to drag the Shogun into this settlement that saved your pile riddled arse from its final conclusion. But Karma is Karma and it can't be changed by mere will and want. It can only be put off until the Kami feel it's been eluted long enough. I'll enjoy my finally victory over your foul carcass when your time comes, and the gods so will it and remove your evil head from Japan's soil at long last." Lord Kawasomeru hissed at Lord Wakatsuki.

"Ieeeee! You're truly a most stubborn man to be forced to deal with, Kawasomeru-sama."   The other warlord complained bitterly as he searched his mind for another way to save both of his provinces. A thought suddenly flashed in his ever sharp mind and he asked Lord Kawasomeru with concern. "Who was the famed Warrior who seems to be so important to your presence and who had successfully killed General Motoshima-sama?"

"Wind-san!" Kawasomeru growled at the other warlord while refusing to look him in his eyes.

"Who? Who was that you just said, Lord Kawasomeru?" The confused Lord Wakatsuki asked as he ignored the insult look he just leveled against him.

"General Wind-san you worthless fool! Yes, the Samurai you want dead is Yuriko Tanizaki-san. Master Trainer Tanizaki-san's honorable Warrior daughter. She is the one who has placed a successful end to your great First General, you great dung heap." Lord Kawasomeru announced angrily to the staring Lord Wakatsuki.

"Ieeeee Kawasomeru-sama!   Then the unbelievable is believable after all, and the foul rumors that I heard uttered over the past year are true, he is a she. This great Samurai of yours who beat back whole charging armies single handed with his sword, is a lowly female warrior. Now I realize General Morimoto-san didn't make a mistake when he first called this Samurai I demanded his head, a her or she. This Warrior is truly female. My great and well feared General by all male samurai was bested by a lowly female warrior. The shame of it all."

"Hai Wakatsuki-sama!   A lowly female Warrior has successfully defeated your great and feared General Motoshima-san." Lord Kawasomeru snapped proudly at the other warlord, for a fleeting moment he was tempted to offer Lord Wakatsuki the section of Shimotsuke awarded him, in a weak attempt to try and save the life of Wind. But he quickly realized if he was to offer this sum of worth for one warrior's life in his army. He would be placing too high a price on her head and worth. Wakatsuki would take further advantage of the offer, and he would seek even more from him, feeling he had something in his grasp he wanted more than his foul province. Lord Kawasomeru's face hardened as he glared at Lord Wakatsuki in controlled anger.

Lord Wakatsuki picked up the sudden change in Lord Kawasomeru's attitude and stance aimed at him, and realized the deal he was seeking from the other warlord, had slipped through his fingers as he growled at his nemesis in anger. "Huh Kawasomeru-sama!   Then I continue to demand her worthless head! If peace is to be restored to this section of the realm of Japan then I want her worthless and evil head resting on the spike to seal our peace terms."

Warlord Kawasomeru wanted nothing more in life than to kill this dishonorable fool daring to stand before him so defiantly, more than he wanted to kill anyone else in his life. But all he could do was reply in anger. "Worthless one, you have been awarded your god cursed pound of flesh so enjoy what you forced from me, now get out of my eyes before I forget that I'm a civilized warrior and I draw my sword and removed your head from your shoulders. The unwanted sight of you makes my stomach ill and growling in disgust. If you remain before me a moment longer, I'll not be responsible for my attack against your foul being."

Lord Wakatsuki bowed as he smirked and left the tent of Lord Kawasomeru's.

General Shimbo saw Lord Wakatsuki stomp away for the covering and rushed in Lord Kawasomeru's tent and asked excitedly. "My Liege Lord. Do we have peace at long last?"

"Hai General Shimbo-san, we have peace in the realm, but at a terrible cost. I must speak to Wind-san privately."

"Hai, Thank the gods for their favor, I'll send General Wind-san in immediately my Lord." The general announced as he quickly left the lord and master's tent.

Seconds later, Wind entered the master's tent still dressed in her armor. Lord Kawasomeru stared at her for a few seconds while trying to find the proper words to tell her she was about to die for the good of the realm. When the proper words would not come to him, he ordered Wind to meet him on the crest overlooking the vast Kugyo Plain, in the early morning hours of the starting of the new day. Everyone in the camp was aware that the lord and master used this special place for meditation and viewing the sunrise. He ordered Wind to appear on the crest twenty feathers of time before sunrise. She smiled broadly, proud she was invited to share the sunrise with her powerful lord and master.

The stunned Lord Kawasomeru decided to allow his female warrior to enjoy her last day and night on earth in peace. So he refrained from informing her that she was about to die so peace could break out over the realm. She left the tent proud and happy.

As she left his side, Lord Kawasomeru called out in a booming voice to the person he was unable to see, but he knew his general was in ear shot of him. "General Kobayashi-san!"

The surprised general rushed in the master's tent, his hand resting threateningly on the hilt of his sword, not knowing if Lord Kawasomeru was in distress. His back was to him and the warlord spoke without turning to face his officer. "General Kobayashi-san! I've been issued an order I'd rather have my right hand chopped from my foul body, than be forced to fulfill this command. The order comes from the Shogun, so I must follow the order to its final conclusion. Even though I detest the order and the outcome." The warlord paused for a moment.

"Hai my Lord and Master? Anything you order of me will be carried out faithfully my Lord." The concerned general replied to his lord.

"General Kobayashi-san! I know how close you are to this female Warrior who has been nothing but problems to my piles. I'm aware of the oath you shared with Master Trainer Tanizaki-san over her protection. But I'm bound by my oath of loyalty to Shogun Ashikaga-sama, to carry out his bidding at the cost of all other. General Kobayashi-san! I have been ordered to take the life of General Wind! It was a direct order from the Shogun himself and I'm honor bound to follow without hesitation, forgive me and my next order."

"God curse Karma and the lowly gods who control Karma and all things that effect the people of Japan. This can't possibly be true my Lord! Why this order to take her life to me my Lord and Master? General Wind-san is one of your most loyal of Warriors. She's the greatest Warrior to have walked upon the sacred soil of Japan. To kill a Samurai of such great worth and respect is to terrible a waste to imagine, my Lord." General Kobayashi replied, stunned by the upsetting words coming from Lord Kawasomeru's mouth.

"General Kobayashi-san! You can't say anything that hasn't been said by me in my attempt to save General Wind's life when General Morimoto-san ordered her death to take place for the sake of peace for the Realm. You're the most loyal of friends and military advisors, you make me envious of such a friendship between two Warriors. But this is the only way to seal the peace pact ordered between Lord Wakatsuki and myself." The warlord offered to his military officer, hating every word he was forced to offer the general.

"This is all the fault of that lowly warlord Wakatsuki. I'll lop off his worthless head from his foul shoulders, and there'll be no more talk of such a wasteful peace, between you and this worthless dung heap of a person, my Lord." General Kobayashi growled as he broke the seal of his sword and pulled the killing blade out three inches to add to his threat against the other warlord before Lord Kawasomeru.

"Ahhhh.... spoken as a true Samurai Warrior you are, General Kobayashi-san. I'm proud of you on this foul day General, but you're not given permission to strike out at Wakatsuki's disgusting neck. That's a pleasure I'll enjoy somewhere along the road I travel on in my future, General. I have a more important mission for you to accomplish for this female Warrior child and myself on this sad day. I'll end Wind-san's life tomorrow morning at sunrise, and nothing you can offer and curse can and will change that faithful decision, General Kobayashi-san. Here is what I want of you, I want you to spend the rest of this foul day looking for a proper cave in which I can bury General Wind-san, her horse and her armor and horde of weapons in. I'll honor her in death as she has honored me in life on the great field of battle.

"I'll order her faithful horse killed and place the animal's body within her tomb so she can ride throughout the Floating World as proudly as she had ridden in the world of now. All her worldly goods will be buried along with her for her personal use in the foul after world of wonder and thought. I'm not sure if the lowly gods who control all things will allow General Wind-san to walk on this earth ever again. But if anyone is offered such a favor by the gods, it will surely be her fine spirit that will have this favor. This is why I want everything perfect for her death and burial that I'll give her in the old way of honoring a fallen soldier, General Kobayashi-san." Lord Kawasomeru finally turned to look at his stunned and angry general after he was positive he had his emotions under control.

General Kobayashi instantly dropped to his knees and bowed when he saw his lord's eyes as he offered. "Hai my Lord and Master, I'll find the proper burial place for Wind-san to rest within peaceably for all times to come. Kawasomeru-sama! I beg a great favor of you."

"Hai General Kobayashi-san! If any one of my officers have that right to ask, you surely do of me. Ask your O negai of me and I'll fill it if possible." Lord Kawasomeru was so disturbed over Wind's untimely death that he overlooked the presumption of his general.

The loyal general bowed lower as he spoke to his master while trying to control his own emotions. "Kawasomeru-sama! I humbly request permission to be allowed to commit suppuku at the feet of General Wind-san, and to be buried within her burial chamber so that I might be of assistance to her in any future wars she is involved in." General Kobayashi dared to look up from his bow to see the reaction from his lord.

The powerful warlord thought for a moment then moaned in astonishment over his general's request. "Ieeeee General Kobayashi-san! What is it about this god driven young female Warrior that commands my faithful General to beg permission to be allowed to follow her to battle even in death? How can I possibly deny your request of me, General Kobayashi-san? But it'll be carried out in this fashion as I order you. General, you'll not be allowed to commit suppuku until General Wind-san's body is set in place for her rest for eternity. Then you're ordered to take a position of kneeling at her head looking down upon her face for all time to come. Then and only then you'll be allowed to slit your belly. You'll not be attended by a second, I order this not as a punishment held against your person, General Kobayashi-san.

"On the contrary my order is a special honor to be paid by you as lasting homage to my Wind. I want you to keep your head so that you can help guide her on her journey to the unknown world of waiting forever and help her in what the gods have planned for her future with them. I'll make a special offering to the gods through their foul priests, so they'll overlook your unattended sacrifice. You'll be greatly honored by future generations of Japan in song and story, General. No greater loyalty will ever be displayed by another Samurai for all times to come in Japan's future. I honor your decision and I thank you kindly for making her death easier for me to endure. Be gone with you now my General and find a secure place in which to bury Wind for centuries to come. She doesn't know she's about to die by my order, and that's the way I want it to remain until her end, General Kobayashi-san. Allow her to enjoy her final hours in happiness and at peace with herself and the world." Lord Kawasomeru watched as General Kobayashi rose to his feet left his tent to begin his task of finding the place to lay Wind to rest.

Again, the angry warlord cursed karma and Lord Wakatsuki for what he was being forced to do to his female general. For the first time in his life he was dreading the sunrise of tomorrow morning to come.

JUST BEFORE SUNRISE ON THE FORTH DAY OF THE FORTH
 WEEK OF THE SEVENTH MONTH OF THE THIRTEEN FIFTY FIVE

The great Lord Kawasomeru was resting peacefully on his large stone crest, solemnly looking over the countless hearth fires burning peacefully in the massive encampment and going up the hillside, long before General Wind made her appearance before him. The smoke from the many fires hung heavy in the long valley, almost like the mist of a dragon's breath as it serenely slept the night away. It gave the ill begotten morning an eerie feeling to the upset warlord. A soaking rain threatened to fill the morning air, and a light mist was already falling on his peaceful realm as he waited for his Wind to join him on his crest of peace.

Strangely, the sky had few clouds blocking the promise of a beautiful, but far off sunrise on this day. From where the warlord sat, he was able to see the Heavens and the earth waging an eternal battle against one another for their battle of dominance of this day. With the sky pounding the earth with blinding strikes of extremely destructive lightening. Then the sky trembled mightily with the earth rattling sound of far off thunder claps. Lord Kawasomeru could not help but wonder if this was an evil omen of the future that would soon rule over Japan's fate with the death of this female warrior? The worried warlord wondered as he thought once Wind was gone from this earth, was the earth and sky going to fight to the death over her untimely demise and wandering spirit taking over the Floating World.

The confused warlord watched the rain fall softly to the earth intensely, and felt the gods themselves were shedding tears of sorrow over Wind's pending death, causing the mist to fall to the earth. But the gods in their infinite wisdom were not allowing the mist to become heavy enough to destroy her view of her last wonderful sunrise on this earth. For the last time, Lord Kawasomeru's mind begged the gods, karma, and whatever else controlled man's destiny, to intercede on this order of death for his female general. But no sign came from the Heavens, and no god chose to answer his silent prayer.

The now angry warlord cursed just as Wind walked proudly out from the light mist towards him. Lord Kawasomeru's breath was taken from him, as he witnessed this stunning young beauty walking up the crest so proudly and respectfully. She looked like a young goddess of myth, dressed so pleasantly in the soft, fine light blue kimono which was the second of the pair he gave her days before, as a special tribute for her great deeds on the battlefield, and in service to him. Her two famous killing swords were nowhere to be seen hanging from her fine young body. No weapons were seen of her person.

The warlord didn't move as she approached him with a pleasing smile. She obviously had no idea of her pending death, there was no display of it on her face or in her walk. The lord saw nothing but a pleasing look on her face, and a calm walk to her body.

"Wind, will you honor me greatly one final time by sitting to my left, and enjoying this mist shrouded but very beautiful of sunrises on this foul day." Lord Kawasomeru grumbled at his female warrior as he gave her a sideways glance and a weak smile of his own.

The young female samurai bowed to her powerful lord and master and then she sat on the same rock he peacefully rested on. Then she turned and stared at the far off distance and slowly rising sun. Just as the crown of the mighty sphere of the sun peeked over the top of the mountains that blocked it from view for the moment. The sky beyond the mountains suddenly erupted in what seemed to be flames and blinding rays of light, and she almost instantly felt the warmth emitting from the growing ball of heat and fire. Its heat felt good to the warlord and her.

The sun's rays reflected off the lifting fog trapped deep in the long valley below them, and gave the appearance of millions of fireflies lighting the way for Wind's spirit to follow them to the next world her spirit would soon inhabit. The puzzled female military officer didn't understand what her master meant with his offer by honoring him one last time. But she knew if she was patient long enough, she would soon find out when the warlord was ready and he decided to inform her of what his troubling words meant.

Lord Kawasomeru turned slightly and glanced at his female general out of the corner of his eye. She was seated peacefully in the proper position of absolute obedience and respect offered to her lord and master by her mannerism. Sitting with her rearend resting lightly on legs crossed at the ankles under her, thus placing her weight on her heels. Displaying to the warlord she was in no position to spring into treachery aimed against him. Her delicate hands resting flat on her knees, palms up and her head bent slightly forward. In case the lord for some reason, decided to lop her head from her shoulders for some infraction she might have committed against him and she was unaware of that crime.

Lord Kawasomeru turned his attention back to the extremely pleasant sunrise. Both battle weary warriors enjoying the wonderful sight until the last of the sun's great sphere finally broke free of the mountain's grasp, and the sun once again soared freely throughout the vast Heavens of the endless earth. When Lord Kawasomeru knew he could not put off his hated order of death for his general any longer. He rose and looked down at his loyal warrior who hadn't made a move and smiling up at him so pleasantly, because she was allowed this honor of sharing the sunrise with her lord and master.

"Wind, my fine young Samurai Warrior unlike any who have served me before in my foul lifetime! Prepare your soul for suppuku, but you'll not commit the sacred act of suppuku in the traditional way the honorable women of Japan usually do. You'll not stab yourself in the throat like a common woman of Japan and slowly bleed to death! No my Wind, my General, you have lived your short life as that of a male Warrior, so it's only fitting that you'll carry out the sacred honor as a true Samurai Warrior born as you have lived out your young life. You'll slit your belly opened as all honorable male Warriors do when ordered to their death by their Lord and Master. You have fought in the world of the Samurai Caste all your life. So it's fitting that you die in that same savage world with the same respect and honor shared by all male Samurai of the Realm. Wind-san, I'll be most honored and greatly pleased if you'd allow me the honor to second your great death, my loyal Warrior ever. This is the least I can do for so loyal a retainer that has served me so well in your honorable lifetime. Bah, to be a slave to Karma and the destiny of my own life to be forced to demand your life so early in your life."

Tears immediately welled up in her lovely eyes as she stared at Lord Kawasomeru while her mind was having trouble understanding what her lord was saying, not understanding the order her master had just leveled against her. She replied in a soft and weak voice. "I'd be honored if you'd second my honorable death as you have just offered me, my Lord."

"I thank you for the honor you have bestowed upon my shoulders, Wind. Prepare yourself then for your death Wind-san! I'll wait until you're properly prepared in both mind and spirit and ready to commit the sacred act of suppuku." Lord Kawasomeru watched in silence as she knelt before him and when through the motions of her ordered death. She slowly opened her kimono and pulled it free of her slender shoulders and down to her waist in what was called the blossoming Lotus. He was surprised she didn't take the time to lock the loose fabric tightly under her legs, to force her body to remain in an honored sitting position after death visited her body. It was insulting if any warrior ordered to death, fell off to his side in that death act. It took his face away if the warrior's body ended up in an undignified position, once death wrapped its chilling hands around the warrior's soul. But it wasn't his place to warn her of this problem she was facing. He was merely her second in her honorable death and was honor bound to keep from offering the one about to die any suggesting she should do in this act.

The powerful warlord continued to silently cursed karma and all the gods of Japan as he looked at the young, youthful breasts pointing upwards. He watched as she removed a small tanto blade carried concealed in the oversized sleeve of her kimono, and unsheathed the blade in one motion. She lightly touched the razor sharp blade to her forehead and offered it to the Heavens and gods in a silent prayer to Lord Buddha. Then she turned the razor sharp knife towards her flat, strong belly. The muscles in her stomach automatically tightened and reacted when threatened by the call of the small but deadly blade's bite. She made certain that she knelt correctly before Lord Kawasomeru's drawn katana sword, and exposed her slender neck to his sword strike. She followed his orders without the slightest bit of hesitation, blindly obeying out of total respect and loyalty for her lord and master.

When she was set in the right position for Lord Kawasomeru to strike her neck with his sword, and she said all the mandatory prayers to the gods of Japan, she dared to turn and ask a question. Stunning Lord Kawasomeru who felt her mind should be so locked in the vastness needed to prepare one's self for taking her own life.

"Did I not serve you well upon the honored battlefield my Lord and Master of all time? Was my service to you displease you somehow to order me to my death, my Lord?" She asked in a trembling voice, scared to death because she was about to kill herself.

"Wind! You have served me far better than any Samurai Warrior who has ever lived, or have ever walked upon this foul earth, or served his Lord and Master proudly in the history of Japan. In your short time of carrying out my orders you have earned my eternal respect. Your loyalty to me is not in question over this order of your death, Wind." Lord Kawasomeru offered to his samurai know to the world as Wind.

"If this is true, then why am I about to die by my own hand and by your order, my Lord and Master?" She asked as her lip slightly quivered and she fought desperately against allowing the tears in her eyes to run down her cheeks. The last thing she wanted to do in her life, was to insult her master and herself, by shedding tears liked a common woman of Japan before his presence. She even tried to bite her lower lip hard, to stop herself from crying in front of the powerful warlord, and to give her the strength she needed to follow out her master's order to kill herself.

"Samurai Wind! Yuriko Tanizaki-san! General Wind! You were picked to die so that Japan can once again have peace restored between the two Great Houses of Central Japan. Enough of this idle chatter! I'm ready to second your honorable death, Samurai Warrior Wind of vast respect and honor." Lord Kawasomeru sadly announced, he was bound by respect for the sacred act of suppuku to answer any question put forth to him, by the one who was about to do the greatest act of obedience to her lord and master.

The well feared and angry Lord Kawasomeru saw her swallow hard and then with great inner strength guiding her hand and mind. She pulled the blade's tooth towards her belly with surprising force, but with shaking hands. Her facial expression barely changed as the blade entered her body and she slowly started to drag the knife through her skin and innards. Blood and guts seeped out of the large slash her small blade opened across her narrow belly.

When she reached the other side of her stomach she straightened her back slightly and then pulled the knife up and after about three inches of further cutting, she turned the blade back towards the other end of her cut stomach. The turning of the blade in her body made her grunt out in pain for the first time during this act of death, and she exhale in a rush of mixed air and blood. She stretched her neck further out in order to give Lord Kawasomeru easier access at her neck and a larger target for him to hack through with is great sword.

The wise Lord Kawasomeru had washed his great blade in pure river water long before he came out to the sitting rock, so it was clean to be used on Wind's neck. When she stretched her neck out, he knew it was his time to act, and his blade whistled through the morning air and easily sliced through her neck and bone as easily as it cut through the damp, heavy air of this morning. As her head fell to the earth, what happened next stunned Lord Kawasomeru even further on the beginning of this most confusing day. That was because he suddenly found himself staring at her body locked in awe and reverence as if some unseen hand was holding her body in the position of respect.

Although she wasn't sitting in the proper position to receive an honorable death, her taught body refused to pitch forward, or fall off to either side. Her body was locked in death in the honored seated position as her life giving blood poured from her body in two longs streams of blood. Fear suddenly filled the warlord's troubled and confused mind, because he felt he might have just committed an enormous error by killing this young female warrior born of the gods and placed on the earth, and known as Wind. As if to add to his growing fear of this once female warrior, a sudden loud crack of thunder rattled the very earth he stood upon, and a blinding flash of lightening ripped across the horizon. As if the earth itself was cursing him for taking the female warrior's life from her and the soil of Japan.

Anger rose in his chest and Lord Kawasomeru again cursed Lord Wakatsuki and all his worthless ancestors, and his future kin to a long and slow death. His mind was racing wildly, trying desperately to decide what way he could further honor this female samurai warrior who laid dead at his feet, because she was guilty of being too loyal and respectful to him and his orders and respects. After much thought, the concerned warlord decided he had to curse her soul, in case she truly was chosen by the gods of Japan for something great, and he wanted to remain on the good side of those gods he barely believed in and respected.

The great warlord drew in a huge gulp of air, and then announced to what he believed was the spirit of Wind, that was still lurking near her body looking in which direction it was going to use to get to the Floating World and grumbled in a very commanding voice. "Body of Wind, I know not what the gods of Japan had in mind when they first allowed life to enter your spirit. But I understand some special hand is at work and is resting and guiding you in this world and now in the spirit world. So I'm going to honor you in your noble death in much the same way you have honored me in your short and obedient life to my will and commands. I'll have you buried in the ways of the old, in the great Samurai Warrior tradition of long ago. I'll bury you in your finest armor; your trusted steed will accompany you on your endless journey to the faithful lands of our ancestors dwelling beyond imagination and thought and wonder.

"Your trusted steed's reins will be held by your worthy hand for all eternity to come. I'll place your head after viewing by the detestable Lord Wakatsuki, dressed in your mighty battle helmet on your chest. I'll order it to be tucked in the great gash of obedience you opened with your own hand across your belly. To help guard your honorable body against all evil and harm for life everlasting. I bid you well and nothing but peace that you have never enjoyed in the living world in the land of wonderment and hope, my beloved Samurai Warrior General Masahiko, Yuriko, Tanizaki-sama, my Wind.

"You have brought great honor and respect in your short lifetime even from your hated enemy to yourself and to your family's well honored and respected name. I must curse your fighting spirit forever to this earth, in case your heart and Warrior spirit and the god's will hasn't yet finished shaping Japan's faithful future and fate by your hand. Soul and spirit of Wind, I order you to be linked to this my sword that has caused your honorable death in body only, for the life of the great blade. Wind! I curse you to this Katana sword of justice forever!

"When the sword is drawn from its sacred sheath, your fine spirit will be called back to the earth in order to carry out the bidding of the owner of my Katana sword. Your heart, you soul, your spirit is too strong to be conquered by the mere gods of wonder, or these lonely moments of death you are experiences at this time. This curse I have just placed upon your honorable head will forever doom your unconquerable spirit to the earth in forever servitude of this, my Katana sword, to be used only in respect and honor, and to the call of the next owner of the sword that took your life. Wind, whoever owns my Katana sword in the future, will be continuing my orders and desires and you are bound by your sacred oath to me, to respect anyone who holds my sword, and calls you back from the Floating World to serve them."

The honoring warlord Kawasomeru had used his great Sugahara crafted Katana sword to dispatch Wind's life, and he held it high over the frozen in death, sitting perfectly body of Wind, as he spoke his words of the curse to her spirit and the gods. He looked at the honored katana sword still locked in his hand, enjoying the sheer power being emitted from the great blade, before he replaced the blood soaked steel shaft back within its wood scabbard prison, without cleaning the blade of Wind's blood from it.

Thus further locking her amazing fighting spirit to the sword's steel and its now wood prison. As he finished speaking to what he believed was the spirit of Wind, another earth rattling crack of thunder suddenly shook beneath his feet, it was followed by a blinding stalk of lightening, as it struck the face of the earth a mere fifteen feet from the body of Wind, and her lord and master.

The loud crash of thunder and blinding lightning bolt made the warlord flinch slightly. Then he thought it was the Kami who came to collect Wind's fine spirit and guide it to the Floating World, and the lord bowed towards the earth where the lightning struck. With this final action for the sake of his dead female samurai, he forever linked Wind's soul to the earth, by allowing her blood to drip from the tip of the sword onto the ground under his feet, before returning the wonderful blade to its sheath. He kicked a fine layer of soil over the few drops of Wind's blood, believing he was further locking her soul and spirit to the land of the living forever.

General Kobayashi, who spent much time looking for the proper Kofun, the sacred burial mound or ancient tomb, in which to bury Wind's body safely in. The wise general selected a few chosen loyal and well trusted samurai to assist him in this task. The warriors carefully picked up her headless body of the female general after the powerful warlord left with Wind's head locked in his hands. The respecting warriors placed the body of Wind in the hastily prepared crypt after dressing it properly in her body armor for the last time.

Lord Kawasomeru ordered her head cleaned and perfumed and then mounted on the honored Gunyoki plate and displayed for the hated Lord Wakatsuki's private viewing.

Immediately upon seeing the fine looking woman's head resting on the Gunyoki plate for the last time in his life, the respecting Lord Kawasomeru snapped angrily at the angelic like face of the young female warrior. "With your proud death, peace has been returned to the great realm of Japan and your Shogun and myself, Wind."

The proud General Kobayashi ordered Wind's horse moved inside the Kofun, and as soon as the horse was inside, he slit the animal's throat and allowed it to slowly bleed to death, while it was held down by other samurai accompanying him preparing the tomb for the female warrior. He discreetly positioned the horse to lay right alongside Wind's armored clad body, and he looped the leather reins around her right wrist and weaved it through the dead fingers of her hand. He then placed the honored sword that had killed Wind in her right hand between the reins, and had the sheathed blade rest perfectly on the center of her right shoulder.

The smaller and matching shorter stabbing blade was placed in her left hand, and the general allowed the sheathed blade to barely touch her shoulder on this side. Wind's mighty strung bow was carefully laid across her body, and her katakama yari spear crossed over her bow and chest alike. All this respect and honor was carried out by the warriors to honor the dead warrior for all times to come inside her burial tomb.

The many throwing stars, skewers, smaller tanto blades, and other fine and honored weapons Wind had accumulated over her short life span were laid about, surrounding her body in everlasting honor and respect to her spirit. Her weapons would forever pay homage to the fallen warrior. Her arrows were laid out in a fan shaped pattern with the hardened brass points barely touching her shoulders where her head should have rested.

Her armor was left unattached across her chest. The terrible gash across her entire belly was exposed, and a series of alternating small silver and gold plates removed from her heavy battle robe, outlined the horrifying gash allowed to gape, so it could receive her head shrouded by her mighty battle helmet. This move would seal the great wound from any and all evil trying to enter her fallen body through the mighty gash.

When the respecting Lord Kawasomeru cautiously entered the crypt as if the interior was going to rob him of his very soul, while carefully carrying Wind's head still dressed in her great battle helmet, resting upon the gunyoki spiked plate. The samurai working inside the hastily prepared crypt, knelt and bowed respectfully towards the head of Wind and their lord and master at the same time. Lord Kawasomeru ceremoniously removed her head from the hidden spike with his bare hands, and respectfully placed it carefully into the open wound. Then the warlord looked at General Kobayashi who was likewise dressed in his honored armor, and slightly nodded his head at him.

Everyone working inside the secret crypt quickly filed outside as General Kobayashi reverentially and slowly approached Wind's lifeless body. He looked deep in the closed eyes of Wind, her face was caked with pure white rice powder, and her lips were covered blood red with paint, and her eyes were circled in the delicate black painted sharp lines, adding to the length of her once beautiful eyes. The head of the young female warrior was delicately perfumed with the finest of scented oils of the times.

The pleased General Kobayashi turned and smiled at his lord and master, not daring to bare his teeth before the warlord for allowing Wind to be buried as the woman she was. He knew it was the polite Lady Yuko who took the time to dress the head of Wind for proper burial, a great honor further offered to the body and memory of the young female samurai. The general nodded his approval of Lady Yuko's handiwork with her head. Then he performed his last duty in life by moving to where her head should have rested on her body, and then went a little further distance from her body to her left, the side of respect and honor to all samurai warriors of Japan. The general next knelt on a short raised natural stone ledge overlooking Wind's body, and then he opened his body armor to expose his belly to the call of the bite of the blade. He took time to tie his legs in place with two rawhide straps, locking his body in the honored seated position overlooking the prone body of Wind and her horse for eternal life.

General Kobayashi said the mandatory prayers to Lord Buddha then he made his final peace with the Heaven and earth and his lord and master. Then he sliced his belly wide with is smaller tanto blade. Lord Kawasomeru moved nearer his loyal general and rested his hand lightly on the honored general's shoulder as he slowly bleed to death before his eyes. The powerful warlord stayed with his general as he suffered greatly through his slow and painful death. When the warlord was certain General Kobayashi was dead, he took a little time to fix the slightly out of place armor on the general's body.

Lord Kawasomeru also took the time and positioned General Kobayashi's body just right until it was sitting protectively, perfectly watching over Wind's body for all times to come. In a private and rare show of emotion, the sadden warlord lightly touched the face of Wind one last time as he bent over her body. Then he stood erect and proud and bowed for the last time in his life, towards the two dead and highly respected and loyal samurai warriors. Then he left the crypt forever. The warlord wanted to get some fresh air in his starving lungs, and put an end to this never-ending nightmare he was living through.

Once outside the burial chamber, Lord Kawasomeru cleared the opening and went a good distance away from the opening to the small cave and looked at General Shimbo, who was assisting the burial procession, and gave him a slight nod. There was a good number of samurai stationed high in the mountains overlooking the narrow opening of the crypt, and once they were instructed by General Shimbo, started a small avalanche. Soon a sea of small and large boulders and yards of loose earth and brush rumbled down the side of the mountain and completely covered over the tiny opening of the tomb, sealing it perfectly throughout eternity.

When the burial procession returned to the massive campsite, Lord Kawasomeru gathered all the samurai warriors who had assisted in the burial of his female warrior, and he ordered every one of the warriors to commit suppuku before his feet, to permanently seal their lips forever on where Wind's body was buried in the mountains. So the secret location of her body and tomb would never be discovered or disturbed by anyone now, or in the future of Japan's great history. The powerful and wise warlord spared only General Shimbo's life, and he ordered the general to oversee the deaths of the samurai who worked on Wind's crypt. Then the exhausted warlord retired to the privacy of his tent to reflect on everything that had transpired on this unending day of sadness and death.

Long before Wind's body was placed in its final resting place for eternity inside her crypt, the despised and hated warlord Wakatsuki and his one hundred samurai guards, along with General Morimoto and his fifty escort of warriors. Left Lord Kawasomeru's encampment to return to their respected provinces and lives. General Morimoto was under orders to report to the Shogun and explain about the agreement he had forced on the two warring warlords of the central provinces. The Shogun was pleased his general was able to force peace between the two Daimyo's and was amazed his general was able to force a peace term between the two warlords.

By the time the once enemy warlord finally returned to his province, the nasty and always angry Lord Wakatsuki's life wasn't as long and peaceful as he wanted it to be. When he had returned to his main province of Echigo, the province was nothing like it was when he left it when he first entered the great war with Lord Kawasomeru and his six ally's provinces. Trying to force his people to his oppressive will again, cost him dearly and in the middle of the night one of his angered generals stealthfully entered his private living quarters of his castle. That general dispatched the warlord's life with a blade while he slept. The warlord's body was collected and then tied to the back of a horse, and the riderless animal was allowed to drag his body through the streets of Echigo until it was ripped apart by the ground and beating hooves of his horse.

The general who had killed the disliked warlord, stepped up and he took over the dead Lord Wakatsuki's position over Echigo and his other province, along with the six other provinces that were once under the influence of the despised warlord Wakatsuki. The new warlord of Echigo was a wise leader and cautious leader and he quickly formed a lasting and trusting bond with Lord Kawasomeru and the provinces under his influence. Thus ensuring peace for the realm for many years to come.